A Change of Regime

J.N. STROYAR

This book is a work of fiction. Places, events, and situations in this story are purely fictional. Any resemblance to actual persons, living or dead, is coincidental.

First published by AuthorHouse 04/20/04

ISBN: 1-4107-9421-0 (e-book)
ISBN: 1-4184-4539-8 (Paperback)
ISBN: 1-4184-4538-X (Dust Jacket)

Library of Congress Control Number: 2003097583

This book is printed on acid free paper.

Printed in the United States of America
Bloomington, IN

To John

and

To all who have shared their stories with me.

Foreword

The fiction of The Children's War, *this book's predecessor, was less fiction than a rewriting and weaving together of various personal histories. The characters are inventions, but in general the events are not. Some of the stories dated from the Second World War from Europe, some from the present from elsewhere. They were all united by the common thread of individuals denied basic human rights and, to a greater or lesser extent, their humanity. Of those who spoke to me personally, many imparted their tales only under conditions of absolute anonymity, for they still had much to fear and did not want themselves or their loved ones to become nothing more than an obscure line at the bottom of a newspaper column. To this end, a fictional tale seemed the best way of telling their stories, of imparting a sense of the humans behind the statistics. Their stories are continued in* A Change of Regime. *As before, the setting within Nazi Germany is a convenience and in no way is meant to reflect upon modern Germany or its people. The Third Reich is used solely to provide the reader with a familiar and historical representation of any number of repressive governments, regimes, or authorities. It is a reminder, too, that no people, no matter how advanced their civilization, should take their liberties for granted.*

As with The Children's War, *a portion of the price of this book will be donated to* The Center *for the* Victims of Torture *and other human rights organizations.*

What Went Before
(The Children's War)

During World War II, Germany never attacked the Soviet Union and enthusiastically promoted a nuclear weapons program. As a result, the war in Western Europe was won by the Third Reich and a truce based upon an unstable nuclear balance of terror was struck between the various surviving regimes: the North American Union, the Third Reich and the Soviet Union. The time is the present and the Third Reich continues its long and harsh occupation of the lands of Europe.

Recaptured after a failed escape attempt from a Nazi labor camp, the English convict, alias Peter Halifax, is sentenced to re-education and forced labor in lieu of death. He endures torture, drugs, and psychological indoctrination which endeavors to make him truly sub-human, and is then released into society as a domestic laborer. He lives out his sentence carefully gathering information about the society around him in order to regain his much-damaged confidence and attempt another escape. He begins his work with the Reusch's who make his life almost too comfortable, but then is inexplicably betrayed by them and forced to work in Berlin for the family of a powerful government official named Karl Vogel. Interwoven into his current story are recollections of his past lives as a child (Niklaus Chase) raised by English parents (Catherine and Charles Chase) determined to integrate him into Nazi society until their mysterious arrest when he was thirteen, and later as a member of the English Republican Army (Alan Yardley) whose entire group, including his beloved Allison, was betrayed and killed, thus forcing him into hiding, both from the authorities and from his own people.

Meanwhile, Richard Traugutt, with the help of his beautiful, cold-blooded daughter Stefi, scrabbles relentlessly up the power ladder, working his way into ever more powerful positions, en route, carelessly toying with others' lives, such as the anonymous English prisoner he casually spares from death. He works his way into Berlin society, ingratiating himself to persons he considers useful, including Karl Vogel. Eventually it becomes clear that his single-minded drive for power is motivated and supported by something greater than Traugutt himself.

Throughout, a remnant of the Polish Home Army works from a "no-go" mountain area to maintain a culture, government, education system, and the other trappings of a normal society and at the same time prepare for the revolution which will one day free their land from occupation. Isolated and insular, their decades of resistance have cost them greatly as shown by the long-suffering Marysia Firlej, her alcoholic daughter Julia, her arrogant son Adam, his manipulative, but charming wife Zosia Król and Zosia's endlessly scheming father, Alex Przewalewski. Julia eventually falls victim to her fears and is murdered by the man she tries to blackmail: Karl Vogel, her one-time lover and the father of her child, Olek. The others work ceaselessly on trying to interest their American allies into taking greater action, only to meet with failure after failure as neither the American government nor the media are interested in the long-standing European question. Finally, the Partisans' lives are struck by tragedy with Adam's arrest and death in custody. Zosia is left alone with her young daughter, Joanna, hopelessly bereaved and more determined than ever to further her cause. Eventually she and her comrades agree that, more than anything, they need one person's story to touch America's heart, a "poster-child" who will personify all that is wrong with the Reich and will give them the opportunity to gain the sympathy of America's people and their money without government interference.

Zosia's hopes are ignited by the unexpected arrival of the desperate and forlorn English-speaking escapee, Peter Halifax, as he accidentally stumbles into their "no-go" zone in the mountains. Not only is his story a compelling tale of the injustices suffered in their land, but his physical resemblance to her late husband stirs a nebulous desire in Zosia of resurrecting Adam. Before she can use him, however, she must save his life, as accepting an unknown stranger into their midst presents an unacceptable risk to the other members of their encampment. Plotting with her mother-in-law Marysia, Zosia brings her captive forward to speak at a trial where he eloquently argues for his life and is granted a place in their Underground society.

Peter settles into his new home in the mountains called Szaflary and run by a council whose leader is an old Holocaust survivor named Katerina. He learns the history and structure of their secret state and eventually works as their cryptanalyst, aided by Julia's son Olek and a teenager named Barbara. Puzzling over an unofficial code, Peter uncovers a conspiracy which ties into information gathered separately by Richard's daughter Stefi. He also realizes, and finally admits, that he is hopelessly in love with Zosia, despite the fact that he is somewhat horrified to find out she is a highly skilled assassin. Though she does not discourage his affections, Zosia refrains from clarifying her own feelings.

In Berlin, Richard finalizes his plans for a promotion by assassinating a problematic rival. Upon his return home, he discovers that his sister Zosia has brought Peter to visit in order to get Richard's support for her idea of making him a spokesman and in order to prove Peter's trustworthiness. At this point it becomes clear to Peter that Zosia's mysterious brother Ryszard Przewalewski has infiltrated into the Reich's government as the ambitious Nazi official Richard Traugutt. Furious that after twenty years undercover, he has been exposed to such a senseless risk, Richard takes an instant dislike to Peter and withholds his support.

After returning to the encampment in the mountains, Peter uncovers more details of the conspiracy and learns that it involves a mass-sterilization program. He and Zosia are sent on a mission to ferret out the details in order to prevent the program from being enacted and to establish further proof of the regime's abuses of human rights. Their mission is successful, but complicated by a chance encounter with Karl Vogel on their return. Zosia saves Peter and in the confused relief and high emotion of their narrow escape, agrees to marry him.

It quickly becomes apparent to all but Peter that Zosia regrets her promise, but she marries him anyway in order to further integrate him into their group and even elicits a promise from him that he will, despite the painful psychological consequences, speak in America on their behalf. Not long afterwards, Peter discovers that he was one of the subjects tested in the initial stages of the sterility program. He and Zosia dispel their fears of the success of that test by establishing a pregnancy. No sooner does the dust settle from that, then Zosia learns that Peter had unwittingly fathered a child by Karl Vogel's wife, Elspeth. His claims, that it was fear rather than love which led him to give in to her demands for sex, do not sit well with Zosia and their already strained marriage is fractured even further.

Nevertheless, Zosia organizes a long visit to her brother Ryszard's (Richard Traugutt's) house in Berlin, where they arrange for Peter to meet his newly discovered baby daughter, Magdalena. Learning that the toddler is little more than the obligatory eighth child for the proper Nazi-Party wife that Elspeth Vogel is, Peter is heartbroken that he can do nothing to alter his daughter's lot in life. He abandons her again to take up his visit to America.

During this time, Richard has used his daughter Stefi to gain the Führer's interest and confidence. He has worked himself into a position of trusted advisor and uses the information that Peter and Zosia discovered about the sterility program to convince the Führer to shut it down and also to gain an edge on his competitor, Günter Schindler, who was directly involved in the now-problematic program. Schindler is less mindlessly cruel, but more cunning than the current Führer, and as the heir-apparent, presents an obvious danger for the future.

With a push from a producer whose family was forced to flee Germany decades before, Peter finally has his chance to present his story, in fluent

English, on American TV. He is an instant sensation and manages to stir up media interest, donations and a genuine political reaction in that America's isolationism is brought to question and the current scandal of a homosexual vice-president is overshadowed, at least temporarily, by a popular demand that the governments of the North American Union do not sign the Helsinki accords which would have accepted the de facto situation in Europe.

While in America, Peter meets his erstwhile boss from his days in the English Underground and learns that the betrayal which cost his friends their lives and which sent him into hiding and eventually into prison, was the fault of a high-ranking official in America. The fact that he had never been under suspicion and that his beloved Allison and all his friends had died due to nothing more than bureaucratic carelessness and a well-connected traitor stuns him and only his darling Joanna, Zosia's daughter and his adopted daughter, is able to comfort him. Eventually the media frenzy dies down, the public turns its attention elsewhere and Peter returns to the mountains and to anonymity with a sigh of relief.

Infuriated by the adverse publicity generated against the Reich in America, the Führer plans revenge, but is stymied by assurances that the unidentified traitor who spoke so freely on American television, would never return to the Reich. Nevertheless, Schindler, who was an acquaintance of Vogel, manages to identify the traitor via his connection to that household.

A visit to a nearby town, alone with his daughter Joanna, leads to disaster as Peter and Joanna are caught in a terrorist bomb blast. While hospitalized, he is identified and arrested. For his later amusement, the Führer has the torture of his nemesis videotaped and as an appetizer, he orders that Joanna be murdered in front of Peter. Peter is rescued, but it is too late to save Joanna. The existence of the videotaped murder comes to Richard's attention and he steals a copy and sends it to his father, Alex, in America. There it is publicized in order to re-ignite popular demands for action and to influence the American elections.

From Berlin, Richard covertly orchestrates a devastatingly asinine reaction from the Reich using Karl Vogel as his spokesman. With each unfortunate statement from Vogel, the American reaction only grows more vehement.

As a response to Peter's escape and the fact that he would now be sought in their region, the encampment council sends him to London, in the company of his starry-eyed young assistant Barbara, to carry out a simple mission of indefinite length. Peter views his assignment as punishment and the fact that Zosia will not accompany him as a statement of his being outcast. While in London, he visits the flat he once lived in just prior to it being torn down and discovers some diaries his mother had hidden in the wall. To some extent these clarify his parents' plans for him and why they were arrested when he was thirteen. He also meets an old lover, Jenny, and in the course of things, must disillusion Barbara of her puppy-love. Her reaction is vehement and she immediately picks up a boyfriend, named Mark.

Meanwhile Zosia is carefully carrying out a series of unauthorized executions of the men responsible for her daughter's death. Back in Berlin an undercover American agent is arrested and Richard is detailed to spring him. He has the agent released, only to have him followed to England and there enlists the help of Peter in trying to determine what is going on. Peter and Jenny discover that the agent unknowingly passed computer files on to Schindler's son, Wolf-Dietrich, but Stefi learns, while in bed with the Führer, that her father is in danger and Richard is forced to give up his investigations.

At the same time, Peter returns to the encampment for the birth of his child. He and Zosia have a fight and she, in reckless fury, takes off skiing through the mountains. Peter chases her down, only in time to learn that she is in labor. In the predawn air, an invasion is launched against the encampment. Ignoring the sounds of battle, Peter delivers the child in an abandoned cabin. He is forced to leave Zosia alone to seek out help. En route, he is attacked by a lone, bewildered soldier, and in self-defense knifes the boy to death. Shaken by his first killing, he makes his way to camp, only to be assigned to carry out a mission to infiltrate the enemy camp.

In Berlin, Richard desperately struggles to convince the Führer to give up his campaign, and after learning that his own son has been killed in the fighting, he has Stefi smuggled out of the mountains (where she is visiting) so that he can use her influence. By the time Stefi arrives, a truce has been declared, but she is put to work by her father finding out about Schindler's smuggled computer files and she manages to learn that they are located in a lab near London.

Peter succeeds in his mission in the enemy camp, even managing to free some prisoners and bypassing an opportunity to kill his erstwhile torturer. As he returns, he is dragooned into sniping and ends up killing dozens of nearly defenseless soldiers – putting yet more blood on his hands. He manages to return to Zosia and his newborn child, and once they have overcome the stress of the last several days, they make peace and Zosia makes it clear she wants Peter to remain at Szaflary. However, the Council and in particular Katerina have other plans and so, with a heavy heart, Peter returns to his assignment in London. There he discovers Barbara is pregnant with Mark's child and wants his help in accommodating their planned marriage. As a gesture of friendship, she organizes a meeting with Peter's brother, Erich, who once betrayed him and whom Peter has not seen since his parents' arrest. Erich proves to be self-absorbed and unrepentant and when Peter leaves, he is sufficiently disgusted that he carelessly walks into a mugging. He is rescued by a Nazi officer whom he, without hesitation, decides to kill, to avoid being arrested again.

Richard contacts Peter and together they inspect the laboratory where the computer files ostensibly are. They discover very little, and Richard returns to Berlin. Peter organizes an unauthorized infiltration of the laboratory, blackmailing his brother into helping him. He discovers the sterility program has been resurrected and there is American complicity. With the help of Richard, Peter returns to the mountains, uses the information to extort the encampment into allowing him to return and giving him a seat on the Council. During his negotiations with the Council, Peter realizes that it has been Zosia, all along, who has been manipulating him. She also admits that she has, despite her best attempts to the contrary, fallen in love with him. The revelations free him from his slavish devotion to her and they are able to start again as equals.

Richard is promoted yet again and fearful that Vogel will reveal Richard's meddling in the American fiasco, decides he must be dealt with. Richard incidentally learns that Vogel was responsible for the murder of his one-time love, Marysia's daughter, Julia, and decides he should be discreetly assassinated. Learning of this, Peter volunteers to carry out the assassination using the cover of being a disgruntled ex-slave. In exchange he demands that he be able to bring his daughter Magdalena back with him to the mountain encampment.

Zosia accompanies him to Berlin and together they execute the last survivor of Joanna's killers. The next night Peter confronts Elspeth and Karl Vogel in their bedroom, and with Elspeth's implicit permission, he kills Karl in cold blood. Finally rid of her sadistic husband, Elspeth verges on telling Peter she loves him, but instead chides him for refusing to accept his subordinate position in the world order. Peter humorously agrees and leaves the room, freed at last from his chains but feeling that with so much blood on his hands and his now almost casual attitude toward killing, he has indeed become less than human.

Table of Contents

Part I

Among the Living

*T*he first thing he did was wash the blood off his hands. The red-tinged water trickling rapidly down the drain should have raised strong emotions in him – revenge, joy, or even just satisfaction – but he felt none of those things. Instead he was preoccupied by a memory of how he had, long ago, washed his hands early every morning after returning from that horrible factory where he had been forced to work all night. Fetid fumes and mind-numbing exhaustion momentarily clouded his thoughts and his hands burned with remembered pain.

Five years, he thought, five years since he had been marched into the Vogel house by Karl and presented to Elspeth as her life-long servant. Well, Karl had been right – it had been a lifetime. Just not Peter's.

Peter shook his head in anger at the distraction. There was no time for such nonsense! He had to get Zosia and the child to safety before the police were alerted. He turned off the water and, drying his hands en route, went to the nursery. Zosia stood ready, a bag of supplies slung over her shoulder, the sleeping Magdalena in her arms. Peter motioned to her and together they went down the steps to the front door. He kissed her, whispering, "I love you."

"I love you, too."

They did not waste time on any further words. Peter opened the door, scanned the street and then ushered Zosia out. He stood there, in the dim light of the Vogel's hallway, watching as Zosia trod down the front path, holding the child close to her breast. She turned left at the street and walked the short distance along the road to the waiting taxi. As she climbed inside, he carefully shut the front door and breathed a prayer into the darkness.

There was still no sound from upstairs, Elspeth was keeping her word, waiting in silence next to a corpse.

He pulled a small tube out of his pocket and went to the hall mirror. He quickly spread the cream over his face and hands, then pulling out another tube, he squeezed a white substance onto his palms and ran his hands through his hair. The white settled unevenly, leaving streaks of brown here and there. He spent a few seconds getting the color right, combing his hair into an appropriate style and checking the back with a hand-held mirror, then he pulled out a bushy white moustache and carefully pressed it onto his upper lip.

He went into the kitchen and fixed a narrow, old-fashioned tie around his neck, grabbed the vest and the hunter-style sports jacket which he had left there, shrugged them on, and then put his coat over top of the ensemble. He pulled a hat on, then reached into the coat's pockets and exchanged one set of papers for another, placing the current set in his breast pocket and tucking the old set into a deep, buttoned pocket. He unfolded a pair of bifocals, put those on, slung a small travel bag over his shoulder, then hunching his shoulders slightly, he walked out the back door. He felt the cream on his face and hands drying as he strode through the back garden, and he squeezed his eyes shut, frowned, smiled and moved his face as he had been taught, in order to establish wrinkles in the appropriate places. By the time he walked out the back gate and into the alley, he had aged a good thirty-five years.

He glanced at his watch as he turned off the alley onto a side street. This was the most dangerous part: he was near the scene of the crime, it was a godawful hour and he would be recognized as a stranger by any wandering patrols. A restless guest of a neighbor was what they had settled on, a father-in-law driven to walk the streets at night by his unsettled sleep. He reached into his pocket and fingered his papers nervously; it would be better if they were not checked at all. If Elspeth kept her word, he would have about half an hour to put some distance between himself and the house. It would not be enough to get him out of Berlin – the city was too large, the exits too easily closed, the hour too unusual – but still it was more than he had banked on.

He had never expected it to be easy to leave Berlin after carrying out such a brazen crime, but he had not mentioned this concern to his colleagues. He had simply taken what he felt were the necessary precautions for their safety. If he was taken, then he would be beyond any help, and anyone associated with him would be lost as well. That was the reason he had insisted on making his way out of the city without help, that was the reason that Zosia had taken Madzia off alone. She would meet Tadek in a car some miles away, they would travel as a family with three other children, one of whom was Peter and Zosia's own daughter Irena, and with luck, the family group would not run into any trouble. The family of six with the tall, lean, dark-haired father would obviously have no connection to the infamous traitor and a kidnapped child. No connection at all.

Peter spared a mental thank-you to his friend Kamil who had allowed his two children to be used in such a manner and to Tadek for the risk he was taking. He felt fairly sure that Zosia and the children would get through to safety; what he wasn't sure of was whether or not he'd be able to escape Berlin once the alarm had been raised. Would the Führer be informed? What would happen to him if they caught him? The questions raised themselves without emotion. The strange coldness he had felt when he had looked at Karl's dead body remained with him as he contemplated his own possible fate. It didn't seem to matter, as long as he knew Zosia and the children were safe.

He reached the main street and turned to walk along it. So far so good, there was even some traffic on the road. He walked past the nearest station, it being far too small and the time being still far too early for there to be any trains, and headed to the next station. By the time he arrived, there were the beginnings of the commuter crowd assembling on the platform: not many people, just bus-drivers and kiosk owners making their way in to serve the morning commuters, but enough.

Despite having lived in Berlin for years, he had never been allowed to use public transit – other than one rather unsettling tram journey – and so now he was studiously casual as he bought and cancelled a ticket in the manner of a normal resident. Once he had the slip of paper in his pocket, he joined the waiting commuters and tried to maintain a semblance of calm and sleepy boredom.

The train from the suburbs got him into the city center just in time to miss a connection to the Ostbahnhof. As he paced nervously up and down the long, empty platform, a light breeze from the tunnel caused a fluttering noise overhead. Peter looked up to see a row of flags decorating the platform. The endless repetition of the red field with its white circle inscribed with a black swastika engendered a familiar dismay in him. God, what he would give to never again see a swastika! He tore his eyes away from the ubiquitous, hated symbol and glanced down at his watch – he would not arrive in time to take the train to Danzig. Well, that was not unexpected. He discreetly reached into his pocket and moved the Danzig train ticket into the lower, buttoned pocket and moved a train ticket to Posen into his breast pocket. Although it was the next possible train he could take after missing the Danzig one, the trains were so infrequent at this hour, that he would have plenty of time to catch it. Too much time, in fact.

At the Ostbahnhof, Peter checked that the Danzig train had indeed already left and then carefully discarded the ticket. He read the board and found the listing for the Posen train and walked to the beginning of that platform. There was no train there and no one was waiting yet. He turned on his heel and scanned the station: the unopened restaurant, the just-opened coffee shop, a dilapidated waiting room with some rather rough-looking men sprawled on the uncomfortable benches. Further along, a couple of policemen patrolled casually along the main hall, stopping to peruse the magazines displayed in the windows of the unopened kiosk. Peter looked up at the station clock. Forty-four minutes to go. It was very likely that by now Elspeth had reported his crime. The police would not take long to recognize the significance of her words and he did not doubt the Führer's office would soon be informed. After that, the Berlin-wide manhunt would be on: twelve million souls – six million males. Half of them adults? Three million men? If he estimated the total number of police or security personnel and the time it took to check each adult male on his way to work...The minute hand on the station clock jumped forward. One down, forty-three minutes to kill. If only he could manage to kill the time without it killing him.

2

*T*he ringing of the telephone was not unexpected, still it annoyed the hell out of Ryszard. He groaned and rolled out of bed, pulling on a robe and his alter ego with it. By the time he reached the hall, he was Richard Traugutt. His servant Leszek was waiting expectantly by the door of the office, but Richard did not even spare him a scowl. He fumbled in the dark with the lock, entered the room, picked up the receiver and growled, "Traugutt!"

The operator advised him to await the Führer and as he did, Richard rubbed the sleep from his eyes and motioned for Leszek to get him a cigarette and to make some coffee. He was in the middle of an expansive yawn when he heard the Führer's voice, "Richard! He's in Berlin!"

"Who?"

"That Englishman, that traitor, that, that, that..." The Führer stuttered in his fury over an appropriate epithet. "He's murdered that idiot Vogel! Right here, in Berlin, right under our noses!"

"Murdered? Vogel? *Who?*"

"That Halifax man! Damn him! Right under our noses!"

Richard groaned away the last of his sleepiness. "Why did he do that?" he wondered, as a last concession to confusion, then more cogently, he asked, "When?"

"Just this evening! He did it deliberately to spite me! That bastard!! Trying to humiliate me like that!"

"The Führer is too great to even notice the actions of such a flea," Richard soothed, rather cynically. "Now do tell me what has happened." He peered at the clock trying to see what time it was as the Führer briefly described the crime.

"...must be still within the city boundaries," the Führer was saying. "I've had them close all the city borders."

"You shouldn't do that. It will create panic."

"I don't give a damn about that!" the Führer snarled. "I want that bastard! How dare he! Trying to make a fool of me like that. In Berlin, announcing his presence for all to know about."

"That's the other reason you shouldn't close the borders," Richard explained patiently, suppressing a yawn. "We have never publicly admitted to this man or the damage he has done us. If we make a fuss now, it will get out that we are seeking only one man and the reason why will not take long to percolate through the population."

"Huh?"

"It will make you look bad, *mein Führer*. And besides, you have no idea what he's going to do. He might just sit tight for days. We can't close the city for days – or weeks." Richard ground out his cigarette and looked expectantly toward the hallway, wondering when his coffee would finally appear.

"Oh." The Führer paused a moment in thought. "Well, we'll just search the city for him. Go house to house."

"The *entire* city?" Richard tried hard to hide his impatience. God almighty, the country was being run by a spoiled adolescent! "*Mein Führer*, please consider the logistics." Richard spent some time convincing the Führer that it was impossible to close the city for days, that it was unwise to inspect every man on the street – after all, what were the police going to do, inspect each other? – that it was unlikely that Halifax would try to leave immediately after his criminal act. "He's not stupid, you know, I wouldn't even bother with public transit – he'll use a car, that's the only way to get out of the city quickly."

"Where would he get a car?"

"He stole Vogel's when he escaped from their house, he could always use that. The border guards and transit police should be on the alert for a Zil, *mein Führer*."

"Ah, good idea."

"And he's got a toddler with him. Surely that will make him easy to recognize."

"Oh, oh, yes."

"That was mentioned to the border guards, wasn't it? To look for a lone man with a lone female toddler?"

"Yes, of course!" The Führer paused as if thinking then added pensively, "I wonder why he stole the girl. That's weird, shows no respect for the family." Richard could almost hear the Führer shaking his head sadly. "Look, I need to see you. I need to discuss this further. Come into the office. No, come to my *Residenz.*"

Richard sighed silently, glancing at the clock again. Not yet five in the morning. "Yes, of course, *mein Führer.*"

"Is you daughter home?"

Richard paused as he considered the likelihood that Stefi's presence in the house had been registered by some observer. Deciding not to lie, he answered reluctantly, "Yes, she's here. I believe she has a very busy day scheduled…"

"Have her cancel it. I want to see her. Bring her with you."

"Yes, *mein Führer.*"

"Oh, and Richard? With this Vogel thing, I think you need a bodyguard."

"Security provides me with full protection anytime I make an official appearance."

"No, I mean someone in the house. I'm going to arrange full-time protection for you."

"No!" Richard blurted unintentionally. "I mean, yes, of course, *mein Führer*, I appreciate your concern, but, um, it's my wife. She suffers some terrible fears of strangers."

"It won't be a stranger – it will be someone I personally appoint!"

"*Mein Führer*, your concern for my welfare has touched me, but it is best if I arrange this for myself. If you give me the budget, I will be sure to arrange a round-the-clock bodyguard, as you have advised."

"Ordered."

"Yes, of course, *mein Führer*. As you command. I will see to it first thing tomorrow."

"Good. I'll see you in a few minutes."

Richard wearily accepted a cup of coffee from Leszek. A few minutes. Did Rudi have any concept of the city's geography? "Yes, *mein Führer*, immediately."

3

Zosia glanced back at the three children in the back seat of the car. Madzia slept peacefully cuddled up against Kamil's five-year-old son. The seven-year-old followed Zosia's gaze to his sleeping brother and the little girl, then glanced at Zosia and smiled indulgently as if to say, "Aren't they cute together?"

The car slowed as they approached the floodlit area of the Berlin border control. "Feign sleep," Zosia advised to the youngster, then she turned her attention back to Irena nestled in her arms. She undid the buttons of her blouse and placed Irena close to her breast, tickling her slightly to wake her up.

"Why are you doing that now?" Tadek sounded annoyed.

"They're less likely to ask me and the children to get out of the car." Zosia then added, quite unnecessarily, "Apparently nursing mothers make some men uneasy."

"They're not going to stop us," Tadek predicted confidently. "There hasn't been enough time."

Zosia twisted her arm to look at her watch. "It's been more than an hour, darling. Believe me, once Frau Vogel reports that crime, the reaction will be fast."

"I thought they've kept the whole thing secret."

"They have, but the local police are aware that Peter escaped from there – that alone will make him worth catching, and don't doubt the ability of gossip to get around. The bosses of that area will certainly be aware that he is important to the higher-ups, though they might not know why."

Tadek drove into the shortest queue and pulled out a cigarette.

"Don't light that! It will annoy the children. We don't want Madzia to wake up."

"Magdalena," Tadek corrected irritably. He put the cigarette back into his pocket and threw back his head. "How is it that I'm always risking my life getting your husband out of danger?"

"Because you are a wonderful, loyal, devoted friend."

"He never even thanked me for getting him out of their hands the last time."

"But I did," Zosia reminded him. "Besides, you were in on this decision. You agreed to this."

"On the assassination idea, yes, but I still think you should have just jumped in a car and driven away together."

"Maybe. But Peter was adamant that no one else should be associated with him."

"Yeah, I know. I guess I can understand, given how much the Führer loathes him. Still, I don't think this charade was necessary. They're not going to check that closely. This," Tadek waved at the queue, "is just the normal border controls."

"I don't think so." Zosia pointed to the car at the front of the queue. "Look."

They both watched as a border guard approached the car and opened the door. The driver stepped out, as he had apparently been instructed to do, and removed his coat and then rolled up his left sleeve. "Shit," Tadek swore as he saw how carefully the border guard inspected the man's arm.

Another two guards came out to the auto. One pushed a strange device which consisted of a mirror mounted at an angle at the bottom of a long handle and set on wheels. The guard rolled the mirror up to the edge of the car and in that manner inspected the undercarriage. The other guard rooted through the trunk of the car and then proceeded to turn up the back-seat bench and inspect under that.

Zosia bit her lower lip and said a quiet prayer. She glanced back at Magdalena. They had not taken the time to change her appearance. Would the border guards have a photograph? She glanced worriedly down at Irena as she snuggled against her mother's breast. What had seemed like a clever idea back at Szaflary now seemed like pure madness.

The wait took ages as each car and truck was carefully searched. Tadek put the car in neutral, turned off the engine and got out, as several others in the queue had already done. He lit a cigarette and leaned against the car, smoking nervously as Zosia huddled in her seat and anxiously stroked Irena's head. Periodically, Tadek reached inside to hold the steering wheel and leaned against the doorframe, inching the car forward.

Finally it was their turn. The border guard approached and asked for their papers. He scanned the back seat and the sleeping children, then asked Tadek to remove his coat. Tadek did so and then rolled up his sleeve as requested. "I've noticed you've done this to everyone," Tadek said conversationally. "What's going on? What are you looking for?"

"A camp escapee. He'd have a number tattooed onto his arm." The young man grabbed Tadek's wrist and gently turned his arm in order to inspect it. "You can put your coat back on, *mein Herr*. I apologize for the inconvenience."

"But why the fuss over one escapee?" They both turned to watch the other soldier go through the routine of inspecting the car's undercarriage.

The young guard sighed audibly. "If I knew things like that, *mein Herr*, I would not be working the graveyard shift." He glanced at the sleeping children again and at Zosia as she cuddled Irena close to her. "Done?" he asked his colleague. The other guard nodded. The young man turned and placed all the papers on a conveyor belt which ran along the strip of road and into a booth further on. "Please drive forward and when you reach the booth, they'll return your papers. Again, my apologies for the inconvenience and please extend my apologies to your wife."

"No problem. We are happy to do whatever is necessary to preserve the security of the Reich!"

Tadek climbed into the car and started it, driving forward the three or so meters that were free in front of him. Zosia could not take her eyes off the conveyor belt. The papers disappeared into a tube and all she could do was watch where she thought they should be. Would the soldier who checked them at the other end note the presence of a female toddler in the car? Would they stop the car at the booth and ask to see the little girl? Did they have a photograph of Magdalena? Did they have a photograph?

4

"**G**ood morning, Günter," Richard muttered as Schindler entered the Führer's foyer.

"Ach, so you've been dragged out of bed as well?" Schindler raised his arms helpfully as one of the Führer's personal guard frisked him.

Richard stood with his arms lazily aloft, trying to ignore the hands which slid down his pants leg in an all too familiar manner. "It seems there is another earth-shattering crisis."

Schindler caught Richard's eye and mouthed, "He's gone insane."

Richard tilted his head in confusion. Had he misread Schindler's words? But the look from his rival was sufficient to confirm that he had indeed read his lips correctly. So, the question was then, why the sudden friendliness? Why the risky confidence? Surely, by now, Schindler knew that Chandler's laboratory had been destroyed, surely he realized the sudden weakness of his position, but it was impossible that he knew how much Richard had in reserve to use against him. There had to be another reason. Richard bit his lower lip, not deigning to respond in any manner to this casual invitation to a conspiracy. The search was concluded and he lowered his arms and turned away to pace pensively.

"Ah, my dear comrades!" the Führer enthused, surprising them both by coming out to greet them. "Please forgive me for this rude interruption of your nights, but duty calls! Come, come into my study!" He turned and strode down the hall to his study, motioning for the two men to follow him.

Richard followed, chewing on his thoughts. Günter was right, Rudi did seem rather unstable anymore – not that he had ever impressed anyone as the most rational of people, but the Halifax affair had placed what may have been the last straw on the rather weak back of the Führer's sanity. It was for Schindler a good time to go on the attack, to drive the Führer ever further into indefensible actions, and clear the way for the next election of a Führer. Schindler would realize that it would be in Richard's interest as well to begin the long process of bringing the Führer down, but the timing for the two of them had to be substantially different. For Schindler, time was of the essence, he already had his well-established power-base and if anything, delaying further would only weaken him. On the other hand, it was still too early for Richard to grab power, he had not been in Berlin long enough and his power-base was not sufficiently broad. Schindler would be aware of these considerations and would therefore try to entice, or even push, Richard into being his ally. Thus his observation in the hallway. Did he really believe Richard was that stupid? Or did he think that the prospect of power would be too alluring for Richard to adhere to his cautious approach? Maybe he thought...

"Richard, are you even listening to me?" The Führer raised an eyebrow inquisitively.

"I'm sorry, *mein Führer*. I have a headache. I, I'm sorry."

"Well, where is she?"

Richard glanced from the Führer's to Schindler's face and back again. Who? Oh, of course. "My sincerest apologies, but I was unable to wake her up. She must have come back late last night. I..." Richard stopped, realizing his mistake. Where had she been? The Führer would want to know. With whom? "I mean, I think she stayed up reading or something. I don't know, I went to bed early. Anyway, I knew you were in a hurry to see me, so I didn't waste time trying to..."

"Waste time?" The Führer's question dripped with sarcasm.

Richard noticed how avidly Schindler was watching their interchange. Well, if it wasn't already known, it was obvious now that Stefi had a so-called "special relationship" with the Führer. "I do apologize. I'm sure my daughter will visit later, whenever you have time today. Just let me know and I'll send her..." He stopped again. The Führer was turning red, clearly angry at the implication that somehow Stefi would see visiting him as a duty. Richard tried again, "She's been..." He stopped to push his hair back off his forehead. He did have a headache and it was only getting worse. "Have the border guards found Halifax yet?"

Schindler snorted. "I heard you advised they only check the transit routes and only stop lone men with toddlers. I've countermanded that – all transit will be searched and all men, regardless of age or companions."

"That's unfeasible," Richard countered. "It will make us look..."

"We are the power here!" Schindler slammed his fist against a table. "Do you want to make the Führer look weak? Afraid of his own people? It is a security matter and all loyal subjects will be happy to oblige the security forces in whatever manner is necessary!!"

Richard offered cigarettes around and lit the Führer's. "Günter," he soothed, "the dignity of the Führer can hardly be under assault from one tiny insect. We'll swat this Englishman in due time, but it would hardly seem appropriate for the entire security apparatus to be seen dancing around the Reich, waving its arms in defense against a single pesky gnat."

"He marched into the center of Berlin and murdered an official of the Führer!"

Richard lit Schindler's cigarette. "He took revenge on a man who had personally tormented him."

"He has issued a direct, personal challenge to the Führer!"

"He satisfied a private vendetta." Richard calmly lit his own cigarette.

"The Führer's dignity..."

"You two talk about me," the Führer interrupted, "as if I weren't even here."

"*Mein Führer*! It is only that..."

"I'm worried by the security implications," the Führer interrupted again. "I care about my people. You, Günter, your new bodyguards will be joining your team tomorrow. And you, Richard, you're going to arrange someone?"

"Yes, of course..."

"Arrange someone?" Schindler pulled a face. "*Mein Führer*, does our dear Colonel Traugutt not trust your selection of a bodyguard?"

Richard's eyes widened with anger. Clearly Schindler was taking his revenge for Richard's refusal to draw the Führer deeper into a chaotic and publicly disastrous response to Halifax's sudden, unexpected appearance in Berlin. Schindler must have felt it was a gift from God, and here Richard was, blowing the calm voice of reason into the carefully worked-up storm of insanity.

The Führer primly pursed his lips. "It would seem so."

"*Mein Führer*," Richard pleaded, "As I said, my wife..."

"Your wife is as loyal as any good citizen, is she not?" Günter asked snidely. "She trusts the Führer with her life, does she not?"

"Of course," Richard snarled, "Still, I think it advisable..."

The Führer was shaking his head. "Günter's right. I can have someone in your office by tomorrow noon. Hell, I can send one of my men over to you tonight! It's silly your wasting time searching someone out when I have my entire trusted retinue at my disposal. In fact, I'll send Mathias back with you tonight. He's the tall one, out in the hall. He'll stay with you twenty-four hours a day. You'll have to arrange some sort of sleeping arrangements in your house, can you do that?"

Richard had to swallow several times before he could answer. Saying "no", he was sure, would only cause the Führer to arrange some housing for him as well – move into the *Residenz* or something horrid like that, so he finally managed to stammer his agreement. "Yes, *mein Führer*, of course. Thank you, *mein Führer*. I am honored by your concern. Truly honored." He glared at Günter as he said that and was presented with an evil, triumphant smile in return.

5

*E*ight minutes to go. His papers had been checked twice, but the security was rather casual, as if routine. Peter downed the last of the ersatz coffee, thanked the waitress for her conversation, and stood to pull on his overcoat. From his vantage point, he could see the train was still not at the platform; nevertheless, the station was beginning to come to life and he felt he could wait on the platform without drawing undue attention to himself.

As he walked along the strip of concrete toward some benches, two young soldiers approached. He cursed and stopped walking so that he could be seen to be cooperative. Suddenly the soldiers' eyes lit up and they veered away from him. Peter turned to see what had drawn their sudden interest. A young man with a little girl, probably three or four years old, was only a short distance behind him. The man stopped in his tracks and awaited the patrol with a resigned expression.

"Not again!" the man lamented as the soldiers came up to him. Without being asked, the man pushed up his sleeve and showed them his left arm. "Look! Nothing! I'm not whoever you're looking for."

Peter's heartbeat quickened as he watched the soldiers inspect the man's arm, but he did not move.

"Your papers?"

The man handed them over wearily. "Exactly how many times do I have to put up with this nonsense?"

"Sorry, *mein Herr*. Orders."

"Orders? Sorry? Harassing citizens on the street! Enough already! You should be out preventing crime or defending our Reich!"

The soldiers looked at each other and seemed to come to some mutual agreement. "Suspicious actions," one stated as he reached for a pair of handcuffs on his belt.

"No! Don't! I'm sorry." The man backed away, waving his hands. The little girl stepped backwards with him, though she looked unperturbed.

"Resisting arrest?" The other soldier reached forward and grabbed the man's arm.

"No! Don't! Please! My daughter!"

The soldiers glanced at the little girl. "Don't worry, it will be an adventure for her."

"We'll let you call her mother from the station. Come along now, don't make trouble. You're already in it deep enough." And with that the two soldiers led away the quietly protesting man and his little girl.

With feigned casualness, Peter turned his eyes away and looked down the track. The train was approaching. It came into the station with a huff of noise and bustle that seemed to overwhelm the aura of fear left by the little scene. As the train stopped, the conductors pushed down the windows of the doors, reached outside the door and used a little key to unlock it from the outside. Then they leaned further forward and turned the handle, swinging the door out and open.

Peter waited nervously as the carriages disgorged their passengers, constantly glancing down the platform to see if more soldiers or police would return, but none did. If only he could manage to board the train, then he'd be clear. After what seemed an eternity, the new passengers began to board. Once the political and military élite had climbed on and settled in and their servants had re-emerged to await their turn, Peter joined the queue to board with the other ordinary citizens. Behind the queue, the various lower castes – subjects, *Gastarbeiter*, apprentices, *Zwangsarbeiter*, and so on, all mingled in their separate groups, waiting their turns.

The queue moved slowly, but at last Peter reached the door. He showed his ticket to the conductor, along with his papers, and was allowed onto the train. Sighing with relief, he settled into his seat and stared out the window. He was safe now – though they were clearly seeking him, he had passed the hurdle of getting on the train. He had made it out of Berlin.

The train came to a stop in Frankfurt am Oder. Seized by a momentary panic, Peter wondered if he should jump out and put some distance between himself and anything to do with Berlin. On the other hand, in a short while they would be crossing out of the Altreich and into territory where there was a substantial A.K. presence. If he could get as far as Posen, he had tickets ready for the next leg of his journey, he would be almost home. Stick to the plan, his training told him, and he decided to obey the diktat. It had been thrown together hastily, that was true, but it only made sense to stick to the plan.

The train chugged out of the station and he settled into his seat, letting the clacking of the wheels soothe him. Out the window the character of the landscape changed as the train left the Altreich and entered the colonial territories.

The compartment door was opened and a border guard entered. "Papers and tickets," he announced in a bored monotone. The woman near the door handed hers over. The guard inspected her papers and handed them back to her without comment. He then turned to the man next to her. After inspecting the man's papers, though, he did not turn around to inspect Peter's. Instead he politely requested to see the man's left arm.

The man obediently removed his jacket. "What's going on?"

The guard shrugged. "Orders, *mein Herr*. Your arm, please."

Peter stood and, excusing himself, tried to edge past the guard to get out the compartment door.

"Where are you going?"

"Toilet. If you'll excuse me…"

"Please wait, *mein Herr*. I'll be done in a moment."

"Can't!" Peter tried to shoulder his way past the guard.

"*Mein Herr*…"

"Look, there's my bag. I'll be right back. Wait 'til you're old, sonny. You'll understand. Now let me out or you'll have an embarrassing mess to explain!" Peter finally succeeded in squeezing between the guard and the seats.

The guard gestured in exasperation toward him, but did not pursue him. Peter strode down the passage as fast as was seemly and at the end of the carriage turned toward the toilet compartment. He glanced back, saw the guard was not pursuing him and went into the next carriage. He stopped dead as he saw another border guard proceeding along the passage. He glanced back the way he had come and then forward. They were closing in on him.

With a confidence he did not feel, he marched down the passage as the border guard ducked into a compartment. But as he tried to pass the compartment, the guard stepped out, "Hey, you! Where are you going?"

"I'm just looking for a restaurant car." Peter pointed innocently down the aisle.

"Stay put. I have to check your papers before you can go further."

Peter waited a moment there in the aisle as the guard finished with one of the passengers in the compartment. He shifted slightly in the direction he had been heading, but the guard looked up and growled, "I said wait! I'll check you next."

"Sorry, *mein Herr*." Peter glanced back down the way he had come. "Look, I'll just go back to my seat." Without waiting for an answer, he strode back down the passage toward his carriage. He stopped in the space between the two carriages and paused to consider his options. He had about two minutes before one or the other border guard would reach him.

He turned back into the carriage he had originally come from and stopped by the toilet, out of sight of the aisle and near the external door. There was, as he expected, no handle or lock on the inside – the door was only meant to be opened when the train was at a stop, and from the outside, as the conductors had done in the station. Peter pushed the window down and leaned out. The wind buffeted his face. The train was moving fast, it would be a lousy place to leap out. Swearing quietly, he reached for the handle located halfway down the door. He had to stretch his arm and the wind buffeted him painfully, but finally he managed to grasp the handle. It did not give way. He felt a bit higher with his fingers. A simple hex lock. He reached into his jacket and pulled out his switch blade, opened it and again reached out the window. With an effort, he managed to turn the lock. He pocketed the knife, reached back out and grasped the handle. He could turn it, but it was so far down, he had to have his full weight pressed against the door. Once he turned the handle, it would open under his weight, and given the direction that the carriage was moving, the wind would catch the door and slam it open, probably smashing it and his arms into the carriage's side. Could he let go fast enough and draw his arm through the window to drop to safety before that happened? Probably not.

Peter hesitated. Was there some other way out? He should have stayed in Berlin, should have had someone drive him out of the city, should have…He swallowed, reached out the window with both arms, the right one grasping the handle, the fingers of his left dug into the lower edge of the window in an attempt to find a good hold, his full weight pressed uncomfortably against the door. He glanced down at the earth flying past below – a steep slope covered in long grass, stones and the occasional bush. It would be a nasty landing. He turned his face into the wind in order to glance ahead. No bridges, no tunnels, but also no better prospects immediately ahead. Taking a deep breath, he turned the handle. The door fell open under his weight, then the wind caught it and he went flying in an arc and slammed violently into the side of the carriage. He felt his right arm crush against the steel sides of the carriage, but his scream of pain was lost in the wind. He let his fingers scrape up along the surface of the door and held himself there for a moment as he braced his legs against the door. Once he was in position, he pushed backward with all the force he could muster so as to avoid being sucked underneath the crushing wheels, and threw himself off the door, twisting as he went to try to land on his hands and feet rather than his back.

The ground met his left shoulder, throwing him back into the air with the impact and sending him tumbling out of control down the slope. He kept his eyes shut, his arms protectively over his head as his body was thrown like a rag doll down the rock-strewn hill, battered and struck and repeatedly bounced. When the dizzying motion finally stopped, he pried his eyes open, blinked away the blood, and stared, unmoving, at the bright dawn sunlight streaming through the black branches of a bush into which his face seemed to be pressed. He moaned and closed his eyes.

6

"*W*hat do you mean, lost?" Zosia screeched over the din. She turned toward Magdalena, "Please! Be quiet!" then looking down at Irena, added, "Oh for heaven's sake, hush!"

Marysia picked up Madzia as Zosia cuddled Irena, but neither stopped wailing. "I said," Marysia shouted into Zosia's ear, "he's gone missing! He didn't show up in any of the destination cities!"

"Did he only have three tickets?" Zosia yelled in return. She tried pressing Irena to her breast, but the baby was uninterested in doing anything other than howling.

"Yes! He couldn't have taken any other intercity trains – at least he didn't have the tickets for them." Marysia reached around to feel Madzia's backside, but that wasn't the problem. "Have you fed her?"

Zosia shook her head. "She doesn't want to eat. I think she's just scared. I guess she doesn't remember me." She shifted Irena in her arms. "And this one is just cranky!"

In desperation, Marysia held Madzia a foot in front of her and begin to spin around. Madzia immediately ceased crying and stared in wonder as the world whirled around her. Marysia stopped spinning. She backed carefully toward the chair and sat down heavily. "Oof! I'm not as young as I used to be."

As if in solidarity, Irena suddenly stopped crying. Zosia stared at the baby, stunned by the abrupt silence. "How did you know that would work?" Madzia was still dizzily staring at the ceiling.

"Oh, I didn't. But Adam always used to like it."

Madzia brought her eyes down from the ceiling and looked into Marysia's face. She reached forward and touched Marysia's nose. "Nose," she giggled.

Marysia smiled and touched Madzia's nose. "Yes! Nose! Nose!" Marysia agreed in German. She studied the little girl, then switching back to Polish, said, "So this is Peter's daughter."

"One of them. Do you think it's possible that the spotters missed Peter at one of those stations? I mean, they were supposed to keep their distance, weren't they?"

"Yes, that's possible. But he should have made it to Neu Sandez by now. There's been no word."

Zosia set Irena down on her thick blanket on the floor. She placed a toy in front of the baby and watched to see if she would grab it. "What should we do? Should we look for him?"

"I don't see how." Marysia let Madzia slip off her lap.

The little girl toddled over to the baby. She pointed at Irena. "Baby!"

"Yes, baby," Zosia echoed dimly. She handed Madzia a rattle and watched as she sat down with it and began turning it over in her hands. Who would have thought that their simple plan would grow so complicated? Madzia banged the rattle against the blanket and giggled. Who would have thought that the Führer would go so far? Zosia reached out and caught the rattle as Madzia hammered it down toward Irena's head. "No, no," she chided gently. "No hit." She shook the rattle and then handed it back to Madzia. "Maybe he saw the fuss being raised and decided to lay low in Berlin. Maybe he took refuge in the pension."

"Maybe," Marysia responded unconvincingly. She sat back in the chair and sighed heavily. "So how did your return trip go?"

"Oh, nerve-wracking, but uneventful."

"I can't believe what they're doing, searching every man in Berlin! Who would have thought the Führer would go so far in looking for Peter?"

"Peter did."

"Really? You didn't tell me that when we drew up the plans."

"He only mentioned it as we left Ryszard's to head to the Vogel's house. I thought he was being a bit paranoid – I had no idea the Führer was such a nut case." Zosia wrinkled her nose at that. "I mean, not in that way."

Marysia nodded her understanding.

"No, Madzia! No hitting! Here." Zosia pulled the rattle away from Madzia. "Here's a nice soft toy. See? Squeeze it."

"You're going to have to find some toys suited to her age."

"And teach her how to be around a baby."

"Yes, I guess she's not used to anyone younger than her being around."

19

"She's not used to much at all." Zosia reached forward and stroked Madzia's cheek. "Elspeth had her cared for by so many strangers, I doubt she'll even miss her mother."

"Mama?" Madzia looked around.

"Here, Mama." Zosia patted her chest.

"No! Nanny!"

"No, Mama." Zosia corrected kindly. "Here's your Mama, honey. Here." She gently grabbed Madzia's hand and placed it on her chest. "Here, Mama."

"Mama?" Madzia pressed herself into Zosia's arms.

"Yes, Mama. I'm your Mama now, honey. I'll take care of you." Zosia stifled a sob as she wondered if she would be the only one. She stroked Madzia's head and held her close. "What about the other information Peter presented to the Council?" she asked suddenly, trying to turn her thoughts away from being left alone yet again. Not now! Not after finally giving in to her urges and letting herself love him. For God's sake, not now!

"We're still working on that. Preliminary indications are that we now have the only copy of the formulae. Schindler was keeping it secret enough that it looks like everything was in that London lab that Peter destroyed."

"Just Schindler? Or was the Führer involved?"

"Don't know yet – we're working on that. We're also having our chemists look at the papers Peter stole to see if they really do contain a workable sterilization formula, and if so, to come up with an appropriate response, just in case there is a copy floating around in Nazi hands. And of course, we know there must be a duplicate of this information in the NAU, so if Schindler's contact still exists, he might be able to get his hands on it again."

"If he can afford it. I imagine the first copy cost a pretty penny." Madzia pulled back from Zosia's embrace and grabbed Zosia's nose, twisting it in her hands.

"Yes, hopefully he or the Führer bankrupted themselves on this."

"What about Peter's brother, Erich? Did anyone contact him?" Zosia gently removed Madzia's hand from her nose.

"He indicated that he preferred not to be involved. Do you think Peter will be disappointed?"

"Disappointed? Maybe. Surprised?" Zosia shook her head. "He said he hoped Erich would do something voluntarily, but that his brother lacked a backbone. He also said we should feel free to blackmail Erich if we have need of him."

Once again Madzia grabbed Zosia's nose. "Nose!"

"We might just do that."

20

"Ouch!" Zosia yelped. "Don't do that!" She pulled Madzia's hand away from her nose and cast about for a worthy toy substitute. "Here! Tweak this." She handed Madzia a rag doll.

Marysia smiled fondly at Zosia. By the time Joanna had reached two, Zosia and Adam had pretty much depended on her to take care of the little girl. She had done so gladly, missing the days when Adam and Julia had been small. But now she just no longer had the time, and with the passing years, she had just that little bit less energy as well. It was a difficult time for Zosia – an unfamiliar two-year-old, a demanding baby, a new and as yet undefined relationship with her husband. She wondered how Zosia would handle it.

Fearful that she might get roped into helping, Marysia stood. "There's a lot to do sorting through all the information Peter brought back, and then there's all the re-organizations necessary now that you've quit and he's joined the Council. I have to put together the application for his candidacy and for his promotion to Major. And we're still having trouble with the supply lines as well. I meant to have you work on that – get the funds and transfer them to the appropriate parties so that we can get some decent food up here. I know you want to spend time with the kids, but are you willing to handle that? You're the best we have when it comes to hacking..."

"Yes, of course, I'll do it," Zosia agreed tiredly. "Tell me, have you taken any action on that leak in the NAU yet?"

"No." Marysia sounded hesitant. "Not yet."

"Any idea who it is?"

"None yet. That'll probably have to wait until after we inform the Americans of the leak." Without interrupting herself Marysia headed to the door. "We can't go poking around their security services without a reason, but we certainly don't want to give away our reasons without constructing a good quid pro quo situation first." She stopped at the door and turned to give Zosia a wink. "Like comedy, it's all a matter of timing."

"Of course," Zosia answered distantly.

"We'll have to see what's to be done with this Underground Railroad idea of Peter's, as well. Once he gets back."

"Yes, once he gets back," Zosia repeated almost as a prayer.

7

*L*eszek saw Ryszard approaching the house and opened the door to greet him deferentially. As Leszek took his coat, Ryszard wearily turned toward the man who had followed him in. "Mathias, this is Lech, he's one of my servants." Ryszard turned back to Leszek. "Leszek, this is Mat–, Herr..." He stopped and turned back to Mathias. "What is your name, anyway?"

"Engel."

"Ach, how appropriate," Ryszard commented grimly. "My guardian angel." He turned his attention back to Leszek, "This is Herr Engel. He is to be my bodyguard and will live with us." He saw the look in Leszek's eyes, but did not react. "You are to follow his orders and serve him, in so far as that does not interfere with your other duties. Understood?" Ryszard raised his eyebrows to emphasize the question.

Leszek brought his expression under control. "Understood, *mein Herr.*" After hanging up Ryszard's coat, he took Herr Engel's and then offered both men cigarettes.

Mathias refused his. "Not while I'm on duty."

Ryszard looked confused. "I thought you were always on duty?"

"Oh, for now, yes, but eventually, I'm sure the Führer will assign someone to join me, so that we can take sleeping in turns, and the like."

"Oh, I'm sure that won't be necessary," Ryszard said, for no obvious reason. His bodyguard would not be the one to make such decisions.

"I beg to differ, *mein Herr.* It is necessary. Herr Vogel was murdered in his own house, in his sleep. It will be necessary for one of us to stay with you at all times – even as you sleep."

"As I sleep?" Ryszard asked in horror.

"Führer's orders, *mein Herr.*"

"Of course," Ryszard sighed. "Of course." He rubbed his eyes wearily. Oh God, who needed to die? He knew what hell was! He felt utterly miserable, his head ached, his whole body felt uneasy with having had too little sleep, and he had no idea when he would be rid of the Führer's stooge! *Damn Schindler, damn him to hell!*

He felt Leszek's hands on his shoulders, massaging his muscles. "Does that help, *mein Herr*?"

Even Leszek pities me! God, I am in hell! "Yes, yes that helps," Ryszard murmured. As he relaxed under Leszek's soothing hands, Kasia came down the steps. She saw the trio of men and raised her eyebrows questioningly.

Ryszard explained the situation, and to her credit, Kasia managed to ask in an appropriately stunned voice, "Karl Vogel was murdered? Oh, my, poor Elspeth!" She sat heavily on the steps, unable to take it all in. "Murdered," she repeated, shaking her head in disbelief. "Murdered by his..., by that...Who would have thought...In our society...Like America." She looked up suddenly at Ryszard, clearly distraught. "Yes, yes, I understand the Führer's concern. Oh, it is unbelievably kind of him to arrange something so quickly. And yes, of course, you must be guarded even as you sleep. Clearly there is danger everywhere."

Ryszard nodded disconsolately. As hard as it would be on his family, Kasia and Leszek and all the others would be free as soon as he left the house in the morning. All but he! He was condemned to this personal hell for twenty-four hours a day, seven days a week. He ordered Leszek to get him some coffee and retreated into the sitting room with his wife. As he saw Mathias take up a position by the door, Ryszard was driven to ask, "Don't you want to go to your home and collect some belongings or something?"

"I was told my things would be sent this afternoon."

Ryszard nodded. He remembered something Peter had told him about living a lie day in and day out. Well, his brother-in-law had managed nearly four years before becoming suicidal. He supposed he could take some inspiration from that. Of course, Ryszard thought, Peter was completely deranged as a result. *That* was rather less comforting.

8

"**D**ad! Dad! Wake-up, Dad!" Joanna's sweet voice prodded him.

He opened his eyes and looked at her. She looked clearer than ever. No wings either. Just Joanna, sitting on the ground in front of him, smiling welcomingly. He was so pleased to see her! "You've decided to visit me?"

"No! You've come to me!"

He frowned in confusion and looked around, but there was nothing. Joanna stood out incongruously in the darkness, as though lit by some unseen source, or as if she were her own source of light. "Joanna, why can't I see anything but you?"

"That's your choice, Dad."

He shook his head. "I don't believe in an after-life."

"Well, that's silly, isn't it?" Joanna seemed as self-assured as when she convinced him that smoking was silly.

"No, honey. You're just a figment of my imagination. I invoke you, apparently whenever I'm under some stress..."

She looked hurt.

"I'm sorry, sweetheart. Look, even if I believed there was an after-life, don't you think it would be impossible for someone like me to make the transition? It must be a phenomenal transformation that takes place – much more profound than being born, don't you think? It's physics beyond normal understanding."

"Like inhabiting one of those extra dimensions you tell Mom about?"

"Well…"

"Or merging your wave function into the vast energy density of the vacuum?"

"Joanna…"

"The spirit – that which makes you human – could dissociate itself from the corporeal *you* and interact with other freed waves to form some coherent field that–"

"Now you're making fun of me."

"No, I'm not. I'm just trying to express the transition to the after-life as a mathematically consistent physical theory. That's the only thing you believe in, isn't it?"

"Joanna, whatever the after-life is – if it is – don't you think that belief would be what the soul needs to make that quantum leap? You could do it, but I don't have that strength, honey. I won't be able to make that leap."

"Does the fetus believe in the outside world?" Joanna asked. "Does the fetus understand the physics of walking in the light?" Tears began to roll down her cheeks, as if she knew she was losing him.

"You're wise beyond your years."

"I'm allowed to be." She wiped away her tears.

"Besides," he argued, while at the same time wondering why he felt the need to debate a figment of his imagination, "if there is an after-life, it can't be like this. It can't be just some sort of extension of what went before. That would be too…"

"Difficult?"

"Unfair."

"What's unfair?" a voice asked.

"You're fading," Joanna moaned.

That was strange, that should have been his line. "You're as clear as ever." He looked around. "Where are the others? Where's Allison? Where are my parents? Where's my grandmother? And my sister? And all my friends?"

"Waiting," Joanna answered. "But first the darkness in your mind has to subside."

"No, this is not possible…" he moaned, turning his head to try to see some source of light other than Joanna.

"Don't move," a voice advised, "You'll hurt yourself."

He ignored the voice. "They're not waiting, Joanna! There is no after-life!"

"I'll wait for you," Joanna cried softly.

"Here, drink this," the voice suggested.

He felt his head being lifted and something pressed against his lips. He took a sip. It was water. He opened his eyes and saw a young girl with stringy brown hair looking at him. Maybe fourteen.

"Where am I?" The light was dim, but he could make out that he was on the floor of a low-roofed hovel. The smell of animals was almost overpowering.

"You're safe. But don't move, you've hurt yourself."

He could feel the throbbing throughout his body, but mostly in his right arm. He tried to flex the fingers of his right hand, but a sharp pain warned him against such folly.

"Stay here. I'll be right back." The girl gently set his head back down and stood. He could see she was dressed in ragged clothing, like the workers he had seen walking along the road years ago when he had first fled Berlin. Berlin? *Berlin!* Oh, God, the train!

She must have seen the panic in his expression because she knelt back down beside him rather than leaving, and stroked his forehead. She turned her head toward the door and yelled out, *"Tatusiu!"*

Two men entered the hovel, one looked to be the girl's father, the other was slightly better dressed and had the air of a visitor. The father spoke to the girl in a rapid Polish which Peter could not follow, though he was reassured by the language. As the girl answered the father's questions, the stranger stooped down beside Peter and asked in German, "How do you feel?"

"I'm alright, I think. Are you a doctor?"

"You could say that." The man tilted his head as if trying to decide something. "The police are looking for you."

With his left hand, Peter reached up to his face. It was smooth, the moustache was gone.

The doctor watched his action with interest. "We've scrubbed that stuff off your face. They're looking for an old man, an assumed smuggler, I gather."

The father spoke up at last. "But you're not carrying anything, are you?"

"We've searched you." The girl blushed as she said that.

Not too thoroughly, Peter thought, as he glanced down at his clothing. Probably frisked him for diamonds or drugs.

The doctor stood up. "So who are you? Why are you jumping off speeding trains? Why are you carrying two sets of papers, a gun, a stiletto?"

"Could I have some water?"

They helped him into a sitting position and gave him some water. After he had drunk a bit, he said, "Look, I want to tell you immediately, if you're found in my company, you're as good as dead."

The doctor sniffed. "We figured as much."

"Your families will be endangered, too."

"So what do you suggest we do?" the girl asked tartly, "Put you back out in that field?"

Peter shook his head. "No, I appreciate your help. I want to thank you, I just–"

"Don't worry about us." The father gestured broadly around the stinking hovel, "This is our life here, we're not risking all that much."

"What is that smell?"

"Oh, the animals. We're adjacent to the barn here. Seems we're not fit to live with the pigs." The father laughed at his little joke. He nodded in the direction of the door. "The big house is some ways away – don't worry, they don't come by very often – seems that it's a bit muddy and smelly for them."

"So you tend the animals for an estate?" The pain in Peter's arm worsened and he gasped involuntarily.

"Not so much an estate, just a big farm. Used to belong to my grandfather. When they started clearing the land, my grandfather handed everything over to his German neighbor, that way it wasn't confiscated by the authorities. In exchange, we got to stay on the land."

"As serfs," his daughter added.

The father shrugged. "Eh, easy come, easy go."

"How do you know the police are looking for me?" Peter motioned for the water and drank some more, trying to drown an urge to groan as the pain in his right arm intensified.

"Oh, my wife serves up at the house. She was there when the police came around asking if anyone had seen anything. Seems they knew you left the train between here and Posen, but they didn't know exactly where. Lucky for you, Jana here," he jerked his thumb at his daughter, "actually saw you leap off that train."

"Some feat!" Jana marveled.

"That's a hell of a way to fare-dodge," the father commented.

"You've broken your arm," the doctor stated, as if in contradiction. "With your help, I'll set it, but I don't have anything sturdy enough to make a cast." He paused and considered Peter as if unsure what to say next.

Twigs and rags, Peter thought, but he knew that was not the answer they were looking for. "Use this." He offered up his left arm. "Use the cast on this arm. It unclasps easily."

26

The doctor stooped down again and pushed up Peter's sleeve so he could see the cast. "We were wondering…"

Without thinking Peter tried to reach for the cast to remove it, but he quickly recognized his mistake. "Take it off, you'll see why it's there."

The doctor removed the cast and all three of them stared at the numbers on his arm. "That still doesn't explain…" the father began.

"No, it doesn't explain anything. But don't be surprised, if in a little while, the police make another visit, looking for someone fitting my description."

The doctor nodded, as if he had expected that.

"You've clearly been well set-up," the father commented thoughtfully. He turned to his daughter, "Jana, get him some food, he must be hungry." Turning back to Peter, he continued, "So why are you on your own?"

Peter smiled wanly. "I'm a dangerous person to be with, easily identified, too. I didn't want to risk anyone else's life."

Jana looked up from the table, where she was cutting some bread. "That's silly! A person always needs help in this world!"

Peter nodded. "Once I got on that train, I thought I was safe. I didn't think it would go this far." None of us did, he added to himself. And what of Zosia? and Irena? and Magdalena?

The doctor looked up at the father and then back down at Peter. "That train was coming out of Berlin. Do you have anything to do with what's going on there?"

"What is going on?"

The doctor shook his head. "I'm not really sure. We've just heard there have been massive traffic jams, roadblocks, police all over, random searches. The whole city is being turned inside-out. At least, that's what the cop said – the one who came by looking for the smuggler. He said the train personnel told him that the smuggler apparently panicked when they started searching the train, as part of this huge effort."

Peter leaned back against the wall and closed his eyes. "Ah, yes, that would be me."

The doctor ran his hand expertly along Peter's right arm, feeling the damage. "You need to get out of here then. They might guess you were the smuggler."

"Yes, they might." Peter could think of nothing more cogent to offer than that. He really had no idea what he should do next. He was in no shape to make his way on his own.

The father looked down at Peter sympathetically. "What do you want us to do?"

Peter sighed. "Can you get me in touch with the A.K.? I need help."

27

"Hey! Over here." Jana paced away a few meters and looked expectantly at the men. They joined her and the three conferred quietly.

Peter watched them as their conversation became heated, as it turned into an argument. Were they planning on betraying him? He'd be worth lots of money, they might be able to buy themselves a decent life. "You know," he called out to them, "if you turn me in, they'll arrest you all. You won't get any reward – no matter what they say."

The three of them looked at him. Jana smiled. "That's not what we're discussing." She turned back to the two men. "It's my decision," she said with finality. The two men looked at each other, the doctor shrugged helplessly, the father nodded sadly.

They approached him and the father spoke, "We'll get you in touch with the A.K. and help them to get you out of here, on one condition."

"What's that?"

"My daughter goes with you."

Peter shook his head. "Didn't you listen to me? With anyone but me! Christ, don't you know what they'll do to her if we're caught?"

"And don't you know the life that awaits her here? We've kept her safe 'til now. My wife, my wife, she..." He stopped and swallowed. "We can't keep her here much longer. Those people," he gestured toward the house, "they're alright, usually, but the boys in the village – they know we're here. They know she's here. We have no right of abode here. If we complain about anything that happens, they'll just kick us all out. We've kept her–"

"I can't keep myself covered in pig-shit and hiding in this hovel for the rest of my life," Jana interjected.

Peter gestured impatiently. "Alright. Look, what I'll do is make sure that something is arranged for her once I'm safe. I'll give you my word."

The father shook his head. "She's just one of thousands. Once you're safe, they'll forget her. She goes with you or you don't go."

"Don't you understand?" Peter pleaded. "If we're found together, they'll think she's important to me! They'll torture her just to punish me. I can kill myself, but she...They'll tear her apart anyway."

The doctor furrowed his brow quizzically. "What exactly did you do?"

Peter shook his head. "I can't explain now. Just trust me, I will make sure that something is arranged for your daughter."

"No!" Jana placed her hands on her hips. "I'm going with you. I'll take a knife and kill myself if necessary, but I'm not going to pass up this chance."

Peter would have laughed at her comically determined pose if the situation hadn't been so serious. "It's too dangerous."

The girl nodded toward his left arm. "You must understand desperation. *Please,* take me with you."

Peter looked down at the numbers. He remembered his feelings in the plaza, when Elspeth had just hit him, in public. When he knew his entire worth was less than that of a dog. He had wanted to die then, to disappear into the earth, and that desire had freed him from his fears. He had accepted the suicidal risk of escape and had found a new life. Could he deny Jana the same chance?

He sighed. "Fine. It's your life. I'm not responsible." He looked at the father. "Did you hear me? Do you understand? I've warned you. Whatever happens, I'm *not* responsible."

The father nodded sadly. He turned his gaze to his daughter and regarded her affectionately, but his words were addressed to Peter. "Whatever happens, I will miss her, she has been the sunshine in our lives. And now, I will trust you, a total stranger, with my little girl." He turned his eyes back to Peter. "Did *you* hear *me? I'm going to trust you."

9

"*H*e made a big mistake leaving that whore-daughter of his at home." Günter motioned for his servant to spread some more butter on his roll as he spoke to his wife.

"Who made a mistake?" Wolf-Dietrich asked as he walked into the room. "Greta." He greeted his father's wife with a slight, ironical bow. "Father." He followed with a slightly deeper, and ever so slightly more sarcastic bow. Having finished with his idea of familial courtesy, Wolf-Dietrich sat at his place at the breakfast table.

"You're up early," Frau Schindler commented snidely. "Do you have a job you have to go to?"

"No, I'm still on indefinite leave. It seems all my positions keep falling apart." Wolf-Dietrich smiled suavely at his step-mother. "It seems Father has trouble organizing anything without it simply going up in smoke." He turned his smile on his father. "Or is it flames?"

"It's that Traugutt," Günter growled. "I'm sure of it! He goes snooping around my territory, and the next thing I know, the shit has hit the fan!"

Wolf-Dietrich motioned toward the servant to bring him a cigarette. He accepted the cigarette, leaned in to have it lit and then used it to point at a man standing discreetly near the door. "Who's that? New bodyguard?"

"Yes, the Führer thinks I need extra protection since that idiot Vogel was murdered."

Wolf-Dietrich dropped his cigarette in surprise. "Vogel was murdered?" He quickly picked the cigarette up before it could burn a hole in the tablecloth.

"Yes, thank God for small mercies."

Wolf-Dietrich noticed how Greta bit her lip at his father's harsh words. With deliberate casualness, he brushed ash off the tablecloth. "When? By whom?"

One of the servants poured out coffee and another presented Wolf-Dietrich with a plate of meats and cheeses as Günter explained the occurrences of the night and the fall-out. "Every time I go there, there's Traugutt. He was there tonight, as usual! Can't get away from that man! Where the hell did he come from? When the hell did he become so damn important?"

Neither Frau Schindler nor Wolf-Dietrich answered.

"I know, it's that damned daughter of his!" Günter answered his own question. "Without her, he'd be nothing!" He turned toward Wolf-Dietrich. "You should have been a girl!"

Frau Schindler sighed and sipped her tea. Wolf-Dietrich broke open a roll and carefully spread some liver-paste on it. "What are you talking about?"

"Oh, Traugutt is pimping his daughter to the Führer. She's got him wrapped around her little finger. Every time I try to put a stop to Traugutt's activities, the Führer prevents me. I'm sure she snuggles up to him in bed and tells him what to do in sweet little whispers."

"In bed," Wolf-Dietrich repeated quietly.

"Otherwise, how can I explain that every time Traugutt noses into my business, he's immune from my retaliations? Damn! I need to find my own woman for Rudi." Günter glanced at his wife, but then shook his head slightly. "A girl."

Frau Schindler glanced meaningfully at the bodyguard. Günter followed her look and groaned slightly.

"How does Traugutt know what you're up to?" Wolf-Dietrich continued to spread the liver-paste back and forth, nonchalantly smoothing it over every crevice of the bread.

"Beats the hell out of me. First he locates that lab outside of Hamburg, then he zeroes in on my scientist in London. And each time everything goes up in smoke. I swear he's feeding information to the Americans and saboteurs just to trip me up. That bastard!"

"In bed," Wolf-Dietrich breathed inaudibly.

Frau Schindler watched Wolf-Dietrich's actions with amusement. "Are you going to eat that bread or stroke it to death?"

Wolf-Dietrich looked down at the liver-paste painted roll he held in his hand as if he had never seen it before. With a sudden motion, he flung it across the room at the servant standing there. It bounced off the young man's chest and landed, paste-down, on the floor.

Both Herr and Frau Schindler looked at him in surprise. "In his bed!" Wolf-Dietrich growled as he stood and stormed out of the room.

Frau Schindler motioned for more tea from the servant who was not busy cleaning up the roll.

"What was that all about?" Günter looked to his wife for clarification.

Frau Schindler shrugged. "Maybe his fiancée is holding out on him. He probably is in dire need of a good lay." She placed her teacup near her lips, but decided it was too hot to sip. "You know," she added casually, "it's bad manners to mention sex in front of celibate men."

"They should set a date. It's high time that he was married. I'll tell him to set a date."

"Yes. High time he's his own man," Frau Schindler agreed with a tight-lipped smile.

10

"*A*h, Herr Traugutt, so you've decided to grace me with your presence." Greta Schindler's gaze turned from Richard to the ornate clock that hung on the restaurant's wall. "It's not polite to keep a lady waiting."

"My sincerest apologies." Richard bowed slightly and kissed her hand before sitting in the chair which the waiter had pulled out for him. "I've had to reorganize my routine."

"So I've heard." She gave him an understanding smile. Her eyes darted to the man standing vigilantly a few meters away. "Is that him?"

"Yes." Richard didn't bother to look at Mathias. "Do you know him?"

"No."

Richard pulled out a pack of cigarettes and offered Greta one, but she shook her head. He placed a cigarette to his lips and dropped his voice. "I suppose lunch is alright, but I won't be able to see you in the hotel."

A waiter approached and lit the cigarette then disappeared again.

"Why not?" Greta asked, rather too loudly.

"He'll report my every move to the Führer!" Richard whispered, holding the cigarette close to his mouth to help hide his words.

"So?"

Richard wished that his head didn't hurt so much. And why were the lights so damn bright? "Well, we won't be able to keep your identity secret indefinitely and the Führer is sure to pass the information on to your husband that we're having an affair."

"Again, so what?"

Richard opened his hands in a gesture of helpless confusion. Greta Schindler had been a handful since the moment he had taken her on, and he wasn't sure if she was worth the effort. It certainly did not feel like it was right now. Schindler confided nothing to his wife, she had been worthless as a source of information.

"Dear Richard! If Günter makes a fuss, I'll divorce him! And you can divorce that mousy wife of yours! We'll make a great team!"

Richard smoked pensively. Still, there was something about Greta which fascinated him. Her drive for power animated her. Her spirit glistened in her eyes. She had passion. Like Julia. Just like Julia.

"Didn't you hear me?" Greta asked petulantly.

"I'm thinking." A passion which Kasia seemed to lack.

"Oh, heavens! Don't tell me you plan to stay with that doormat? Even you daughter thinks you should dump her!"

"My daughter?"

"Yes. By the way, you didn't tell me she was having it on with Wolf-Dietrich."

"I didn't know." Richard's thoughts strayed to Kasia. Doormat, Greta said. Brood-mare was what his sister Zosia called her.

"Well, Günter let on this morning that Stefi and the Führer were an item and, my God, you should have seen the color Wolf-Dietrich turned! I think he's in love."

"I feel sorry for him," Richard responded distractedly. Good, sweet, reliable Kasia. Loyal, clever, someone he could count on. Someone he bet his life on.

"No you don't. You set it up! You had her pump information out of Wolf-Dietrich, just like you have her feeding little stories to the Führer! You're quite despicable!"

"Am I?" Was he? After more than twenty years as Traugutt, had he lost all of himself to his alter ego?

Greta leaned back, her eyes widening ever so slightly. Her breasts rose provocatively as she sucked in a deep breath. "Me, too? My God, is that what all this is about?"

Richard forced himself to shake his head, but his heart wasn't in it. "No, I've never once asked for a single detail from you about your husband's doings, now have I?"

"You've never had to ask!" Greta sneered. "I've volunteered everything to try to help your career!"

"My dear, you know nothing about your husband's activities. The secretaries know more about him than you."

"Be that as it may, you are only interested in me because of my husband!"

"Greta," Richard soothed unconvincingly, "we both know what we are, we both know what sort of relationship this is…"

"Don't you–"

"Listen!" Richard snapped, his patience at an end. "You'd have no interest in me without my having prospects. Don't pull the blushing virgin act with me! You're as much a whore as I am!"

Greta placed both hands flat on the table and began to rise. Richard jumped to his feet and came around to her, gently placing both his hands on her shoulders. "Greta, please forgive me! I'm sorry! Oh, darling, I didn't mean that. I, I admit my interest in you at first was because of your husband, but that's long in the past," he whispered desperately in her ear. "Please, you don't understand, I've fallen so deeply in love with you, it terrifies me. It was my fear speaking! I'm so afraid of losing you!"

"Then divorce your wife," Greta responded calmly, as she sat back down.

Still holding her shoulders, as if afraid she'd run away, Richard leaned forward and kissed her cheek. "I'll make it to the hotel today. I promise."

"I said, divorce that cow."

"Greta," Richard whispered pleadingly, "I can't. Not yet. The time's not right!"

"Why not?" Greta stared coldly forward.

"It's your husband. He'll take it as a personal insult – and I don't have the power to take him on yet!"

"So, your love is rather cowardly, isn't it." Greta turned her head to look up at Richard.

He shook his head helplessly. "You make me a coward! I can't bear the thought of something happening to you! Don't you realize, he might take revenge on you, rather than me?" Richard leaned forward again and kissed her lips. "I'll make it to the hotel, I promise!"

"You better, if you know what's good for you."

She let him cool his heels for half an hour in the hotel lobby before she deigned to show up. He was on the verge of leaving, but he knew she would be furious and vengeful, so he sat, impatiently tapping his fingers on the coffee table, and waited. Finally, precisely thirty minutes late she bustled in, full of smiles but no apologies. They kissed, as a husband and wife might, and then went up to the room which Richard had arranged. Mathias followed them into the room, inspected it thoroughly and then went to stand by the window.

Hiding his irritation, Richard walked over to him. "You can wait in the hall."

Mathias shook his head. "That would be dereliction of duty, *mein Herr*."

"You've checked the room, now go guard the door – from the outside!"

"Can't, *mein Herr*." Mathias pointed to the windows. "This room is not secure."

"I'll take that chance."

Again Mathias shook his head. "Sorry, *mein Herr*. Führer's orders – full protection, as I have been carefully trained to do. I know what that means and I can not disobey orders from the Führer."

In an involuntary gesture of surrender, Richard closed his eyes. "Neither can I."

Greta gave him a kiss on the cheek. "Come on." She pulled him toward the bed. As Richard reluctantly followed her lead, she gestured toward Mathias, waving her hand in the direction of the window. "There's no need for you to watch, young man. Keep your attention on the door and windows. Understood?"

"You're used to this, aren't you?" Richard asked numbly, as he sat on the edge of the bed.

"But of course." Greta stroked her hand along his face and seductively down his chest. "Günter's been under the Führer's surveillance for years, and besides, there're always servants about. But you should be flattered, it's not many men who threaten the Führer enough to merit his personal bodyguards."

"This is all because of Vogel's murder." Richard felt how Greta loosened his tie and undid the top buttons of his shirt, but he still could not bring himself to move.

"Oh yes, of course!" She laughed, nuzzling his neck as her hands began gently massaging the muscles of his back. "I think it was a bombing which earned Günter his little keepers. The one that killed Schacht, I think."

"Hmm."

"But I must admit that until you get used to it, it can be pretty off-putting. Especially for peasant-types who aren't used to ignoring the lower orders as they carry out their duties." Greta turned her little kisses into teasing licks with her tongue and worked her way up his neck to his ear. "Your wife must be appalled! I can't imagine she's consented to sex yet, has she?"

34

Richard felt truly annoyed by Greta's words, but he answered her anyway. "No, you're right, she has been put off." He tilted his head in response to her tongue teasing his ear, but even he did not know if it was out of pleasure or irritation.

"Of course, she might be right in this very hotel having it on with my husband!" Greta giggled, clearly feeling giddy with her woman-of-the-world role.

"No," Richard disagreed wearily, "she's supposed to be visiting Vogel's wife or, I suppose, widow. Comforting her." And checking her story. Prodding her to find out how much she knew, how much she had guessed, how much she might say.

"How very wifely!" Greta grabbed Richard's face and turning it to her, kissed him on the lips, long and passionately. Her tongue worked its way into his mouth and he found himself gasping for air, and perhaps for something else as well. When she pulled away, she smiled and winked at him. "I guess I'm just not as wifely as your little *Hausfrau*. I can't imagine wasting time on such distractions, but then I can't imagine Elspeth Vogel needs much comforting. I think Karl was becoming a genuine burden for her. And that guy, that servant was screwing her as well. At least, before he left, anyway. I think they were in love." She leaned back a bit and looked at Richard expectantly. "Still, it's strange he did that."

"Did what?"

"Risked everything to come back and kill Vogel. It didn't seem like him at all. I wonder if there was some other motive."

"No, just vengeance," Richard swiftly assured her. "It can make people do odd things."

"Still, after all that song and dance on American television, you'd think he wouldn't have dared to show that side of his personality." Greta had switched tack and was now undoing her own buttons. Slowly, languorously. Richard could see how her breasts rose and fell with each breath.

"I guess he didn't care. Probably figured they'd never find out." He reached tentatively up to touch the exposed skin above her slip.

"Well, we could tell them!" Greta laughed. She parted the blouse and let it slip off her shoulders. "Now wouldn't that destroy his credibility!"

"No!" Richard hissed, his hand withdrawing from her as if she were burning hot. He wished he had never mentioned Vogel.

Greta glanced down at his hand, then into his eyes. "Hell, we could really stir up the pot and let them know that he and Elspeth were lovers," she suggested maliciously. "Now wouldn't that make a great story! That would throw everything into a different light! And that kid, Jesus Christ, kidnapping a child. Well, I suppose it was probably his – but still, it can't look good for him, that poor martyr, murdering his mistress's husband and

35

stealing her child. Oh, poor Karl. Poor, poor Karl Vogel. Cuckolded and murdered and deprived of his heir."

Richard leaned forward to hug her. "Please shut-up," he whispered desperately. "Everything you say could help Rudi, and we don't want that now, do we?" He felt the muscles of her back, the lace of her slip under his fingers.

"I don't know," Greta whispered in reply, arching her back at his touch. "Maybe we do. The Führer's been taking a hammering at Günter's hands recently. He blew this American video thing. He's falling fast – and you're not ready yet. You've said so yourself."

"Yes, but, we can prop him up in other ways," Richard murmured as he nibbled her ear. His fingers moved upward to the straps of her slip. He pulled them gently downward. They slid onto her arms, the silk of her slip dropped a few inches in response. "I don't want to stir up that horrid video thing. It's messy. And no matter how bad we make that Halifax guy look, it won't really help us: the tape still exists, the Americans have proof of Rudi's mad predilection for filmed torture."

Richard shuddered slightly as he said those words. He noticed Greta shuddered too and they both glanced warily at Mathias as he stood impassively staring out the window. Everyone knew that the great lacuna in the Führer's tape collection was the torture of a high-level official or, say, the wife of an official. "We're never going to save him from that," Richard said, with determined calmness. "There'd be no point in pursuing your idea."

"But no harm either." Greta shook her shoulders slightly, causing her slip to drop down a bit further. It hung precariously for a second and then fell to her waist. She deftly freed her arms from the straps. "You can ingratiate yourself to Rudi and slow Günter down a bit."

Richard felt her bare skin pressed up against him. Despite himself he gasped with pleasure. "No, I don't want to do that. Please, just let this one drop, Greta. As a favor to me, okay?" His hands moved of their own accord to hold Greta's breasts, to close convulsively over her soft flesh.

"If that's the way you feel," Greta sighed. It was not clear whether she sighed with pleasure of exasperation. "Alright. But I expect you to be extra nice to me in return. Extra nice."

That evening, as he returned to kith and kin, Ryszard felt even more depressed than usual. He could not shake the feeling of how much he had enjoyed Greta's attentions. Despite her cold-blooded scheming. Or perhaps because of it? He chewed his food in silence, nodding occasionally at Kasia's conversation to show that he was indeed listening. She was telling him about her visit to Elspeth, he should listen to find out what she had discovered, but he already knew, by the tone of her voice, that there were no serious concerns there.

He looked up from his food to Mathias, who sat at the table, supping with them, as if a guest. Leszek stood near the door, moving now and then to serve them or to fetch something from the kitchen where his wife, Lodzia, prepared the courses. The children sat, grimly mute, silently chewing their food. Ryszard scanned their faces: there was Stefi, stuck in Berlin now that her presence had been noted by the Führer. Well, she would be useful to have around in any case. His eyes strayed to Pawel, returned from Szaflary after his brother's death. "I'll take my risks where I choose to!" he had stated defiantly to his father, and after the fiasco with Andrzej's death, there had been nothing Ryszard could say. Pawel had been seeing that Vogel girl quite frequently. What was her name? Teresa, yes, that was it. The excuse had been to provide Madzia with company. Ryszard wondered if Pawel would continue to see Teresa now that the excuse had been kidnapped. Pawel had gone along with his mother to comfort Elspeth. Had it been a farewell visit?

Ryszard worried about Pawel. Was his son going native? He took a bite and almost laughed aloud – he was one to think such thoughts! He turned from Pawel's grim visage to the empty chair. Andrzej. So young! It had been Kasia's only gesture of grief: she kept an empty place ready for Andrzej at their table. A place which would never again be filled. Ryszard sighed and looked to Jan and Genia. Still children, hardly touched by all that went on around them, yet so solemn! They were condemned by the bodyguard's presence to a charade they could hardly understand. Only nine-month-old Piotr was oblivious as he squirmed and fussed on his mother's lap, preventing her from doing more than grabbing a bite of her food every once in a while.

"Here, let me hold him. I'll take him into the playroom." Ryszard wasn't hungry anyway, and he was clearly unwelcome at the table. Even his children found his presence burdensome and he looked forward to the chance to interact with the only person who did not view him as if he carried some horrible, contagious disease.

He stood and felt some degree of satisfaction as he saw Mathias hurriedly shove in a few last bites of his dinner. Kasia handed the baby to Ryszard, whispered a relieved "Thank-you" and began to eat her food. Ryszard left the room, followed by a clearly annoyed Mathias and went upstairs into the children's room.

A prisoner in my own house, Ryszard thought, as he helped little Piotr learn how to walk. Peter, he chided himself. The baby's name is Peter for as long as the guards were in their house. Just like his other living sons were named Paul and Johann, and his dead son was named Andreas. No whiff of esoteric names in this patriotic family! The baby took a step, struggled free of his father's hands and promptly tumbled to the floor. Even the baby must wear a mask.

Ryszard pulled the child to his feet and they repeated the process over and over. I'm like a leper, Ryszard thought, as Piotr took two steps in a row before grabbing onto the edge of a table. The baby turned around, grinning, and took the three steps into Ryszard's waiting arms.

"Good boy!" Ryszard praised, as he had heard Kasia do on other occasions. "You're so strong! Such a good walker!"

"Ga, ga, ga, ga, ga!" Piotr yammered with excitement.

Ryszard picked him up and held him aloft, above himself, bouncing him in celebration. "Good boy!" he enthused even as Piotr burped up a mess of milk right into Ryszard's mouth. Wincing with disgust, Ryszard clapped his mouth shut, and glanced around for somewhere to eject the vomit, but he did not want to spit on the carpet. Still holding Piotr, he got up and shoving his way past Mathias, who stood in the doorway, he went down the hall to the bathroom and spat into the sink. Mathias followed and took up a position in the doorway as Ryszard set Piotr down by the sink. Ryszard grunted his annoyance but did not protest – he had already learned that it was useless. The foul flavor was still in his mouth, and keeping one careful hand on Piotr, he filled a glass of water and used that to rinse out his mouth.

Still, there was a funny taste, and carefully holding Piotr with one hand and keeping a disapproving eye on Mathias, he viciously scrubbed at his teeth with a toothbrush. Only as he was spitting out the toothpaste did he realize what he had done, but it was too late – he watched in paralyzed horror as the tiny capsule washed down the drain with his spittle.

He continued to stare at the drain, but there was nothing he could do. He looked up cautiously at Mathias, but his face betrayed no emotion, clearly he had not noticed what Ryszard had done. Ryszard turned his attention back to the sink as if he could will the poison capsule back into it. It had been unbroken, of that he was fairly certain. Nevertheless, he poured himself another glass of water and carefully rinsed his mouth. Several times. When he was satisfied that he was not going to die, he reached with his tongue back to the tooth that had held the poison and felt carefully around it. The thin top was missing and the hollow was deep and empty, but otherwise the tooth felt normal. He must have broken the top off earlier in the day – perhaps on one of the innumerable occasions when he had grit his teeth in frustration. Or possibly with Greta...

Damn! He should have noticed! It was the sort of thing he usually checked routinely. Damn it! Well, he thought, the dentists had warned him often enough about punctual maintenance. It seems they were right. He shook his head in disgust. His carelessness could have cost him his life! It was sheer luck that he had not killed himself while eating.

Once his initial shock at nearly killing himself had passed, he felt an overwhelming tiredness. He grabbed a cloth and cleaned Piotr's face and hands, running water the entire time so that he could be sure the pill was truly washed down the drain and would not reappear later in some back-flush that could cause it to end up in one of the children's hands.

He picked up Piotr and walked him back into the children's bedroom. He set the baby down among the toys and rubbed his face. Not only had he nearly killed himself, but now his only escape route was gone. He needed to go to Szaflary, or at least see one of their dentists, before he could get the tooth reset. He could not get a replacement for the poison until he was free of his bodyguards – and that was not for the foreseeable future! After Greta's words in the hotel, it was clear that the Führer now feared him as much as valued his advise. It was not unlikely he would get arrested on a trumped-up charge, maybe something to do with Vogel, maybe something manufactured by Schindler. Whatever the source of the disaster would be, he now lacked his only sure way out. He might well provide Rudi with that last, long-sought-after tape.

Ryszard closed his eyes. There in the comfort of his own home, in the warmth of his family, surrounded by servants and bodyguards, protected and cosseted, his every whim catered to, there he felt as trapped as any prisoner in a Gestapo cell. It left him exhausted and disheartened. *And it hasn't even been a full day!* So this is what Peter had felt day in and day out for years. *Only worse.*

Piotr made a noise and Ryszard opened his eyes to make sure all was well. Why, he wondered, had his thoughts turned, once again, to his brother-in-law? Was it the revelations he had made to Peter only last night? They had spoken about much; much more than was wise. He had told Peter about Julia – not only about Karl's casual admission to killing her, but everything else as well. It had been insanity to admit so much. Utter weakness. In Peter's place, Ryszard was sure he would have heaped scorn upon such raw emotionality. Indeed, that is exactly what he had done about Peter's love for Zosia and that other woman, the one who had been killed. Yet Peter had treated Ryszard's information considerately, responding thoughtfully, and respecting Ryszard's confidence. Even as he had bared his soul, Ryszard had marveled at Peter's demeanor – both sympathetic and detached. As if there was no history between them, as if Ryszard had not publicly humiliated Peter, tearing into his deepest fears and worst memories in front of everyone at the encampment. *I knew what they had done to you, yet I did it anyway.*

39

Piotr dropped a ball and it rolled away. He crawled after it but it had gone under the cabinet. Ryszard reached underneath to get the ball and handed it back to Piotr. The baby gleefully grabbed the ball and Ryszard stroked his face fondly. *I gave you a chance for revenge, why didn't you take it?*

11

*T*he grim-looking man shook his head in rejection of Jana's presence. "Our orders don't say anything about a girl."

His companion gestured toward Peter. "We were told to look out for someone fitting your description, escaping from the authorities, and to assist him in whatever manner possible. Nothing about a girl."

Peter looked at Jana. This would be the perfect opportunity for her to back out. They stood, the four of them, in the cellar of an enormous apartment block. The floor was wet, the walls damp, and there was an abiding smell of mold in the air.

"Then your orders are incomplete," Jana boldly asserted.

The grim man ignored her. "She's local. We were told to help you, and only you."

Again Peter eyed Jana, but it was clear she would not be dissuaded. "You were told to assist me in whatever manner necessary. That includes her."

Jana smiled at him gratefully. The two men stepped back and conferred. Then the grim-looking man looked up. "No. We don't know what dangers or risks she'll introduce to this mission and we will not accept the responsibility of violating our security on her behalf."

Peter turned toward Jana and shrugged apologetically. It was for the best.

She shook her head violently. "No!" she begged in a whisper. "You promised!"

I'm going to trust you, he heard her father's words echo in his head. Her father was right, if Peter left her now, she would be taken back home and left there. No matter what promises he elicited, she would be forgotten. He stroked his chin worriedly. Jana looked at him pleadingly. That must have been how he looked to Marysia as he had begged her to give him a chance. After so many years where he had prayed in vain for help, Marysia had taken the risk of letting him live, even as he pointed a gun at Olek. And Zosia had let Tadek into Szaflary, violating every rule in the book to do so.

They had defied authority to show their humanity. They had given someone else a chance at life, could he do any less?

He turned to the two men. "I'll take the responsibility. I think you know, I have that sort of authority." He doubted that he did.

Again the two men conferred in whispers before the leader answered, "I'm sorry, sir. We weren't told anything about you. Just told to help you."

"Then go find out. Tell them I've found..." Peter glanced at Jana, then dove in, "I have someone with essential information and I must bring her back to be debriefed. Tell them to give me clearance to do that."

The leader looked dubiously at Jana, but then shrugged. "Okay. We'll put you in hiding while we check it out."

The clearance was received and the two of them became a package, passed from one sector to another, handled as carefully as if they were phials of deadly toxin. Only when they reached the last village before the first base camp, did Peter stop to question Jana's intentions.

"You do realize," he said, as they were left alone to finish the small supper they had been provided with, "that there's no returning past this point. This is your last chance. You can pull out here. I'll make sure someone gets you a decent identity, and you can make a life for yourself here or in one of the nearby cities. How about it?"

Jana shook her head in confusion. "I don't understand. Aren't you heading into a city? Are you leaving the country?"

"Sort of. I'm heading into the mountains. Into the free territory there."

"I didn't believe it really existed," Jana breathed.

"Oh, it does," Peter assured her, intrigued by her response. "The problem is, once you've been inside, you know too much to ever leave. That's okay if they decide to let you join up, but I can't guarantee that will happen."

"Then what would they do?"

The vote was six to four against... In his mind's eye he saw the barrel of Tadek's gun pointed at his face. He shook his head to clear away the images. "What do you think?"

She chewed silently on her bread and cheese for a moment, staring grimly at her plate. Then she looked up at him. "Please, don't abandon me now. I'll take the risk. I'm not afraid. Please take me in with you. I want a chance to fight."

He studied her, but her gaze did not waver.

"I haven't had a single chance in my life at anything," she said softly. "I couldn't even attend the illegal school because it was too far away. I don't know how to read, I don't know anything. I've slaved away all my life tending other people's animals, scurrying out of their way so as not to offend them, hiding like some sort of rat that will get stomped on if it dares

41

show itself in the light of day. My mother has worked at the house, being especially nice, if you know what I mean, just so that they don't ask for me. Do you know what we have to go through to stay alive? Do you have any idea?"

He wiped at the tears that streamed down her cheeks. "I have some idea. Don't worry, I won't abandon you. I'll take you in and I'll fight for your right to stay. I just want you to know, I can't guarantee what they'll say."

"What the hell were you thinking?" Marysia yelled at him. She paced angrily around her small flat, stopped and turned to look at Peter as if seeing him clearly for the first time. "Who the hell gave you the right? This isn't your personal playground, you know!"

"She saved my life."

"Saved your life! And now you've gone and destroyed hers! We can't keep her here! We have no place for an illiterate teenager! For Christ's sakes Peter, why'd you bring her all the way into the Central region?"

"She begged me. She didn't want to be left behind with people she didn't know. I could understand that – I didn't know what would happen to her if I left her at a partisan camp."

"You idiot!" Marysia gestured angrily and resumed her pacing. "What are we supposed to do now? Where is she supposed to stay?"

"She could stay with us. Zosia and I could use help with the children."

"Zosia quit specifically to spend more time with her family. Do you begrudge her that?"

"No, not at all. But you know Zosia, that won't last long. She'll get involved with something and then she'll be running all over trying to do everything, exhausting herself. Just this week I've been away, you can see she's stressed out. With my work on the Council now, and with this..." he raised his right arm slightly to indicate the cast on it, "We'll need help. Jana could take care of the children..."

Marysia came to a stop at the far end of the room and threw him a contemptuous look. "Maybe, Peter, you've forgotten, that on this side of the border we don't have personal servants at our beck and call. Maybe, you'll even recall that that is at least one of the reasons you are here now!"

"It'll be temporary. Until I can teach her how to read, teach her some skills–"

"And when exactly do you think you'll get time to do that, eh?"

"Oh, Marysia! It's just one more person. A slip of a girl."

Marysia crossed the room to stand directly in front of him. "Yes, just one more person! One more person, *you* chose to favor. One kidnapped daughter, one girl you stumble upon in a field. When do the rest of us get to

42

go out and save our one favorite person? Eh? Or do we just exist to cater to your omnipotent whims of granting life to this or that supplicant?"

Peter shook his head, confused by the turn the conversation was taking. "I think this is being taken all out of proportion–"

"Don't you lecture me about proportions! Do you have any idea what it takes to keep this place running smoothly? Do you have any idea what just one extra person costs in terms of supplies? Do you know how many people are out there," Marysia pointed angrily in the general direction of the nearest border, "scrabbling for life? How many millions? Do you think we are heartless? Wouldn't each of us like to bring in a few poor souls? Maybe a hundred, maybe a thousand, hell why not millions? What makes any one of them less worthy than your girl?"

"Marysia, I'm sorry. They made a deal with me. She saved my life. I gave my word–"

"*Your* word? You gave *our* word! You lied to us, you told us there was important information to be had, and then you present us with this fait accompli! My God, Peter! I was warned. Even Katerina roused herself to warn me not to grant you clearance to bring back an extra person. But I trusted you. *I trusted you!!* Against everyone's advice, I gave the clearance and you were lying. You betrayed me!"

"Oh, Marysia, I'm sorry. I didn't know what else to say right then. I couldn't explain what had happened. You *know* that. I didn't realize–"

"Of course, you didn't *realize*, because you just don't *think*, do you?"

Peter was taken aback. "I'm sorry. I didn't mean to–"

"If we keep her here – if we were to keep *your* word, how the hell are we going to clear her?"

"That shouldn't be a problem," he answered, quite relieved by this turn in the conversation. "Even the local A.K. contact recognized her as a local. And she's only a kid."

Marysia shook her head in disbelief. "Are you really so stupid?"

Peter looked around helplessly, but there was no one else in the room, so she must have been talking to him. "I don't understand."

"She's sixteen. Your wife was an assassin already. What makes you think they couldn't come up with something similar?"

"Yes, but we know this girl's a Pole."

"So was the boy who betrayed my son," Marysia said sadly. "Do you believe the Nazi's racial theories? Do you think you can trust someone because it's in their blood? Haven't you learned anything?"

"Marysia…"

"Think Peter, for once stop and think. You were out for at least an hour. This girl sees you come flying off the train. She turns you in for the money, or out of fear, or whatever. She's convinced to play the part of your savior, to win your trust and then to extract a promise from you to take her with you, wherever you go. To meet every single agent along the way who escorts you. Even if they didn't know your end destination, that alone would be worth a lot. But, lo, you go one better for them and bring her here. All the way to Central. And we're supposed to just let her live here among us, memorizing faces, learning aliases, finding out about our people in the field."

Peter stared at his feet. Why had he been so sure of her? Intuition? Could he possibly say something so irrational and expect Marysia not to laugh at him?

"Now tell me, seriously," Marysia said into his silence. "Didn't anything about them make you suspicious? A doctor? Where'd he come from? And they just happened to have heard about you. And the girl, why did she insist on sticking with you the entire way? Huh?"

"She said her life was so hopeless, she saw it as her only chance–"

"She could have worked her way up the ranks!" Marysia nearly shouted.

Peter shook his head slightly. An insider all her life, Marysia could not understand the desperation of an outsider. He could, but he could never explain it, instead he said, "Marysia, the Führer wants me so badly, he'd have never set this thing up. He'd have never taken the chance of letting me get away."

Marysia pursed her lips as she considered this. "You have a point there. But maybe he wasn't the one giving the orders. He might be fuming about your 'escape' this very moment, and meanwhile, someone in Berlin is rubbing his hands in glee that you've fallen into his trap. You're a fool if you think that each official doesn't have his own personal agenda. The number of people who would love to bring down the current Führer–"

"And the easiest way to do that would be to give me to him and then let the news slip out about what happened to me. Geez, you know I'm driving him nuts and all sorts of people are using that to their advantage–"

"Some are. But others might have a different agenda."

"Alright, alright. You're right, that's a possibility. But the one thing I know something about is acting, and Jana's not acting. I'm sure of it. She's genuine. Every bit of your scenario could be true, but maybe she set them up? Maybe it was her way of getting out? She's not going to betray us. Please–"

"If you know so much about other people's motives," Marysia interrupted to ask, "how did you miss Elspeth Vogel's agenda with you? Eh?"

So Zosia must have confided the details to Marysia about Magdalena's existence. Peter fell into an embarrassed silence. "Alright, maybe I can't

44

read other people's minds," he conceded at long last. "But don't you think you're being paranoid? Not just with Jana, but–"

"Paranoid?" Marysia hissed. *"Paranoid?"* It looked as though she would explode and Peter took a tentative step backward, as if she were Elspeth. As if she would slam her fist into his face and he would be obliged to do nothing but bear the humiliation. As if she...But, of course, she wasn't Elspeth and he wondered at the intensity of his reaction to her gesture. She did nothing more than raise an angry finger and shake it at him. "You're supposed to be numerically literate, but maybe you have trouble with what a million means. Think about the numbers! This country had thirty-six million people in 1939. Do you know how many we have now?" Without waiting for his answer, she said, "Eighteen, maybe twenty. Does that mean anything to you? Can you understand that? Huh?"

He winced at her anger, but could find no words to repel it.

"Within the first six years we lost six million people. Six million! A million a year! *A sixth of our population!* Do I need to interpret that in terms of roomfuls of little fingers? Tons of hair? What will it take for you to realize what we've suffered here? Civilians! Murdered! *Three thousand a day, every day for six years!*" Marysia stopped suddenly, but only to catch her breath. "Only with England's capitulation and the armistice did it begin to slow down, but we were a growing country. Let's be conservative," she fumed, suddenly sounding analytic, "Let's assume in two generations our population would have doubled. We would stand at seventy or eighty million now, but no! Twenty! How many lives lost? How many lives not lived? You tell me." She waited a moment and then yelled, "Tell me!"

Like a schoolboy who had fluffed a lesson, he answered, "Fifty million."

"Now what was that word you used? Paranoid? You saw with your own eyes what they did to Joanna. Do you think that was unique? Do I have to show you the pictures of the tiny burned corpses? Or the children hanging from ropes? Do you think any child here would be spared? Do you?" Marysia motioned with her head back toward the pictures of Adam and Julia on the wall. "I've lost both my children to this war, Peter. Both of them. I've lost my only granddaughter, and my only grandson is now a cripple. Now you ask me to risk everyone here, every single person, for your whim."

"Not for a whim – for humanity! Jana was en route to being a statistic. I wanted to drop that horrendous number by one. Just one! I was inspired by you all. By Zosia, by how she saved Tadek, against orders..."

Marysia was shaking her head.

"By *you* too! You saved me! *You* took a risk. You risked Olek. You risked everyone here! Please, Marysia! There must be a way. You did it for me."

"That was a phenomenal effort which we indulged in only because of your skills and the possibility that you might serve our purposes. And don't bother to look bitter about it!" she snarled. "I'm fed up with that. You have no idea what you cost us and yet you expect it to have all been for free! We'd have to lose at least two full-time people to keep track of one illiterate, unskilled girl."

"You let Tadek in!"

"Just. Also Tadek was skilled, and we could check him and his story. He was already involved in a local group, he had been cleared and was on his way up within that hierarchy." Marysia spoke softly, her voice having gone hoarse from yelling. "If he had been an infiltrator, there would have been no reason for him to give up his position like that. He could have worked his way in here within a matter of years."

"I didn't know that."

"There's a lot you don't know."

And a lot you've lied about. Peter took a deep breath as if preparing to argue, but he could think of nothing more to say. He looked down at the floor trying to gather his thoughts. All he had wanted to do was give someone the chance he had been given, to pass on hope. But Marysia had already told him that was foolish.

Marysia was shaking her head in exasperation. "Damn it! We're having to re-organize every agent that accompanied you two or sheltered you on the way back. Every single one uprooted! And we have to track anyone the agents may have been in contact with since then. Shit!"

Peter bowed his head, bringing his uninjured hand up to rest his forehead. He pressed with brutal strength against his temples, trying to force the pain out of his head so that he could argue coherently. "Marysia, you're right. I'm sorry. I'm an absolute idiot and I didn't think through my actions at all. I was injured and confused, I wasn't thinking clearly." He looked up at her and gave her a pleading smile. "But it was *my* mistake. I'm the one who should be punished. Jana didn't do anything wrong. Please don't take it out on her."

Marysia shook her head. "Do you think I'd do this to punish you? What do you think I am?"

Peter shook his head vigorously. "No, that's not what I meant. I'm sorry–"

"She's a security risk! This is a decision I have to take!"

"I understand. I understand. But can't you decide to let her stay with us? Part of my punishment could be to give up my time to ward her."

"You mean take her to Council meetings with you? Let her know even more of our secrets?"

"No! I'll quit the Council."

"And the cryptanalysis office?"

"I, I don't need to be there–"

"Yes you do. You're too valuable for us to have you wasting your time in this manner. She should have never been brought here." Marysia's voice had grown cold.

"I realize that now. It was a mistake, but it was my mistake. I disobeyed orders! She's innocent. Don't kill her. Please. Please let her live!"

"It will be quick and painless. She won't even know we're doing it," Marysia assured him in such a businesslike tone that it made him shudder.

How had it all gone so wrong, so quickly? "Marysia! No! You can't! Please!" He stepped up to her and grabbed her arm, shaking her slightly as he pleaded. "It was my mistake! I'm sorry! Don't do it, please!" As he saw the determination in her face, he slid to his knees, pressed his head against her. "Please, Marysia! Ma! I'm begging you. I don't know what else to do. Let the girl live!"

Marysia shook her head. "I can't. Can't you understand that?"

"Oh God, don't kill her! I'm sorry. I'm sorry I brought her here."

"So am I." As if exhausted, Marysia shook his hand from her and stepped back, leaving him there on his knees, begging in vain. "I don't want your apologies. You've wasted her life." She walked to the door but stopped in the doorway and turned back to look at him. "You betrayed my trust in you. You've forced me into a decision I never wanted to face, one which will torment me for the rest of my life. You've risked everyone's life here. You may have betrayed everyone who risked their lives to get you home safely. You've thrown away a young girl's life. All just to prove how noble you are. I hope you feel good about yourself."

"Marysia," he moaned hopelessly, "The girl is innocent. It was my fault, I should be punished."

"I don't doubt you will be."

"Can't I do anything to change your mind?"

She paused to consider. "Yes. Give me a viable alternative. I'll give you twenty minutes." She left the room.

Peter lowered himself to sit on his heels. The seconds ticked past. His brain worked feverishly, but he had no viable alternative. The minute hand moved inexorably forward. What viable alternative had Zosia offered about Tadek? None. Five precious minutes went by and still his mind plotted. What viable alternative had Marysia offered when she had saved him? None, none at all. Ten minutes disappeared into the void, his strategies with them. Marysia and Zosia had disobeyed orders, had shown their humanity despite the danger, despite the risk. The hand slipped past the fateful twenty minutes and his thoughts scrabbled for an answer like fingers clawing at the loose dirt of a cliff. He had been inspired by them, he had believed he could risk human kindness as well. But he had been wrong. Dead wrong.

12

*R*yszard marched up the path to his house, his two bodyguards walking vigilantly next to and slightly behind him. The door opened and Leszek greeted him, took his coat, removed his boots, lit a cigarette for him and then went to fetch a drink as Ryszard retreated into the sitting room. Mathias took up a position just inside the door of the sitting room as the other bodyguard, Jörg, proceeded through the house, checking it out for anything suspicious.

"Once Jörg is done," Ryszard suggested to Mathias, "you can take the rest of the evening off."

"I appreciate the suggestion, *mein Herr*," Mathias answered with a slight bow, "but I'm on duty until seven and it would be derelict for me to leave early."

"You've stayed late on nights I've worked late, make up for that time by leaving a bit early now. I'm home for the evening, there won't be a problem."

"I'm sorry, *mein Herr*. I must follow my orders."

"Yes, of course," Ryszard sighed. He lowered himself wearily onto the couch. It had only been a week, but already he felt like he was falling apart. Every action of his was observed, every minute of his time was accounted for. Oh God! He felt like dying.

Kasia came into the room holding the drinks which Leszek had prepared for them. "Would you like some company?" She handed Ryszard his glass.

He looked up at her, his expression an unguarded plea for help. She smiled at him sympathetically, then bending down to kiss him, she whispered, "Have patience, my dear *Ryszard.*"

Usually any such breach of security would have earned her a warning scowl from him, but this time he just pressed his cheek against hers, silently begging for comfort, for some acknowledgment of the person who was trapped inside. Kasia pulled away and stroked his cheek with the back of her hand. "Tired, my dear?"

"Headache." With an effort he pulled himself together. "I've got some work to do. After dinner, I'll need to go into my study for a few hours."

"I understand." She did as well. It was a kindness on Ryszard's part. His guard would follow him into the study and the rest of them in the house would breathe that bit easier.

"I'm sorry to deprive you all of my company," Ryszard added bitterly. "But duty calls."

He kept himself busy and the guard out of the family's way until nearly midnight. When he emerged from his study he saw that although Kasia had prepared for bed, she had waited up for him, sitting on the couch, quietly reading a novel. He was aware of how Jörg waited in the hall as he paused in the doorway of the sitting room to contemplate his wife. "You look beautiful," he said uneasily. It was not his usual manner with Kasia, but nothing else was working, so he thought he might try seducing her.

She looked up at him, somewhat suspiciously. He smiled hopefully and walked over to her. He sat down next to her and gently removed the book from her hands. "Inspiring," he whispered, aware that Jörg had taken up his post in the doorway.

He leaned in to kiss her ear, but Kasia pulled away slightly. "Ryszard," she protested softly.

"Ignore him."

"I can't."

"Yes you can. You have to, or else..." He stroked her cheek. "My dear, beautiful Kasia. I so want to hold you and touch you and have you." He let his hand move down her face onto the soft fabric of her nightgown, but she reached up and grabbed his hand, stopping it from moving any further.

"Let's go to bed," she suggested ambiguously.

After they had all settled into their respective places, after the lights had been turned out, after a decent interval of at least thirty seconds, Ryszard turned to Kasia again. In the privacy of the darkness, he whispered his devotion to her in her ear. He kissed her longingly, and slowly, gingerly, he let his hands reach out to touch her.

He felt her fingers close over his hand. He felt the way she squeezed his hand, as if trying to convey a torrent of emotions, and then he felt how she picked his hand up and placed it a safe distance away from her. "Kasia, please..."

"He'll hear," she returned softly.

"Just forget he's here. He'll ignore us. I promise. He's used to such things."

"Is he?" Kasia asked, coldly.

49

Ryszard sighed and rolled onto his back. He stared up at the ceiling. It would be pointless lying to her. Pointless and insulting. She knew. She had known all along. They had both chosen to ignore that aspect of his life and he wondered why she now chose to make an issue of it. "You know what my life is like," he said at last.

"I know what Richard's life is like."

"Then you'll know I've never enjoyed it," he muttered. "Do you have any idea what it's like to get mindless women to confide their boss's secrets? I spend the entire time making *them* feel special. I get nothing out of it!" It wasn't fair – to be condemned for an activity that was part of his work, a charade which he did not enjoy in the least. He got nothing out of all those women. Nothing at all! Not since Julia, and then again, not until Greta. She made *him* feel special.

"I know what Richard's life is like." Kasia rose on her elbow and leaned over so that she spoke directly into his ear. "But I love Ryszard and I cannot make love to any other man."

"You might have a long wait before you."

Kasia lowered herself back onto the bed and rolled so that she was on her side, facing away from him. "I think you know that I am a patient woman."

13

*I*t was the first proper council meeting since his return. Peter forced himself to attend, and as he took his seat, he felt sure that those already in the room were watching him. He nodded at the few greetings, muttered one-syllable answers to the questions about how he was doing. Tomek came over to look at his arm and ask how long he would need to wear a cast. Peter answered but kept his attention on the files and papers and agenda which he had set on the table in front of himself. How, he wondered, could he face them all?

Once everyone had arrived, Marysia made a move to open the meeting, but Peter stood up and interrupted her. "If it pleases the chair," he said, with unintentional formality, "I would like to address the group as a whole, before we begin the meeting."

He managed to look up from the table long enough to see her nod, almost imperceptibly. He looked back down at the papers in front of him, touching them with his fingers as if preparing to put them in order. He took a deep breath, placed his uninjured hand on the table to steady himself and then looked up to meet the curious stares of his comrades.

Still, though, he could not speak. He swallowed, looked at them all again, and then let his gaze drop back to the table. As if reading notes, he began, "I want to apologize for my actions this past week. What I did was dangerous, irresponsible, and unforgivable. It had painful consequences which I should have foreseen, but didn't..." He closed his eyes as an image of Jana came to mind. "I am sincerely sorry. I also recognize that the only reason I have a seat on this council is that I blackmailed my way onto it. Clearly your judgment about me was far more reliable than my own: I don't deserve to be here."

He looked up at Marysia. She was studying him with interest. They had not spoken since their argument in her flat and had studiously avoided each other since then. Now he held her eyes as he spoke, "I hope you can accept my resignation in the spirit it is intended. I am not in any way trying to distance myself from you or the Council's actions. Indeed, I am grateful to you all for having shouldered the burden of handling the fall-out from my actions. I also appreciate that my resignation should not in any way affect whatever sanctions I am due to receive. I'm not doing this to lighten my punishment. Whatever I receive, is more than due and less than adequate. It's not that." He shook his head as if arguing. "I simply don't belong here."

Using only his left hand, he clumsily gathered the stack of files together and picked them up. He did not even know why he had brought them. Maybe, he thought, he should leave them, he had no right to them anymore. He set them back down and stepped back from the table in order to make his way out of the room.

"Peter." It was Marysia who broke the stunned silence. "I appreciate your gesture, but there is no reason for you to leave. If each of us quit any time we made a mistake, there wouldn't be any council members left."

I hope you feel good about yourself. Though it had been a week, Marysia's words still rang through his mind and Peter shook his head. "This mistake killed someone."

Tadek snorted. "Try getting four people killed." Peter looked at him, confused, but then he remembered Zosia's story about how Tadek had convinced some friends to attempt to free his wife from a military brothel. And they had all been killed, all but Tadek.

"This was different–"

"It's not a competition on whose mistakes are the stupidest," Konrad asserted. "Your actions have not merited a motion for dismissal – you'll note it's not on the agenda – nor do they merit a resignation. If you feel uncomfortable with how you obtained your seat, I suggest you step into the hall and we can have another election. This time, free and fair."

Peter looked around in surprise. "Would you do that?"

Marysia took a poll of expressions. "I don't see why not."

Peter left the room and closed the door behind himself. Well, this was an unforeseen turn of events! He had been sure that someone would move to dismiss him and he would have been obliged to listen to an endless catalog of his failings. Instead, there seemed to be a chance that he might win a seat through a fair election!

God almighty, what sort of person was he? He leaned against the wall, furious with himself. His words had been sincere, his distress over Jana genuine. Was this all it took to put her death behind him? If they elected him, he would have to turn the seat down. It was the least he could do for the girl.

Tadek opened the door. "Congratulations." He motioned Peter back in.

Marysia greeted Peter as he entered the room. "Now that you have been fairly elected, you understand, you'll have to go through the same approval process I outlined last time–"

"Marysia, I can't do it. I meant what I said. I don't deserve–"

"Nonsense!" Hania sputtered. "If you want to see a priest, do that. This isn't a confessional. We need your talents and we have offered you a place on our committee. We have a job to do. We don't have time for your soul-searching. Do that elsewhere. So, sit down, shut up and start working. Okay?"

He didn't know what to say to that, so he just said, "Okay."

"So how did it go?" On the third time Zosia said it, Peter managed to hear every word over Madzia's boisterous singing. Irena was watching Madzia's loud performance and giggling with delight.

"I didn't know they did that sort of thing so young," Peter marveled. Madzia was so involved in her performance that she had not even noticed his returning.

Zosia threw a benevolent smile at the girls. "So how did it go?"

"Oh, that. They re-elected me to a seat." He still was unsure about how elated he should feel.

"So you didn't resign?"

Madzia suddenly noticed him and stopped singing. She ran to him and threw her arms around him. "Papa!" It hadn't taken long after his return for her to accept him as her father. Clearly Karl had left the position quite open.

"No, I mean, yes," Peter answered Zosia, while stooping down to give Madzia a big hug. "I quit, but they invited me back on." He wrapped his left arm around Madzia and carried her over to Irena. Lowering himself carefully, he bent down and kissed Irena hello. "The commission is in the toilet though. As Marysia said, she could hardly recommend a promotion right after I had flagrantly disregarded standing orders."

"Fair enough," Zosia chuckled. "There's tea. I made it earlier, but do you want some anyway?"

"Yes. Ow!" Peter yelped as Madzia managed to kick his right arm. "Be careful, sweetie." He set her down next to Irena.

"Did you get sanctioned?" Zosia poured Peter a cup of tea and he sat down to drink it.

"It'll go on my record." Peter sipped the tea, it was already tepid.

"Any punishment?"

He shook his head. "I talked to Marysia about it afterwards. She said she could not think of any adequate punishment. She said extra duty was out as long as I had my arm in a cast, since I'd be more trouble than help, but maybe, once my arm is healed, I might have to put in some unpaid overtime on the sewage works."

"That seems appropriate. You create shit, you can help clean shit up."

Peter threw Zosia a glance, thinking of all the times she had brazenly disobeyed orders, but he did not comment on that. "She also said that she knew that I would more than adequately punish myself." He turned back toward his daughters and took on a distant look as he watched the antics of his two beautiful little girls. "I wonder how they did it," he said almost to himself.

"Did what?" Zosia settled herself on the floor near Irena. She picked up some blocks and began to build a tower. Madzia watched entranced.

"The girl. I guess they got one of the kids to march her into the woods…"

"Oh, they'd never do that!" Zosia carefully balanced the last block on the tower. "Just like they didn't ask you to do it – even though, to be fair, you should have been the one to clean up the mess you made."

I was just trying to give her a decent chance in life. But there was no point in saying that, so he said, "I know. I appreciate not being involved. But why not one of the partisan guards?"

Madzia reached for the tower and sent the blocks tumbling. She giggled in response.

"They're too impressionable. It would be cruel to force that sort of job on just anyone." Zosia began to rebuild the tower.

"Then who?" *Why this fascination for the macabre details. Penance?*

Madzia swiped at the tower and it tumbled to the ground again. One of the pieces landed on Irena and Madzia began to laugh as Irena stared wide-eyed at the gift from heaven. Zosia tilted her head as she plucked the block

53

off Irena. "Be gentle," she cautioned Madzia and then began building the tower for her to knock down again.

Peter noticed that Zosia hadn't answered him. It was like she had buried herself in the children. "You?"

Without looking up from the tower, Zosia nodded.

"Why you?"

"I volunteered."

"Volunteered?"

"Yes, I'm experienced, so I knew it wouldn't traumatize me, though I must say, it's never an easy thing to do." Irena turned her head away from the tower and stared across the floor as if to take a break from such fascinating things. "Also because I'm good at what I do." Zosia put the last block on top of the tower. Madzia sprung and knocked it down before Zosia had even pulled her hand away. "She didn't see it coming," Zosia assured him over Madzia's loud laugh.

"Oh, Zosia, I'm sorry."

"You should be." Zosia's attention seemed absorbed by the blocks as she collected them together. She spoke as if in a trance, as if she had no choice but to release the words into the room. "We went for a walk in the woods, I chatted with her, pointed out a hawk circling above, I gave her a hug, and then..." she sighed heavily. "Then she gasped as if an insect had bitten her."

Peter buried his face in his hands. "I'm sorry."

"You should be," Zosia repeated. Unerringly she stacked one block on the other. "Tadek carried her back. He said she was very light."

"I'm so sorry. I..." he looked hard at Zosia. Despite her experience, despite her words, she seemed terribly affected by it all. "Zosia, you should have had me do it. It was my fault. You shouldn't have done it."

"What's done is done," Zosia said, icily. "Anyway, you would have reneged at the last minute and made a mess of it. Better to leave such things to someone who is experienced, someone who won't be touched by it all, someone like me." Again she finished the tower. Again Madzia sent the blocks flying.

The cold distance in Zosia's words sent a chill up his spine. "Was this last week? After Marysia summoned me?"

"No, yesterday evening."

Madzia tugged on Zosia's arm to get her to start building again. "If you collect the blocks for me," she told Madzia.

"Yesterday? But Marysia said..."

"We didn't want to be precipitous. We were all hoping for some solution to suggest itself."

Madzia began picking up the blocks, bringing each to Zosia like a gift.

54

"But…"

"We kept her down at one of the camps. Since we knew the delay was likely to be pointless, we figured there was no point in prolonging your agony." Zosia accepted each block and piled them on her lap.

"Oh God, if I had known there was time – I might have thought of something." Peter stopped. They had done it to protect him and he changed tack accordingly. "I had no idea! You shouldn't have shielded me like that. I don't deserve such protection."

"No, you don't." Zosia accepted the last block from Madzia, but did not move. Madzia waited expectantly, then tugged on Zosia's arm and pointed at the blocks. "We spent the time researching everything we could about her, but we still couldn't answer the two crucial questions."

"Which ones?"

Zosia placed the first block down and carefully balanced the next one on it. "What were her motives and what were her plans. That was the problem. With dubious motives, we couldn't trust her, and we couldn't watch her, not for the rest of her life." She stacked each block on top of the other, adding conversationally, "You do realize, Marysia was right – if she had been desperate, there were other avenues into the Underground. Certainly much safer ones than running off with a wanted criminal."

"I know, I tried to tell her that."

"Not very successfully."

"I don't think you understand how desperate someone like that can feel. You don't know what it's like to be entirely alone. Without friends or support or anywhere to run to."

"And *you* do?"

He was surprised by the question. Wary of what she might read into his words, he answered carefully, "I think so. When you see a chance – however risky – you take it. I did. And you and Marysia gave me hope."

Zosia turned to look at him, her eyebrows arched contemptuously. "So, you decided to pass on the favor."

He felt suddenly nauseous, and he wished he hadn't spoken. Deciding not to risk any further confidences that would draw her scorn, he simply repeated, "I'm sorry, Zosia."

Zosia finished the tower. Giggling with anticipation, Madzia swung at it and sent the blocks flying around the flat. Zosia looked at Madzia's triumphant smile and she smiled affectionately in return, reaching up to stroke her face, but her words were directed to Peter. "You should be," was all she said.

14

"*O*f course, you should be," Greta assured Elspeth, offering her a comforting hand.

Wolf-Dietrich rolled his eyes. Another bout of tears was sure to follow and he did not know which was worse – the perpetual whining of Frau Vogel or his step-mother's hypocritical reassurances. His father had forbidden them from attending the funeral – Karl Vogel's reputation had been rather too iffy, he had assured them, but Greta had insisted that a visit, after the fact, was necessary, though she herself had referred to Elspeth as a "flighty cow" and all the troubles which had befallen the family as "well-deserved."

"There, there, darling," Greta soothed, "I'm sure everything will work out for you."

Frau Vogel looked up at Frau Schindler and sniffed noisily. Despite all the crying, and handkerchief-dabbing, her eyes were not red, her face not puffy. In fact, Wolf-Dietrich thought, for all the bluster, he had not yet noticed one real tear.

No great surprise there. Karl Vogel would be missed by no-one, least of all his family, whom, by all accounts, he had alternately ignored or terrorized. Wolf-Dietrich remembered a long-ago meeting with Geerd Vogel and how much the lad had hated his father. Driven the elder son insane, Geerd had opined. And apparently the servant as well, Wolf-Dietrich thought. What other excuse was there for such a risky and unnecessary action? He tried hard to remember something of that man who had caused so much turmoil for so many, but though he knew he had seen him, he could remember nothing except someone wearing gray-blue. Nothing distinguishing about the boy at all.

Well, in any case, Frau Vogel would clearly be better off without her lumbering husband now that the Führer had personally extended his guarantees to her. It had been a bit touch-and-go there for awhile – nearly every official had missed the funeral – Traugutt's family being a notable exception. Stefi had told him that her mother considered it the only decent thing to do and her father was not one to disagree with her mother on points of etiquette. Once the Führer had learned how many people had snubbed the funeral, he had made a special effort to contact Elspeth Vogel and extend his sympathies. He was personally aware of the treacherous nature of that Halifax fellow, and he could truly sympathize with Elspeth in her hour of need. The Party would forgive the remaining mortgage on the house and Karl's pension would reach her intact, he had personally assured her. After that, Elspeth's fortunes had revived and her popularity as a distraught hostess was unparalleled.

Elspeth sighed heavily as though dropping the curtain on her act, and asked, "Would you like some wine? I think it's late enough."

Wolf-Dietrich nodded eagerly, but Greta placed a kind hand on his knee and assured Elspeth, "No, neither of us wants anything other than tea, right now. Isn't that right, dear?" She turned to Wolf-Dietrich for confirmation.

He grimaced and nodded.

A blank-faced man poured more tea for them and then retreated to the kitchen to refill the tray of pastries. Greta picked up her teacup, but did not drink. "Where did you get him? I thought you had a woman working here."

"Oh, the woman was on loan from my sister. Once the Führer heard of our tragedy, he sent over one of his staff for us. Said we could have him as long as we want, so I sent my sister's girl back to her. Wasn't that unbelievably kind of him?"

"Yes, he's taken a real interest in you," Greta commented sourly. She was obviously going to say more, but a young woman stepped tentatively into the room. Wolf-Dietrich immediately rose to his feet.

Elspeth glanced up at the girl and smiled. "This is my daughter, Ulrike," she cooed to Greta, and especially to Wolf-Dietrich. Both of them had met Ulrike before, but this was the first time that Wolf-Dietrich had seen her as a woman. He bowed and kissed her hand. She blushed becomingly.

He straightened and scanned her appraisingly. Not bad, in a sort of plain way. Round face, pale skin, her long, straight, bleached blond hair was pulled back into a braid, though some strands had strayed from their bonds and hung becomingly loose about her face. Even more attractively, the Traugutt family kept some minor contact with the Vogels and Stefi would definitely hear about a newly established friendship between himself and Ulrike.

"Pleased to make your acquaintance," Wolf-Dietrich said, not quite accurately.

Ulrike did not remark on the fact that they had previously met. She grinned, glanced down at the floor like a school-girl and giggled. "The pleasure is all mine." She seated herself and waited patiently as the servant set down the new tray of pastries and poured her a cup of tea. Once the servant was no longer in the way, she picked up her teacup delicately, her little finger carefully projecting outward. Wolf-Dietrich smiled at her as he reseated himself.

"So everything is settling back down," Greta commented, as a sort of question.

Elspeth sipped her tea before answering. "As much as is possible given the traumatic events we've endured."

"Yes, such an odd thing to happen, going through all that trouble to come back, taking all that risk. And then stealing your baby! I can't fathom why he would want to do that."

"He said it was in retaliation for the authorities having killed his daughter." Though Frau Vogel spoke to Frau Schindler, her eyes did not stray from Wolf-Dietrich's face and the way he was looking at Ulrike. "A daughter for a daughter, or something like that, is what he said."

"He had a daughter?" Greta tapped her chest in histrionic astonishment.

"It would seem so. She was five."

Greta furrowed her brow. "How is that possible? Wasn't he working for you then?"

"No, she was five at the time she was killed. He would have been working for the people before us at the relevant time, or I guess, he was in a prison of some sort then."

"Well, that still makes it impossible."

"Or at least illegal," Wolf-Dietrich corrected.

Ulrike looked as if she were waking from a dream. "That means he had a baby when he was here!"

"No," Elspeth sighed. "I gather she was adopted." Her expression darkened and she added, as if realizing it for the first time, "I guess that means that there was some woman he married or, er, whatever those sort of people do."

"Marriage! Adoption! Who the hell does he think he is?" Greta Schindler was so angry she nearly slammed her teacup down into its saucer. "My God! These people think they can–"

"Funny, I don't even remember what he looked like," Wolf-Dietrich said, mostly to shut his step-mother up.

"I'll show you a picture." Elspeth turned to the servant. "Go into my husband's study and get that folder off his desk. The big one stuffed with papers."

When the servant returned with the large folder, Elspeth carefully paged through it. "I guess this is the information my husband was using when he was working as a spokesman for the Führer. The police located it in my husband's study and said I should hand it back to the security services, but nobody's come to pick it up yet." She pulled out an American magazine article and handed it to Wolf-Dietrich.

Wolf-Dietrich was surprised by the strangely slick pages. Despite the smooth texture, the ink had not smudged on the paper, and Wolf-Dietrich was sufficiently impressed by the unexpected quality of the magazine that he almost forgot to look at what Elspeth was showing him.

"It's on the next page," Elspeth offered helpfully.

A half-page, color picture of a man in normal street clothes, sitting casually in a leather armchair, greeted Wolf-Dietrich. The man had a bemused smile on his face, a knowing expression in his eyes. It couldn't be! He looked so normal, so much a part of the world! An intelligent expression, fine features – handsome even – and not in some dark-skinned, exotic-native sort of way. No, the man could easily pass for Aryan. Wolf-Dietrich scowled. "Did he really look like that?"

"Yes." Elspeth's answer was matter-of-fact.

"Yes," Ulrike echoed dreamily.

Wolf-Dietrich frowned in thought. It was true he had seen the Vogel's boy infrequently, maybe three or four times altogether, but still, how was it he had never noticed what he looked like? Hell, if the Vogel's servant walked into the room now and sat down and had tea with them and talked about Party politics, nothing would seem out of place! Wolf-Dietrich glanced in confusion at the servant who stood wearily by the door but Wolf-Dietrich saw nothing more than a mindless expression and a gray-blue uniform. He handed the magazine to his step-mother. "Interesting."

Frau Schindler glanced at the picture and tossed the magazine onto the table. "Still with that know-it-all expression!" She laughed, unaware of how Elspeth Vogel was studying her. "I warned you all along he'd be trouble."

"Yes, you did," Elspeth agreed, unperturbed.

"Still, this sort of thing, coming back like that, that surprised me." Frau Schindler picked up the magazine and studied it a moment. "You would think that he'd have had his revenge, laying out how horrible his life here was for all to see."

"Horrible?" Ulrike sat upright, her eyes growing wide.

"Oh yes!" Greta shoved the magazine at her. "Read away! Any paragraph!"

"How do you know what he said?" Elspeth asked suspiciously.

Greta laughed. "Oh, Günter showed me the files. He's the one who identified Halifax at a meeting the Führer had once this horrible thing happened. It's all in there." She gestured toward the magazine Ulrike held. "Read it!"

Ulrike looked in confusion at the words. "I don't read English."

"I didn't realize you did," Elspeth commented to Greta.

"Oh, yes. Went to school there. America, I mean."

"School? How was that possible?" Elspeth and Ulrike asked in concert.

"I grew up in Switzerland. Swiss citizenship. My mother thought it would be a good experience for me to study abroad. What a mistake. Ugh! Horrible place! I'd never go back to that cesspit!"

"So how did you end up here?" Ulrike asked, clearly intrigued.

"Oh, my father was a Reich citizen. Diplomat. That's how he met Mother. I met Günter at a ski resort, and he convinced me to come here. Come home, as he put it." Greta laughed. "Anyway, if you can't read the English, look at the translations – they're stapled on the back. You'll see, he whines on and on about how horrible you all were to him. Like you were Cinderella's ugly step-sisters. The poor thing. And then he goes and proves exactly what we said all along – he was a criminal with a defective sense of morality! Murdering a noble German man in cold blood, in his sleep! Stealing a German child. God Almighty, what a degenerate!"

"Yes, degenerate," Elspeth echoed quietly, her eyes straying to the magazine which Ulrike held.

Ulrike stared disconsolately at the words on the page. "Someone should tell the Americans what a nasty man he is. It wasn't like that. We weren't like that. We're not horrible."

Greta reached across to touch Ulrike's knee. "No, of course you're not, dear."

"Father wasn't like that at all. He was a good man. Stern, but good." Ulrike's voice choked with tears. "He just tried to do what was right. To keep *him* doing what was right." She tapped the magazine to emphasize who *he* was.

"Discipline and a sense of order were important to your father," Wolf-Dietrich suggested, sympathetically.

"Yes," Ulrike agreed, gratefully. "And look what it's got him! Someone should tell those people! It's not fair! Someone should tell them!"

Wolf-Dietrich looked thoughtful as he agreed. "Yes, someone should."

15

A scream emerged – a shriek of instinctive terror that cut through the night and sent him tumbling from his bed and to his feet. Peter stumbled to Madzia where she lay in her little cot. She threw her head around and screeched again, but she was not awake. He knelt beside her bed, stroking her forehead, whispering calm words in her ear, and she slowly settled back into a peaceful sleep.

He kissed his little girl's cheek, then sat back down on the edge of his bed. Only then did he realize that he was bathed in sweat and trembling violently. Madzia's screams, but his memories. But what were they? What caused him to shudder so?

"Is Madzia okay?" Zosia's voice came out of the semi-darkness, tired but awake.

"She's fine. I guess it was a dream."

"What's the matter?"

Peter opened his mouth to tell Zosia about his strange terror, but her contemptuous words from the afternoon ran through his mind. "Ah, nothing."

"Nothing?"

Eyes stared at Peter through the dark quiet. Motionless, sightless eyes set in a pale, young face with the wisps of a beard. Death scented his thoughts. "I was just thinking that maybe I'd have a drink."

Zosia got out of bed and lifted Irena out as well. She carried her over to Madzia's cot and tucked her in next to the toddler.

"Why are you doing that?"

"I have a better idea than your having a drink. Irena can sleep there for a while – it'll give us more room." Zosia kissed the two little girls and then came around the bed to sit next to Peter. "What do you think?"

Peter tried to look at her in the dim light, but all he could see was a stinking pile of bodies and staring dead eyes. Burial duty. There had been more to it than that, but he couldn't remember what. He didn't want to remember.

Zosia stroked his hair, let her fingers trace a pattern down his face. "You're sweaty. What's the matter? Headache?"

"No." Worms and maggots and rotting flesh. But something else, too.

"Does your arm hurt?"

"No." The older bodies, the ones on the bottom, stinking and bloated. But what else?

She grabbed his left hand and pressed it to her chest. She leaned into him and kissed him on the cheek. "So?"

"Not now," he sighed, letting his hand drop off her chest. *Just forget it.*

She pulled back, stunned. *"No?* Why not?"

"Just not now, Zosia." Never before had he said no to her. Never before had she even needed to ask. He rolled into the bed. They were dead. Jana was dead. Everyone was dead. *Just forget it. None of it matters.*

Zosia continued to sit on the edge of the bed, then she turned and crawled in next to him, pressing herself intimately against him. He was forced to put his arm around her to keep her from falling off the edge. She adjusted her precarious position by climbing on top of him. He had to readjust himself to prevent her from putting pressure on his broken arm.

Her hand reached downward and she began stroking him. "Not interested? That's never happened before."

"Well, it's happened now. Some other time? Okay?" He could see she was beginning to grow angry, and within seconds she would begin screaming at him, but he preferred that to confiding in her. He just couldn't bring himself to tell her about the eyes, about that pile of bodies. He didn't want to risk her derision. *So, you decided to pass on the favor.* He could still hear the scorn in her voice. He might forget the words, but it would be a long time before he would forget that tone.

"What's the problem? Is it the extra weight? For Christ's sakes you carry and nurse a baby and see what it does to your body!" Already the pitch of Zosia's voice had risen considerably.

Without meaning to, he spoke even more softly in reply. "It's not that. You are as beautiful as ever. It's just me."

"But it's been such a long time! We haven't done it since—"

"Since before you sent me off to London," he finished dryly.

"What?"

Since before you clung to Tadek at Joanna's funeral. But he didn't say that.

"What are you trying to say?" By her shrill tone, he knew that she did not really want to know. What she wanted was an apology.

Since before you called me Adam at our daughter's birth.

"Are you saying somehow it's my fault we haven't been together?"

Since before you admitted it was all a lie.

"Peter?"

None of it mattered anymore. He tried to see her face but the stinking pile of corpses and those disembodied eyes obscured his view. He hesitated, then risking the truth one last time, he softly explained, "Madzia's screams…They provoked…I've just had a nightmare. I feel…" What did he feel? Fragile? Distant? Disembodied?

"A nightmare?" Her voice was sharp with disbelief.

Cold? Clear-headed?

"You're rejecting me because of a stupid nightmare?" It was a genuine shout. Right in his ear.

Peter looked past her, in the direction of the children, but they were sound asleep. Yes, that was it. Rational. How rare – to feel in control of his thoughts while in her presence. Her hands should have inflamed his passion, her words – so carelessly demanding – should have angered him. But he felt very little emotion towards her. Not anger, not desire, not much at all. As if her explosive revelations outside the Council chamber had blown out the fires of his passion. As if Jana's death had killed his desire to feel any human emotion. *Just forget it. None of it matters.*

"Peter." Surprisingly, she said it in a quiet, bedroom tone. She didn't say more and he didn't ask. Eventually, as if confessing, she added, "I love you."

"I love you too." But he felt so cold! Cold, distant, *safe*.

She continued to lie there on top of him, her hand moving gently over his body, her face pressed next to his. I should feel something, he thought. But he didn't. He pushed her hands away and gently rolled her off him and back onto her side of the bed. "I do love you. I'm glad you love me. But right now I just can't."

"Oh, Peter! For heaven's sake, you could do it with–"

"Is *that* what you really want from me?"

She fell silent. After a moment, she ventured, "Can't?"

"No, not *can't*. I just don't want you." He winced at this slip of the tongue and quickly amended, "That's not what I mean. I mean, I don't want to. Not right now. Maybe later. Just give me time. If you really do love me, you'll give me time."

16

"*G*ive me time," Richard begged, "Just give me a bit more time!"

"I don't understand why you're hanging on to her!" Greta stopped kissing his lips and slowly began working her way down his naked body. "What do you get out of it?"

"Greh-taaa" Richard drew out the syllables as if her name were a song. He could feel the way her breasts caressed his skin as she moved on down. His hands reached to stroke her shoulders, to encourage her. "She gave me six children, I want them to have a proper home…"

"Why six? For heaven's sake, does she believe all that crap about making babies for the Reich?" Greta planted a kiss on his stomach, right where the thin line of hair began its march downward. "You could be free if she had stopped at two, but no! She goes and ties you down with baby after baby!"

"I love my children," Richard protested weakly. It didn't help that Greta had moved even further downwards and was now using her tongue to excite him. "Oh, woman!" he moaned, unable to say anything more coherent. Kasia never did that sort of thing. Not ever! Hell, anymore she wouldn't do anything. Nothing at all! "Oh, Greta, how am I supposed to have a conver–" He couldn't go on. It wasn't the presence of the bodyguard in the room – that didn't matter anymore, he was used to it. Nor was it that their conversation had reached the same stonewall that it always encountered – she demanded he divorce Kasia and he could not explain why he would not. No, it was none of that, it was simply that his brain had ceased to function the way it was supposed to.

She knew he would do that, simply turn off all higher order functions, and she used her power exquisitely. At her prompting, he moaned as if in pain, groaned that he would do anything for her. He whispered hoarsely how much he wanted her, how he could never leave her and then, just at the right moment, she moved upward and sat herself on top of him, letting him slide into her, grasping him with her muscles, making him feel he would go mad if she let him go.

Ah, she thought, the Führer doesn't know what he's missing by insisting on young girls! A woman with experience, now that was something no nubile body could beat! But the Führer had his tastes, strange as they were, and they did not include the likes of her. So, she was reduced to hanging on to her husband and his prospects of advancement, or of attaching herself to this man and following him on his way up.

The trouble with Günter was that he was no longer so easily manipulated. He had lost interest in sex, at least sex with her, and since he refused to view his wife as a worthy partner in any other way, she had lost her hold on him. He was a mean-tempered sod as well and she was weary of his petty vindictiveness. Richard, on the other hand, was a worthy partner – still virile, and therefore still manipulable. The poor man thought that he was calling the shots! She watched as her victim writhed in agonized pleasure. He would make a good partner, attractive and good-tempered as well. His intelligence and strength were a good match for Günter's experience. No wonder Rudi had so carefully set them in opposition to each other: it would be a long battle, they would do each other down and he would sit safely watching from the sidelines. Unless, Greta thought, unless someone tipped the balance.

Richard's groans reached that pitch that let Greta know it was time. She began to pull away. He grasped her convulsively to him. "No! Don't go!" he implored. "Don't leave me!"

Compliantly, she settled back on to him even more intimately, driving him deeper into her, tightening her hold. Richard jerked uncontrollably, moaned expressively, with a death-like finality, and then collapsed, spent, onto the bed. Greta leaned forward, placing her chest on his and, embracing him, whispered, "Richard, I love you."

"I love you, too," he responded mindlessly.

"Let me be your wife," she murmured. "Promise me that."

"Anything," he exhaled. "Anything you want."

* * *

64

"What do you mean, divorce?" Kasia asked angrily.

Ryszard glanced backward to make sure that Mathias was sufficiently far behind them as they continued their stroll along the street. "It won't be for real," he assured her. "And once I'm Führer, I'll divorce Greta and remarry you."

"Oh, Ryszard, how could you suggest such a thing?"

"It's for you and the family. You won't have to put up with my bodyguards, and if anything should go wrong, you'll be safely distant from me. You can go to Szaflary."

"You know we won't be able to do that!" Kasia wailed. "We can't just disappear! We'll have to stay in that house and live our fake lives and you'll go off and live you double life with Frau Schindler. My God, Ryszard, have you gone mad?"

"No, it's just necessity. I need her on my side."

"Why? She has no power!"

"But she does! She has a lot of connections and influence. She will expand my power base, and it works the other way as well – if she doesn't help me, she can hurt me. She knows how to make mischief. If she feels vindictive, she could make a lot of trouble for me."

"And why might she feel vindictive?" Kasia asked bluntly.

They were walking past the Vogel's house and Ryszard spared a glance at it before answering. "You know what my life is like, Kasia. You know what I have to do…"

"No," Kasia shook her head vehemently. "No, this is a problem of your own invention. You had no need to get involved with her. And now you want to organize a divorce just so that you can stay near her. My God, Ryszard, she's a viper! How can you want to wrap yourself in her embrace?"

"Kasiu," Ryszard snarled, "you know how much of my life I've given to this. You know the people I've had to involve myself with. You know I've had to completely immerse myself in this role just to keep us all alive. And now, with these shadows…" He jerked his thumb back in the direction of Mathias as he followed them. "Now I don't get a single moment's peace. Not one minute! I'm trying to spare you from that, put some distance between you and them and all you can do is question one connection I've made, simply because you're jealous. For Christ's sake, woman, don't you know what I've given to reach this point?"

"Yes, you've given up your soul."

"Don't give me that trite shit," Ryszard growled, working hard to keep his voice low. "How the hell do you think I'll ever get that top position?"

"For what, Ryszard? What good will it do? You've become one of them."

They walked on in silence through the park that led to the square. They stopped at the duck pond and Kasia pulled some dried bread out of her bag and threw it to the creatures. They quacked noisily and flapped their wings excitedly, some of them even coming up to Kasia's legs, raising their beaks expectantly.

"As your commanding officer, Kasia, you know I can order this," Ryszard said under his breath.

Kasia continued to drop bread for the ducks, but her attention was directed out across the water. "If that's what you feel, Ryszard, then I guess an order won't be necessary."

17

*G*reta looked around appraisingly. "Not a bad place, you have here. How long did you let it for, Richard?"

"Until the end of the year. Renewable." A furnished flat in the center, walking distance from the Ministry. How convenient. Restaurants, nightclubs, cafés all within a short distance. Not like the stultifying suburb where the house was. Here the evenings were lively. Well, as lively as any place in Berlin nowadays.

"That should be long enough to get all the paperwork done." Greta glanced into the bedroom and kitchen before entering the living room.

"I don't know." Richard followed her, motioning to Leszek to join them.

"And you brought along one of your servants. How very clever of you."

"Yes," Richard agreed sourly. Kasia had intimated her concerns to HQ and the result was that Leszek had taken up residence with him when he separated from her. And now he had to put up with Leszek's interminably patient expressions. Take the poor man away from his wife, condemn him to sleep on a cot in the hall. One would think Richard had committed some great crime against Leszek! For Christ's sake, he found excuses often enough for Leszek to visit the house – and what soldier got to see his wife at regular intervals anyway? How many soldiers throughout history would have killed for a comfortable cot inside a warm apartment? Their situation was never intended to be cozy! For heaven's sake was he the only one who could remember that this was all for a purpose? That they were fighting a war?

"...and after I get everything sorted out with Günter, you can move into the house." Greta glanced out the living room windows, then turned her attention back to Richard. "You can bring him with you, perhaps."

"You're sure he'll let you keep it? The house, I mean."

"It's mine," Greta laughed. "The house and all but two of the servants." She motioned toward Leszek to light a cigarette for her.

"*Was* yours. Marriage put everything in his name, you know." Richard accepted the cigarette that Leszek offered him and waited impatiently for him to light it. "That's the law."

"Two points, Richard dear." Greta grabbed his face and planted a smoky kiss on his lips. "First of all, it's traditional that the man gives up the house, whatever his rights in law. Secondly, laws like that are meant for little people. I made sure everything stayed in my family name. Don't you worry, I'll get to keep my house."

"Maybe you should take this a bit slowly." Richard lowered himself into an armchair. "We don't want to be precipitous. Wait a bit."

"Why?" Greta looked at him suspiciously. "What do you have in mind?"

Richard called her over to his lap. As she sat down, he wrapped his arms around her and whispered in her ear. "I think I can force Günter to be my ally, or rather, my lieutenant. I might need your help – from the inside, so to speak."

"You have something on him?"

Richard nodded. "I think so."

"Does it have anything to do with that London fiasco?" Greta pulled back enough to look him in the face.

He did not meet her gaze. "Could be." Why, he wondered, had he even mentioned it?

"Richard dear, if you want my support, I expect your trust. Now, answer me, does it have anything to do with the London lab?"

He supposed there was no harm in telling her, she would find out soon enough. "Yes. I've gotten hold of information about what he was doing there. It should be enough to bring him down, at my leisure. I'll offer him an alternative: he can be loyal to me."

"Us," Greta corrected. "To us."

"Yes, to us," Richard agreed, uneasily. He looked across the room at Mathias, as he stood there, ever vigilant. "Let's go for a walk," he suggested in a normal tone of voice. "It's Sunday, after all, what better thing to do?"

"Yes, let's. Günter never goes out with me anymore."

"Where is he now?"

"London. I think there's a problem there," Greta confided, with a wink.

Richard liked her sense of humor, her spirit of conspiracy. Like Julia, he thought. Always like Julia. Whatever had happened to them, he wondered, as he gave his arm to Greta so they could walk out the door together. Why had Julia so decidedly refused to work with him? She was young, yes, but they had thought at the time that the assignment would be temporary. Why not a jaunt with him in Kraków? Why had she applied to work in Berlin, removed herself from him like that? And why, he wondered, had he compromised and married Kasia? Good, old, reliable Kasia. Part of the job, he thought, even then, it had been nothing more than a marriage of convenience. It was a cruel thing to have done to the poor girl. It was good to finally make a break from her. She needed the space to grow. She needed to be without him.

They waltzed down the stairs and out the door, held open for them by the porter. They only had to walk a few meters along the street to reach Unter den Linden. Turn right and they could walk up to a small park near the museums. But Greta pulled him to the left. "I want to walk to the Tiergarten."

So, they went to the left along the grand street. Funny, the street had once been famous for its linden trees; now it was cold, empty, desolate. Filled with guard boxes and clumsy stone monuments. Even the name was changed to forever obliterate any memory of the trees, as if they were enemies of the state. But that had never taken. It was still, to all and sundry, Unter den Linden. Maybe, Richard mused, just maybe, there was hope for this culture. Maybe Europe would emerge from the mire and rebuild itself.

A patrolling soldier saluted as he walked past. Richard returned the salute with a brief wave of his hand. He was not wearing any sort of uniform – what, he wondered, had tipped the soldier off? Was he already recognizable as a prominent resident of the area? Or was it the bodyguard? A couple, walking in the opposite direction, carefully moved to the side as Richard's group approached. The sidewalk wasn't that narrow, but still the couple gave Richard and his entourage plenty of space.

He sniffed his amusement. What hope? he thought as he lit himself another cigarette. They were all too ready to be obedient, all trained to hierarchy. To salute and command and grovel and snitch. At least those who were left. Anyone with any spirit was gone, driven out or murdered. There was no hope that change would come from below. If he gained power he would have to drag the Reich, kicking and screaming, through the changes that he planned. The battle would only have just begun. And, he wondered, as Greta clung to his arm, was he really the one to do it? He had no understanding of democracy, did not, in fact, really trust it. His entire life, he had experienced nothing but military discipline and a war-footing.

What could he hope to accomplish? Capitalism? Free markets? Democracy? None of it meant anything to him. His father assured him, it was the way to go – the way to wealth, equity, peace. But how? He didn't even know what the words meant!

They strolled through the Brandenburg gate and across the road. A sentry checked Richard's documents, then smiling and bowing slightly, gestured the entire group through the entrance into the well-groomed section of the park reserved for Party members and their guests. As they walked along the path, a worker who had been picking up some of the numerous cigarette ends, moved deferentially out of their way. Richard glanced at the insignia on his uniform. A French political prisoner. Goodness, they really were scraping the bottom of the labor pool!

Greta clucked disapprovingly. "They shouldn't have him working here on a Sunday."

Yes, even forced-laborers could do with a day off, Richard thought, as he flicked his cigarette end into the grass.

"After all, that's when everybody is out walking – they get in the way! Surely they could find some work for him somewhere out of the way."

"Surely."

They stopped at a park café. Since it was in the reserved section of the park, there no lines and it was reasonably clean.

The maitre d' bowed slightly. "A table for three, Colonel?"

"Two."

Greta shivered slightly and said to Richard, "Indoors."

"Indoors," Richard dutifully added.

Mathias stepped up to Richard and said something. "Oh, alright," Richard agreed testily. "And not by the windows."

They were led to a quiet table in the corner and with no view. Richard found himself scanning the restaurant. Was it really so dangerous? Or was it all part of a charade that was intended to keep him on a nice, short leash for the Führer? Clearly Rudi's watchers didn't prevent conspiracies – Schindler's activities in London were sure proof of that. Or was it? Was the Führer aware of the activities in that laboratory? Had it all been at his behest? If that was the case, then the information that Peter had uncovered was not particularly useful for blackmailing Schindler. Indeed, if that was the case, then if Richard handled the information badly, he could actually injure himself more than Schindler. Before he did anything, he decided, he needed to know more about what the Führer already knew, and for that he needed Stefi.

"Well?" Greta prompted.

Richard looked up, confused. A waiter waited patiently for his order. Richard scanned his uniform. Though it was discreetly worked into the design of the uniform, there was the insignia of a forced-laborer on his shoulder. Were there, then, no jobs left for decent hard-working German citizens?

"Coffee," Richard finally ordered.

Greta raised her eyebrows. "No cake?"

Richard pulled out his pack and offered Greta a cigarette but she waved it away. He pulled one out for himself and the waiter promptly lit it. Well, the service was always better from the *Zwangsarbeiter*. He supposed the threat of being beaten was always more convincing an incentive than a low wage and a miserably tiny flat in a concrete tower.

"Richard?" Greta pressed.

"No, no cake." It didn't make sense. So much cheap, almost free labor, should make life much better for all those who benefited from their work. That's the way it used to work. The Greeks with their life of leisure and deep thought, surrounded by their slaves, carrying out the boring, daily chores. Or the Romans. Or the aristocrats of Europe, served by armies of serfs. The indentured servants, the African slaves, the virtual slavery of the industrial revolution. Massive wealth and leisure supported by armies of anonymous people toiling away. Or had it been like that? In each of those societies there were the peasant farmers, the money-lenders, the innkeepers and the artisans, merchants and traders. Their lives were not interesting enough to ever be separately chronicled, but they had existed, and it was they who had carried on the society, they who made the economy work. And, he thought, it was the societies that allowed those people to grow wealthy that were the strongest. Decrease the size of the slave-class by making it possible to leave it, either by education or hard-work or whatever. Decrease the strength of the parasitic warrior class by denying them their unique access to wealth and power. Empower that middle group by allowing them to accumulate worldly goods, by making their lives and old-age secure, by giving them the leisure to be educated and inventive. Could it work?

"A penny for your thoughts."

Richard smiled at Greta. "Just thinking about the nature of our society."

Greta fingered one of the little flags which formed their table's decorative centerpiece. "Yes," she sighed dreamily. "Our orderly society is the envy of the world. And you and I are at the pinnacle of it!"

The day had grown chillier and Greta leaned into Richard's embrace as they walked back. He could feel the curve of her waist under his fingers and it made him feel rather inspired. The doorman opened the door to his apartment building, they climbed the flight of steps and then, at last, they achieved the relative privacy of his flat. Jörg was off duty, so they had a few seconds alone as Mathias searched the flat for anything suspicious.

Richard used the time wisely, kissing Greta passionately in the hallway, slowly walking her toward his bedroom as he worked at the buttons of her blouse.

"*Mein Herr*!" Mathias called out, as if alarmed.

Richard groaned and went to see what the problem was. Greta followed him, carefully doing up the buttons of her blouse. Mathias was standing in the kitchen, holding some papers in his hand. Leszek was there as well, looking somewhat worried.

"Is it a bomb?" Richard asked, sarcastically.

"He had it hidden, there." Mathias pointed excitedly toward a cupboard. "Under the dishes."

It was clear they had come in earlier than Leszek had expected; indeed Richard had noticed that he had not even managed to open the door for them. Nevertheless, there was no excuse for such a blatant breach of security. Grimacing, Richard put his hand out so Mathias would hand him the papers.

"It's in some sort of code!" Mathias looked menacingly at Leszek.

Richard scanned the documents. "It's written in Polish. Though the modern linguistic abilities of our security personnel are rather limited," he glanced pointedly at Mathias, "it hardly qualifies as a code."

"You know the language?" Greta peered over his shoulder.

"I can certainly recognize it."

"I thought it was officially banned." Greta touched the paper gingerly with one finger.

Recognizing her implication, Richard took his attention off the pages to look at Greta. "Current law is that the written word is. Nevertheless, when people are plotting revolutions, they rarely stop to think about whether or not they are violating language laws. And it would hardly do for me, heading up the security in that region, not to be able to recognize the language in print."

"So, it's a revolutionary tract!" Mathias trumpeted.

"It's a letter to his woman." Richard felt exasperated by the circus. "See the salutation? That's her name."

"His woman?" Greta pursed her lips, disapprovingly.

Richard pulled out a cigarette and Leszek stepped forward to light it, but he did not look up enough for Richard to see his expression. "You remember," Richard patiently explained, as he scowled angrily at Leszek, "the other servant in our house is female. Obviously, the two maintain some sort of correspondence."

"But, isn't that illegal? It's certainly improper!"

"Yes, yes," Richard agreed tiredly. "As long as they did their work, I didn't make it my business to interfere in what they did in their spare time."

71

"Richard! That's so, so..." Greta was hardly able to contain her shock. "Well, this is certainly too much! Letters! Writing! Illegal communications! Relationships! What are you going to do?"

"I'll deal with it." Richard looked threateningly at Leszek.

"He must be punished!"

Mathias nodded his head in agreement. "Yes, *mein Herr*. It wouldn't do to let this sort of thing go unpunished."

Between the two of them, they would know that he had done nothing. And given Mathias' words, it was clear that the Führer would hear about it as well. Richard frowned and stared at the floor. He was furious with Leszek. What in God's name did he think he was doing? Such an unforgivable breach of security! Such senseless risk! Couldn't he go a week without his wife? Had he forgotten he was a soldier? That they were at war?

Richard sighed heavily. What could he do? He supposed, with some effort, he could manufacture something. Send Greta and Mathias from the room, make a lot of noise. It would be difficult to pull it off. And risky. Was it worth it? Richard glared at Leszek. He deserved whatever happened.

Richard turned to Mathias. "You discovered it. You handle it." He ignored the look of glee on Mathias' face and motioned for Greta to join him as they left the kitchen. Before they had even reached the door, Mathias swung his fist at Leszek's face. Richard quickly turned around, "Just not the face."

Mathias looked at him, clearly surprised, but he readily agreed, "Yes, *mein Herr*."

Greta tugged at Richard's sleeve and whispered something in his ear.

"Really?"

She nodded. "They have no concept of the problems it causes."

"Ach." Addressing Mathias again, Richard added, "And no broken bones." The look of disappointment on Mathias' face told him the warning had not been unnecessary. "In fact, nothing visible – understood? I don't want people talking." He left the room with Greta, closing the door behind them, and retreated to the apartment's balcony.

"Let's go back into the bedroom." Greta pressed herself provocatively against his back as he stood at the railing.

Richard looked out at the street. There was a patrol of soldiers. A few couples walked along, one family group. Across the road and down a bit there was a hotel with large windows. He saw how two *Zwangsarbeiter* were carefully cleaning the glass. Another was polishing the marble statue which stood in front of the hotel's entrance. He thought of the demographics he had mentioned to Peter. Official numbers. Peter was right though: the numbers didn't seem to match with experience. Were the numbers wrong? Was it incompetence? Deliberate misinformation? He sighed heavily.

"What's wrong? Didn't you hear me?" Greta's hands wrapped themselves around him.

What was wrong when even someone as highly placed as he could not believe the statistics that he was shown?

"Richard?"

Though they had pulled the door to the balcony shut, he could still hear some noise from the kitchen. What was wrong, Greta asked. Lots, he thought. Lots.

18

"*L*ots! Lots, lots, lots!" From her vantage point on Peter's shoulders, Madzia squealed excitedly, pointing toward a patch of berries and prodding with her feet.

"Careful there, sweetheart, don't kick your sister." Peter glanced down at Irena snuggled on his chest in her little papoose. She gave him a toothless grin in response. The papoose had been sewn by Marysia for her son Adam to carry his daughter Joanna, and as Peter smiled down at the baby, he felt a pang of regret that Irena and Madzia would never know their older sister. He supposed Joanna would have only been a half-sister to Irena and was not even related to Madzia, but that seemed a tediously pedantic point for three children who would have been such a natural family.

"Go, horsie! Go!"

Imitating a whinny, Peter did his best to gallop over the thick, thorny underbrush so that he could safely deliver his daughter to the berries she had spotted. He scanned the patch, and, seeing nothing suspicious, set Madzia down. Though it had been several weeks since his cast had been removed, he still enjoyed the sensation of having full use of both his arms and appreciated the ease with which he could do such things now.

"They all look good, pick whatever you want, sweetie. Just be careful of the thorns." He swatted at some of the bugs which seemed particularly heavy in the humid June air and added, "and don't get bit." Oblivious to his words Madzia wandered directly through a swarm to get to her beloved berries. Peter chuckled and settled himself on the grass, letting his mind wander even as he kept an eye on both his girls.

Despite the relaxing sunshine and Madzia's antics, shoving more berries into her mouth than into the bucket, it was the encampment's computer system that dominated Peter's thoughts. It needed to be completely redesigned both to fit in with the changes in the Reich's systems and also to better communicate with the Americans. The question was: how to do it? Warszawa had already indicated that there was no one available for the job, so Peter was left considering the practicality of his doing it himself. With patience, determination and a bit of instruction from afar, he might just manage to learn enough to restructure everything. The thought of learning something new and expanding his skill set pleased him, and the prospect of working alone, without having to interact much with other humans, had a strong appeal.

A bee buzzed near Irena and Peter lazily swatted it away. The more he thought about it, the more he was convinced he could do it. He'd get the information from Warszawa and the North American Union and get someone who could be called upon to offer instruction when necessary. But then, to whom should he suggest the idea? Wanda, as his superior officer, would be the natural one to hear his plan, but she would reject it reflexively. So, he would have to convince Marysia, as only she could override Wanda's veto.

Peter looked down at his watch but instead his eyes lit upon the numbers tattooed on his arm so long ago. He wondered if they really were as irremovable as the physician had told him upon his arrival at Szaflary. It was something he should look into – but the opportunity of visiting a proper facility, as well as the money required, was a severe hindrance, and rather than fret over the impossible, he had simply put their existence out of his mind. He ran his fingers lightly over the skin. It had seemed a vanity to worry about removing them – a vanity they could ill afford given the greater need all around them, yet if those numbers hadn't been there when that bomb exploded last September, he might never have been discovered, and Joanna wouldn't have been...*No, mustn't go there!*

It was time to head back – Irena would be needing Zosia's milk soon, and even more pressing, Zosia would be needing Irena to relieve her of it. Peter called to Madzia, accepted the berries she had picked, hooking the little bucket onto his belt and lofted her back onto his shoulders. Thus encumbered with two children and the fruits of their labors, he began the long walk back through the woods, warmed both by the sunshine and Madzia's continuous barrage of chatter. It reminded him of the tiny window in his past when all was going right with his family. His little sister's babbling speech, his mother so happy at the birth of her daughter that she greeted the antics of her children with a contagious laughter that simply

74

filled the room with joy. Someone had once told him, long ago when he still laughed out loud, that his laughter was like that.

I should find that part of me, he thought, and resurrect him. It would be a good trait to add to the personality he was constructing and it would fit so well. He felt supremely happy with his life, surrounded by the beauty of the mountains, with a family he loved, and work which kept him busy and feeling needed. And he felt balanced – he was able to approach life with a rationality and coolness that had long been absent. Zosia's tantrums left him unmoved and unhurt, a distinct courtesy and careful friendliness in his relations with others kept him safely distant. He rarely lost his temper anymore, or more precisely, he never lost his temper. There was nothing worth losing his temper about – he just occasionally used a display of anger to a well-calculated advantage.

He had everything under control, his life was running like a program where unwanted input was simply ignored. It was almost like the old days. Zosia's revelations and Jana's death had taught him much, or rather, had reminded him of lessons learned long ago. He again understood his place in society and just how much he could engage himself emotionally. And that was not much at all. Beyond the narrow world of his children, he knew better than to care a great deal. *Just forget it, none of it matters*, had returned as his leitmotif. It left him remarkably calm, pleasant and helpful, and on those occasions when he wanted to disengage, he was able to erect an invisible wall almost instantaneously. It worked wonderfully – everyone agreed he was doing well now. Everyone saw his ready, relaxed smile exactly as he intended them to see it – as a sign that all was fine. He was happy and secure, and if he needed to manipulate his actions to reflect that, or suppress unruly emotions to achieve such a state, then so be it.

"Go horsie! Go!" Madzia spurred him on with her heels and he dutifully attempted to gallop. Madzia swayed precariously from side to side, too excited by the ride to sit still. A sudden sharp pain tore through Peter's leg and his knee buckled. He felt himself falling and panic-stricken he threw one arm protectively around Irena and held onto Madzia's thigh with the other. With nothing left to break his fall, his shoulder slammed into the earth. Madzia held onto his head, straining his neck, herself unharmed. Irena cuddled against him, utterly unperturbed by the entire event.

Peter lay unmoving on the ground, feeling extraordinarily foolish for having been so careless. It was one thing to project a happy normalcy, it was quite another to believe one's own bullshit. "Damn," he muttered, using English, as he always did when cursing himself. "I'm such an idiot!"

"Damn. I'm such an idiot!" Madzia gleefully echoed as she climbed off her father's shoulders.

Peter covered his mouth to keep from laughing out loud, but Madzia knew he was amused. "Oh, fuck!" she added helpfully. "It's this fucking computer!"

Her accent was perfect and unmistakably his. That did him in and he began laughing uncontrollably. "You know, little girl," he said in English, once he had regained his breath, "I think you spend too much time in my office." Madzia looked at him uncomprehendingly and he leaned forward and kissed her. "I'm going to have to teach you some better English."

Madzia giggled at his alien words, Irena yawned and burped her disinterest. Peter climbed to his feet, adjusted Irena's position, hefted Madzia onto his shoulders and strode, somewhat more carefully, off toward the camp. As they crested a hill, he took a small detour and stopped to rest under a great pine. Joanna's stone was there, next to Adam's. A bit further away, where the roots were not so thick, was Andrzej's grave. Of the three, his was the only one with a body.

Peter counted backward. Nine months since Joanna's murder, not even five months since his nephew had been killed in the fighting. Poor Ryszard and Kasia had not even had a chance to see the grave, much less their son's body. Since Ryszard's controller was based in Warszawa, the Szaflary council was not generally informed of his doings and Peter had heard nothing about the family since he had been there in March and he wondered how they were doing. At the time Peter had visited, Andrzej had been dead only two months and Kasia was still clearly distraught, but Ryszard had seemed almost unconcerned, consumed as he was by his discovery that Karl Vogel had murdered Julia. Eh, unconcerned was the wrong word. Ryszard did care about Andrzej and was obviously deeply hurt by his son's death. It was just not his style to betray any of his emotions to anyone. A fact which had made his heart-wrenching confessions about Julia all the stranger to Peter.

Peter's eyes strayed from Andrzej's grave back to the stones directly under the pines. Behind Joanna's and Adam's white stones, Peter had privately placed another, much less remarkable one. He had put it there for Jana. He didn't know where she was, didn't know if there was a marker for her, and he didn't dare ask. Instead he had placed a stone under the tree so that he could always be reminded of another girl who had senselessly lost her life, and so that he would not forget the lesson her death had taught him. He had been forced to give his word to her and her father in order to get their help, but no one said he had to keep it. He should have abandoned her when they had made contact with those two men in Poznań. It was that simple – he should never have tried to help. Zosia's scornful words remained with him. She was right – he had never been in a position in society where he could do anyone any good, and it was stupid and vain to have tried.

Madzia tugged at his hair. *"Tatu,* I'm hungry!"

Peter turned away from the memorials and began climbing back to the encampment. "Me too, *Mäuschen.* Let's get home and have some of that stew I made. I bet it'll be yummy!"

"You ate all the stew?" Though there was no hope, he scratched forlornly at the dirty pan that still sat on the stove.

"I was hungry." Zosia settled herself in with Irena.

Peter sighed, put some butter into the bottom of the stew pan, turned the flame on low and began cleaning mushrooms as the butter melted. "I guess Madzia and I will have some of the mushrooms we picked. Just as well, they're all broken anyway."

"Didn't you pick up any rations?"

"Those *were* our rations." He sliced the mushrooms and tossed them into the already browning butter and breathed deeply, savoring the pungent smell.

"You forgot to take the trash out before you went off this morning."

The trash was a genuine nuisance – it had to be carted and buried quite far from the encampment, and ever since he had moved into Zosia's flat, she had happily assigned that job to him. "Sorry. I'll get it after we eat. I have to go back out anyway."

"More work?"

"Yeah, there's some things I have to sort out. I can take Madzia with me, if you want."

"You'll get a chance to clean up the kitchen before you leave, won't you?"

"Of course. It'd be my pleasure." He turned to look at her to see if she'd understand the irony. He had really looked forward to that stew!

She smiled at him. "You people like working, don't you?"

Peter laughed to himself and took the bait. "Who are 'you people'?"

"The working class! It's in your genes, I think. This work ethic. Makes you feel needed."

"Needed. Yep." Peter turned his attention back to the mushrooms. He had heard this one too many times to be amused, and he hoped that agreeing would be sufficient to spare him Zosia's theories. It wasn't. As he fried the mushrooms, Zosia waxed poetic about her lineage and how it made her special and, predictably, meandered onto her theory of how all the truly genetically talented had shaken themselves out of the proletariat, thus establishing a hierarchy which, if not exactly fair, was at least natural and efficient.

77

"Uh-huh." Peter nodded his head in an imitation of agreement.

"Don't you think?" Zosia queried, clearly looking for a more active response.

"We've gone through this before."

"Well, yes, there are exceptions – like you. I mean, you're clearly quite talented even with your background, but see – you've immediately moved out of your old milieu and into your appropriate class."

"So did my father." Was that the reason his father had worked so hard to belong to the Party? To escape the working class label which would otherwise drag him down for the rest of his life? *Yes, guv'nor, pleased to be of service, guv'nor...*

"Your father was a Nazi!"

"I know. Interesting that if you're right and the cream naturally rises to the top, that they're the ones running this society and you and yours are cowering in the mountains." He didn't look up, but he could feel the intensity of her anger.

"It's the prols," Zosia fumed. "It seems to me that anytime the prols grab power, things get murderous – not just in the Reich, I mean, look at China's revolution. And Russia – how many years did it take before they stopped murdering their own people en masse? Forty? Fifty?" Zosia shook her head in dismay. "Tch. There's no end of examples. Something violent about the lower classes – maybe it's in your upbringing."

"I thought you said it was genes."

"Whatever. Something separates you people out from us."

"Or *you* out from us." Peter gave up on his attempt to avoid the topic, endeavoring instead to lighten the tone. "Unfortunately, after a while you all get inbred. Then we need a revolution and have to lop off a few heads to clean things out."

"Peter! That is in truly poor taste!"

"Well, yes, there are exceptions – like you." He winked at her as he used her words. "Your mother was clever enough to outbreed – to a low-class mixed-blood mongrel of all things! But at least it saved her children from–"

He was saved from saying more by a knock at the door. He turned down the flame and went to answer it. A young soldier greeted him, holding a note. Peter accepted the piece of paper wordlessly.

"What's it say?" Zosia was intent on Irena and did not even look up.

Peter unfolded the note even as he wondered how Zosia could be so calm about official notices. Of course, she had not grown up in a society where unexpected knocks at the door were *always* bad news. "Marysia wants to see me as soon as convenient." He glanced back at the stove then at the courier. "Please tell her, I'll meet her in the council room in thirty minutes."

"Sir..." The messenger hesitated, looking down the hall.

"Go now," Zosia advised matter-of-factly.

Though Zosia wasn't looking at him, Peter nodded his recognition of the implicit order in the request and said to the messenger, "Two seconds while I turn off the gas. Where is she?"

"In her apartment, sir." The courier nodded with his head to the room only two doors away. "Shall I escort you?"

Peter shook his head at the silliness of the suggestion. "That won't be necessary." He dismissed the boy, turned off the stove and, after heaping a mound of mushrooms into Madzia's bowl and arming her with a spoon, he went down the hall to Marysia's. He greeted her with a kiss before asking, "So, you couldn't come knock on our door?"

"I sent the message out when I was in the Council chambers," Marysia explained, somewhat embarrassed. "But I guess you were out then. By the time they located you, I was back here."

"What's up?"

"We need you to go to England."

"England?" Peter raised his eyebrows histrionically. "Isn't that exactly where the Nasties have been looking for me?"

Marysia shook her head. "No, Berlin, ever since your escapade there."

Peter glanced around the empty room. "Wanda's not here, so I'll play her part. Now why in the world would you send me to England, with what I know, with my infamy? Isn't it sort of stupid to take that kind of risk? Wouldn't anyone else do?"

He said it as a joke but Marysia recognized the truth in his humor. "Yes, you're right, normally this sort of thing would cause conniptions."

"*Yes!* I might get captured and betray everything as soon as they stick a pin in my finger. You know what we English are all like. Faint-hearted! Can't be trusted! Born traitors! Doubtless I've been working for them all along and will use this opportunity to betray you all!"

Marysia looked slightly pained. "We'll work on the assumption that you're one of us."

"Should I take that as a compliment?" Peter asked wryly.

"The highest."

Peter laughed. "It *must* be important. Why me?"

Marysia smiled wanly.

"Money?"

She nodded.

"Now how did I know that? Let me guess: A celebrity magazine wants to do an interview and photo-shoot of me in front of Big Ben. Funding will skyrocket and we'll overthrow the Reich within days. Am I right?"

"Would you just shut-up long enough for me to explain?"

"They do know that the clock is now topped by a swastika and eagle, don't they?"

"Peter." Marysia did not need to say more to exhibit her exasperation.

"And it doesn't keep time anymore."

"Peter, please!"

"Alright, what's up?"

"Several things. We need you to get in contact with Barbara – I'll explain why shortly. We also need you to try to recruit your brother."

"I thought he said he wasn't interested."

"He's in a very useful position at this moment. We're hoping you can work on him."

A gleam came into Peter's eye. "It'd be my pleasure. And the real reason?"

Marysia sighed and paced away from him. She stopped and looked up at the photographs on her wall. Her wedding photograph with Cyprian, her husband, now divorced and as good as dead. Below that, she had photographs of her children: Julia, the alcoholic daughter who had gotten herself murdered by her erstwhile lover, and Adam – buoyant, proud, reckless. Beloved Adam, brutally tortured to death, the son Peter would never replace. Beneath those photographs were the grandchildren. Adam's child, beautiful Joanna, taken at such a young age, strangled while under Peter's care. And Julia's illegitimate son, Karl Vogel's progeny, Olek, crippled by a mine, the only survivor of Marysia's pathetic family.

Peter waited in respectful silence and eventually Marysia turned away from the photographs and faced him squarely, her attitude completely businesslike. "It seems there has been a series of suicide bombings in and around the London area. The group responsible is a splinter group from the English Republican Army – your old gang. They have apparently grown fed up with the status quo and are trying to ignite some sort of violent confrontation. Unfortunately, they have chosen to use random terror as their weapon. They strap bombs to volunteers and send them into crowded shops, government offices…Whatever. Usually they choose targets frequented by occupation colonists, but they have managed some English victims. Conciliators, mostly."

Peter nodded but did not comment.

"Obviously the Toronto government is not pleased by this turn of events. The ERA is, of course, in a minority position in government and is thoroughly embarrassed by this group."

"Naturally."

"The activities of this group are costing them an inordinate amount of money. Funding is down because people are being confused by the names and by the various goals."

Peter raised an eyebrow. "What are they calling themselves?"

"The *Real* ERA."

"Charming."

"This is the first group to openly break with the 'United Front' policy in years and the cracks are causing a slowdown in funding for all groups – not just the English."

"I see."

Marysia eyed him as if looking for sarcasm in that answer. She finally seemed to accept his comments at face value and continued. "They claim that they were inspired by your words. That you advocated a 'revolution of any sort' as being preferable to the stalemate that we currently have."

"I didn't say that."

"I know. Even Toronto is aware of that. They asked Alex if he could possibly get in contact with you–"

"They don't know where I am, do they?"

Marysia shook her head. "No, but after that thing with Joanna, they know you two are connected, that you married Alex's daughter. That's all."

"Good."

"Anyway, they want you to personally go over and talk to some representatives of this group to try to dissuade them from their tactics."

"I see."

"They promised funding to Alex's group – as they called it – if he managed to get you there, talking peace."

"I see."

"It's worth it to them. They're not only losing money, they're losing political clout."

"Of course."

Marysia paused, perturbed by his brief answers. She tilted her head slightly, as if taking his measure. "Will you do it?"

"I owe nothing to the government in Toronto."

"I know that."

"In fact, those bastards are responsible for everything I suffered."

"I know that."

"And for the deaths of my friends."

"I know that."

"And they laid the blame for everything at my feet. They implied I did it."

"I know that."

Peter smiled unkindly. "Now they want my help."

"Yes."

"They want my help to dismantle a group that is fed up with them?"

"Yes."

Peter paced over to where Marysia stood. She turned so that they were both facing the photographs.

"Their victims are random, Peter."

"Aren't we all?"

"They've blown up children."

"Children?"

"Yes, children."

Peter remembered the dark-haired little girl who lay motionless on the pavement near the store where the bomb had exploded. He could still see how her mouth, slightly agape, had filled with something dark and wet. What had her death achieved? What had she done? What had Joanna done? What had any bright and happy five-year-old done?

"Okay, I'll go."

Marysia looked at him, surprised by the speed of his decision. "It's risky for you."

"You knew that before you asked me."

"I know." Marysia bit her lip. "I just wanted to give you a chance to back out."

"No you didn't. You just wanted to *say* you gave me the chance, in case anything happened."

Marysia smiled ruefully. "Maybe you're right. I couldn't live with myself if anything happened to you."

"Now you can – you gave me the chance to back out and I didn't take it." Peter smiled at her. It was one of his best – a calculated smile that implied cheerful good humor and an obliviousness to any duplicity that had come before. "Whatever happens now is my fault."

"Really, Peter. It is very risky. You don't have to go." Marysia tried to hold his eyes – there was so much she wanted to say.

Peter refused to be drawn. He leaned down to kiss her forehead, and in so doing, casually broke off eye contact. "You know that's not true."

19

*T*hough she had resigned from the Council, Wanda was still head of security, and therefore, she was, along with Hania, responsible for prepping Peter for his adventure. Whereas Hania, who authorized the various identities used by their agents, was aware that she was dealing with an experienced agent and had delegated the task of presenting Peter with his credentials and legend, Wanda felt the need to personally attend to the security issues raised. Peter sat patiently through her tedious and repetitive lecture on procedure, using exactly the same neutral expression which had worked so well through the initial phase of his re-education as he let his thoughts wander freely.

"Are you even listening to me?" Wanda's sharp voice cut through his thoughts.

He looked at her in sincere astonishment. "Of course, Colonel!" With that he repeated her last several phrases verbatim, all the while wondering how there could be so many colonels. He should have stuck with demanding that promotion to major. After all, that thing with blaming him for Jana was quite stupid. Over the years with his rank as a captain, he had successfully completed several risky missions, had decoded and analyzed mountains of data, had organized the cryptanalysis office entirely on his own, had successfully carried out a fund-raising and publicity drive in America that had raised millions, and was currently redeveloping their entire communication network – it was worth at least a promotion to major and was a hell of a lot more than Wanda had ever done...

"Captain Halifax!"

"I *am* listening, Colonel."

He was sitting, like a schoolchild, and she was pacing around him, explaining things that any first-year student would know. Even in the somewhat less intense atmosphere of the English underground, the procedures she was stating were trivial doctrine.

Suddenly exasperated, aware that she was talking into a vacuum, Wanda sighed heavily. She pulled a chair over to where Peter was sitting and sat down opposite him.

"Captain." She sounded as though she had reached the end of her tether with an extremely stupid and recalcitrant young recruit.

"Yes, Colonel?" He was a model of military courtesy.

"I hear you're drinking again."

"Are you spying on me?"

"I keep a watch on all my people. Is it true? Are you drinking?"

"Wouldn't your time be better spent watching our borders? Or supporting me in my efforts to upgrade our encryption technology?" It rankled that, though he had been handed the portfolio for secure communications, everything still had to be run through Wanda since she was head of overall security. And she did nothing to make his job easier.

"Is it *true*?" Wanda snapped angrily.

Peter shook his head. "No, it's not true. I drink no more than most people here."

"Liar."

"Colonel, it's the truth."

"You've lied since the day you've arrived. You've lied and lived while my two sons—"

"Yes, your two sons were killed and I'm sorry about that. I really am. But I didn't do it," Peter stated through gritted teeth. "In fact, I had nothing to do with any of you when it happened. I did not even know them!"

Wanda drew herself up, clearly angered, but he decided to continue. "I never knew your sons, I did not know *you* then. In my entire life I had nothing to do with you, or your children, or their deaths and I am sick and tired of being blamed for what happened to them!"

"Captain Halifax!"

"What is it? What is it you hold me responsible for? You *had* your chance! You could have had me shot when I arrived! But you heard my story and you voted to let me live among you. *Why*, then? Why this continual harassment? Why have you *never* given me a chance?"

"You deceived us!"

"About one small personal fact that was – to be honest – none of yours or anyone else's goddamned business! You take my statement after I've just escaped years of slavery and abuse, when I'm held at gunpoint and threatened with death – as if you all had the right to decide who lives and who dies – and then you expect me not to protect myself. *Everything* told to me at that time was a lie, *every* gesture of kindness was an act, and yet you expected me to throw myself and every detail about me to you and simply trust you!"

Wanda glared at him, her face suffused with an irrational anger. "You're an abomination."

"So why did you let me live? Why didn't you vote for my death when you had a chance?" As he said that, he wondered if perhaps, he wasn't going too far. For all he knew, Wanda could still cause him no end of misery.

"You Nazi-fucker! You and that Frau Vogel woman."

"You hated me before you knew about that. What is it, Wanda? What do you hate? That I'm not one of you? My blood? Is that it? Do you believe that someone's worth is in their blood? Or the culture they're raised in? Is that it? Are you—"

"Shut-up!"

"You're as bad as the Nazis! You're a hypocritical, nationalistic—"

Wanda stood so suddenly she knocked over her chair. "You've been briefed," she stated coolly and left.

Peter remained sitting, his expression calm as he mentally replayed and analyzed their interchange. He had not asked for Wanda's enmity, but once

84

it was undeniable, he was not going to let it destroy him either. If anything, he would turn it on her and strangle her with her own hatred, if that's what had to be done.

"I heard you and Wanda had a bit of a tête-à-tête."

Peter looked up at Tadek, then back down at Madzia as she played in the little pool at the base of the waterfall. It was nice being able to come here. One of these days, he promised himself, he'd make the trip in winter – whatever it took. For now though, it was beautiful enough seeing it in summer when it was easily accessible. The only problem with summer was that there were always too many people around: the young soldiers smoking their illegal cigarettes, the youngsters playing war, Tadek...Peter glanced down at Irena, sleeping in his arm then back up at Tadek. Tadek still stood there, eyebrows raised expectantly.

"Use English." Peter was in no mood to wade through Tadek's rapid and complex Polish.

Surprisingly Tadek was not deterred. "Will you settle for German?"

Peter motioned to the ground next to him.

Tadek accepted the invitation. "Where's Zosia?" he asked, letting the question of Peter's conversation with Wanda drop.

"Well, I guess she's not with you." Peter glanced down at his watch. He had about forty-five minutes until he needed to get Irena back to Zosia's breast.

"Zosia seems quite tired." Tadek scanned the trees as if talking to no-one in particular. "She seems, well, rather distracted, wouldn't you say? As if..."

"Zosia is Zosia. If she feels the need to sleep sixteen hours a day, I'm not going to interfere."

"Maybe it's her way of communicating..."

"We have three languages in common. If that's not enough..." Peter shrugged, his attention on the trees which clung precariously to an escarpment. How did they manage to grow and survive in such conditions?

"It's just that, there are some things that–"

"Let me remember here, a moment." Peter tapped his temple in satiric imitation of deep thought. "Oh yes, now I remember, you were the one who wanted to shoot my face off, isn't that right?"

"Isn't it time to forget about that?"

"I believe the phrase is *forgive* and forget. But we all conveniently ignore the first part of that, don't we?" That, Peter was sure, would end the conversation.

"Alright then. I'm sorry."

"Fine. It's forgotten." Peter said it with about as much sincerity as Tadek's apology.

"Now–"

"Not so quickly. What about the malicious lies you and Ryszard spread about me to try to ruin my marriage to Zosia?"

Genuinely perturbed, Tadek looked sharply at Peter. "How'd you know about that?"

Peter didn't return his look. "For all the evil things you both said, neither of you claimed I was stupid."

"Alright. I'm sorry about that, too. It was unfair."

"'Twas nothing."

"I wanted to talk to you about Zosia."

But I don't want to talk to you. Was Tadek being deliberately obtuse? They had worked together on several occasions; Tadek had accepted Peter's presence at the encampment and had stopped deliberately trying to sabotage his life; Tadek had even, once or twice, been genuinely helpful – but none of that could obliterate all that had gone before, none of it amounted to friendship, and certainly none of it gave Tadek the right to mix into Peter's personal life!

"I care about Zosia…"

As if I don't.

"…and she told me that you two–"

"Comrade." Peter pointedly turned to look at Tadek. "I have never asked what you and my wife do with your time together. That she can find so much time for you is, in and of itself, quite an irritant which I have chosen to ignore. I will tend to my job and the children and our home while she indulges her need for sleep or your companionship, but the one thing I will not do is discuss our private life with *you*. Do you understand that or do I have to draw you a picture?"

Tadek finally stopped studying the trees and turned to look at Peter. "I'm worried about her, Peter."

"I have too much to take care of," Peter tossed his head in an arc to include Madzia and Irena, "to fret about my aristocratic wife's angst of the day. Physically, she's fine. And emotionally, she has her *ghost* and her *friend* to see to her needs. I've learned I can't compete with that and I'm not going to try anymore."

"She loves *you* now."

Peter sputtered a short laugh.

"She really does!"

"Then she needs to show it. She needs to learn that love is something more than an excuse to be adored. Until she shoulders a part of the burden of our life together, her love for me is nothing more than an adolescent's raging hormones, and is about as useful."

"Don't you love her anymore?"

Peter leaned back against the slope and looked up at the sky. Did he love Zosia? He cared deeply about her, wished only the best for her, he would even – he was fairly sure – lay down his life for her. But he was also wary of her and what she could do to him. Was it possible to love someone you were wary of? He sighed. "That's none of your business, my dear comrade."

Tadek stood. "I heard you're leaving for England soon."

"Yes, this afternoon."

"It's a dangerous mission. You're well known and wanted everywhere – especially London. There's a price on your head."

"I'm aware of that."

Tadek remained uneasily silent, as if debating whether or not to wish Peter luck.

Peter rose to his feet and called to Madzia. As she scrambled up the hillside to him, he thought, I should tell Tadek to take care of them – Zosia as well as the children – in case I don't come back. Peter shifted his weight uneasily from one foot to the other. As Madzia reached him, she threw her arms around his thigh and hugged him. Peter leaned down to hug her. Then, straightening, he turned to Tadek. "I've got to go – it's a long walk with the children." And without mentioning his concerns or hopes, he grabbed Madzia's hand in his, wrapped his arm more firmly around Irena and headed back to the encampment.

20

"*L*ong time no see."

Peter looked down at the diminutive woman and smiled. "Not as long as either of us expected." People flowed around them down the long platform, heading for the exit of the station but the two of them remained still, contemplating each other like old lovers. "Not quite three months, isn't it?" He glanced down to see if Barbara's pregnancy was visible, but she was wearing a long raincoat that effectively hid her figure.

"I missed you."

Peter nodded noncommittally. "That's not what you're supposed to say to the husband who not only abandoned you, but plans to divorce you."

A loud whistle echoed down the platform and the doors of the train near them slammed shut. Barbara looked up in surprise, as if she had forgotten she was in a station. They both watched in silence as the train chugged slowly out from under the roof. The train from Dover had finally emptied and with the departure of the neighboring train, they were suddenly alone on the isolated concrete stretch. Barbara reached out and gingerly touched the jacket of his suit. "Are you going to be Niklaus Jäger the entire time?"

He shook his head. "Only long enough to sign the necessary papers."

"Thanks for coming back to do that. I didn't realize it's so much quicker if the husband files. But why did they decide against the suicide idea?"

"Hania was advised that leaving clothes on the beach and claiming Jäger was dead was very likely to lead to a criminal investigation. And she thought having you and the bookstore investigated would not be wise."

The girl Peter had known back at Szaflary would have greeted his words with a titter of adolescent bravado, but the woman who stood before him now blanched with fear, and he felt a wave of pity for the difficult isolation of her current position. "It's hard, isn't it?"

She nodded. "I thought I was brave – when I used to patrol the woods, I'd risk being shot by any encroaching enemy. But I had a gun as well, and I always felt that I had a chance to fight back. I knew what was going on, I knew what to do. Here..." She raised her hands in a gesture of helplessness. "Here, I'm surrounded. There's no way to fight back. You never know what's going on, you never know *when* to fight. If a policeman approaches me, I don't know whether he's going to offer to help carry my groceries or if it's the beginning of the end for me."

"Keeping us in ignorance and the arbitrary enforcement of the law are their strongest weapons. That's why there are so many laws." Peter stroked her cheek with the back of his hand. "You have to use other weapons now. And believe me, you are not defenseless. The smile of a beautiful woman can be quite powerful."

Barbara shook her head. He could see tears gathering in the corners of her eyes. "I didn't want to be like that! I know how the others work, those who infiltrate, but I didn't want to have to be like that!"

"It's a police state and the bullies are running the schoolyard." Peter gestured toward the crowded front of the train station. "They all have to do it. And so do you."

"I don't think I can."

"I know you can. You did it when we were working together here."

"Then I thought it was only temporary. And..." Barbara looked away, embarrassed. A tear escaped and slipped down her cheek. "I had your help then. I knew you'd cover for me."

Peter smiled fondly as he remembered all the nonsensical risks that Barbara had taken back then. A married German woman who went out partying with an English lad! How often had he pleaded, requested, ordered her to be careful? And all to no avail. But now it was no longer a game, now she was the senior officer, now she was expecting a child, now she was responsible for her life. He picked up his bags. "We should get going before someone grows suspicious."

Together they walked along the platform toward the exit. Barbara detoured to read a sign on a post. Peter came up behind her. "What's it say?"

"Oh, nothing important. You know, I have to keep an eye on the regulations. They change so frequently."

"I know," Peter laughed. "We used to say that the only people who followed all the laws were those in the resistance." He read over her shoulder and saw that the poster was advising a change in policy on the usage of taxis by non-residents of the Greater London Administrative District. Henceforward, all non-residents would pay a premium since they did not pay local taxes to maintain the roads. This meant of course, that residents would need to show proper identification and payment of taxes to their local officials in order to receive the chits which could then be given to the taxi drivers to avoid the extra fee. A list of addresses and a schedule of when the chits would be doled out was given below the announcement.

"I guess that explains why the fare was so high when I came here." Barbara began digging in her purse, "I don't have much money left, shall we take the subway?"

"That wouldn't be wise. Don't worry, I can pay the taxi."

"Okay. Where to?"

"Well, since I'm Jäger for the next several days, our flat, my dear. Is Mark living there?"

Barbara nodded.

"He's going to have to go live with his parents or with friends for the next few days." Peter considered for a moment. "Do you think the neighbors have noticed?"

"I don't think so. You know, with that separate entrance, and all the businesses on that street." She shook her head as if convincing herself. "No. I don't think so. We keep to ourselves when we're there."

"It probably doesn't matter anyway."

"Why not?"

They stopped walking and Peter set down his luggage. Barbara faced him and he placed both his hands on her shoulders, "Because I'm divorcing you. It seems, while on my long business trip, I met someone and fell in love." Peter pointed at one of his bags. "Most of the paperwork has been

89

drawn up already – it weighs a ton! The story is that I've had a lawyer in Leipzig organize everything and informed you by letter at least a month ago. We'll take this stuff to a lawyer here in London – his name was given to Hania by the English, he does a lot of work for them – and in his presence we'll sign about five thousand forms and then he'll handle the rest and I'll run back to my new love in Leipzig, never to be heard from again."

"What about the bookstore?"

"The owner has agreed to have you manage the store. Of course, that's another five thousand forms. The special permission necessary to have a woman run a business and all the other details are also in this suitcase. Once everything is signed and witnessed, processing the divorce application will still take a year or so, but it can all go through without my being here. You can pick up the final papers and send them to me and I'll sign them and send them back. Then you're done."

He picked up his luggage and they continued along the platform in silence.

"What about the baby?" Barbara asked suddenly.

"Childless marriages are much easier to terminate, so we're ignoring your pregnancy for now. Once the final papers are signed, there's the five year waiting period to make the divorce official–"

"Five years?"

"Don't worry, officials and the wealthy bribe their way past that. We'll just forge some appropriate papers. When we get the waiting period waived – or more likely, shortened – we'll include the necessary papers for you to maintain custody of the child."

"But it will remain yours?"

"Jäger's, yes." Peter shifted a suitcase so that he held both with one arm. He placed the other arm around Barbara's shoulder. She was so delicate! How, he wondered, would such a small body cope? "I'm sorry, but it's almost impossible for a German father to renounce a legitimate child, especially if the woman is of pure blood as well. Jäger has no Party or government affiliations and, so, no strings he can pull. Also, having the baby adopted by Mark would go against the purity laws."

"What about claiming Mark as the real father?"

"That could be disastrous." Peter shook his head. "You don't want to do that."

"Why are we going through all this? Why not just plant the relevant documents–"

"Barbara, that's not going to happen. Too much risk. You know, this is a personal favor being done for you. No one is going to risk breaking into government offices in London and Berlin just to sort out your personal life."

"I understand. I'm sorry I asked."

"After we've seen the lawyer and the papers are signed, I'll move to a hotel room and change personalities, so that if anything happens, it'll be that much harder to trace me to you, but I want you to be vigilant. You know I'm here for something much riskier than a divorce, and I can't guarantee that if I'm taken, your name won't pass my lips. You know that."

Barbara's face was drawn with worry. "I know. Are you carrying poison?"

"Yes, in my tooth – but still, I'll try to avoid killing myself, and if I know you're safe, that will make it easier for me to stay alive. Do you promise if anything happens to me, you'll go into hiding immediately?"

Barbara nodded. "I promise."

"Good. I'll need you to arrange a meeting for me. With Jenny. Can you do that?"

"Of course."

They had reached the main section of the station and Peter dropped his voice to say, "You know, a lot of people have worked very hard to set you up here with Mark. I hope it's what you want." He raised his voice back to normal and scanning the station entrances asked, "Now, where the hell are the taxis?"

21

"*A*lan! Peter! Oh, whatever the hell your name is now..." Jenny hugged him enthusiastically, but then suddenly moaned in frustration, pulled away and glanced quickly around the hotel room. There was nobody else there.

Peter took her raincoat and welcomed her into the room. "My papers say Adolf."

"Adolf! Jesus Christ, why that name?"

Peter shrugged as he hung her coat on a hanger. "I'm a Major as well."

"Yes, I noticed they kitted you out very nicely." She surveyed him. Blue-gray eyes, dark brown hair tinted with gray at the temples. Was that genuine or part of his disguise? Still fit, still handsome, his eyes had that distant, sad look that was alien to the man she had known so long ago. Or was it? He had always been a bit of a puzzle to her, even when they had been lovers. That had been part of the attraction. But the distance then had been controlled, now it seemed to control him. The way he held himself suggested an iciness that placed a frozen wasteland between him and the rest of the world. Jenny looked at the impressive black uniform he wore and realized that it looked very natural on him now. "Why not Colonel?"

"Too rare. Majors are high-ranking enough to get royal treatment, but thick enough on the ground not to draw undo notice."

"I see." Jenny glanced back toward the door through which she had come. "When your friend asked me to meet you, I didn't expect...Did her group, I mean, the A.K., did they organize all this?"

"Partly. One of their representatives got in touch with me and asked me to come here. The A.K. is serving as a go-between."

"Between you and whom?"

He shrugged again. "If I were privy to such things, I'd know more than was good for me. All I know is I've been asked to talk to the Real ERA. Try to dissuade them from blowing up innocent people."

"Why?"

"Bad publicity, I gather."

"No, I mean, why you?"

"Oh, that. Apparently they took some of their inspiration from my words. Or rather from what they thought I said. It was hoped I could set them straight."

Jenny did not bother to ask who had hoped. She had caught the slight admonishment in Peter's tone for asking too many questions and now decided to concentrate on the task at hand. "Do you intend to talk to the Realies personally?" She said, "Reh-ah-lees" almost as if the word were German.

"Do you have any other ideas?"

Jenny shook her head slowly in disbelief. "Do you have any idea of the price on your head?"

"Two million marks the last I looked."

"When was that?"

"Oh, I guess in March – just before I left."

Jenny laughed. "Well, then, your stock has climbed steeply. Did you do something to drive up your price?"

"How high is it?"

She noticed that he had not answered her question, but she didn't press. "Eighteen. I don't imagine that your people were told that little fact when your presence was requested."

He laughed slightly. They knew, but they hadn't told him. "I would guess not."

"Gauleiter Schindler is desperate to get his hands on you. I don't know why, it must be pressure from above, but he's convinced you're in London and he's been doing everything in his power to ferret you out. Including offering big money. That's enough to buy a nice flat in the center of town!"

"Only if you have the right papers."

Jenny rolled her eyes at his obstinacy. "Don't you realize what that sort of money can do to someone? I mean, when your friend got in touch with me and said you needed to talk to me – hell, even I had a moment's thought!

Peter smiled at her fondly, "But I knew it wouldn't last more than a moment. You're a brave woman, and noble, and I trust you with my life."

Jenny blushed and dropped her gaze, embarrassed by the compliment.

Peter placed two fingers under her chin and gently lifted her face. His sweet, little Jenny with her dreams of being an artist, now a matronly nobody whose career in the Underground had degraded into that of an errand-runner. She deserved better, but would never get it.

"Maybe you can trust me," she admitted, "but do you think every Realie is trustworthy? All you need is just *one* of these characters to *french* you and that'd be it. You'd be dead."

"Well, that's why I came to you. I wouldn't trust the current Underground leadership here to be able to organize a piss-up in a brewery, but I know you can arrange something."

Jenny shook her head in confusion. "I'm a woman. Who's going to listen to me?"

It was one of the long-standing problems of the British Underground: the machismo. Out of sheer desperation the A.K. had been forced to accept and acknowledge the full participation of women in their ranks, but the British had never suffered the devastation visited upon the Home Army and could cling to quaint prejudices, whatever the noble words of equality printed upon their various decrees. Along with ill-tempered, violent, chain-smoking alcoholics, Peter thought, he should have added the word *sexist* to the description of the British Underground he had given to Graham's friends so long ago. "Is that why you quit last time?"

She nodded. "Maybe. I wanted to have a life – and they seemed to think that was only an option for men. If you were a woman and wanted a family, then you weren't committed to the cause."

"Like Allison," Peter whispered. He realized he had spoken aloud, so he explained, "She came after you."

"I know." Jenny looked away, embarrassed. "I kept tabs." After a moment, she brought her gaze back to him. "Did she have children?"

Peter shook his head. "She always said that it would ruin her chances of promotion." He sniffed. "Didn't help. They were willing to promote Graham over my head, but they ignored her, even though she was much more highly qualified."

"Graham?"

"Some idiot." Quite abruptly he changed the subject. "Anyway, I don't expect you to convince anyone of anything. The leadership already knows

93

I'm coming. I told them I'd send my contact to them to make arrangements."

"And I'm the contact?"

He grinned winningly at her.

Jenny contemplated the charming plea for a moment, then caved. "I never could say no to you." She did not bother to say that he had never asked enough in the first place. "What do you want to do?"

"I thought of luring the Real leadership to a meeting on the pretext that the ERA wants to do a bit of power-sharing…"

Jenny shook her head.

"Why not?"

"You want to talk to the rank-and-file. As many as possible."

"Why not just talk to the leadership? It'd be less dangerous – less people, each with more to lose. And they're the ones making the decisions – you know about bombing, et cetera."

Jenny nodded her understanding. "I know, but I think you'd have no luck convincing them."

"Why not?"

"Just a feeling."

A feeling? Peter studied Jenny for a moment. "What can you tell me about these people?"

"Not much." Jenny saw Peter's look and realized that anything she offered would be useful. "What I know is, they say there was a big bust-up at one of the leadership meetings a few months ago – March or April, I think. Not long after you left. Anyway, a part of the executive walked out and made a general call to the membership to join them in a 'Real' fight against the Nazis. Hence the name. I got a flyer, but I ignored it. I guess others didn't. Altogether I'd say maybe ten percent of the group walked out. The remainder of the leadership claims it is much less than that. Two percent, at most. Anyway, in May sometime the breakaway group started their bombing campaign. I don't know how much of their membership is for that sort of thing, but that's the path they've chosen."

Peter nodded but remained silent. Though few were privy to such statistics, he could guess that there were about two thousand or so full ERA members. That would mean up to two hundred committed terrorists had left the group to form the breakaway Real ERA, possibly with a few more drifting in from the Monarchists, the Socialists and the Communists.

"I don't know anything more about them than that."

"Do you think you could get your hands on some of their literature for me?"

Jenny nodded her head emphatically, "Oh, yes! They're really keen on flyers and such like. I've still got the original one they sent me, and I know where I can get copies of the others." She paused and shut her eyes as if recalling what she had read on the sheets. "They quote you a lot. I think they *have* chosen you as their spiritual leader."

He laughed at her choice of words, "So, I finally get to found my own religion, and I'm not even here to enjoy being worshiped."

Jenny giggled.

"At least I didn't have to get crucified."

Jenny shook her head, laughing. "That's not what I meant."

"I know what you meant," Peter responded, trying to be serious. "But given their devotion to me, why do you think I shouldn't bother talking directly to the leadership? Maybe I can get them to call off the bombing campaign with just a few quiet words."

Jenny furrowed her brow as if trying to gather her own nebulous thoughts into a cogent answer. She shook her head a bit and said, "You're going to laugh at me, but maybe it's just intuition."

"Intuition usually has a basis, maybe you can work out what your feelings are based on?"

She smiled almost sadly, "You always were the rationalist. Okay, if I think back to the brochures, they had the basic history right – including your tour of America. But they quote you saying things that…well, since I know you personally, I knew they couldn't be right. I think they are deliberate misquotes, or taken way out of context."

"So you think they already know my views on these things and would not be interested in being corrected?"

"Yes! They've built their entire power base on delivering results. *Real* results! And that means bombs. They're not going to stop because you tell them they're misquoting you."

"Ah. How about if I try to get the Real leadership to call a general, mandatory meeting? If they don't give away my name before the meeting, I should be safe. Then I can address the rank-and-file directly and disabuse them of this philosophy."

Jenny turned a bit and leaned into Peter so that her back rested against his chest. He looked down on the brown roots which extended several inches into her bleached hair. "You've stopped dyeing your hair." She had lost weight as well, but he decided it would be unwise to comment on that.

She sniffed a little laugh. "Yeah, I thought your friend Barbara looked so beautiful with her natural color – *and* her self confidence." She paused as if weighing the wisdom of speaking, then added softly, "And I remember the tone of voice you used when you commented on my new color."

"I didn't mean to be judgmental."

"I know. That made it all the more important to me." She pressed herself against him and he put his arms around her. "I'm worried about you, Alan. I don't trust these guys – these Real ERA people. I think if you go to them and ask for a general meeting of the membership, they'll know that you're going to contradict them. They'll *french* you both to get rid of you and for the money. And I'll lose you forever."

He recognized the risk in her words. She was turning back into the Jenny he had known so long ago – the hair, the figure, the sense of adventure. He had enjoyed that woman, but he had not loved her then, and he knew he would not love her now, either. He bent down and kissed the top of her head. It was the only acknowledgment he would give to her admission, thus he would give her an easy retreat and a way to save face. "It would never work." His meaning was deliberately obscure.

She tilted her head back to look up at him. "So?"

"So, maybe we can advertise directly that I'll talk to the membership. I think they'll be intrigued enough to come – at least some of them. And I can try and disabuse them of the philosophy their leaders claim I espouse."

"Dangerous."

"Well, how about if we tell them that I will address them, but then lead them to a location which is different from the one announced. Obviously, we'd have to be very careful, but if we could filter them out in small groups to the secret location–"

"Better yet, start off with small groups in different locations, then lead each to the meeting."

"Yes, that'd work. They'd have to be screened–"

"With the new hand-held devices, that shouldn't be so hard."

"During the meeting, there would, of course, be a closed-door policy, and afterwards, I'd be the first to leave."

"Do you think you'd have any chance of walking out of such a meeting?"

Peter shrugged. "Maybe a sixty-forty chance of getting out of there alive. Or even better with devoted friends."

"Do you really want to take that sort of risk?"

Peter thought of Joanna and the dark-haired girl and smiled wanly. "I don't have any choice. I don't want random murder to become one of our tools. And I owe it to my children to hand them a world that's just a little better than the one I was born into."

"Or die trying?"

"If that's what it takes."

22

*T*he rain came down in sheets and the man hurried along the pavement, rushing to the taxi stand before the last cab was taken. Peter fell in step next to him, taking shelter under his umbrella. The man thought Peter was a queue-jumper and brusquely thrust his shoulder forward, trying to edge his way past.

"Erich, I want to have a word with you."

Erich stopped dead. He stared straight ahead, watching as if in a trance as the last taxi was taken, unwilling to believe what his ears told him.

"Erich, I want to have a word with you."

"Go away! I don't know you!"

"It's not that easy, brother. If you don't talk to me now, I'll come to your home – and you don't want that, do you?"

The wind grabbed Erich's umbrella, turning it inside out. He turned away from the wind to fight his umbrella down. The rain lashed at both of them. The wind shifted suddenly and collapsed the umbrella back to its original shape. Erich closed it and as he wrapped the strap around the outside, he gestured with his head across the street. "I'll meet you there, in the pub. In the back, by the bar. Standing."

"We'll go together," Peter suggested, unwilling to give his brother the opportunity of betraying him. He motioned along the road. "There's a café up ahead. We can speak German there without drawing attention." He grabbed Erich's arm and began walking toward the café.

"You're wanted!" Erich hissed. He pulled his arm free, but fell in step with Peter. "I've seen the poster."

"And could you recognize me from it?"

The wind had dropped and Erich opened his umbrella again. He shook his head to rid himself of some of the accumulated rain, then turned to look at his brother, studying him silently. "Not really." Having conceded that point, his voice took on a slightly more conversational tone. "Someone just pointed out how much they were offering for this Halifax fellow and I looked closely at the picture." He laughed. "I thought if maybe I, you know–"

Peter nodded, "Yeah, I know."

"Anyway, once I looked closely at it, and putting that together with what you told me last time, I realized it was you. You never told me–"

"Yes, I did. I told you that I had spoken out in America and that I was wanted. Remember?"

Erich sighed, "You also told me you were from some office or other and referred to yourself in the third person."

Peter laughed. "Well, now you know. I told you it was a dangerous game, but you were interested anyway. What's happened?"

They reached the door of the café and Erich paused to close his umbrella again. "I had no idea how dangerous. Do you know how much they're offering for you?"

Peter nodded. "I should feel honored."

"I'd feel scared."

"That too."

Erich gestured toward the inside of the café. "I would think you'd feel safer in an English pub than a German café. Are you sure we should go in here?"

"They'd expect me to hide among the English, so this is much safer than the pub. Come on, you'll see – no one will recognize me."

"But if they do, I'll be arrested!"

"Yeah, and they'll probably torture you just to get me to talk." Peter grabbed Erich's arm and opened the door. "But don't worry, I won't say a word – no matter what they do to you."

Erich failed to see the humor in Peter's words and Peter had to tug at him to get him inside and to a table. The café was done in a Viennese style and between customers buried behind their newspapers and the thick cloud of smoke, they were quite well hidden. They were also, in keeping with custom, completely ignored by the waiter.

Finally overcoming the semi-paralysis brought on by fear, Erich removed his coat and used the conveniently placed hook to hang it up. He then reached for his brother's. As Peter removed his coat, Erich's mouth fell open. He didn't say a word, he just stared at the black uniform. Finally he found the wherewithal to accept the coat from Peter, hang it up, and seat himself.

Peter picked up the tattily photocopied, folded sheet of paper that sat in the middle of the table, but he did not bother to scan the offerings. "I imagine they have coffee."

"Probably. Tea, at least." Erich continued to stare at his brother's uniform. "An SS major?"

Peter smiled. "Hey, if you don't want to be beat by them, join them!"

Erich's eyes wandered upward to Peter's hair. "It's lighter in the poster. Which color is natural?"

"The poster. It's useful, since no one expects this color." Peter indicated his dark brown hair. "After all, no sane person in this society would dye his hair *darker*."

Erich nodded slowly. "And the gray?" He moved his chin upwards to indicate Peter's temples.

"Makes me look distinguished, doesn't it?"

Again Erich simply nodded. "The poster claimed you were a murderer and a kidnapper."

"And guilty of crimes against the state."

"Is it true?"

Peter made a face. "Technically, yes."

Erich shook his head in dismay. "What sort of people have you fallen in with?"

"The question, dear brother, is what sort of people have *you* fallen in with?"

"Me? I'm just trying to make my way in this world. Just trying to get along. I haven't hurt anyone."

Peter snorted his rejection of that. "*They* have, and you're part of them. They killed Mom and Dad. Is that what you wanted?"

Erich shook his head. "That's not fair! That wasn't my fault."

"No, it was theirs. And you just want to get along with them. You told me you wanted to help *us* out, but you turned away the contact sent to you."

"You told me I had a free choice!"

Peter shrugged. "I was wrong. They need you now."

Erich's eyes widened with a combination of fear and anger. "You can't force me–"

"Yes, we can." Peter found the smoke irritating, making it hard to breathe, so he coped with it in the only way he knew worked: he lit himself a cigarette. He offered Erich one and lit it for him. "Do I need to tell you, dear brother, of all the ways we can blackmail you?"

Erich shook his head. "What do they want?"

Peter leaned forward and dropped his voice, but it was at that very moment the waiter decided to notice them. "Have you decided?" The waiter's tone balanced nicely between being bored and being snide.

"Waged labor," Peter muttered, just loud enough for the waiter to hear. He eyed the waiter carefully as if searching for hidden crimes.

The waiter glanced at Peter's uniform and stiffened. "May I take your orders, *meine Herren*?"

"Coffee," Peter grunted.

"Real?"

"Of course."

"*Mein Herr*, I'm very sorry, but we're out of real coffee, I can offer–"

"Find some!" Peter ordered.

The waiter snapped his head in acknowledgment and turned his attention to Erich.

"The same."

"Could I offer *meinen Herren* any of our cakes?"

They both shook their heads and the waiter disappeared to find real coffee. Once he was out of earshot, Erich said, "The Gauleiter is trying to introduce more of that here."

"More of what? Rude waiters?"

"No, what you said – *Zwangsarbeiter*. For the uneducated jobs, to free up the Germans and the English for the more technical work." Erich sounded as though he felt the idea had merit. "They're going to import some continentals–"

Peter laughed. "At first, maybe. Give it a couple of years and I'm sure there'd be a reasonable pool of English among all those benighted foreigners."

"Never! The people would never tolerate that!"

Peter raised an eyebrow. "Oh? They already send their sons away for six years to slave on the continent."

"Those boys are paid."

"Not all as highly as you were."

Erich reddened at Peter's reference.

"And in any case," Peter said quickly, wishing to avoid a confrontation over ancient history, "paid or not, they have no choice about going. Just imagine if some of them were assigned locally, and then, for the miscreants, their terms would be extended. Perhaps indefinitely."

Erich breathed deeply, so busy calming himself that he could not argue.

"Or there could be a program to put criminals into useful employment. Their wages, naturally enough, would go to the State, to pay for their room and board and to compensate society for their crimes. Then, perhaps, there'd be a program to clean up the streets, get those sniveling orphans and ne'er-do-wells into gainful employment. Teach them a skill..." Peter paused long enough to take a drag from his cigarette. "They'd have to work a few years to pay off their apprenticeships – after all, such training doesn't come cheap. Then there are the few gypsies still roaming the countryside. Who would disagree to finally getting some useful work out of those tramps?"

"They're not English, anyway."

"No, of course not. But the Cockneys are – and everyone knows they're just a bunch of thieves. And God, there's all those perpetually drunken northerners. Mancunians, Hartlepudlians–"

"They hang monkeys there, don't they?"

Peter laughed. "Hell, they can't even speak English properly!"

Erich smiled as he recognized one of their father's tirades. "Alright, I get your point. But it would still take an inordinate amount of effort to

100

change things. I mean, as it is, there's so few *Zwangsarbeiter* here – mostly just the household help that the colonists bring with them and the road crews from the prisons. Why would the Gauleiter want to change everything?"

"Practice."

"Huh?"

"Schindler got the Greater London Administrative District, what, about twelve years ago?"

Erich nodded.

"He then managed to get the rest of England, Scotland and Wales about two, three years after that."

"Yes, I remember. That was the first time the same man ran the entire group – since the ceasefire anyway."

"He's also Reich advisor to the Irish Autonomous region and he's head of security in the *Niederland* region of the Reich. So, he has this entire corner sewn up."

"Yeah, so?"

"With so many responsibilities here, where does he spend all his time?"

"Berlin, I gather."

Peter rested his chin on the heel of his hand and waited patiently.

"Oh, I see. Next step, Führer."

Peter leaned back into his seat as he saw the coffee arriving. The waiter placed their cups in front of them, then set the tray of sugars, milk, cream and chocolates in the center of the table. Without even tasting it, Peter could tell from the smell that the coffee was real.

After the waiter had left, he leaned forward again, ground out his cigarette and picked up the cup. "You see, England has been blessed with a true believer." Peter sipped the coffee. It tasted good. "Schindler thinks that the way this place is run..." he gestured with his free hand to indicate England, "is a crime against pure Nazi philosophy. Too much mixing, the hierarchy is unclear and semi-permeable, too many people are loyal to the system simply because it's easier than fighting it. He wants to return the Reich to its original course, as laid down by Hitler."

"And what would that be?"

"The natural pre-eminence of Germans over all the other European 'races' – even those who are nominally Aryan." Peter did not comment on how frequently the list of Aryan races changed, Erich would already be quite sensitive to that fact.

"But they do get preference here!"

"Not preference, pre-eminence. The existence of you and your sort are a thorn in Schindler's side. You shouldn't exist."

"What do you mean?"

"I mean, he believes the philosophy exactly as it was laid out to him in the Hitler Youth. The Germans are superior and the natural master. These practical detours that the Reich has taken – like accommodating collaborators and granting honorary Aryan status to various groups like the Japanese – that bothers him. Especially the special treatment the English have received. He figures we're the lowest sort of traitors on this earth and our place is very clearly at the bottom of society."

"How do you know so much about him?"

Peter coughed, then sipped some more coffee to try to wash down the smoky atmosphere. "A few years ago, I was, uh, employed by an official in Berlin, as domestic labor."

Erich furrowed his brows slightly.

Peter coughed again, tried some more coffee, then gave up and lit another cigarette. "This fellow, the official, he was trying to work his way up the political ladder, and one of the VIP's he regularly invited to dinner was Schindler. I overheard their conversations."

"Overheard? They talked strategy in front of a foreigner?"

Peter laughed. "I was a slave, a subhuman, Schindler's a true believer. He never figured I was capable of understanding what he said, and even if I was, what would I do with the knowledge? He made no secret of the fact that he loathed us lesser beings. In fact, sometimes, speaking very simply, he would tell me that to my face."

Erich raised his eyebrows in surprise. "What did you do?"

"Nothing, of course."

The hot-headed, proud younger brother who would fight anyone, anywhere at any time just to defend his honor had done nothing. *Of course.* Stunned by the implication, Erich stared into his brother's eyes. "What did they do to you?" he whispered, appalled.

"The question is what is Schindler going to do to all of you."

"Us? I don't understand."

"Whatever Schindler plans to do as Führer, he's going to start here, where he already has power. And one of the things he wants to do is re-establish a proper hierarchy. He hates the English, he *really* hates us. And he hates that there are people like you, people who have moved up the system."

"Even if that's true. Can he do anything about it?"

Peter shrugged. "Who knows? He can try. If he succeeds he could make millions of lives very much more miserable. And if he fails, he might provoke civil unrest, even war. I don't want that. Not for our people, not for anybody."

Erich narrowed his eyes as he thought about what his brother had said. "But Niklaus, I thought...I thought you wanted to overthrow the government."

Peter shook his head. "Not that way. Too much bloodshed and the outcome would be very uncertain." He hesitated a moment, then added, "Besides, I've made a promise I'd like to keep."

"But what do you think Schindler would do here?"

"Well, he's trying to get a new legal code passed, one that would make a lot of jobs illegal for anyone who couldn't come up with a reasonable pedigree."

"What sort of jobs?"

"Yours, for instance. He'd like to eliminate the Conciliator class. He thinks you should all be kept in low-class work, or even forced labor."

Erich shook his head. "He can't be serious."

"I agree. He's run into a lot of hurdles. The Führer, for one, doesn't want to upset the status quo and has effectively blocked most of Schindler's moves. But that would change if Schindler became Führer. Also, we have every reason to believe Schindler is determined enough about this, that he's developing alternate strategies."

"Alternate strategies?"

"Remember that laboratory we broke into?"

Erich glanced nervously around them. "What about it?" he whispered angrily.

"It was a sterilization program, remember? And do you remember it was not an injection – it was not meant for people already at the Reich's bottom rung. After all, they can be surgically sterilized, or just killed. It was intended to be unnoticeable. Do you see what I'm getting at?"

Erich shook his head slowly from side to side. It was not clear if he was saying "no" or if he was simply rejecting the implications as too disgusting.

Peter decided to be explicit. "We think Schindler figured if he couldn't legislate you..." Peter gestured as he looked for a politer word than *collaborators*. "If he couldn't outlaw an English middle-class within the Nazi hierarchy, he could just wipe you out, physically."

"No!"

Peter shrugged. "Why else all that research effort?"

"But it was destroyed. Wasn't it?"

"Yes. And that gets me to why I wanted to talk with you. You see, after we destroyed that section of his laboratory and the whole program was brought to the Führer's attention, Schindler felt the need to lay low. He's transferred most of his efforts to the Institute. The one you're working in."

Erich shook his head. "You have the wrong impression there. There's nothing going on in my lab."

103

"Not in your section, but the Americans believe that there are biological agents being developed somewhere in England, and the English Underground believes that your laboratory is one of the places these weapons are being developed."

"I'm a chemist. I have nothing to do with biology!"

"I know. But you're in there. Make some friends, find out what's going on."

Erich shook his head vigorously, "I can't do that. I can't start asking questions! It's dangerous. They'll suspect. I can't take that sort of risk. I have a family!"

"So do I. And I don't want to see them fall victim to smallpox or bubonic plague or anthrax."

Erich sat back in his seat and surveyed his brother in silence. After a moment, he leaned forward, resting his elbows on the table and clasping his hands together. "I thought that we were talking about an attack on my cohort."

Peter recognized Erich's suspicions. "Erich, I'm not making up the threat to you or your family. We simply don't know what's going on." He opened his hands as if opening a book, "Here, I'll lay it out for you: the Americans believe that the Reich is redeveloping its bioweapons program. Back in the sixties, there was a bit of a truce on this stuff and both sides agreed to stop development of these weapons. Since then the NAU has continued some research, solely, they claim, as a defensive measure. The Reich responded by continuing their so-called defensive research. Now the Americans have reason to believe that the research has become more aggressive, with attack mechanisms being worked on. This involves diffusion techniques and might well enter into your section of the lab – or the physics section. They think that most of this work is taking place in England and the Underground here thinks that it is your institute that is handling the bulk of that."

Erich rested his chin on his hands as if listening, but reluctantly.

"The Americans are afraid the weapons will be used against them, against the civilian population there."

"Why would anyone do anything so stupid?"

Peter shrugged. "I can think of a dozen reasons ranging from sheer idiocy, to ideology to strategy. For instance, if Schindler wanted to get the Führer deposed, that would be one way to destabilize him. Or he might do it just because he hates the Americans so much. Thinks they're undisciplined and immoral."

"Why are the Americans so certain they'll be the target?"

"Because that's who they care about! You could be the target here. Schindler might institute a vaccination program only for the élite, or perhaps distribute preventative doses of antibiotics, and then release something really nasty into the city. Just to test what happens. We simply don't know."

"I thought it was the Führer who was reputedly a nut case."

Peter looked off to the side as he tried desperately to suppress the memory of Joanna's murder. He read the headline of a newspaper held by another customer. *New fertilizer factory will boost agricultural production of southeast region!* After taking a deep breath, he turned back to his brother. "Yes, his personal tastes are insane. He enjoys inflicting pain, he may even enjoy receiving it. But he's pragmatic too. He knows better than to kill the goose that lays his golden eggs."

"And Schindler?"

"He's a true believer. His personal tastes are much more normal – he isn't particularly given to enjoying torture or murder, but on the other hand, he honestly believes that there are lives in this Reich which are worthless. If torture gets him what he needs, then fine. If it's murder, then fine." Peter shook his head as he tried to find the right words to explain what he had slowly come to understand through his observations. "To him, there are lives that are simply expendable. And if he destroys them because they annoy him, well, that's no worse than, say, swatting a mosquito or killing a rat."

"So you're fairly sure it's Schindler's program?"

"No. It could be the Führer simply beefing up his arsenal. We don't know. That's why we need you to sniff around a bit. Find out who's being promoted or transferred. Which labs have been renovated, which doors are being locked. Get your hands on supply lists–"

"Whoa!" Erich threw his hands up in the air. "I'm not going to get myself arrested!"

Peter very deliberately ground out his cigarette. He continued grinding it into the glass long after it had stopped burning, kept twisting the end until it was completely smashed into bits of paper and tobacco. He stared at the broken bits of the cigarette, mindlessly pushing them around the bottom of the ashtray.

"Niklaus?" Erich sounded afraid.

Without looking up, Peter spoke. "I knew it was a mistake trying to explain anything to you. I knew you wouldn't take it seriously. It's just other people's lives." Finally Peter looked up at his brother. "If you don't do exactly as you are instructed to do, evidence against you will be given to the Gestapo. I personally will see to it. Do you understand?"

"But I didn't do anything!"

Peter wondered why Erich thought he needed to actually be guilty of anything. Still, there was no reason not to have a little fun at Erich's expense. "Have you forgotten? You broke into Schindler's laboratory."

"You held a gun on me!"

"And after we released you unharmed, you went straight to the police. Right?"

Erich shook his head. "You have no proof I was there."

Peter laughed harshly. "Once they take you in for questioning, I think we can safely assume that you'll give them all the proof they want."

Erich stared wide-eyed at his brother. "You wouldn't, not to your own brother!"

Peter cocked his head. He was bored with tormenting Erich, and besides, a loyal agent would be more effective than a terrified one. He softened his voice considerably. "Erich, you didn't see the way Mom and Dad were pushed and shoved and thrown into the back of that van." Peter looked down at his fingers and absently began rubbing the ash off them. "I'm giving you an opportunity to make up for what you've done. Take it. Work with us." He hesitated a moment, then looked up to add, "Please."

It was clear Erich was still terrified, but he forced a small smile onto his face. "Okay."

23

*E*ighteen million marks! Peter paced nervously in the small living room of Jenny's flat. He could hear a baby crying, but it was not Jenny's – the noise came through the walls from a flat down the hall. Eighteen million marks! Even though any rational person would know that the government would never pay out the entire sum – and indeed, was likely not to pay a pfennig of it to an informer – the number was so fantastic it was almost irresistible. Eighteen million marks!

Peter sat on the couch and rubbed his eyes. As far as his brother was concerned, he was reasonably safe. He had told Erich he was leaving London immediately and, as added security, had promised that if he were arrested, the first name he would mention would be Erich's. It was the others who worried Peter and made his gut ache. Eighteen million marks! For his own part, there was not so much to fear. If someone succumbed to the temptation and he was betrayed, he would bite down on his poison and die. But what of his comrades? If the police invaded the meeting, they would all be arrested. Those who simply attended would face crippling fines or imprisonment. Those who helped organize the meeting could be imprisoned for years or even sent to re-education. If anyone talked and pointed fingers, Jenny and Barbara would be implicated as ringleaders and could well be sentenced to death for treason. Barbara's baby would never be born, Jenny's children would be motherless. Even worse, if the Führer felt cheated of his revenge by Peter's suicide, would he turn to one of them as a substitute? Would Peter condemn his friends to a month of torture before their executions? He closed his eyes in dismay at the thought that any of his friends would ever experience what he knew so well. God, please, no.

"Would you like a cuppa?" Jenny stood in the entrance of the kitchen niche with a small tray. Peter nodded and she brought the tea over to a little table and began pouring. "Milk?"

He shook his head even though her back was to him.

She turned around at the silence and then laughed, "Oh, that's right, dark and bitter."

He smiled wanly as she handed him a cup of plain, black tea.

"You look nervous." She sat down on the couch, next to him.

"I am." He sighed heavily as he set the cup down. "There are so many people involved whom I don't even know. Any one of them could destroy us all. I can't stand the thought of being responsible for you or Barbara or anyone else being arrested."

"You wouldn't be. Each of us makes our own decisions. After all, you're taking the greatest risk, why shouldn't we take a risk as well?"

"Ach, in my case..." Peter waved his arm dismissively and fell silent.

"What? Are you saying your life's not important?" Jenny furrowed her brow as her lightly offered suggestion was not answered. "Alan?"

He picked up the teacup and stared at its contents. It was odd how she always called him by his old name, yet it also felt right. It made him want to answer her honestly, but he did not know how to express what he truly felt. He wasn't even sure what it was that he felt.

"Don't you care about your life anymore?"

He shrugged. "I'd just like to sort of get it over with. You know, without cocking up again, or causing anyone's death."

"What? Over with? Are you thinking about suicide?"

He shook his head. "No. That'd make a mess of things. I think it would be awful for my children to know that their father had killed himself."

"Is that the only reason you want to stay alive?"

He set the teacup down again, still without having drunk a drop. "Essentially."

Jenny shook her head slowly. "I don't understand. That's not at all like you. You were always so..." She searched the room as if looking for the right word hiding in a corner. "Resilient."

"Yeah," he grunted with amusement. "That was me alright."

"And now?"

"Now?" He turned his head to stare out the one small, sealed window. He could see nothing but the gray wall of the apartment block opposite. The room was rather like a prison cell. How, he wondered, did Jenny keep herself from going mad? He turned away from the window to give her one of his most convincing smiles. "Now I've got what I always wanted. I belong, I have an important job, my wife loves me, I have adorable children and a wonderful home."

She wasn't buying it. "And?"

In reply, he let the smile drop. He studied her, trying to imagine the desire he had once felt for her, or for Allison, or Zosia, or anybody. It was pointless. He felt nothing except a vague dread at the thought of things spinning out of control again. "I have things under control."

Jenny looked ready to question that, but there was a sound of someone in the hall and a key turning in the lock. A man stepped into the room. He wore the blue overalls that were the usual uniform of a manual laborer, on the upper left strap was the insignia of his company and below that he had pinned his badge. Jenny stared at him in astonishment. "What are you doing back already?"

The man took in the scene with a glance – his wife sitting on the small couch, an unknown man sitting next to her. He scowled. "Me? Why are you home? Why haven't you gone into work?"

"We have a guest." Jenny nodded with her head toward Peter.

"And he's going to pay your missed wages?"

"We're conducting business!" Jenny took a deep breath to calm herself, then indicating her husband with her head, said to Peter, "Adolf, this is my husband, Edmund."

Peter stood to greet Jenny's husband, offering his hand. Edmund ignored it.

"He's with the organization," Jenny explained carefully.

Still Edmund did not take the offered hand and Peter finally withdrew it. "The organization will pay your wife's missed wages," Peter ad-libbed. He pulled out his wallet and turning toward Jenny, asked, "How much?"

Jenny shook her head slightly, but Edmund said, "Five hundred."

Jenny spat a laugh. "I wish!"

Peter pulled out a thousand mark note and laid it on the table, then he resumed his seat.

108

While Edmund stared entranced at the note, Jenny ducked her head in embarrassment, but then she looked up and mouthed the word, "Thanks."

Out of the corner of his eye, Peter saw how Edmund's hand reached slowly for the note – as if he were a child trying to sneak a bit of cake.

"Hands off! That's mine," Jenny barked.

Edmund withdrew his hand guiltily. He smiled sheepishly, set down his lunchbox and finally answered his wife's original question, all the while staring curiously at Peter. "There was a bomb alert at work. They had us wait in the street, but they'll never sound the all-clear before shift's end. So I came home."

"They keep attendance!"

"Yeah." Edmund threw himself into the only vacant seat. "Carter said he'd punch my card. I did it for him last time."

"You know you could get the sack for that."

Edmund sighed heavily. "Yeah, I know."

Jenny turned to Peter and explained, "It would be the third time and after that no employer would take him on." She turned her attention back to Edmund and added, "You'd be unemployed – unemployable. And you know that it doesn't take much after that to get arrested for something or other and from there on it's a downward spiral."

Edmund did not answer. He stared at the wall opposite, drawing a breath as if that alone took sufficient effort to consume all his mental strength.

"You want some tea?"

Edmund nodded wearily and Jenny stood to get the tea for him, but not without first picking up the thousand mark note and tucking that away into the pocket of her dress. The dress was one of those ill-fitting floral prints which, along with a headscarf, seemed to be ubiquitous off-hours uniform among the working women of the Reich. Peter's mother had once worn something rather more stylish while grocery shopping. The gauntlet of stares and comments she had received had been sufficient to prevent a repetition of her display of frivolity and individualism and had led to a weeks-long diatribe from her about how they simply *had* to move to a better neighborhood.

Suddenly, grunting something like "excuse me" Edmund got up and left the flat. Peter felt a sudden surge of fear as he realized that he had been recognized and Edmund was going to betray him. He looked to Jenny but she had her back turned to make the tea and did not seem to notice Edmund's departure. Not notice? Certainly she heard the door open and shut. Was she in on it?

Peter stood and walked over to her, pressing himself intimately, almost intimidatingly, close. "What's going on?" He managed to keep the accusation out of his voice but he could not suppress the urgency.

"What do you mean?" She leaned into him slightly but did not turn her attention away from the tea.

"Edmund. He left the apartment."

Suddenly she realized why he was concerned and she turned to smile at him. "Oh, that. He's gone to use the loo."

"Your loo is outside the flat?"

"Yes, of course! Isn't everybody's?"

He thought back to the private shower and toilet of his parents' flat, but said, "Yes, of course, I just forgot, it's been a long time since I lived here with English papers." He hesitated, then added, "And I assumed things have got a little better since then."

"Maybe they have – we only share the toilet with two other families."

That left him wondering what sort of conditions she had lived under as a child, but his more immediate concern prevented him from asking. "Can you trust him?" He jerked his head in the direction that Edmund had gone.

"Don't worry. He doesn't know who you are. Anyway, he's not that sort."

"Eighteen million marks."

Jenny closed her eyes and nodded. "I'll go check." She returned several moments later, smiling. "He's in there. Grunting and groaning. He'll be another twenty minutes." She laughed lightly and added, "I guess I should feed him something other than bangers and mash every day."

"You have sausages every day?"

"No! But the old name sticks. I guess I should say 'mash and mash'. If I were concerned about his health, I would give him more beans, but hell, I've got to sleep with the guy."

"Maybe you should try some good German bread."

Jenny laughed, shaking her head. "Works too well! The boys don't have much opportunity to use the loo at work – so that would be disastrous."

Peter nodded, reassured by the senseless conversation, but still he felt an ache of fear deep in the pit of his stomach. If only he could get this meeting over with and be heading home.

"You have no idea what it's like!"

"We want action, not words!"

"We've had enough waiting!"

"Yeah, it's alright for you, you get to go touring America – but for us rank and file, all they want us to do is pay our dues and collect money from other people! At least the Real ERA is doing something!"

Peter looked from one side of the room to the other as the comments flew through the air. Had they heard even a word of what he had said? He felt a sudden exhaustion sweep through him. The adrenaline from the early part of the meeting, when he feared betrayal at any moment, was evaporating and there was nothing left but an overpowering sadness and this dreadful tiredness. He remembered when he was imprisoned in the camp, if a prisoner was punished by flogging, the prisoner was required to count the strokes. A miscount required a recount, starting from the beginning, so despite the pain, despite screams and exhaustion and dizziness, those numbers kept emerging from the prisoner's mouth. Not because he wanted to count, but because the alternative was worse. And so it felt to Peter now. He had to explain, yet again, what was wrong with blowing up innocent kids in the name of freedom. Even the enemy's kids. He had to explain how tactically stupid it was to lose support among the international community and especially America, from which they received so much money. He had to explain not only that it was useless and counterproductive, but wrong as well. And each and every word he said would be wasted.

"There are casualties in every battle, in every war!" someone was saying.

Indeed, and once again, Peter would have to explain the difference between such unavoidable civilian casualties in a full-fledged hot war and the deliberate targeting of innocent lives just to make a political point. And not even a very good point. After all, what were the Realies saying? Let us run England because it's our birthright and otherwise we'll blow you up? What alternative were they offering to Nazi rule?

"And no one in the NAU is even paying attention to us. We'll get their attention!"

Yes, they would. Maybe. It depended crucially on the media's mood whether or not England's struggle would become the flavor of the month. It wouldn't last more than a month or two in any case and then the island could settle in splendid isolation back into its squalid mire. Peter felt depressed as he waited through the worst of it in order to respond. They were such an unpleasant group of people – almost uniformly young, aggressive men, spouting slogans and shaking their fists and a few rail-thin, intense women. None of them had any clue about strategy or planning or even what they wanted out of this struggle. All they wanted was action. They wanted revenge for years of humiliation. They wanted somebody to notice them. They were frustrated and acting out blind aggression.

Peter had felt the same potent urges and he knew they were not something to be easily defused in a simple half hour of rational debate. It was also pointless repeating to them that a well-presented hour on American TV was worth far more than any suicide bombing because that was only partly true. There was no new information to impart – it was all already there, in books, magazines, newspapers. But nobody wanted to hear about it. It was simply *too depressing*, as one person had explained to him. Rather than do something about it, or even write a lousy cheque, the man had simply stood up and left, refusing to hear the rest of what Peter had to say.

And I cleaned it up for them. Peter laughed to himself as he remembered the incident. The Realies were right, a bombing *would* have gotten that man's attention. Especially one in his own backyard. And he might then have recognized that ignoring depressing news did not make it go away. Indeed, it often only exacerbated the situation enough to bring the bad news closer to home.

And that was a problem, for the Realies were as aware of that as he was. They *were* succeeding in instilling fear in the colonists and Conciliators. They *were* spreading the misery, from the oppressed parts of London, from the prisons and displacement camps and shabby tenements, into the affluent gated suburbs and controlled tower blocks. Even Berlin was taking notice. If the bombing campaign lost the Realies support among a rather disinterested American population, that was a price they were willing to pay. And if they took their struggle further afield – to Berlin, or America, they might well cause some big changes. Probably not for the better, but that was hard to predict, and after decades of waiting, it was difficult to claim that they had not been patient or given the nonviolent approach a chance.

Peter read the anger and emotion in the faces around him. It had been a mistake setting the meeting for the evening. What they had gained with the cover of darkness, they had lost to alcohol. Nobody was going to be convinced of anything tonight. These boys would continue with their bombs. He had said it all and they had not heard him. He could say it all again and they would still not hear. He was wasting his time and with each passing minute the risk to Barbara and Jenny and the others who had helped organize the meeting only grew.

Peter stood and motioned for silence. "I am *not* your conscience. Do what you think is right, but I'm warning you – I want my name removed from any of your actions, and if you continue to use it, I will not only publicly denounce you and humiliate you for your cowardice in needing to prove yourself by blowing up children, but I will use my personal connections to have you hunted down and exterminated. Tell you leaders that. Is that understood?"

There was a barrage of shouts and replies, none of which he could understand over the din. He made his way out of the room and left.

24

"So, we meet again." Arieka approached the table. It was set back from the crowded room, near the window, overlooking the sidewalk and the steady flow of pedestrian traffic that streamed along 57th street.

Alex stood and grasped her hand. "So glad you could make it!" Arieka's long, bony fingers wrapped themselves around his gnarled hand and then she surprised him by draping her other arm around him and hugging him. He felt the disturbing thinness of her frame, the surprising strength of her emaciated muscles. He looked up at her – she was taller than he – and kissed her cheek. "Really glad."

Arieka pulled back and surveyed Alex from her haughty height. Her clothes hung loosely on her – casual jeans, an unexceptional tee-shirt. Nothing like the fashionable rags from which she made her living. She had no make-up either, and without it, without the practiced look of other-worldliness that she carried with her on the catwalks and in magazines, she looked young, almost girlish. She also looked worried, and before she had even seated herself, she asked, "Is he alright?"

She must mean Peter, Alex thought, and he rushed to reassure her, "Yes, had some adventures, I've heard, but everything's fine with him."

"And how's the baby? Your granddaughter?"

"Doing well, I've heard. Haven't seen her, of course. Peter's adopted a daughter as well, a two-year old."

"Oh! Why?"

Alex wondered why he had mentioned Madzia and now he debated about telling Arieka the truth. He offered Arieka a cigarette, lit it for her, then lit one for himself. Still he was undecided.

"Off the record?"

Alex nodded. "Off the record, he had an affair with the woman who…" he sighed, unsure of how to describe Elspeth Vogel. "She had a baby by him."

"Ah-hah. He does get around, doesn't he?" Arieka commented slyly. Or was there something else to her tone?

"He claims it was under duress. I guess I can see that. She controlled everything – his food, the amount of work he had to do, whether or not he was punished…" Alex wondered why he was essentially defending Peter's actions. Maybe it was in response to Anna's furious reaction to the news. She had finally accepted him, learned to trust him, genuinely begun to like him, and then this. It was as though he had betrayed her personally and Alex could not even rationally discuss it with her anymore.

Arieka pursed her lips. "Do you think he fell in love with that woman?"

"Pff. Not to judge from his words. But who knows? I don't think he interacted with anyone but her. I suppose he was lonely and she was there. The fact that any affection that he could give her would make his life easier must have had its influence."

"He certainly didn't mention that during his visit."

"No. Of course not. Even I didn't know. I guess my daughter only found out when she learned about the child. The two of them decided to keep it a secret."

"Well, it certainly would have cast his words in a different light." Arieka held her cigarette in front of her and looked at the smoke as it danced heavenward. "It certainly couldn't have been that awful for him, if he was screwing the lady of the house."

"Yes, it could have been! The woman's husband had bought the legal right to do whatever he wanted to Peter. He could beat him, beat him to death if he wanted. In fact, he nearly did. And he crippled Peter. He clearly had no moral aversion to violence. He may have had a financial incentive not to kill Peter, but that was all that stood between Peter and a brutal death. The woman could have invented any story she wanted to about him – and it would have been enough to have him tortured or killed. His word counted for nothing, not in that house, not with the authorities. He had no legal rights at all. If she wanted him to sleep with her, then it was a very wise idea for him to find her attractive. End of story."

Arieka closed her eyes as if in pain. She nodded slowly. "Yes, of course," she whispered. "It is certainly a story as old as time. And I suppose the fact that we are immune from such things, does not make it any less painful for those who are not."

"Also there was no way he could have mentioned the child when he was here without endangering both the mother and the child. She might have been arrested for miscegenation, and God knows what they might have done with the kid."

Arieka opened her eyes, but she did not look at Alex. She focused on something across the room as she sucked on her cigarette and then exhaled a stream of smoke. The waitress came with an ashtray and kindly asked them to extinguish their cigarettes as smoking was not permitted in restaurants. Arieka sheepishly ground hers out, but Alex smiled broadly as he smashed his into the ashtray, exclaiming with a heavy accent, "Sorry! Didn't know!"

The waitress nodded wearily and took their orders. By the time she had moved away Arieka had shaken off her mood and in a business-like tone of voice asked, "But how was Peter in a position to adopt the child? I don't understand."

"Ah, well, he kidnapped her."

"Kidnapped?" Arieka sounded alarmed.

Alex shook his head. "It's not what it sounds like. Given the way the parents ignored that girl, I'm sure he would have won custody if there had been a court he could have gone to. But there isn't. That's the way our life there is, we sort things out for ourselves."

"Of course, of course," Arieka said, distantly.

"I wish there was some way you could see it for yourself."

Arieka laughed lightly. "I will. I mean, a little bit anyway."

"What do you mean?"

She grinned, flashing incredibly white, perfectly straight teeth at Alex. "You're looking at the new ambassador of Kivu to the Third Reich."

"You?"

"We have diplomatic relations with them. Remember? Have to keep that aid money flowing!"

"Yes, of course. But why you? Why there?"

"Me? Because I asked. I'm one of the élite of my country – given my money and my connections here."

"Yes, of course, I didn't mean it like that. But why there?"

"Because I asked. I'm curious. The position was open, so I let the embassy here know that I'd be willing to take up the post. I'll even pay my own expenses, so they couldn't resist that offer. Anyway, most of our people aren't too enamored of the idea of going to a place that prides itself on its lily-whiteness. Cold and rainy too. No night-life. The place is a drag, I've heard."

"You've heard correctly, though I gather there is some sort of nightlife in the clubs, for the élite. Do you think you'll be in that group?"

"Hard to say. Maybe I'll be exotic enough that they won't hold my ebony skin against me."

"More likely, your wealth will be sufficient to lighten your tan," Alex joked.

Arieka laughed. "But this isn't why you asked to meet. What's up?"

Their orders arrived. Alex noted that though he had a full lunch, Arieka had nothing more than a cup of coffee. He raised his eyebrows and suggested, "You should eat something. You're going to make yourself sick."

115

"Sick and rich. Fashion likes famine victims. Don't worry, after I finish up this shoot, I'm going to eat a bit – in preparation for all that cold rain I'll encounter in Berlin."

Alex nodded. "We talked to Peter about your donation. He has two purposes in mind. The first is personal: he wants to use a small part of the donation to help a kid get some artificial limbs. Legs – two of them. Good ones. The sort you can only buy in America."

"Who is this kid? How did he lose his legs?"

"A mine," Alex answered the last question first. "The kid's name is Olek." He paused as he thought about how he could explain Olek's relationship to Peter. "You remember Joanna? My granddaughter?"

"Of course. The girl who was murdered."

"Yes. Her father, Adam, was Olek's uncle. Olek's parents are both dead, his grandfather…Anyway, I believe he looked to his uncle Adam as a father – all the other men in his life were absent. After Adam was killed…"

"You do tend to hemorrhage people, don't you?"

"It's a dangerous business we're in. Anyway, at that point my daughter married Peter. Olek was assigned to work with him decoding stuff and I guess they became good friends."

"And this Olek looks to Peter as a father?"

Alex shrugged. "Quite likely."

"Well, I have no objection to using the money in that way."

"Good. The second part, the majority of your largesse, Peter would like to use to establish a sort of Underground Railroad."

"Too bad I'm not an African-American, the irony would be glorious!" Arieka laughed. "As it is, I think my people were more involved in the profitable end of the slave trade. But we won't talk about that." She gave Alex a wink.

"Yeah, portions of my wife's ancestors owned more than their share of serfs, too."

"So, how is he going to set up this Underground Railway?"

"Ah, good question. The reason I wanted to talk to you, assuming you approve this use…"

"But of course."

"Good, the reason we need you, is these people need a destination. He'll work on the mechanism of spreading the word, and getting the escapees to a border, but after that, they'll need passports to get them out, and visas to get them somewhere safe. We'll need money for the papers to get them out, such things don't come cheap, and we'll need influence with the American government to give them visas and a place to settle. They'll need some start-up help as well. They'll need English classes, a place to live, most will have to be taught how to read and learn some useful skill. Some of them will need psychological help, counseling or something."

Arieka pulled back from the table. "Geez."

"Yeah. I was hoping you'd—"

"I can't afford to increase—"

"Oh, heavens no! You've been incredibly generous! What I was hoping was that you might lend us your voice. We could organize a campaign to raise funds here and also to twist the government's arm into helping us a bit."

"And it wouldn't hurt to embarrass the Reich just a bit further?" Arieka guessed. "Publicity for the arms funds?"

"If that's a side-effect," Alex admitted, almost as an afterthought. "Well, it wouldn't be all that awful, would it?"

Arieka sipped her coffee. She looked off into the distance as if seeing her answer printed on a menu held by another customer. "I come from a group of people who, a few hundred years ago, moved in on the natives of a region and lorded it over them. We still pretty much run things. Periodically the lower classes rise up and slaughter my people, periodically we get the upper hand and keep them calm. Some would say oppressed. Colonial powers, our neighbors, despots have all used this constant feuding to good effect. The end result is usually an incompetent and corrupt government keeping an uneasy peace which is regularly interrupted by tribal war, slaughter, and famines. We're always begging for aid, thinking we're clever because we can play the Reich off against America or the Soviet Union. It all ends up in Swiss banks or buying arms made in the Reich, or America, or the Soviet Union. Our so-called politicians use the deaths of our people, and our neighbors, to funnel money from taxpayers in rich countries to arms-makers in rich countries, skimming a bit off for themselves in the process. Clever, isn't it?"

Alex shook his head.

"We're always thrashing, drowning in a foot of water." She looked at Alex and smiled sadly. "I always wonder what we could have achieved if things had been, if they were, otherwise."

"So do I."

"This is why I insisted Peter have a right to decide how my money would be spent. I don't want to see it going to arms. I like his idea. I'll support it. I can't publicly lend my voice to it – that would ruin my diplomatic career before it even started, but I can get you in touch with some people who can. And, privately, there are a few arms that I can twist."

"We'd be extremely grateful."

Arieka nodded. "As long as it's not buying guns, okay?"

"Promise."

117

25

*M*arysia ladled out the mushroom soup. "Berlin? You've only just got back! Are you nuts?"

Peter glanced across the table at Zosia before answering. She smiled her encouragement. "I don't think so, but I wanted to check with you first, before even bringing the idea to the Council."

"Peter, you of all people should avoid that city! Why would you want to take such a risk?" Marysia doled the last of the soup into her bowl. It wasn't even half full.

"Have some of mine. You've given me too much."

"No, no! I had some while I was making it. Anyway, they're your mushrooms – yours and Madzia's."

He didn't insist. Marysia's soups were exquisite, and it had been a long time since she had invited them to dinner. Though Zosia had made a half-hearted attempt to learn to cook, too often he came back to the flat from a busy day working only to find her too exhausted to have made anything, even something mediocre. So they nibbled on whatever was available while running themselves ragged keeping a two-year-old and a baby simultaneously happy. Only Olek's generous offer to watch the children gave them enough peace to enjoy Marysia's efforts.

Marysia cut into the fresh bread she had baked, they took a moment to say grace, and then once she had settled into her seat, she repeated, "Why?"

Peter postponed answering to taste the soup first. "It's my idea of helping the slave labor – those who want to get out. I need to lay the foundations of an escape network."

"You *are* an adrenaline junky!"

"It'll be less dangerous than London was."

"London was important."

Peter's eyes narrowed slightly. "Because that involved money but this just involves people's lives?"

Marysia shook her head, but did not debate the point. "Look, Peter–"

"Marysia, *this* is important. At least to me."

"The risks–"

"To hell with the risks!"

Zosia agreed with one of her favorite phrases. "Life without risks is not worth living!"

Marysia looked at her askance. "Sensible risk, perhaps."

Peter smiled fondly at his wife, but spoke to Marysia. "Risk is risk – you can only append the word sensible or senseless after the fact."

Marysia rolled her eyes in annoyance.

"Really, I don't think this is a senseless risk. I want to learn what I need to do to get this idea working."

"Pff! Don't you think a mechanism and a destination would be the first things you should establish?"

Zosia dabbed at her mouth with her napkin. "Father is helping with that. He's talking to that woman who donated most of the money to see if they can raise more funds and maybe get a pressure group together to organize asylum for these people once we've spirited them out of the country."

Marysia turned from Zosia back to Peter. "But why do *you* need to go, why not someone else?"

Peter slurped some soup before answering. He felt ravenous. "Two reasons: no one else seems really interested – it's dangerous and I wouldn't want to coerce anybody into doing this who isn't absolutely committed to the idea. But the main reason is that these people aren't going to trust just anyone. I need to be the one to make first contact, because they know me. Maybe later, I could work through representatives."

Marysia absently spread some butter on her bread. "Okay, but why not wait a bit? A year or two won't matter and it will be much safer then."

"I might not have that sort of time."

Marysia gave him a sharp look. "Why not?"

Peter turned toward Zosia, "You didn't tell her?"

"Tell me what?" Marysia set the butter knife down.

Peter turned his gaze back toward her. He looked at her a long moment, almost as if savoring the view. "The doctor thinks I might soon lose my vision altogether."

"What?"

"You know the question of my sight has always been unclear. The original problem was probably caused by…" Peter made an abrupt motion with his hand toward his head as words seemed to fail him. "You know, all that…all those impacts. Either that or the chemicals caused some deterioration and the violent jarring exacerbated the problem." He waved his hand in annoyance at the imprecision. "Whatever it was, anyway, since then, I've had a few more occasions to be banged around – and well, after knocking myself out when I jumped off that train, the problem's worsened. When I was getting my arm treated, the physician–"

"The upshot is," Zosia interrupted, "that there's a chance Peter will go blind soon, and he wants to set up this system while he's still able to infiltrate Berlin."

Marysia looked in horror from one to the other. "Don't you think," she said, releasing each word carefully, "that you should be tending to this problem first?"

Peter shook his head. "There's no point. No money."

"What about the money raised in America?"

"You know, it's all been spent."

"Even the collection taken up specifically for your medical expenses?"

Peter glanced at Zosia as he answered. "I left everything in Alex's hands. Has he told you that he held anything in reserve for me?"

Marysia shook her head. "But what about this current largesse?"

"No, I want to help the others, the people I left behind. And, well, and I wanted Olek to have a new set of legs. You don't want to deny him that, now do you?"

"No, of course not, it's just..." Marysia floundered, waving her hand uselessly toward Peter's eyes.

He shrugged. "Look, they probably can't do anything to prevent it anyway. And my bet is that natural healing will be better than any intervention, but if I'm wrong, all I'm asking is that I get a chance to do something for those people before it's too late. Whatever the limits on my own time, Marysia, you have to understand – a year or two in their hands – that's a lifetime. Please, can I go to Berlin?"

Marysia hesitated a long moment as she considered his request. "Where would you plan to stay once you're there? You certainly can't go to Ryszard's."

"No, of course not. It would be far too risky for me to ever go there again," Peter agreed readily, relieved that she seemed to have accepted his plan.

"That isn't what I meant. While you were away, Peter, I've been in contact with Warszawa and I've been informed of a few things with respect to Ryszard. They updated me on his situation and were looking to see if we could provide any useful feedback."

Zosia raised her eyebrows. "Oh? What then?"

"Ryszard is under constant surveillance by the Führer. Ever since Vogel's murder."

"Is he under suspicion?" Zosia asked in alarm.

"Probably not. It looks like the Führer is just using Vogel's murder as an excuse to shorten Ryszard's leash a bit, but it's not only that, Ryszard has separated from Kasia. He's living in a flat in the center of town."

"What?"

"As a prelude to divorce. Seems he wants to link up with Frau Schindler..."

An image of that woman came into Peter's mind and he nearly shuddered with revulsion. What could Ryszard possibly see in her? Even if Ryszard were only using her, it seemed impossible to believe he could get close enough to plan marriage. Peter remembered how Frau Schindler, while visiting Elspeth, would look at him as if he were truly less than human. She always talked about him as if he did not understand and ceaselessly goaded Elspeth into treating him more sternly. And when Frau Schindler addressed him directly, it was in a contemptuous, harping tone, and always with the intent of chiding him for improper behavior.

On the other hand, there were the dinner parties, and how Frau Schindler behaved with the men there. Not Peter, not the other servants, rather the guests, those with status. He remembered how her eyes lit up, how her hips swayed provocatively, how she laughed merrily at their jokes. He remembered that she had quite a wit – one which often involved humiliating the lesser beings in her presence but which was nevertheless clever. He nodded his head. Yes, perhaps Ryszard would appreciate such charms.

"...We're getting only indirect news about him because of the surveillance." Marysia was explaining. "HQ is afraid he's gone renegade."

Zosia slammed her spoon down. "Ryszard? Never!"

Peter used his napkin to wipe up the drops of soup she had sent flying. "What does Kasia think?"

"This surveillance has been rough on him, she's afraid he might be losing his grip. Even worse, he apparently lost his poison, so now all he has is cyanide capsules."

"Which is useless to someone like Ryszard, given the number of times he's searched," Zosia interjected.

"Yes, and in any case it'd be stupid of him to poison himself immediately upon being arrested so the capsules would be confiscated before he genuinely needed them. He's essentially unprotected, and if he's interrogated, he could ruin us all. As you know, he's privy to a lot more information than is normal for a field agent. HQ is thinking of pulling him in."

"Oh, good Lord!" Zosia banged a fist on the table, again sending a bit of soup sloshing out of her bowl. "They can't do that! Not after all the work he's done!"

Marysia shrugged. "His actions leave his motives unclear. Can we risk having him out there when we don't know what he's doing?"

Peter placed his hand gently on Zosia's fist and stroked it soothingly as he spoke to Marysia. "Whatever he's doing, he's still working his way into being Führer. If he's working for us, then it would be criminal to destroy what he's achieved because of rogue suspicions. And, if he's working only for himself, then we can do as much damage to him as he can to us. And he knows that."

Marysia pursed her lips, intrigued. "So you think we could eventually blackmail him, if nothing else?"

"Yes, of course."

Zosia shook her head. "He's not gone renegade. He just knows what has to be done. He's playing the game. What else did we expect him to do?"

"But leaving Kasia…" Marysia protested.

Zosia huffed. "Since when do Nazi marriage laws mean anything to us? He was married to her, by a priest, here! That's the only thing that matters. If Kasia doesn't recognize that, then she's a fool."

Peter resumed eating his soup, returning an air of calm to the discussion. "He probably feels he's protecting her as well. He knows that divorcing her, or at least being separated, means they probably won't touch his family if they haul him in."

Marysia nodded thoughtfully. "Yes, I think he was quite disturbed by Andrzej's death. And by what happened to Joanna. You may be right. I'll at least pass on your comments to HQ."

Zosia managed to unclench her fist. "Tell them, if we go to Berlin, we could see if we can't find out a bit more. I could go and see Kasia personally, get her feedback. Maybe time my visit with one from Ryszard. He must come and see the children now and then."

"Yes, weekly, we're told." Marysia looked at Zosia appraisingly. "Yes, that would be good if you could talk to her personally. Currently she's the only one who can tell us anything about his state of mind. She and Leszek."

"Leszek?"

"Yes, HQ insisted he go with Ryszard to keep an eye on things. But Ryszard is never forthcoming, even at the best of times, and now…Well, all Leszek's noticed is that Ryszard seems truly enamored of this Schindler woman. That, and that Ryszard let his bodyguard beat him up."

Zosia furrowed her brow questioningly. "Beat who up? Leszek?"

Marysia nodded. "Apparently as punishment for some indiscretion on Leszek's part. The bodyguard discovered a letter Leszek was writing to Lodzia and Ryszard let him mete out an 'appropriate' punishment."

"Oh, God!" Zosia covered her mouth with her hand to contain her horror.

Peter stood and paced to the family portraits which Marysia had on the wall. He stared into the eyes of the woman he had never met, Marysia's daughter, Julia. Olek's mother, Julia. Karl Vogel's lover, Julia. *Ryszard's* Julia. "You know," he said, without taking his eyes off the picture, "that probably isn't as bad as it sounds."

Marysia turned in her seat to look at Peter. "Why do you think that?"

"Just basing it on my own experience. You see, Karl not only had rights over my labor, he was accountable for my actions. Many times he was unnecessarily cruel, but sometimes even I had to admit he was obliged to discipline me – especially if there were any witnesses involved." Peter turned away from the picture to survey the two women. "Don't you see? With the bodyguard there, apparently reporting his every action to the Führer, Ryszard would have had very little choice in what he could do. Ryszard is legally responsible for everything Leszek does – if he hadn't taken some sort of action, it would have been as if he condoned the crime or had committed it himself. Public behavior is very constrained, and now Ryszard is living every moment of his life in public. Leszek should have known that."

Zosia raised her eyebrows in surprise. "I would have thought *you* would have had more sympathy for Leszek."

Peter shrugged. "I am aware of the realities of life out there. It all ticks along just fine, letting you believe it's a normal society, but just take a tiny step out of line, and you realize that the whole culture is psychotic. Especially the closer you get to the core of power."

Marysia nodded. "You may be right. In any case, we clearly need more information about what Ryszard is up to. He's always been a bit of a wild card." She glanced over at the picture Peter had been staring at. "It's the reason I advised her to stay away from him."

Zosia gaped at Marysia in astonishment. "And did you advise Adam away from Ryszard's wild sister?"

Marysia looked stunned. "Zosia! What's come over you?"

"Ryszard and Julia would have been happy together!" Zosia snapped. "Instead he married a woman he didn't love and Julia got herself knocked up by one of her targets! She never was happy after that! My God, no wonder she–"

"Don't blame me for her mistakes." Marysia intoned ominously. "I gave her my advice, nothing more. She made her own choices."

Peter walked over behind Zosia's chair and gently massaged her shoulders. "So, what do you think about us going to Berlin?"

"That? Oh, yes. Both you and Zosia?"

"Yes, and the children. We'll be much less suspicious as a family and we can stay longer. A month or two."

"Don't you think it's dangerous?"

"We've discussed it." Peter leaned forward so he could see Zosia's face. She still looked angry and he continued his impromptu backrub. "Berlin is a huge city and word is they aren't looking for me there anymore – not since it leaked out that I was in London, talking to the Real ERA. The

123

only time I'll be taking any risk is when I go to talk to my old comrades. At that time I'll make sure I carry papers that don't in any way associate me with the address that Zosia and the kids are at. And if I get picked up, I'll just opt out before I can do any damage."

Zosia looked uncomfortable but didn't say anything. She resumed eating her soup in silence.

Marysia grimaced, "Be careful about how you plan to use that poison. It's not guaranteed to work. We've had occasions where it has failed to kill, like with that Vogel fellow."

"I probably placed that badly," Zosia volunteered. "Into muscle."

"And he had been drinking," Peter added.

Marysia looked quizzical. "So?"

Peter shrugged. "Slows the metabolism, maybe it affects the uptake."

Marysia nodded noncommittally. "It's not clear what's going on – maybe the adrenaline of such situations, or something – obviously we can't test this sort of thing."

"Why not give out larger doses?"

"I gather it's not that simple. And with each tooth we fill, there is that much more risk of an accidental poisoning. But that's not the point, the point is, it's not infallible and I don't want you to bank everything on it."

"I could carry cyanide."

Marysia sighed. "That's easily detectable and would remove the implication that you are acting alone and unsupported. Do you want that?"

Peter shook his head.

"How about you just stop planning your own death? Hmm? No idiotic risks, okay?"

"When," Peter asked with exaggerated seriousness, "have I ever done anything stupid?"

Marysia snorted slightly. "Maybe I'll support your plan. But won't this cost a lot? You'll be wasting the money that you were given."

"We'll only use a tiny bit for start-up funds. Since Zosia has to take care of some financial transactions in any case, we'll just establish an extra account to cover our costs once we're there."

"But shifting funds into a personal account is risky. They might track you down with that!"

Zosia shook her head. "Don't worry, I know what I can get away with. We'll keep the sums low and we'll be long gone before they catch up with us."

Marysia considered her, as if weighing her words against her earlier anger.

Zosia bit her lips, then reluctantly said, "I'm sorry about what I said." She seemed like she was going to say more, but instead she turned her attention back to her soup.

Marysia continued to watch her, but when Zosia failed to say anything more, she looked up at Peter. "When would you leave?"

"We can leave anytime. What do you say? Do you mind if I put this idea to the Council?" He gave her a broad, charming smile.

"Will anything I say stop you?"

The smile slid from Peter's face. "Yes. I'm sincerely seeking your advice, and if you say 'no', then I won't bring the idea up again. I haven't forgotten Jana, Marysia. I'm not that shallow."

Marysia nodded, satisfied. "Give me a bit of time to think about it. I'll tell you tom–"

Madzia's intense, sudden screaming from down the hall caused all three of them to pause and listen. Before Marysia or Zosia could react, Peter was already at the door. Once he had left, Marysia turned to Zosia. "Now, child, what was that all about?"

"I'm sure Madzia wasn't allowed to stick her fingers in Irena's eyes, or maybe Olek stopped her from throwing herself off the top shelf of the bookcase. Something draconian like that."

"Is that why you're so on edge? Is the two-year-old getting to you?"

Zosia's spoon hit the table again. "I'm not on edge!"

Marysia smiled gently. "That thing with Julia and Ryszard. And guessing that I said something negative to Adam about you. You know better than that. What's wrong? Is everything okay with you and the children and Peter?"

"Pff."

"I thought you two had finally settled down. He's so calm and relaxed now."

"Oh, if it's settled down you're looking for – goodness yes!" Zosia agreed sarcastically. "He goes off and handles this and that with the Council and still mixes in with Olek's cryptanalysis office, and now he's training Jurek to take over, and then he has to organize this 'Underground Railroad' and then off to London for a few weeks...and there's always something going on."

"You know what it's like. When you were on the Council, you were always busy too."

"Meanwhile," Zosia continued, not even noticing Marysia's comment, "I'm left to care for two kids, one of whom is not even my own, the other a new baby for Christ's sake, and he's never around to help, and I'm trying to carry out my duties – do you know I haven't even embezzled the funds to support our local bribes? If I let that go much longer, we'll never re-establish good supply lines and we'll be eating cabbage and potatoes for the next year here! It's as if my work isn't important! And Magdalena, my God, she's always into something! I just get Irena to sleep and she'll start singing at the top of her lungs or screaming for something or, oh God…"

Marysia raised an eyebrow.

"Yeah, I know, two-year-olds are like that. And with a baby around, and well, I guess I thought Peter would do more. I mean, before he took care of everything, but now he's always busy with something else."

"He seems to do quite a lot." Marysia picked up a slice of bread and broke off a piece. "He's still doing most of the cooking isn't he?" She put the bite into her mouth and chewed thoughtfully. "And I've seen him hauling in supplies late in the evening and hauling out the garbage and anytime he's home he handles the kids and I've seen him walking Irena around at night so you can sleep–"

"Sleep," Zosia muttered sarcastically. She picked up her bowl and drank the rest of the soup.

Marysia broke off another bit of bread and ate that. "And you still seem to find plenty of time alone for your long walks with Tadek."

"As if I'm supposed to give up every aspect of my life! Damn it, I quit the Council–"

"You didn't have to quit the Council. It was not only your idea, but you specifically said you wanted to spend time with your family. You've got what you want–"

"No lectures!" Zosia snapped.

"Sorry, it wasn't a lecture. Come on, tell me, what's really the problem?"

Zosia pushed her empty bowl out of the way and then quite theatrically dropped her head onto her arms. She said something incomprehensible.

"What? I didn't hear you." Marysia set down the remainder of the bread as if to indicate that she was giving Zosia her full attention.

Zosia looked up so that her chin rested on her crossed arms. "We're not having sex."

"What? Since when?"

"Since when? I don't know. Since he's come back. But you know, with everything that's gone on, with his being away and Irena's birth, my God, it's been since before Joanna's mmm…Since September."

"September? That's…" Marysia paused to count. "That's over nine months!"

Zosia nodded and buried her head back in her hands.

Marysia narrowed her eyes. "Are you telling me, he's been *refusing* you?"

"Well, not exactly. He's just not interested. I mean, he's kind and considerate and friendly, but…Well he used to make me feel so wanted! He'd look at me so longingly, I could say no or push him away or yell at him and he'd just keep coming back. He'd cajole and flatter and give me gifts, and, oh, all sorts of things. Now…It's not like it used to be."

Marysia smiled knowingly. "Ah, the honeymoon's finally over."

"No. It's more than that. He's become really cold. And the worst part is, I don't think it's intentional."

"Has he told you why?"

Zosia shook her head. "No. He won't talk about it. About anything, really. I get angry and yell and insult him, and he just shrugs it off. He soothes me! It's like nothing I say matters anymore."

Marysia averted her eyes to look at the wall as she thought back to Zosia's behavior when married to Adam. "Have you expressed your frustration physically?"

Zosia snorted her amusement at Marysia's diplomacy and shook her head. "I'm not that stupid!"

"When did this all begin?"

Zosia thought back to all those times Peter had opened himself to her. They had talked like best friends as well as lovers. Argued, too. Now she lived with a polite and helpful stranger who reacted with calm sympathy to her tantrums. "Right after that thing with Jana." I mocked him, Zosia thought, but she didn't want to admit that to Marysia. "I guess I came down on him a bit hard about that."

Marysia sniffed. "Me, too. I so much wanted to blame someone else for my decision." She looked off toward a corner of the room, biting her lip. "I don't know, maybe he was right. Maybe it wasn't necessary…"

Zosia seemed unaware of Marysia's words. "It's as if he's a stranger in my house."

Marysia drew her attention away from the past and back to Zosia. "He doesn't trust you."

"I don't see why not!"

"You don't?" Marysia tilted her head and waited, but Zosia didn't answer. "My dear, that thing with Jana followed right on the heels of his returning from England. You know, when he found out the truth about your clever plan. Did it ever occur to you that you can't jerk someone around – from the moment you meet them – for nearly three years, continuously deceiving them and then expect to have their complete trust?"

Zosia raised her head to look at Marysia. "It wasn't like that. I loved him."

Marysia raised her eyebrows and pursed her lips in disbelief.

"Well, I love him now. Isn't that enough?"

"With time, probably."

"How much time?" Zosia whined.

"How long has it been? And I don't mean altogether. I mean, how long have *you* been willing to let him near?"

"Well, ever since he got back from Berlin. And I even suggested it to him once."

"How daring of you," Marysia remarked snidely.

"Marysia! He actually turned me down! Me! Just because of some stupid nightmare."

"Do you think you used him badly all these years?" Marysia asked, ignoring everything else. Before Zosia could answer, she added, "Be honest."

Zosia shook her head slightly. "You know what was going on, Marysia. For heaven's sakes, it's not that simple! I always cared about him, I always tried to make things easier for him, but—"

"Do you think you were using him?" Marysia repeated.

Zosia stuck out her lower lip. "Whose side are you on?"

"Does there have to be sides?" Before Zosia could answer, Marysia added, "I know this is hard to believe, dear, but even men have feelings. Inscrutable lumbering beasts that they are, God only knows what they feel until all of a sudden they just explode – like Cyprian just packing up and leaving – but even so, if you want to live with them, you have to take into account that they do feel things. And rarely on the sort of time-scale that one would expect. I mean, it took Peter over two years to really understand that you never stopped loving Adam. That's finally hit home, and it hurts him. Now, tell me the truth, what were you thinking when you married him? Did your thoughts turn to Adam during the ceremony?"

Reluctantly Zosia nodded.

"If Peter had guessed that then and gotten angry, would it have been understandable to you?"

Again Zosia nodded.

"Then don't you think his anger is justified now?"

"He claims he's not angry." Zosia stood and walked to the doorway, glancing nervously down the hall toward their apartment, but there was still no sign of him.

"Maybe he isn't. Maybe he's just protecting himself. There is nothing in his background to suggest he's ever had any reason to trust anyone. Then he goes and violates all his instincts and experiences and trusts you completely. And see how he was rewarded."

"He trusted you, too!" Zosia shot back angrily.

Marysia nodded sadly. "I don't think he does anymore. I can't say I blame him."

"So do you think he feels betrayed?"

"Betrayed, angry, cautious...I don't know. Whatever his reasons, you can react in two ways – you can resent what's going on and watch your marriage fall to pieces – the way mine did, or you can take some action and try to undo the harm you did."

Zosia shook her head. "I didn't do any harm! Damn it, I've been good to him!"

"He absolutely adored you, Zosia, and you used that against him. You never once stopped to think if you were being fair. The adoration is over, he's become his own person again. It's up to you to decide what you want to do with that fact. Was it only his total devotion to you that attracted you to him or is there something about *him* that you love?"

Zosia continued to stare down the hallway. "The latter," she whispered forlornly.

"Then the usury is going to have to stop. Old habits will have to change, and it won't be easy. You're going to have to make an effort."

"What do you suggest?"

"For starters, apologize."

"Apologize? Me?" Zosia squeaked. "I did nothing wrong! It was for the Cause!"

Suggesting that Zosia become considerate of another's feelings was like telling the sea to settle down. Marysia shrugged tiredly. "I don't know then. Try to seduce him?"

Zosia snorted at that suggestion. "He jumps if I so much as touch him unexpectedly."

"Really? Still?"

"Here he comes." Zosia turned back into the room. "Just watch."

Peter entered the room and kissed Zosia as she stood there. "Done already? Sorry, I took so long, but I needed to put Madzia to sleep." He sat down to finish his soup.

"No problem." Zosia silently walked up behind him as he ate and, as Marysia watched closely, Zosia planted a light kiss on the back of his neck. Peter flinched sufficiently to spill the soup from his spoon, but rather more disturbing was the fleeting expression of unmitigated hatred which marred his features before turning rapidly into a look of embarrassment. Marysia realized she was shivering.

"Sorry," Peter muttered as he wiped his chin, though he did not indicate to whom he was apologizing or for what. He gave her a charming smile. "Pity to waste even a drop of your delicious soup."

"No need to apologize," Marysia assured him, her eyes searching his face for an indication of where that hatred had come from, to whom it was directed, where it may have gone. There was no sign of it though – it was as if she had imagined it.

26

Stefi moaned and stretched backward, letting the towel she had casually held over her stomach, drop lightly onto the bench as she moved. The men in the sauna threw sly glances at her, but with the Führer there as well, they were quite discreet. She loathed saunas. The first five minutes or so were okay, the warmth felt good, but then it grew rapidly hot and boring. Still Rudi wanted her along, to enjoy her company, he said, though it was clear he was just showing off his prize possession.

She bent one of her long legs seductively, but otherwise lay prone. It was really the only acceptable position for a naked woman – sitting up forced one to be uncomfortably stiff in order to avoid incidental rolls of flesh at the stomach. A fine point which the men seemed to miss entirely. All of them, no matter how flabby, sat upright, some even leaned forward, carefully shielding their delicate bits – especially those who had just come in from the cold water and wanted to hide the unfortunate effects that had upon their anatomy.

Stefi sighed. Even the view was loathsome! As a light dew covered her artfully displayed body, she could stare at rolls of grotesquely sweating male flesh. Ugh! And she was hot! Still, she knew it would not do to leave. Besides offending Rudi, she would miss the gossip – or was it called strategic discussions? She rarely said anything – she was the dumb woman who just looked pretty – but she took it all in and organized it for later use.

Gracefully, she swept her legs to the bench below and stood. She stepped down to the floor, delicately avoiding stepping on anyone's hand, saying "excuse me" as she brushed by the men. All eyes rested on her as she left the room. Werner Büttner went so far as to actually give her a small smile. Powerful, relatively young, he ran the Neureich territory of the Warthegau and had extended his power base up into Denmark and Norway. He would naturally assume that she would find him attractive, what with his inordinate height, his blond hair and blue eyes, but she found his type quite loathsome. For one thing, he lacked a chin; for another, his hair was miserably thin and creeping ever-backward from his forehead. He had no build either – his height only emphasized the narrowness of his back, and worst of all, he was pompous!

She walked to the shower, doused herself in cold water and then, just as casually re-entered the room. An attendant handed her a towel and she used it to wipe her face, but otherwise let the water drip down her body. This time she seated herself on the step below the Führer and leaned backward, resting her head against him. In response, he fondly stroked her hair. Stefi looked across the small room and caught her father's uncomfortable expression. He looked even more annoyed than when he had first entered and noticed her presence. He quickly hid his expression by wiping some sweat off his face with the back of his hand, but the Führer could not have failed to notice.

Good! Stefi thought. Her father's genuine discomfort would please the Führer, letting him feel his power over his subordinate, his sexual prowess at nabbing a younger man's daughter. Not only that, it was good for her father to squirm a bit. His behavior had been incompetent and unprofessional recently. Not that he had separated from her mother – that she understood as a necessary tactical move, but that he seemed genuinely enamored of that Schindler woman. Just like her idiotic aunt Zosia, suddenly all moony-eyed over her husband and spending her precious time raising children. "I need to live my own life a bit," was what Zosia had said to her in explanation, when they had discussed her quitting the Council. "Peter's taught me a lot about taking time out for the little things," she had added, all dewy-eyed. Little things! God Almighty! What was happening to that generation? Were they all losing their cool? Getting old?

Stefi noticed that her father had shifted his position slightly so that his eyes naturally fell onto the glowing stones rather than across the room to his leader. She smiled her amusement. It couldn't have been better if they had planned it! Nothing could more clearly indicate that her love for the Führer was genuine and not part of a plot that her father had concocted. Nothing would more thoroughly convince Rudi that she was devoted to him even over her loyalty to her father. He would trust her now, more than ever.

Her eyes strayed to the man across the aisle from her father – pudgy little Frauenfeld, head of *Komsi*, communications security. The sweat accumulated on his bald spot, making it shine like a halo. Interestingly, he too had averted his eyes from the Führer's mistress. Was it terror or modesty? With Frauenfeld, probably loyalty. Dutiful little loyal man, the eternal number two. Always promoted to the next level simply because every boss enjoyed his fawning devotion. Lord of no territory whatsoever, happy only to serve, he would never amount to anything. Quite in contrast to Schenkelhof, sitting next to him, who, if nothing else, had sheer bulk to his credit. Rolls-of-flesh Schenkelhof, taking a rare break from running the *Wehrmacht* to be in Berlin, was not a pretty sight and Stefi quickly averted her eyes.

The Führer's hand slipped downward, gently fondling Stefi's breast as he casually addressed Büttner. "Werner, how is it going with my palace in Posen?"

Poznań, Stefi mentally corrected, then chided herself for doing so. The palace, *Rudi's* palace, had been built by Kaiser Wilhelm II to solidify Prussia's claim to the troublesome city that it had annexed at the second partition of Poland. Despite the *Kulturkampf*, despite the palace, Germanization did not succeed and the province reverted back to the newly independent Poland at the end of the first World War. Thus, when Hitler again claimed the city for Germany, he determined to make the province entirely and solely German, expelling all the Poles and confiscating their property so it could be given to newly arriving Germans. He charged Speer with designing an appropriately impressive residence for him in the palace and even contributed some of his own capital to the project. Stefi sniffed slightly at the thought – no one asked *how* their devoted and hard-working Führer had come into so much private wealth! Speer's design had been predictably grandiose and the building was used as one of the Führer's main residences until the late sixties when local riots, bombings and a poison gas attack on the palace convinced the Führer's security detail that a strategic withdrawal to Berlin was advisable. The palace in Potsdam was redesigned and modernized and the Führer hunkered down in his new *Residenz*, avoiding the problems of the wider Reich by remaining firmly in the heartland.

Now it was Rudi's goal to reassert his authority over the Warthegau and move back into the Posener palace. As Gauleiter of the region, Büttner had been tasked with making the residence more secure and clearing out the last of any resistance in the region. He was none too happy with the idea of giving up his headquarters and as he finished sourly describing the arduous work involved in making the palace invulnerable, Rudi pointedly asked, "If it's all so insecure, how have you managed to stay safe there all these years, Werner?"

Büttner's eyes met Stefi's and he gave her a conspiratorial smile. "I am not such an august personage as *mein Führer*, and therefore the terrorist scum have less interest in attacking me."

Schenkelhof dabbed at some sweat with a towel, his massive rolls of flesh wobbling with the movement. "What I want to know is why there is 'terrorist scum' there in the first place. Don't you keep a clean house, Werner?"

Büttner gave Schenkelhof a poisonous look. "Perhaps you are unaware of the political realities, comrade. I've inherited an extremely complex situation in that region."

Frauenfeld poked his head out from Schenkelhof's shadow. "How so?"

Stefi glanced up at Rudi and they shared a smile at Frauenfeld's charming naïveté. Büttner leapt at the opportunity to validate his rule. "Ah, Seppel, you see, back in the forties, there was a huge population in that region of mixed blood. In that we were fighting in the west and had to defend our eastern frontier against a Soviet invasion, we were in great need of soldiers – and that meant new citizens to the Reich."

Frauenfeld's eyes glazed over as he realized that he was being lectured to like a schoolchild, but he was far too polite to interrupt and Büttner continued, "So Reich citizenship was offered not only to full Germans living in the reclaimed lands, but also to those who could prove a partial connection. I'm afraid, at times, the definition of what it meant to be *Volksdeutsch* became rather loose." At this point Büttner stopped and twisted around so that he could look at Traugutt. "Ask Traugutt – his wife is one of those."

Richard casually brushed his hand through his hair, pushing a few sweaty strands off his forehead, but did not otherwise respond.

"But that doesn't answer the question," Frauenfeld insisted, clearly annoyed by Büttner's unprovoked attack on Traugutt's sweet and gentle wife. "I thought your region had been purged of all foreign elements."

"Initially, yes, but some have been readmitted as guest workers." Büttner smiled evilly and Stefi thought sadly of the grandparents she had never met, living in a dilapidated tenement as *Gastarbeiter* in their home city.

"Are they the problem?"

Büttner shook his head. "No, it's not that easy – if it were, we'd just throw them back out. The problem is the *Volksdeutsch*. It seems that generations ago, a number of them accepted Reich citizenship without truly feeling that they were part of the *Volk*. Some of them even had bloodlines and histories as impeccable as yours or mine – yet they adopted Polish citizenship when that monstrosity was created, and didn't give up their loyalty even when it was destroyed again twenty years later! Thus we have traitors among us who are indistinguishable from truly loyal Germans. We never know when one of these vipers have crept into one of our organizations."

"Aren't they a bit old now to be causing trouble?"

"They've passed their treachery on to their children! Someone as unimportant as a construction worker, *mein Führer*–" Büttner made a point of directing his comments to Rudi again, "could be one of these people and who knows what danger he could build into a newly renovated residence!"

"Um?" Rudi shook his head slightly in confusion. He had clearly been daydreaming.

133

"What I want to know," Schindler asked into the lull, "is why would anyone who has been blessed with German blood voluntarily choose to betray their heritage?"

Büttner nodded his agreement and turned his attention from the Führer to Richard. "Maybe you can tell us, Richard. Your wife is *Volksdeutsch*, but as far as I know, her family isn't. What are they thinking? Hmm?"

All eyes turned to Traugutt – even Rudi showed keen interest in his answer. Stefi wasn't surprised that her father was suddenly under attack – his power and influence had grown considerably over the past year and Büttner, in particular, was feeling threatened by this strong new rival and would feel it was time to bring him down. What did surprise her was how absolutely unruffled her father seemed by it all.

Richard smiled at his colleagues, then pointedly turned his attention directly to the Führer. *"Mein Führer*, I have always been aware of the difficulties suffered by my unfortunate colleague in his province and from early on, have taken action to prevent the disease from spreading eastwards into the Göringstadt region. You will note, we do not have the same problems there – and if you wish to establish a new residence in a rebuilt royal palace near the ruins of Warschau, we would be most honored by your presence and could assure your safety."

Rudi looked intrigued. "Why's that, Richard? And what's this have to do with your wife's family?"

Richard cast a glance at Büttner, then turned his attention back to the Führer. "My wife's family are truly loyal to you and have given up that most precious right to be full citizens of the Reich, just so that they can use their historical connection to our advantage. They work as my agents infiltrating into the resistance and in particular, a number of them hold a rank within the Home Army."

There were gasps of surprise from around the room. Stefi was shocked by her father's bold move. Not only would Warszawa be furious with him for requiring yet more control over their resistance activities, but by making his power so explicit, he had also created dangerous new enemies in the room.

"Your wife's family is in Posen!" Büttner nearly shouted. "Are you poking around my territory?"

Richard tilted his head bemusedly. "Werner, you know so much about me, and I don't even know your wife's maiden name. I do feel ashamed of my social ineptness."

The others laughed. Rudi grinned at Richard. "Very clever, Richard. It's good that you have these agents. You should have told me about them earlier."

"My apologies, *mein Führer*. It's only recently that they have achieved positions of significance in the organization. I was waiting until I could offer something truly useful to you." Again Richard turned to Büttner to give him a polite nod, "And with Werner's permission, I would like to offer their services in vetting the workers on the Posener palace. Then he can see that the work is carried out quickly, efficiently, and loyally."

"It will still take years," Büttner muttered, only barely managing to contain his fury.

"Of course, Werner." The Führer stretched and yawned, having lost interest in the subject. He motioned toward one of the servants to throw some more water on the coals and they all fell silent as the hissing cloud of steam spread through the room. Stefi used the opportunity to dab herself with a towel. The Führer turned his attention to Schindler and asked him about how things were in London. As they talked about the deteriorating situation there, Stefi's mind wandered onto the implications of her father's brazen actions. There would be a lot of communication necessary with Warszawa to get all the after-the-fact permission for this move. It was so typical of her father! And what of the enmity he had created between himself and Büttner? She supposed it was inevitable in any case. Being the youngest, Büttner was the first to be shoved aside and already his daughter's engagement to Schindler's son, Wolf-Dietrich, was coming into question. Now, Büttner could not fail to know that the winds were shifting against him.

"I don't think we're going to find him in London," Günter was saying, when Stefi reminded herself to listen.

"Yes, we will. That's his base – he can't stay away long," Rudi countered. "Keep up the searches – he'll be there."

"They're disruptive! I'm supposed to be managing that territory and in my opinion–"

"I said, keep searching. Keep up the pressure!"

So, they were talking about Uncle Peter again. Stefi felt proud of herself. Schindler had thought he was being clever by driving the Führer into ever more hysterical reactions to Peter's crimes, so rather than fight the trend, Stefi had turned it against Schindler by convincing the Führer to focus his searches on the greater London area. It wasn't difficult to convince a Nazi that nationality was the most important thing to any human and therefore it had been fairly trivial to get Rudi to believe that an Englishman would be based in and inevitably return to England. Not only did the continuous harassment of Londoners embarrass Günter and make his job more difficult, but it protected Peter and took some of the pressure off their own people near Szaflary.

"Have you done any bulldozing?" Rudi was asking.

135

"Yes, we've taken out some apartment blocks where known members of the Underground lived."

"That was in response to the laboratory bombing?" Rudi asked pointedly.

"Well, yes, but it served the purpose."

"You're not being severe enough in this search!" the Führer snarled.

"We have a lot of things to keep under control," Schindler replied almost as angrily. "We have to relocate twenty-five thousand residents to put in that new military airfield you were so keen on; we had that nasty chemical spill into the Temms, and that leak from the nuclear plant north of London is still causing problems–"

"Has the population been informed?" the Führer asked in alarm.

"No, of course not. But there's been a rise in local cancer deaths, and illnesses keep cropping up. Deformed babies, shit like that. The Underground has published some sort of propaganda claiming they have proof of the leak. It was written by someone who knows what he's talking about – it's hard to refute. The people in that area are getting angry–"

"If it's beyond your capabilities to handle that region–"

Richard stood suddenly, interrupting the argument. It was a well-timed interruption, pre-empting a confrontation which he could not, at this time, utilize. He bowed slightly in the Führer's direction. "I have an appointment." Though it wasn't phrased as a request, he naturally waited for the Führer's answer.

"Oh, Richard, yes, of course. Don't let our small talk keep you!" Rudi cheerfully waved him out of the room.

Stefi watched her father as he left. Of the men in the room who counted, that is, ignoring the sundry bodyguards and attendants hanging around, he was the handsomest. Of course, excluding Büttner, he was the youngest as well. She cast a glance up at the Führer. He wasn't too bad looking for his age, still it required all her acting skill to have sex with him, his hair was perilously thin, his muscles sagging. She looked over at Günter. He was even older than the Führer and even less kempt in his appearance. Ugh! Thank God she didn't feel any need to soften him up! Or rather, harden him up! She giggled privately at her little joke, then turned her attention back to the boys' conversation.

"Ach, she'll be back from her holiday in about two weeks, I think," the Führer was saying about his wife, apparently in answer to Günter's question. He seemed annoyed, as if the question had carried the implication that he was indulging in some sort of impropriety as his hand absently stroked Stefi's body. "And how is *your* wife doing, Günter? Getting around, I hear."

"She's in Berlin," Schindler answered deadpan. "Doing God knows what. Probably shopping. Spending my money."

The Führer chuckled. "She's a pretty woman, Günter, you ought to pay more attention to her. If you don't, she'll get bored with you. Pretty women are like that, aren't they, *Schatz*?" He brought his hand up under Stefi's chin and turned her head upward to address the last part to her.

Stefi smiled enigmatically. "I wouldn't know, I'm just a girl," she answered, slyly reminding the Führer of Greta Schindler's age.

He laughed and placed his hand in front of her mouth. She kissed it and then let her tongue slide along his fingers. "And speaking of bored, enough of this heat! I think I have something better in mind to do with my time. What about you, *Schatz?*" The Führer rose to his feet and looked down at Stefi for her answer.

Stefi stood as well. "Your wish is my command, oh gracious one."

After a servant had helped them into their robes, they walked out together, followed by the various hangers-on that the Führer's august person required, and withdrew to the relative privacy of his bedroom.

Stefi rolled onto the bed, letting her robe fall open in the process, but the Führer ignored her and walked over to his wall of videos. She sighed silently to herself. She had rejected the idea of watching his torture videos four out of the last four times he had suggested it. It was time to bite the bullet and sit through one of the horrible things. With luck, she could distract him before it had finished. She stood and walked over to join him as he perused the titles.

Her eyes skimmed over the single word titles, pausing only briefly at the one labeled "Halifax". Anything but that, she prayed. She did not want to listen to those brutes murdering her dear little Joanna nor did she want to witness Peter's torment. Seeing it etched into his face, months after the crime, was more than her heart could bear. "What's this one?" Her fingers delicately caressed the spine of one of the videos.

"Ach, that." The Führer furrowed his brow in thought. "Some Spaniards who were discontented with their government's lack of independence. Protested by marching through the center of Madrid carrying anti-Reich slogans. We got them extradited to us."

Stefi wondered at the naïveté of people who would blatantly protest against their government's policies. "What happened to them?"

"Oh, it's boring." Clearly distracted, the Führer continued looking at the titles, "I was looking for something recent, from London...Maybe I left it on the shelf in the main library." He clucked his tongue in irritation. "Damn it, I can't remember the stupid name!"

"There's been a lot of trouble there recently, hasn't there?" Stefi asked innocently, as she helpfully searched through the titles looking for one that might be English.

"Yeah," the Führer moaned. "That spill, and the leak, and that traitor hiding out there…"

"And a laboratory was blown up?"

"Not really blown up. Just a bit of it was set on fire. Arson, I guess."

"Terrorism?" Stefi asked, worriedly, "Or was there a particular target they were aiming for?"

"I guess a section of the lab works on weapons." The Führer continued to scan the titles. "But the idiots got the wrong part. Amateurs!"

Now, Stefi wondered, was he engaging in disinformation or did he really have no clue? She decided to press a bit further. She moved close to him, reached over and untied his robe and pulled it open. Then opening her robe she slid between him and the wall of tapes and pressed her body against his. "I'm chilly," she explained as their bare flesh touched, "Can I hug you?"

"Oh, my little girl," the Führer sighed, stroking her hair, as she buried her face in his chest. "You are so dear to me!"

Stefi pulled her head back so that she could gaze lovingly into his eyes. "And I love you so much!" She embraced him even more warmly and pressed her cheek against his chest. When enough seconds had passed, she added, very softly, "And I worry about you."

"Me? Why?"

Still keeping her head against him, she answered, shyly, "I'm so afraid something will happen to you!"

The Führer laughed lightly. "Oh, little one, don't fear for me! I'm well protected!"

"I'm afraid Günter's plotting something."

"Günter's always plotting."

"I don't trust him."

The Führer laughed. "Neither do I, but he's useful to have around." He paused as if reconsidering that statement and amended, "Or rather, he's hard to do without. Even harder to get rid of!"

"He means to harm you! I think that's why he had that laboratory burned."

"How would that harm me? There was nothing there!"

"Really?" Stefi's voice nearly choked with tears of worry.

"Really. I mean, unless…Do you think he had the laboratory burned?"

Stefi sniffed back her tears. "I don't know. He just acted so strangely when you mentioned it, I had a flash of intuition, a vision almost, of him destroying it – as if it were important to you."

"No, no, no, no." The Führer patted her back comfortingly. "There wasn't anything there important to me. Maybe to Günter though. Maybe, you're right. Maybe he was intending to harm me and had to cover his tracks. Hmm."

Stefi sighed her relief. "Well, if so, at least you're safe!"

"Yes, don't worry child," he responded, clearly touched by her display of concern. "No one's going to touch me."

27

"**I**'m still not comfortable with the idea of our staying here," Peter confided to the old woman, as he set the last of their luggage down in the room. He watched as the old woman spread yet another comforter onto the bed, carefully arranging it so that the pattern was properly aligned. "It's so dangerous for you and your husband."

She looked up at him and smiled, even as she continued to smooth the blanket. "As you have discovered, short-term housing in Berlin is difficult to get. This is a practical solution to your housing problem." She patted the bed, satisfied with her efforts. "And we so welcome a visit from our goddaughter and her family, that we will happily tolerate any risk to see her!"

Chrzestna, godmother, was what Zosia always called her, and for the longest time, Peter had thought that impossible word was the woman's name, so he was rather relieved to learn he could call her Alisia. That name reminded him of Allie, his dear Allison, and though the physical similarities between the old woman and his long-dead love were minimal, the old woman somehow resembled Allison. He imagined if Allison had grown old, she might have risked her life supporting the work of others, protecting them, providing a safe-haven in the same no-nonsense, caring and comforting manner of this woman.

He paced over to the window and looked down at the street far below. An attic flat in the pension. He had to admit that he was actually quite relieved that they had decided upon using this place. He felt safe here, he had strong memories of being safe in the care of these fine people. These two brave old people who carried out a risky yet thankless job. They had been here when he had narrowly escaped Karl on the train, they had tended his injuries and given up their bed to him as he and Zosia had remained in hiding through that day. He had been lying in their bed when Zosia had declared her love for him, when she had agreed to marry him.

Without meaning to, he frowned at that memory. *All a lie.*

Alisia saw his frown, walked over to where he stood, and stroked his cheek with the back of her hand. "Don't worry, your family will be safe here. This little flat is often rented out for months at a time – it won't raise any suspicions, and being up here, out of the way, not many people will see you. Plus you'll have us to help look after the children – that way you can both pursue your business."

He smiled wanly at her reassurances, embarrassed that his worries had been different from her assumptions, but before he could say anything, a moving swathe of color on the street below caught his eye. Peter tilted his head to get a better look. A small knot of people were approaching along the street. The group had a woman in the fore and very oddly, she was not white. She wore a long, multi-colored robe, belted at the waist – it looked almost like traditional garb except that there was a slit up the side of the robe which caused it to catch and sway with each step, revealing a very long, painfully slender leg. The commanding stride of the woman, the confidence with which she marched through the streets of Berlin, her very presence in a racially-cleansed city, told Peter that she was, by some measure, important. He narrowed his eyes to get a better look. The woman and the people with her went into a building almost directly opposite.

"What building is that?" He pointed to the one into which the woman had disappeared.

Alisia leaned forward to get a better look. "The building has various offices. The separate entrance, the one with the awning–"

"Yes, that one."

"That holds a number of embassies."

"A number?"

"Yes, that door leads to a group of embassy suites from several places." She paused to remember. "Siam, Liberia, Ceylon, Kivu, and Paraguay."

"Kivu?"

"It's in central Africa. One of those tiny, poor places always at war or being absorbed or spat out by someone else."

"I know," he said, as if in a dream. "I met someone…" He scanned the street again. "Is this area full of embassies?"

She shrugged. "We're in the center of a capital, so of course. But we're a humble neighborhood, so only poor countries have their offices here. Why do you ask?"

He shook his head. "I just saw some people go into the building and there – you can see the security in the street." He pointed out some obviously undercover police. "I wanted to be sure they were there for a reason."

Alisia glanced down at the undercover police. "Yes, they keep an eye on that building. Foreigners, you know. Don't worry – they don't even look over here."

He nodded but was unconsoled. It had been Arieka, he was sure of it. She must have linked up with one of those diplomats that she partied with in Manhattan, or maybe she had been appointed to an office herself. Her fame and wealth in America would make her a ready candidate for a government position. But why Berlin? Had she deliberately chosen it? He felt his heart quicken at the thought of meeting her again. There had to be a way. His mind worked through a dozen possibilities, but none would work. As a foreigner, she would always be watched and anyone who met up with her, accidentally, deliberately, however – that person would be carefully observed, probably questioned, possibly arrested. He couldn't risk talking to her. It was just too dangerous.

He continued to stare out the window. Far too dangerous.

"What's the matter, son?"

He drew his eyes away from the window and to Alisia's kind face. "Do you think you might do me a favor? You know, without telling Zosia?"

"As God is my witness!" Josef breathed.

Martin was patting his chest as if trying to calm his heart.

"My God, man, were you trying to scare us to death?" Roman's expression was only just changing to astonishment as his fear abated.

Peter laughed. "Sorry about sneaking up on you like that. I knew you'd scatter, if you saw someone in street clothes approaching."

"Is it really you?" Josef tipped his head up to look at his friend. "Peter?"

"In the flesh!"

"But how…?"

"Where…?"

"What happened?"

"Why are you here?"

Peter patted the air with his hands as if physically restraining the questions. "All in good time, lads. All in good time." He glanced around, double-checking that he had not brought anyone with him, then settled himself on the ground, his friends ringed around him. "I have a lot to tell you, and there's a lot I want to know."

It was a good conversation, a wonderful feeling. His friends' obvious joy at his successful escape touched him. He did not tell them any of the details in between, and so they only saw that he had left and was now well-fed, well-dressed and moving about freely, and therefore assumed that there was nothing but joy in his recent past.

He learned that Josef's wife had a young child now, though Josef had, unfortunately, not been transferred to that household. He learned that Roman had been moved yet again, but this time he was directing the youngsters who worked under him. "A real boss!" Roman thumped his chest jokingly. "I cuff the young bastards anytime they get out of line!"

"What about Elda – has anyone seen her?"

There was a momentary silence, then Roman said quietly, "No one knows what it was. She just got weaker and weaker and was always in pain. When she started coughing blood, her mistress handed her a knife."

Peter shuddered.

"At least they let her decide," Vasil soothed.

"Yeah, as if she had a choice!" Roman agreed sarcastically. "Why didn't they take her to a hospital?"

Peter rubbed his forehead as he thought about her. He remembered how she had struggled against all odds to learn how to read.

"Do you know, there's a reward for you?" Vasil asked, in an attempt to break the silence.

Peter nodded. "I guessed as much. A large one, I imagine."

Vasil nodded enthusiastically. He seemed proud to know someone with a large reward on his head.

Peter noticed Martin chewing his thumbnail, contemplating him. "You won't gain anything by turning me in, Martin. So don't even think of it."

"I wasn't!"

"No, I'm sure you weren't. But I just wanted to warn you all, that money isn't for the likes of you. And even mentioning my name might get you extensively questioned – and you know what that means for our sort."

"Yeah, they have to prove we're telling the truth," Roman agreed, directing his comments at Martin. "So no rewards – just you in a room alone with the boys."

"I wasn't thinking of saying anything!"

"Good!" Peter gave Martin a broad smile. He turned to Vasil, "And how have things been with you?"

Vasil chuckled. "You're asking me? Shit, you know, nothing changes. I'm a good boy, I get fed, I don't get beat. End of story. But tell me, how the hell did you pull it off? What in the world are you doing here now?"

"All will become clear, but first, has anyone seen Konstantin recently?" Peter turned to Roman, since he was always the most likely to make contact with anyone else.

Roman shook his head, looking somewhat worried. "Not recently. Not since the police came around asking about you."

"About me? When? After my escape?"

"No, not then. Just a little while ago. Beginning of April, I'd say. Wouldn't you, boys?"

"End of March," Vasil corrected. "I remember because I had used up my rations and nicked a bit of food, so I thought they were coming after me for that."

"Yeah," Martin chimed in, "It was really weird – I mean, they didn't ask anything about you when you escaped, but then years later they come back and question all of us. Luckily, nothing forceful."

"And we had nothing to say in any case," Vasil agreed.

"Konstantin may have been picked up then," Roman guessed. "Maybe he was arrested."

Peter grit his teeth. "I hope not." Damn! If his adventure had caused Konstantin to be arrested, that was…"Roman, have you tried to see him?"

Roman shook his head.

"Can you do me a favor? Can you find out if he is still around? If so, let him know I'd like to talk to him. Tell him, I know he'll be released soon and that seeing me would be dangerous and so I'd understand if he'd prefer not to. But if he wants to, then see if he can set a place and a date."

"I assume you'll be in touch?"

"Yeah, if not me, then someone will carry a message for me."

"Messages? What's up?"

Peter glanced around again. "Do you guys have some time?" When they agreed that they did, he told them what had happened to him since his departure. He gave no information about where he had found refuge, but was quite explicit about his tour of America. "The upshot is, I've gathered enough money and connections that I may be able to arrange passages out of this country for people like us. What do you think?"

Martin was shaking his head. "It wouldn't be proper."

Peter waved his hand in exasperation. "How the hell do you justify skiving off to come here? Huh?"

Martin raised his eyebrows in surprise. "I have permission! My mistress just warns me not to get picked up. Don't you guys?" He looked to the other three. They cast dubious glances at each other but did not answer his question.

"Fine, you stay," Peter scoffed. "What about the rest of you? What about the people you know? What do you think? Could we get the word out? Would people take the risk?"

"Risk?" Vasil looked nervously around, as if expecting that the word itself would draw the police.

"Of course," Roman answered for Peter. "Did you think he's going to snap his fingers and you'd be in America?"

Vasil was shaking his head. "I'm too old to try out a new life. And the thought of getting caught. Jesus! Do you realize what they'd do to us?"

Peter nodded. "Yes, I know. That's why I wanted your opinions before I even tried to organize anything." He turned to Josef. "What about you?"

"Maybe before," Josef said, thoughtfully, "But now, with the child. I don't think I want to risk that sort of thing."

"Roman?" Peter asked despairingly. Well-established, comfortable, even bossing other people around now. What chance was there that his friend would throw away everything, would risk arrest in order to flee to a land where he did not speak the language, had no prospects, did not know a single person?

"Count me in." Roman smiled. "I want to see what it's like to be free. But I'll tell you what. Why don't I stay on, working at the bakery for a while first? I can pass on the message easier than anyone around – and I'll send word to the other bakeries and in a matter of weeks or maybe a few months, everyone in Berlin will know. For those who are interested, I can give out the first step in the directions."

"That would be incredibly dangerous!" Peter warned.

Roman shrugged. "Someone has to do it. And hey, Vasil and Josef and a few others will be sure to take vengeance on anyone who might snitch on me – if you take my meaning." He looked at Martin meaningfully.

"You guys! I'm not going to say a word! I swear!" Martin scanned their faces. "I wish you'd stop looking at me like that."

"Don't worry, Martin," Josef assured him. "Since you know what we'd do to you if Roman was suddenly arrested, we know you won't say a word!"

Peter grabbed Roman's arm. "I really don't think you should take that sort of risk. Go first, you can help us establish the route."

"No. I want to help." Roman looked thoughtful, then added, "You know, the delivery vehicles go outside Berlin. I could probably even spread the message outside the city. Just let people know they have to get to Berlin on their own…"

"Roman! You can't take this risk!"

"Hell, you took the risk of coming back here to help us, why should you be the only one who can feel noble? Someone's got to do it and I'm the best man for the job. After a while, after it's all working smoothly, I'll train a replacement and then I can go too!"

"I can help out, too," Josef volunteered. "And when the kid is older – if this thing is still in place, maybe then the whole family can go. How about that? Do you want my help?"

Impressed and grateful, Peter looked from one to the other. "Yeah, I need you all. I can't do this alone."

28

"**G**od Almighty, I hate this place," Günter Schindler grumbled to his son as he scanned the bleak streets of London. "Does the sun never shine in this godforsaken land?"

Wolf-Dietrich looked up at the heavy gray clouds and squinted as some drizzle covered his face. "My guess is not." A heavily-laden lorry lumbered along the road, sending up a spray of dirty rainwater and both he and his father stepped back from the curb only just in time. The stench of its fumes mingled with the noxious pollution of the stuttering cars and with the ever-present chill dampness into a foul-smelling fog which permeated everything. Behind them, the blank walls of Green Park prison loomed menacingly, reflecting the noise and smog from the street back at them.

They had been at the palace to check on affairs. Günter had irritably turned down the formal luncheon in his honor and had stomped off alone with his son and his small retinue in the direction of some restaurants. They had passed through the prison to avoid the rain, and though their route had taken them through well-appointed, carpeted hallways, hung with paintings and mirrors and nowhere near the stinking cells, Wolf-Dietrich was, nevertheless and despite the rain, glad to be back outside its oppressive walls.

"Can't stand the English either," Günter continued. "What in God's name made us ever think we could incorporate such a slovenly, violent people into our finely-tuned culture?"

"Don't know." Wolf-Dietrich knew it wasn't just the obstreperous English – it was a concatenation of things which was fuelling his father's bad mood. The Führer's shrill insistence that Schindler must somehow track down Halifax in London, the various environmental disasters that had been causing popular disgust, the relocation of twenty-five thousand residents on the northern outskirts to make way for an unnecessary and expensive airfield, instituting the new taxes that were, as a result, necessary. All of it was contributing to a growing sense of mayhem, to a feeling that his father was losing control. And if he couldn't even keep the Greater London Administrative District under control, what in the world made anyone think he was ready to rule the Reich?

As Günter instructed one of his men to stop the traffic so that they could finally cross the road, Wolf-Dietrich felt a sudden revelation. Stefi Traugutt! Of course! Everything his father did to weaken the Führer's position and strengthen his own, she turned around to Schindler's

145

disadvantage. She had admitted it herself: her father needed time. Her clever plan to liaise with Wolf-Dietrich to strengthen both her and his fathers' positions had metamorphosed as she had become the mistress of the Führer. She was working for her father alone now, and every bit of damage she could do to his main competitor was an advantage for her father – even if it meant propping the Führer up a bit! And even if it meant betraying her lover. Despite the chill, damp wind, Wolf-Dietrich felt his cheeks grow hot as they marched across the street.

They ducked down a small street away from the stink of traffic, into another sort of stench: that of uncollected rubbish and raw sewage. The English were a filthy people, he thought irritably. Filthy and treacherous. They stepped out of the alley into a cobble-stoned area of quaint buildings and cozy restaurants: one of the few *gemütlich* areas of London around, hidden away there behind the monstrous apartment blocks that the common people called home. Ugh, how could they live in such ugliness? Didn't they have any pride in their Fatherland?

They entered a tiny, crowded restaurant and Wolf-Dietrich listened in amusement as his father demanded a table and gave the maitre d' exactly one minute to clear one for him. As Günter theatrically raised his wrist to time the reaction, the maitre d' did not even blink in response. "But *Herr Gauleiter*, please follow me," he said as he suavely gathered together a special set of menus. "*Mein Herr* surely knows that the best table is always on reserve for his use!"

They were led up the stairs and into a well-set private room attended by three young women, very-fetchingly dressed as wenches. Clearly, someone had informed the restaurateurs that Schindler was in town, or more likely, someone from Green Park prison, just across the way, made a habit of visiting the area. Well, if it kept them all on their toes, ready to serve their superiors properly, so much the better. As the maitre d' opened each menu for his guests, he explained that there were no printed prices since everything was, naturally, courtesy of the house in gratitude for the honor of their visit. Of course, Wolf-Dietrich knew it was nothing more than a blatant bribe, but nevertheless, it was so marvelously worded, so suavely carried off, that even he felt proud of his father's and, by extension, his own power.

The gracious service did nothing to improve his father's mood though. He eyed the young women, but did not even suggest that one of them sit on his lap. Instead he waved his hand petulantly at the nearest one and said, "Get their orders," as he pointed to the two bodyguards who had accompanied them up the stairs. "Something you can eat standing up," he ordered the bodyguards, "since we don't want you to be derelict in your duties." Then he turned his attention to the second waitress, "And a *Maß* beer. Good German beer – none of your English crap. And one for the boy here. Understood?"

She nodded and left.

At that point Günter turned his attention to his son. Wolf-Dietrich cringed, wondering what in the world he would be denounced for at this point in his father's bad mood, but his father surprised him by sighing heavily and saying, "How are things with you and your fiancée?"

Wolf-Dietrich bit his lip. Was now the time to make his bid for freedom? Gathering his courage, he answered, "I want to break it off."

His father raised an eyebrow. If one didn't know him, the expression would look curious, but to Wolf-Dietrich it was ominous. "It serves no useful purpose anymore," he explained hurriedly. "Her father has been losing ground recently, there's no real point in our families being linked. And I don't like her." He looked at his father's reaction but there didn't seem to be any, so he added, rather timidly, "She doesn't like me either."

There was a leaden silence as his father surveyed him sourly. "So, you too," he said at last.

Wolf-Dietrich glanced guiltily down at his menu but he couldn't read any of the words. If only he could offer up a match with Traugutt's daughter as an alternative! But no, the whore had to go crawling into the Führer's bed! Damn her! Damn her, damn her, damn her to hell! Wolf-Dietrich looked back up at his father and lowering his voice almost to a whisper said, "I think we can solve at least one of your problems here."

"Which one?" Günter was clearly annoyed that *problems* was in the plural.

"The Halifax one."

"How? How the hell are we supposed to find him in London when he isn't here?"

Despite his father's loud tone, Wolf-Dietrich continued to speak quietly. "My idea is to make it so the Führer no longer wants to find him. Or at least doesn't need to. Let's destroy the man without arresting him. That will get the Führer off your back and maybe even allay some of the suspicions he's been voicing to you about that laboratory of yours."

"Why would it do that?"

"It'll prove your loyalty to him by destroying his number one enemy."

"And how are we going to destroy this man without finding him?" Günter asked, his patience at an end. "He's probably not even in the Reich. Probably back in that cesspit over there." He gestured broadly out the restaurant to indicate *over there* was across the ocean, in America.

Wolf-Dietrich smiled. "The Führer doesn't hate the man – hell, they've never even met. He hates what the man has done to him. Ruined his reputation, besmirched the Reich, gained support for rebel and terrorist organizations–"

"You don't need to tell me about that."

"But think about how he did all that," Wolf-Dietrich whispered eagerly. "By going public with all sorts of information about how he was mistreated, about how he was innocent of any wrong-doing yet was mishandled by the Reich and the Führer's regime."

"Yeah, so what?"

"He banked everything on his innocence! Don't you understand? All the sympathy he got was what fueled all those reactions. But no one is sympathetic to a murderer and a kidnapper. For heaven's sake, if we advertise what he's done recently, we'll destroy his reputation and everything he achieved during his month tour of America. Hell, we don't need to arrest him. In fact, it'd be better if he's on the loose and a danger to society. That'll show the Americans what sort of degenerate they've supported. That'll show them that we had a reason for keeping him, and all his sort, under control!"

Günter shifted in his seat as he considered Wolf-Dietrich's words. The waitress returned with the beers and placed the huge glasses on the table. There was a large head of froth on each – clearly the beer had been poured too hastily in the rush to serve their petulant client, but neither father nor son commented. They gave their orders for the food and still Günter didn't respond to Wolf-Dietrich's idea. The fact that his father hadn't immediately dismissed the idea as crap was quite a hopeful sign to Wolf-Dietrich.

Günter tapped his finger thoughtfully against his lower lip, making a slight popping noise with each tap. "And I suppose, in gratitude for this idea, you want me to bless your breaking off the engagement?"

"The marriage is unnecessary," Wolf-Dietrich replied hopefully. "And there's the Vogel girl – Ulrike. She's a nice girl, I've talked to her. She can help us with this. Initiate the outcry maybe. She'll help us, I'm sure, if I have a chance to, you know, be nice to her."

Günter returned to tapping his lip.

"And the Vogels still have connections. Any support we generate for them, will flow to us. Besides, the mother, Elspeth, she's got her family connections. Karl Vogel never used them, but with him out of the way, maybe they'll throw their weight behind you."

Ever so slightly, maybe even approvingly, Günter nodded his head. "Tell me more."

29

"Oh, my God! I..." Arieka looked around at her companions and fell silent. She looked back up at the man who stood at their table. In the flickering, romantic candlelight of the restaurant she could barely make out his face. Dark hair, dark eyes. Only the voice, only the voice. She raised her eyebrows, waiting for him to take the lead.

He smiled at her. "Would you be willing to step into the lobby for a minute?" he asked in highly accented English.

"But of course." She excused herself from her friends and together the two of them walked out of the hotel restaurant and into the dimly lit lobby. Once they had seated themselves in the comfortable lounge chairs and ordered two drinks from the bar, Arieka turned to Peter. "I hardly recognized you! You don't look anything like yourself."

"That was my intent. Still, I can't talk for too long."

"How are you going to escape being interviewed by those goons?" Arieka tilted her head in the direction of the undercover security policeman who had indiscreetly left the restaurant to follow them into the lobby.

"You'll see. But tell me, what are you doing here?"

She explained her new position, and added, "I didn't figure there was any chance of seeing you, but I thought I might learn about where you come from."

Peter smiled, flattered. "So what do you think of my homeland?"

"Everyone is so ill-tempered! Snapping, snarling, growling, tears...It's like a wild dog pack."

Aware of his audience, Peter choked back a laugh. "Yeah, that sounds pretty accurate."

"I thought you people were reputed to be cold and unemotional."

Peter found it amusing that Arieka made no distinction between the various European national groups. *You people*, all of them. "Maybe before all this Nazi stuff we were, I don't know. All I know is, all my life everyone has been very edgy. And here in Berlin, it's worse, since on top of the stress, there's all the petty power battles going on." Peter sighed heavily, "It's the culture now – if you have the power to do so, you berate someone. Politeness is viewed as weakness, silence is subservience. Everyone defends their place in the hierarchy. Unless, of course, you're at the bottom – then you just stay very, very quiet."

Arieka nodded. "Or leave. I talked to Alex, he told me what you wanted to do with the money. I think it's a good idea."

"I want to thank you for all you've done." He wished he could kiss her, or at least hug her. He couldn't though, and so he maintained an official-looking distance. "I'm afraid I haven't found much time to learn how to play your guitar yet."

"Yes, I've heard you have two kids keeping you busy now."

"You've heard?"

"Alex told me. Don't worry, it's not common knowledge."

That wasn't what he was worried about. He studied her face but saw no sign of condemnation there. Why, he wondered, would it matter? Why did his heart pound when he was near her?

They chatted for some time, about what each had been doing, and all the while he wondered why he was so attracted to her. He hardly knew her, nor was her thin frame the sort which excited his urges. Was it the smooth, dark skin? The kind, open acceptance of him for who he was? Or her very inaccessibility? Whatever it was, it was driving him mad with desire. He shifted uncomfortably in his seat and glanced around. "I'd better get going."

"What can I do to help?"

"Just remember the story I gave you. And...wish me luck."

He stood and gave her a slight bow, clicking his heels as he did so. "Gnädige Frau." He spoke rather more loudly than they had been speaking. "Thank you for your help." He turned and strode toward the lobby doors.

Before he had reached them, the undercover agent approached him, asking to see his papers.

With a snide smile of pleasure, Peter pulled out a set of papers and handed them to the man. "You'll see, that I am from the Führer's office. I was interviewing this lady because she is acquainted with an enemy of the Führer and may be of help to us."

Almost without reading them, the agent quickly handed the papers back. "My apologies."

"Now let me see your papers!" Peter demanded. He grabbed them from the agent and opened them. "I want to be sure to note your name."

"*Mein Herr?*"

"You incompetent fool! Look!" Peter gestured angrily behind himself toward Arieka. "Our foreign guest can clearly see your actions. Do you wish our visitors to realize that everyone who talks to them is interviewed? Do you?" He glared at the man. "Not only have you interfered with the Führer's business, but you have carried out your duties incompetently!" He smacked the man across the face with his own papers. It couldn't have hurt, not in the least, but for Peter it was cathartic. He tossed the papers back into the man's hands, threw a glance back at Arieka, winked at her, and then stormed angrily out of the hotel and into the street.

He walked along, flushed with success. He took a very circuitous route back home to be sure he was not followed, stopping for a coffee in a café, visiting a park, then finally meandering back to the pension. God, he felt great! And so incredibly alive! And horny! What was it about that woman?

He stopped in at Alisia's to pick up the children since Zosia wasn't back yet. He had a cup of tea there and then returned to their room so that Irena could nap. While the baby slept, Peter played a game of keep-away with Madzia, using the balloon which he had bought her in the park. Time after time, she leapt up after the balloon or chased it down and brought it back when it had escaped. Over and over he sent it back up into the air with a light tap, and stared into the distance, thinking of Arieka.

"What's this about?"

Peter spun around in surprise at the sound of Zosia's voice. In her hand was the leather wallet with the papers he had just used. Oh God, he had forgotten to give them back to Alisia! He had left them in the pocket of his jacket which he had idiotically left hanging on the rack in the hallway of Alisia's private apartment.

He stared at them for a moment before asking, "Why are you going through my pockets?"

"You went to see that Arieka woman, didn't you?"

So she knew Arieka was in Berlin! "*Why* are you going through my pockets?" He tapped the balloon into the air and Madzia skittered after it, oblivious to what they were saying.

"Just as well I did! Some field agent you are, leaving incriminating documents in your jacket. All so that you can pull off some childish stunt. For Christ's sake, Peter, how could you take such a risk?"

"I risked no one's life but my own," he replied evenly as he again hit the balloon. Madzia managed to bat the balloon immediately back to him and without meaning to he slammed it across the room. Madzia giggled uncontrollably and ran after it.

"You risked the life of Madzia's and Irena's father," Zosia hissed furiously. "Have you no sense of responsibility?"

Peter replied calmly, "You're going to have to use something else. I'm not buying into that blackmail anymore." Madzia tossed him the balloon. Whap, he hit it across the room again.

Zosia walked up to him, shaking the leather wallet in anger. "You had no right to use these papers! You did not ask permission!" Without warning she smacked him in the face with the wallet.

Absolutely shocked by her outburst, Peter stared at her. Only when he saw her take a step backward in fear did he realize that he had in that brief moment felt something much more potent than surprise.

151

But the feeling was gone. All feeling was gone.

Madzia pressed the balloon against his legs and gently he took it from her and sent it back into the air. Completely without emotion, he said to Zosia, "I didn't ask permission because I knew I wouldn't get it."

The balloon floated down onto the bed. Madzia screeched her delight and went scrambling after it. Peter stooped down and picked up the papers Zosia had dropped, placing them safely on a table.

Zosia went to Irena as she lay asleep on the bed and brushed the balloon away from her, onto the floor. She sat forlornly on the edge of the mattress, her body protectively placed between Irena and Madzia. "I don't understand," she sighed. "I just don't understand anymore."

He could see tears running down her cheeks. Zosia did not cry easily and he knew it embarrassed her to show such emotion. He felt saddened by her despair, saddened and touched, but in an intellectual sort of way. He no longer had a visceral response to her – not to her anger, nor her condemnations, nor her love.

He was truly free.

Along with Zosia's tears, that also saddened him. Though he had longed for his freedom, fought for it, now that he had it, he missed the bonds which had held him for so long. He missed the excess of emotion, the highs and the lows that his love, his absolute adoration of her, had inspired. He felt cold and distant.

Cold, distant, free.

Madzia had clambered off the bed, following the balloon, but she did not retrieve it. She had lost interest and was pursuing a more intriguing line of research: following the trail of some ants as they disappeared into the wall.

Irena was asleep, Madzia was absorbed in her studies. He had not touched Zosia for ages, months, a lifetime. It was, he supposed, remotely possible that she was not sleeping with Tadek, that her relationship with him was entirely platonic. Funny, he no longer really cared about that either. Still, if she wasn't sleeping with Tadek, then she had remained untouched by anyone for so long. Too long. It wasn't fair to treat her in such a shabby manner, no matter how badly she had treated him. The desire which Arieka had inspired in him was still there – he should use it to comfort Zosia, to show her that she was beautiful, that he did still care.

He sat down on the bed next to her and gently touched her cheek where the tears had wet it. "I'm sorry, I'm sorry I've been so distant."

She had exquisite cheekbones – like Arieka's he allowed himself to think – and the arch of her eyebrows, that was similar too. His fingers traced a pattern along her face, he let them stray down along her neck. "You deserve better than that," he whispered as he leaned in to kiss her. He kissed the tears on her cheeks, kissed her eyelids, kissed her lips. He thought of all their wonderful times together, of walks in the woods and falling asleep under the stars. Of passionate embraces and tender words. He whispered to her that she was beautiful, that her skin was soft, that he missed her, wanted her, needed her. He let his hand stroke downward, finding the buttons of her blouse, undoing them slowly. He felt the wonderful curves of her body; excitement traveled along his fingers and up his arm as he caressed the deep arch of her waist. He brought his lips close to her ear and suggested that they shuffle the children downstairs.

She turned her face away from him, reached for his hand and roughly pulled it away. "So, this is how you managed it with Elspeth."

He pulled back from her. At one time she had had the power to devastate him with such words. He would beg for forgiveness for whatever wrong he had done her – real or imagined. He would cajole and flatter and plead with his goddess. Even argue with her to gain her love, or at least her acceptance. He would feel lost, alone, and desperate in the face of her rejection.

But those passions were gone, and there was nothing but emptiness in their place. "Zosia…" he began, unsure of what he wanted to say.

"I'm not interested in *that* sort of approach. I'm not interested in your services!"

"What *do* you want from me?"

"Damn it, Peter! I *hit* you. The least you could do is be angry with me! *Feel* something!"

He looked at her, at the lines which had set around her eyes, at the memory of devastating loss reflected in them. *Feel something!* But what? All emotions were dangerous. Love left him vulnerable, hatred was self-denigrating, and even simply caring brought death. What could he dare to feel? He took her hand in his and leant forward to kiss it. "I know I'm not the person you want me to be."

Zosia furrowed her brow in confusion at this strange response.

He brushed his hand gently across her cheek and added, somewhat sadly, "I never was." He kissed her again, this time on the forehead, then he stood and walked over to Madzia to see what she was doing. He sat down next to her on the floor and, stroking the child's hair, asked, "What have you found here, sweetheart?"

Zosia stared at him, but he didn't turn back to look at her, so she rolled onto the bed and cuddled up with Irena and took a nap.

30

"*A*lex, what is the meaning of this?" Anna shouted out from the living room of their flat.

Alex groaned to himself. God almighty, when was Anna ever going to learn the damn language so that he didn't have to spend all his time translating for her? He backed away from the closet shelf he was attempting to put up and spit the nails out of his mouth into his hand. "I'm busy!" he shouted back. It was Anna's stupid idea to put in another shelf and even worse, she had single-handedly decided that it was his job to do it! Shit, his thumb hurt from the number of times he had pounded it, the plaster was a mess from all the hammer marks, and now she wanted him to drop everything and come read some idiotic advice column to her about how husbands should do more around the house!

"I really think you should look at this," Anna advised in an aggravatingly calm tone. "But if you don't want to…"

The threat of his future ignorance was enough to get Alex moving. He flung the loose nails onto the bureau, ignoring how three of them rolled off onto the floor, and set down the hammer on the edge of the bedside table before stomping impatiently into the living room. "What's so all-fired important? Eh?"

"Look," Anna suggested, pressing the newspaper into his hand and pointing at a paragraph.

Alex read the news item. The Nazi government was pressing the NAU for the extradition of Peter Halifax, a one-time celebrity and now a suspected murderer. Though there was no extradition treaty between the two governments, there were grounds to believe that this case was different in that the suspect was not only hiding in the NAU but had been explicitly supported by the NAU government in his criminal actions and therefore, though his actions had been personal, criminal and non-political, the NAU government's harboring of him was a political act which would have serious consequences for relations between the two governments.

Alex flung the newspaper down. "Shit!"

Anna looked up at him. "The NAU would never give him up – even if he were here."

"I wouldn't be so sure of that. Besides, that's not the point, is it?"

"What do you mean?"

"They're trying to destroy our credibility! We built our publicity on Peter's innocence and now they're publicizing that he's a murderer. Shit!

Who the hell thought of this propaganda move! Clever bastard – better than I expected from them. It was an idiotic idea anyway, having Peter do something so publicly."

"It took the pressure off our son," Anna reminded him. "They had to act fast."

"Yeah, I know. Ryszard was in real danger. I guess he still is."

Anna nodded worriedly. Alex could see there were tears in her eyes. She was thinking of Andrzej and Joanna. And she was worried. Her children, her grandchildren, all of them, at risk. "I wish it would end already," she whispered.

"There, there," Alex soothed, patting her head, rather too roughly. He saw Anna wince at his indelicacy and he pulled his hand away. "Don't worry, they'll be okay. Ryszard is used to this sort of thing."

"Even for one as strong as Ryszard, I think it can be too much. And poor Stefi, my God, she's…" Anna's voice faltered. What could she say about her granddaughter? She shook her head in disgust. It was too much, just too much. She should have called a halt to it years ago. Should have forced Zosia and Peter to stay in America after his visit. Now it was too late.

Alex walked over to the television and put it on. "Let's see how widely disseminated this piece is. Maybe it will just go away from lack of interest."

No such luck. One of the "Little Brother" organizations, that is, one of the political fronts which promulgated National Socialist propaganda within the NAU, had picked up on the story, presumably under orders, and was publicizing it. After several hours of checking one news channel after another, Alex determined that the story was not going to be allowed to die. He rubbed his forehead in dismay, wondering how they should deal with this new development. Ignore it? Deny it? Justify it? He went to bed that evening still wondering and awoke the next morning with no clear answer.

Still yawning, he wandered into the living room and put on the television. He had to watch the news for over an hour – it was still a minor item – nevertheless, it was reported.

Alex sighed. Shit. Whoever had organized it had done a reasonably good job. Informing the government and press simultaneously, keeping up the pressure through a Little Brother. All that was missing was a sympathetic victim.

Even as he had the thought, the newsreader introduced a video clip. Alex watched in fascination as a young woman with bleached blond hair was shown. At the bottom of the screen was her name: Ulrike Vogel. She was speaking German, her voice strained, tears streaming down her cheeks. Unusually, sub-titles were used rather than a voice-over, so that the emotion in her voice was not lost on the viewer.

"My dear father, my wonderful little sister..." she was saying. She held up a photograph of a young child – presumably Magdalena. "We took him in, offered him a chance at rehabilitation, but rather than accept our kindness, he abandoned his job, left us, maligned us! And then, that wasn't enough," she nearly howled, "then he returned, in the dead of night and murdered my father! As he slept!" Ulrike stopped speaking as she struggled to regain her self-control. She slurped noisily, wiped at the tears on her face.

Alex wearily accepted the cup of coffee that Anna offered him. He felt sick.

"Then he stole away my baby sister!" Ulrike continued, still sobbing. "For no reason, no reason at all! After all we had done for him, it wasn't enough to drag our name through the mud..."

"He didn't mention your name," Alex muttered, as he slurped his coffee. He only half-listened as Ulrike carried on her denunciation, as she appealed to the American people to reject this murderous thug, to return him to the Reich to face justice for his crimes. "There was no political motive," Ulrike was saying as if she had carefully memorized not only the words, but even the tone and her expression, "He cannot claim that this was anything other than personal vindictiveness! It was a crime carried out by a murderous criminal – one who has deceived everyone into thinking he was something else. He is nothing but a killer, a deranged psychotic..."

Alex glanced away from the subtitles so that he could listen directly to the words without interference. Who wrote such a well-considered script? Who knew the right sort of words to direct at the Americans? Presumably one of the Little Brother organizations had lent a hand. Damn it! Ulrike's appeal could do them real damage.

Anna chewed her thumb nervously. "Thank God they've waited this long to organize a response. At least enough months have passed that our cause is not as linked to Peter as it was back in the autumn."

"Yes," Alex muttered, still trying to hear every word Ulrike said. She carried on and on and the news was showing every bit of it. Who had made that decision, he wondered? And why?

There was an appalling habit in the American media to over-emphasize one point of view and then precipitously switch to the other point of view as if this in some way constituted fair and impartial reporting. He had seen it often enough: Intervene in this civil war! People are dying!! they scream into their microphones. Our government is letting the situation here slide into chaos! No one cares!! Weeks later, once the government had decided to take action, the same reporters would bellow about the devastating effects of the American militaristic action. There would be sympathetic footage of enemy losses, an academic explaining how the NAU was acting only in its

156

own imperial interests, interviews with disgruntled troops, confused and weary, as they were thrown into a situation that could never be solved by ignorant outside forces.

Yes, he had seen it all too often. They had ridden the upside of such a wave, now it looked as though they may be on the way down. The question was, what to do about it?

There were, Alex thought, certain causes which never underwent this terrible so-called impartiality. Usually all-American issues. Race relations was one. Any right-thinking person knew exactly what to say on the issue of race relations – whatever the news event, whether black violence on white or white violence on black – the commentary never varied. There was a thin line of acceptable thought on the subject and anyone who stepped off that line was shunned as intolerant and intolerable. Tolerance had become an increasingly intolerant religion, with its own high-priests who shifted policy at whim. The fact that most of the population did not buy into it was fairly irrelevant. Though they might be more inclined to view individuals as individuals, a person's actions as the actions of a person, they rarely voiced that opinion publicly for fear of being pilloried. They kept a discreet silence or toed the party line as necessary.

Drugs was another, he thought. And less defensible, too. Drugs will ruin your life, was the refrain, and then the proof would be that you end up in prison. Never was the question raised as to exactly what was ruining the prisoner's life: the drugs or their illegality? He sighed heavily. There was a whole industry devoted to keeping drugs illegal – not least the drug mafias themselves. Prison guard unions, legislators who wanted to sound tough, scared parents...

That's what they needed. They needed to isolate their cause. To remove it from the nebulous world of foreign policy where right and wrong could be switched from one week to the next into that world of sureties: bigotry is wrong, drugs are evil, abandoning the resistance movements is unthinkable. Unthinkable because the resistance movement is unmitigated good. There is no in-between ground: the Reich is evil, Resistance is good. If there is any evil committed, then it has nothing to do with the Resistance. End of story.

Alex nodded to himself. "We have to throw Peter to the wolves."

"What? Huh?" Anna looked at Alex in confusion.

"They're trying to do us in, by destroying him. We can't hesitate. We have to cut him loose – deny anything to do with his actions and make it clear that any further destruction of his character does not reflect on us."

"Alex!" Anna breathed in disgust. "How can you think such a thing! That's unfair. I mean, I know he hasn't been a saint, but after all he's done for us? And he did this for your son! Have you no loyalty?"

157

"Loyalty? Pff! This is a war, Anna! Besides, it won't do him any harm. We'll issue a statement distancing ourselves from him and the whole thing will die down and soon be forgotten."

"Do you really think that's wise?" Anna asked, clearly worried. Despite her occasional misgivings about her daughter's choice of husband, she still felt that he deserved to be treated fairly.

Alex nodded. "Yeah, we'll make it clear, whatever the merits of their case, *our* sort of people don't indulge in that sort of thing. Peter's a free agent and we take no responsibility for his actions."

"I don't think you should do that. Not yet, anyway. Nobody's pointed a finger at us. If you jump up too soon, they'll think you're reacting out of guilt."

"Nonsense. The connection is obvious. I was his handler, Peter mentioned our fund explicitly, and you heard that girl – she was already pointing a finger at us, at least indirectly, telling the Americans they had been misled. We can't hesitate. We've got to be as appalled as everyone else is, and that means, denying any knowledge of his actions, denying any complicity. Immediately."

Anna shook her head. "They have no proof! We could deny it happened. Say the whole thing is manufactured."

"Too dangerous. Who knows what proof they could find – given it's true, we could paint ourselves into a very tight corner if we go that route. Sort of what Ryszard had that Vogel character do. No, we're better off dumping Peter immediately. He's served his purpose and it does no good keeping it his personal cause. In fact, this is actually good, we can distinguish between a small, personal crusade of limited interest and our great cause which is ongoing and should never be forgotten."

"I don't think it's wise."

"Eh, who cares what you think?" Alex huffed. He was fed up with Anna's negativity. "It's the people midtown I need to talk to."

"I know, I'm nobody here. Just your loyal wife."

Alex looked up at her. Something about her tone surprised him. "What are you saying?"

"I'm saying, I'm going home, Alex. You don't need me here, and I am needed there."

"Anna! I do need you! For heaven's sakes who's going to…"

"Cook and clean for you?" Anna raised an eyebrow scornfully. "Frankly, Alex, after an entire lifetime of seeing to your needs, I don't care. Maybe you'll do your own laundry for once. I'll leave you a stack of two dollar coins."

"Coins?" Alex asked in confusion.

But Anna refused to be drawn. "Be as helpless as you want. I'm going home."

"Home?" Alex repeated helplessly.

"Home," Anna stated definitively.

31

German Folk, defend yourselves! Now there was an idea, Ryszard thought, as he glanced up at the sign. It was spread in large, permanent letters across the top of the building. They were running out of enemies against which they could defend themselves, but still the sign warned them, commanded them rather, defend yourselves! After all these decades, they still needed to be told. In familiar speech, as well. But, of course, the command was meant paternally, from Father-State, from their beloved Führer, to his dear, albeit apparently moronically forgetful, children.

Ryszard lit a cigarette and went into the restaurant. Stefi was waiting in the lobby. She saw him and smiled. She had just come from spending time with her beloved Führer, and Ryszard noted that her smile carried a hint of sadness. She looked weary. Or was it impatience?

They were seated at a table in a dark corner and Ryszard immediately ordered a bottle of wine. Dry white in deference to his daughter's tastes. Jörg stood a discreet distance away, looking ever vigilant. What is he watching for? Ryszard wondered. Danger? Or conspiracies? He scowled his frustration at his keeper.

"How's it going, Papa?" Stefi asked innocently.

He turned his gaze toward her. Papa. She was sleeping with a man thirteen years *his* senior and she referred to him as Papa. As if she were five years old.

"Oh, come now, it's not that bad! Certainly your little Greta is keeping you happy!"

"You're one to talk."

"I haven't lost sight of my goal. If you think that a huffing piece of flabby flesh, sweating and stinking and grabbing at me, is something I look forward to or enjoy, then you've lost your mind."

"Maybe I have," Ryszard muttered. "But you didn't have to go so far, you know."

"No? And where should I have gone? Maybe I should have joined the women's auxiliary of the Party and worked my way up the hierarchy as a secretary? Hmm? Or, I know! You introduced me to Rudi so that I could endlessly tease him. Yeah, that would have worked," Stefi scoffed, "I'm sure he would have waited patiently for a pious virgin, in the meanwhile confiding secrets to me and taking my advice as we sipped cups of tea with long white gloves on!"

"*Dość już!*" Ryszard snapped. *Enough already!*

Stefi's eyes widened and she glanced fearfully around at her father's uncontrolled use of Polish. Neither said a word as the waiter arrived with their wine. Ryszard inspected the bottle, sipped the wine and pronounced it acceptable. The waiter poured a glass for Stefi and then filled Ryszard's glass. Once he had done that, he asked if they were ready to order and dutifully listed the available dishes, emphasizing which ones were specialities of the chef.

He was good at his job, Ryszard thought. A German. A paid employee. Probably free to quit his job – if he dare – with only a month or two notice. Of course, once he had quit, it would be noted in his work documents and he would be dogged by questions for the rest of his life. Was he work-shy? Was he a malcontent? Why had he quit a good job? After conscription, he would have apprenticed for this position – a year or two. A year or two of abject obedience to some senior employee. A year or two earning a pittance. But now, at last, the pay-off. He would earn enough money to live in a boarding house, or if he were married and had children, in a State-subsidized flat. Separate bedroom for the parents and ever-present baby, fold-out beds for the children in the living room. State-provided daycare in a squat building on the premises. School for the elder children. A proud position on a waiting list for an automobile. The ideal family life. No, he would not quit his job.

"What news do you have?" Ryszard asked after the waiter had left with their orders.

Stefi sipped her wine. "Good news. Olek is going to be in Berlin for a while."

"How so?"

"Ah, somehow they've found the money to get him a decent set of replacement legs. They're setting him up as wounded in West South Africa while working as a military advisor to the government there. The hospital is being paid dollars so that they can fit him with the best limbs available – from America."

"Good. So you'll get to see him?" Ryszard lit another cigarette. He didn't even touch the wine.

Stefi grinned. "Better than that! Seems his parents were old friends of the family, but poor Olek is now an orphan, so we're going to be putting him up in our house throughout his recovery. It will take months, what with the physical therapy and all."

"Ah-hah. And who will handle the cryptanalysis at Szaflary?" Not that he really gave a damn.

"I gather it's mostly automated and the inter-office memos are quite routine to translate. Uncle Peter said he'd help out if things ever got more complicated than what Jurek can handle."

"Wanda's husband?" Ryszard asked in surprise.

"Yes, I guess he's Olek's understudy," Stefi answered impatiently. "But never mind that, my big news is that we're going to arrange the marriage while he's here. The banns have already been posted."

"Your marriage? Here? In Berlin?"

Stefi nodded happily. "Otherwise, we'd have to wait forever for me to get a good chance to get to Szaflary and this way everyone in the family can be there."

"Everyone but me," Ryszard corrected bitterly. He turned his head to exhale a stream of smoke away from their table. Across the room, a family gathering, apparently some sort of celebration, caught his attention, and he stared jealously at them.

Stefi tilted her head and frowned sympathetically. "I know, Dad. But you wouldn't be able to come to Szaflary either. Not until you lose your keepers – if even then."

Ryszard's eyes strayed from the table to his "keeper" then back to Stefi. "All along I've been fighting for our right to exist, to maintain our culture. And now I can't even attend my own daughter's wedding."

"I'm sorry, Dad. But we just don't want to wait. It might be years..." Stefi began, but seemed to think better of it. "Look, maybe you'll be able to come to my wedding after all, I..." she saw her father's sharp look and hastened to amend, "I don't mean the real thing, but Olek and I thought we could have a wedding under Reich law as well. Then you could attend."

"What about Rudi? He'd never allow that."

Stefi shrugged. "I don't know. If I put the idea to him in the right manner, maybe he'd even support it. I could imply that Olek's injuries extend all the way upward, if you know what I mean..."

"Do they?"

"No, fortunately! But it'd be a good way to assuage any sexual jealousy Rudi might feel, and if I'm married, he can feel sure that I'm not trying to trap him into marriage."

"He doesn't feel trappable."

"I could paint it as a patriotic act – one of our boys, wounded in action, taken in by a loyal German woman, blah, blah, blah." Stefi wagged her head in imitation of some yammering propaganda broadcast.

"He won't allow it."

"And I could point out how the French aristocrats did this sort of thing all the time – had married women as their mistresses."

"He's more like an American gangster, sweetheart. He doesn't think of you as an equal – you're his possession, and if you suggest marrying another man, you will make him angry. Not only is that going to possibly get you thrown out of his bed – which, I must admit, would relieve me – but it could put you in serious danger. Please! Don't do this! It's a bad idea."

"But I want to be able to be seen with Olek publicly!" Stefi wailed. "I want a life."

"Don't we all?" Ryszard looked across the room at the celebrating family. An older man and woman sat centrally placed, apparently it was their anniversary. An anniversary. Friends, family, a little celebration. The distant husband and wife kissed each other and there was approving laughter at the table. Ryszard closed his eyes against the warm family scene. "Don't do it, Stefi. It could be dangerous."

"Well, I know Rudi better than you, and I don't think I'll have any problems, if I handle it correctly."

Ryszard turned his attention back to his daughter and studied the small lines of determination that had set in around her mouth. The one thing his daughter had definitely inherited from him was his stubbornness. Unless he could offer new information, there was no point arguing with her. "Alright, do what you think is best, but please, Stefi, remember what happened to Joanna. Don't be misled by his buffoonery. The man is a monster..." He stopped speaking as their appetizers arrived.

Stefi delicately took a bite of the toast with its artfully displayed salmon, nestled cozily on a thin slice of cucumber and decorated with a bit of sauce and a sprig of dill. "Eh, tasteless."

Ryszard looked down at the wafer thin slices of beef and horseradish sauce that was on his plate. He had been only a youth when Szaflary had suffered through an attempt at an invasion and a siege. All supply lines were cut-off with a prolonged attack on the surrounding area. There had reigned a ceaseless feeling of hunger, of worry, of near desperation. Even as he sat in the dim and smoky atmosphere of the restaurant, he could smell the fresh air of the woods, the damp leaves underfoot as he had led his siblings on long hunts for mushrooms, berries, even, when they were lucky, rabbits. Anything to help, anything at all. His mother inventively used the fruits of their labor to enhance the cabbages and potatoes and beets that formed the staples of their diet. Never once, had any of it been tasteless.

He missed Szaflary terribly! He had not been there since Zosia's wedding, more than a year ago, and now, it was possible he would never be able to go there again. Not as long as he remained under the Führer's thumb, not even once he was Führer. He would have to keep up this impossible act, even then. God, he missed his home! He missed his parents and his family – the family as it had been then: full of a sense of purpose, committed to their cause, to each other, appreciative of the flavor of a wild mushroom. He looked up at his daughter, at the beautiful, pampered young woman who risked her life by prostituting herself to a monster, who bit into her appetizer and groaned that it was tasteless. It was no longer her role – it was who she was. Even if they got exactly what they wanted, they had lost their own lives in the process.

Stefi caught her father's intense gaze and smiled wanly. "I need Olek here. I know it's risky. I know that we shouldn't taint our family by adding any unnecessary connections, but I asked that it be arranged this way, because I need him."

"I understand. Just please, please, be careful."

"I will, Dad. More careful than you, anyway."

"What's that supposed to mean?"

Stefi sputtered. "Have you forgotten who your little Greta is married to?"

"It's a tactical maneuver," Ryszard snapped. "You've seen the sort of shit I put up with because of your mother's background. The further I progress, the less appropriate our marriage is. She's holding me back."

Stefi picked up her wine glass and sloshed the wine around a bit. "What do you plan to do, divorce her and marry Greta?"

"Maybe. I need to strip away as much of Günter's support as possible. She'll bring her family ties with her if we marry."

"I don't think it's worth the risk. Günter is a dangerous man – he's not going to take this lightly."

Ryszard shrugged.

"It's not the tactics, is it?" Stefi asked, her eyes narrowing. She leaned toward her father and hissed, "You like fucking her, don't you? She excites you, is that it?"

"Let me have what little life is available to me," Ryszard sighed tiredly.

"Your life? What about Mother's life? What about us, your children?"

With deliberateness, Ryszard directed his gaze at Jörg. "That's not available to me, right now, in any case. I'm letting you all off the hook by staying away." He raised a hand to stop Stefi from interrupting him. "And besides," he added angrily, "your mother, my dear wife, won't let me touch her as long as they are around. Shall we guess how long that's going to be?"

Stefi wet her lips. "I didn't know that."

Ryszard lit another cigarette. The waiter arrived with their meals and looked questioningly at Ryszard's untouched plate. Ryszard nodded, waving his hand to indicate that he could take their appetizers away. Let someone in the kitchen enjoy his untouched meat, he didn't want it.

* * *

They emerged from the restaurant in a sour mood and into a light, uncomfortable, evening rain. Ryszard paused at the entrance and scowled at the sky. He wasn't that far from home, but if he wanted to get a taxi for Stefi, they should go back into the restaurant and have one ordered.

Three businessmen walked toward the entrance of the restaurant. The foremost of them boldly approached Ryszard and holding a gun in one hand, flapped open an identification wallet in front of his face. Ryszard glanced back at Stefi – she was under the guard of the second man. He turned his head the other way to see that Jörg was already being disarmed. "Fucking lot of good, you are," he snapped angrily at Jörg.

He turned his attention back to the man in front of him. "Let me see that!" he ordered, grabbing the identification wallet. Führer's Special Services. "What do you want?"

"You're under arrest, Colonel Traugutt."

"On what charge?"

"Secret indictment." The officer gestured toward a car. "Come with us."

Ryszard looked down at the gun pointed at him, he turned his head and looked again at the one pointed at Stefi. Three, possibly four, against two. Rather risky, he thought. Besides, if he and Stefi – especially Stefi – exhibited the sort of talent that would allow them to disarm and escape three armed men, that would blow their cover. Better to find out what it was all about. "Alright. If you let the girl go."

"Naturally, Colonel. Just come with us."

Ryszard allowed himself to be frisked, disarmed, and escorted to the car. He settled into the back seat and watched out the open door as the other two men carefully backed away from Stefi and Jörg. Along with his escort, they jumped into the car, the door was slammed shut and Stefi and Jörg disappeared behind the impenetrably dark glass of the auto.

As the car drove off, a partition went up between the front seat and the back. So, he would not even get to see where they were taking him. Ryszard could not help but wonder how many days it would be before his badly-decomposed body would be found floating in the Spree. The battered corpse would be too far gone for there to be any indication of cause of death. Bruises, burns, knife-wounds, strangulation marks – all would be indistinguishable from the depredations of decay. Suicide, they would say. Family problems, the story would go. A recent separation from his wife, obviously depressed behavior. Clearly, the simple arrest and investigation into corrupt activities had been the final straw. Released after a short interview, he had disappeared, and then, evidently distraught, jumped into the river.

Suicide. High level officials always committed suicide.

32

Stefi watched as the car disappeared into the distance. She had to get to the Führer – the sooner the better. Nevertheless, she hesitated. It was unlikely that she could get access to him tonight – not without there being something important involved, and unfortunately, he was unlikely to view the simple arrest of a subordinate as sufficiently important to interrupt his evening with his in-laws. She bit her lip and thought. He'd see her tomorrow, of that she was sure, but her father probably wouldn't have that long. They might hold him through the night, getting whatever they wanted out of him, but they almost certainly wouldn't let him live into the morning – it would be too dangerous. She had to act now.

Ignoring Jörg, she walked back into the restaurant and had them call her a taxi. Then she made a telephone call to her father's flat. "I'll be there in a few minutes," she told Leszek. "Meet me at the front door and bring your papers with you." She made several more brief calls then went outside to meet her cab.

Jörg was still standing by the door, as if undecided about what to do. When he saw Stefi, he looked relieved and came forward as if to accompany her.

"Get lost!" Stefi snapped. "You were worse than useless!"

"But they were the Führer's men!"

"How do you know that?" From her angle Stefi had been able to see at least a part of the identity badge that had been thrust in her father's face, but she doubted that Jörg had.

"I saw their documents," Jörg argued unconvincingly.

"You surrendered before they showed any identification. They could have been any gangsters. You gave my father up to the first set of thugs who came along. Without a fight!"

"But they were the Führer's men!"

Stefi paused to consider if she could in some manner make use of Jörg. "We still don't know that for sure. Go back to the Führer's office and make sure he agreed to this arrest. They may have been using fake documents."

Jörg agreed and Stefi stepped into the taxi, ordering it to take her to her father's address. There she had the taxi stop and Leszek joined them, sitting up front, with the driver. She then had the cab drive to a public building near the pension, all the while checking that there was no one following them.

She and Leszek walked through the public building, crossed the street, turned several corners and finally, sure that they were alone, went into the little hotel. The old woman greeted them formally and showed Stefi and her servant the way up to the top floor.

"Is my Mom here yet?" Stefi asked Zosia as she scanned around the room. Two bumps on the bed told her that her little cousins were sound asleep.

"Obviously not. What's up? Why this breach of procedure?"

Stefi's surveying stopped as she looked at Peter. "You've changed your eye color."

"Ah, yeah. Contact lenses." Peter self-consciously turned away from her steady gaze. "We got enough money for me to buy the sort that doesn't cause me pain. At least not too much."

Stefi wondered how much pain her uncle would define as "not too much", but that wasn't the sort of question one could simply ask. There was another knock at the door and Kasia and Pawel came in.

Pawel kissed Stefi in greeting. "What's going on?"

"Dad's been arrested."

Kasia moaned, her hand moving unbidden to her heart. She turned pale, and Pawel reflexively reached out to hold her. "Mom? Are you okay?"

"When?" Kasia stammered.

"By whom?"

"Why?"

Stefi waved her hands to suppress the questions. "All I know is we came out of a restaurant together about half an hour ago and three men came and took him away at gunpoint. They showed him identification that seemed to say they were from one of the Führer's offices. They drove away in an official car – here's the license number." Stefi handed the slip of paper to Zosia. "I want you to see if you can trace who they are. I'm going to take a taxi to the *Residenz*. Rudi is supposed to be there tonight – I've got to get in to see him and see if I can't convince him to put a stop to it before it gets nasty."

"Why didn't you just go there immediately?" Pawel asked. "Aren't we wasting time? Something could be happening to Father at this very moment!"

"I know but I won't get into the *Residenz* tonight – not without something earth-shattering."

"Isn't Father's arrest enough?"

Stefi shook her head. "I doubt it. Even if he didn't order it directly, Rudi would think it's sort of funny. He likes to keep his people at each other's throats – it weakens everyone else and keeps him powerful. If Dad ended up dead, he'd say, 'oh, bad luck' or something like that. He'd probably even be genuinely upset, but by then it'd be too late."

"Isn't his door always open to you?" Zosia asked, clearly out of curiosity.

Stefi shook her head. "No, the other way around – I'm always available for him. Tonight he has a dinner party with his in-laws followed by a night in bed with his wife. It is essential that appearances are maintained. On such nights I'm explicitly told to stay away, and the orders at the doors are that no unexpected visitors are admitted under any circumstances. And that includes me, with or without urgent business."

The pained look on Kasia's face only deepened, but she didn't say anything.

Stefi turned back to Pawel. "Did you bring the car?"

"Yes, as you said."

"Give Leszek the papers. He's going to drive Mom to Posen."

"Posen?" Pawel raised his eyebrows in surprise.

"Poznań," Kasia corrected irritably.

Zosia smiled at her sister-in-law's one persistent concession to patriotism. "Why?"

"I want Mom to pick up her sister and brother-in-law."

"Dorota and Feliks?" Kasia made a face in surprise.

"Yes, I'm going to use them to get Dad sprung and if Mom goes to get them, she can fill them in on the way back. Dad's car is fast – it shouldn't take too long to get there, and his papers should prevent any problems en route." Stefi turned to Alisia. "I'll need you to inform Warszawa of what's going on and have them contact Posen and relay their orders to them before Mom arrives."

Alisia nodded. She didn't bother to ask questions, knowing from experience it was simply quicker to wait for instruction.

Kasia gently brushed Pawel's hand off her shoulder, indicating that she no longer needed his support. "Why my sister and her husband? Why not someone already here in Berlin?"

"Dad's already invoked them in front of Rudi, and we know they're loyal. Now Zosia and Peter," Stefi spun around to face her aunt and uncle, "I need you to establish a computer trail. Bank accounts, telephone records, anything you can manage in the next couple of hours. Can you do that from here?"

Zosia pursed her lips. "Depends on what you'll be wanting. If we need to do any direct intervention, I'll leave Peter working from the cellar connection and I'll do the break-ins."

Stefi glanced at Peter to see his reaction to Zosia's automatic assumption of command, but his expression remained completely unchanged. Stefi turned to her brother, "Pawel, get hold of Stefan. You two are going to help Warszawa construct a suitable background for Feliks. After that, you'll have a very special assignment."

"What are you planning?"

Stefi grinned. "I'll tell you. As you'll see, timing is absolutely crucial. Unfortunately, we'll have to wing some of it as information becomes available, and I don't know how much I'll be able to keep in touch with any of you once I've gone to talk to Rudi. Also, of course, everything depends on what's happening to Dad right now."

"I shudder to think about it," Zosia said.

Kasia discreetly made the sign of the cross.

33

*T*hey had to be well outside of Berlin, Richard thought, as the car finally came to a halt. Either that or they had driven in circles. He had initially attempted to note the directions that the car was taking, but that had rapidly proved useless and frustrating, so now he waited in complete ignorance for them to open the door and give him a view of his whereabouts.

They stepped out into the darkness of the countryside. A momentary panic gripped Richard as he thought they were just planning to shoot him dead, then and there, in a field outside of town, but then he noticed the lights of a large house not too far away. He glanced around and realized that there were dim lights along a periphery as well. Apparently they were on the grounds of a country estate used for military or governmental purposes.

One of the men accompanying Richard brought out a pair of handcuffs and approached him.

"Put those away!" Richard barked. "Unless you plan on wearing them yourself!"

The man glanced at his companions, then at Richard's expression. There was no denying which one of them was used to giving orders and which of them was used to taking them. The guard put the handcuffs back on his belt.

Together they marched into the manor. The foyer was large and well-appointed, with a huge chandelier casting its light on the plush oriental carpet underfoot. Period furniture was set against the walls under large, ornately framed mirrors and paintings. On the left, a wide marble staircase with an exquisitely carved banister swept grandly upwards. To the right, the hall continued back into the depths of the house, and presumably to the much less imposing staircase which would lead into the cellar.

Richard swallowed nervously, wondering which direction he would be taken.

He was led into a room on the ground floor, furnished like some sort of small dining room. There was a gleaming mahogany table, six chairs, a sideboard and a small side table. There was no-one in the room, of course, and as his escort withdrew, Richard paced to the window to look outside as it seemed silly to sit down and wait expectantly.

Within ten minutes a young man came into the room. "Ah, Colonel Traugutt!" he welcomed smilingly. He set down a stack of papers and documents and walked up to Richard, thrusting his hand out expectantly. "My name is Jung, Georg Jung. A pleasure to meet you, *mein Herr*! Welcome!"

Richard turned his attention from the window to the young man's hand. After a moment, he looked up and asked, "Why have I been brought here?" He deliberately used the passive voice as he did not credit the young man with any authority.

With a weak smile, Jung withdrew his hand and walked over to the stack of papers. "Oh, just a minor administrative matter. Sorry for all the cloak and dagger stuff, that was not how our men were instructed to handle this. Over-enthusiastic, you know," he apologized unconvincingly. He picked up one of the documents. "It's just that we have been carrying out an investigation into certain, er, activities among our Party faithful, and, well..." He waved his hand in a gesture of dismissal, as if the whole thing were really rather trivial. "Your branch, I mean...Just a few indiscretions. Nothing serious. Here." He walked back to Richard holding just one document. "It's all laid out here. Your signature. That's all we need."

Richard took the document. He turned back to the window, unlatched it and opened it. Somewhere in the distance he heard an alarm go off, but he ignored that as he crushed the document and threw it out the window. Calmly, he closed the window and turned back to the young man. "That's what I think of these bullshit accusations."

Jung's eyes narrowed in anger, but he managed to calm himself and took the rebuff in stride. "Fortunately, Colonel Traugutt, I have a copy."

"I'm not putting my signature on anything. Go tell your master that!" Richard pulled out a cigarette and held it up expectantly. It wasn't the Führer, of that he was fairly sure. The Führer might have agreed to some part of this, perhaps in order to once again tug on his lieutenant's leash, but the man pulling the strings was someone else. Someone who wanted to see him dead. Günter perhaps? That didn't make much sense. Günter was in the RSHA as well and if it were Günter, Richard should have recognized at least one of his minions by now. Besides, Günter had a better claim to the throne than he did and this wasn't really his style. Unless, of course, he was jealous.

Reluctantly Jung lit the cigarette. Then, returning to the stack of documents, he began digging, looking for the copy.

"If your master was intent on a political murder," Richard explained casually, as Jung continued feverishly to dig through his stack, "he should have had it carried out there on the street. There was no point in kidnapping me, because I'm not signing anything."

"There it is!" Jung trumpeted as he pulled out another document.

"And, in abducting me, he has made a serious error."

Jung feigned disinterest. "Now, if you would be so kind as to review this document rather than litter our lawn." He walked back to Richard with it.

"You see, your master's thugs abducted me in front of my daughter. She, no doubt, will have the license number of the vehicle and this action will be traceable to you."

"As you can see, there has been an extended investigation into–"

"What your master no doubt knows, but I'm sure, didn't bother to tell you, is that my daughter has a very special relationship with the Führer."

Despite himself, Jung looked up with interest. Richard nodded. "Yes. Now that his goons made the mistake of letting her witness this so-called arrest, there will be no denying that I ended up here. When the Führer starts asking about my health and wonders aloud about my suicide, your master will deny any knowledge of what happened to me. And you know what that means, don't you?"

Jung looked somewhat pale.

"That's right, boy, you're going to be fingered for my murder. You and you alone." Richard gave him a long, almost sympathetic look. "And *murder* it will be called. No matter what you've been told. You'll be hauled into the RSHA and questioned. Questioned about the murder of a *superior* officer. Questioned by people who are my friends, do you understand? After you confess, and you *will* confess, believe me, then you will be tried and executed. Do you understand that?"

Jung turned away and paced to the table, to the stack of documents. He began fingering them as if he could read his response there on their pages.

"Your only hope is to release me immediately. And I expect to be transported back to Berlin." Richard paused long enough for his words to sink in, then commanded, "Go arrange it. Now!"

Jung continued to stare at the papers, then suddenly, he looked up at Richard. "Please wait here." He immediately left the room.

Richard felt sure there was no point in trying to leave, so he did wait, hoping that Jung had the authority to arrange his release. The problems with his strategy crowded his mind: if Jung's boss was on the premises, then he would not be able to release his prisoner. If they took his threats seriously, then Stefi's life would now be in grave danger.

Richard finished his cigarette, then pulled back the drape and looked out the window again. There were half a dozen armed men in the yard below, apparently summoned by his having opened the window a few minutes ago. He stared past them into the darkness, at a fence on the periphery, at the woods beyond that. If his sense of direction was correct, then he was looking east, toward Poland, toward home. A home which had vanished from the earth, a home which suffered interminably, screaming in silent agony. A home which he had never seen as a free land, probably never would see as a free land. A home for which he had risked everything, given everything.

He was here, far from home, far from everything and everyone he loved, posing as a scheming Nazi official, risking his life in the deadly power game which was played out at the top of the Reich's hierarchy, and there they were, the Warszawa headquarters, wondering about his loyalty! Stefi had told him that he was under suspicion. That his actions were considered questionable. *Out of control.* Those were the words she had used, quoting. Out of control. There they sat, twiddling their aristocratic rings on their fingers as they plotted their pointless revolution; there they sat, doubting him! The only one who was actually accomplishing anything! And now, now he might die. His daughter might be killed, and they would lose their only genuine opportunity in decades. Richard pulled out another cigarette and lit it. Would they even notice in their profound self-absorption? Or would they be relieved?

The door opened but Richard did not turn around. "Is it all arranged?" he asked imperiously.

"Ach, Traugutt. Always the little Napoleon."

Richard spun around. It wasn't Jung, it was Kraus. Adolf Kraus. A nobody from the Interior Ministry. The *Interior* Ministry! "You? You're behind all of this?"

"Just doing my duty." Kraus grinned malevolently.

"Release me immediately, and I won't have you hanged." Richard calmly took a drag from his cigarette.

Kraus shook his head sadly. "I don't like your threats, Traugutt. First you threaten my subordinate, and now me. If you had taken the time to read our charges, rather than rudely throw them out the window, you would have seen that it is quite a complex scheme you've been running. Bribery, corruption, funneling money out of the country. The usual." Kraus paused dramatically. "Only one small, extra thing. You see, what we've found out, my dear colleague, is that apparently you've been funneling all these monies through your daughter into foreign accounts. It seems your daughter must be investigated as well."

"You leave her alone!"

"Too late. She's already been indicted. She should have been picked up along with you. It was an oversight that my men did not recognize her, but that was only a temporary set-back. We picked her up outside the *Residenz* and she is now safely in our custody and will soon be joining us here."

Richard was speechless with horror.

"You see, Traugutt, I *am* going to get your signature. I know you're a coward, I know you're going to cave. The only question is how fast."

"Go fuck yourself."

"Ah, and crude as well. But we knew that – after all, you've even used your daughter's cunt to scrabble to the top. Now, you'll get to see it being used another way."

"I'm warning you, leave her out of this!" Richard noticed the end of his cigarette was shaking and he quickly brought it to his lips to hide his trembling.

"In fact, I sort of hope you don't give in. I'd like to see how much you enjoy watching your daughter being..." Kraus pursed his lips in pleasure, then slowly, as if savoring its taste, released the word, "...questioned."

Richard paused, swallowing his anger and fear. "Fine. Say you succeed. Then what? You'll have to kill both of us. How the hell are you going to explain two suicides? You'll never get away with it."

Kraus smiled. "Suicides? Goodness, Traugutt, what do you think of us? Don't you know your daughter has a boyfriend. That little fact has emerged in our investigation since, it seems, she's using him to get your money out of the country. After our little question and answer session, she will know that it's only a matter of time before everyone knows about him, and fearing retribution from her lover she will flee the country. She'll be spotted in Switzerland, I believe."

Richard felt quite sick.

"Ah, I see that one hurt, didn't it?" Kraus laughed. "And you realize now that I've told you all this, I have no choice about what's going to happen next. You see, you should have accepted our first offer and signed on the dotted line. Then all you would have had to do is resign in dishonor and disappear from public life."

"I'm not signing anything, you puffed-up worm."

Kraus shrugged. "It's not all that important, you are clearly depressed enough that even the hint of an investigation will put you well over the edge.

Hey, but what the hell, it will be fun breaking you, anyway. You've always been an arrogant son-of-a-bitch and I'm going to enjoy watching you fall." Kraus snapped his fingers in the direction of the door and two men entered.

Richard walked up to Kraus and waving a finger in his face, said, "Whatever you do to me, you're going nowhere. You think this will move you up the ladder? Well, think again! You're nobody and you always will be."

"We'll see about that. Or rather, I will," Kraus gloated, gesturing toward the men to come forward.

"You will pay for this, you know." Richard blew the last of his cigarette's smoke into Kraus's face. "If I don't get you, one of my people will." Then motioning to the two men and snapping a "come on, already," at them, he walked out the door so that Kraus would not have the satisfaction of seeing him dragged out.

34

*R*ichard paused in the hallway. "Well, gentlemen, where to?"

One of the two men gestured to the right, down the hallway and away from the grand staircase. "This way, *mein Herr.*"

Richard followed them, mulling over his options. He sort of wished he had fought the abduction on the street, taken his chances then, but it was too late for that, he had stepped into Kraus's trap, and now he had to find his way out. He could attempt an escape now, but he suspected that it would have very little chance of success and if he made it as far as scrabbling about outside, trying to scale the fence, then he would lose any semblance of his position and would be clearly nothing more than a prisoner. It was probably better to run through the motions. There was still a possibility he could get out of this alive.

They turned a corner and went down a flight of stairs into the cellar. Richard grimaced his irritation. The first priority was to keep up his appearance of authority. He had to prevent them from striking him even once – for once the spell of his hierarchical position was broken, then anything was possible. The cellar was, therefore, not a good place to be.

They reached the bottom of the steps and walked through a large room. What sort of game was Kraus playing? He couldn't possibly believe that shuffling one competitor out of the way would forward his career enough to offset the risks involved. Or could he? One of the men opened a door at the far end of the room and the three of them entered a long hallway. Was it possible that Kraus was working for someone else? Someone clever enough to keep his distance from the entire proceedings? Günter? Seppel? Werner? Schindler made no sense, Frauenfeld – well, it wasn't his style, and Büttner? He was angry and desperate. He might be the one.

The two men stopped in front of a door. One of them opened it and gestured Richard inside. Richard glanced inside the room, then casting a scornful look at his guard, entered. The door shut and locked behind him. He stood still for a moment, suppressing an urge to kick the door.

The room had the drab, gray stone walls and low ceiling common to cellars. It was simply furnished with a table and a couple of chairs. He was relieved to see that it was not specifically outfitted for torture, although he knew it did not take much to turn an interview room into a torture chamber. Still, it was something – they intended to begin with the usual civilities. He walked over to the single window in the room. It was set high in the wall, against the ceiling, but he was tall enough to see through it without difficulty. He wiped away some of the dirt and squinted past his reflection. On the other side of the thick panes of glass was a hefty iron grill and beyond that was nothing but darkness.

He paced back into the room, angry at himself for having let it go this far. He should have demanded a different room. He should have sat down in the little dining room and insisted on conducting their business there. The atmosphere always mattered, it determined how fast things would degenerate. In a room like this, it would take less than an hour. He lit a cigarette and paced nervously. He was hot and he debated the merits of removing his suit jacket. It would not do to look disheveled, but on the other hand, it was not wise to sweat either.

He walked over to the window and leaned against the wall there, where it was a bit cooler. When he finished his cigarette, he lit another one and watched as the smoke curled upward toward the ceiling, bounced off it and then came back down again, interfering with the new upward stream so that the whole was a chaotic and unpredictable dance. Sort of like life, he thought whimsically. Yeah, that was it, the secret of the universe, the answer sought by mystics and religious since the beginning of time: life was a stream of cigarette smoke bouncing off the ceiling of a prison cell where you are likely to be tortured in the near future. He laughed at himself, at the way he had spent his life, at the likely end to it, and was still snickering when the door opened.

"I knew it'd be you," Richard laughed. "My dear Herr Jung."

"Herr Traugutt, you seem to be in a good mood," Herr Jung replied as he set his stack of papers down on the table.

"Yes, I was just thinking of all the years I've had that you're not going to have."

"Me?"

"How old are you, Jung? Twenty-five?"

"I'm thirty-two, *mein Herr!*"

"Thirty-two! Good God! I was giving commands at that age, not taking them. And look at who you're taking commands from. A loser! A sleaze-bucket."

"Mein Herr, I–"

Richard waved his hand dismissively. "You think I'm in trouble? Hah! At least, no matter what happens to me, I know it will be less disgusting than what's in store for you – and, my dear young Jung, I've spent my years well, it has all been worth it. I've had a good life: power, money, wife and children, a fine house, servants...What have you had? You're a lackey! And now you're a fall guy!"

Jung shook his head. "I'm not! Look, all I need is your signature on these papers, indicating your agreement–"

"Pff! You know as well as I, that whether I sign that crap or not, Kraus intends to have me killed. He even wants to enjoy it, and that's why you've been told to move me into a room with a camera as soon as things get ugly, am I right?"

Richard didn't wait for a reply. Jung's look of surprise was sufficient. "A camera," Richard emphasized. "Doesn't that tell you something? He's afraid to be around. Doubtless he's already headed off to an important meeting in Berlin at..." Richard consulted his watch, "...it's nearly midnight now, so let's give him two hours. Two in the morning?"

Jung picked up a stack of papers, "Colonel Traugutt, if we could please discuss these charges."

"My guess," Richard interrupted, "is that he's actually quite close. Maybe giving a dinner party. He left for a few minutes, but nobody would find such an absence unusual. Now he's back there, chatting with friends, drinking champagne, and you're left here to carry out the dirty work. You get to call in the goons. You're the one giving the orders."

Finally losing patience, Jung slammed the papers down on the table. "Nobody is going to trace you here!"

"My daughter." Richard reminded him.

"Is in our custody!" Jung shouted.

"Then where is she? Do you think Kraus would pass up the chance to have me see her suffer? Do you?"

"Colonel Traugutt, you misjudge us. We have no interest in harming either you or your daughter. But I know, for a fact, that she is in our custody."

"Okay. Just for the sake of argument, let's say you're right." Richard pulled out his cigarettes and offered Jung one, then lit it for him. "Let's say

175

that no one will trace me here. And let's acknowledge what your orders are: after all, Kraus told me to my face he plans to see me dead." That wasn't true, Kraus had been very careful in his wording, but Richard saw no point in letting Jung know that. "So, you carry out your orders, I'm interrogated, tortured a bit, maybe you oversee my daughter's torture." Richard raised a hand to prevent Jung from objecting. "Let's not waste time denying things that we both know are true. Now, maybe you get a good signature out of me. Even a videotaped confession. I conveniently commit suicide and my daughter disappears." Richard paused just long enough for Jung to digest the scenario. "Everything goes exactly as planned. Exactly. What do you get out of it? A promotion? Money? Hmm? You curry the favor of a nobody?" He shrugged. "Who knows. Something, anyway, right?"

Jung remained silent, smoking his cigarette thoughtfully.

Richard took a drag off his cigarette and blew a stream of smoke into the air. "My dear, young Jung. I know Kraus. He couldn't organize this. He really has nothing to gain from removing me – he's not well-enough placed to properly utilize my sudden absence. Do you realize what that means?" Without waiting for an answer, Richard explained, "Someone else is behind this, using your boss as his front man. Someone who is so far out of the picture that he'll never be fingered – except by one fellow: Kraus himself. How do you think he's going to deal with that? Hmm? Undying loyalty to a subordinate who can blackmail him? Hmm?"

Jung paced across the room to the window and stood there as if looking out, though he could only see the reflection of the room in the glass.

"I'll give you a rather quick lesson in Realpolitik." Richard paused only long enough to draw some smoke. "Kraus's puppeteer will uncover a terrible conspiracy which led to the unfortunate demise of a highly-placed, loyal official and his beautiful daughter, much beloved by the Führer. The trail will lead to Kraus, who will then squeal like a pig that he had nothing to do with it. But there will be undeniable evidence – the car, the paperwork, all of it will point to him. Ah yes, he'll admit that there was an investigation, that I was arrested under his orders, that he even spoke to me in the dining room of this estate. A friendly little chat where he urged me to co-operate and to trust his subordinate, a certain Herr Georg Jung. And guess what, my dear young Jung. Can you guess?"

"He leaves to attend to business and the next he hears is that Colonel Traugutt was released after questioning, disappeared, and is later found dead."

"Precisely. But now there is a suspicion of foul play. A few thugs are brought on the stand, and guess who they point at as having been present when I was tortured and murdered?"

"Me," Jung answered, dismally. He swallowed.

"And do you know what they do to men who murder their superiors? Eh?" Richard paused to enjoy his cigarette. He inhaled deeply, letting the smoke fill his lungs, holding it there a moment before releasing it in a satisfied exhalation.

Jung nodded. He was staring at the floor, but Richard could see that his face was ashen.

"All you have to do," Richard suggested gently, "is have me released. Believe me, Georg, when I take my revenge, I won't come after you. In fact, I'll welcome you into my fold. You'll be under my protection."

Jung looked up. There were tears in his eyes. "I can't do it," he moaned. "I don't have the authority to release you."

"No?" Richard was surprised.

"I imagine the story would have to be that Kraus had left your release papers with me, and I destroyed them. Or something like that."

Richard licked his lips. "Who *does* have the authority to release me?"

"No one," Jung wailed. "No one but Kraus!"

Richard finished his cigarette and carefully ground the end out on the wooden table. "Ah, that is bad news."

35

*Z*osia and Stefan walked along the brightly lit avenue, attempting to look casual, and perhaps slightly tipsy. It was late, much later than was normal for decent people to be out and about. A policeman eyed them from his guard post, but apparently decided that Stefan's uniform was sufficiently impressive that he need not ask to see their papers or curfew passes. He gave them a slight bow of the head as they went past, indicating that he was there – ready and willing to defend them against the predators of the night.

Zosia sighed her relief. They had not taken the time to construct more than the flimsiest of stories to explain who they were and where they were going, based upon the papers they already had in their possession. A pick-up in a club. Which club? That little one, on the corner of...? Well, there had been several. She'd have to look to Stefan to name them. Friends, yes. Just tonight – they didn't know all that much about each other, they were walking to her place, or was it his, to find out more. Actually, neither of their official addresses would suffice, they were heading away from both of them. A hotel then. Or maybe just a walk around the town. Yes, to the river – that would be the right direction – to the river to spend some romantic time alone together. Her bag? Oh, nothing much. Yes, it looks heavy, but she always carried lots of junk. Did he want to search it? Oh, no, well, good. Thanks. Late? Yes, they knew that they should not be out at this late hour without a good reason, yes, they'd turn around and go home immediately. Zosia grit her teeth and walked on.

They turned a corner and headed down the street into the shadow of a huge building. The windowless concrete rose above them in an unbroken wall, like that of a prison. High above, gargoyle-like figures perched on top of swastikas set into the edge of the roof and scowled at the petty mortals below. Zosia could not make out the shapes from where she stood, but she knew who they were: past Führers, Party leaders, Bank directors. Deutsche Bank's main building. Anybody who was anybody, anyone who was loyal kept his money here. Ministries kept their accounts here, officials kept their earnings here, foreign transactions took place here and through it all was the careful segregation of private and official. Drug money, arms deals, corruption takings, bribes, and kickbacks – almost all of it was handled within these walls. No other bank had the authority to deal with foreigners, no other bank had the power to resist almost all subpoenas – as rare as they were, no other bank could so easily crush an official who dared deal through someone else. Leave the savings-banks and the people's-banks to the workers and the small businessmen. If you wanted to deal in real money, you did your business here.

They stopped at a break in the concrete. It was a small doorway, guarded with an electronic lock. Stefan leaned against the building and lit a cigarette as Zosia fumbled in her purse for the meter and a screwdriver. She pried off the face of the lock and placed the probes of the meter on top of two contacts. She pressed a few buttons and a series of numbers flashed on the screen, but there was no tell-tale pulse to let her know that the right number had been selected. She furrowed her brow and looked at the contacts. There were more than two – in fact there were about ten places that might possibly serve as contacts.

Damn! She wished she could have brought Peter along. He was good with these sorts of things, taking an almost child-like pleasure in conquering locks. Indeed, he had suggested that he should be the one to risk breaking into the bank, explaining that he could probably establish an external link in half an hour, then they could do the rest safely back at the pension, rather than her spending hours in danger. She had not bothered to critique his plan or offer one of her own, instead she had simply told him to stay put, adding, in a huff, "That's an order!" He hadn't liked that – she could see it in his face, but he hadn't said a word more.

She looked to Stefan. "Do you know anything about this type of lock?"

He peered at it, then shook his head. "Sorry."

She tried a different set of contacts and had the machine run through its trials. Then another and another. A dangerously long time passed with her and Stefan stuck outside the door. Finally, on a pair of contacts, the green light flashed and over a period of a few seconds the code appeared on the little screen and the lock opened. Zosia removed the device, replaced the plate on the lock face and then carefully opened the door. She listened but did not hear any alarms, and so, deciding to throw caution to the wind, she motioned to Stefan that he could leave and she slipped inside.

The door clicked shut behind her and Zosia took a moment to catch her breath. That took much longer than it should have done, she was already behind schedule! She walked along the corridor, worked her way through two more locks: one electronic, the other mechanical, and within a few minutes was on familiar turf: the office she had infiltrated in order to carry out her refinancing of Szaflary and the re-establishment of the complicated series of bribes and pay-offs which kept the place safe and supplied.

She glanced around but saw no sign of a security guard. Using a small, shielded flashlight, she went over to a filing cabinet, pulled out several forms, and seating herself at one of the desks, began filling them out. She had not had much time to prepare, so she invented names and places quite whimsically, aware that they would not make sense when checked. That wouldn't matter – she had no interest in framing anyone in particular. It would be enough to imply that money had been transferred to Kraus, from somewhere outside the Reich, with Soviet agents as the likely culprits.

She worked in absolute silence, keeping her ears peeled for the sounds of a security guard. Eventually she heard what she had been expecting and she turned out the light and lowered herself under the desk. She heard his humming as he peremptorily paced around the room, poked his nose into some offices and then proceeded on his way. She checked the time, counted out two minutes, and then emerged from under the desk to continue her paperwork.

After filing the forms in the appropriate drawers and secreting the customer copies, Zosia set about amending Kraus's accounts accordingly. That took some time as she had to dribble the payments in and make sure that she did a reasonable duplication of the handwriting and signatures of various clerks. The security guard returned and Zosia hid herself again, trying not to breathe too noisily as he paced right past her desk. He stopped there. She looked at his legs as he stood immobile. Was he looking at the papers she had left on the desk? Could he smell her fear?

It was only to light a cigarette. He exhaled a stream of smoke, sighed noisily and continued his pacing. Zosia waited a short time, then climbed out. She checked her watch: if he kept to a regular schedule, then she could expect him to return every half-hour. Reasonably infrequent, but then, there was no money in this office and precious little of value to an average thief.

She continued writing up the deposit slips, dropping down to take cover through several more visits of the security guard. When she finished, she stored the originals in her purse, filed the copies and re-locked the drawers. She glanced again at her watch. Time was passing far too quickly. She looked around the office and decided that she had done enough with the paper files, they could always add more later.

The next bit was more complicated but also more in keeping with her expertise. She headed down a series of corridors and through two more locked doors and slipped into the dark room with its lumbering computer. Zosia shut the door behind her, leaned against the wall and took several deep breaths. Never had she been so nervous! What was wrong with her? Perhaps it was the lack of preparation, the absolute speed with which they all had to move. Maybe she feared for her brother's life. Whatever it was, she felt inordinately uneasy, and that worried her – not least because it could cause her to make mistakes.

As she stood in silence by the door, she heard the approach of the security guard. She snapped on her flashlight and quickly scanned the room for a likely hiding place. No desks, open-space tables, a few filing cabinets. She swore quietly.

Zosia switched off her flashlight as the door opened. The guard reached for the light switch. Zosia ducked under his arm and managed to squeeze herself out of the room without touching him. She fled down the corridor to a closet and hid in there, her heart pounding with terror. How, in God's name had she let that happen? She closed her eyes to calm herself and forced herself to forget her fear. Szaflary. The mountains, trees, glistening sunshine, noisy bubbling streams. The welcome smells of home: damp concrete, Marysia's bread, the faint whiff of the past from her great-grandmother's carved cedar chest. Zosia touched the gold band that had belonged to her, saw in her mind's eye the delicate lace of the curtain which had hung in her window, remembered the photograph she had seen of that building, with its balcony overlooking the town square.

And now it was all so different! Wasted lives, unnecessary and unending privations. Even those who managed to get on with their lives, the ones who avoided hunger or forced labor or imprisonment – even they endured a lifetime of shortages, of snooping, of mind-boggling bureaucracy, of a complete lack of privacy or dignity. They found their joys and they smiled at the birth of their children or the first snow of the year, but it never lasted long and soon their faces fell back into their hard lines of care and worry. It was for them, she reminded herself. For all the people who had not benefited from the gangster regime which raped the continent. Given her work, she hardly saw these people, the ones for whom she was fighting. Though they were the vast majority, they were unimportant, and so she and the others mingled with the oligarchs, their work kept them immersed in the highly-placed sleaze that ran the society, and so she and the others came away with misimpressions, with a sense of hopelessness and a fear that it was all quite pointless. It wasn't. If only they could re-enfranchise the lost multitudes, re-invest their lives with the happiness that came of being human. If only she could hear occasional, unconcerned laughter or see easy smiles on the people here, the way she had in that Manhattan coffee shop. It was hardly the rhetoric of revolution, but it was, in the end, what they were fighting for.

But now, to work. The images of the room played through her mind: computers, filing cabinets, a few tables, a copying machine. Ah, that would do. If she had a moment or two to prepare it, she could move the shelves inside the bottom of the machine and dive in there anytime the security guard paced through the room. She opened the closet door a bit and checked the hallway. All was quiet.

Once she was back in the computer room and had prepared her hiding place, Zosia set about breaking into the computer. It was a fairly standard system and she had some familiarity with it, but again she was hampered by her lack of preparation. Still, her heart was now calm, and she worked silently through the night, hacking into the records, amending them to include the transactions that would implicate Kraus and shifting some other monies around to suit her needs.

Once that was done to her satisfaction, she downloaded as much information as she could for later use, packed up her computer and made her way out of the building. Next was the *Reichstelekom*. That would be a lot easier since there was nothing of value in the building and it was not as closely guarded. She walked along with instinctive caution, but otherwise relaxed. It felt good to be involved again, invigorating. Once she had conquered that alien fear, her confidence had returned, and with it, her skill. But where, she wondered, had the paralyzing fear come from? Peter? Ever since she had met him, he had had an unusual effect upon her. First the dizzying confusion of his presence, then the constant conflict of their marriage, and now this, this love that dominated her and kept him always in her thoughts. It weakened her, left her vulnerable. It was, as Stefi had put it, *impossible.*

That thought brought a smile to her lips. She remembered how she had calmly crocheted a blanket as Stefi attempted her first assassination all those years ago. Seven years. My, how Stefi had grown! Then she had bungled the kill and nearly vomited at the result. Now, she was giving the orders and chiding her aunt for having withdrawn from active duty. All Zosia's arguments about taking a break, experiencing life instead of work, and so on...all of them had failed to convince Stefi, and, Zosia had to admit, herself as well. There was no denying it – the children were tedious, the baby in particular. How could one spend all one's time being interested in wiping up spittle and changing nappies? God, she felt she was going to die of boredom! Only pride had stopped her from admitting it before now. Only pride kept her from crawling back to the Council and begging for her seat back.

Something had to be done! She should take things back to the way they were before. That had worked well. With Peter handling all the tedious details of life, she could devote herself to the important things. Just like before. He could contribute, of course, but it would be clear whose work was more important. Just like before.

But that was impossible. Things *had* changed, and it could never be like it was before. It was clear she could still use her rank and her seniority to order him around, at least when it came to their official tasks, and she could still depend on his innate sense of responsibility toward the children to be sure that everything at home would be well cared for, even if she did absolutely nothing. But unlike before, she now paid a price for such services – and she had seen it explicitly in his face as she had issued her order this evening. He might just as easily have said, "Fine, but don't expect me to care."

Zosia turned a corner and strode purposefully down the street. Somehow, somewhere along the line, she had lost control of the situation. She had lost control of him. How had that happened? Why did she now feel confused, pulled this way and that by her heart? *I know I'm not the person you want me to be. I never was.* The words echoed through her head as she walked along. He had said that in answer to her demand that he feel something. What sort of an answer was that? It didn't make any sense! Feel something! *I'm not the person you want*...Why not "I feel angry," or "I feel confused"? Why *I'm not the person*...?

She stopped dead in her stride. Because he had known. He had known that she did not want him to feel *something*, she had wanted him to feel guilt. Guilt that he wasn't Adam. Guilt that he was a disappointment to her. Guilt that he wasn't the person she wanted him to be. The better for her to control him with. But he had refused to feel guilt, he had simply stated it as a fact. *I'm not the person you want me to be. I never was.* Was it then true? Had she, by constantly insisting upon it, *made* it true?

She glanced around herself to see if she had drawn any notice and then started walking again. It was, she supposed, just possible that she bore a tiny bit of the blame for his current aloofness. Marysia seemed to think so. Apologize, she had said. Zosia snorted to herself. Apologize! No way!

She had done it for the cause! Still, she felt she loved him. Maybe she *could* do something. Perhaps show a little more consideration? It had worked well enough when she had had a motive and wanted to manipulate him. Could she do it without a motive? Should she?

Now that was an intriguing idea.

36

"*N*ow this is intriguing," Richard commented sarcastically. He sat in the chair, relaxed and in command. "You want me to sign documents admitting to crimes I haven't committed."

Jung nodded wordlessly. He was becoming irritated, that was obvious.

"I'm not signing anything," Richard repeated. There really wasn't much else to say. So far, he had managed to maintain his air of authority, so far, he had kept Jung at bay by virtue of his rank, but he could tell it wasn't going to last much longer. Jung was under pressure and growing impatient. The thug at Jung's side raised his fist threateningly, but was interrupted by the sound of the door opening. Kraus strode in, smiling broadly.

"Ach, my dear Kraus. So you've reconsidered your rash actions," Richard predicted with a smirk.

"Ach, my dear Traugutt. It's better than that." Kraus's smile broadened into a grin. "We know who you are. We know all about you."

Richard let his gaze slide away, disinterested. It meant nothing, they knew nothing, it was a bluff.

"To use such a name." Kraus shook his head mournfully clicking his tongue.

Though it was unwise, Richard looked up at him. What was he talking about?

"Did you think we didn't know? Did you think we are so unaware? Look!" Kraus flung down a very old manual. "It's there in the Gestapo manual from 1939 – your famous Polish patriot, Romuald Traugutt. *R. Traugutt.* Leader of the secret underground state. Rebel. Hanged by the Russians! You're a fool, Traugutt. Worse than a fool – you're scum. A traitor. An *Untermensch.*"

Richard let his breath out slowly. Kraus seemed very sure of himself. But how could he know so much?

"Your people are fit for nothing more than slavery, and you – ah, you, *Ry-szard*," he drawled the name out as if the sound gave him pleasure. "You are going to suffer…"

"What's going on?" Jung asked, utterly confused.

"He's a colonel in the Home Army, an infiltrator, an *Untermensch*," Kraus clarified. He turned his attention back to Richard. "Born Ryszard Przewalewski, in that terrorist enclave called Szaflary, twenty years working your way through our system. Your father, Alex Przewalewski, a half-Jew, a diplomat in America, your sister, Zofia Król, called Zosia, one of the Home Army's best assassins, Adam Firlej's widow, now married to that English traitor, Peter Halifax. And your daughter…Well, well, well. We've got you, boy. We've got you good." His whole body shook with mirth. "God, I'm going to enjoy this!"

So much! How the hell could they know all that? Richard's tongue probed back to the tooth in his mouth which had carried poison for him, but it was empty. Nothing but an unusually deep hollow met his tongue.

"You're going to scream, you Slav-Jew, capitalist-imperialist pig. You're going to scream a lot!" Kraus giggled.

Richard felt sick. How did they know so much? And if they knew so much, then they would know Kasia was involved. Oh God, what they would do to her! What they would do to his children! How could he have ever left them?

"We know so much, boy, we're not even going to question you," Kraus explained, as a camera was set up in the room. "All the Führer wants to hear is your cowardly screams."

Kraus looked at him expectantly, but he had nothing to say. How in God's name, did they know everything? Stefi? Oh God, what had they done to her to get her to say so much? His little girl! His free-spirited, dark-eyed little girl, running through the park with flowers in her hand, her dark hair streaming joyfully behind her.

He felt like vomiting.

"What? No defense? No explanations? No comment?"

Richard sputtered his disgust. "I know you intend to murder me, Adolf. What do I care what fairytales you invent to cover yourself? They won't work!"

At a motion from Kraus, two of the thugs grabbed Richard's left arm and held it pressed against the table. Another grabbed his right and twisted it behind his back, pulling it painfully upward.

"You'll pay for this," Richard gasped. "That's all I'm going to tell you. The Führer will see you hanged!"

Kraus picked up a crowbar. He laid it across Richard's left forearm and then using both hands, leaned his weight on the bar. It pressed excruciatingly against Richard's flesh. Richard squeezed his eyes shut against the pain, grit his teeth to keep from screaming. Kraus threw his full weight against the bar, but it was insufficient. He motioned with his head and together he and one of the thugs threw their weight onto the bar. There was a cracking sound and the bar suddenly dropped a bit.

Richard sucked in his breath noisily. He felt a sharp, stabbing pain and then a flood of warmth where his bone had snapped, but he managed to keep silent.

Kraus looked surprised. He pulled back, motioned for the thugs to pull the bar away.

Richard kept his eyes on the wood of the table, on the drops of his sweat which wet the planks. He kept his teeth gritted, he kept his silence.

Kraus motioned for Richard's right arm to be pinned to the table, his hand dangling free over the edge. This time they used a lighter and burnt his fingers, one after the other, and this time, Richard screamed.

The scream woke him up and he stared upwards, panting with terror in the darkness.

There was an intricate molding where the ceiling met the wall and he let his eyes focus on its dim outline as he took stock of his situation. He was uninjured, lying on a divan in the room Jung had given him for the night. His left arm ached, but he suspected that was from how he had lain on it.

He must have fallen asleep. He shook his head to rid himself of the images from his nightmare. He was annoyed at having succumbed. Annoyed and worried. If such thoughts were that close to the surface, they might emerge under more dangerous circumstances.

Down, down, they must go. He had to bury the thoughts, bury the nightmare, bury the truth of who he was deep within. Down, deep down. He must bury Ryszard, the *Untermensch*, the Slav-Jew, completely.

He stood and paced the finely appointed room, stopping to contemplate the fancy ironwork covering the window. It had obviously been placed there for security, to keep prowlers out, but it was equally effective at keeping him in. He reached his fingers through the opening and wrapped them around the grill. It was quite decorative, beautifully made. Strong, too, he thought, as once again, he tightened his grip and pushed. There wasn't the slightest indication of movement. Yes, a nice room, a comfortable bed. Jung had delayed having him questioned, which was no small mercy, but had been unable to manage anything more than a comfortable room in which he could spend the night.

The clock struck three and Richard reached into his jacket and removed his last cigarette. How appropriate, he thought. It was unlikely that Jung could keep him alive much longer anyway. The only mystery remaining was how they would do it. Strangled probably. That was the easiest. Of course, if they feared a serious investigation, they might decide to drown him. A rather undignified way to go, having one's face shoved into a tub full of dirty river water. How many men would it take to hold his head underwater? If they tied his hands behind his back, probably one, but maybe, just maybe, two. Would the IQ of his executioners add up to even half of his? Such were the equations of power.

It was annoying. He was going to be killed and he didn't even know by whom or even why. Presumably, power was the reason or a vendetta by one of his numerous enemies, but that still left the question, by whom, unanswered.

He sighed. He had always suspected his death would be stupid and pointless. After all these years, he had achieved nothing more than to be within reach of the brass ring. And now it would fall out of his grasp and all his effort would be wasted. Not that that was an unusual story.

Unbidden, his mind listed the untimely deaths of his political comrades. Though there were a fair number of inexplicable suicides, unfortunate accidents, and unsolved crimes, none were considered overly suspicious. Few rated even two lines in the international news. Sad – murder was such an accepted part of the Reich's political reality, and the rest of the world happily swallowed the propaganda. Even the most intrepid reporters within the NAU did little more than add the word "suspicious" to the all-too-brief obituary of a possible opposition figure.

I'm going to die, and I've achieved nothing. He paced the room and returned eventually to the window. *Nothing.*

My time could have been better spent. Writing history. Living at Szaflary, digging into dusty archives, interviewing people, organizing a coherent history of the Underground.

His thoughts turned again to Kasia and the children. He would miss them! Oh, how he would miss them! Of Greta, he thought not at all. Funny that – when she was around, he was utterly enchanted, but now, as he faced the end of his life, the absolute negation of all his work, it was only Kasia who came to mind. God, how he loved her! How he missed her! How could he have ever left her? And the children? How could he have given them up so easily? He was so proud of them all, they were marvelous! Stefi, in particular, was unbelievably talented. He sniffed his amusement. Even if he had achieved nothing, he would leave his legacy – especially in her. She would make an impact. Somehow she would achieve what he had failed to do.

There was a noise outside the door. Richard listened, heard the key turn in the lock, but he did not turn to face his visitors. He winced as the lights were turned on, but continued to look out the window at the heavy darkness of the brief summer night. It would be dawn in only an hour or so. But would he see the sun rise?

37

"**R**udi! Please! Every moment we delay could mean death for my father!" Stefi begged as the Führer directed his servant to pull out a reasonable suit of clothing for him.

The Führer shook his head and pushed back the few strands of hair that had fallen onto his forehead. "Why do these things always happen at night? When did you say this happened?"

"This evening, after we had dinner together."

"Ach. Why didn't you come to me then?"

"I tried, but they wouldn't let me in."

"Well, you must understand my dear, my in-laws are very influential. On nights like this one, I have to leave standing orders. It would hardly do to have them make an exception for my mis... What did they say?"

"They said I had to wait at least until your guests were gone. They wouldn't even listen to my news."

"Why didn't you go through channels?"

"I tried, but your office claimed the people who arrested Father were working under your orders. I know that's not true. I know that it's more than that, but they wouldn't listen!"

"Of course, *Mäuschen.*"

"So I came back here."

"Ach, *Schätzchen*, my guests just left. I'm tired. And you know, I was planning to spend the night with my wife, in her *bed*, you understand." He said "bed" as though the word itself contained visions of hell. "She demands that of me now and then," Rudi offered by way of apology.

"I understand," Stefi whispered, trying to keep a balance in her voice between injured love and genuine understanding, "but we must hurry now, before they hurt my father. Please come!"

He waved his hand at her and then nodded at the suit that had been brought out. "It will only take me a few minutes to dress. I'm not going to be seen wandering around in my robe like some sort of demented Caesar."

"Of course, darling." Stefi knew she should carry on about how dignified he was in any situation, in any clothing, but she decided instead to begin explaining what had happened. Once she had laid out the base details, she continued, "I don't know who did this, of course, but I did get the license plate of the automobile. And they were working, at least nominally, under your authority..."

"Ach, there are many investigations, dear. I have to give them some authority, otherwise they'd never be able to act, and, of course, I can't keep track of every detail." Rudi turned to Stefi and kissed her sweetly on the cheek. "You do realize, that you should have waited until morning with this. It is, after all, just a normal investigation."

"I don't think so. As I tried to tell your staff, I'm sure it's much more than that."

"I know you worry about your father, *Schätzchen*, but I can't have you storming in while my in-laws are here." The Führer gave her a look of affectionate annoyance. "I hope you appreciate that."

"Oh I do!"

"Bad enough you convinced them to pull me out of my wife's bed. She'll make me pay for that later, you know."

Stefi nodded solemnly.

"Though I must admit..." But the Führer didn't bother to finish his thought other than to give Stefi a leer.

Stefi risked ignoring it. "We can find out exactly who it was via the number plates, but I think I have a better lead."

"And what is that?" The Führer helpfully raised his arms to slip them into the sleeves of his shirt. He tilted his head back slightly as the servant did up his buttons.

"Father told me at dinner that he had an important meeting with one of his agents. He was en route to that meeting when he was arrested."

"Oh." The Führer sat down to have his trousers slipped onto his legs. He stood to have them pulled up and zipped. To Stefi, it looked a lot like the way her little brother Piotr was dressed by his Mommy.

"I don't know what was so important that this agent had to meet with Father personally," Stefi explained as a belt was slipped through the loops of the Führer's pants and buckled for him, "...but luckily I know who he is. Doubtless, whatever he has to say, it's the reason Dad was arrested."

"Hmm." The Führer pursed his lips. "So you don't think it was a legitimate arrest?"

"No!" Stefi snapped, only just managing to stop herself from adding: *you idiot!* Taking a deep breath, she said softly, "Someone grabbed my father because of his loyalty to you! They're going to kill him because of what they think he knows!"

"And where is this agent now?"

"My mother is bringing him here." At least the hours Stefi had wasted trying to get in to see the Führer had given Kasia enough time to pick up Feliks and his wife so Stefi was spared spinning any stories about why they weren't present. They would be arriving at the *Residenz* within minutes.

"Your mother?" The Führer sat down again to have his shoes slipped on and the laces tied.

"Yes. You remember, my mother is *Volksdeutsch*—"

"Um. Speaks with a Slavic accent even." The Führer leaned back and sighed, "Gives her words an exotic lilt, I find."

"Yes, yes," Stefi agreed impatiently. "Well, you'll remember her family never accepted Reich citizenship."

"No? Oh, oh yeah."

Stefi wasn't sure if Rudi truly remembered the conversation in the sauna or if he was only placating her, so she explained, "As my father told you, it's so they could more efficiently work for *you, mein Führer*. After my father met my mother, he convinced her family not to change their status so that they could spy for him. My mother's sister and her husband, in particular, have infiltrated deep into the Home Army. My father has been overseeing their careers for years – you see, they've provided him with much valuable information and as they've worked their way upward, my father was hoping to have them infiltrate all the way into the top of the organization so that he could finally break it!"

"That is quite brilliant!"

Stefi grimaced.

The Führer stood. Again he co-operatively held his head high so that his tie could be put around his neck and knotted. He waved away his holster, shrugged his jacket on and strode over to the mirror. He sucked in his breath, threw back his shoulders and surveyed his image. "Good enough." He nodded his satisfaction, then turned to Stefi. "Shall we go?"

As they strode down the hall to his office, a minion approached and informed the Führer that Frau Traugutt was at the front gate and had asked to see him. "She has two people with her, a man and a woman."

"Ach, as you predicted, my sweet!" The Führer grinned at Stefi. He turned his attention back to his subordinate who scurried along sideways in order to keep up with the Führer while still facing him. "Yes, of course. Have them frisked and brought to my office immediately."

"Yes, *mein Führer*."

"Oh, here," the Führer added, motioning to Stefi to hand him her slip of paper, "check out this license number. See what office it belongs to and contact whoever is responsible immediately. I want him in my office within the hour."

"Yes, *mein Führer*!"

The minion disappeared to carry out his orders and the Führer, Stefi, and assorted personnel continued down the long hallway. The clock chimed and Stefi counted: one, two, three, four. Oh God, four in the morning already.

More than six hours since her father had been arrested. A lot could happen to a person in that length of time.

They went into the Führer's office and he threw himself tiredly down into an armchair. "Come here, *Schätzchen*." He beckoned to Stefi.

She sat down on his lap and he embraced her, nuzzling her neck with his unshaven face. It scraped her neck painfully, so Stefi pulled away, then to cover her indiscretion she kissed him. He responded enthusiastically and began caressing her as they kissed. His hands wandered along her body as his tongue probed deep into her mouth.

"Rudi..." Stefi gasped. She managed to make it sound like passion though it was nothing more than a gasp for fresh air. In his rush, Rudi had not bothered to clean his mouth and the stench was overpowering. Controlling her revulsion with some difficulty, Stefi pulled back from him and smiled sweetly. "My mother is going to be here soon."

"Ah, yes, I've heard she's an upstanding woman." The Führer released Stefi and she climbed out of the chair.

A few minutes later, there was a knock at the door and Kasia and her two companions were escorted into the office. Kasia rushed over to Rudi as he stood to greet her.

He reached out his hand to her and she grasped it in both of hers and pressed it to her breast. "*Mein Führer!*" she breathed, her voice laden with awe and devotion. "Thank you for seeing us!"

Stefi was impressed by the depth of her act.

"But of course, my dear Frau Traugutt." The Führer pressed his free hand reassuringly against hers so that all four of their hands were resting as a great lump on her breast. "I see you all too infrequently, and I would have certainly hoped to have seen you in better circumstances than these!"

"Oh, yes. Dear Richard, arrested! It's terrible!"

The Führer shook his head. "Yes, I had no idea that it would all be so complicated when I approved...I mean, you know, investigations are rather common for our higher-level officials, but this sounds much more serious. Your daughter said something about *my* life being in danger?"

Kasia turned to her two companions, motioning them forward. "This is my sister, Dorota. And this is her husband, Feliks. I'll let Feliks explain. He's the one who..." She stopped, obviously distraught, and motioned to Feliks to pick up the thread.

Feliks stepped forward and bowed formally. "*Mein Führer!*" He sounded genuinely in awe.

Stefi certainly could hear a tremor in his voice. She looked at Dorota and back to her husband. Both were pale, obviously terrified. It didn't in any way detract from their roles, but she knew it was genuine. She glanced at her mother and saw the tiniest smirk of satisfaction on her face. At long last, Kasia could have revenge upon her sister for the years of rejection she had suffered! Poor Dorota and Feliks had never infiltrated – they were part of the education network and had no need for such duplicity. And now, suddenly they were thrust into this incredible game, speaking their lines on a deadly stage, their only support, a woman they had scorned for twenty years.

Stefi moved closer to the Führer, ready to distract him if Feliks or Dorota fluffed their lines. He placed his arm fondly around her shoulder and let his hand rest familiarly above her breast. Kasia's smirk disappeared.

With careful precision Feliks explained how he was in the Home Army, how he had worked for years under Colonel Traugutt's direction, moving up the hierarchy. He explained that his wife was also involved and paused momentarily as the Führer sputtered his disdain. "Using women like that! How uncivilized!"

Feliks agreed and continued his story. His words came out woodenly, as if memorized. Stefi heard her mother's voice in them, but Rudi would be ignorant of such subtleties, and indeed he nodded his head with interest, unaware of Feliks' nervousness, or more likely, completely aware of it and appropriately pleased. A conscripted member of the Home Army speaking in a theater where the next scene might be death, or a lowly Nazi infiltrator finally able to meet the omnipotent and godly Führer? What did it matter? Both would be equally terrified.

Feliks paused to swallow at the point where his boss, Colonel Traugutt, had moved to Berlin and he had been told to stay in the area of Posen so that he would be close to Berlin.

"So this so-called Home Army have no agents here in Berlin?"

Stefi stiffened, but Feliks avoided the mistake of giving information which he could not know. "Not that I know of."

The Führer walked over to Dorota. He placed two fingers under her chin and gently lifted her face so that she would look at him. "Don't worry, my dear. It is unbecoming for a woman to involve herself in the matters of war, but I understand you did it out of loyalty." He turned toward Feliks and added, "I've heard the Americans put women in uniform. Ugh." He shuddered with disgust.

He turned his attention back to Dorota. "A fine woman like you should be producing children to populate our Reich. Do you have any children, my dear?"

Dorota nodded. "I had two." She turned her eyes downward rather than gaze directly at the Führer.

"*Had?*" The Führer furrowed his brow.

Stefi could see that Dorota was shaking, but she did not know if it was fear or anger that made her quake so.

191

"Yes, *mein Führer*," Dorota answered, with some effort. "Our first child was taken from me by the police, I guess to be adopted, or something." She paused, then raising her head she looked directly at Rudi. "You see, in order to maintain our cover, we were never declared *Volksdeutsch*. We, my husband and I, are not legally married according to Reich law, and that means, our children can be seized."

Taken into care, Stefi mentally corrected, but otherwise she thought Dorota had managed her answer well.

"Oh, my!" the Führer exclaimed. "Well, we'll have to do something about that!" He paced back to Stefi and put his arm around her shoulder. "Do you know what happened to this child? We should get him, or was it a her, back for you."

Dorota shook her head. "Colonel Traugutt felt that it would be too suspicious if our child was traced."

Stefi looked at her mother. Though her expression was calm and sympathetic, she could see her mother was seething. Even after an abduction, Dorota and her family had not sought Kasia's help. Their rejection of her had been that complete!

The Führer was nodding his head. "Ah, Richard is indeed loyal, but still, I'm sure we can do something about this. I'll have one of my staff work on it for you. And, of course, we must make this marriage of yours legal. It isn't proper for a woman to shack up with a man without the blessing of the State."

Dorota nodded. Feliks cleared his throat and the Führer turned to him. "Oh, yes, but you were saying?"

"*Mein Führer*, we, in any case, cannot return to our undercover work. I blew my cover by coming to Berlin to see Colonel Traugutt personally. We were supposed to meet a few hours ago, after he had dinner with his daughter, but he was arrested before I could talk with him."

"Oh? And what was so important to make you give up everything you've achieved?"

"Your life, *mein Führer*."

"My life? Not Traugutt's?"

"No, I've uncovered a plot against *you*. I felt it had sufficient chance of succeeding that it was imperative that I talk to Colonel Traugutt and have him warn you immediately."

"Ah? Who's plotting? The Home Army?" the Führer asked, his eyes already lighting up at the thought of revenge.

Feliks shook his head determinedly. "No. No, they don't have that sort of power."

Stefi held her breath. This was the most delicate phase as Feliks had to strike a careful balance between a credible threat to the Führer's life and yet avoid retaliations against their people.

Feliks glanced at Kasia as if seeking strength from her, then he dove in, explaining how certain members of the Nazi government had approached the Home Army in order to enlist their aid in contacting members of the Soviet security services. "They knew the Home Army existed on both sides of the Soviet-Reich border and therefore could convey information seamlessly from one side to the other," Feliks explained. He continued, telling the Führer that these government officials had apparently wanted to organize an assassination attempt on the Führer during his upcoming visit to Moscow, and expected Soviet help since they knew that there were elements within the Soviet Government that were disgruntled with certain of the Führer's recent actions – most notably his siding with Japan on the issue of who owned certain islands off the Soviet Pacific coast. The Home Army had refused to be involved as they saw no particular advantage for themselves in this conspiracy, but from information Feliks had received, it seemed apparent that the conspiracy had gone forward anyway.

"What is most disturbing, *mein Führer*," Feliks continued, "is that we have reason to believe that they may have decided to relocate the attempt from Moscow to Berlin. When I learned that, I decided that I must immediately warn you. After all, with the combination of the Soviet Security Services and some of your own people, there is a possibility that they could succeed in placing your life in danger!"

"And who is involved?"

"I don't know the full extent of the conspiracy, but I heard two names – Colonel Zhivkov, head of the Soviet secret police in Minsk–"

That name was genuine and Stefi had planted it deliberately, since he was responsible for the torture and deaths of several individuals she had known. She looked at Rudi to see if he was already plotting a revenge.

"And the other?" the Führer asked.

"Adolf Kraus. My guess is that he is also the one who had Colonel Traugutt arrested."

The Führer nodded. "Interesting. He has been carrying on an internal investigation – maybe that was just a cover for..." He turned to the phone and picked it up himself. He barked a name into it and when the connection had been made, asked, "Has anyone traced that license number yet?" There was a short pause and then he shouted, "Keep checking. Meanwhile, get hold of Kraus. Immediately!"

The Führer slammed down the receiver and walked up to Feliks. "That's quite a tale you've told me, young man." Stefi saw how Feliks' Adam's apple rose and fell as he swallowed nervously. "Strong allegations against some of my people," the Führer continued ominously. "I hope you can prove some of it."

"I believe if your people look into Kraus's activities, you will find bank accounts, foreign messages, and other evidence which will support what I've said," Feliks replied stiffly.

Stefi indeed hoped that was true and imagined that Zosia and Peter were still feverishly at work adding whatever they could to the body of evidence.

The Führer nodded, then turning to his private secretary, ordered, "Contact my office, have some of my people on this immediately. Also," he paused and eyed Feliks, "check this fellow's background. Everything you can dig up. And contact the Soviet embassy. I want to have a chat with their diplomat tomorrow afternoon. Understood?"

"Understood, *mein Führer.*"

As the private secretary picked up the telephone, the Führer added, "And don't forget to trace that child. It is a tragedy for a good German woman like this to be denied her child!"

The secretary nodded forcefully, "Of course, *mein Führer.*"

The Führer turned to his guests and suggested, "Perhaps we should have some coffee and pastries – it is nearly breakfast time, after all."

Before the others could answer, the private secretary looked up from his telephone conversation to say, "*Mein Führer*, they have Herr Kraus on the line. Do you want to speak with him?"

Rudi walked over to the telephone. "Adolf! Sorry to get you out of bed so early." He nodded his head as he listened to Kraus's assurances. "Yes, well, I'm sure the young thing will wait for you!" There was another pause and the Führer giggled appreciatively. "No, no, but look, I've got another young lady here, terribly worried about her father. Seems he was arrested last night and whisked away to God-knows-where." There was another pause, and then, "Yes, I know. You're doing good work. But do you know anything about Traugutt? Richard Traugutt?" Again a pause. The Führer furrowed his brow as he listened, nodding his head intermittently to what seemed a very long answer. "So that was you? Just a minute."

The Führer pulled the phone away from his face and covered the microphone with his hand, but he did not say anything, he just looked surprisingly thoughtful. After a moment he put the phone back to his ear and said, "Have you seen him personally?" Again there was a long pause, then Rudi asked, "Yes, but have you seen him personally?" A short pause, then, "You have?" Another long pause, then the Führer said, "I see. Released already." Another pause. "Oh, you think. That was your orders?" Again a torrential explanation, then Rudi reiterated, "So you did see him, and ordered his release. Yes, I understand." A few words were said, then Rudi agreed, "Yes, you never expected them to pick him up. Of course.

Over-enthusiasm. Hmm. So where is he?" The Führer listened some more and then repeated, "Jung. I understand. Okay, we'll check into that." He listened and added, "Yes, of course! Look, I want you in my office – there are a few things I need to discuss with you." A further pause, then "Yes. Now." The Führer slammed the phone down.

Stefi looked at him expectantly. "What did Kraus say?"

"Ach, you heard. His office was behind your father's arrest. Claims that he did not expect them to actually haul him off the street. Was supposed to be an interview in the office tomorrow – at a civilized hour. Once Adolf found out what his subordinate had done, a fellow named Jung, well he left a party to go and have a chat with Richard. They had him in an estate outside Berlin. Very civilized. They talked a few minutes, Adolf apologized to your father and ordered his release. He left before the car had been organized for transporting your father back into town. That's all he knows. He's going to check with Jung to make sure that is what happened."

"Oh God!" Kasia moaned.

"Our only hope," Feliks offered, clearly warming to his role, "is that they thought I had already talked to him and they kept him alive long enough to try to find out how much of their plot has been uncovered."

The Führer looked in surprise at Feliks. "Oh? You think they're still holding him then?"

"Yes, *mein Führer*."

Stefi moved close to the Führer. "Rudi, now that they know you're on to them, if Dad is still alive, they'll kill him!"

The Führer raised his eyebrows.

"Even though he hadn't yet talked to Feliks, he now knows what sort of questions they've been asking him. He's dangerous to them!"

"And he might have information from other agents," Feliks suggested.

"Yes!" Stefi agreed. "He might have valuable details! You've got to call Kraus back and tell him that if my father doesn't show up alive somewhere, he'll be held personally responsible! Not this Jung character. He's hiding behind him. You've got to make it clear that you're not accepting any stories. My father didn't meet Feliks yet, he doesn't know anything about the assassination plot – Kraus must realize that by now, so he can be stopped from silencing my father – but only if he's convinced that he'll be held responsible for whatever happens. Please! Call him back now and tell him that!" Stefi begged, her hand on his arm. She was so close to him that their bodies touched.

The Führer paused, looking at her as if surprised at her sudden involvement in the manly art of strategic planning.

195

"Don't let Kraus know you know about the plot. Just tell him you want Traugutt back here, safe and sound and as lead investigator, it's his responsibility to see that that happens."

Still Rudi hesitated.

"Rudi, my father has been your loyal lieutenant. For him, please. For me," Stefi whispered intensely. She let her body brush against the Führer's, enticingly reminding him that there was more at stake than one subordinate's life. "He's one of the few men you can truly trust! His life is on the line for you. All you need to do is demand that he show up alive and it will happen."

"And will I get a thank-you present?" the Führer asked softly, nuzzling Stefi's ear.

From her position, Stefi could see how her mother turned her gaze toward the wall, how Feliks shuffled nervously, how Dorota blanched at this putrid display of affection. Stefi ignored them, the cowards, leaned into the Führer's affectionate embrace and murmured, "Of course."

38

*J*ung ran his hand through his hair and repeated what he had said numerous times already. "Please just sign – the charges are minor. I'm sure nothing will come of it. Your worries are groundless, I can assure you."

Richard did not respond. He was sitting on the couch, leaning back, his arms folded in a gesture of stubborn patience. Having determined that Jung had no authority to free him, Richard's strategy had been reduced to simply waiting until his time was up. Though he didn't know how long Jung had been given, Richard knew that it was best to carry out certain actions under the cover of darkness.

Richard could hear the twittering of birds. Incautiously, he let his gaze stray to the window. There was a hint of gray.

Jung twisted around to follow Richard's glance then sighed. "Ah, yes. I'm afraid we're out of time." He stood and walked over to the door and opened it. Three thugs waited outside.

Richard stood and went to the door as well, but he ignored Jung, addressing the thugs instead. "Get me breakfast!" he ordered. "And make it something nice. I'm hungry." He turned and strode away, clearly expecting his orders would be obeyed.

The thugs looked at Jung, who simply nodded in response. Once one of the thugs had left, Jung addressed Richard. "I'll be back after you've eaten." He left without waiting for a response.

Within ten minutes, Richard heard the key in the door again. That was quick, he thought grimly. He hoped they were bringing food and not a tub of river water. God, what a mess that would be...

Jung came into the room but he had no food with him. "Colonel Traugutt," he said, his voice carrying a note of confusion, "there's a phone call for you. From Kraus."

Richard raised his eyebrows but otherwise did not comment as he followed Jung from the room. "What have you told him?" he asked, just before picking up the phone.

Jung shook his head. "Nothing. He just said he needed to talk to you immediately."

Richard picked up the phone. "Kraus? Good of you to call."

"Ach, Richard! I'm glad to hear your voice, dear friend. I'm afraid there's been some sort of mistake! I gave my lad orders to release you, but I've found out that he kept you overnight! I hope you were comfortable?"

Richard snorted. He could hear the tell-tale clicks which warned him the conversation was being recorded. So, Kraus was in denial already. Interesting.

"Richard? Are you there? Did you hear me?" Kraus sounded somewhat desperate. "Look, I realize that I may have said some things last night that sounded a bit rough. I mean, I was drunk, I really don't remember everything that went on. Jung pulled me out of that party, I didn't expect...Well, anyway, I was a bit angry about that stunt you pulled with my men, last week. I know I shouldn't have been, but, well, we're all human, aren't we?"

Richard left the pause hanging.

"Richard? You are there? I was saying, I'm sorry if things got out of line. Are you alright? I assume you were well treated. I mean, I know my people should have never held you...You are alright, aren't you?"

"I'm fine," Richard assured him. "Just get me out of here now and we'll call it quits."

"Yes, of course! I'll have Jung arrange a car to take you back into town."

"Jung himself will drive me wherever I say," Richard corrected. "And only Jung."

"Yes, of course, wherever you want."

"And I'll be making several phone calls before I leave, understood?"

"Oh, but of course! Don't tell me they haven't let you call anyone?"

Richard handed the phone to Jung. "I think your boss has some instructions for you." He walked across the room and sat in one of the armchairs. Kraus had telephoned and acknowledged Richard's presence at the estate – that meant, Kraus had every interest in getting Richard outside its gates, safe and sound, and there must be witnesses to the event so that he could wash his hands of Richard's fate. But what would happen outside the gates?

Richard rubbed his forehead. He felt exhausted and unable to think clearly. When Jung hung up the phone, Richard asked that his home number be called. The connection was made and Lodzia picked up the phone, formally announcing the Traugutt residence.

"Lodzia, get my wife on the line," Richard demanded.

"They're not here, *mein Herr*. They've gone to the *Residenz*."

"They?"

"Your wife, your daughter Stefi and the agents you were planning to see," Lodzia answered obscurely. "I've been asked to tell you, *mein Herr*, to call the Führer's private number."

The agents he was planning to see? Clearly things had gotten rather complicated and Lodzia was warning him to play along, but he certainly could not ask for more information, not over an insecure line. "Fine. I'll call there. And just for the record…Ah, is Paul there?" There was no point saying anything to Lodzia, she could not legally testify in a court.

"He's, er, out, *mein Herr*. Will Johann do?"

Richard waited for Jan to come to the phone, then quickly explaining his situation, said, "I want you to know that I'm at the Interior Ministry estate near…" he looked up questioningly at Jung.

"Southwest of Erkner."

"Near Erkner," Richard repeated. How convenient, a stone's throw from the river Spree. "I was arrested and detained under a secret indictment which Kraus ordered. He has already stated it was in error and I'm being released. Do you have that?"

"Yes. And Dad…"

"What son?"

"Are you coming home now?"

There was a pause as Richard wondered what exactly Jan's question meant. In the background he could hear Piotr crying. "Yes, I'm coming home."

He called the Führer's private number next and was let through immediately. "Ah, Richard!" the Führer's jovial voice greeted him. "You've cost me some sleep you know!"

"My apologies, *mein Führer*. That was certainly not my plan." Richard struggled to keep the irritation out of his voice.

"I gather you've had a bit of an adventure? What? No missing teeth, I hope? Heh?"

"No, I'm fine." Richard grit his teeth. "It was Kraus..."

"So I've heard, so I've heard. Well, look, I imagine you're rather tired, and in fact, I could do with some sleep myself. Why don't you get yourself home and cleaned up and rested and then after you've talked a bit with your man, come and see me. I want your take on what all this means."

Not knowing what Rudi was referring to, Richard simply answered, "Of course, *mein Führer*. Always at your service." If there was some way he could have sent acid down the phone line, he would have done it then. No missing teeth, the man asked. If they had tortured him, all Rudi would have wanted to know was whether or not there was a videotape available!

"Oh, yes, your daughter wants a word with you. She's a devoted girl, do you know that?"

Without waiting for Richard's answer, the phone was handed to Stefi. "Are you alright?" she asked, a tremor in her voice.

"Yes, they didn't touch me. Just tired, that's all. I'm going to get the assistant here to drive me into Berlin."

"Don't do that. You may hit trouble on the road."

Richard recognized her concern. "I have reason to believe I can trust him. I'll give you his name so–"

"Please, Father. Take the train in from Erkner to Friedrichstraße."

Why, he wondered, was she announcing his plans in advance? It didn't make sense. "Stefi, that doesn't–"

"Stefan, Mathias and your agent Feliks will meet you at the station."

"Feliks?" Richard was completely confused. Was this one of the agents Lodzia had mentioned?

"Yes, he's alright. They didn't get him."

"Oh. What about Jörg?" he asked, to mask his ignorance.

"He's under arrest. The Führer doesn't know yet whether it was incompetence or complicity, but he's been relieved of his duties."

"Ah. Stefi, I still don't see–"

"Please. It'll be safest that way."

He could hear the tension in her voice. "Okay, honey. As you insist."

It was a long wait for the train and a long ride into the city. The entire time, Richard expected one of Kraus's thugs to attack, but nothing happened. There were several policemen on the platform and several more on the train, and perhaps even Kraus realized how suspicious an assassination attempt at this juncture would be. Yes, Stefi was right, it was probably safer on public transport. Witnesses around, no possibility of the driver suddenly turning onto a dirt road in some woods. Of course, they

199

might have done better coming to pick him up at the gate, but perhaps they knew he wanted to get out of there as soon as possible.

The train arrived and Richard stepped off it into the welcoming bustle of the already crowded station. He breathed a sigh of relief as he saw Stefan and Mathias approach him. There was a third man with them whom Richard did not know, and he assumed this must be Feliks. Stefan and Mathias placed themselves protectively on either side of Richard and fell into step with him, Feliks walked behind. "Where's everyone else?" Richard asked Stefan.

"I believe your son and daughter are en route," Stefan assured him, glancing nervously in every direction.

They walked to the steps and were just about to descend when Feliks suddenly threw himself against Richard knocking him to the ground. Almost simultaneously there was a shot. Then another. Stefan and Feliks both fired off toward one of the other platforms. In the great hall of the station the echoes made the shots sound like a barrage. The crowd on the platform was scattering, there was shouting and some screams, various people had taken cover on the ground and behind walls.

Suddenly it was quiet. Richard looked up and saw that police were everywhere, pointing their weapons at everyone. Feliks rolled off him, but stayed in a low crouch. "Stay down," he warned. Richard did. He could feel his heart pounding. God almighty, hadn't he endured enough for one night? An assassination attempt! Stefi had been wrong, she should never have…Or had she been wrong? He saw police approaching and he climbed to his feet and presented his papers.

"It was aimed at me," he said coolly. Stefan and Feliks had climbed to their feet unharmed, Mathias wasn't moving.

One of the policemen inspected Mathias. "He's dead."

Richard glanced down at the corpse. "He's one of my bodyguards."

There was a minor commotion along the platform and Richard looked to see Pawel arguing with a policeman. Stefi was with him.

"He has a gun," the cop announced to his comrades.

"That's Colonel Traugutt's son and daughter," Stefan explained. "Bring them over here."

Once Stefi and Pawel had brusquely greeted their father, Pawel showed the police his gun permit and then explained, "I saw the bastard aiming at my father. I got off a shot, but he got away, down that platform." He pointed to the adjacent platform along which both Stefan and Feliks had aimed.

The police conferred with them for several minutes, interviewed a few witnesses and agreed that a least one person had fired at Richard. His bodyguard Mathias had been hit, while his other bodyguard Feliks had saved his life. Stefan, Feliks and Pawel all gave a brief description of the perpetrator. Richard was told that all the station entrances had been closed, all persons leaving were being carefully inspected, and the station itself was being thoroughly searched.

As they discussed the details, Richard took the two steps over to where Mathias lay. He stared at the body on the ground with casual disinterest, not even bothering to feign concern. Leszek will be pleased, he thought.

One of the policemen came to stand next to him, and together they watched as the corpse was wrapped and carried off. "We'll find the bastard," the policeman assured him. "A number of our men headed down that track – whoever it was won't get far."

"Your men saved your life," another one said. "They've done a good job," he added, offering up what was apparently a professional opinion of praise.

"Yes, Father," Stefi agreed, joining them. "Their loyalty to you and the Führer is beyond doubt." She linked her arm in his and said to the police lieutenant. "Could you escort us out, please?"

They went, as a group, down the steps and into the hall, heading toward the exit.

Richard watched, in a trance, as the police lieutenant explained who they were and saw them through to the street. The lieutenant took his leave of them, promising that they would be contacted as necessary for further details. Richard turned to watch him go, then he looked at the faces that surrounded him. Stefan, who had convincingly fired at nobody, his son Pawel, grinning smugly, proud of his precise aim, this unknown Feliks, obviously a part of the plot, and his dear daughter Stefi who had saved his life.

He turned to Feliks and extended his hand. "Have we met?"

Feliks shook his hand warmly. "Ah, Colonel Traugutt, I am your trusted agent, come in from the cold."

"From the cold," Richard repeated numbly. The fear of the previous night, the shock of gunfire, and now all these strange events left him feeling almost dizzy. He summoned up enough energy to reply, "I guess we have a lot to discuss."

"Yes, *mein Herr*. And I guess we owe you and your wife an apology."

"We? An apology?" Richard repeated, confused. An apology?

"All in due time," Stefi interrupted, reminding them they were still in public. She gestured toward Feliks, "The Führer is impressed by our Feliks here, trusts him, it seems. I suggested he take Jörg's place as your bodyguard. He's agreed."

A replacement for Jörg. A trusted replacement for Jörg. He would be free! "And is there a replacement for Mathias?" Richard asked slowly.

"As it happens, *mein Herr*," Feliks volunteered, "my wife, that is, your wife's sister…"

Kasia's sister. An apology. Of course!

"…is very well trained with weapons and could serve as your bodyguard at your house while I will accompany you, along with Stefan here, on any outings. That is, of course, if you will accept such unconventional protection."

"Oh, I have no problem with it." Richard began relaxing somewhat, as the ingenuity of Stefi's plan was slowly becoming clear. "But will the Führer approve?"

Stefi grinned. "Oh yes, I'm sure he'll be amenable. He was impressed by the professionalism of both your agents, and he has much to thank them for. They've given up their positions to protect him – I'm sure he won't object to their both being employed by his most loyal and dear Richard."

"Loyal and dear?"

"Yes, it seems the whole attack was precipitated by your loyalty to Rudi. Terrible, isn't it?" Stefi gave him a wink. "Kraus was involved in a plot on the Führer's life, and you and Feliks and his wife all risked your lives to warn him. He is indeed grateful to all of you."

"Kraus, eh? Anyone else?"

"I'm sure he'll tell us. Poor fellow has a lot of questions to answer. Then I'm afraid he won't be long for this world."

"No great loss." Richard felt rather amused and quite curious as to what had been happening in his absence. Before anyone could say more, he saw Leszek opening the door of their car and Kasia emerging from within, coming toward him. They embraced tenderly.

"*Moja kochana Kasiu!* I'm back! I'm free!" he whispered in Polish. "Oh my love, I've missed you so much."

"I've missed you, too," Kasia whispered in reply.

"Can you forgive me?" How could he have ever left her?

"Of course, I understood: you did what you had to do."

He stroked her hair, bent down and kissed her warmly, hugged her again, and with his lips pressed close to her ear, asked, somewhat rhetorically, "How about I move back home?"

Kasia pulled back to look at him with those beautiful, liquid brown eyes of hers. "No, Colonel," she whispered coldly. "You were right – it is good strategy, and we certainly can't let emotions interfere with strategy."

*A*lex glanced along the dim tunnel that was the entrance of the building. Fifth Avenue huffed and puffed noisily outside one of the openings, people streamed along the other passage, the one that let into the subway. Lots of people, but no one obviously associated with the balding man who stood before him. "Don't you guys have any real news to report?"

"We only want your comments, sir. In the interest of fairness."

We? We the people? We the press? We – me and my tapeworm?

Alex sighed his resignation. They had managed to trap him at the entrance to the American Fund headquarters five out of the last ten times. Was he really so popular? Why not call his flat? Perhaps it was more exciting this way, more up to the minute. "Alright," Alex conceded. "But let's go somewhere where we can talk – this waterfall is driving me nuts." He gestured at the pathetic, albeit noisy, stream of water that ran down one of the tunnel walls. Doubtless it was supposed to be artistic, or was it healthful? Freely flowing water, refreshing the air, soothing the soul. It was all somewhat pointless, as this was the place the smokers chose to have their cigarettes. They huddled there, as close as possible to their offices and workstations, the addicts, those poor benighted souls who still could not wean themselves from their drug. It made Alex long for a cigarette, but he had promised Anna he would quit, and it had been…He consulted his watch. Ah, six hours now. He was doing well, he should stick with the program. Besides, she had thrown all the cigarettes and his ration card away, and so he'd have to go begging for one, again. He ground his teeth in annoyance. God, how many days until the first of the month? How many more days of scrounging cigarettes?

They walked up the street to a hamburger joint. It was only four o'clock, so it wasn't very crowded, and they were seated immediately. The waitress gave them a broad smile as she shoved huge menus in their direction.

Alex didn't even look at his. Since Anna had decided to prepare him for her departure by ceasing to cook for him, he had become quite familiar with this menu. He knew what he wanted: special number five with coffee and, oh God, if only they'd offer it, a cigarette.

"Okay, so what's up?" he asked the reporter. Then before the man could answer, Alex added, "You have a copy of our statement, don't you?"

"Oh yes! But there are still some things that need to be clarified."

"Such as?"

"Where is Halifax?"

"We don't know," Alex stated wearily. He looked down at the menu, as if reading it.

"Is he in America?"

"We don't know."

"How does the Armia Krajowa feel about Halifax being extradited for trial?"

Alex was surprised that the reporter not only used the appropriate title of the Home Army, but also pronounced it correctly. Clearly, this was more than the usual ignorant hack. "No comment."

"Don't you assume any responsibility for his actions?"

"No." Alex continued to stare at the menu. "As it says in our statement, we hosted his visit here and then parted company."

"But he's married to your daughter. Have you no ties to her?"

The waitress returned and they gave their orders. After she had walked away, Alex remained silent.

"It was your grandchild who was murdered," the reporter whispered intensely. "You explained Halifax had adopted her after marrying your daughter. How is it you know nothing about him now?"

Alex stared across the room. He was quite sick of this. It had been easy for the office to throw Peter to the wolves, they didn't know him. And it was, after all, only figuratively. Peter remained in blessed ignorance of the continual attacks on his character, on his motives, on all the words he had spoken. But it was beginning to have an effect on their fund-raising. Donations were down, engagements had been cancelled. They had supported a murderous criminal. A kidnapper. Were they worthy? Or were they no less disgusting in their tactics than the Reich itself?

It was a question that he had never wanted to hear asked. He tapped his fingers and, without looking at the reporter, answered, "Officially, we have no knowledge of his actions and bear no responsibility. Personally, well, my daughter's private life is private."

"Why did he kidnap the girl?"

Alex shrugged.

"I mean," the reporter said, quite conversationally, "I understand why he'd want to kill that bastard, but why steal the girl? That's so..." He hesitated, apparently genuinely at a loss for the correct word.

Still without looking away from the far wall, Alex heard himself saying, "You have no idea what it's like over there. No idea. They steal children from us all the time. To be adopted, to be worked liked slaves, to be murdered." He blinked his eyes, trying to keep them dry. "My son's wife – her two brothers were taken, and to this day, no one knows what happened to them."

He turned suddenly toward the reporter and looked him in the eye. "They treat it as normal to steal children. For decades now, they have taken our children and no one says a word! They murdered my granddaughter in cold blood – just one of so, so many! And all we hear about is why did Halifax kidnap a child. I'll tell you this: if he did take that child, it would not be surprising." He reached out and plucked an invisible object off the reporter's shirt. He repeated the gesture angrily, over and over, until the reporter felt compelled to shift uncomfortably in his seat. "They grab and grab and grab and grab! Is it any wonder we react?"

"Sir…"

"Don't 'sir' me! You want to know what it's like? Go live there! If Halifax grabbed that child – and that has not been verified!" Alex reminded him. "If he took a child, you can bet at least one thing: that child is better off in his care than it was in that household. It wasn't kidnap, it was…" He stopped, suddenly aware of what he had said.

"Was it his daughter?"

Alex returned to staring across the room. "No comment."

"It's what everybody is guessing."

"No comment. Read the statement, it's all in there."

The reporter pushed aside his notebook and pen. He hadn't written anything in any case. "Look," he said, lowering his voice to imply confidentiality. "Off the record." He gestured broadly toward the crowd of people downing their hamburgers and nibbling their french fries. "Most of these people couldn't give a damn about foreign policy. They liked Halifax, they trusted him. He spoke from the heart. Now, all of a sudden, there is silence, nothing but a guilty silence. We want to tell his side of the story, we really do, but you people just ignore these accusations from the Reich. You do that at your peril. You linked yourself to Halifax, to his story, now you want to disavow his actions. You can't do that."

The waitress arrived with their food and still smiling broadly, set the plates in front of them. Alex looked at his special number five, but somehow he had lost his appetite.

Once the waitress had left, the reporter continued, "People don't care about you. They're not giving to you or your cause. They're giving to him. To that decent guy who spoke to them. Now, all of a sudden, there are all these accusations. Murderer, terrorist, kidnapper. And there is no response! For Christ's sakes, we can't ignore news like that. You know, especially the tabloids. Jesus, we've got to make a living! As long as they keep saying salacious things, we're going to print them. Then when we look for a response, you guys say, 'no comment.' You can't do that. You've got to give us something to write. Let Halifax speak. Maybe through you, maybe some other way, but you've got to let him say what you just said. Explain why he did what he did. People here want to believe in him. They'll listen."

"I doubt that a written statement could convey the complexity of the situation or do justice to his motives."

The reporter raised an eyebrow. "How about speaking directly to us?"

Alex rested his elbows on the table, and his chin on his hands. "How can he speak? You saw what happened last time."

"So he's in the Reich?"

Alex scowled at the reporter. "And you'd report that, wouldn't you? You don't give a damn if the man is torn limb from limb, as long as you get your story out of it. Go to the zoo and throw some meat to the hyenas – there's a story for you."

"I'm sorry, I didn't mean it like that." Even the reporter looked surprised by his apology. "But there must be some way that he can give a statement. Maybe, I mean, I know you have nothing to do with what went on, of course, but maybe you could offer some speculation? An exclusive interview?"

Alex was still thinking about what the reporter had said, but he was not so distracted that he missed the sudden change in emphasis. He smiled at the fellow and shook his head. "Sorry. No. I'm afraid I have to run. Got to take my wife to the airport." He stood and without offering to pay, left his unfinished meal and the reporter and headed for the door.

40

*P*eter leaned back in the comfortable armchair of the Traugutt living room and watched with a sense of ease and satisfaction as someone else served drinks and brought in the trays of food. It was a co-operative effort, mostly among the women, he noted, although now and then he saw Pawel ferrying something into the living room, and Leszek was helping out as well, probably under orders.

He saw how Kasia picked up a squalling Piotr and handed him to Ryszard with an exasperated, "Here! Can't you hear your own son?" She walked off before Ryszard answered her. Peter watched how Ryszard handled the boy, as if he were still rather unused to fatherhood. It was in such sharp contrast to the way Peter interacted with Madzia who was even at that moment straddling his leg, being bounced up and down on an impromptu leg-horse, or Irena who had worn herself out exploring on all fours and now huddled sleepily in the crook of his arm.

"Ow!" Peter yelped. "Madzia, don't do that. It hurts."

Madzia giggled and ceased trying to bite his knee. "Faster!" she ordered and he dutifully bounced her up and down faster.

Zosia perched herself on the arm of his chair. "Doesn't that hurt?"

"Not really," he answered over the sound of Magdalena's pleased giggles. "Nothing hurts me anymore."

"Indeed," Zosia replied obscurely. She looked across the room and Peter followed her gaze. Olek had just come in the door, a crutch under each arm, proudly walking on his new legs. According to the therapists, he would eventually be able to walk with only a cane, perhaps even without that.

Olek hobbled over to Peter. "So, how do you think I'm doing?"

"Great! I had no idea you'd be up and about so soon."

"Hasn't anyone been telling you of my progress?" Olek asked, clearly surprised.

Peter laughed. "Shit! Everyone has! Still, there's nothing like seeing it for myself. Though I still can't believe you guys invited me here. You've lost your collective mind."

"Hey, I'm not going to get married without my best man."

"Anyway," Stefi added, as she joined the little group, "as Olek's physical therapist, we can do no more than trust your papers. If you're found here, it just proves how determined the terrorists are to destroy my ever-loyal father."

"Ah, so none of your elaborate plots to free me, if I'm caught?" Peter jested.

"I don't do miracles," Stefi retorted.

Peter grabbed each of Madzia's hands in his to steady her. "Can't say I really care anymore."

All of them looked at him in surprise. "Are you saying you're suicidal?" Olek asked cautiously, using that tone of voice which one might use with a physician when asking about a beloved, but very fragile, grandmother.

Peter shook his head. "Nothing so active. Just tired, that's all. That thing with…"

Madzia's giggling filled the silence. Zosia stroked Peter's hair affectionately, soothingly.

"Never mind me. I don't know what I'm saying." Peter returned Madzia's broad grin with a silly face just to amuse her. "As usual."

"Well, don't fret about it, you're not a target right now," Stefi assured him breezily. "Not only is Rudi out of town, but Günter's managed to convince him you're in America after all."

"Why'd he do that? I thought Schindler enjoyed goading the Führer with my existence within the Reich."

Olek laughed and pointed at Stefi. "Blame her. She's a bloody genius! She convinced *Rudi* to hound Günter into wishing you out of the country." He said "Rudi" as if the name were a private joke and Peter marveled that there seemed to be no hint of jealousy or even competitiveness in his voice. Just pride, pure pride.

At the thought of supportive spouses, his eyes strayed across the room to Anna as she huddled in conversation with Marysia. He wondered how Alex was doing on his own. Had he worked out that there was silverware in the kitchen drawer or did he exclusively use the plastic utensils that came with his delivered meals? Funny, Peter thought, in the needing-support stakes, it went in a line directly from Alex down through his children and into the grandchildren. Zosia was doing her best to buck the trend, but he suspected it couldn't last – it just wasn't her.

As he watched Anna, he saw how she wiped some tears away. She must be talking about Andrzej. She had not even had a chance to see him since they left for America and now her grandson had preceded her in death. He remembered how his own grandmother had reacted to his sister Anna's death. As bitter as it was for a parent to lose a child, it was against Nature, she had said, using her usual euphemism for God, against Nature itself for a grandparent to bury a grandchild. Not even in her advancing senility, not even then, had he believed she could be so naïve about the state of the world.

Marysia wiped some tears from her eyes as well and glanced across at Olek. The last surviving member of her family. Julia, Adam, Joanna...All of them lost. He saw how Marysia mouthed the words "Thank-you" to him and he realized that she must be talking to Anna about Olek's legs. He nodded his understanding. He had received a lot of gratitude for Arieka's gift. Odd that people wanting to take Arieka's photograph meant Olek could walk again. What a funny world it was.

"...not a word yet," Stefi was saying. "He claims they worked through an intermediary whose name he never learned. Naturally, he claims no knowledge of the plot to assassinate Rudi, denies any communication with the Soviets, says he thought it was solely aimed at Traugutt. Didn't even know the reason why, whether a power move or a vendetta or what. So, either Kraus really doesn't know anything or..." she pursed her lips, "Well, I can't come up with an 'or'."

"That's too bad," Zosia commented. "It would help to know who had it in for your father."

"Not really. It could have been anyone – they're all snakes. Actually, it works out quite well this way. All the evidence you and Peter planted is consistent with Kraus not knowing who's behind it all. That means, we can slot in a name whenever we wish – some incriminating evidence – and get rid of an enemy at will."

"Schindler?"

"No, Dad doesn't think there's any point yet. It would just create a vacuum that would be filled by another competitor."

"I mean, do you think it was Schindler behind the whole thing?"

Stefi shook her head. "It doesn't seem likely, but who knows. Anyway, ever since Dad managed to walk out of this thing unscathed, he's been almost fireproof. He doesn't need bodyguards anymore – everyone knows not to mess with him."

"Poor Kraus is providing an object lesson in how not to advance oneself."

"Yeah, I guess he's not a happy camper," Stefi agreed. "Of course, Rudi's having selective bits taped. I guess I'll get to snuggle up with him and watch it later. Ugh!"

With practiced precision, Olek propped one of his crutches against the other and then used the freed arm to wrap it around Stefi's shoulders. "Poor baby."

Zosia glanced down at Peter with an indulgent smile. "Aren't they sweet?"

Somehow it sounded like an accusation to him, as in: why can't you be like that? Magdalena decided to climb off his leg and he breathed a sigh of relief as she ran off across the room.

"Was she hurting you?" Olek asked.

Peter nodded. "It was excruciating, but she likes it, so what the hell."

He did not notice the sharp look of surprise which Zosia gave him as he was too busy watching Magdalena. It was Genia who had caught her attention. She threw her arms in greeting around her cousin and Genia tried to pick her up in response. Genia lifted her off the floor and gave her a big kiss.

Peter could not look at Ryszard's child without thinking of Joanna. During their visit to the Traugutt household – what was it, just over a year ago! – Genia and Joanna had been inseparable. Now Genia stood there without her cousin, without her best friend. Brown curly hair instead of blond, brown eyes instead of blue. Otherwise the resemblance to Joanna was striking, overwhelming. They had both inherited the high cheekbones which Anna had passed on to Zosia and Ryszard, they both had incredibly delicate features, long lashes, bright eyes, sensuous lips which moved from a precociously mature pout into an incredibly infectious little girl grin almost without transition.

Quite in contrast to Madzia's rather stodgy features, he could not help but think. Thin lips, narrow eyes, straight, dirty-blond hair that would soon lose what little color it had. He could see traces of Elspeth in her round face, in the muddy brown eyes, in the shape of her eyebrows. Of himself, he saw very little. Perhaps a tendency toward moodiness, perhaps sudden, uncontrolled rages. Or maybe, he thought, that was simply that she was only two. He smiled fondly at her. For all her two-year-old tantrums, she was incredibly sweet, utterly determined to be loved by someone.

Irena fussed in his arms and he looked down at his other daughter. Though she was barely half a year old, he could already see that she would have fine features, like Joanna, like her mother. High cheekbones, long lashes, ruby lips drawn into that distinctive pout. She had his eyes, perhaps; the lower lids almost as defined as the upper, but Zosia kept promising that that would disappear.

"She's hungry," Zosia said, taking Irena from his arms.

Freed of children, he stood. "Here, you have the seat. I'll get you some water, if you want."

"Eh, make it wine." Zosia settled in and opened her blouse. "And refill Stefi's glass."

He returned with white wine for both women and saw how the entire little group stared at him. "What? Did you say red?"

"No, it's not that," Olek explained. "It's just that Stefi was relaying what her grandmother told us earlier. It seems there's a bit of a fuss about you in the NAU."

Peter handed Stefi her wine. "America? What's the problem?"

Stefi grimaced. "Seems that your murder of Vogel has made the news. They have a sob tape with his daughter Ulrike and everything. There's even a small movement pressing for your extradition – since they think you're in the country…"

"We don't even have proper diplomatic relations, and they're talking about extradition." Zosia laughed as she accepted her glass from Peter.

Stefi shrugged and continued, "…so that you can be tried for murder."

"Now there's the pot calling the kettle black," Peter commented bitterly. "What are they doing about it? Alex and co., I mean."

"Oh, denying any responsibility for your actions."

"So they're not denying the murder or my complicity?"

Stefi took a sip of her wine. "No. Just distancing themselves from you. No comment on the rest."

Peter shrugged. "Well, it's what I suggested, though I thought it'd be trouble from this end they'd be fending off – not the Americans."

Zosia set down her glass and stroked Irena's head. "I don't suppose it'll make much difference."

Stefi gestured with her chin in Anna's direction. "Grandma's not so sure. She's been talking to Dad about it all. Even grandpa might be having a change of heart about the 'no comment' routine."

Zosia waved her hand in dismissal. "I think it's best to ignore it all. We'll just wait it out and it will die down. I do suppose, though, that it might make you less welcome on your next visit, Peter."

"Yes, I guess I'd better delay getting these numbers removed." He glanced ruefully down at his arm.

Olek looked surprised. "Were you planning on doing that?"

Peter nodded. "If I can find the money. I've been told it may be possible after all, though there may be scarring."

"Still scars are more easily explained away than that," Zosia reminded him, unnecessarily. "You should have had it done the first time you visited."

"It didn't seem so important then, remember?" he retorted, a bit sharply. "In fact, *we* decided that it would take something away from my story if they were removed. *Remember?*"

Stefi and Olek gave each other one of those knowing, we'll-never-be-like-that-glances.

"Find me a snack," Zosia ordered, as she glanced around the room. "The trays seem to be empty in here, maybe there's something in the kitchen."

Lodzia and Leszek were working in the kitchen, putting together trays of food for the party. "On duty?" Peter asked, jokingly, as he reached for one of the snacks on a tray.

"Get the hell out of here," Leszek growled, smacking Peter's hand, the way a mother might do to a child. "We're busy."

"Hey!" Peter raised his arms in mock submission, "Just looking for food for my starving wife and child. Give me a break!"

Leszek looked up from the tray he was preparing. "I heard," he said, his voice threateningly low, "you said it was appropriate that the Colonel had me beat-up. You snake!"

"That's not what I said. I said, I understood his decision. He's got to maintain a very delicate balance here."

"At my husband's expense?" Lodzia asked pointedly. "You have no idea–"

"Oh, I don't? Remember, for me it was for real. I couldn't just leave."

"Neither can I," Leszek responded sourly. "We've tried for over a year now to get transferred, but they just keep putting us off."

"Then quit," Peter suggested, not in the least concerned.

"Quit? Knowing what we know?"

211

Peter shrugged. "Eh, life's tough all over."

"My wife and I are talented, we have skills! We joined up to fight the occupation of our homeland and here we are putting together canapés for the stinking Colonel and his stuck-up brood!"

"Sorry," Peter said, unconvincingly, "I'm having a really hard time working up a tear for you two. Shit, you have a job, you're well fed, well housed, together, among friends, and you know that what's going on here is important. You also know that eventually you'll be moved to some other assignment. Until then, why don't you just do your job right and quit the whining? Hmm?"

"He still had no right to–" Lodzia began.

"Who said anything about rights? Ryszard made a judgment call. He's got to make fifty life-and-death decisions a day. We're not strong enough to fight all this directly, so we have to resort to subterfuge and Ryszard is actually making progress in the hierarchy. If he survives, he could well change things. And have you forgotten that they need changing? Eh? You should count yourselves lucky that one afternoon's discomfort is the worst thing you have to bitch about. Hell, look around you. Lodzia, you could have been snatched and put into a brothel. Just because we don't mention them, just because they're out of sight at military installations, doesn't mean they've gone away. Those women are there day in and day out until they collapse from disease or exhaustion. How's that for a sacrifice? And the camps. Commit a minor crime, offend some petty bureaucrat, and they have you slaving away 'til you drop. Or what about all the genuine *Zwangsarbeiter?* Do you spare them a thought when you're having your pity parties?"

"I've tried to get permission to do some work among them, but *he* refused," Leszek retorted bitterly.

"Oh?" Peter raised an eyebrow in interest. "You want to make some contacts?"

"I thought I might set up a school, but the Colonel said it was too dangerous." Leszek pronounced the words "too dangerous" with a snide precision that quite nicely imitated Ryszard.

"He's probably right, you know," Peter said, somewhat more gently. "Even if his cover holds, his enemies would grab at anything to bring him down. It really is a snake-pit. But look," he added after a second's consideration, "I could really use some help with my Underground Railway. Maybe I could convince him to let you work on that. Are you interested?"

"Anything," Lodzia sighed. "Anything to break the monotony."

"Yeah, it's boredom and fear here. Nothing else. We really need to accomplish something."

"Okay, I'll see what I can arrange." Peter picked up one of the trays and added, "I'll shuffle this into the living room – I can use the practice."

Casually balancing the tray on one hand, he carried it in and, bowing slightly, presented it to Zosia, *"Gnädige Frau,* your choice?"

As Zosia selected a morsel for herself, Olek plucked one off the tray and presented it to Stefi. She accepted it, as if it were a gemstone. Both Zosia and Peter burst into laughter.

Zosia eyed the two in amusement. "So are you going to make it Reich-official, this marriage?"

Stefi's eyes did not stray from Olek's face. "Sure."

"And just how do you plan to tell your dear Führer about this?"

"Pff. He thinks it's his idea." Stefi took a tiny bite from the canapé which Olek had given her and very seductively offered the rest to Olek.

"I told you, she's a bloody genius." Olek accepted the offering and took his own nibble.

Zosia reached for her wine in defense against the schmaltz. "You guys are going to make us puke, you know, with all this lovey-dovey crap."

Still dreamily surveying Olek, Stefi chided, "You and Uncle Adam were worse!"

Silence fell upon the group like a stone. It lasted only a few seconds but it was leaden. Olek gave Peter a quick she-didn't-mean-it-like-that-smile. "Rudi's wife gets on his back about Stefi, and, I gather, others, so he's decided her being married will prove that his wife has nothing to worry about."

"Why would he care what she thinks?" Peter asked, feeling somewhat strange. What was that sensation in his chest? Pain?

"Oh, the family connections. He doesn't dare offend his in-laws."

"It's more than that though," Stefi clarified. "What I did was point out how he had chided Dorota for not being sufficiently feminine and I fretted that I should have children, too. You know, he's wanted a boy, and, as he puts it, his wife's not up to it."

"Is that really the case?"

Stefi shook her head. "Doubtless her only fertility problem is being too terrified to sleep with anyone else. Anyway, Rudi thinks an heir would be nice, someone to inherit his throne."

"An heir? Now? My God, exactly how long does he think he can hold onto power?"

Stefi shrugged. "Forever? Actually, though, that's not his concern. What bothers him is that it's not all that usual for these things to go dynastic – after all, he managed to wrest power from the last Führer even though he had a son all lined up."

"Fair point. We have a real democracy here," Peter commented sarcastically.

"Yeah, so he not only needs a son, but he needs one in a strong position to inherit in his own right. That means: born of a young woman, like me, good family on both the mother's and the father's side..."

"That explains why you had us beefing up Olek's past. Hapsburg blood, of all things!" Zosia scoffed.

Olek jerked his head back in surprise. "Hapsburg?"

"Yes, I'll tell you all about it later," Stefi laughed. "You'll have plenty of time to learn your life story."

"Good switch on the first name," Zosia praised, "Ole Karlsson – makes him sound positively Scandian!"

Peter selected one of the hors d'ouevres from the tray he was holding. "I thought it was a bit rich, calling yourself Karl's son."

Olek frowned. "It wasn't my idea. I'm no relation to that murderer."

Stefi laughed. "It's a joke!"

"You're not your legend," Zosia advised rather more seriously. "You should feel no attachment to any part of your persona, otherwise, you'll fall into bad habits, isn't that right, Stefi?"

"Absolutely! If the name annoys you – all the better. Take it from a pro: the only person you want to be is Oleksander Firlej, the rest is an act and you must never forget that."

"How far along is the planting of the paper documentation?" Peter asked, trying to push the subject along. He was feeling more and more uncomfortable with the conversation.

Stefi draped her arm over Olek's shoulder. "We're doing fairly well. Dad's handling some of it directly. He and Stefan are 'inspecting' various records and when the files are returned, well, they're a bit thicker."

"Ah. Is Olek going to be working for him?"

"You bet. Nepotism is traditional. Anyway, getting back to what I was saying: the kid will have appropriate parentage, it will be raised for power, and perhaps related to someone who might, just for a while, step into power between Rudi and his boy."

Zosia raised her eyebrows. "Your father?"

"Yeah. The babe will be Traugutt's grandson, so there'd be an alliance between our family and the Führer, but no official dynasty, so to speak. Rudi thinks the sprog would also cement my father's loyalty to him, which he now believes is quite important."

"Why does he think that? I mean more than before?"

"Feliks and Dorota. They've brought in all sorts of information, including some indication of my father's network of agents in the east."

Peter plucked another hors d'ouevre off his tray and handed it to Zosia. "But how is the Führer going to believe any child is his?"

"Ah, yes, that part." Olek glanced downward, clearly embarrassed.

"Olek, it seems, is..." Stefi looked at him and giggled, "...well, I've told Rudi the damage was a little more extensive than it actualiy is. So, I'm being nice to the boy next door, a real patriot at that, and keeping myself, um, pure for my true love."

Zosia carefully detached a very sleepy Irena and throwing her head back, sighed heavily. "Take her, Peter. She needs burping."

Peter handed the tray to Stefi and picked up his little girl. He placed her on his shoulder and gently patted her back. "I'll walk around with her a bit, that always helps." He paced away, glad for an excuse to leave the conversation. He needed to be alone, his feelings were in a muddle and he wasn't sure why. Was it Stefi's comment? But why should that matter? He knew better than to care about such things.

Was that the problem? That he was beginning to care? Zosia had been more affectionate lately – like the way she had stroked his hair to soothe him. It was both something he longed for and feared. What was her motive? If he succumbed to allowing himself to feel something, would it all careen out of control again?

Already, things which should not have mattered bothered him. Not so much Zosia's habit of issuing brusque commands when a normal person might simply make requests – he was used to that and used to ignoring it. More like the sly way Zosia had implied he was responsible for not having his numbers removed when he was in America. It shouldn't have mattered that it was she and Alex who had insisted on "not wasting money on something so stupid," when he had suggested exactly that. It shouldn't have mattered that she was rewriting history to cement his guilt about Joanna's death.

So why did it? Because he cared what she said? And if he opened himself up to caring and therefore made himself vulnerable to hurt, could the anger be far behind? Dare he let that demon loose?

Better not to care, it was all in the past. The distant past. Yet it had been less than a year since Joanna's murder, since he had been injured by the bomb, bound into that chair in that cellar, stabbed in the leg, threatened with weeks of horror, forced to witness...He let his mind move away from that time, backward. Only three years ago, he was still at Elspeth's beck and call, obliged to obey her whims, in fear for his life if he disobeyed her, in fear for his life if he obeyed her. It was a bit further in the past, but there were also those months of torture which he could not so easily shake.

Everyone seemed to think he should be over all that, so he told them he was. But was it really possible to simply erase such deliberate

215

dehumanization? Beatings, sleep deprivation, pain-inducing drugs, overwork, exhaustion, hunger, thirst, the repeated, endless, unprovoked assaults. Gangs of them attacking him, brutally sodomizing him with whatever was on hand. Over and over.

He stopped walking. Oh yeah, he had forgotten about that, hadn't he? But his torturer had made no secret of his cover story; despite the lack of a pink triangle, he had been labeled homosexual and every damn sadist in the place had felt the need to teach him exactly what that meant. Over and over. As one went at him with some implement or tool or device, the others – and there were always others – they kicked him, choked him, screamed abuse at him. And then the next took his turn.

He shifted Irena from one shoulder to the other and resumed walking, patting her gently on the back. Gently, gently. He had thought at times they were sure to rupture something vital, he had thought at times, as he lay there, finally abandoned, still in chains on the floor, that he would bleed to death. He had hoped that he would. Close his eyes and never wake up. But he hadn't, he had just withdrawn into an exile within himself. They hated him and his body was theirs, he could do nothing more than try to save his soul.

Peter sat down in the hallway, in a chair near the door, and pressed his cheek against Irena's hot little head. Her hair, what little there was of it, felt as smooth as silk. It had been difficult being so hated. So righteously loathed. So evil and despised that he merited anything – everything – no matter how awful. And it had become so easy to hate in response. To find comfort in unmitigated, irrational, overwhelming hatred. To find salvation in hatred.

He turned his head a bit and looked out the thin window that abutted the door. He could see down the path and to the street, could see how the leaves of the trees rustled in the fine summer breeze. He hated it all – the warmth, the sun, the tree, the twittering birds. It was all nothing but twisted blackness…

Irena burped and dribbled milk onto his shirt. Peter, shaken from his reverie, smiled fondly at her as he wiped the burble off with his handkerchief. The darkness eroded as light streamed in. None of it mattered, none of it was real, he had no past. His life was now, it consisted of his family, his work, nothing else. He did not hate them, because he had no reason to hate them. He did not hate them…

"A penny for your thoughts." Ryszard leaned casually against the wall, holding a drink.

Peter looked up at him, surprised by his presence, unable to determine if it had been sarcasm that had motivated his words. "Eh, they're not even worth that much."

Ryszard tilted his head in that way he had of wordlessly asking questions.

After a long moment, Peter gave in. "I was thinking..." He sighed and pressed his head against Irena's. "I was thinking I must learn not to hate them."

"Who?"

"Them."

"But who are they?" Ryszard asked suggestively.

Peter shook his head slightly. He was well past that point. "That doesn't matter."

"Then what does?"

"The hate. Just the hate." Peter caressed Irena's silky soft hair with his cheek. "One of these days it's going to..." He fell silent. He didn't say what the hate would do, nor did Ryszard ask.

41

*T*he old shed stood outlined in the yellow-orange light of the security lamps that littered the train yard. Peter stopped and carefully surveyed the surroundings. He ran his hand through his hair, brushing out the water which had accumulated from the light, misting rain. Too dangerous, Zosia had complained. No more trips out, that was an order, she had added, then immediately amended that to say it was a request. A cat yowled and Peter jumped with fright. Damn it! She was making him unnecessarily nervous. What in God's name had gotten into her? Ever since Ryszard's arrest, she had been different – or rather, more like her old self. Like the Zosia he had fallen in love with. And that scared him.

He paced a few steps to the next shadowed area and scanned a bit more. She worried about him, she said. But life without risk was not worth living, he had reminded her. Yes, she had agreed, but he was so wanted, so infamous. It was more than ordinary risk.

Still no sign of anyone, the place looked quiet. As quiet as it had been on all the nights he had come here and met up with his students. Then, he had felt a purpose, even as a slave he had felt his life had meaning. It had been worth the risk then, and it was now as well. Why did Zosia want to deny him that wonderful sense of purpose?

In the privacy of the darkness, he had to admit, though, that her concern was touching. She hadn't just ordered him around the way she used to, hadn't simply insisted that if he loved her, he would do as she demanded.

Nor had she attempted to manipulate his actions through Council orders. She had said she wanted to convince him personally. She wanted him to know how much she loved him, how much it worried her every time he waltzed around Berlin, how the children needed him and would miss him if anything happened. And, she had added, quite sadly, how his words at Stefi's wedding, about not really caring anymore, had hurt her and worried her terribly. Was it true? Had he lost all feeling?

Though genuinely touched by her pleas, he was very careful in his response. He had not been immediately moved to adoring obedience, instead, he had told her he would give serious consideration to her words. He had to meet with Marta yet – she had wide connections due to her mistress's constant travels, but he would forego talking to the Schindler boys. Even though they were clearly chomping at the bit, he recognized that meeting them would be too dangerous. So, after this meeting with Konstantin, one with Marta, a few more outside of Berlin to handle the establishment of a safe path, then after that, maybe he would let emissaries handle the rest. Roman had already been given a password, he would know that someone other than Peter might return to guide him. Would that be enough for her?

It would, she had admitted, sounding relieved. A rat scurried out from the darkness and Peter watched as it crossed the wet, oily dirt of the rail yard. Within seconds a cat shot out after it in hot pursuit. He watched the life-and-death drama disinterestedly, thinking only of Zosia. Her face had been drawn in poignant lines of worry for him, her eyes carried a tenderness that he had hardly ever seen. It was one of the rare times they had settled an issue without her screaming abuse at him and he had been drawn to her by her tenderness, by the absolute lack of acrimony. They had embraced warmly, he had felt his desire for her reawakening, his passion stirring. She had been receptive, unaccusing, forgiving. An entire evening of passionate love-making had followed, breaking their self-imposed abstinence with tender words and gasping need.

He smiled at the memory, savored the last vestiges of the physical sensations of her body. He could still smell her lingering scent, could taste her skin, felt the heat of her thighs against him. He began to feel an urgent need for her, and he shifted uncomfortably as he stood there in the darkness. He could, of course, turn around and go back. Ah, but Konstantin had taken some risk to agree to meet him here. Business first, he could make it brief, and then, he could return to more pleasure. With that decided he turned his attention to the job at hand.

With practiced ease, he dodged across the last open expanse to the shed and tried the handle of the door. The wet metal gave way easily and he slipped inside.

"Peter?" Konstantin's voice greeted him.

Peter squinted into the darkness. "Yeah, it's me. Are you alone?"

A small lamp was lit and Konstantin's face emerged, strangely shadowed by the low-held light. "Welcome back." Konstantin extended his hand. The two shook hands, then embraced, overjoyed at seeing each other alive and well. Peter opened the small bag he carried and presented Konstantin with some gifts: cigarettes, two bottles of brandy and some money.

"Money?" Konstantin raised his eyebrows as if in alarm.

"I know you're allowed to have some, so I thought it might come in handy."

Konstantin thanked him, hid a bottle of brandy and the cigarettes among the equipment, and then opened the second bottle. "Let's drink."

They turned down the light and huddled in a corner, passing the bottle back and forth, conversing as they had done years before, like conspirators, like two friends, adrift on a raft in a sea of totalitarian insanity. Just as he had years before, Peter felt that strange balance of emotion: tense with the risks he was taking, exuberant at the expression of freedom, of doing what *he* wanted to do. He told Konstantin a bit of what had happened to him, but was careful to leave out details which could be dangerous. Konstantin explained that his life had been tediously uninteresting.

"At least you'll be free, soon," Peter reminded him, taking a deep drink from the bottle.

"Ah, 'fraid not. I got another eight years lumped onto the original ten." Konstantin grabbed the bottle back and downed some of the brandy.

"Whatever for?"

"Oh, when they came around questioning everyone about you – well, one of our loyal students must have let on about the school we had. You see, I kept it up for some time after you left."

"Oh, God, I am sorry! Any idea who it was?"

Konstantin shrugged. "No point even guessing. They're all cattle. Show them a police badge and they'll turn in their mothers."

"So, I guess you won't be interested in helping me organize an escape route for them?"

Konstantin's eyes lit up. "An escape route? Yes! I'd be very interested!"

"But you just said…"

"Oh, don't mind me," Konstantin scoffed, waving his hand in exasperation at himself, "I know it was only one person who got scared. Anyway, now I have lots more time to kill and one helluva grudge against the bastards who keep us here. So tell me all about it."

Peter had to admit that not much had been set up yet. He had organized the first stage with Roman, but there were no safe houses established. What he was looking for was how much interest they could expect, ways of publicizing it, guides to take people to the first house and possibly beyond. "It'd be right up your alley, but I can't guarantee the quality of the clientele. If one of them betrayed you, it wouldn't be just another eight years that you'd get."

Konstantin nodded. "I understand. But tell me, is that really all you've established so far? You haven't done anything else with your time?"

It sounded ever so slightly like an accusation and Peter squinted in curiosity at his friend. "I'm afraid so." He handed the brandy back to Konstantin. "It's almost empty, why don't you finish it." He was feeling slightly woozy with the combined effect of the alcohol, the closed room, and the inexplicably tense atmosphere.

"I need some air." Konstantin abruptly rose to his feet, walked to the door of the shed and opened it, then stepped out into the darkness of the rainy night.

Confused, Peter rose and went to the door to see what Konstantin was doing. When he reached the threshold, each of his arms was grabbed by assailants who had waited, hidden, just outside the door. Peter realized, belatedly, that he had stepped right into a trap. He struggled against his captors but could not break free.

With a great effort of will, he forced himself to stop. As a man frisked him, finding his gun and removing it, Peter peered into the darkness. He could see at least sixty security police loosely ranged in a circle around them and the shed. Konstantin stood a few meters away, his back toward Peter, lighting a cigarette for himself.

"Why?" Peter asked, when he finally found his voice.

"It's not eight years for teaching," Konstantin answered, over his shoulder. "You should know that. After what I did for them, the scum went and turned me in! That makes twice!"

"But, but how could you help *them?*" Peter gestured with his head toward the cordon of police.

Konstantin turned around to face him squarely. "Not help, my dear friend. I've joined. They've offered me everything – freedom, a career, a rank, money. Everything, if only I handed you to them."

"I don't understand," Peter said helplessly. He had trusted Konstantin so completely, he had walked right into their arms! He felt quite sick at the thought.

"I was tired of being on the losing side. I want to be with the winners. I'm sorry, you were a good friend. But a deal's a deal." Konstantin wiped some of the rain from his face, then suggested, "You know, maybe they'll work a deal with you, like they did with me."

Peter shook his head, dismayed by Konstantin's naïveté. "No. They're going to kill me. They're going to torture me – I've heard for at least thirty days, if they can keep me alive that long – then they'll kill me." And given the information he had so blithely passed on to Konstantin, Roman would be arrested, tortured and killed as well. Of that, he was sure – at least as long as he was alive to witness Roman's agony. The only hope for Roman was that Peter not allow himself to be taken alive.

"Aren't you being a bit melodramatic?"

Peter looked down at the ground, then back up at Konstantin. Peter motioned with his head toward the vast array of police surrounding them. "Why so many police?"

Konstantin turned his head from one side to the other, surveying the crowd. He then looked pointedly at the officer who was in charge of the group, but the officer, who had remained aloof, standing back with his troops, only smiled slightly, as if amused by the theater he was watching. Konstantin turned back to Peter, his face betraying confusion. "I don't know."

"And I bet you had orders to make sure I wasn't harmed. Can you guess why?"

Konstantin shook his head. Droplets sprayed from his hair. "No. Why?"

Ah, so it was true. That *would* complicate matters. "The Führer, *your* leader, wants to make sure I'm in good shape to amuse him with my prolonged and agonized death. And given how instrumental you've been in my capture, don't be surprised if you're invited to view the proceedings. And remember, you'll be expected to *enjoy* them."

Konstantin threw another glance at the surrounding policemen, then looked worriedly at Peter.

"Welcome to the winning side, Konstantin," Peter sneered. "I hope you enjoy the company you've chosen."

"What on earth did you do?"

"I spoke the truth. And that's always a crime here, isn't it?"

"The truth about what?" The rain dripped down Konstantin's face. "To whom?"

Peter did not answer. As he had stood, unresisting, talking with Konstantin, the grip of his guards' hands on his arms had loosened considerably. Peter looked down at the ground again, as if considering his answer, then without warning, he twisted violently, dropping down as he did so, and slipped free of the men holding him. He rolled out from under their befuddled attempts to grab him and bolted for the corner of the shed, turned it, and ran straight at the cordon. The guards in front of him had pressed themselves together, forming an effective wall, but at the last second he veered suddenly and threw himself at the surprised guards who stood more loosely spaced to the side. He rammed into them; they slipped and skidded on the mud and the whole group tumbled to the ground. Peter scrambled to his feet, yanking away someone's rifle that was caught on his arm. Somebody lunged for him and caught his clothing, he swung around, slamming the rifle into the policeman's head. Somebody else clung to his arm, there was another on his back. Four or five of them managed to grab him, hold him, drag him back, but they had been too well instructed to take the bait of his near escape: nobody dealt a killing blow.

Peter fell to the ground under the mass of bodies. He rolled, kicking and fighting. He tried to grab the stiletto he had hidden in his boots, but it was out of reach. He fought wildly, trying to hurt them, trying to cause them to overreact. It wasn't working, and as he felt a rifle butt slammed against his back in an effort to subdue him, as he felt the hands pinning him down, as he felt someone throw their weight onto his head, he snapped the top off his tooth and worked the capsule out of the hollow of the molar. As he struggled though, it dropped unexpectedly forward, out of his mouth and onto the oily mud. It glistened in the dirt – his only hope for freedom! Peter lunged at it, bit into the earth and sucked the tiny capsule back into his mouth. He crushed it with his teeth and as he felt it slide down his throat, he ceased struggling.

For a moment nothing happened and he was only aware of the absolute weight of humanity holding him still. He began to panic as he realized that it wasn't going to work, that somehow he had failed to swallow the poison. Then, there was a sudden, terrifying pain in his chest and along his arms. His heart thundered with some great effort, his body flushed with warmth and he could not catch his breath. His muscles seized up and he went rigid. He struggled to breathe, felt how his head throbbed with the lack of air. He tried to raise himself up, fought against an insurmountable weight. His sight dimmed and the throbbing in his ears drowned out all other sound. Oh, God, I'm dying, he thought. *I'm dying.*

So, this was all there was to it. Dying here, on the greasy, poisoned earth of a rail yard, under the harsh security lights, surrounded by the ever present darkness. He wouldn't get to see the end of the story. Like Allison, like Adam, like his mother...Cut out in the middle, fighting, struggling, dying uselessly...His efforts to do something meaningful had gained him nothing more than this chance to crumple in pain on the filthy ground, suffocating under his enemies. He felt his body weaken to the point where he could not respond, could hardly perceive the din of voices, the way they lifted him up and moved him into a vehicle. He felt himself drifting away from among the living. He could see nothing, could feel nothing, could only hear a waterfall of noises through which one sweet voice rang ever more clearly.

"*You made it, Dad! I knew you would!*"

Part II

The Führer's Wishes

1

"*A*ch, so you've made it!" the Führer absolutely beamed at Kasia, grabbing her hand and pulling it upward to kiss it. "My dear Frau Traugutt, it is such a rare pleasure that you come to one of my parties."

Uncouth. That's the word that came to Kasia's mind. A gentleman bows to kiss a lady's hand, he doesn't haul it upward! She smiled in response to the gesture and even managed a becoming blush as she ducked her head slightly in modest acknowledgment of the Führer's flattering attention. "*Mein Führer*," she cooed, keeping her eyes shyly averted, "you do honor me so."

"Ah, dear Frau Traugutt, it is we who are honored," the Führer insisted, raising his voice slightly to compensate for the music which had just started again. "After all, you are so rarely here." Without even asking, he pulled her into an embrace and swung her around to join the other dancers in a waltz.

Murderer, Kasia thought. My poor Andrzej rots in his mountain grave because of your bloody orders! But what she said was, "I'm sorry that I have been ill so often. This last child has been difficult. I'm afraid as a model mother, I'm a failure."

"Nonsense! The quality of the children you have produced more than compensates for any lack of quantity. Why, your first-born alone is such a treasure, that I will make sure that you are awarded a Mother's Merit Medal, even though you have only had six children."

"And now I have only five," Kasia sighed.

"What? Oh yes, your son. Andreas, wasn't it? Sad. How did it happen?"

"Some military activity, out east," Kasia answered in a dead tone.

"Oh yes, Richard mentioned something about it. He was so young."

"Our boys serve the Fatherland as soon as they are able," Kasia explained mechanically. "Active service in a military academy. Richard insists on it."

"Yes, yes. Your husband is very loyal, very loyal." They danced in silence for a few moments but then the Führer must have noticed Frau Traugutt's pained expression, for he added suddenly, "Oh, that was quite thoughtless of me, wasn't it? You're living separately, aren't you?"

Kasia nodded. "Yes, though we came here together, we're living separately. Richard needs to be near his work, and I have much to do at home."

"Especially now, with a new son-in-law?" The Führer subtly turned the subject away from Frau Traugutt's embarrassing situation with respect to her husband and his mistress. His eyes strayed toward Greta Schindler as Frau Traugutt answered him. Traugutt was dancing with her even as they spoke. A handsome couple, almost regal in their mutual arrogance, Rudi thought to himself. Good connections on both sides as well. She would make a powerful ally for Traugutt, not like this poor little churchmouse that he had married. Ah, the mistakes of young love!

The Führer brought his eyes back to Frau Traugutt's face. What had Richard seen in her? A lot, he supposed. She had those lovely, sad eyes. And somehow she managed to look mysteriously alone even in a roomful of people. Alone, not lonely. She seemed to prefer the solitude of her thoughts to the company of the beautiful people who mingled at his parties. Yes, Frau Traugutt was quite seductive in her own strangely sad manner. If she were younger, he could find her quite attractive.

He searched her face for some sign of her daughter's features but there weren't many. Stefi resembled her father – the high cheekbones, the sharp looks, the ill-contained arrogance. In the beautiful young woman, it left him breathless and occasionally desperate for her attention; in the father, it gave him cause to worry. Was Richard the sort of man who could ever be truly loyal to anyone other than himself? As Rudi spun Frau Traugutt around, he again caught sight of Traugutt and Greta Schindler. The two of them were up to something. It couldn't be love – not with those two. It had to be power.

And there was Günter Schindler, obliviously boring some poor, young thing trapped in a corner. He was so busy weaving his own schemes he was completely unaware that his wife intended to desert him and take all her connections with her to Traugutt. The idiot! Well, Rudi mused, time to tip the see-saw in the other direction for a while.

The music came to a conclusion and Rudi spun Frau Traugutt around with a flourish and embraced her as the echoes died down. He then pulled back enough to look sincerely into her eyes. "Frau Traugutt," he said, with deep sincerity, "It pains me to see you like this, living apart from your husband."

Kasia looked away, embarrassed.

"My dear lady. I will order your husband to move back home. He should set an example for the populace and live with his wife and the mother of his children. On his behalf, and speaking as a man, I beg his forgiveness from you. We men are weak and fallible, and we need a good woman to look after us and forgive our failings. Accept him back, forgive him. Will you do that for your Führer, for your people?"

Kasia went from looking at the wall to staring at the floor. "But of course, *mein Führer*. Of course," she agreed, her voice trembling.

The Führer spied Stefi entering the room with a young man on crutches. "And now, perhaps you will introduce me to the brave, young Herr Ole Karlsson – I see he has arrived, with his young bride."

Kasia and the Führer made their way over to the pair and Kasia introduced her new son-in-law to the Führer, giving only the briefest of biographies before being interrupted by the Führer's assurances, "Oh, but I have already heard a lot about you, young man. Heavens, but I am impressed by your loyalty and the sacrifices you have made to the Fatherland." Eyeing Stefi slyly, he added, "Enough to invite you to a soirée which, I am afraid, you might find is over-stocked with boring old men." He gestured around the room and added, almost wistfully, "But such are the grandees of our fine revolutionary National Socialists. We are aging..." The Führer paused, smiled at Olek indulgently and concluded, "We need men like you. Young men of good blood."

"I am honored, *mein Führer*," Olek intoned with convincing deference.

"Yes, yes," the Führer agreed incongruously, "I know that my dear Richard will have examined every detail of your background before letting his beloved daughter marry you. And, of course, since you will now be working in his office, you must have one of the highest clearances available. He and his assistant have been personally scouring the records and interviewing your acquaintances, and my dear Richard has assured me that you have a most impressive record and family. Odd that we haven't heard more from your family before this."

Olek smiled broadly. "If you are aware of my history, then you are aware that my family had to abandon nearly everything they owned to escape the Soviet invasion. They settled quietly in Croatia and kept a low profile after being forced to flee Lithuania. The Soviets, after all, carried out a ruthless depolonization of the territory."

"And how is it you came to know the Traugutt family?"

"Colonel Traugutt's father worked in Croatia before moving to London. My father worked for him. My parents died and I joined the army, but I kept in touch with the Traugutt family. After I was wounded, Frau Traugutt insisted I come to their home to recuperate."

"And there you met our lovely Stefi?"

Olek smiled fondly at his wife. "Became reacquainted, yes."

The Führer chose to change the subject. "So your family was German but belonged to the Polish gentry?"

"Yes. The culture of that territory was very heterogeneous. We had Austrian, Polish, Lithuanian and Hungarian roots."

"Indeed. A descendent of King Jan Sobieski, I was told. The savior of Vienna. Sad, isn't it, that so much has changed since those times, no? The union of good Aryan nations against the heathen Turk." The Führer shook his head sadly. "Yes, I believe that there were possibilities there that were missed. Maybe we'll do something about that, eh?"

He looked expectantly at Olek, who quite surprisingly seemed to have followed a thread in these rambling words. "I agree, *mein Führer*," Olek said with vigor, "Indeed, one may suppose that after all these decades, what shall we say, two, maybe even three generations of Poles have reached maturity in a Jew-free land. Perhaps they have regained their true Aryan character and that long lost purity."

The Führer turned his attention to Kasia. "Frau Traugutt, you know these people, don't you? What do you think?"

Kasia took a deep breath, then very quietly said, "I cannot deny that part of my lineage hails from that land. Indeed, you are well aware that, from the very first, many of the Third Reich's best officers had undeniable connections to Poles and the erstwhile Poland. They…we provided the first defense against the Asian invaders for centuries, against the Mongols, against the Russians, against the Communists. In this, we have served European civilization loyally and often paid a very high price. Ever since the first German colonists were invited in to repopulate the land and establish new cities, ever since Saxon kings were elected to the Polish throne, ever since royal Prussia chose to remain a fief of Poland, or large segments of the Polish population lived under Prussian or Austrian rule, ever since then, we have been inextricably bound together. Whatever name they carry, whatever language they speak, the people there are part of the *Volk*."

"Ah, but Frau Traugutt," the Führer argued, "we were spurned in our initial offer of a union. Our armies were resisted fiercely, though uselessly."

Kasia looked as though she was having trouble maintaining her composure at the words *offer of a union*, and Stefi quickly stepped in for her mother, saying, "Yes, but at that time, there were so many foreign elements in the population! Jews! Ukrainians!" Stefi waved her hand in dismissive disgust. "All that has been swept aside and the remaining population has been disciplined. They have learned their lessons, I am sure."

Olek shifted uncomfortably on his crutches and Kasia seemed to have fallen into that lonely silence that was her favorite refuge, but the Führer did not notice as he was too busy beaming at Stefi and she at him. "Yes, yes! They have been whipped into shape! Horse-whipped!" He laughed at those words and as his thoughts turned inward, his eyes glinted with pleasure and anticipation. After a few seconds, he regained his presence of mind and turning to address Olek directly, said, "Maybe it is time to change our strategy there. Traugutt's office is the perfect place to research this – what with his being responsible for most of that area. And he's always nagging me about restructuring things there. I want you to undertake a review of our policies in that region and see what you come up with. I'll let him know that I've put you on that job. Are you up to it, lad?"

Olek bowed slightly. "Yes, *mein Führer*. It is a great honor you do me."

"Now, if you will excuse me, I'm afraid there are some things I must attend to before the evening is done." Ever the gentleman, the Führer kissed the ladies' hands and bowed slightly to the young man, then strolled away. Horse-whipped! Ah, that sent a shiver of pleasure along his spine. What would it feel like? Would he find the pain intolerable, or would it be like a beautiful, naked young woman, in the throes of passion, drawing blood as she dug her long fingernails along the skin of his back?

He stopped for a moment in his stride to discreetly rearrange his increasingly erect genitalia into a more comfortable package, but he noticed that his hesitation drew an immediate response from nearby guests who wanted to have a chance to speak to him. Grunting at the inconvenience and slight pain, he started walking again with that purposeful gait that warned people not to bother him. Once he had managed to leave the room for the relative privacy of the hall, he stopped again and shifted everything, trying to calm his thoughts with something boring. At his age! That brought a proud smile to his face. Such virility! Complete and absolute ruler of the vast millions of the Reich! My God, but he was great!

By virtue of his having left the main room and entering the hall, he picked up another half-dozen attendants of varying description. He waved them all away. He wasn't leaving the reception, he just had a bit of business to conduct, and he always preferred privacy. So, with only two bodyguards, two servants and a recording secretary, he walked the short distance down the hall to where the various non-entities were killing time while their betters attended his party.

Altogether there were only six men he felt he needed to keep a close eye on and all six were at the reception tonight. He called over Büttner's personal bodyguard first. He always did it alphabetically, it was easier to keep track of everyone that way. As he walked with Büttner's bodyguard to his private chambers he wondered if he should extend his circle of surveilled subordinates. Kraus hadn't been one of them, and clearly he had been involved in something quite important. On the other hand, it was tedious work – he had to do it all himself as there was no one to whom he could delegate this task. Besides, though Kraus was the fall guy for Traugutt's arrest, it was clear he was working for someone else. The question was, who? Probably one of the six, maybe even Traugutt himself. He could have organized the whole thing to enhance his importance. Or it may have all been genuine. Rudi felt he really would have to get to the bottom of that sordid little affair.

They reached his apartment and he carefully interviewed the bodyguard about Büttner's activities, then sent him back to the room to fetch the next in line. By the time Traugutt's bodyguard came into his room, the Führer was feeling a bit edgy and ready for a drink.

"Here, have a drink with me," the Führer suggested to Feliks as he motioned for his servant to pour each of them some vodka. He sat back in his leather armchair, relaxing a bit, and beckoned Feliks to come stand closer to him. He quite liked Feliks – he wasn't the usual sort of simple, thuggish type who found work as a bodyguard. But, of course, Rudi thought, proud of his deductive reasoning, Feliks hadn't chosen this line of work, it had simply fallen into his lap after his infiltration had been broken.

While they had their drinks, Feliks described what Traugutt had been up to in the past several days. He mentioned several meetings with Schindler which quite surprised the Führer. Immediately suspicious, Rudi demanded to know, "Why didn't Schindler's guard mention this to me?"

"I don't know, *mein Führer*. Perhaps it was while the other man was on duty."

"They're supposed to exchange information," the Führer growled.

"Or perhaps they were told not to, *mein Führer*. I don't know why that would be – the topics were very innocuous."

"You heard what they were talking about?"

"Yes, *mein Führer*, I managed to overhear key words. I would say they talked about economics and possible ways of solving the labor shortage in various sectors. Colonel Traugutt seemed particularly concerned by the problems the farmers have been giving you, their demands for extra farm labor and the like."

The Führer nodded his head. Yes, the farmers. Salt of the earth, backbone of the Reich. Always whining about how hard they worked, always demanding more agricultural workers. If they didn't burn through the people they were assigned, there wouldn't be such a problem. And their wives! With their polished nails and high-heeled shoes! Using the workers as their servants rather than for food production. Those women were spoiled! They should be tending to the chickens rather than wasting agricultural workers. What had become of the hard-working German peasant woman?

The Führer scowled at the thought of how much trouble the farmers were giving him. He had been raised in a city, what did he understand of all these *Land* issues? He had sought some clarity from his advisors. His agricultural minister had suggested that they needed to increase tractor production. So, they needed more industrial workers. Schindler had told him to increase the number of round-ups, but Traugutt had resisted the idea, calling it asinine and pointing out, quite rightly, that they could not harvest the entire population of menials if they wanted workers available in the future. Traugutt had had some idea involving changing the nature of conscription and paying some sort of wages, of motivating workers and importing necessary equipment – and that involved earning money through foreign sales, which meant opening up their markets…All very complicated and when told that, he promised to present the Führer with a well laid-out plan that could be studied, revised, and eventually instituted. It would change the nature of their very society, Schindler had argued. All to the good, Traugutt had answered.

That must have been what the two were discussing. The Führer looked up sharply at Feliks. "Anything else? Has he been seeing Schindler's wife?"

Feliks nodded. He sounded slightly embarrassed as he reported, "They met four times in the past week."

"What about sex?"

"Six times."

"Six?" the Führer asked, sitting upright in his chair.

"She apparently inspires him, *mein Führer*. All four meetings took place in his apartment."

"So at least he's saving on hotel bills."

"Two at lunchtime," Feliks continued, "one in the evening, and once when Herr Schindler was out of town, she came in the afternoon, greeted him when he came home from work and stayed the night, leaving after Herr Traugutt had left for work."

"So she has a key."

"My wife let her in, *mein Führer*. She guards Herr Traugutt in his home."

The Führer motioned for cigarettes. He smoked in silence for a moment, slumping back into his seat. Feliks remained standing, shifting his weight from one leg to the other as the Führer smoked his cigarette.

The Führer casually tapped some ash into the ashtray. "So, tell me, what sort of sex do they have?"

Feliks looked at the Führer in surprise, then remembering his place, dropped his gaze to the carpet. He cleared his throat, then answered, "I guess I'd call it normal, but enthusiastic. Very passionate."

"Handcuffs?"

"No."

"Ropes?"

"No."

"Whips? A riding crop? Anything?"

"No. Nothing as far as I know." Feliks added, somewhat hesitantly, "My wife carries out the majority of internal guard duties. We tend not to discuss unimportant details."

"Ah, how very polite of you," the Führer commented snidely. "Tell me, do you think they're in love?"

Again Feliks looked up in surprise. This time the Führer caught his eye and smiled encouragingly, like a friend inviting a confidence. Poor fellow is embarrassed, he thought.

"I don't know."

"What about Frau Traugutt? She's your sister-in-law, isn't she? Doesn't it bother you to see how her husband behaves?"

Feliks shifted uncomfortably. "I don't really know the woman. In order for her family and myself to maintain our ability to infiltrate into the Underground, we had to..." he paused, as if distracted by memories, "we had to ostracize her and her husband completely. I only met Herr Traugutt a few times, secretly, to pass on information and receive instructions."

"Ah, yes, of course, the Poles would view her as a traitor, would they not?"

"Yes." Feliks sounded almost sad, or perhaps somehow contrite.

"Do you miss your work?" the Führer asked, sympathetically.

"My work?"

"Yes, infiltrating."

"Oh, that. Yes, I guess I do," Feliks answered, then he recovered enough to add, "But of course, I wish to serve the Fatherland wherever I am needed and am proud to be able to work for you directly."

"Hmm. Still, it's too bad about you having to give up your position there. What exactly did you do?"

"I worked in education, acquiring and distributing textbooks."

"Political tracts? Traitorous works?"

Feliks sniffed his amusement and shook his head. "No, just reading, writing, and arithmetic. They were meant for children."

The Führer laughed. "That's the sort of thing Traugutt's always trying to get me to reform. He claims that change is coming sooner or later and we'd be well advised to institute reforms before they are forced upon us by events. What do you think? You worked with those subhumans, do you think they're capable of being educated?"

Feliks grimaced but answered simply, "Yes."

"Do you think they'd co-operate with us if we established an educational system?"

"Re-established."

The Führer raised his eyebrows.

"I'm sorry, *mein Führer*," Feliks rushed to say. "It was a slip of the tongue. I spent years undercover and I had to thoroughly inculcate myself into their propaganda. My point was that they would say that they had a very long and illustrious educational system – having established the very first national education ministry in Europe back in the eighteenth century and having had some of the finest universities on the Continent before they were destroyed..."

"And the point is?"

Feliks wet his lips. "I guess there are divergent opinions in the underground government. Some will not work with the Nazi government under any circumstances, others are more realistic about making changes for...for the betterment of their people."

"And what do you think?"

"I think..." Feliks swallowed, as if forcing the words out. "I think the Reich would be well-served by an educated population and the more the people of the Fatherland learn, the more they are capable of supporting it."

"So you would–" the Führer broke off his sentence as a messenger was admitted to the room by one of his attendants. "What is it?" he asked, clearly annoyed by the interruption.

The messenger approached, clicked his heels and bowed slightly. He leaned forward to impart quietly into the Führer's ear, "*Mein Führer*, word has been received that Peter Halifax was arrested this evening..."

Arrested! The bastard was caught! In their power! In *his* power!! Rudi's heart pounded with excitement. He had the traitor! He breathed deeply, in, out, in, out. Had to calm himself, there were lots of plans to be made. Let's see, where should they do it? When? How long? Thirty days? Could he find someone clever enough to cause that evil man to stay alive for thirty days? Oh, how he would love hearing his screams for mercy! His pleas to be killed! He'd have to attend these in person, it was worth the risk to his reputation. There'd be tapes as well. In stereo, surround-sound! He could show them to Stefi later. Or maybe she'd sit in on the live performances with him? No, she seemed a bit squeamish at times. Fair enough, she was, after all, only a woman. But who could he get to handle the job? And be discreet? Couldn't have any more propaganda fiascoes like last time. No, officially Halifax would be arrested, disappear into the prison system and conveniently die of a heart attack, sometime early on. A heart attack? *A heart attack!*

He turned his attention back to the messenger. What was he saying? How could that be? "A heart attack?" he asked, infuriated. "Those bastards! They've fucked up the arrest and they're covering their tracks!" he raged, not waiting for the answer, "I'll kill them! I will have their heads for this!" He stopped, collected himself, then motioned to Feliks, "You! Out of the room!"

He breathed deeply some more as Feliks bowed and left. In, out, in, out. Calm that heart, calm it right down. There, that was better, that was less uncomfortable. Now that he was back in control, he could get the details. Find out what had happened. Find out what went wrong. Find out who was responsible. He turned to the messenger who stood trembling in terror. "Okay, give me the details."

2

"Couldn't you give us more details?" the reporter asked plaintively.

"We've given you all the details we have," Alex's colleague answered wearily.

Alex glanced down at his watch. Eight o'clock already. It would be dark when they left. He could never get used to that, these early Manhattan nights. It was the latitude, so southerly – the same as Naples! And being on the eastern edge of a time zone as well, that didn't help. It was also, he thought with a sigh, nearing the end of summer. Not that there would be a break in the damn heat. Oh no, that would continue well into September, probably October. Ugh. The air-conditioning never quite made it feel right. It was a swampy, hot, and dark city, tropical even. With its humidity, its sudden torrential rains lasting only minutes, with its alien voices speaking incomprehensible tongues on every street corner, in every taxi, sometimes it felt like he was in the third world.

"Is it true, Mr. Przewalewski, that Halifax's wife, your daughter, not only has some contacts in the Underground, but she's actually a member?"

Alex looked in alarm at the questioner. Where in the world did that come from?

"Is it true she's in the security service of the Home Army?"

Alex shook his head in dismay. "Where in the world do you people come up with this stuff?"

"Then you deny the rumors?"

"What rumors?" Alex snapped. "Are you just making things up to see my response? I'm not going to divulge details of any sort to deny or confirm such nonsense. People's lives depend on my discretion and I resent your attempts to get me to say things which could possibly place my daughter's or other people's lives in jeopardy."

He pointedly turned his attention to another member of the small group who had attended their press conference and asked, "Do you have a question?"

"Yes, sir. What do you or your colleagues have to say about the report that the young girl – your granddaughter – was killed in a bomb blast and not by the security police. And is it true that the bomb was planted by Mr. Halifax and exploded prematurely?"

Alex dropped his head into his hands. He heard his colleagues deny both parts of the question, explaining in detail how the question of the validity of the videotape had already been settled, how this story could not possibly be true under any circumstances, and if no other proof was accepted, it was sufficient to note that no one had given this spin to the events months ago when the tape had originally surfaced.

When he had the strength to look up, Alex added, "Isn't it enough that his little girl was murdered before his very eyes? Now you want to turn him into her killer? What's wrong with you people?" He felt how his colleague gently kicked his ankle, trying to remind him of the necessity of a civil response to the vultures.

"But was it really his daughter?" someone asked. "After all, reports are that the paperwork for her adoption wasn't finalized here in Manhattan until well after the incident. Wasn't she just a decoy, used by him as he set the bomb?"

"No!" Alex snarled. "He loved that little girl! If there were any delays in the paperwork, it was…" He paused as he tried to decide whether or not to admit that it had been his own doing. "It was just bureaucracy. My granddaughter was a wonderful little girl, and Peter loved her dearly. I know that for a fact."

A woman from the back of the room stood. "Excuse me, Mr. Przewalewski, but there are also reports that the officers responsible for your granddaughter's death have all met with untimely deaths since that incident. One, it appears, was quite brutally murdered in Berlin the night before Herr Vogel's murder. Did Mr. Halifax have anything to do with that?"

Alex narrowed his eyes at the woman. "Now," he said patiently, "let me get this straight: you said something about the officers responsible for my granddaughter's death. Is that right? Does that mean that the bomb theory has been abandoned? Or that the Reich is generating so many idiotic lines of propaganda that they can't even keep their own stories straight?"

The woman glanced down in embarrassment at her notes. "I'm sorry, I may have misquoted the information. I believe the original report said something about the officers who had been falsely accused of causing your granddaughter's death, that is, after the bombing..."

Alex sighed heavily. "Young lady..." He felt his colleague kick his ankle again, this time not very gently. He fell silent. His friends were right – he was not in the proper frame of mind to answer these accusations. He had lost his steely approach and was giving in to emotion and anger. He listened to his colleague as he blithely denied any knowledge of the alleged incidents, and then added, for good measure, that it was not only untrue, but even lousy fiction.

"Is it true," someone asked next, "that Peter Halifax's real name was Alan Yardley?"

Alex saw no harm in acknowledging it. Someone at England House must have recognized him and sooner or later blathered it to someone until it was eventually leaked to the press. "It was the name he used just before his arrest."

"Then is it also true that he was not married and that he was having an extra-marital affair with the woman he claimed was his wife?"

Alex sighed. Someone at England House had a big mouth. "I don't know what his personal situation was at that time. I imagine it was possible that he was not legally married under Nazi law. Many people aren't – the laws are racist and marriage is particularly discouraged among certain peoples in order to accelerate the degradation of their culture and family life." He thought about his answer and realized that this was the sort of thing they should have been emphasizing all along. If only they could get Peter to speak again! He added, "Indeed, the difficulty or impossibility of obtaining a legal marriage causes many children to be technically born out-of-wedlock and therefore they are subject to seizure by the government as so-called orphans or children of unfit parents."

"Is that why Mr. Halifax kidnapped the little girl?"

"We don't know that he did that."

"But if he did, was it because it was his daughter?"

"She may have been," Alex admitted.

"Does that mean he had an affair with Mrs. Vogel?"

"That would be a possible explanation," Alex said, rather sarcastically.

"So he killed Mr. Vogel out of jealousy?"

"I doubt it." Alex felt tired. He had blown that round and he feared what the next question would be.

A hand went up and the reporter stood to ask, quite solemnly, "Sir, Mr. Halifax spent some time explaining to the American public about the brutality of his, er, employer – whom we have since learned was Mr. Vogel. Given these conjectures about Mr. Halifax's sexual misconduct with the lady of the house, is it now possible to re-interpret Mr. Vogel's actions in a different and more understandable light?"

"Aren't you putting the cart before the horse there?" Alex asked sharply. "Mr. Halifax was not employed by Herr Vogel, he was *bought* by him. Do you understand what that means, my man? He was treated brutally for years and if there was any 'sexual misconduct', as you so strangely phrased it, then it most likely occurred near the end of his tenure there and was almost certainly the reason he took the suicidal risk of leaving. Frau Vogel was no blushing teenager – she was the matron of the house and in a position to get what she demanded from her forced-laborer – whatever that might be!"

Alex's near admission caused a buzz among the reporters and it took a moment before they settled enough for one of them to be selected for the next question. But Alex didn't hear what was asked. His attention was caught by a woman from the office who came in the back door and walked up past the reporters to come straight to him. Something in her expression warned him and when she leaned over to tell him the news, he was not too surprised.

He rubbed his forehead and stared disconsolately at the table as he listened to the few details that were available. It would be two in the morning there. "Just tonight?"

The woman nodded her head.

"Just him?"

"We've been told everyone else is safe."

"Any confirmation?"

She shook her head. "Not yet. The news just came in." She reached a hand tentatively toward Alex, then glanced at the roomful of now very quiet reporters. Deciding to ignore them, she touched his shoulder and whispered, "I'm sorry."

She left the room and Alex remained in silence, his head resting on his hand, his eyes fixed on the table. It had been at Ryszard's – the first time Alex had seen Peter. Zosia had brought him there, defying orders and advice. Peter had not known anything about her actions, had innocently entered into their presence, perhaps expecting a welcome and a chance to join them, but instead encountering inexplicable and unmitigated hostility.

Alex remembered how Peter, sensing their animosity, had shifted nervously in his seat, had suddenly risen and walked aimlessly around his chair. Then, when he had realized that everyone was staring at him, he had smiled nervously – wistfully, even – and, aware that there was nowhere he could go, had sat back down. Trapped and at their mercy. Alone, powerless, and completely aware of that fact.

Alex looked up. Everyone's eyes rested on him. He took a deep breath, then said in a businesslike tone, "I've just received an unconfirmed report that my son-in-law, Peter Halifax, was killed while resisting arrest this evening in Berlin."

There was a momentary silence, then a sudden buzz of questions. Several hands shot into the air, several reporters stood to make their determination to ask a question more obvious.

Alex ignored them. He stood, breathing deeply, trying to control his sudden dizziness. He looked at the eager faces, at all the people wanting news. Details. Gruesome details, if possible. They didn't care. Not one little bit.

He felt nauseous. He took a deep breath, then said, "Now, if you'll excuse me, I need to leave."

3

*U*tter darkness. Like in that box, when he was bound and gagged and suffocating. Maybe that's where he still was. Maybe he was dying, hallucinating, inventing entire lives. Years of life lived in the delusional minutes leading up to death. He knew that wasn't true though. He was alive. He could no longer hear or see Joanna. He could still feel the warmth of her hand in his, but even that was fading. He was alive.

He felt his chest moving up and down as he breathed, he heard the echo of his heartbeat in his ears like the thunder of the surf on the shore. Oh God, he couldn't even kill himself right! Once he had broken free of his guards, he should have grabbed his stiletto and tried to use that. A quick jab, from below, directly into the heart. There had been time. Why had he used the poison so stupidly? In front of everyone with quick transport available. Doubtless when they had realized that he had collapsed, they had rushed him to the hospital, slammed some device onto his chest, and jump-started his heart.

What an idiot! Why the hell hadn't he waited until some quiet moment in the depths of a prison cell? He could have done it then, quiet and alone, he would have been cold before they found him. He would have succeeded.

Or was that the point? Had he sabotaged his own suicide attempt? Katerina had hit the nail on the head: he had an incredible and almost inexplicable desire to stay alive. Was it because, all his life, no one else had acknowledged his right to live, not to mention the desirability of his continued existence? *Love yourself,* he had told Emma. He had not added, *because no one else will.* Had he then, in some way, taken upon himself the entire burden of family and friends? Or was it because, for him, there was no other choice?

He remembered once asking about death, about what happens afterwards. It was shortly after his sister Anna had died and his mother had offered some vague but comforting words about heaven. Her confusion, her lack of conviction had left him unsatisfied and he had gone to his father and asked the same question.

"What happens when someone dies?"

"Don't."

It wasn't clear whether his father had meant don't die, or don't ask the question. So he had asked, "What do you mean?"

"Don't!" his father had repeated angrily. Grabbing his shoulders and shaking him, his father had almost shouted, "Just don't!"

And that had been his philosophical underpinnings for the rest of his life.

There were people in the room, he could hear them now. He remained very still, hoping to preserve the protection of sleep for a bit longer as he thought about what he should do. There weren't very many options and his mind wandered onto other things, like how he would miss his family and how the forest smelled in autumn. It would be September in about three weeks. September first, the anniversary of his birth. His real birth, the one marked on Niklaus Chase's papers, the one that determined his real age. He thought for a moment and realized that if he managed to survive the next three weeks, he would, at his death, still be a year younger than his parents had been when they had died. He wasn't sure of what significance that was, but it made him sad. His parents had died so young and now he could not even manage to live as long as they had. Would Irena and Madzia have longer? Given that one of his grandfathers had died in combat, that would make three consecutive generations of violent death. Would Irena or Madzia add a fourth, or would they be the first to live to a ripe old age and die peacefully in their beds? Oh God, oh God, Joanna already was the fourth generation sucked into oblivion by this endless war. Oh God, would it ever stop?

He turned his thoughts away from death. There would be time enough for that later. Thirty days he had been promised, or, since August was a long month, maybe thirty-one. What sort of mess would be left of him on that last day? Would he even be capable of feeling pain by then? Would the Führer personally attend, watching as they let him slit his wrists on that last day, watching smugly as he committed that final act of self-defilement? Would he be able to cheat them of a few days of his life? He doubted it. They could be subtle when they wanted to be. Still, there was no accounting for sudden anger, for a miscalculated blow – he would have to watch for his opportunity and seize it whenever it became available.

Oh God, what his life had come to. Eagerly seeking his murderer. Where had all the hopes gone to? What had happened to the little boy with all his dreams and plans? Gone, all gone. All a waste. Now, he knew what lay ahead: he had been here before, and though he tried to shield himself from the reality by focusing only on his eventual death, he knew, deep down how much he would have to suffer before they would let him die, and he knew real fear.

"So you are awake," a voice said, not unkindly.

He opened his eyes and looked up at the face of an older man, probably a doctor. Everything seemed very bright – much brighter than usual. He blinked a number of times and realized that his contact lenses were gone. Without the familiar brown filters, everything looked remarkably brighter.

"I'm the one who saved your life." The doctor glanced around behind him at some guards who stood on either side of the bed and added, "From what I've heard and observed, I can guess that you're not going to thank me for that."

Peter remained in silence. He had forgotten that there was also the possibility that he would be questioned. Oh God, there were so many people he might betray in a moment of confusion or agony. If they even guessed at the things he knew. How could he have let himself be taken alive? How could he have botched his suicide?

He caught his breath and concentrated on his situation. He was lying down, in a hospital room with guards on either side of him. His wrists were bound to the metal frame that ran along the side of the bed. His ankles were tied as well. There was a strap across his neck, another across his chest and another at his hips. He was so constrained he could do little more than turn his head.

The doctor was still looking at him. Peter moved his lips and whispered inaudibly. The doctor leaned forward and Peter panted, "Kill me. *Please.*"

The doctor's expression grew pained. "I can't," he replied sadly. "They would know."

Peter closed his eyes, exhausted by the effort of speaking. His chest ached and his entire body felt weak. Maybe if he just relaxed enough he could slip away.

The doctor turned away to address an aide standing next to one of the guards. "He needs food. I want to remove some of the restraints so he can eat."

"I'll check with the commanding officer." The aide left the room.

A few minutes later, the back of the bed was raised and Peter's right wrist was released. A moveable table was put in front of him, and on it was placed a glass of water, a spoon and a bowl of some sort of oatmeal-like concoction. Peter stared at it, unmoving.

"Remove the neck strap as well," the doctor ordered.

Again the aide disappeared. This time the officer returned with him into the room to confront the physician personally. "What do you want?"

"His neck strap should be removed, so he can eat more easily."

The officer eyed Peter and the restraints, then shook his head. "He's fine like that."

"But..."

"And make sure he eats!" The officer left the room again.

Joanna obediently eating oatmeal with a woman standing behind her, holding a piano wire, ready to strangle her. Peter closed his eyes, rejecting the memory, rejecting the food, rejecting the entire situation. Maybe he could will himself into death.

He heard the doctor approach. "Please eat. If you don't, we'll have to force feed you. I don't want to do that. It's very unpleasant. Please eat."

Peter opened his eyes, picked up the glass and drank the water. Then he picked up the spoon and ate the porridge. Maybe someone had managed to poison it for him. He finished the bowl and closed his eyes again, waiting for the effects of the poison, but nothing happened. Maybe no one was even aware that he had been taken yet. He opened his eyes and scanned the room. There was no window. "What time is it?"

The physician looked at his watch. "Nearly ten."

"Morning or evening?"

"Morning."

Morning. Damn. Then another thought occurred to him. "Which day?"

"Sunday."

Ah, so he was right – only nine or ten hours had passed. Still, it was plenty of time. Zosia had expected him back at two or, at the latest, three. He was seven hours overdue. She would know something was wrong and she and the children would be long gone. And anyone else he might betray would have had plenty of warning. Peter breathed slightly easier.

The officer returned to the room and glanced down at the empty bowl. "Good. Is he ready to travel?"

The physician shook his head. "He needs several days of bed rest."

"No way. I'm getting him off my hands as soon as possible. Can we move him?"

"No. The exertion might kill him."

"What about this evening?"

"It'd be too strenuous. His heart–"

"We'll carry him!" the officer snapped. "All I need to do is get him to the *Residenz* alive and then I can wash my hands of him!" He stopped to calm himself, then said, much more patiently, "And, once he's off my hands, he will cease to be your responsibility as well. You do understand that?"

The doctor nodded.

"Now, if we carry him, will it hurt to transport him this evening?"

The doctor looked at Peter. He shook his head sadly. "No. He should be alright as long as he doesn't have to exert himself."

The officer nodded, satisfied. Then he turned to the aide and ordered gruffly, "Find someone to get that dye out of his hair. Bleach it or whatever. And make sure his clothes are laundered. The Führer wants him looking like this." The officer reached into his jacket and removed a folded up piece of paper. As he unfolded it, Peter recognized it as a page from an American magazine. One from a year ago. One that had his picture in it.

There was a loud sigh of relief from the officer as Peter was handed over to the security detail at the *Residenz*. Peter sat impassively in the chair the attendants had dropped him into and waited while the paperwork was finalized. The officer and the physician apparently had not bothered to convey any concerns about his health, for once they had left, he was pulled to his feet and was expected to walk. He had no objection to that. He felt healthier than the physician had indicated, and if there was any weakness left in his heart, he could hope that a brisk walk down the palace corridors might provoke a fatal attack.

It wasn't a brisk walk, though. His feet were bound by a relatively short chain and he had to walk slowly, with small, awkward steps. His hands and arms were held bound by a strait-jacket and so he hobbled down the corridor, disoriented, apprehensive, constrained, looking for all the world like the madman that he was supposed to be.

When they reached a checkpoint, his restraints were removed, and he was stripped and searched as thoroughly as he had ever been in his life. Once they were satisfied that he was clean, he was permitted to dress himself and the strait-jacket was put back on, but the ankle chains were left off. They then stepped into a section of the *Residenz* which seemed to be the Führer's living quarters.

An exquisite, thick carpet ran along the length of the hall, period furniture was set against the walls, richly framed portraits hung above the settees and tables, soothing chamber music emanated from discreetly hidden speakers – giving the overall impression of a rather tacky, overdone show of good taste. Peter was hustled along the display to an ornately carved door and then he and his escort were admitted into the Führer's private chambers.

It was large – the size of a small banquet hall – furnished somewhat like a very expensive hotel room. There was a suite of furniture: a couch and several armchairs ranged about a coffee table. Off to the side was a television set atop a machine which Peter recognized as the Reich standard player of videocassettes. Along the walls of the room were heavily curtained alcoves which contained various useful annexes: a bar, a piano room, a library area with a writing desk, another with a dining table and chairs, a dressing area and leading off from that, a large closet. In the main room, but set against the far wall was another cluster of furniture: a dressing table and some chairs, a bed with a canopy that had curtains which could be lowered for privacy, though at this point they were not, bedside tables and the like.

The walls were half-paneled in a heavy, dark wood. Above the paneling was a pale red wallpaper embossed with a dark red velvet pattern that looked like a coat of arms. Sconces held candles that provided the only light in the room, and Peter had to peer into the darkness to detect that various people stood in the corners, waiting to attend to the Führer's needs.

A movement at the far side of the room caught Peter's attention, and he realized that there was someone sitting in one of the bedside chairs, facing the bed. Presumably the Führer. His attention was on the woman lying on the bed and Peter squinted, trying to make out her features as she sat up. She pulled the covers back and stood up and he saw that she was completely naked and that it was Stefi. The Führer stood as well and handed her a long, white satin robe which she wrapped around herself, and then once she had finished doing that, he extended his arm to her.

The regal couple approached him. The Führer was completely dressed, obviously expecting his visitor; Stefi looked stunning as she glided across the floor, the satin which draped over her doing nothing to hide her curves. Peter allowed himself one look at her face, but she showed no sign of recognizing him, and once he had firmly established that she had nothing to communicate to him, he was careful not to notice her further.

The Führer motioned for the men holding Peter to back away and they did, retreating to a position near the door. "So, Herr Doktor Halifax, you delight us with a visit," the Führer said with a diplomatic grin, speaking with sufficient formality to let Peter know that he was no longer considered Karl's runaway chattel but was a political prisoner.

"I'm not insane. Get this thing off me."

The Führer raised his eyebrows in surprise, looked as if he were growing angry, but Stefi whispered something in his ear and his look of anger melted into a smile. "Yes, of course." He indicated that the strait-jacket should be removed.

As the sleeves were untied, Peter silently thanked Stefi. The entire time he had been forced to wear the thing, his hatred of such an inhumane and humiliating form of constraint had dominated his thoughts and muddied his thinking. He found it worse than handcuffs and he imagined that any sane person forced into such a device for long enough could easily be driven mad by it. Indeed, given the grotesque images which had flashed through his mind ever since they had forced him into the jacket, he suspected that he was more familiar with the device than any sane person should be. He wisely decided, however, not to pursue that thought at the moment, as he needed to concentrate on the difficulties at hand.

"Have a seat." The Führer gestured helpfully toward one of the comfortable armchairs. "I want to ask you some questions before we proceed with your punishment."

"You're a murderer. I have nothing to say to you," Peter snapped angrily. The armchair the Führer had indicated was angled to face the video-player. Is this where the Führer sat to watch Joanna's murder time and again?

"*You* are calling *me* a murderer?" The Führer laughed.

Peter ignored the Führer's reference to Karl's execution. "Of at least one innocent five-year-old girl."

"Oh, that." The Führer waved his hand dismissively. "He was acting outside of orders. He was upset – his own niece had been blown to bits by that bomb, and he thought you were responsible. Sorry about that."

Peter was taken aback. He remembered the little girl lying near to him after the bomb had exploded, blood dripping from her ears, her eyes staring and glassy.

"But five-year-olds die all the time." The Führer brought his hands together in a gesture of mock sincerity. "I don't see you moaning about some child in the Horn of Africa. There's a drought there now, or a war, or something. I'm sure even you could manage enough money to save one child's life. In fact, you could have raised money on American television for that. Could have saved hundreds of children. Maybe thousands." The Führer opened his hands and looked heavenward. "Don't they count?"

Peter sifted through his memories. There had been every indication that the order to murder Joanna had come down from the Führer directly, and it was standard practice to blame subordinates for unseemly acts; yet, he had never bothered to establish the Führer's guilt beyond a reasonable doubt. And the Führer had apologized; however brusquely, he had apologized though there was absolutely no need to do so.

The Führer returned his gaze to earth and assumed a more businesslike tone. "It's not even that they're black-skinned, is it? After all, the Soviets are in the middle of stomping on some rebellion in the Caucasus right now. Kids are dying by the hundreds, I'm sure, yet no one bothers about them. They're white there – did you know that? The original Aryans, I'm told."

Peter tilted his head with interest as he realized there was a point to all this. He was being asked about strategy. As an experienced speaker, as someone who had impressed the American population, his advice was being sought!

"Why us?" the Führer wailed. "Why do we always get the bad publicity? We never stop hearing about those Jews we whisked out of the way. On and on they yammer about it over there. Children killed, babies...Not that anyone was willing to take them off our hands. Hell, we'd have been more than happy to just throw the lot of them out of the country – the disloyal scum. No! We're supposed to keep them here, letting them destabilize and pollute our society. So, we solve our own problems and we're still hearing about it. Hell, they'd be dead of old age by now anyway. At the same time Stalin wiped out most of the Ukraine. He outdid us by millions! And they weren't oriental or dark-skinned or alien, they were white people, Europeans, *Christians!!* Kids starved there – someone said the *whole* country looked like a concentration camp. You know, an extermination camp, I mean. And that's okay with the world? Too far in the past to care about, it seems. Hell, Stalin still has his defenders! No one has apologized to the few survivors or made reparations, yet the Soviet government can deal directly with the NAU government. Why?" The Führer gestured with his fist toward the ceiling as if calling on God to redress the wrongs of centuries. "Why are *we* singled out?"

"Do you really think I'm going to offer you my help?"

The Führer brought his gaze down from the ceiling to look at Peter indulgently, almost fondly. "Yes, I do. You see, there's a friend of yours, implicated in your crimes. A nobody named, er..." the Führer bit his lip in thought, "Ah, yes, Roman. He's not going to be missed by anyone. His fate will not cause a stir in America. You'd rather he not suffer, wouldn't you?"

Peter sucked in his breath. He remembered Zosia's admonition that day he had arrived in Szaflary: *You can't give in to blackmail, it just gets used against you more and more if you do.* But Ryszard had argued on another occasion that the Poles should have never resisted the original invasion. They knew the odds against them, he had said, they knew their allies would have to abandon them, they knew the Soviets were waiting to strike, they should have thrown open their cities, worked with the system, diluted its virulence, changed it from within. Instead of fighting bravely, dying uselessly, they should have established a Vichy government, they should have had their own Quisling. It would have saved millions of people untold suffering.

Who was right? He had heard the two argue the point endlessly every time they were together. But that wasn't the issue right now. The question was did he want to let Roman suffer on a point of his own pride?

"What will you promise if I co-operate?"

The Führer shrugged. "I couldn't care less about this so-called friend of yours. Tell you what, I won't even have him arrested. We'll leave him completely alone. Let him get on with baking his bread. How's that?"

"How will I know that's what you'll do?"

"You have my word."

"How do I know you'll keep it?"

The Führer looked annoyed. "You don't have any other options but to believe me, now do you? Take the deal or leave it!" He gestured impatiently toward the chair.

"Okay. I'll take it." Peter seated himself. "On your word as an officer, a gentleman, and leader of our great nation that Roman will not be arrested or in any other way harassed or harmed."

The Führer smiled at the sudden change in Peter's tone. "Agreed." He seated himself in the other chair, also facing the video player, but angled such that the two of them could converse easily. Stefi seated herself on the arm of his chair and whispered something into his ear.

"Richard?" The Führer pursed his lips. "Ah, yes, I suppose you're right. And Günter as well."

Peter saw how Stefi's smile wavered only slightly at that. He also noticed that the Führer had not deigned to introduce her.

The Führer directed one of his aides to contact the two men and tell them their presences were required. Then he ordered drinks for the three of them and offered cigarettes, though only he chose to smoke.

"Tell me," Peter said, as he sipped the cognac he had been given, "do you still intend to have me tortured and killed after this?"

"Oh yes!" the Führer laughed. "I'm not offering *you* any amnesties. But," he added with a wink, "we don't care for your terminology. It's not 'tortured and killed', it's only a just punishment for crimes committed."

"But I haven't even been formally indicted, not to mention tried and found guilty," Peter argued as if he were debating the chances of Borussia making it to the finals. The whole encounter had taken on such a surreal quality that he felt himself responding as if in a nightmare: aware of the horrors which lay ahead, but unable to give credence to them. He had certainly felt more genuine apprehension when Karl had approached him, his fist raised, than he did now, with the promise of being tortured to death hanging over him. Perhaps the threats had crossed some line of believability and left him in a cocoon of shock.

The Führer flapped his hand. "Yes, you have. Last year, in absentia. Sealed indictment, secret court, guilty."

"Ah. Good. Hate to violate procedure," Peter commented sardonically.

"I should have you questioned, you know," the Führer added, conversationally. "You seem to have friends who provide you with papers, money, and so on. I really should find out about all that."

"But?"

The Führer chuckled. "But my pet here warned me I wouldn't get a word of truth out of you, now would I?"

Stefi nodded. "He's the clever sort who would name someone like Schindler, just because he's met him."

The Führer regarded her fondly. "Yes, my pet. Maybe he'd even name you."

"You haven't told him my name," Stefi reminded him. She looked at Peter and said, "It's Stefi. I'm Richard Traugutt's daughter and Ole Karlsson's wife." She smiled and looked back at the Führer. "There. Now he can make up wild stories about me as well."

Very clever, Peter thought. Stefi had covered herself, Olek, and her father quite well. He downed the rest of the cognac in a gulp and set the glass down with a thunk. "You do realize, that with such a fate awaiting me, I might have trouble concentrating. You really are more likely to get sense out of me if I knew that my future was a little less grim."

The Führer clucked his tongue and wagged his head emphatically. "No, no, no, no, no! I'm not *that* interested in what you have to say! I've already promised you your friend's life. Be satisfied with that. You have violated the Reich's laws, repeatedly, blatantly and publicly. You must be punished. Severely punished. There is no alternative."

"I see."

The Führer waved for Peter's glass to be refilled. "What I want to know is why do the Americans care about what happens to you. You're nobody. Why you?"

"They think the way I was treated was unfair."

"Unfair? What's fair about the world? What's fair about disease?"

"I think they concentrate on human actions–"

"Human? What's fair about war? Do they think the brave, good soldier is never outnumbered? That innocents don't die?"

"On ugly things, like torture."

249

"Torture? *Torture!* That's utter nonsense! If they cared about torture, I could find them a hundred victims this very minute, all outside this Reich! Go to Africa, you have despots there who eat people, for heaven's sake. And they have diplomatic relations with America!"

"They seemed upset by these." Peter pushed his sleeve up, showing his tattooed number.

The Führer snorted. "We didn't cut off your hand, did we? They have diplomatic relations with people who cut off hands, you know. We don't execute people in public, we don't beat up women for showing their ankles, we don't flog people for spitting in the street. We don't stone adulterers or put tax dodgers to death. All these things are tolerated in other regimes."

"The Reich has instituted a form of slavery–"

"As if that hasn't been the natural human condition for millennia! I could name fifty regimes that have unofficial forms of slavery. Chinese prison labor, Mexican peons, illegal immigrants in America...Go ask the Indian untouchable what sort of opportunities he has. Go ask a Turkoman woman. Or the starving Somali peasant. They'd kill to be as well fed as our *Zwangsarbeiter*." The Führer tapped some ash from his cigarette. "It seems if you have oil on your hands, then it's alright to have blood as well. Or better yet, claim it's part of one's religion. That excuses anything. I know, that's it! Nazism isn't a political philosophy, it's a religion." The Führer took a deep, satisfied draw from his cigarette.

"And it has carried out genocide."

The Führer blew a stream of smoke into the air. "Every regime begins with violence. Even the pious little Americans. I've heard that a third of the population fled to Canada after their revolution. Do you think they went for the better weather? Eh? Sounds like they had a lot to fear, doesn't it? But the Americans view their revolution as noble, bloodless almost. And they don't even mention how the Indians were shuffled out of the way. They seem to have been pretty efficient at establishing *Lebensraum* there, wouldn't you say? Suddenly the American continent is simply empty!" The Führer took another puff from his cigarette. "And they think that the French chopping off aristocratic heads was justified and a sign of egalitarianism."

"Perhaps they are more forgiving of politically inspired murders. The Reich's were ethnically motivated."

The Führer whistled derisively. "I couldn't count the number of ethnic-cleansings which have taken place elsewhere since then. And political murder is usually just a thin veil for ethnic or class warfare. What I want to know is why was that one so important?"

It was not unlike a question which Arieka had put to him when they had spoken after the late-night talk show. Peter had not had an answer for her then. To the Führer he said, truthfully, "I suspect because the survivors and the witnesses are vocal."

The Führer threw his hands up in the air in a flippant imitation of having received a revelation. "So the lesson is, don't kill well-connected people. Stick to peasants or remote corners of the world – brown-skin, poor – and it's alright. Or be a darkie yourself and no one gives a damn what you do to others. I know, maybe it's don't touch people who have connections in America – to newspapers or news organizations or publishing. That seems to be the lesson that the Americans wish to impart. Everyone is equal, they all deserve human rights, isn't that what they say? Yet, somehow the tragedies that befall some people are just less important than those that befall others, have you noticed that? Have you noticed any correlations between the backgrounds of sorrowful victims and the backgrounds of government officials and reporters, eh? And they wonder why we refer to conspiracies!"

Peter stopped listening. Clearly the Führer was doing nothing more than amusing himself. Peter felt embarrassed and dismayed – for a moment there, he had been misled into thinking that what he said might matter. He looked up from the Führer, as he continued his lecture, to Stefi, perched there on the arm of the Führer's chair. She gave him a look which was hard to read. Sad, in part – as if sorry that she could do nothing to prevent the horror which lay before him, but also her expression urged him not to give up. She seemed to think that his words somehow would have an impact, however improbable that might be.

Well, Peter thought, if anyone knew the Führer's bizarre way of thinking, it would be Stefi, and if she thought it would do some good for him to discuss the rights and wrongs of the Reich with the Führer, then it was certainly worth the effort.

It occurred to him that the Führer had phrased the question as why he was so important to the American populace. Clearly Stefi had coached the Führer into thinking he could gain some propaganda expertise from his prisoner. Her intent though, must have been to have the discussion move into a comparison of the two systems – one which would make the Reich not so very different from America. A comparison which might make the Führer more open to changes which could improve the Reich and lead to better conditions for its people. That would follow Ryszard's agenda that improvements were to be welcomed and would lead to genuine changes faster and less violently than resistance and revolution.

Peter had always balked at the thought, terming what he wanted not "revolution", but "liberation." Nevertheless, given his current circumstances and the short span of days left to him, if he ever did want to make a difference, he had no choice: Ryszard's and Stefi's agenda was the only option. So, the point of the discussion was to make the Führer feel a keen embarrassment about anything which drew the Reich along the wrong path: Joanna's murder, the torture of prisoners, and so on, and at the same time to encourage a sense that there had been changes which should be continued, changes which were genuinely progressive, which would bring the Reich back into the fold of civilized nations.

When there was a pause in the Führer's diatribe which was sufficiently long that Peter could interrupt without appearing rude, he said, "I agree completely. To be honest, I think the only reason the Reich is singled out for criticism is that the Americans expect better of us than they do of the rest of the world. They know we are a civilized people with a rich culture and a long history. Most Americans are Europhiles and they want to look up to European civilization and are therefore singularly disappointed that we are at war with each other."

"That isn't what you said when you were there."

"I know, and I am quite sorry about that. But once I was there, I had access to a free press, and I learned that much of what I thought was tainted propaganda wasn't. What you've said about the depredations of other rulers in other parts of the world is true – and it is equally true that they come in for faint criticism from the Americans. If we allowed a free press here, then the people would see…"

The Führer's expression told him that he had presumed too much. To suggest a free press! Was he mad? "The people here are told exactly what they need to know. Only renegades like you have a problem with that!"

"Yes, of course," Peter agreed, with a weak smile. He definitely needed more time to hone his skills before he played this game in earnest, but there wasn't time. He glanced up at Stefi, hoping she might guide him a bit with her expression. She raised her head, ever so slightly, indicating, he guessed, that he was on the right track and that he should continue, albeit gently.

So he did. As he drank the Führer's cognac and ate the hors d'ouevres which were offered to him, he and the Führer talked at length about American society, about the common roots of the two lands, about free markets and free expression and created wealth. As time passed, Peter determined that the Führer had no real understanding of economics or ethics or any of the mundane subjects necessary to the day-to-day running of an empire. He delegated everything to subordinates and only interfered when necessary to either maintain his power or indulge his whims. Therefore, he was most open to what Peter had to say when it had a clear political use, and so Peter was careful to structure his ideas in terms of power – how a just Reich would be stronger, how fair treatment of its peoples would build up its economic base and make the Führer both richer and unassailable.

Peter reminded himself now and then that he was talking to Joanna's murderer, to a man who planned to have him gruesomely tortured, but the admonitions remained theoretical. Somehow this mildly intelligent man seemed too banal to be a threat to him. *I must be in shock or perhaps I can't accept the danger because I so desperately don't want it to be true*, he thought, indulging in a bit of self-psychoanalysis. It was the "good tsar, bad advisors" syndrome, this wanting to believe that if only he could get the Führer to listen to him sincerely for an hour or two, then the man would undergo a conversion and reform the entire society, naturally commuting Peter's sentence in the process.

It was clear, though, that the Führer could never be genuinely converted, because he had no fundamental morality. He was making it up as he went along, based upon his life-goal, which was to keep and hold power, and his tastes, which tended to the bizarre and sadistic. He would treat Peter well, chatting to him like a benevolent uncle, determining what he could from him, as long as that served its purpose, then when he had exhausted that vein, he would turn in the other direction – exacting his revenge and treating himself to an orgy of sadism.

Their conversation approached its end as the Führer exhausted his attention span. Peter ran his hand over his face as if trying to induce words which would hold the Führer's interest and therefore prolong his own life for a little longer. Like Scheherezade. He felt a growing dread as the reality of his situation hit home, and he looked at Stefi, almost openly, seeking something from her, but unable to even guess what she could offer him. She gave him a fleeting, sad smile that offered no hope, only sympathy and a hint of admiration.

The Führer yawned and turned to Stefi. "Well, I've had enough. It looks like Günter and your father aren't going to make it here in time to meet our guest."

Stefi leaned into him. "Let's give them a little more time."

"No." The Führer yawned again. "I'm tired and…" he leered at her, "…I have other things on my mind, right now."

Peter felt overwhelmed with grief. To be at the whim of a lunatic. To die for such a stupid reason, and so horribly. Before he could think of anything to say to delay the inevitable, the Führer looked at his watch and said, "It's late. I'll give the preliminaries a miss." He turned to one of the officers who had stood the entire time, quietly waiting by the door. "Take him downstairs and have them start on him. I'll stop by tomorrow morning to see how it's going."

The officer nodded and approached Peter, indicating with a gesture that Peter should stand.

"And make sure every minute of action is recorded."

The officer solemnly nodded.

"You know," Peter said, as he stood up, "other countries put their political prisoners in jail for long prison terms."

"Yes." The Führer stood as well, as if taking proper leave of his guest. "And as long as they're there, they are a thorn in the government's side, providing a focus for foreign protest and for domestic opposition. Have you ever noticed how often the imprisoned opponent ends up running the country ten years down the line?"

Peter nodded noncommittally. The officer grabbed his arm and snapped a handcuff around his wrist. It felt like a lead weight. His whole body felt like lead, his muscles paralyzed with dread. It was as if the blood had drained from his body into the floor, rooting him to the spot, to the only safe place left to him.

"No," the Führer continued, as if lecturing on practical politics, "it's much better executing the bastards straightaway. You put up with a few days of fussing from foreign governments and then it's all over with. No one can maintain interest in a corpse. No one."

Peter swallowed as his wrists were chained together behind his back. It was difficult even drawing his breath. "Then shouldn't you just have me executed right away?"

"Always worrying about the Reich's reputation, eh?" the Führer scoffed. "How considerate of you. Too bad you weren't so considerate last year." He stepped up to Peter and tapped Peter's nose with his finger. "You hurt me. For an entire month you hurt me. Day in and day out, I suffered through your denunciations. No one-off for you, no op-ed piece in one of their newspapers and then disappear into obscurity. No, you had to drag it out, going on television, talking to reporters, moaning on and on and on. You had to be a *celebrity*!" The Führer turned on his heel and walked back to Stefi's side. "You dragged out my suffering, now I'm going to drag out yours."

"I'm sorry about that. That wasn't my intent. I just thought I could help make things better."

"Are you *really* sorry?" the Führer asked slyly.

What Peter said was true: many of his words had been twisted to make everyone in the Reich a caricature of a human – either unmitigated evil or blameless lamb – and he regretted that. He also regretted the money sent to the insanely violent groups which had attached themselves to his name. And, naturally, he regretted what had happened to Joanna. Nevertheless, he felt ashamed of his words and how they could be misinterpreted.

He looked at Stefi, but there was no judgment there. She recognized that he was fighting for his life, or at the very least, a dignified death, and she encouraged him with her eyes to say whatever was necessary. He recognized then the inordinate bravery of what she did day in and day out with the Führer. Using her bravery as inspiration, he agreed, "About some of it, yes."

"Good! Then I'll let you make a tape for me, where you explain the error of your ways."

"And then?"

"Then?" The Führer snorted. "You get to go to your punishment with a clear conscience. Did you think I'd commute your sentence? Do you think I'm an idiot? Do you think I'd let you get away with all that you did just because you're willing to say you were sorry?" He shook his head vehemently. "No! No way. I want anyone who hears about you to know what happens to people like you. I want to make you a lesson for everyone else."

"What about the Americans? If everyone knows what happened to me, then they'll also know."

"Don't worry. They will hear a different story – they'll hear it and believe it, because it will be convenient for them: tried and executed. The objective reality will agree with the subjective reality in, oh, thirty days." The Führer paused and furrowed his brow. "Oh, yes, thirty-one. August is a long month, isn't it?" Without waiting for an answer, he continued, "The Americans won't know about the fun and games in between and your death will be forgotten before your body is cold."

"But executing political prisoners…If you want to impress them…"

"Political prisoner? You're a murderer!" The Führer laughed. "Even the Americans execute murderers. All the time. And if they're poor, then I don't think they even have to be really guilty." He smiled broadly at Peter. "Whatever reason you had for killing Vogel, I can't thank you enough. You've made it so easy for us!"

Peter cast a last, desperate glance around the room. "That's a beautiful piano, you have there." He gestured with his head toward the instrument. "Do you play?"

4

*T*raugutt looked up as Schindler entered the foyer. "Finally! Where the hell have you been?"

Schindler smoothed his clothing. "Why? Were you waiting for me?"

"Yes! I wanted to have a word with you before we went in to see Rudi." It was the only place they could talk without Schindler's bodyguards in attendance – this no-man's land between the security check and the Führer's private apartment. Even here was not completely secure as there were guards scattered at various strategic locations along the hallway. "Come on, we can walk slowly." Richard picked up his briefcase and started down the hall.

Günter fell in step with him. "Do you know what this is all about?"

"He's got his hands on Halifax."

"Good! He can do the man in and finally get off my back about him."

Richard shook his head. "That's not what I want. He's already embarrassed the Reich with his treatment of that man, do you want to drag the Fatherland through the mud again?"

Günter graced Richard with a broad smile. "The Führer is not the Fatherland. And if our dear Rudi manages to destroy his internal support by aggravating foreigners with his treatment of one famous prisoner, then..." He shrugged. "Who am I to question his orders?"

"We need to stop him acting like a madman. And I want your co-operation."

"Pff. Why would I help you?"

"Because I'll denounce you if you don't. I know all about that sterility program you resurrected in London. I have the documents to prove it."

Günter's eyes widened. "How did you...? Were you behind its destruction?"

"Don't be idiotic. No, apparently I wasn't the only one who learned about what you were up to. Your security there has more holes than a sieve."

"My people in London sold me out?"

"London, America," Richard replied coolly. "Seems your agent in the ASA has been rather promiscuous. If I were you, I'd ask for my loyalty payments back."

"My agent in the..." Schindler glanced around nervously.

"Re-establishing laboratories directly against orders? To work on a program which Rudi staked his international reputation on preventing? Even Rudi would recognize that as a challenge – or rather, a threat. And your very own agents right inside the ASA which you didn't tell him about? Tch, tch, tch." Richard wagged his head in mock dismay. "He won't be pleased. You've been a naughty boy, and if he finds all this out, I think he might just be fed up enough to get rid of you."

"He wouldn't dare touch me! Not with my connections."

"Three quarters of which are your *wife's* connections. Have you kept an eye on who she's been spending her time with recently?"

Schindler gave Richard a sharp look. Richard responded with a broad, guilty grin. "You've been ignoring her, you know. Is it any wonder she seeks comfort elsewhere?"

"You son of a–"

"Now, now. Be civil. All I want is your help."

It only took a few seconds as Schindler processed Richard's threats and came to his decision. "What do you want?"

They were already at the door. They could hear piano music through it. Bad piano music. "Just follow my lead." Richard knocked lightly at the door. "When I say that you agree with me on something, back me up."

They were admitted to the room and were greeted by a strange tableau. The Führer sat at the piano, furiously pounding the keyboard, Stefi, clothed only in a white satin robe, stood in rapt admiration, Peter stood next to her, his hands bound behind him, also apparently listening to the impromptu concert. Their backs were to the door and though Peter turned and gave them a quick glance, the others did not even seem to notice their entrance.

Richard set his briefcase by the door, and then he and Günter joined the little group. When the Führer had finished the piece, all who could applauded enthusiastically. The Führer stood, gave a small bow to his audience, and then said, "Ach, so you've both made it in time to meet our dear, famous guest, after all."

Schindler turned toward Peter and eyed him disdainfully. "I told you he was in Berlin all along."

"No I wasn't," Peter disagreed. "I was in London."

Schindler snorted angrily. "Where?"

"With your chief of police. I stayed in his guest room."

"Liar!" Schindler raised his fist threateningly.

The Führer raised his own hand in a gesture of restraint. "Günter, calm down."

Schindler glanced at his audience and lowered his fist. "He's lying!"

"We know, we know." The Führer waggled his fingers whimsically. "We're not going to get sense out of him, that's obvious."

"He should be questioned. Find out who's been hiding him. Find out how he's been traveling to and from England."

The Führer shook his head. "I'm not going to waste time on that sort of nonsense. He's got a debt to pay to me and I'm going to see that he pays it. I don't give a damn who he's been staying with. Anyway, he's not going to tell us."

Using just two fingers, Schindler tapped Peter's cheek threateningly. "Oh, he'll talk. His sort always does."

The Führer smiled at Schindler's act. "He managed to go through, what was it, three months of re-education?"

257

"Four," Peter corrected.

"Four months with some of our best, plus weeks of interrogation at his recapture, weeks of interrogation at his original arrest, years in a labor camp, and all those years that he was right inside the household of an official of the Reich's security headquarters, yet in all that time, he didn't even let on he was in the English Underground." The Führer laughed. "You all took him for some common criminal. So much for your detective abilities."

"He's scum," Schindler snarled. "What more do we need to know about him?" He turned his attention back to Peter. "You weren't even a competent servant for the Vogels, you're just scum."

"*Scum?*" Peter spat in disbelief. "In the name of your asinine racial theories, you and your ilk laid waste to half of Europe, murdered millions of people, destroyed any semblance of culture or learning. You condemned half of Europe to live under Nazi slavery and betrayed the other half into Communist slavery. You so destroyed our civilization, our economic might, that even your much vaunted Master Race is forced to live in penury compared to the Americans. You've looted a continent, reduced free peoples to subservience and poverty, ruined our futures, and *you* call *me* scum?"

They were all so stunned by his audacity that none had found the wherewithal to interrupt him. The Führer glanced at the myriad faces in the corners, his officers and servants, as if afraid that Peter's words might be contagious.

Schindler, finally regaining his composure, struck Peter hard across the face. "You never did learn to keep your foul mouth shut in the presence of your betters! Let me teach you now–"

"Oh, that's right!" the Führer laughed, recovering himself and pre-empting Schindler's next blow. "You've met him before, haven't you?"

"Met? No. I've seen him working. Or rather, more often, *not* working, at the Vogel's. He's a worthless, insubordinate..." Schindler lowered his fist.

"What about you, Richard?" the Führer asked suavely, "Have you met our guest before?"

"I believe our paths have crossed," Richard replied obscurely. He looked at Peter. "Yes, in fact, I remember you served a dinner at the Vogel's once. I tried to have a conversation with you. Asked you where you were from. In English. Do you remember that?"

Peter shook his head.

"You screwed up, answered London. Luckily no one in the room understood and so no one noted the contradiction when Herr Vogel claimed you were born in Halifax."

"No one but you," Schindler noted sourly.

Richard shrugged. "I figured he was answering the question where he grew up. He was obviously exhausted and not thinking clearly."

"His sort is incapable of clear thought."

"Except when it comes to deceiving you?" the Führer asked. "You visited the Vogel's frequently, didn't you? And you didn't realize he had a whole secret life, did you? He even organized a school for his fellow workers. Right under your noses."

Schindler scowled but did not respond.

The Führer goaded Schindler further. "He's not even named Halifax. Did you know that?"

"He's got a number, what does he need with a name?"

"Yardley, wasn't it?" the Führer asked Peter. "I've had some of my people look into your story. Alan Yardley. That's the name they came up with. More or less matches all the details of the story you told to the Americans. Except, oddly, that it seems we marked you as dead."

Peter didn't say anything.

"But that's not your real name either. Tell me, what is your name? My people couldn't come up with anything before Yardley – the trail was completely cold."

Still Peter didn't respond.

"Oh, you can tell us. It doesn't matter. It's just curiosity on my part. I could have my people track down every married couple arrested in the London area when you were between ten and fifteen, then see if any of those had a lone son. We'd probably work out who you were then."

Schindler crossed his arms impatiently. "Assuming *that* bit of his story was true."

The Führer ignored him. "But why not save us the trouble? Tell us what name to put on your headstone. There's no reason not to."

"Who are you going to have handling him?" Schindler asked, apparently fed up with the Führer's silly games.

"Heinrich Lederman. I've pulled him off his punishment detail to come here." The Führer turned back to Peter. "You remember him, don't you? Or maybe you don't recognize the name. It's your old friend – the one who oversaw your original re-education."

"Torture," Peter muttered.

The Führer ignored that. "I'm letting him have another go at you, to redeem his reputation after his abysmal failure." The Führer winked at Peter. "He's waiting downstairs for you at this very moment. It'll be like old times."

The Führer seemed to expect a response but Peter had nothing to say. The Fuhrer studied Peter for a long moment, then added, "I'm afraid it's going to be unpleasant for you. But you're already aware of that, aren't you?" The Führer glanced at the others as they stood in uncomfortable silence, then he looked meaningfully back at Peter. "I would guess you're the only one in this room who knows what it's all about. I envy you, envy you your knowledge."

Again some sort of reply seemed to be expected. Peter remained silent.

"It's amazing what these boys can do nowadays to a human body!" the Führer enthused, as if carrying on a dialog. He smiled winningly at Peter and added, teasingly, "Though Lederman did say he could do better if I might provide him with an auxiliary – like your friend perhaps?"

"You will keep your word?" Peter asked worriedly, "About my friend?"

"That?" the Führer mocked. "I suppose so. But you do realize that your promise of co-operation extends through the entire thirty-one days? And you owe me thirty-one entire days. If I get anything less out of you, then I will have your friend finish off the term, do you understand?"

"That wasn't part of the deal!"

The Führer sniffed his amusement. "You're in no position to dictate terms."

Stefi touched the Führer's sleeve. "Rudi…"

"What is it, *Mäuschen?*"

Stefi let her delicate fingers stray along the fabric of the Führer's shirt. Though she touched nothing but his arm, there was something very indecent in her gesture. "Do you think this is wise? You know…"

"My daughter's right," Richard agreed in a businesslike tone. "*Mein Führer*, Günter and I need to discuss this affair with you, before you take any further action."

Günter looked surprised but did not disagree.

"Oh?" the Führer asked, rounding his lips in an exaggerated and rather effeminate gesture of interest.

"This is an important opportunity, we can't afford to miss it." Richard gestured with his head toward the sitting area and led the way. The others followed and took their seats: Richard in one chair, Günter in another, Rudi on the couch and Stefi curled up next to her lover. Only Peter remained standing by the piano, consigned to ignorance and silence as the others sat down to discuss his fate.

The Führer placed a protective arm around Stefi. "Richard, you better have a good reason for this."

"I assure you, *mein Führer*, I do. As I've mentioned before, I have some agents infiltrated into the Home Army in our eastern territories, and these agents maintain contact with their counterparts on the other side of the Soviet-Reich border–"

"So the Soviets haven't managed to wipe them all out?"

"Not quite. Some of the major Polish cities there still maintain their character and a rump population. Lwów, for example."

"Where?"

"Lemberg," Richard amended, rather annoyed at himself. "The Russians call it Lvov." Luckily neither Günter nor Rudi noticed the slight shift in pronunciation from the Polish *Lwów* to the current Soviet designation of *Lvov*, though Stefi did arch an eyebrow ever so slightly. The problem, Richard knew, was that though he could work Peter's arrest into his strategy, he was ill-prepared to do so. It was forcing him to make moves earlier than he had planned and as a result he was making most of it up as he went along and was consequently more inclined to err.

When they had first heard the news about Peter's arrest, Stefi had assured him that she could convince Rudi not to bother questioning Peter for information – Rudi was, she said, far too emotionally charged by the thought of punishing Peter to want to do anything so sensible. Consequently, Ryszard had felt no particular danger to himself or his family and therefore his first inclination was to leave Peter to his fate. But then Zosia had come to him and literally thrown herself at his feet begging him to do something to save her husband. She claimed she had the outline of a plan, based upon Anna's reports about what was happening in America, and he could work that into his overall strategy.

It was too risky, there was too little time to plan and organize all the essential elements, and besides, Peter's gruesome murder, if publicized appropriately, would work well toward Zosia's goal of garnering American support for armed insurrection, Ryszard had pointed out, rather unkindly.

Forget all that! she had cried. She offered Ryszard a deal: save her husband and she would throw her support to his strategy, working however he wanted in order to further his goals. She would be obedient to his political commands, she would collaborate, argue his brief to the Councils, do whatever he said, if only he would do this for her.

So, our little Zosienka is in love, he had teased her, as he had done so many years ago. This time, she had not disagreed, and he had given in to her pleas and agreed to try to save Peter. That had meant he had spent the entire day organizing the necessary background. He had sent Stefi to the Führer to be sure he saw Peter personally, preferably in a day or two, before anything was done to him. When they had learned they only had until the evening, he had left her with instructions to keep Peter there with the Führer for as long as possible while he covered the last details such as planting evidence, rehearsing stories, and forcing Schindler's support.

"Richard? So what are your agents saying? And what does it have to do with him?" The Führer waved his hand at Peter, standing alone by the piano.

"Sorry." Richard rubbed his forehead. "Their information is still incomplete, and I was just trying to organize it mentally so that I could most cogently present it, together with my suspicions."

"I see."

"From what we've learned so far, it seems the Soviets may have been encouraged in that assassination plot which was aimed at you and which I uncovered earlier."

"By whom?"

"The Americans."

"The Americans?"

"Yes. I've brought some documents with me that support that assertion and we can go over them if you like. They're in my briefcase…"

The Führer shook his head vigorously, "No! Just tell me what's going on."

Of course, Richard thought. If he hadn't bothered to manufacture paper evidence, the Führer would have demanded to see it. He ignored his irritation and continued, "After that market crash a few months ago and the downturn in their economic figures, they're feeling more edgy, poorer, and even more inclined to isolationism."

"Good," Günter commented.

"Some of their policy experts realize, however, that the appropriate response is to open up their trade and become less protectionist, rather than more. They also know that if things continue on this downward trend, they won't be able to cover their defense costs and so they'll have to scale back."

"Even better," Günter grunted.

"The problem is, such economic conditions as might be created are exactly those which give rise to demagogues and militarism. There is already an extremely vocal and increasingly influential branch of the Christian Right which wants to, as they say, reconquer Europe for Christ. They recognize that the remaining established churches here are kept under the government's thumb and they know that proselytizing is illegal – thus they feel that the Continent has returned to paganism and they have a moral duty to save it."

The Führer chuckled with amusement and motioned for drinks. "Good idea! Another Thirty Years War to let foreign armies lay waste to Germany in the name of God."

"All joking aside," Richard continued, "this is not a group we want to see get into power. In fact, any sort of militarism on the part of the Americans is bad news for us. As in '39, our continued success is dependent on their unwillingness to act. Chaotic, corrupt and economically troubled as they may be, we are currently no match for them."

"Nonsense!" Günter sputtered. "You're speaking treason!"

Richard let his breath out slowly. "My dear colleague, if you think back, you will remember that we've discussed this point in some detail, and after looking at the *facts*, you came around to my point of view. Remember?"

Günter stared at Richard for some seconds before conceding, "Oh yes. That's right. I forgot."

The Führer looked surprised at Schindler's admission but did not comment. "If that's so, why don't the Americans invade and 'liberate' their allies?"

"Two reasons: the first is, they believe a pre-emptive strike is not in keeping with their democratic principles. Many of them believe it would be immoral to strike us unless provoked." Richard paused to let that soak in, then added, "The second is more understandable. They fear the human cost. They know an invasion, or in fact any armed struggle, will lead to enormous losses, both for us and for the people they claim to represent here. They are also loath to expend American lives for any cause other than their own defense. So, as long as they're not led by fanatics, we're safe."

"And you think there is a chance of fanatics gaining the upper hand?"

"What I think is irrelevant. What matters is what these policy experts think. They feel that the best way to avoid such a scenario is to open trade relations with us. They think it would help both our economies – and rich countries are always less likely to make war than poor ones, so an economic recovery for us would be good news for them."

The Führer looked intrigued by that thought and nodded for Richard to continue.

"And it would also serve to de-vilify us a bit – thus making us a less likely target for a propaganda war."

"So how does this tie in to the plot on my life?"

Richard looked obviously embarrassed. He cleared his throat before answering, "It seems, *mein Führer* – and remember, I am only reporting *their* opinions! It seems they think you are too…"

The Führer leaned forward slightly, raising his eyebrows and pursing his lips in interest. "Too what?"

"Unpredictable," Richard said, clearly compromising.

"Unpredictable?"

"Yes. Though your political abilities are not doubted, there are those in the American government who feel uncomfortable dealing with you because of what is known there of your personal tastes." Richard gestured broadly to the wall of videotapes. "They feel they need someone who is more in control of their…er, passions. And they know that even if these things are not a stumbling block in their ability to work with you, they would still be viewed with a great deal of suspicion by the American people."

"Unpredictable," the Führer repeated, as if reciting a foreign phrase for later use.

"That thing with the little girl, last year..."

"Ah..." the Führer said, as if waking from a trance. "So these people encouraged a plot against me?"

"Apparently. They assumed that you would be replaced by someone they could deal with."

"Who?"

Richard shrugged. "Perhaps Günter here. He appears very statesmanlike."

"And I don't?"

"I am only reporting on the enemy, not defending them."

"I see," the Führer said, distinctly offended. "So what does this have to do with him?" He tossed his head vaguely in Peter's direction.

"Well, first of all, we must recognize the facts. Our economy is a shambles. We can't find enough workers to do work that needs to be done, we spend vast resources on defense and police, our industry is crumbling and the infrastructure is deteriorating." Richard spoke rapidly, hoping to prevent Schindler from interrupting. "Agriculture has gone backwards, we still have areas of famine now and then, we have environmental disasters with depressing regularity, child mortality has *increased* over the last thirty years, and there is unrest seething beneath the surface in nearly every province–"

The Führer turned to Schindler. "What do you think, Günter?"

Richard answered, "We've spoken about these things and Günter is in agreement–"

"Let him speak for himself," the Führer snapped.

Richard turned to Schindler and waited. Schindler shifted in his seat, looking from one man to the other, then reluctantly said, "Richard and I are in complete agreement on this."

"That's unusual." The Führer raised an eyebrow sardonically. "What has made you change your mind?"

Again Schindler hesitated, then said, "I've had some discussions with Richard. He's made some interesting points. We now see eye to eye on these issues."

"Hmm. Alright Richard, get to the point."

"The point is, we need to open up relations with America. They have the technology that we need and they have markets for our products. If we could sell them French cheeses and Polish hams and German wines–"

"But what does this have to do with Halifax?" the Führer interjected impatiently.

Richard cleared his throat again. "Do you see that we need to talk to the Americans?"

"Yes, yes, yes! My God, but you've nagged me enough about it. Reform this, restructure that, talk to the Americans. Damn it Richard, I know it all by heart!"

"But you agree, it is important?"

Again, the Führer turned to Schindler. "What do you think? You're always countering what he says. Tell me why it's not important. Tell me why we should stand alone."

Schindler looked from the Führer to Richard and back to the Führer again. "It is important," he stated dryly.

The Führer drew his head back in histrionic surprise. He turned to Stefi. "Have I heard right? Are my two dear advisors in agreement?"

Stefi nodded.

"Oh, don't look so solemn, *Mäuschen*! What's on your mind?"

"I think my father is right, Rudi. I think we need to change our policy and I believe a great leader like you is just the man capable of doing it." She managed to press herself more closely to him as she said that, and he smiled warmly in response.

"Alright, Richard, I can't disagree with all of you. So what's the next step?"

"In order for there to be talks with the Americans – under your great leadership – we must improve your image in the Americans' minds. We all know that you are a noble ruler and an excellent statesman, but somehow the Americans have fixated on one or two personality traits which they find…"

"Tasteless," Schindler suggested, suddenly warming to his role. "That leaked videotape! My God, Rudi, but it makes you look like a brute!"

"A brute?" the Führer asked, clearly disturbed.

Richard continued, "And when it gets out that you have that sweet little girl's father–"

"Who?"

"Halifax. He's her father," Richard explained patiently. "It'll look–"

"He'll be tried for murder and executed in accordance with laws even the Americans approve of!"

Richard shifted in his seat. "You plan to have him tortured, don't you?"

"Oh, don't go telling me the Americans don't torture people. I know they do."

"If they do, they keep it very quiet. No one there hears about it."

"Well, they won't hear about this either!" the Führer snarled.

Schindler leaned forward in his seat. "Yes, they will. There's always someone willing to talk. And if it's taped, you can bet they'll probably even get their hands on some footage."

"You can imagine what that would look like on American television," Richard added, wondering slightly at Schindler's enthusiasm. He supposed that since Schindler had no choice but to agree with him, Günter had decided to make the most of his situation: he could get the Führer into talks with the Americans and then, when they failed, as Günter was sure they would, he could step in to rescue the Reich and its reputation and put its policies back on the proper, rigid path.

The Führer looked thoughtful. "Well, what am I supposed to do? I can't just release him!"

"If you kill him, you make a martyr out of him," Richard explained. "Günter's been doing a great job in America destroying his reputation. He's of more value to us alive and well, then tortured and dead."

The Führer shook his head, quite angry. "I am not giving up my chance to punish him. He deserves to be punished. He *must* be punished!"

"Rudi," Richard said, very carefully, "you killed his daughter. Every day he is alive, he feels her absence. He has been punished. Believe me."

The Führer looked confused by this. Then he shook his head, "No, he doesn't understand that sort of loyalty. That's an Aryan trait."

"You know he does understand." Richard spoke very softly, not only in an effort to convince the Führer, but also fearful of crossing that invisible line that would mean he had gone too far and could himself be sacrificed to some god of vengeance. "You just used his friendship for someone to blackmail him. Imagine how much more strongly he felt about his daughter. You can see it in the tape if you watch."

Rudi pursed his lips. Stefi leaned toward him and kissed his cheek. Then she whispered softly, "I know you are courageous and strong. You are a great leader and will do what's right for your people, even sacrificing your own right to vengeance. He is nothing but a gnat, and your actions will prove that his words were lies and that such miniscule creatures as he are irrelevant to one as great as you."

"What about the murder of an official?" the Führer asked, decisively. "I can't let that go unpunished. Whatever else you say, we can't start letting murderers just walk free."

Richard allowed himself a silent sigh of relief. "No, but if he is tried here, his defenders in America will claim he did not get a fair trial."

"So?"

"So, I suggest we give them exactly what they claim to want. Give him to them."

"Huh? I don't understand."

"Well, as long as we have him, he can be a martyr – whether tortured. dead or imprisoned. We can't just release him, not with the charges against him; so, give him to the Americans on the promise that they'll try him for Vogel's murder."

"What? That's idiotic! We can't surrender our sovereignty like that! He's a Reich subject–"

"Not even," Schindler corrected. "He's *Untermensch* category."

The Führer scowled at the interruption. "Subject, chattel, whatever! He's one of *ours* and he committed a crime in *our* territory against one of *our* citizens! What business is it of theirs?"

Richard opened his hands expressively. "It's a gesture on our part. A gesture of goodwill. We know they have a special interest in this man, and we are so sure of the justice of our case against him, that we are willing to have him tried by outsiders, just so that they, too, can see the evidence against him. We can suggest an international tribunal – a special court convened just for this case, in some neutral country, say Switzerland."

The Führer was shaking his head. "Are you mad, Richard?"

"When they see you willing to give up someone they thought you would never let go, as a completely voluntary good-will gesture, then there will be no doubt about your statesmanship. They'll be willing to deal with you and we can open talks with the Americans. Meanwhile, we can foist this troublesome man on them. There, in their limelight, on trial for kidnap and murder, they'll see him for what he is: not some sort of saintly martyr, but a thuggish terrorist, willing to do anything, even murder an innocent man in his sleep."

The Führer tilted his head with interest.

"Günter has already done an excellent job laying the groundwork – the man's reputation is already in tatters. Now, all we have to do is let him out among them, trying to defend the indefensible and he will be ruined entirely and all the people who supported him will end up looking like the fools they are." Richard smiled broadly. "We couldn't have arranged it any better if we had tried."

The Führer twisted around to look at Peter as he stood alone by the piano and the others followed his lead. Peter was too far away to hear any of their conversation and was staring at the piano, wrapped in his own thoughts. He must have noticed the sudden silence though, for he looked up at the little group, his face completely expressionless. After a brief moment, he pointedly returned to looking at the piano, as if indicating his complete disinterest in them and what they might be saying.

The Führer turned his attention back to Richard. "Alright. I'll think about it anyway." He stood suddenly and the others rose quickly to their feet. The Führer turned to one of his officers and directed, "Send Lederman home and put the prisoner somewhere safe for the night. Here, in the building. Make him comfortable, and make sure no one touches him or talks to him, understood?" Not waiting for an answer, the Führer turned his attention to Richard and Günter to add, "I'll see you both at noon tomorrow. Now leave, I'm going to bed." And with that, he wrapped his arm around Stefi's shoulder and walked with her to his bed.

5

"*I*n all my years on the beat," the reporter announced breathlessly into his microphone, "I have never seen security as tight as this in Washington." He gestured behind himself at the crowds lining Pennsylvania Avenue. "Crowds of protesters have assembled along every conceivable route from the airport to the White House. DC police are having trouble maintaining order as rival groups have occasionally clashed and..." He stopped and looked heavenward as a heavy thump, thump, thump interrupted his speech. Then, turning back to the camera, he brought the microphone in closer to his face and began to shout over the noise of the helicopter. "We can assume that this is them now. Ladies and Gentlemen, we are witnessing the first visit of a high-level official from the Third Reich since..."

A rising howl of anger detonated from the crowds swallowing his words.

"...unusual distance – presumably to prevent snipers or any other attacks against...Oh, there, we can see them now. They will be escorted to the White House and will meet directly with the president in a diplomatic move which has been highly criticized in Congress and by foreign policy..."

With an effort Alex found the mute and hit that. He looked at the right side of the screen, past the reporter with his mouth moving silently, at the White House lawn where the helicopter had landed. As if reading his thoughts, the cameraman managed to zoom in on the little group emerging from the chopper and Alex was able to make out Ryszard's tall, lean frame. He rubbed his face as if exhausted or exasperated, shook the proffered hand of some low-level official, then draping his arm protectively over Kasia's shoulder, motioned to his little group to follow him as he and Kasia accompanied the official toward the great looming white building.

It wasn't going to work, Alex thought, as they disappeared into the building. All his life he had supported all his children in their endeavors, but especially Zosia and Ryszard. He had helped Zosia organize Peter's direct assault on the Reich's reputation, the fund-raising for arms, and the rhetoric of armed struggle while at the same time supporting Ryszard's infiltration and his unceasing drive to the top. He had, somehow, always imagined that the two strategies would coalesce once Ryszard had attained his goal: that he would be interested in destroying from within that which they had failed to destroy from without. Ryszard would, as Führer, ruin the Reich, driving a stake through the creature's heart so they could nail the coffin shut once and for all. Or so he had thought, and so it had begun.

But things had changed with time. Ryszard spoke ever more frequently of evolution, of peaceful transitions, of reform and restructuring. The word "liberation" barely crossed his lips anymore and others had begun to doubt his loyalty to the cause, to the nation, and to the overthrow of the German occupiers. Indeed, even Ryszard seemed conflicted, as he had assiduously worked on publicizing the videotape of Joanna's murder and set up Karl to make one idiotic mistake after another in the Reich's defense – something which had hardly furthered his overall goal to normalize relations between the two powers. Yet, he had explained that even that had served his purposes – that he had to fight battles on two fronts: one to win over the Americans and another against the non-reformist elements of the current government. If a serious embarrassment could push the Führer to begin instituting the policies which Ryszard would later bring to fruition, then it was worth the minor damage done to American-European relations.

Judging from the angry crowds and the political denunciations, though, it wasn't minor damage. Rather unusually, the American people were in no mood to deal with torturers and murderers, and Ryszard's ground-breaking visit seemed both ill-timed and doomed to failure. How in the world was he going to walk the tight-rope between pleasing his political master back in Berlin and sucking up to the Americans enough to begin talks on normalizing relations and the establishment of a peace treaty? Ryszard's enemies back in Berlin would have their eyes wide-open for any sign of disloyalty, however slight, and the Americans would refuse to hear him, opting for mindless denunciations of past evils over any hope of dialog.

It didn't have to be like that, Alex thought, as he reflected on the brutal regimes with which the Americans happily and routinely dealt. But it was that way, because they themselves had helped fan these flames and now Ryszard was walking right into them, hoping to calm them down and to make progress in NAU-Reich relations.

Or was he? Alex suddenly wondered. No one knew what his son was thinking anymore. He had been on his own, up to his neck in the Nazi hierarchy, living the lie for more than twenty years now. Was Ryszard simply planning his own coup? Was he trying to fan the flames even further to provoke some sort of crisis which he would use to his own personal advantage?

Alex shook his head at the thoughts. Such ideas were planted by people who did not know Ryszard. It wasn't like Ryszard. He knew his son, he could trust him. Though Ryszard kept his emotions to himself and his words short, when he spoke, it always got to the heart of the matter, and as Alex thought back, the reason Ryszard had prompted Peter to speak out, as opposed to Zosia's and his own motives, had been to counteract the terrible effects of torture.

As long as you remain silent, you remain their tool...Though he had not said so at the time, therein lay his motives: it had been neither a plan to use Peter to raise money for resistance, nor had it been part of a convoluted plot to further his own career. He had simply found Peter's torture abhorrent and his enslavement equally so, and he had wanted someone to speak out against it, because he could not. He may have even surprised himself by his eloquent speech, for up to that point, he had given no indication of doing anything more than silently acquiescing to Zosia's scheme.

And now? Ryszard's heartfelt actions, his revulsion at the Reich's methods and cruelty, might well have sabotaged his own goals of reconciliation, restructuring and reform. How in the world would he get the Americans to accept the Reich after the negative publicity barrage which it had just endured? And how would he counter that barrage when he himself had been behind so much of it? It couldn't work. It was too soon, the ground was not ready. Peter's capture had precipitated Ryszard's actions and in the end that would lead to their failure. Still unsure of whether or not he approved of his son's strategy, it nevertheless saddened Alex that he could do no more at this point than watch the sad tale of failure unfold. A failure which could, ultimately, cost his son his life.

Alex sighed expressively. He wished that Anna or someone would bring him a sandwich and a drink because he did not want to move away from the television, yet he was quite hungry. Damn that woman and her sudden surge of independence, he thought, as he pressed the button which brought back the reporter's voice. He listened to the yammering with a sense of dismay. The reporter knew nothing yet felt obliged to speak – and here he was, desperate enough for information that he was listening! What he would give to be able to be present at the meeting between Ryszard and the President. The real meeting, not this introductory crap which the news had cut to. Still, it was fascinating, and Alex watched, intrigued, as he saw his son play out his role.

The protocol was awkward, the two men completely ill-at-ease with what they knew of each other's culture. The cameras which had been allowed inside the White House recorded how Colonel Traugutt and the President approached each other; Traugutt stiffened, brought his heels together and seemed to bow slightly, but straightened immediately to shake the President's hand. The President said something and gestured toward the press. Traugutt cast a contemptuous eye at the cameramen then nodded. Still holding hands as if they were glued together, the two men turned to face the cameras and smiled artificially into an onslaught of photographs.

The handshake was repeated even more heartily, then they released hands and the president stepped forward to welcome his guest. Even as the President spoke, the cameras focused on Ryszard's face, on the look of arrogant disdain which he barely held in check. Alex shook his head in recognition. It was Anna's look – that display of aristocratic superiority. Though she had cast herself in the role of the family's servant, slaving away for her husband and her children all her life, she had never lost that look – that statement that the blue blood in the family came from her veins. What was he? A mongrel mix of Polish and Jewish and English – none of whom had ever attained anything. But she, though she might scrub the floors and cook their food and wash their clothes, she did it as a noblewoman. As *Szlachta*. Her family had been citizens of the Commonwealth, had voted in the election of the Kings, had been a part of that Noble Democracy. A branch of her family had also been fabulously wealthy, but that was neither here nor there, according to Anna – the Commonwealth did not recognize degrees of nobility – only the brotherhood of the *Szlachta* and their equality under the law. The fact that the Magnates, with their private armies and personally owned estates larger than some countries, might be rather more equal than the other gentry was an irrelevance.

As the cameras continued their harsh dissection of Ryszard's flawed democratic tendencies, his face suddenly softened and a smile played across his lips. He was looking off to the side, at someone, and the camera angle changed to show that corner of the room. It was where Ryszard's entourage stood, and there, centrally placed, was Kasia. The view shot back to Ryszard and as the President finished his speech, Ryszard gave him a polite nod, then gestured encouragingly toward his wife. She came forward, looking abashed, beautiful in her timidity. When she had reached Ryszard, he bent formally to kiss her hand, then straightened and kissed her cheek with a smile of fond familiarity, then he put his arm around her shoulder in a protective, yet respectful, manner and introduced her to the President.

Damn the man! Alex thought. It had all been an act! He knew the Americans would expect certain behavior and he had dutifully provided it, but then he had broken the ice with his spontaneous invitation to Kasia to join him in his talks with the president. He had also managed to show that despite a reputation to the contrary, women were taken seriously in the Reich, at least by him, while at the same time displaying, for all to see, that he was a loving husband, a caring human being. With his spontaneous gesture he had dispelled in a few seconds, decades of distrust. Here was a man who could be human, here was a man with whom the Americans could deal. The reporter announced it as breathlessly as one would expect and the on-the-spot analysis was followed by a buzz of agreement from experienced political commentators as the small group smiled naturally into the incessant flashing of the cameras.

Ryszard struggled not to wince at the irritating flashes of light as he stood with Kasia and the president for yet another photo-op. Why, he wondered, wasn't a single official photographer sufficient? But he knew the answer, or rather Peter had told him. In fact, Peter had prepared him exquisitely, scripting every move, from beginning to end. Their conversations had been exceedingly useful and Peter had been very co-operative, at least in the end. That hadn't been the case at first – but that was the Führer's fault. After about two weeks of patience, and at the insistence of several of his other advisors, the Führer had broken his word and had Peter interrogated. Nothing strenuous, in fact, quite gently, the Führer had insisted. Even so, once Ryszard had found out what was going on, he had rushed down to the cells to keep an eye on the proceedings.

They were only just beginning. Peter had been seated in a chair at a table, not even handcuffed. There was an empty syringe on the table in front of him and he stared at that as he spoke. Whatever they had given him, Peter had not succumbed, for though he looked a bit disoriented, he showed no signs of straying from the legend he had been taught. He dutifully relayed the details of his life to his questioner from the point where he had left the Vogels. He had headed south, into the Balkans, he reported. There he had been picked up by some mountain bandits who kept him in their camp as a sort of prisoner. He could give no details as he had not known where he was or what they did, nor did he speak their language; he just did their bidding and was permitted to live among them.

Then, one day, he was told that his services were needed. He was taken through Turkey, into Iran, and from there to America. At the airport, in New York, he had been handed over to a representative of the Governments-in-Exile and told to be cooperative. So, he had given interview after interview, relaying only the truth. At this assertion, there was a grunt of anger from his interrogator. He reached toward a small black box, the size of a pack of cigarettes, that sat near him on the table, but Ryszard interjected from his position, standing aloof, leaning against the wall, that the Führer was not concerned with the prisoner's opinions of his own veracity, and the interview moved forward.

Büttner wandered in and joined the little group, leaning casually against the wall next to Ryszard and offering him a cigarette. Together the two men smoked and watched as Peter explained how he had met the daughter of the representative who had guided him through his American tour, and how they had fallen in love. Along with her daughter, they returned to the Reich together, and carefully avoiding any contact with the Balkan bandits who had sold his services, they headed north into the Tatra mountains.

He explained how he had no idea where he was or why they were there, and in fact, he and the little girl were left behind in a village while his wife tried to make contact with someone in the Underground. She had little success, being told that he was too much of a provocation to recruit into their fold. Nevertheless, in gratitude for the work he had done, they were provided with identity papers, clothing, and enough money to rent a house. They had settled into a hotel in Neu Sandez and were in the process of exploring the housing market, when the bomb had exploded and caused him to be arrested.

At that point he stopped speaking and simply stared at the syringe. His interrogator gruffly ordered him to continue, and once Peter had taken a moment to compose himself, he did, saying, "After they strangled my daughter, I collapsed…"

The interrogator glanced down at his notes and shook his head. "Liar! She was killed in the bomb blast!"

Peter looked up at his interrogator. It was clear he knew there was no point arguing; nevertheless, he said, "She was strangled in front of me. It was filmed and your Führer has the videotape." He gestured with a finger toward the two men who were observing the interchange. "They know, ask them."

Bloody-minded fool, Ryszard had thought.

The interrogator grasped the small black box and snarling, "You will not lie!" pressed a button on it. To Ryszard's amazement Peter cried out and leapt to his feet, knocking over his chair as he did so, doubling over and dropping down in agony. Only then did Ryszard notice the belt-like device that was strapped snugly around Peter's waist. Büttner whispered into Ryszard's ear that, though he had heard of the belt, it was the first time he had seen it used. American, he had intimated. Quite effective, Ryszard returned, drowning out whatever Peter said to provoke its use a second time.

There was a pause and the prisoner remained in a defensive crouch, one knee and a hand on the floor. He was breathing heavily, obviously quite stunned by his brief ordeal. Nevertheless as soon as he found his voice, he asserted, yet again, that his daughter had been brutally murdered. Ryszard and his companion watched impassively as he was punished a third time. He writhed in uncontrolled agony, his mouth stretched in a silent scream.

Once the shocks had stopped, he remained in silence, glowering angrily at the other men in the room like a vicious dog which had only temporarily been beaten into submission. The interrogator obviously disapproved of this

273

unspoken recrimination and, holding the remote control threateningly in his hand, insisted, "Now, tell us the truth about what happened to her."

Before Peter could reply, Ryszard stepped forward to whisper into the interrogator's ear, "He's suffered one heart attack already. If you kill him, you know, the order is that you'll take his place."

The interrogator looked up in alarm. Ryszard shrugged, as if to say, it wasn't his place to question the Führer's orders, and then casually returned to stand by the wall. "Anyway," he said, in a normal voice, "the details of her death are irrelevant, so move on with it."

The interrogator nodded, a guard helped Peter into his chair, and the interview continued. Peter continued to relay the story he had been taught, one which carefully matched up to the information already known to the government. He explained that he knew very little, pleading ignorance of the language and a dependence on his wife. His wife must have bribed the guards in the hospital, he guessed, and feeling that they could obtain new papers and hide best in the multitudes of the great city, his wife arranged their flight to Berlin. He gave few details, but all the details he did give, Ryszard knew, had been carefully organized so that the background would be in place by the time they were checked out.

In February, a chance sighting of Karl Vogel had set Peter's blood boiling. By March, he was unable to control his urge for revenge and he climbed into the Vogel house and murdered the brute. At the harsh wording, the interrogator reached impulsively for the remote control, but then decided better of it.

"On an impulse, I kidnapped the daughter as a sort of compensation for having lost my own," Peter reported, his eyes fixed on the interrogator's hand and its proximity to the remote control. "I brought her back to my wife and she screamed abuse at me, told me I was insane, that I should have never done anything so risky and cruel."

"Cruel?" the interrogator repeated.

Peter's lips twitched and his eyes strayed to the recording secretary. He clearly disagreed with the wording he had been obliged to learn, but he had stuck to his orders. Finally he clarified, "She thought we wouldn't be able to give the girl a good home since we were on the run." He looked down at the table, clearly embarrassed, and continued, "The next morning, she and the girl were gone. I haven't seen either since."

"What then?"

"I didn't have any money, just the papers she had left me. I lived rough, broke into basements, stole food. Eventually I thought I could con my old mates into helping me. I met up with them and fed them a long story about..." He waved his hand in exasperation. "You've heard it all – I'm sure Konstantin told you everything."

The interrogator nodded as if not interested and asked, "So you were never in London?"

Ryszard sighed his relief. It was nothing more than Schindler trying to prove he had not been derelict in his duty! They had bought the story and the questions would be innocuous from this point on. His relief was rudely interrupted by Büttner whispering in his ear. "I think he's lying. I'm pretty sure we had him cornered near Posen, after he murdered Vogel."

"What? How do you know that?"

"He was found in a field by one of my officers. We didn't pick him up, instead we ordered some local illegals to help him and for their girl to accompany him. I wanted to see where he'd go. I was sure he'd lead us to someone important."

"And?"

"And he did. He sought out the A.K. and they led him and the girl south. Unfortunately my men lost them, the girl might have deliberately given them the slip. The girl was supposed to report back as soon as possible, but we haven't heard a word from her."

Ryszard whistled. "Just as well!"

"What do you mean?"

"I mean, if you found out anything that you had to report to Rudi, then he would have learned that you had Halifax back in March and *let him go!*"

"I figured getting one of our agents into that mountain enclave was worth it," Büttner returned somewhat irritably. "After all, he was all agog about them."

Ryszard snorted. "That was in January. You must have missed most of his rantings about Halifax before and after that."

"I guess I did," Büttner agreed sullenly.

"If I were you, I wouldn't point out the inconsistency. It's probably meaningless anyway – they probably refused him entry and he just went back to Berlin."

Büttner nodded.

Ryszard nudged his companion and added sardonically, "And don't worry about me, dear comrade, I would never betray your little secret to the Führer. You can rest assured of that."

Büttner's face turned beet red in fury. But there was something else there and Ryszard recognized it as chagrin. He knew with a sudden certainty that it was Büttner who had ordered his arrest and he didn't hesitate to add, "And, by the way, I do hope you realize that if you ever try another *stunt* with me, dear comrade, you *will* be hanging from a lamppost by the next day."

Büttner had sputtered something about nonsense and had stormed out. Ryszard had filed away the interchange for later analysis and returned his attention to the interview, studying Peter, trying to gauge his mood, but Peter had kept staring at the syringe on the table, answering in mono-syllables, and would not look up.

"Halifax!" Ryszard had called out, to get Peter's attention. Peter had looked up then and the look of pure hatred Ryszard had received had sent shivers down his spine. For a moment he was sure Peter would betray him. But then Peter brought his gaze back to the syringe, as if staring down hell, and continued tersely answering the questions put to him.

Ryszard had found himself studying the empty syringe as it lay innocently on the table. What had been in it?

The irritating flashes of light stopped and Ryszard woke from his reverie. Later, with the appropriate prompting, the distant look on his face would be described as that of a man with a vision for the future. Kasia kissed him lightly on the cheek and he smiled with genuine pleasure. The admiring and happy grin which he gave her would be splashed on newspapers around the country the following morning and even as the three of them retreated into the President's private conference room, the press was already abuzz with this revelation about Richard Traugutt's inscrutable character.

6

*T*he cock crowed. It did it every morning and for hours afterwards. Irritatingly so. Peter opened his eyes and stared at the ceiling for a few moments, then he turned his head and looked out the window, at the golden leaves of the birch tree. Day six and sixty. Sixty six. What could one do with that number? Well, at least it sounded nice. And in either direction it was six and six. That must mean something – perhaps it was a prediction of his day. Forward or backward, in English or German, it would be the same.

His eyes strayed from the window to the video camera mounted in the corner of the room. One of four in this room, another two in the bathroom. Doubtless with infrared capabilities as well. He smiled a greeting at his unseen keeper, mouthed "good morning," then rolled his eyes upward and looked at the clock. Half past six. In another couple of weeks it would be dark when he awoke, or maybe he wouldn't wake up so early. Or maybe he'd be dead. It didn't really seem to matter. Everything had drifted into one indeterminate and indefinable being. He existed. He existed in relative comfort. He existed in relative comfort in a vacuum. An absolute vacuum. A vacuum of unknowing and unbeing.

Tired of resting, he rolled out of bed, and went into the adjacent bathroom suite. When he emerged, he glanced at the clock again. Six forty five. He spent the next forty-five minutes exercising, doing whatever he could within the confines of his room to strengthen his muscles and relieve his boredom. At seven-thirty, he went to stand by the window. He stared out at the view, contemplated the leaves on the trees, noticed that there was a light fog – or was that just his eyes?

At eight-thirty a servant brought breakfast into the room. Peter thanked him, he always did, but he never received a response. It had become clear within the first few days, that he was considered too treacherous, too dangerous, too full of hatred and lies to be spoken to or listened to by any of the lowly and impressionable sorts who dealt with him on a daily basis. He was served three meals a day and taken out for fresh air usually twice in the day, but never, not once, had he received a response to any comment, query or request. It was as if he had not spoken at all. As if he spoke in barks and growls. As if he were not really human. Nevertheless, he never failed to thank the servant for bringing the meals or the guard for taking him out. Even if they would not acknowledge that he was human, he would not forget.

He ate the breakfast slowly, enjoying it. It was a good breakfast, though always the same: pâté and ham, cheeses, jam and butter, fresh bread and coffee. Real coffee. He poured the last cup out of the small pot and savored its flavor. Real coffee. If only it would remain hot. But it didn't. It grew warm, then tepid, then cold. He glanced at the clock as he downed the last of the now-cold coffee. Nine o'clock.

There was nothing to read in the room, no pen nor any paper to write on. Peter went over to the mirror and breathed on it, forming a cloud on the surface. Long ago when he was being held for interrogation, he had been kept in a dank prison cell, also without pen or paper. Nevertheless there had been something to read – previous prisoners had scratched their messages on the walls of the cells, often using their own blood as ink. Words of despair, pleas to God, messages to loved ones. There had been a political tract advocating revolution and resilience. Another had advised *kill them all*. Someone had scribbled the word *freedom* and drawn a picture of a bird escaping its cage. Back then Peter had written nothing at all, but now he had an urge to leave a message. The only question was, to whom? The fog on the mirror would soon clear, leaving only the faintest outline of what he traced, and then the mirror would be cleaned and even that would be gone. To whom should he direct his ephemeral message?

He touched the mirror and began drawing a heart. In it he would write *Zosia and Peter*, carved in mist instead of wood. As he had done a hundred times before, he stopped drawing before he had even completed the curve of the heart. They knew he was married, but it would not do to let them know his wife's name or that he loved her. His finger remained poised as he decided how he should complete his aborted drawing this time. He swept his finger down and crossed the line to make an eff, then finished the word *friede*. Peace.

He smiled at his message, but could not shake his irritation at the small eff – the grammatical error was typical of an English pupil and guaranteed a sharp smack with a ruler across the back of the hand. Better no peace than to get it wrong, he thought, and with a sweep of his hand he wiped out peace. He glanced over at the clock again. Nine fifteen.

He went over to the chair and sat down to look out the window. It was an old-fashioned window that opened wide. Wide enough for a full-grown man to easily climb through and down the three floors to the enclosed courtyard below. He had thought about it often enough, but there seemed no point. There was always a guard posted below and on the walls around, and even if he could get out of the courtyard, he had no idea where he could then go. The *Residenz* was the most secure building in the Reich. He got the impression that even well-known visitors such as Traugutt and Schindler always underwent a search as they entered or left. There would be no point in even trying to pass as someone else – his face was known to all and sundry.

He supposed he could throw himself out the window in an attempt at suicide, but if he succeeded, he was sure Roman would be made to pay a price. More likely, though, he would not succeed. It was only a three story drop onto grass and it was very likely that even a head-first dive would end in his instinctively trying to save himself. He would probably do something idiotic like break his back. The thought of being paralyzed *and* in the Führer's control was more than he could stomach. No, suicide was not an option. There was no way out for him. None at all. He was the unwilling guest of the Führer awaiting the whim of his keeper and there was no point in denying it.

Indeed, his boredom was quite nicely balanced by his terror. He had no information about his status. He had watched from afar as Ryszard had spoken with the Führer and Schindler, presumably about him, and then the next thing that had happened was he was led away. Not to the thirty or so days of torture then death which he had been promised, but to this room, this hotel-like room, with its tasteful furniture and its impersonal comforts and its reasonably nice food. And here he sat, day after day, awaiting his fate, whatever it was. He had heard no word. Not from Ryszard, not from anybody. He had simply been left alone, not spoken to by the servants, the guards. Nobody.

After two weeks of silence and without warning, he had been led out of the room and down to a cell. He had expected the worst, but he had only been interrogated. Gently, he would say. One nasty injection, and there had been that conflict over what exactly had happened to Joanna, but after three excruciating presses of that little button, Ryszard had whispered something into the ear of the interrogator and they had moved on. Peter had dutifully repeated his story, but that had not prevented him from seeking solace, or information, or something from Ryszard.

Ryszard had appeared suddenly, shortly after the interview had begun, out of breath and apparently taken by surprise, but then he had taken up a relaxed position leaning against the wall. Peter had tried repeatedly to catch his eye, to get some hint as to how Zosia and the children were doing, but Ryszard had been adamantly cold, chatting informally with the official who had joined him. After a number of rebuffed attempts at eye contact, Peter had withdrawn and had been quite surprised when Traugutt had shouted out his name, as if trying to gauge his reactions. By that point, he had nothing left but hatred and he had let his face express exactly that and had been quite gratified by Ryszard's obviously perturbed reaction.

Weeks more had passed after that. He overheard one exchange of comments in the hall and observed a few other things which led him to surmise that one officer had been given responsibility for keeping him alive and well. As an incentive the officer had been promised that if Peter did not survive or somehow escaped then the officer would take his place. His keeper was then given a staff to care for his prisoner and authority to approve or disapprove anything – up to all levels save the Führer himself. His control over his staff was complete since he had been given one additional responsibility: before he was offered up as expiation for Peter's escape or death, he would name the punishment for all his subordinates. That kept them all scrupulously unbribable: there would be no cyanide capsules, no smuggled stilettos, no secret messages. The silence was complete, his exile from any and all help – unbreachable.

One day, the tedium had been broken, and he was unexpectedly led from the room. Peter felt himself growing almost weak with fear as they walked him, without explanation, down the stairways and through various hallways. He was pushed through a door and into a room which had only a table and two chairs. In one of the chairs sat Traugutt. Though Peter had never been impressed by Ryszard's warmth, he was immediately aware that the cold and inhumane man who presented himself that morning on the far side of the table held no hint of Ryszard's existence.

Traugutt formally introduced himself and explained that he had been given permission by the Führer to interview Peter. Peter's usual guard stood nearby, Traugutt's bodyguard stood close and attentive behind him. With the witnesses and probably with the ubiquitous listening devices, it was clear that Ryszard would not impart any information to Peter, but still Peter had looked for something – a gesture, a sideways glance, anything! There was nothing. Traugutt scrutinized him as curiously and coldly as if he were looking at a rat in a maze, and Peter had realized then just how far from friends or hope he was.

"I want information on America," Traugutt had stated with rude brusqueness, "And I expect you'll give it to me."

"What makes you think I'd care to help you?" Peter had asked, though he knew the answer well enough.

"There is your friend. He is still well and alive."

Peter shrugged. "That's been overused."

Traugutt's eyes narrowed in anger. He scrutinized Peter as if trying to bore into his soul and there was a long, tense silence. "It's for the good of *your* country," he said at last, with a meaningful emphasis on "your".

So it was an order. And so Peter complied with the request and told everything he knew about America, everything he had learned about American public opinion. Over a period of weeks, he described American life and the American media in detail. He scripted useful sentences which would convey the essence of Traugutt's message – explaining that such sentences were called "sound bites". Peter conducted mock interviews – providing appropriate responses to awkward questions. He invented spontaneous situations which would go down well with the press and the people. In essence, he mapped out the strategy for Traugutt's entire visit.

After several weeks, the interviews suddenly stopped. And now he was alone again.

Peter's thoughts were interrupted by the servant returning to remove the tray. That would mean it was nine-thirty. The servant carefully counted all the items on the tray, then picked it up. Peter thanked the man and was ignored. He asked if he could have more coffee but the servant did not appear to hear him. He followed the servant to the door and looked out as the door was opened, but he did not attempt to follow the servant out. The door was closed and Peter stared at the wood for a few moments before turning on his heel and returning to the window.

He remained standing. It was time to talk to Joanna, and it wouldn't do to be too comfortable. Funny, he could never bring up Allison or anyone else he had known – maybe he really did believe what he had said in his dream: of all the people he had known, only Joanna had had the strength of spirit to survive the transition through death. With little effort, he conjured her up and imagined her antics as she bounced around the room and told him about what it was like to fly or to dance from one cloud to another or to be a leopard. She giggled, said she was a rabbit, and jumped up and down on the bed, commenting that it was nice and soft and bouncy.

When he heard the ten o'clock bells from the clock tower, he forced himself to stop the imaginary conversation. He didn't want to drift from it being a diversion into madness. Only once had he allowed himself to violate this rule – on the anniversary of Joanna's death. On that day he had allowed his little ghost to curl up on his lap and keep him company for hours, and, despite the cameras, despite the comings and goings of his warders, he allowed himself to weep.

The next hour was hard to fill. He had determined that it would be used to keep his mind as sharp as possible, but it was getting more difficult with each day to construct a mental puzzle or series of self-asked questions that were sufficiently challenging without being tedious or impossible. Worst of all, yesterday, he had actually given up, deciding that the entire exercise was pointless. He thought of revising his opinion that he should not review his Polish vocabulary, and indeed should avoid anything that caused his mind to focus on those unrevealed aspects of his life. After a moment's consideration, he decided to continue that bit of self-censorship. Whatever he thought of, it would have to be relatively innocent as well. He picked two random numbers, repeated them to himself and then multiplied them together. He memorized the answer, remultiplied the numbers and compared the two answers.

He looked at the clock. Five past ten. That would never do. Far too slow! He paced up and down, continuing the mental games, switching at half past from numbers to words. As the clock slowly approached eleven, he felt himself grow more and more restless. Like Pavlov's dog. The clock struck eleven and he stopped in mid-stride and turned to look at the door. He stood there, stock still, and waited. One minute past eleven. Three minutes. Five minutes. *Oh God, please, let them come.* Please don't let it be one of those days when, for whatever reason, he was not given time outside.

The handle moved and Peter walked over to the door. He greeted the guard with a relieved half-smile and accepted the shackles that were handed to him. He stooped down and placed the metal rings around his ankles, then stood to wrap the chain around his waist and placed his left hand in the manacle that was attached to the chain. The guard finished the process by chaining his right wrist into place and then kicked the short chain between Peter's ankles as a means of checking that the ankle rings were securely attached. Together the two of them walked out the door and down the corridor, Peter trudging along with necessarily small steps, the guard stopping periodically so that he did not get too far ahead of his prisoner.

Initially the chains had been placed on him at the entrance of the courtyard and the guard had stooped to fasten them around his ankles, but after a few days, Peter had protested against the chains, arguing that they were completely unnecessary. The guard had not said a word, he had simply turned around and walked his prisoner back to his room. Three days later, after not having had a single opportunity to leave the room, when Peter was offered the shackles at the door, he had gratefully put them on and since then he had not questioned his keepers' methods.

The garden was laid out beautifully in a large, completely enclosed courtyard. There was, as far as Peter could see, no way out of the courtyard and he had long ago given up thoughts of escape. A small stream ran through the center of the garden, appearing out of a grate in a tall brick wall and disappearing through another grate. Plum and apple trees lined its banks, a willow draped its branches gracefully over the water. Peter hobbled over to the willow and after dropping carefully to his knees, rolled into a sitting position under its branches. Initially he had taken to lying down, staring up at the unfettered sky, but with a wordless nudge from the guard's foot, he had been warned that such behavior was inappropriate and disrespectful, so now he sat with his knees drawn up and his arms draped casually over them, tilting his head upward so that he would not see the walls.

Though the ostensible reason for his being taken out was to get exercise, the chains made it difficult to walk around and he often spent the entire time rooted to this one spot, enjoying the sight of the birds as they flew freely overhead, listening to the burbling of the brook as it echoed with the laughter of his children, and letting the willow brush against his face as if it were the gentle touch of Zosia's loving hand. He wondered how they were doing, Zosia and the girls. It must be hard for Zosia alone with them, trying to work as well. Marysia would hardly have time to help out, Olek and Stefi were in Berlin, but maybe Anna would lend a hand. Or maybe even Tadek. Peter felt so incredibly sad about having inadvertently left Zosia alone with the children, that he did not even mind if Tadek was helping out – there was no jealousy at the thought, just gratitude that someone was there for her, since he so obviously was not.

He wondered if Tadek and Zosia would finally marry once they learned of his death. He assumed so, and decided that it would probably be a good idea. They seemed to understand each other so well. Doubtless, all those long walks, he thought, with a quiet chuckle. And Tadek's attitude toward children as intolerable nuisances had seemed to mellow enough that Peter felt sure Tadek would be a reasonably good father. Better than none at all, which seemed the only other alternative.

He sighed at that thought. God, he missed them! But it seemed unlikely he would ever see any of them again. It was a sad thought, and as much as the prospect of being tortured to death dismayed him, the thought of never seeing any of them again, hurt even more. He wished he could hear some news about them. A muttered "they're okay" from Ryszard would have meant the world to him, but Ryszard had given no indication of knowing who he was. Clearly Ryszard's survival instinct was superbly developed. Even so, Peter had been happy to see a familiar face – even Ryszard, even knowing that Ryszard would sacrifice him without hesitation if the situation merited it. But now even Ryszard was gone and Peter felt that not only his only possible connection with the outside world had been severed, but also his only possible defense against the Führer's sudden mad whims had been removed.

The guard approached and nudged Peter with his foot. Peter struggled to his feet and followed the guard back to the door leading inside and to his room. It had been a relatively short outing, but he did not dare complain. If he obeyed the subtle commands immediately, his chances were better that he would be able to go back outside in the afternoon. Back in the room, he would do more exercise, the barber would come to shave him, then he'd have his lunch. Then, all he would have to cope with was the afternoon and the evening before he could lie back in bed and await the dawn of day sixty seven.

7

*"D*amn that bastard! What the hell does he think he's doing?"

Stefi sighed slightly at the familiar sound of Rudi's angry shout. She stood patiently by the bath to let the servant slip a bathrobe onto her and wrap a towel around her wet hair. Whatever it was, it could wait a moment more.

"I'll kill him, I swear, I'll kill him!"

The "him" was good news. One of these days it would be "her" and that would be trouble. Besides Stefi, Rudi interacted with so few women – his wife, the few young things who occasionally caught his eye – that Stefi was fairly certain that the phrase "I'll kill her" would refer to herself and she would then feel that maniac's wrath. Now she could only assume that the offending man was some chef who had prepared a lousy breakfast, or perhaps some underling who had misdirected a ministry.

Stefi studied herself in the mirror and smoothed her eyebrows, but the effect was still not right. With a wave of her hand she indicated the silk robe and the servant obediently removed the terry-cloth robe and picked up the silk one. Stefi cast an eye at her naked figure in the mirror. Still no sign of the pregnancy, but it wouldn't be long before her belly would begin to bulge. How in the world would she maintain her control over Rudi at that point? Maybe an extended holiday in the south of France. She could send him steamy letters and keep him panting back in Berlin, picturing her with a nubile figure, blissfully unaware of the rigors her body was undergoing. Well, she'd worry about that later. She still had a couple of months to think of something.

Once she was swathed in her fine white robe, Stefi removed the towel from her hair and laid it on the sink. She artfully arranged her wet hair, picked up the towel, and then carefully grabbing just one lock, began to stroke it dry as she stepped out of the bathroom into the Führer's bedroom. He wasn't there, he was at the far end of the huge room, in the area he used for entertaining guests. She walked over to Rudi, waiting to catch his eye, but he was engrossed in the television.

"What's on?" Stefi skillfully placed herself just to the side of the television so that Rudi could not help but notice her, but also so that she was not in any way blocking his view.

Rudi looked up at her and smiled sadly. He beckoned. *"Mäuschen,* they all betray me! Every last one of them."

Ach, another paranoid fantasy of betrayal! As she approached her Führer, a look of understanding and sympathy pasted on her face, Stefi threw a quick glance back at the television and saw, to her horror, that it was a videotape of an American news report. Using her most tender voice, she purred "What's wrong, darling?" as she nestled herself onto the Führer's lap, curling up like a kitten and placing her head comfortingly on his shoulder.

"See for yourself." The Führer gestured angrily toward the television. A servant responded immediately, touching a control and setting the film on rewind. "This is from yesterday, but it's the same every evening."

Stefi turned her attention to the television and watched as the American news played on the screen. There was a reporter speaking of the visitor from the Reich. There were pictures of her father, snatches of him speaking to an obviously pleased audience, a few seconds of his appearance at a formal dinner, another few seconds of him spontaneously greeting people on the streets of Washington D.C. – *black* people even! There was a thirty-second direct quote from Richard which seemed to be effective – the newscaster nodded his head slightly at the pat phrase, finished the report, and then turned to his script to continue with the other news.

Rudi gestured brusquely and the servant stopped the tape. "That's just the most recent! I've been watching the news reports all the while you were in the bath and every day is as bad as that!"

"Did you only just get them?" Stefi asked in order to divert Rudi's attention for at least a few moments. She needed to determine what he was mad about, and what she could do about it. And she feared she only had seconds.

Rudi looked at her in surprise. "No, of course not, I've just been too busy to watch."

"Things seem to be going well," she ventured timidly.

"Well! Well for whom?" Rudi screeched. He pushed Stefi off his lap and jumped to his feet. "I want that traitor summoned home immediately!" he bellowed to an officer standing near the door. "Have him arrested at the airport!"

"Rudi!" Stefi tugged at the Führer's sleeve.

"Throw him into interrogation. I don't even want to see his face!"

"Rudi," Stefi begged softly, reaching a hand around to stroke him soothingly.

"And videotape it!"

The officer saluted briskly. "Yes, *mein Führer.*"

"Rudi, please wait."

"What?" The Führer looked at Stefi as if surprised by her presence. One of her hands was on his cheek, the other had reached somewhat lower and was doing something rather pleasant, rather calming. "Wait a minute," he said to the officer.

The officer nodded his head and returned to standing at attention by the door.

"What is it, *Mäuschen?*"

"Before you do anything, please tell me what is wrong. I'm worried – you seem so upset."

That hand! It continued to gently touch him, stroking him, soothing him, like a soft leather whip across the fine skin of a beautiful virgin! He felt the whisper of a kiss on his jaw, raising the down on his cheek. Tendrils of agonizing pleasure spread through his body. He felt himself growing stiff. A man of his age! Such virility! Ruler of the third empire! The most powerful man in the world! Such virility! And soon to be a father! Yes, virility, strength and discipline: he must not let himself be waylaid from his duty as Führer. There was time enough for beautiful, young women later. He forcefully grabbed her hand and pulled it away. "Not now, you little minx! I have to deal with your father first."

"But what has he done?"

"Didn't you see?"

Stefi shook her head helplessly.

"He's trying to usurp my position! He's making himself the personal representative of the Reich! And the Americans, they love him!"

"Oh no, no, no!" Stefi wailed. "He's only doing what it takes to represent you, he's being completely loyal. Don't you know how much he loves you? You *are* the Fatherland! How could he ever do anything to harm you?"

The Führer pulled his head back in histrionic disbelief. "We'll see. I'll have him interrogated–"

"Haven't you been listening to his words?" Stefi interjected desperately, her eyes glistening with tears of tender love and affection.

"His words?"

"Yes, he's been praising you! That applause that you saw from the audiences, that was when he was telling them what a great leader *you* are!"

The Führer grimaced. "I wasn't listening carefully, but I thought…I know, let's listen together."

Stefi gasped, then sighed seductively. "Isn't there anything else you'd rather do?"

The Führer held her shoulders and surveyed her sadly, "Oh, my little one, how I long to hold you close, but affairs of state beckon. I'm sorry, that's the way it is with men. You have no idea of these things, but I know I'm being betrayed."

"Yes, yes – there are traitors everywhere! Snakes and vipers and you must always step carefully, but my father is not one of them. He has protected you – don't you remember?"

The Führer eyed her sharply. "And is your loyalty with your father or with me?"

"With *you,* of course! You are the father of my child. But can't you see that Richard is loyal to you as well?"

Rudi scratched the back of his neck. "I don't know, I don't know. He's setting up this deal where we'll trade that traitor to them for some stupid talks. I mean, the man hurt *me,* and Traugutt doesn't seem to care at all!"

"You mean Halifax?" Stefi's mind raced ahead with a number of plans. Which had the best chance of success, which would most surely save her father? Rudi clearly needed to attack someone – the question was, who could take the place of her father?

As the Führer nodded, Stefi studied his face and came to her decision. With a slight twinge of regret, she said, "It's him you want: Halifax. That was a mistake on my father's part. But, of course, he does not possess your strategic genius. You're right, darling. Halifax must not be allowed to get away with what he's done. He's the traitor, he's the one who should be punished."

The Führer's eyes glistened. "Do you really think so? What about your father's plan?"

"Your plans, *your* needs are paramount. My father has erred, it is time for you to set everything right."

"Yes, and imagine Richard's face when he returns and finds I've ruined his little bargain! That will teach him to run off with his grand ideas!"

"Yes, of course, you'll show him who's in control."

"He'll appreciate the lesson!" the Führer giggled.

Stefi nodded. "It's an important lesson for him to learn, but you are a father to us all and it is your duty to show us the way."

The Führer turned his attention to the officer by the door. "Cancel that last order. Instead, go fetch Lederman, I have some work for him."

The officer nodded and left.

The Führer turned toward Stefi and stroked her face gently. "My little treasure, do you want to come along with me? I'm going to personally inform Halifax of the service he will perform for me today. Today and for the coming month."

Stefi licked her lips. Hers would be the last friendly face Peter would see before going to his death, to a horrible death. She should at least bear witness. She could risk giving him a faint, fleeting look of solidarity in recognition of his sacrifice: it would mean a lot to him, and she owed him at least that. But he might recognize her complicity in his murder, and then his ghost would haunt her dreams for the rest of her days. It would be more than she could bear. She shook her head. "No, my love, I'm just a fragile woman – a woman with child – and I'm afraid such a scene might be upsetting."

Rudi gently patted Stefi's abdomen. "Yes, of course. We must protect the little one."

He prepared himself for his long-awaited revenge and from the happy grin on the Führer's face and the comments that he made as he was dressed and shaved, Stefi knew that her father was safe. She did not dress, she just watched the Führer as he prepared himself. She was always careful to have a look of adoration on her face whenever he noticed her, but when his back was turned, her face betrayed concern. Several times she opened her mouth to say something, but each time she glanced worriedly at the television and closed her mouth again without speaking.

Lederman was shown into the room. He bowed deeply, intoning, "I am at your service, *mein Führer!"*

Stefi eyed him curiously. Tall, finely built, handsome in a somewhat effeminate way. In one hand he carried a file, with the other he fussed at his moustache. He noticed Stefi and returned her intense gaze with a look of smug confidence. Yes, he thinks he's quite a catch, Stefi thought. The

Führer noticed the interchange and immediately came to stand by Stefi, placing an arm possessively around her. Stefi noticed Lederman's sudden nervousness. She laughed lightly and whispered in Rudi's ear, "You've scared him!"

The Führer laughed in response and turning Stefi's face to his, kissed her full on the lips. Lederman shifted uneasily.

"Sit down, sit down!" Rudi gestured jovially toward the armchair and Lederman went to stand by it, but carefully waited until Rudi and Stefi had seated themselves on the couch before seating himself.

The Führer pulled Stefi in close to him, letting his hand run absently along the smooth satin that draped her shoulder. "I've called you here," the Führer began, addressing Lederman, but still cuddling Stefi, "in order to finally deal with this…, this…, this miscreant. But first, I want to know more about him. He's done me more damage than…Oh, you have no idea how much he has made me suffer!" Stefi noticed how Rudi's fingers dug into her shoulder, but she did not react. "You knew him personally, didn't you?"

Lederman looked rather contrite. "Not personally." At the confused and almost angry look the Führer gave him, Lederman hurried to add, "He was indeed under my control and I dealt with him on occasion – that I know from my notes – but he was just one of many and I had no particular reason to remember him once he was released. Not until later, of course."

"I see. But you have notes?"

"Yes, I kept very careful notes on all the early prisoners. We were still in the testing phase then."

"So what do your notes say?"

"Well, he suffers from sluggish schizophrenia," Lederman stated pompously. "Most acutely in the delusion of equality – that we are all created equal and therefore should have equal rights and equal protection under the law. He is infected with a particularly virulent belief in individualism – that no group or nation or race is more important than the individual's own sense of morality as evinced by that individual's behavior, so he is obviously unsuited to National Socialism. In fact, he is not easily co-opted by any group, even groups with the same overall goals. He's a loner, the sort of person who knows how to live among other people, but not with them."

The Führer furrowed his brow in confusion, but did not interrupt.

"He was a very difficult subject. A pathological liar, very clever in his deceit, but we did manage to prise some background information out of him – especially when we had him doped up."

The Führer tilted his head, "Why did you care what he said? I thought you did re-education, not interrogation."

Lederman leaned back in his chair and breathed deeply, like a professor preparing for a long lecture. "We have an overriding interest in using every being in our society to the maximum possible benefit of the Fatherland. To your benefit, *mein Führer.*"

"That's obvious."

"Of course, with loyal, pure Aryans, there is no problem – they naturally recognize the natural order and obey every command. With inferiors, it is sometimes more difficult: they are stupid and do not understand their place in society. In the past we would simply use them however we could, but that was often inefficient. We spent so much effort on forcing work out of them, that it hardly paid a dividend. When our only goal was to rid our society of them, that was not a problem, but now that we need their labor, then we must find new methods to get the most out of their existence. My thesis was, if we could find a way to make them work – perhaps spending a bit of effort at the beginning for a large pay-off later, then we would have a loyal, well-behaved and *productive* workforce, even among the inferior races. To that end, I experimented on the worst of the lot – the proven individualists. If we could break them, then we could mold anybody to our will."

"But that doesn't explain why you wanted to know what *he* thought."

"These creatures are sick, their thinking is *wrong*. But..." Here Lederman raised a finger instructively. "But we don't a priori know *where* they've gone wrong. Once we have determined that, we can remove the flawed thinking and use the remaining patterns to mold their behavior to that appropriate to their status."

"I see. And that's what you did with Halifax?"

"Yes. It took some time – about a month, but finally the psychiatrists thought they had corrected his thinking and deemed him fit for release, though that wasn't at all the case."

"Then why did they say he was ready?"

"I told you, he's a pathological liar. He knows how to *feign* obedience, to feign everything, in fact. Frankly, I don't think the man really has a personality he could call his own. He's a complete individualist, totally lacking in discipline or natural submission to the group. To get along, he just designs whatever seems appropriate to his situation – and so, in our program, he came across as submissive and obedient. He had the staff completely fooled. Only I saw through him. Rather than release him when the psychiatrists deemed him fit, I moved him onto a more stringent program."

"And what exactly did you do?"

Stefi breathed deeply and stared at the leather of the sofa as Lederman read from his notes, embellishing now and then from memory or conjecture.

She tried not to remember that it was a human being they were talking about, but even that did not help – it would have pained her to hear of any animal treated so brutally. Finally she gave up. Ignoring it would *not* make it untrue. Indeed, ignoring it made it all the more possible. Too many people said it was too horrendous to hear, too awful to believe, and with their deliberate blindness, they empowered evil.

Stefi decided she was not one of *those.* She was tough, she had to be tough. Tough and professional, and it would not do to show weakness – even to herself. She must take inspiration from Lederman's words to fight him with every means available to her, she must remind herself of the justice of her cause. She listened to what he said, let herself imagine the situations, played the details through her mind, let herself see what Peter must have looked like, let herself feel what he must have felt. The pain, the humiliation, the unutterable aloneness...She stood suddenly. "Excuse me, morning sickness," she muttered and fled to the toilet.

The Führer watched her go, then he turned back and smiled indulgently at his guest. "Women."

Lederman stroked his moustache. "Delicate creatures."

"So, after a month, you gave up on using your initial approach of thought redirection, and instead opted for this three-month program of personality obliteration. But obviously, it didn't work."

Lederman shook his head defensively. "It would have worked with others. With him – well, there was little hope to begin with. Indeed, given his personality profile and his persistent refusal to accept treatment, I was fairly sure he'd never be released, and by the end, I was simply toying with him – er – I mean, planning to test new methods on him, until such time as he ceased to function as a viable unit."

The Führer looked momentarily confused, then muttered, "Ah, you mean died." He contemplated what Lederman had just said, and then asked, "Why did you change your plans?"

Lederman tapped his notes, "I was convinced by a visitor. A senior officer. In fact, your aide: Colonel Traugutt."

"Traugutt? What did he have to do with that operation?" The Führer threw a glance back at the bathroom, but Stefi had not re-emerged.

"Nothing at all. He was just visiting, on an inspection tour – as part of some grander scheme, I gather. Anyway, I showed him the prisoner and he insisted that he was completely broken and I should release him immediately. 'To someone important' he said. See, I've written it right here."

The Führer leaned forward and looked at Lederman's notes. How very intriguing! Traugutt had ordered the prisoner released back then, back when he was nobody. And Traugutt insisted on keeping the prisoner alive and unharmed now. The same prisoner who had then proceeded to provide him with a wealth of information about the Americans. He furrowed his brow and turned again to look at the bathroom. Stefi had come out, but she was remaining by the bed, out of earshot. Was there some connection between Traugutt and the prisoner? But what could it be? And what did each get out of the association? How very odd!

They talked some more, but at long last Lederman departed. Stefi gathered her strength and went over to Rudi.

"What are you going to do?" she asked softly, hopefully. Maybe he was sated?

Rudi turned to her. "I'm going to order the prisoner's execution." He studied her face as he said that, trying to discern her thoughts.

She smiled at him in response. "It's the right thing to do."

Rudi was pleased by her words, relieved even. He closed his eyes as a wave of ecstasy washed over him. "Oh, I feel so…" He opened his eyes and smiled at her. "Thank you, *Schätzchen!* My loyal little one. Once again, you knew exactly what I needed." He stood and hugged her tenderly. "You know me so well! Wait for me, just like that. I'll be back in, oh, about an hour. Then we'll celebrate before I go and watch it all." He shivered with excitement. "Oh, this is going to be great!"

Once Rudi had left, Stefi went to her dressing table and picked up her hairbrush. A servant came over to assist, but Stefi waved the help away. She pulled the brush through her hair slowly. It was a rarity, but she allowed her guard down for a moment so that she could think about her purpose, her goals, *the Cause.* She had saved her father, she had prevented disaster. What she had done was justified.

She pulled the brush somewhat less gently through her hair and stared into the mirror, imagining her father's face, his pride in her for having, once again, saved his life and rescued their plans. But she didn't see her father. What she saw was the look of happiness on Olek's face as he was able to walk again – on the artificial legs Peter had bought for him. She saw her brothers excitedly telling her how Peter had taught them all sorts of new things during his month visit to their house and how he had even managed to get their father to open up a bit. She heard Genia tell her how Peter had comforted her, only two months ago when he had attended the wedding. No one else had noticed the way Genia left the festivities – only Peter. He had quietly followed her and discovered her crying over Joanna's absence and had then sat with her, talking to her, as she had tearfully hugged him and told him about her lost cousin and friend.

Stefi tugged relentlessly at her hair. Peter had only been in Berlin to spend the money his friend had given him – not on himself, but on setting up an escape route. He had taken an enormous risk in order to help the vulnerable people he had left behind. And he had been betrayed. Betrayed by a friend. Stefi dug the brush deep into her hair so that the bristles scraped painfully across her scalp. The strategy her father was using in America had been designed by Peter as well. He had done a good job, an excellent job. It was apparently very successful – too successful, it would seem. Stefi huffed with the effort of brushing her tresses. So successful was the strategy that it would cost Peter his life. He had designed the very plan which would kill him. But that wasn't true. Stefi stopped brushing suddenly and stared at her reflection.

It was me. I've arranged his execution.

With an abrupt sweep of her arm, Stefi violently swung the hairbrush into the mirror and shattered the glass.

8

*D*ay seven and sixty. *Oh, for Christ's sake, use English!* Sixty seven. Six, seven. Six, seven, eight, nine…Peter pried open his eyes and noticed that the breakfast had already been delivered. He had not even heard the servant enter the room. Good Lord, the man could have walked over to him and slit his throat! But what did it matter?

Day sixty seven. Ah hell, he thought, turning over in the bed, maybe he could just skip this one. Like Marysia's cat Siwa sometimes did – just sleep through the whole damn thing. Eventually though, boredom overcame him and he threw the covers back and got up. It was quite chilly in the room – although it was mid-October, the heat, apparently, had not been turned on yet. Perhaps, the *Hausmeister* was reacting to the unusual daytime warmth. Still, the nights were cold and the *Residenz* hardly seemed the sort of place that worried about energy conservation. Peter pulled on his clothes and went to the window. It had rained heavily last night and was still drizzling now: it was unlikely he would be allowed to leave the room today.

Someone was coming down the hallway. The servant, no doubt, coming to fetch the tray. Peter debated whether he should rush to eat a bit before the tray was taken – he was sure that he could not convince the servant to break his routine and leave the tray a few minutes longer – but then decided there was no point. He wasn't all that hungry anyway.

The door opened. Two men swept into the room, grabbed him and began frisking him. Even as they carried out their thorough search, two more men entered, then, with regal splendor, the Führer pranced into the room. He seated himself in one of the chairs and watched avidly as the probe continued, and Peter had a sudden, overpowering fear that the humiliating search was only a prelude to something much, much worse. But when the two men had finished, they escorted him the few steps to the Führer's chair then stepped back so he stood alone. There was no doubting the Führer's intent – his eyes glimmered with gleeful anticipation.

Despite an intellectual fear of what was to come, Peter felt fairly numb. He stood, not three feet from the man who had ordered Joanna's murder, and patiently awaited the words that would let him know he could join her in a month.

The Führer stood and paced around him. Peter turned his head slightly to watch his progress, but did not otherwise move. He could still see the plea in Joanna's eyes, the way the capillaries had burst, turning her delicate little face red and blotchy. How many other children, he wondered, how many innocent faces had perished at this man's command? How much sadistic misery had been caused by this man, hidden behind his buffoonish behavior?

"My aide," the Führer stated suddenly, "I think you met him – well, I know you met him, maybe you remember it? My aide, Traugutt, convinced me to spare you." He was behind Peter's back, and Peter cocked his head to indicate he had heard, but did not otherwise respond. "He promised me you could be useful. He said that I needed a respite from my reputation as a…" At this the Führer looked to his men. "What was it, now? What sort of reputation do I have?"

None of the men caught his eye. All of them shuffled nervously, staring at their feet as they declined to answer.

"A brute," the Führer answered his own question. "It appears that the Americans think I'm something of an uncouth peasant. The sort who might beat a raving dog to death with a stick. Can you believe that?"

"No, strangling newborn puppies is more your style."

The Führer missed the point. "Yes, even that, even ridding the world of unnecessary vermin, is now viewed negatively. No doubt there's a 'Save the Rats' foundation somewhere!"

"If you're so good at ridding the world of vermin, why haven't you managed to strangle yourself, yet?" That, Peter supposed, would earn him a heavy blow.

But the Führer laughed instead. He finished his circuit around Peter and stood before him to confront him directly. "I've had some time to learn more about you, you know. I've studied your record, in preparation for finally getting some satisfaction out of you. I must say, anticipation has made my appetite even keener!"

Peter rolled his eyes.

The Führer either missed or ignored his gesture. "According to Lederman's report, you were a hard nut to crack: resilient, self-reliant, determined." The Führer raised his eyebrows in appreciation of Peter's talents. "He said you withstood a lot – an incredible amount – simply by disappearing into some void within yourself. He even thought we'd lost you – that is, your obnoxiously insubordinate personality – forever. And that's why he certified you as acceptable. Clearly, he was wrong – you slither out of sight only to reappear when everything seems safe again. Fascinating. I look forward to studying that response. And I'm intrigued by your motives as well. I've learned that your problem – or maybe it has been your strength – is that you don't understand hierarchies. You think we're all equal!" The Führer laughed and turned to his men to see their appreciative smiles. Then he turned back to Peter to expand upon his thesis, "You've never learned your place. Born in the gutter! You never learned when to keep your mouth shut and obey your betters. Even now you don't know enough not to look me directly in the eye!"

Peter did not avert his eyes from the great man's face. At the questioning look from the Führer, he shrugged.

"You've never learned that the world is structured according to might, power, and natural right. You see, I have all three, and you have none of these things!"

"As if your opinion meant something to me."

The Führer's eyes widened in anger. "It *will* mean something!"

"You're a worm!" Peter announced, suddenly feeling freed of any constraints. They had nothing to hold over him, nothing but Roman, and their word about him was meaningless anyway. "And these lackeys who tremble at your command – they're worm-shit! They'd betray you into the hands of the first person who could seriously outbid you for their services!"

"I am Aryan might! I am the *Übermensch!* I am *the Führer!"*

"But the one thing you are not, is smart. That's something I have that you will never possess," Peter taunted. "Brains! You can destroy them, but you will *never* get them. You're an idiot, and you always will be. All you know how to do is scheme and kill and it's only your complete lack of morality that let you get where you are. And now you're there, you don't know what to do. You haven't a clue about how to run an empire. You're stupid and that's why you hate me and anyone like me. You hate anyone who thinks for themselves."

"I am the power here!" the Führer nearly shouted in reply.

Peter saw Joanna's tiny fingers clawing at the huge hands of the brute who had strangled her at this man's order. Was that what the Führer thought power meant? *"Power?"* Peter asked, his anger growing into that irrational torrent of energy that sometimes overtook him. "You're a pathetic weakling!" On an impulse, he decided to prove his point, and he surged forward and, wrapping his arm around the Führer's neck, twisted him around to face his minions, holding him in a powerful stranglehold.

"So much for power," Peter stated dryly. Only as he heard the choked response of his victim and saw the confused alarm of the other men in the room, did his furious anger subside enough for him to realize what he had done. He tightened his hold on his captive's neck and the Führer coughed and flapped his arms uselessly in response.

Peter reached with his free hand to the Führer's jacket and found the gun hidden there. Peter removed the gun and, jerking back on the Führer's neck, whispered, "Open your mouth." The Führer obeyed automatically and Peter pushed the muzzle of the pistol into the Führer's mouth. The Führer shivered with fear as he felt the metal forced between his teeth. Peter calmly turned his attention to the other men in the room. "I have a few requests to make of you gentlemen. And you're going to grant them."

What could they do? They had been disarmed by the Führer's paranoia – few, if any, of them, were allowed weapons. To take any action would gamble with the Führer's life, and even if it were successful, they would face his wrath afterwards. Any action opened them up to denunciation. Docile obedience to the kidnapper's demands was the only option. It was the only way to show complete loyalty. No one would take the chance of assigning a sniper to shoot Peter from a rooftop, no one would risk the Führer's reaction to that. Obey the kidnapper's commands: that would show loyalty to their cowardly leader. Take no initiative that could be misinterpreted! Let the kidnapper go! And if the Führer survived, then it was proven to be the right strategy. And if he did not, well, then it didn't matter, now did it?

Still holding the gun on the Führer and half-dragging him out the door, Peter carefully approached the car that had been prepared for them. He stopped a few meters away and gestured to one of the officers who had followed them out into the courtyard. "You, there. Start the engine."

The officer looked completely stunned by the command. He shook his head in horror at the idea.

Peter laughed and whispered into the Führer's ear, "It looks like they were willing to blow us both up."

"No!"

"See for yourself. Look at his face. Now, if you want to survive this ordeal, it looks like you're going to have to help me get out of here. Which way do we go to leave on foot?"

The Führer told him and together they progressed through the *Residenz*. At each gate, the Führer demanded that they be allowed to proceed unhindered, and in that manner they eventually were outside the main compound. They were still, however, well inside secure territory. Peter stopped and loosened the stranglehold on his hostage's neck. "How far until we reach a public road?"

The Führer choked and sputtered. "I don't know. I've never walked!"

Peter decided they had gone far enough, and he pulled the Führer over to one of the cars parked near the entrance. He opened the door and ordered the chauffeur out of the car and told the Führer to take his place.

"I don't know how to drive!" the Führer protested convincingly.

Peter sighed and ordered the chauffeur back into the car. He forced the Führer into the back of the car and sat next to him, holding the gun on him all the while. He had the chauffeur drive the two of them out of the compound and along the *Landstrassen* through woods and past fields until they reached one of the *Hauptstadt* borders. The entire way, they were followed by a cavalcade of automobiles which only grew larger with each mile. He snickered at the thought of all the bickering that was probably taking place among the various services, officers, heirs-apparent and so on. They were waved through the border post and drove slowly along the long corridor of blank walls that surrounded each side of the road. Gun emplacements were scattered along the way, but Peter had chosen well – he not only had a hostage, but the car had opaque glass and bulletproof shielding.

He settled into his seat and relaxed a bit, holding the gun more casually on his hostage. With the dark glass of the windows, he was fairly sure that his actions were unobserved and so he did not need to maintain a tense, close hold on the Führer. He kept the gun pointed at Rudi's head, staring at his cowering profile, and wondered what he should do next.

He supposed they could drive to an airport and demand a plane. There was, however, the question of where they could go. The Soviet Union was out – he had no idea of what their current relations with the Reich were but he knew they could not be trusted to offer him a safe haven – not with his, now public, associations with the Home Army. He feared the NAU would not welcome him either. The general public might support his cause, but the administration could refuse entry to their aircraft long before any public outcry could be mounted against such action. Too much of a provocation, they might say. Or some other politically-inspired shit.

So, major powers were probably out of the question. Also their allies. They could drive to Switzerland, but his previous experience there left him doubtful: just one official sympathetic to the Reich, and his entire escape could be ruined. That left the few non-aligned tin-pot countries around the world. Now which of those might he trust? He sputtered at the thought. None were truly independent, and the politics of all of them were rather obscure to him. It wasn't like he had been able to follow international news recently. He thought of Arieka's homeland, but from what she had said, it would be a complete gamble, depending on who was currently in power and whether or not the country even existed anymore. Anyway, she had said something about them receiving substantially more aid from the Reich than from the NAU. So that place was out as well. A totalitarian theocracy? That was a possibility, but other than his distaste for such places, he suspected he would be as likely as the Führer to be arrested on some charge of having violated God's law.

There was also the overriding problem that he did not trust any transit provided by the Führer's minions. The more time they had, the worse it would be – and an aircraft with pilot could take a reasonable amount of time to arrange. They could easily supply a jet which would plunge into the earth not long after take-off. He imagined Günter Schindler's feigned sorrow at the news of the Führer's demise and just how fast the election of the new Führer would take place afterwards. More to the point, though, was that Peter wanted to go home. He had not escaped in order to condemn himself to an exile from his family in some unfamiliar land. He would go home. If he could manage to keep the Führer alive, they could use him as a useful bargaining tool and Szaflary could gain some advantage from his action. It was decided then, he would go home.

They were heading southwest and through the next several junctions he directed the chauffeur to the southeast and then eventually due east toward Hitlerstadt. He decided to skip the beautiful, undestroyed city which had once been called Praha and skirting around it as evening fell, they headed toward the region of Slovakia. This area was rather more familiar to him – he often dealt with the villages to the south of Szaflary – and he had also made his exit from Szaflary through the south, but still they were far from anywhere he could call home.

They needed to fill the tank with petrol and Peter directed the chauffeur into a *Tankstelle*. There were no problems and Peter noticed that the chauffeur was more than co-operative. Perhaps he had his own grudge that was being satisfied by this little theater. They drove on, into the foothills of the Carpathians. As far as Peter knew, they were still well within Reich-controlled territory, nevertheless, he noticed that the number of cars willing to follow them was thinning itself considerably. Of course, they had no idea where the real border with Szaflary lay. After all, it was not something that was printed on maps, and they would all know that whatever information they had about the "terrorist controlled territory", it was very likely deliberately misleading or just plain wrong. They were certainly not interested in taking the chance of being captured by partisans just because they had decided to loyally follow their Führer.

He laughed as he realized that their tail had thinned itself to two police vehicles. Poor sods are under strict orders, he thought. They were getting near to where he guessed the nebulous border might lie, but he also was unaware of exactly when he could expect partisans to attack their vehicles. He wanted to avoid a direct confrontation. Unless he happened to know the partisans personally – and that was very unlikely here – then he couldn't guess what their reaction to his presence might be. They were under orders to simply shoot interlopers, but the impressive line of autos might be allowed to pass. Then again, it might not. Or they might encounter bandits who would kill them for their possessions, unaware of any significance they had as possible hostages for either side.

He was uncomfortable with the risk and rather than let the first group of people that stumbled across them make the decision about their fate, he decided that it was better to take control of their situation. It had already grown quite dark as they entered a woods which seemed to be uninhabited. Peter had the chauffeur slow the car and then stop it on the narrow road. The two vehicles following stopped about a hundred meters behind them. He ordered the chauffeur into the passenger seat and agilely rolled out of the back seat and into the driver's seat, twisting around as he landed to point the gun at the Führer, just in case he had gotten any bright ideas in those few seconds. He hadn't. He looked stunned by Peter's maneuver.

"Open the glove box," Peter ordered the chauffeur. When it was opened, Peter said, "Take out the documents for the car. Yeah, those. Okay, open the docket and pull out a sheet." The chauffeur did that. "Fold it in half."

The chauffeur folded the paper. It looked like a message.

"Do you have any reason to believe anybody might ransom your life?" Peter asked, as he continued to point the gun at Rudi.

The chauffeur hesitated a number of seconds then answered, "No."

"Then get out here. If you go any further, you won't be allowed to live."

The chauffeur stared at Peter in amazement.

"What I want you to do is get out and walk down the middle of the road toward those police cars back there, waving that piece of paper. Walk slowly." That would do it: under the pretence of following orders to save the Führer's life, the chauffeur was being given the opportunity to help Peter escape. And under the pretence of learning what important information might be contained in the note, the policemen were being given the opportunity to avoid pursuing the Führer and his kidnapper into dangerous enemy territory.

The chauffeur exited the car, and waving the note in the air, slowly approached the police cars. "Get into the front," Peter ordered to the Führer. "Now!"

The Führer obediently clambered over the seat and crawled into the passenger seat. Before he had even settled, Peter sent the car speeding down the narrow, muddy road. It was rather difficult driving while holding a gun on his passenger, but it was a better car than the police vehicles and with the delay caused by their waiting to see what the chauffeur had in his hand, they fell far behind. Peter crested a hill and lost them from view. He noticed a small road off to the side, but drove past it. The police vehicles reappeared in his rear-view mirror and he drove even faster, turning bends at a dangerous speed, putting some distance behind them and losing them from sight.

He turned into the next small road he found and cut the engine and lights. He waited the few seconds until he heard the vehicles speed past on the main road, then he backed out and headed without lights toward the first small side road he had noticed. He drove along that for a few miles, then pulled into the trees and stopped.

The Führer glanced nervously all around. "What are we doing?"

"We're going to walk from here." Peter climbed out of the car.

He ignored Rudi's "Walk where?" and went to the trunk to inspect its contents. Unfortunately there was nothing that would serve as a rope or handcuffs in the car. Nor was there anything which could remotely keep them warm. He cursed at the thought. It was already bloody cold and it would only get worse as the night deepened.

He ordered the Führer out of the car and, waving the gun into the woods, told him to start walking.

"Don't kill me!" the Führer pleaded as he realized they were abandoning the car. "Oh, please, don't kill me! I want to live! My wife – my poor wife! Oh, you can't kill me. I'm important!"

Peter snorted his contempt, but did not otherwise answer.

Once they had walked for a bit, Rudi finally became convinced that he was not being marched to his execution. "Where are you taking me?"

Again Peter did not bother to answer him.

"My legs hurt." The Führer began to limp theatrically.

"Mine don't. You should walk more."

"The Führer does not walk!"

"Weakling," Peter scoffed. "Anyway, I thought you were fascinated by pain. Now you feel some – enjoy it."

"Not this sort," the Führer muttered. "This isn't interesting – it just hurts."

"Ah."

They continued their march. Over the hours the Führer continued to complain. As Peter maintained a stoic silence, the Führer whined endlessly about the cold, about the pain in his legs, about how sore his feet were, about how he should be obeyed, about how he should not be treated in such a disrespectful manner.

"Shut-up, or I'll blow your fucking brains out!"

The outburst had come without warning and the Führer fell into a stunned silence. Peter grit his teeth and trudged on. He was having a difficult time controlling himself. Time and again Joanna's last minutes played themselves out in his mind, and here he had the bastard responsible for it all, alone, at his mercy, in the deep forests of the mountains. He could do anything to him!

They stopped to rest, and as Peter breathed on his hands to warm them, he contemplated his prisoner. The Führer sat on the ground, huddled against a tree, shivering with cold. He looked up at his captor, but the situation seemed utterly beyond his comprehension and eventually he turned his gaze away to stare blindly into the gloom of the woods.

The Führer looked pathetic, an old man pushed well beyond his limits, but Peter did not forget the gleam he had seen in the Führer's eyes only hours earlier. I should hang you, Peter thought. Stop at the next village, find some rope and hang you so that you slowly strangle. Or maybe, break your kneecaps, then drag you, screaming in pain, the rest of the way to Szaflary.

Peter breathed again on his hands, but his breath felt chill.

"Are you going to kill me?" The Führer did not look at Peter, he simply asked the question. His voice was different from usual – the petulant, snapping tone was gone, as was the leering sarcasm. He simply spoke as an older man to a younger one.

Peter set the gun down and walked over to the tree. He leaned forward and placed his hands around the Führer's throat. The Führer did not attempt to resist, he simply continued to stare into the woods.

"Do you know what it feels like?" Peter whispered into the Führer's ear. "Do you know what she felt?" He tightened his grip.

The Führer's hands reached instinctively for Peter's and he weakly tried to pull them away. "I didn't–" he choked. Peter held his grip for a number of seconds. The Führer's color changed, his nails clawed into Peter's hands. Veins stood out in his forehead, his mouth opened wide in a desperate bid to get air.

"Do you understand what you did? To a little girl?" Peter loosened his grip slightly so the Führer could answer.

The Führer gasped and sputtered and coughed. After a moment he croaked angrily, "I didn't order that!" He took another noisy breath. "My

God, what do I care about a kid? I just told them to make sure you showed up in Berlin in one piece. It's you I wanted, damn it!"

"They invoked your name. Read from an order you sent."

The Führer tried to shake his head. As a punishment, Peter dug his fingers into the Führer's neck. The Führer gasped with pain and then Peter loosened his hold again so that the Führer could speak. "It was pure theater! I didn't send any orders about the kid. I didn't even know there was a kid at first!"

Lies, all lies. Peter's fingers tightened again and he felt the Führer's nails clawing at his hands. Like Joanna's clawing at that brute's hands. Weak and helpless, fighting against merciless strength. Peter didn't like what he felt and without coming to any decision his hands loosened their grip.

The Führer took several deep, painful breaths. Undecided, Peter continued to hold his throat loosely and the Führer rotated his head backward to look at his tormentor. "Think about it," he rasped. "Have you ever heard anything about me and kids?"

Peter had to admit that he hadn't.

"I'm no different than dozens of world leaders, allies of your pious American friends. We all run our prison systems in the same manner. Suspects have to be interrogated, confessions need to be obtained. Terrorist enclaves must be subdued and civilians get hurt in the process. Do you think the other leaders don't know what happens when uprisings are crushed? When tanks roll on villages? I'm just honest enough to acknowledge what goes on." The Führer lowered his head so that Peter could no longer see his face. "I've never orchestrated anything for my videos – they're all events that would have happened anyway. Like they do in police stations and prisons and occupied territories all over the world. I had nothing to do with your daughter's murder."

Murder. He had called it murder. And he had apologized, even though there had been no need to, back when Peter had been first captured. Was it possible that he was speaking the truth? What if it was true? But that wasn't important. What mattered is what Peter had felt as his hands had closed around the Führer's throat. Something odd. Not joy at revenge, or justice, or whatever. Something much more destructive. Something inhuman. If he gave in to it now, it would own him. Justice was possible, the Council could convene a court.

He released the Führer's throat and straightened. He stood for a moment towering over the man, then walked back over to his gun and picked it up. "Get up, we need to move."

The Führer climbed to his feet and they continued their journey into the darkness.

At some point the clouds grew thick enough that Peter could no longer navigate. He didn't really know where he was, but he had decided to keep a steady course to the north east, hoping they might eventually stumble across familiar territory. Now, though, without the night sky, without a compass, they could easily wander in circles. Rudi was exhausted, he was constantly tripping and falling and each time it took longer for him to regain his feet. It was time to stop.

Peter turned back toward a village they had skirted a quarter of an hour earlier. He chose a shed on the outskirts of the village and they approached it cautiously. He had no idea whose territory they were in, but he warned the Führer that these were partisans who would string him up immediately if they got their hands on him. "If you're lucky." He was going to elaborate, in order to more thoroughly cow the Führer, but then he remembered Stefi's words about the man and changed his mind. It wasn't clear if Rudi was not also a masochist and he might well betray them – possibly even inadvertently – if there was the promise of someone being tortured, even himself.

They crept into the shed and shut the door. There was a cow stabled in the corner, and a few implements, but otherwise there wasn't much of interest. Peter indicated some of the straw on the floor and said, "Sleep here – it'll be warm enough."

As Rudi lay down, Peter sat on the floor nearby, leaning against the wall, holding the gun loosely on his hostage. Despite his fear, it didn't take long for the exhausted Führer to fall into a deep sleep and once Peter was convinced that his hostage was asleep, he stood and inspected the shed. He found some rope and took that, and he found a small knife, which he decided would be useful as well.

He was hungry, thirsty as well, but there was, unfortunately, no food secreted in the shed nor was there any clean water in sight. He looked at the cow, cocking his head, as he weighed the risks versus the rewards. There were villages, mostly to the south of Szaflary which he had often visited in order to buy food and distillery products, and he had, out of sheer curiosity, learned from one of the peasant women how to milk a cow. Then, however, it had been the appropriate time of day and the cow had been in the presence of a trusted human. What luck could he expect as a total stranger in the middle of the night?

He picked up a bucket and approached the animal. He stroked her face and she turned her large brown eyes upon him. "How about it, old girl? I could really use something to drink, and you're already awake. Any objections?" She seemed a calm enough animal, and he decided to give it a try. He grabbed the stool, placed it near the cow's hind legs and sitting down, put his foot in front of her hoof, to prevent her from kicking the bucket. He stroked her flank and cautiously placed the bucket underneath her. So far, so good. He reached gingerly toward her teats, placed his hand on one of them and the cow let out a loud moo.

Peter pulled his hand away. That was exactly the sort of protest that might well wake up an alert farmer. He removed the bucket, stood up, and backed cautiously away from the cow. "Alright! Sorry for the imposition."

He sighed. He was still hungry and still very thirsty. He turned to look at Rudi sleeping on the floor. He had probably walked more that day than in the last year altogether. Peter snickered his amusement at the poor, weak, superhuman sound asleep in the straw. He walked over to him, removed his boots, and then carefully frisked his sleeping prisoner. He took his lighter, watch, and pocket knife, but found nothing more of interest and the Führer did not awaken. He rolled the Führer onto his stomach and tied his hands behind his back, then he tied his feet as well. With his tired hostage safely immobilized, he felt free to leave the shed and he wandered into the darkness of the surrounding night to find some food and something to drink.

He returned sated and with a few supplies for the morning. He noticed that the Führer was shaking with cold, so he threw an old blanket over him, then he sat on the straw near his hostage and leaned against the wall to relax and wait out the night. As he sat there with the gun resting casually on his lap, watching the Führer snoring soundly, he was reminded of all the times he would sit, late into the night, in the Vogel's hallway, waiting for someone to return to the house. It had always been a strange time, full of dark thoughts, as he rested there, exhausted but not permitted to sleep. He remembered how he had incessantly questioned the point of his life, the relevance of staying alive. How very odd it had all been! The whole bizarre charade had started with his joining a cause which he thought would lead him into a brave fight against evil, but instead he had ended up lighting cigarettes, opening doors and tolerating endless abuse.

It had been such a lonely time. Not just the incessant work and orders and insults from Elspeth and Karl and their children, but even his friends, when he was able to see them, even they, had left him feeling strangely alone. It wasn't the abuse or the torture or the imprisonment, he had realized. Some, if not all of that, was an expected risk of his profession; it was the unexpected risks that had slowly eaten away at him. He had expected his torturers, during his re-education, to denounce him as worthless; he had expected the minions of the Fatherland to denigrate the value of his resistance and therefore his own person. The petulant scolding of the Vogels, though often difficult to accept in silence, had nevertheless fallen into the category of understandable. What he had not been able to accept, though, was how his comrades had accepted the status quo and thought he was rather crazy for fighting it.

When everyone around him – every single person! – in some manner or another, had let him know he was a lesser being, how could he then believe in his own worth and equality? Was it not the vanity of a madman to believe that everyone else was wrong and only he was right? Had he not been insane for insisting that he was the only one who understood the way the world should be, contrary to what everyone else said, contrary to whatever happened around them?

At first he had held out against the onslaught, using memories from long before, using the image of his Grandmother's frail figure and strong spirit to bolster his beliefs. But as time had progressed, the memories had faded, the ancient voices of dead friends no longer carried any weight, and he had begun to believe that he was, like so many others throughout history, worthless, in debt to others for his right to live, destined only to serve his betters, born to be a lesser being.

He laughed at the thought. At least now, as he waited for the dawn, he knew it would be different. He wasn't waiting to open the door to an ever-surly Karl, or a drunken Horst, or even jovial Geerd. He wasn't waiting for some brute to drag him out of his cell to face whatever sadism was on the agenda for that day. When the time came, he would kick the Führer awake, pull him to his feet, and lead him on through the woods until they met up with a partisan group he trusted. Then he would leave his hostage in their care and return to the central sector of Szaflary to present himself, tell the story of his miraculous escape and offer them the wonderful gift of a hog-tied hostage who just happened to be the Führer of the Third Reich! He chuckled quietly at that and let his thoughts drift into the wonderful greetings he would receive, and the congratulations, and the warmth of the hugs of welcome from people who understood what it was to fight for freedom and who did not believe in lesser beings.

9

*G*ünter Schindler had been in the *Residenz* at the time of the Führer's kidnapping. He had been impatiently awaiting the Führer as, yet again, Rudi was late for an appointment, busy being obsessed by something stupid. According to the staff, it was that idiotic *Untermensch* prisoner this time. Günter had sighed heavily, put up his feet and ordered a drink for himself and his son, Wolf-Dietrich, who had accompanied him. The boy was turning into a fine man: very cooperative, helpful, full of ideas. Some great change had come over him and he no longer rebelled against the idea of helping his father or advancing himself. True, the marriage to Büttner's daughter was off, but that didn't really matter – he seemed to be doing well on his own, and there were possibilities with that Vogel girl. Goodness, but she could act! Or maybe it was genuine?

The staff had come running in to him with the news of the Führer's abduction. Günter had carefully suppressed a smile and ordered that absolutely no risks be taken with the Führer's life: and if that meant letting the prisoner escape with his hostage, well then, so be it. He and Wolf-Dietrich had gone down to the courtyard to watch the departure of the parade: the prisoner and his hostage, the security details that were sent to follow at a safe distance. Oh yes, Günter had agreed to the cortege – it wouldn't do to let the Führer go too easily. But he had also strenuously reminded them: the Führer's life was sacred and nothing should be done to risk it!

Günter stood staring into the distance once the parade had left. He was still seething about the explosives placed in the getaway auto. Luckily the prisoner had been clever enough to detect the trap. If he hadn't – well that would have shuffled Rudi out of the way, but it would have almost certainly caused Günter's downfall as well, as he would have been immediately suspect and no amount of denials would have sufficed to clear him when faced with the roomful of sharks who would be his judges. Whoever had ordered it was clever: destroy Rudi and depose Günter with one fell swoop. Günter ran through the likely candidates: not Traugutt, he was still in America. Who, he wondered.

"Büttner," Wolf-Dietrich said.

"What?

"Büttner put the explosives in the car. He probably is the one behind the attempt on Traugutt's life, as well."

"Why do you think that?"

"He hates both of you. Traugutt for moving in and usurping his position, you for letting me out of that engagement. He knows he's being displaced and so he made a desperate move." Wolf-Dietrich did not look at his father as he spoke, he stared off in the direction the cars had taken. "I know he was here – I saw his car as we came in earlier."

Günter motioned to one of the Führer's staff officers. "Find Büttner and put him under arrest for suspicion of plotting the Führer's murder."

The officer hesitated only a second as he weighed up the merits of obeying, then clicking his heels and bowing his head slightly, he said, "Immediately, *mein Herr!*"

"You'll need to deal with Traugutt right away, as well," Wolf-Dietrich advised.

"Why? Traugutt will be good to have around – he's a good strategist. All I'll have to do is tighten his leash a bit to make sure he knows who's running things, and he'll be quite useful."

"You need to move against him now – there's no time to waste."

Günter shook his head. "He's in no position to be elected Führer. I'm already here, taking control as the emergency situation merits, I still have Greta with all her connections legally married to me. I'm a shoo-in! Hell, all I need to do is wait for that thug to murder Rudi and I'll be home free."

"He's not going to murder Rudi."

"Why not? He's not afraid of killing. And he certainly has a motive."

Wolf-Dietrich shook his head. "I don't know what happened with Karl Vogel – but the more I talk to his daughter Ulrike, the more I'm convinced that there was something strange about that murder. It just didn't seem like the man she knew or talks about."

"Why not?"

"Apparently he was more self-controlled than that. Gentle even."

Günter snorted. "Is she in love with him?"

Wolf-Dietrich shrugged. "I guess it's at least possible."

"What is this world coming to!" Günter moaned. Well brought up German girls giving their hearts to *Untermensch* slaves! May Hitler forgive her! "Well, if she loves him, why is she doing such a nice job tearing his reputation to pieces for us?"

"Hell hath no fury like a woman scorned." Wolf-Dietrich did not bother to add that a man scorned was not a particularly pleasant adversary either. If only Stefi had waited for him to become his own man!

"What do you think he's going to do with Rudi?" Günter asked, breaking into Wolf-Dietrich's thoughts.

"Halifax?"

"Who else?" Günter snarled.

"He's not going to kill him."

"He'd forego revenge? Impossible!"

"Very possible."

"Why?"

"I think he's going to use him as a bargaining tool." Wolf-Dietrich stopped watching the road and turned to look directly at his father. "He knows getting out of the country is impossible and crossing the channel is too risky, so he'll head back to those bandits in the Balkans. The ones who kept him captive. But this time he has some leverage and might be able to organize a better position for himself. Or maybe he'll head to the Tatra mountains. His wife's father had some association with them."

"They refused him entry last time."

"Yes, but now he has something to offer them. In any case, he'd be stupid to kill Rudi."

"He's not a clever man. He's an *Untermensch*, remember."

Carefully, Wolf-Dietrich said, "Yes, Father. He is truly an inferior, you only need to look at him, to listen to his words, to review his background and his accomplishments to see that." Wolf-Dietrich paused only slightly to see if his sarcasm was recognized, but, as expected, his father only nodded his head in agreement, so Wolf-Dietrich continued, "But that only means he can be even more sly and devious. He's not held back by any morality."

"Good point." Günter paused a moment wondering if he should really take the next step. His son seemed to have a keen eye for strategy, but if he asked his son's opinion, then Günter would be admitting his own weakness.

Fortunately Wolf-Dietrich pre-empted his father's painful decision by volunteering, "If Halifax does what I expect he will, it will take several days for him to reach his destination and negotiate his way inside. So what you need to do is have Traugutt summoned back from America – by Rudi's order. While he's en route, declare the Führer dead and arrest Traugutt's daughter. She must be complicit in this whole thing: after all, it was she who convinced Rudi to keep Halifax alive. She probably also convinced the Führer to see Halifax personally and thus exposed him to the danger of being kidnapped. And doubtless she did it all at her father's behest. Of course, it was timed so that Traugutt was out of the country so that he could deny any knowledge of the kidnap."

Günter looked at his son in amazement. "But how would it have helped Traugutt to have the Führer kidnapped?"

"I don't know. But does it matter? The point is, you have to discredit him immediately so that he doesn't contradict your declaration of the Führer's death, or worse, save Rudi's life in some manner. Once Traugutt is under arrest, with Büttner already in custody, you're the sole power. Then, whatever Traugutt says is irrelevant – and who's going to hear him? Just your own special investigators."

"Of course." Günter nodded his head in approval. He continued to nod as the plot worked through his mind. "What if Rudi shows up alive?"

"Father," Wolf-Dietrich drew the word out. "With the other players under arrest, who are the bandits going to negotiate with?"

"Ach, yes, me of course."

"Exactly! You can quietly bargain for Rudi's life and then quickly end it. The point is you must take action now and get Traugutt back on Reich soil so he can be arrested and you're the sole power."

Günter nodded. "You're right, boy." He paused, then amended, "Son."

10

"Don't go, Ryszard!" Kasia pleaded. "Something's not right. It's some sort of trap."

Ryszard was annoyed by Kasia's use of his name. Doubtless the Americans had the room bugged, it was then quite likely the subtle shift from *Richard* to *Ryszard* would be noticed and the information could filter back to Berlin. Or maybe he was just getting paranoid. After all, in some German dialects, the two names were indistinguishable. And the Americans seemed pretty thick about such subtleties. Still, Kasia should know better.

"Ryszard," Kasia wailed, apparently upset by his lack of response. "He wouldn't have summoned you back unless he's angry with you."

"Of course, he's angry with me. I haven't been there to keep him calm and Stefi can't fight off all the venomous attacks that my absence will have provoked."

Kasia threw pleading glances at Dorota and Feliks, as if begging them to participate in the argument, but they remained in stony silence in their respective places. "He's going to have you arrested."

"Maybe, but I don't have any choice." Ryszard made a slashing movement across his throat, trying to shut her up.

Kasia ignored him. "You can stay here."

"If I do that, then I'm sure to be arrested. Look, if he's angry, the last thing I can do is ignore his summons. I'll go back and calm him down. Ole and Stefan need to return with me, and I'll take Feliks. I'll leave Dorota here to guard you."

Kasia shook her head sadly. "Don't go. We can seek asylum here."

"Have you forgotten that our children are there?"

"But if you go, you won't live long enough to do them any good! I'll go back and fetch them. He'll let me leave – the Americans will embarrass him into that. You stay here."

"You want me to give up absolutely everything? Everything we've worked years for?"

"Please, Ryszard, after last time—"

"Stop being so god-damned paranoid! I don't know what Rudi is up to, but I can't afford to ignore a summons from him now. I'd lose everything – you know that. And I'm not giving it all up now."

Kasia sniffled noisily. "But Ryszard..."

"Damn it, we've been through all this. You knew this job was dangerous – now stop your incessant whining and help me plan."

Kasia's face froze into pained obedience. "Yes, Colonel."

Ryszard sighed heavily at Kasia's meaningful use of his military title. Luckily it was coincident with his SS rank. He gestured helplessly toward the walls, silently begging Kasia to be more careful. "Wife, are you going to help me, or are you going to stand there like a silly puppy whose nose has been smacked?"

Kasia began to weep. Her whole body shook and tears streamed down her face, but she didn't make a noise.

"Fine! Have it your way." Ryszard motioned toward the door and Feliks stepped cautiously outside, checking the hall. Just American Secret Service personnel.

Feliks nodded to Ryszard that all was clear. Ryszard holstered his gun and pulled on his jacket. The Americans had been pleased that he had brought so few people with him: just two assistants, his wife and two bodyguards. In exchange, Ryszard had demanded that he be allowed to wear his weapon. The Americans had acceded – just as long as he was willing to give it up in certain circumstances, and as long as he was discreet about it. Ryszard glanced in the mirror to check that the gun was unnoticeable.

"I've got to have a quick meeting with the Americans, tell them I've been ordered back, see if they'll give me any information about what's going on." He glanced at Kasia but she did not respond, just continued to snivel silently. "Then I've got some arrangements to make. When you manage to get control of yourself, pack my bags." He stormed out of the room.

He replayed the scene as the endless concrete sprawl of Berlin came into focus. God! If only there was some meaning in his life. A Jesuit. That's what he should have been. A learned Jesuit who wrote histories. Yes, a Jesuit, ah, what the hell, a Jesuit with a mistress or two on the side. Ach, but that wasn't really their tradition, was it? He reviewed what little he knew about those "soldiers of Christ" but he couldn't come up with anything except an image of Loyola's self-flagellation. Well, that wouldn't do! He'd have to settle on something else. A Trappist? Brewing beer to praise God. Yes, maybe that should have been his calling.

But no! He had been called to a more earthly soldiering. Fighting for a chimera of a country, a vestige of a people, a wisp of hope for a culture. And how was he fighting? By flattering and grinning and bowing. Ugh! Rudi better behave himself this time, or he was likely to fall victim to Ryszard's growing impatience. Let that little weasel say one stupid thing, Ryszard thought, just one stupid thing and, this time, I will strangle the slug!

Ryszard felt the slight thrust backward as the plane touched ground and hurtled to a stop. It was at this moment that Kasia always reached out and grasped his hand, as if offering thanks to God for their safe landing. He missed her touch, but she had wisely stayed behind, to attend the evening dinner, to make apologies for his sudden absence, to avoid whatever unpleasantness Rudi had cooked up in order to summarily summon his subordinate back from his great American tour.

The honor guard that greeted him as he stepped off the plane was impressive. And it was Günter, not Rudi, who came forward to shake his hand. But Günter did not shake his hand. Instead Günter motioned with his head to the soldiers standing to either side of them, and the soldiers dutifully moved in. Feliks, Olek and Stefan began to react, but Ryszard stopped them with a gesture. There was no point in committing suicide.

"You're under arrest," Günter announced solemnly as the soldiers grabbed Ryszard's arms and frisked him. They removed his weapon and one of them drew out handcuffs, but Günter magnanimously suggested, "That won't be necessary. I'm sure Colonel Traugutt won't give us any trouble."

It was said with such malevolence that Ryszard knew they already had Stefi.

Stefan was taken into separate custody, but Olek and Feliks were allowed to accompany Ryszard to their home in Schönwalde. Günter was even kind enough to let them enter with dignity, without a guard.

Lodzia greeted them, her face strained. She whispered something to Olek, who immediately disappeared down the hall, then she turned and awaited Ryszard's instructions. He stood stock still in his hallway, surveying the house, thinking about his last words with Kasia. Months ago, at the Führer's insistence, he had moved back in with Kasia, and since the Führer had naturally assumed that she wanted him back, Kasia had been obliged to allow him to return. It had been an awkward time. Kasia had greeted him at the door, like a visitor, and coldly informed him he was welcome to use the guest room. He had felt like a stranger in his own house. Now, it was even worse – he was a prisoner.

"Welcome back, *mein Herr,*" Lodzia prompted after several minutes. She helped him remove his coat.

Ryszard shook his head to dispel his dizziness. "Who's all here? Johann? Paul?"

"No one has entered the house, *mein Herr.*" Lodzia cast her eyes around meaningfully. "And we have diligently cleaned the house."

"Fine. Speak freely."

"Genia and the baby are upstairs. Your sons are as well. They've stayed indoors, but no one has shown any interest in them one way or the other. Including Pawel."

Ryszard breathed a sigh of relief. Perhaps Pawel was young enough he would be spared. "Is Stefi here?"

"Yes, *mein Herr*. She's under house arrest, *mein Herr.*"

"So am I. What's your situation?"

"That's unclear, *mein Herr*. Leszek and I have not been formally arrested and we are free to leave the house to carry out our duties; however, I am closely watched when I fetch the bread, as is Leszek when he runs errands." Lodzia gestured toward the window. "As you can see, the house is also under constant surveillance and there are armed guards at every entrance."

"I guess they figure they can intimidate you and Leszek into disobeying any orders I might give. They won't assume I command much loyalty from you."

"Indeed."

"Where's Stefi?"

"In the library, I sent the young master to her."

Lodzia led him into the library with Feliks following. Stefi sat in an armchair by the window, staring out at the sky. Olek was on his knees at her side, holding her hand as though he had been pleading with her. She did not react as Ryszard entered the room. Olek scowled at Ryszard and stood. "She won't say a word."

Ryszard was struck by her pallor. "Are you alright?"

Lodzia tugged at his arm and he leaned toward her. "She was arrested at the *Residenz*, by Schindler," Lodzia whispered. "They took her to a hospital and aborted the baby. Then they brought her here. She won't speak to anyone. Not even Genia."

Ryszard gasped with anger, hurt...Or was it fear? His precious Stefi! He looked to Olek, but Olek had turned his attention back to Stefi. She was still ignoring him.

"Leave us," Ryszard ordered.

Olek squeezed Stefi's hand, seeking her intervention, but she seemed uninterested. "I'll be back in a few minutes," he assured her, and sparing an angry glance at Ryszard, he left.

Lodzia and Feliks withdrew as well, shutting the door behind them. Ryszard walked over to Stefi's chair and gently placed a hand on her shoulder. "Stefi..."

"Seven years bad luck."

"What?"

She turned from the window to look at him. Her eyes were red, her face drawn. "Seven years bad luck. Isn't that what you get for breaking a mirror?"

"What are you talking about?"

311

"I sent him off to torture and kill! I told him to do it!"

"Who? To do what?"

"Rudi! To kill Uncle Peter. To torture him and kill him!" Stefi hissed. "That's worth seven years, isn't it?"

Ryszard grabbed his daughters shoulders. "Stefi! What is going on? I've been arrested by Günter. Where is Rudi? What is going on? I don't know anything! Get hold of yourself and tell me what is going on!"

She did. Slowly, haltingly, her voice choked with tears of anger and frustration, she told Ryszard how she had sent Rudi off to kill Peter, how Rudi had been taken hostage, how Peter had escaped with his hostage, how Günter had taken control and had her arrested and the baby aborted, how she could not face Olek or anyone else in the family. "Only you, Father. Only you know what I have done."

Ryszard shook his head. "I don't understand. Why'd you do it? Why'd you defy my orders? I told you to keep Peter safe – I was going to use him as a bargaining chip. You knew that! Why did you deliberately defy me?" He realized he was shaking her and he stopped.

Stefi stared up at him, her eyes narrowing with disgust. "Whatever my reasons – if it had worked, if Peter had been killed, or was dying in agony at this very moment – you wouldn't give a shit! The floor could be slick with his blood and that wouldn't matter – just don't slip on it, just don't let it stain your pretty uniform. Just as long as *you* were safe!"

"Safe? What? Stefi!" Ryszard begged. "Please tell me, why? What happened?"

"It's always you, isn't it? You're the one who's important! You're the one who's going to change everything! Any sacrifice will do! Any *body* thrown on the pyre, as long as *you* are safe! Even a man who has been your friend, the only friend your children ever had. Someone who has exposed himself to enormous risk, who has killed for you – so that you would be safe. You save his life as a 'joke' and you expect gratitude. He saves your life and you expect him to be thankful for the opportunity to be useful. You really do believe you're an *Übermensch*, don't you!"

Ryszard dropped to one knee, pulled Stefi toward him and hugged his daughter tightly to his chest. After a moment, he repeated softly, *"Why?"*

"Rudi was jealous of your success in America. He ordered you to be recalled and interrogated. You would have been found guilty of treason, and hanged. I diverted his attention the only way I knew how."

Ryszard stroked his daughter's hair. "Oh, my child. Oh, my little girl..."

"I encouraged Rudi to torture and murder the bravest person I have ever met. I betrayed him to save you. It was me. You didn't do anything. It was me. I'm a monster."

"Oh, little girl…"

"Then I broke a mirror, so they killed my baby…"

Ryszard hated superstitiousness and he knew Stefi did as well. He wanted to tell her to at least be rational in her self-denunciation, but he bit his tongue. He was completely at a loss for what to say. Clearly what Stefi had done had been right, but it had also traumatized her. Thoroughly unprofessional, he thought, but he cleverly managed not to say that. He let his fingers stroke soothingly through her hair as he wondered what he should say. "There, there," was all he finally managed. Then, with a bit more inspiration, he added, "I'm sure Peter wouldn't have minded the sacrifice, if he had known what it was for. And he got away, didn't he? See, it's okay. It'll all be okay."

He paused a moment, continuing to stroke his daughter's hair, then standing again – his knee had begun to hurt – he asked gently, "Do you have any ideas how we might handle Günter?"

11

*B*ogdan made a rough motion to return the guard's salute and bowed out of the wind, into the Council tent. "Sorry I'm late. Is he here yet?" He glanced around the tent. There was an animated debate but no sign of Halifax. Must be the Americans. "Have we decided what we're going to do with those Americans yet?"

Marysia rubbed her forehead wearily. "We have bigger problems than that right now. Here." She handed him a sheaf of papers. "Everyone else has already read it." Outside the tent, the wind whipped wildly around, making a haunting whistling in between the banging and snapping of the canvas.

As Bogdan took the report and sat down at the table to read it, the other Council members excitedly continued their discussion over its contents but were almost immediately interrupted by a soldier entering. "Captain Halifax is here for his final debriefing and to answer any questions you may have on his report." The soldier stepped outside the tent and motioned to Peter that he should go in.

"Do you have any idea what you've done?" Wojciech said before Peter had even finished ducking through the entrance. The wind, which had been ripping around only a moment before, dropped suddenly as if on command.

"You've ruined everything!" Wanda hissed into the sudden chilling silence.

Taken aback by the greeting, the happy grin melted from Peter's face. Perplexed, he looked to Marysia. She motioned somewhat confusedly toward Bogdan, at some papers he was reading. "I'm afraid we've just learned that the disappearance of the Führer has caused many problems. Schindler's taken control. He summoned Ryszard back from America and had him arrested the moment he arrived. He's declared the Führer dead and with all the opposition under arrest, he'll be elected the new Führer."

Before Peter could respond to that, there was an explosion of words from all sides.

"Didn't you realize, the Fuhrer is not a useful hostage for us to have!"

"Why didn't you release him immediately?"

"This is absolutely horrible!"

"Did you hear–"

"Your both disappearing like that–"

"Everyone thought the Führer was dead!"

"How could you not know how important he was?"

"You've thrown everything off! Ryszard's position was so delicately balanced!"

"Do you know what happened to Stefi?" Wanda was shouting at him over the din. "She was forced into a hospital and her baby was aborted!"

Peter spun around to face her. "Aborted?"

"Olek's been arrested as well. He, Stefi, Ryszard – they'll all be hanged for treason!"

"Arrested?"

Marysia watched as the color drained from Peter's face. His gaze turned inward as he absorbed the information being hurled at him. The incoherent commentary went on unabated, the accusations continued to fly, growing louder as the wind picked up again.

"My God, we're going to lose everyone there."

"All those years of hard work!"

"Poor Ryszard!"

"I'm sorry," Peter said quietly, almost to himself, "I didn't think…"

"Of course not!" Wanda hissed, "You never think of anyone but yourself!"

That brought everyone up short and they looked at Peter to witness his scathing response, but he didn't say a word. He scanned each of their faces and the look of confusion vanished as his expression hardened. He sniffed as if amused – either by them, or perhaps himself – then he turned on his heel and walked out.

The wind caught the tent flap and it banged noisily, filling the edgy silence that followed Peter's departure. Marysia stood and looked at the Council members who sat around her. What the hell had happened? They met her gaze but no one said a word. She placed her hands on the table in front of her as if ready to address them earnestly, but words failed her. *What the hell had happened?* Hania lowered her head and rubbed her temples.

Marysia singled out Wojciech. "You couldn't wait ten seconds until I had said welcome home?"

Wojciech grimaced guiltily in response. Everyone knew he had vied for the chair upon Katerina's retirement and it wasn't the first time he had pre-empted Marysia's lead.

Marysia shook her head in disgust and left. She walked aimlessly, heading first toward the bunker, undecided about what to do. For heaven's sake, what was wrong with her? Why hadn't she demanded order? Why had she let things get out of control? She sighed heavily. I'm too old, she thought. Old, slow and ineffectual.

After a few minutes, she decided to find Peter. He hadn't been cleared yet to enter the bunker so he would have to be somewhere among the trees. She went through the woods to the escarpment which she knew was his favorite retreat. She saw him sitting there and approached, but he did not hear her over the rustling caused by the breeze.

She stopped and surveyed him, looking at the slope of his shoulders, at how he ignored the glorious vista before him and stared down at the dirt. He ran his fingers along the surface of the rock and picked up a handful of the nearly worthless soil. Nothing would grow in it, it was too thin, too exposed, too stony. He sifted it through his fingers, letting the wind scatter individual grains, and then he pressed his hand against his face, wiping the rest of the dirt onto his cheek.

Marysia muttered a prayer under her breath and then cleared her throat.

Peter looked back over his shoulder at her and gave her one of his fleeting smiles. "Hi."

She approached and sat down next to him. "How are you doing?"

"Fine," he answered, without conviction. "How are you coping?"

"Me?"

"Well, I believe I heard that Olek is under arrest. He could be hanged."

"I know," Marysia said grimly.

"And you've lost your great-grandchild. I'm very sorry."

"Oh, yeah. If it was Olek's. Even Stefi admits it's hard to make sure of paternity."

Peter cast a glance at Marysia, then looked back out toward the trees. "Well, whoever the father was, it was certainly Stefi's baby."

"Pff. Julia had her pegged! She's such an icy creature, I doubt that it will matter to her."

Again Peter threw a glance at Marysia. "I suspect it does."

"Peter..." Marysia paused to tuck a lock of hair which had blown into her face back into place. "About what happened in the meeting..."

"Yes?" He continued to stare out at the trees.

She reached over to him and brushed the dirt off his cheek. "Look, I'm sorry about all that. It's every soldier's duty to escape – and you did that. We should have congratulated you. We were so happy when we heard the news, we should have mentioned that when you finally got up here. We *did* miss you and we, all of us, are truly glad you made it back. We got off to a bad start there..."

"Marysia."

"What?"

"There was a time when I cared."

"What do you mean?"

Peter shook his head. "Never mind. I was told that Zosia took Irena out east, along with Tadek – is that right?"

"Yes, she's carrying out some work contacting some of our people in the Soviet Union. All part of that elaborate plot Stefi set up to free her father. We figured that since we had so much in place, we'd work on using it to our advantage, and so we're firming up the eastern end of the story."

"Good idea. Are you going to tell her about my return?"

"She's essentially out of touch until she comes back."

"And that's supposed to be in about a week?"

"Yes."

"I was told Madzia is staying with Kamil and his family?"

"Yes. It was felt that it's too dangerous for Zosia to take her out of Szaflary," Marysia explained, in case Peter might think Zosia had shown some favoritism for Irena.

"I understand. But Kamil and his family are down south for the day. They won't be back until tomorrow, right?"

"Yes."

"Well then, do you think you can delay any punitive action against me, say, for a week or so? When Madzia comes back tomorrow, I'd like to take her to one of the border camps. We could just live among the partisans for a while, get to know each other, away from all...from all this. Then I'll come back and you guys can take whatever measures against me that you think are appropriate."

"Oh, Peter! There's not going to be any punitive action. We're pleased you escaped."

"Oh? That wasn't at all clear to me, but alright. That's good. Thank you. Still, I'd like a week alone with my kid, down there. Down among the commoners. Would that be okay?"

"Of course it would!" Marysia was perplexed by his strange wording. "But it's rather cold at night, you know. And this wind…Wouldn't you rather stay up here, where it's comfortable? It's your home, after all."

"Home. Yes, of course," he agreed perfunctorily. "Still, I think she'd enjoy camping." He glanced up at the sky, "The wind won't last and the days are warm. At night, we'll use a tent and warm sleeping bags. And we'll be back before Zosia and Irena return. Do I have your official clearance?"

"Of course." Marysia worried that somehow she was agreeing to something entirely different. "Of course. But before you go, I want you to have the physician check you out."

"Looking for implanted electronics?"

There was a pause, then Marysia reluctantly agreed, "Among other things."

"What other things?"

"You swallowed that poison, didn't you?"

A sudden gust ruffled Peter's hair. "That's what I explained in my debriefing. You read the report, didn't you?"

Marysia pushed a few strands of hair out of her face. "Yes, of course, just a couple of hours before you got up here."

"Well, did you think I lied?"

"No, no, no! It was just a faint hope on my part that somehow you were mistaken."

He tilted his head at her questioningly.

"Well, it obviously didn't kill you, but it may have caused permanent damage to your heart."

"I feel fine."

Marysia didn't though: his practiced air of unconcern disturbed her. *There was a time when I cared.* God, but it reminded her of Julia! Marysia studied Peter, trying to determine what lay behind his flippant disregard for his own health. What had lain behind Julia's virtual suicide? "Peter, go to the physician. That's an order."

"Okay." He gave her an easy, agreeable smile, "I'll see what the physician has to say about me and take whatever precautions he advises. Good enough?"

"Yes." Marysia bit her lip, then ventured to add, "Your report didn't say much about how you spent those months."

Peter shrugged.

"What happened?"

"Like the report says, nothing much: I spoke with the Führer, later I was interrogated – with reasonable civility – then I spent time alone, then I was interviewed by Ryszard, then a bit more time alone."

"Were you tortured?"

He stiffened at her question – as if the words themselves were painful. Or as if somewhere, deep in his past, he had heard them before. But then all he did was shrug noncommittally. "Not physically. And that's all that matters, isn't it?"

Marysia didn't answer. She wondered at the strangely detached person who sat next to her, reacting almost as though he were running one of those complicated programs of his rather than feeling anything. The Council had clearly wounded him with their words, why did he show no sign of injury? Why no anger? Who was this man?

"Do you have any other questions about my report?"

Marysia shook her head, then nodded. "Yes, just one. And it's just curiosity on my part."

"What's that?"

"When you were first taken to see the Führer, you were alone with him, weren't you?"

"Stefi was there, and there were a few guards."

"But he was within reach, wasn't he? I mean, later you managed to take him hostage and escape. Why didn't you try that when you had your conversation with him? Was he too wary then? Were you too weak?"

"Too wary, no. Too weak, maybe. But neither of those is the real reason." Peter laughed quietly. "The real reason is rather more stupid. You see, I simply didn't think of it."

"Why not?"

"Good question." Peter sighed heavily. "I would guess that a lifetime of propaganda has its effect, even on a rebel. You see, every child is told, continuously, that the Führer is invincible, almost godlike. I heard it all my life. I probably, deep down, believed it."

"So how did you manage to attack him later?"

"I was overwhelmed by pure hatred. Afterwards, I was no less surprised than he by my action. And by my success."

Marysia nodded thoughtfully. "That's certainly worth knowing. If someone as bright as you…"

Peter snorted with amusement at her assessment of him.

She decided to change the subject. "Do you know, when Olek left for Berlin, he gave me his medal. He wanted you to have it when you returned. Of course, he didn't know at the time, that you would end up in the *Residenz*…"

"I couldn't possibly accept it."

"He said you'd say that, and he also said that I was not allowed to take 'no' for an answer."

Peter laughed good-naturedly. "I don't deserve anything."

"Olek thinks otherwise." Marysia wanted to add: *and I do too*, but somehow the words would not emerge. If only he made it easier for her. If only Julia hadn't always resorted to those icy stares of contempt anytime Marysia had tried to bridge the gap. "I didn't get to ask him about it, he just left it in an envelope with a note."

"I won't accept it, but I wish I had known he had done that when I saw him. I would have told him how honored I felt just by his friendship." Peter stared off into the distance, then added, "Julia raised an incredible boy."

Marysia nodded sadly. "Yeah, somebody should have told her that when she was alive."

"How have things been going otherwise?"

"Oh, more or less okay. Wanda rejoined the Council."

"I noticed. How did that happen?"

"Once you were gone..." Marysia turned away, clearly embarrassed. "She asked to rescind her resignation. You know we hadn't elected anyone to take her place yet. She's been loyal for many years and with..."

"...the loss of her two sons."

"Yes, well, you understand."

"Of course. So she took up her old seat. What about my seat?"

"Zosia's sitting in for you."

"Sitting in?"

"Well, she's been...You know, Peter, no one thought you'd make it out of there alive."

"I understand."

"I'm not sure what we should do now. Hmm. I guess we could add another seat, or maybe Zosia should resign..."

"Nonsense." Peter picked up a pebble and cast it over the edge. "Let things stay the way they are. I'll resign my seat – if it's still mine to resign."

"But Peter, you earned your place, you deserve a seat."

He shook his head. "I wouldn't be comfortable. And I don't want another confrontation with Wanda. She is, after all, still my superior officer, and it was really awkward when I was on the Council and she wasn't. I could imagine having both of us on the Council would be a recipe for continuous bickering and not much work getting done."

Marysia sighed. Peter was right, when the political and military hierarchies clashed, it made things difficult. Someday, when the war was over, someday the military could take a backseat to the civilian government, but for now that was not practical.

"Speaking of Wanda, how are things in her section? She must have spent a few peaceful months without me around to annoy her – and with her husband working cryptography..."

"Ach!" Marysia groaned. "That was a mistake."

"Why?"

"Oh, Jurek's having so many problems and Wanda doesn't know what to do about it. I'm sure Jurek would like to talk with you. With both you and Olek gone, he didn't have anyone to turn to."

"You mean our all-knowing Wanda couldn't handle that for her husband?" Peter joked.

"No," Marysia answered testily.

"Alright. I'll stop by. I'll go there as soon as the Council is finished with me." Peter got up from the rock. "I'd better get back to them before Wanda orders my arrest for desertion or something stupid like that."

Somehow all the words Marysia had meant to say seemed inappropriate. *There was a time when I cared.* Did he mean that? What did he mean by that? Was he telling her that her concern was unwelcome? Or was he just trying to protect himself? Feeling unsteady, Marysia stood as well. "Tell the sentries you've been cleared. Go see the physician, then after that, go straight to see Jurek. He's really quite desperate. You don't need to go back to the Council now, I'll collect whatever details we need from you later."

"Good, I didn't really want to hear any more right now, anyway. After all, a guy can get embarrassed hearing so many effusive greetings."

Marysia did not laugh at his joke. She studied him for a long moment as an idea formed in her mind, then, having come to a decision she said, "Peter, there's one more thing."

"What's that?"

"I'll give you clearance to go down to a border camp on the condition you talk with someone."

"Who? Another psychiatrist?"

Marysia took a deep breath and braced herself, "An American. He's here studying...He's supposed to be looking into the social problems created by the violence of our society, you know, on a personal level. He's supposed to interview people who might have been traumatized by all the..." Marysia noted the way Peter stiffened, but he did not interrupt. "I want you to talk with him, answer his questions. He's here with his wife—"

"His wife?"

"Yes, she's part of his cover story – from the American side of things. Anyway, I want you to get to know him, or rather, them."

"What are his credentials?" Peter asked warily.

"I don't know. He just needs to explore our society and report back. There's funding involved."

"There always is. Does he speak German?"

Marysia nodded.

"Well, he obviously didn't come here expecting to talk to me."

"No, of course not. He doesn't even know you're affiliated with us."

"Then let him talk to someone else. There's lots of people who could give him a good perspective on this society. Take him into one of the camps."

"We plan to. I still want you to talk with him." Again Marysia corrected herself. "Them."

Peter stifled a yawn. "I did my time. They've heard it all. I don't want to bore anyone, now do I?"

"I don't want you to mention what happened after your arrest. I want you to talk about *before* your arrest. We can give them perspectives on this society, here east of Berlin, but things are different in the west – and they need to hear about that. They need to hear that although things are different there, they're not necessarily better."

"Marysia, that was long in the past."

"But it shapes us, as a people. Your upbringing was not all that unusual and the regime passes it off as completely livable."

Peter looked off into the distance. "It was."

"But only just. There are so many things which were worse than they had to be. So many negatives."

"Maybe, but I've already told the American public a cleaned up version of it all – at Alex's insistence. It wouldn't be wise to suddenly change my history."

"This won't be a public report. He's reporting to the government, the wife's got some charitable affiliation. Just tell them what it was really like. He's a former refugee – he'll sympathize, and you have some feel for American culture now, so you'll know what the differences are, how our National Socialist upbringing and philosophy have scarred us all. Tell them how the wrecked economies and the lack of opportunities hurt normal people. How your mother's talents were wasted, how your father resented the burden of an extra child, the omnipresent gangs..."

Peter turned to look directly at Marysia. "How do you know about that?"

Marysia bit her lip.

"Marysia! How do you know about all that?"

"I read your mother's diaries."

He took a deep breath. "You had no right."

"I'm sorry. We all thought you were dead."

"We?"

"Zosia suggested it. She thought..." Marysia seemed stymied.

He laughed bitterly. "I thought I could convince her I was human, and not just somebody set on this earth to serve her needs."

"Zosia?"

"No, Frau Vogel. But you see, it was an impossible task. I was too useful to her as a lesser being. She could never stop using me – she was addicted to her power. But I'll tell you this, Marysia," he leaned toward her menacingly, "Elspeth at least knew enough to leave my parents out of it!"

Marysia drew back.

"You've been using me since the day I arrived. Now you want even my mother for propaganda purposes. God damn it, this system killed my parents. *Let them rest in peace!*"

Marysia felt affronted by his tone, by the implied threat. "It's an order, Captain," she stated coldly.

There it was! That look – that fleeting glimpse of somebody Marysia did not recognize, someone quite terrifying. But then it was gone as quickly as it had appeared. He blinked slowly, then casually turned his head to look out into the distance. "You know," he said, his voice almost toneless – unnervingly so, "I know you're lying to me."

"Peter! I'm not–"

"I'm not blind. My sudden reappearance has given you an idea, an opportunity you didn't expect. There's something behind this charade, this talking to these Americans, but you're not going to tell me, are you? You want me to do something for you, but you won't trust me enough to tell me what." His voice dropped as he added, "It's just like last time."

Marysia shook her head. "No, no, it's not like that."

"Don't you understand? I've *joined* you. You don't need to manipulate me." He sighed slightly, as if forced to continue despite the uselessness of his words. "Please. Treat me as a human – your comrade, not an *Untermensch*. Not your tool." He continued to study the lay of the land as he added softly, almost hopelessly, "And maybe then, I could allow myself to be human."

Marysia bit her tongue. Her pride had been wounded by what he had said, but upon reflection, perhaps it was justified. More to the point, though, was how could she tell him what she wanted, when she herself did not know? She took a deep breath to calm herself, then said, "I need your help on this. Get to know them, give me your feedback. Would you do that?" It took a moment before she could add, "Please?" She saw a wry smile appear on his face at that last word. She wondered momentarily if she had ever said it before to him. She didn't think so.

"Fine. Where are they?" He said it without looking at her. He just stared into the distance, like an artist memorizing the landscape for later use.

"They're down at the border right now, but they'll be up here late this evening–"

"Up here? In Central? Who the hell cleared that?"

"Wanda. The Americans were insistent."

"Why? What business do they have coming up here?"

"I don't know, but it's hard to tell the Americans we don't trust them."

"Why not? They don't trust *us* with any information."

Marysia sighed. "That's different—"

"Why? They have their security concerns, we have ours."

"That's got to be the most irritating thing about you – the way you feign this belief in equality."

"I do believe it."

Marysia snorted. "I know you know better than that. They're rich and powerful so their security concerns are important. We are poor and weak, so ours are not."

"Tell them they are to us! Tell them you *kill* innocent young girls who are foolishly brought into Central by irresponsible do-gooders!" Peter nearly snarled. "Tell them, it's *not* possible!"

"Peter…"

"Don't tell me you don't take security seriously, Marysia. Don't you dare tell me that!" He gestured angrily toward the border. "What sort of vetting does this clown have?"

"He's from the American Security Agency. We have to trust their procedures."

"The ASA are the people with the security leak! Don't you remember what I discovered in London? The files? *Don't you remember!*"

Marysia sighed. "Yes, I know. The files you decoded, translated and sent to the ASA turned up in a Reich laboratory in exactly the format you sent them. And yes, I realize, that means there is a problem there. But what are the chances this guy would be the one who stole the files?"

Peter threw his hands up in exasperation. "Huge, I would guess! Any self-respecting spy would leap at the opportunity to get inside here."

"He's not your spy."

Peter stopped. He surveyed Marysia sadly, shaking his head slightly in disbelief. "Jana's story was better than that–"

"And yours was worse."

He ignored that. "Those files were passed on by someone, this man may easily be connected to that."

"It's not even clear…" Marysia looked away.

"What? What are you saying?"

"Look, it's not me. It's just that, it has been suggested that you added those files to your presentation to us – just to make it look more impressive. I mean, after all, you certainly had access to them. And you had your computer with you."

"Marysia!"

323

"I don't believe it, Peter. But you must see, that it is a credible alternative to your version of events. You gave us files that were exact copies of what you already had, that could be read by your computer, but not – according to your own testimony – by the machine on Chandler's desk. The files alone proved nothing. There may not even be a spy!"

"They weren't exact copies. I told you that."

"You told us they were exactly the same."

"The information content, yes, but you know that they had been reformatted exactly as one would expect if they had been routed through a number of marginally compatible systems. There were even some unnecessary changes." Peter's voice grew strained with irritation. "I *told* you all about that."

Marysia waved her hand dismissively. "Frankly, you can say whatever you want on this stuff. I just don't understand the details."

"Then believe *me.*"

"I do. Others don't. What can I say?"

Peter shook his head sadly. They were sufficiently unfamiliar with science, with computers, with cryptanalysis, with research, that they might well believe Chandler's lab could have completed the sterilization work on its own. It seemed unlikely he could overcome this perverted version of events with just his words. "Alright. I'll talk to this fellow. Why don't you have them rest down at the border for a day or two. When Madzia and I go down, we can accidentally stumble across them. I can talk to them down there and we can slowly wend our way up here together. With a local guide leading us, I'm sure we can make the journey last a few days."

"Do you want to admit to an outsider that Madzia is here?"

Peter shrugged. "I don't want to spend the time without her."

Marysia looked thoughtful. "Do you think they'd believe the journey could be so arduous?"

"What do you care what they believe? At least this way, we'll delay their arrival and maybe somehow we can prevent it altogether."

"They still have to come up here sooner or later. I don't like it any more than you do, but I'm under orders and politically, it'd be disastrous to deny access to someone the ASA has vetted."

Peter nodded his head slightly. "You know my story, Marysia. Politically it was disastrous for my superiors in Toronto to arrest a suspected spy with royal connections. You know what happened. All my friends and colleagues were killed. Everyone but me – and I was on the run for years, hunted by both sides, with no where to go, no one to turn to. I don't want to lose everything again to political expediency. Please be careful. You *know* I'm not lying about this American spy. *You know that!* And you had Jana

324

killed – you were strong enough to take that decision. Please stand up to the Americans. My family is here. My children. Don't let this fellow ruin us!"

"Don't be melodramatic. We've had visitors before. We've even accepted random English escapees into our fold and nothing has happened. You've had a very stressful time of it these past months, you were betrayed by a friend, and now you're seeing enemies and phantoms even among–"

"Please don't say it, Marysia. Don't mock me with my experiences."

"Oh, Peter, that isn't what I meant."

"You were quoting Ryszard – back when he was trying to convince the encampment I was insane. Insane and cowardly."

"That isn't what he meant."

"It isn't? Well, I suppose you would know better than anyone. You spoke to him privately before that great, public therapy session, didn't you? Tell me, what kind and understanding words did he impart to you about me before that meeting?"

Marysia reddened as she remembered how they had blithely discussed how they could most effectively make use of Peter. Ryszard had joked about taking Peter as a personal slave, called him a "wreck" and some torturer's "pet." Wanda had categorically stated her lack of trust in him. Marysia had argued for Zosia's plan, not once bothering to counter Ryszard's gratuitous slander. Katerina had listened dispassionately, weighing nothing more than the risks.

No one had mentioned the psychiatrist's report – the one which lay buried in the thick folder that had sat on Marysia's table. No one had asked if Peter's being forced to present such a sanitized version of events would in any way degrade his sacrifices. No one even thought to ask his opinion of the idea. He had been present in their minds only as a tool to be used or discarded and no one had given even a moment's pause to the idea that he might have some say in the matter or could, in some way, be harmed by the decisions they had made for him.

"Shall we walk back together?" Peter asked, rescuing her from answering his question. His tone had changed back to that calm and detached air he had held only a moment before.

Marysia felt shaken by the suddenness of the transition, but did not resist as he gently took her arm in his and helped her down the path.

12

"**S**o what's the problem?" Peter casually picked up a piece of paper and scanned it.

Jurek petulantly snapped it out of his hands. "It's not that!"

"Didn't mean to pry." Peter knew Jurek would miss the irony in that, and indeed he did.

"It's this," Jurek stated gloomily, as he turned toward the computer. "I can't get anything to work right!"

Peter watched as Jurek tapped a few keys and drew up a screen of obscure text messages. "As you can see, anytime I try to run this program – I get this message. Errors! I don't understand. I thought this was all automated!"

"Automated, yes." Peter perused the messages. "Unfortunately, there's always a bug hiding somewhere." He pulled up a chair for himself, sat down at the computer, and typed in a few commands. He read through the diagnostics, tried a few things, pointed out a few key phrases to Jurek and then entered the appropriate changes. "Ah-hah! There! I've changed the formatting to cope with the different standard used by the Americans. It should work alright now."

"Why didn't you do that before?" Jurek asked, sourly.

"They never used to send things in that format. They've changed their conventions."

"But how was I supposed to know what to do?"

"You weren't!" Peter laughed. "I mean, I guess they should have told you, but getting information out of these people…Anyway, sooner or later you'll stumble across every sort of problem, and sooner or later you'll have a clue how to solve anything that comes up. It's all trial and error and at first you'll spend hours solving problems that later will take only seconds to sort out. That's why experience is so important. That and communication."

"What do you mean?"

"Oh, nobody can keep track of everything – that's why it's good to talk to the others, in Warszawa, even in the NAU."

"I don't speak English."

"Ah. Well, I'll warn you now – everyone changes conventions with some regularity. There are updated machines, more secure protocols, better ways of handling things. Even stylistic changes. Most aren't important, but they can foul up any routine machine translation. Whenever stuff doesn't run smoothly, you need a human to look at things and recognize what's going on. A trained human."

Jurek grunted.

"For instance – there was a complete change in what the security services do here, about five years ago. Anything from before that time, you have to handle differently – otherwise you'll get gibberish out of the machines."

Jurek screwed up his face with something like interest.

"And there are even varying styles among the different regions. Dialects you might call them."

"Such as?"

"Well, a long time ago I worked with coded documents, mostly inter-office memos from within England but every now and then something came to us from France, and it was quite different. Same security service, different styles. And now the stuff out of England is almost unrecognizable. I would guess that when Schindler took over he replaced all the top people in London with his own cronies and they had their own conventions, so the old ones were supplanted."

"I still think you should have set it up to cope with the different format," Jurek mumbled.

"Yes, of course." Peter felt annoyed that he had deluded himself into thinking he was having a reasonable conversation with Jurek. "I should have foreseen every eventuality. Just like when I made my escape and took the Führer hostage."

Jurek missed the sarcasm. "Yes, you really did wreck things there, didn't you?"

Rather than argue, Peter stared blindly at the screen. "They'll sort it out when they want to."

"Who? How?"

"The Council. Once they settle down, they'll realize they can turn this whole thing to their advantage."

"How so?"

Peter mindlessly typed in a few commands and watched as the resultant information flowed reassuringly across the screen. "Lots of ways. For example, they could send a hint from some external source – maybe the Americans – to the respectable German press, letting them know the Führer is alive and in command, then a few hours later, once the press realizes that it's in their best interest to support Rudi, they could have a statement from Traugutt leaked, defending the rightful Führer and denouncing Schindler. Shortly after that is published, and before Günter can react, the Council can openly announce to all and sundry that they have the Führer, alive and well, and they will release him to a neutral representative – say the Ambassador from Kivu."

"Why Kivu?"

"They know that the country is a trusted Reich ally and they also know their American representative – that is, Alex – has worked with the ambassador and trusts her personally. They'll release Rudi into Arieka's protection and just to be sure Ryszard remains safe, they can demand he attend the handover. Rudi can return to Berlin in triumph, toss Günter out, possibly imprison him for treason, and Ryszard comes out of the whole thing as a truly loyal son of the Reich, ready to take the reins of power whenever Rudi must step down or dies of an unfortunate accident or whatever." Peter casually typed in a few more commands.

Jurek was staring at Peter, clearly intrigued.

"And hell," Peter added, getting into the spirit of his script-writing, even as his fingers moved over the keyboard, "if they want to prove that they are truly not in any way associated with my murderous actions against Vogel, they could ingratiate themselves to the Reich government by throwing me in as a special, complimentary prize! Bundle me off, back to my well-deserved fate, as a goodwill gesture, then everything would be back to the way it was before I messed it all up, but even better." Peter stopped typing and turned to Jurek to bestow a broad grin on him. "That's just one scenario. I could devise a dozen others – I'm sure they could as well." Then, turning his attention back to the desk, he asked casually, "Now, what other problems have you been having?"

"Nothing that can't wait. I promised I'd meet Wanda for lunch. Do you think you could stop by later? I have a few more things I need help on."

"Sure. Later this afternoon. Tomorrow I'm going to head down to do some camping with my daughter."

"Camping?"

"Yeah, down with one of the partisan groups. Sit by the campfire, sing songs, dance to the music. She can fall asleep in my arms while I drink and talk with the others. I think she'll enjoy that."

Jurek nodded disinterestedly. "Of course. Now, if you'll excuse me, I have to go."

"Me too, I don't want to miss my welcome back party." Peter laughed and turned his attention back to the keyboard.

An hour later he walked the corridors to his and Zosia's flat. When he had been escorted into the Central region, they had taken him directly to the Council, and so he had not yet been to the apartment. Fatigued from maintaining a tight control over his emotions, he was relieved to at last be alone. As he approached the door, it occurred to him that he might not be alone, there might be some sort of genuine welcome awaiting him. Despite himself, a faint hope glimmered in the back of his mind, but he recognized immediately that it was only tiredness that was causing him to let his guard down. He took a deep breath, annoyed that he had entertained such a notion even briefly, coldly extinguished the flicker of boyish anticipation that had been ignited, and entered into the dark and empty flat.

It was not completely dark – the night lights which he had rigged with timers were on. The day lights should have been on, but Zosia had probably shut everything down to night-time lighting while she was away. Peter put on the light and walked through the flat, casually taking in the scents and sights of home. Even empty, the rooms were welcoming: Irena's blanket, Madzia's toys, Zosia's books. He noticed that this time – though there was no realistic expectation of his ever returning – this time, Zosia had not removed his belongings. His clothes were in the closet, his books on a shelf and his letters and his mother's diaries in their drawer. As he shut the drawer, a smile of relief on his face, his eyes lit upon an unfamiliar book. It was part of a stack that he recognized as belonging to Tadek. Peter walked through the two rooms again, this time looking at things more carefully. It was clear Tadek was spending considerable time with Zosia. Doubtless helping out with the children. Peter laughed silently and turned his thoughts to other things.

Uppermost in his mind was food. He searched the cupboards and found the makings of a nice meal. After that he showered, shaved, and changed clothes. Feeling refreshed and somewhat relaxed, he finally set about looking up the information he had mentioned to Marysia. Of course, once he had given up his position in the cryptanalysis office, he had lost "his" computer, but he had kept a copy of his files, and he grabbed that and went to the cryptanalysis office to use the computer there.

Jurek was out and so he had the place to himself. He inserted his disk and called up the files he had saved: both the version he had found in Chandler's office back in March, as well as the original that he had translated with Olek and Barbara more than a year before. He wanted to refresh his memory on what exactly the differences were that he had detected.

He sighed as the files appeared on his screen. The finished formulae which he had found in the laboratory had been his ticket home, the existence of these files was of secondary interest: they had indicated the presence of a spy in the American Security Agency and had given Ryszard a tool with which he could blackmail Schindler. Surely the idea that he had invented their existence was unnecessary paranoia. Either that or Wanda's inexplicable distrust and hatred of him.

329

It was one thing, putting up with her constant jibes and petty tyrannies, but this time she had gone too far. This time she was risking the entire encampment's safety. Apparently the Americans had yet to be informed they had a spy. Apparently Ryszard had yet to use the information against Schindler, thus proving its worth. Apparently no one else took his information seriously. But he did. He remembered ever so clearly that moment when he had discovered his very own work in a file drawer in Chandler's office. Peter remembered how his brother had leaned over his shoulder asking what was going on, why he look so perturbed. He felt again the burning sense of betrayal, the salt on the wound of seeing his own entry there on the computer in that laboratory. The information about his life which had been so blithely traded around, like the veterinary record of an animal bound for the slaughterhouse. Again, as though bewitched, he found the cursor straying to that part of the file. He typed a command which deleted the line, watched with a sense of relief as that episode in his life disappeared, then chiding himself for his stupidity – he was tampering with the very file he wanted to inspect for changes – he typed another command and the line magically reappeared.

As part of his mind reminisced about how he had found the files and why Wanda hated him so much, another part studied the work of some unknown hand and wondered what clues could be found among the subtle changes. The width of the margins had been changed – that was natural enough, the Americans used a different sized paper, so if they wished to print anything they would change it. Oddly, they had opted for the longer length of the two sorts of paper they used – fourteen inches instead of eleven. Peter had been fairly sure that the standard was eleven, but then it was possible that a government bureaucracy such as the ASA might have a different house style.

He typed a few commands so he could look at the hidden characters. Several lines had been added to the beginning of the document – probably automatically by some machine as it translated his computer's code to fit its own standard. He didn't explicitly recognize most of it but that didn't surprise him, he was not particularly familiar with all the subtle differences between various bits of American office equipment. One set of lines did surprise him though – they were the sort of translation instructions he used to put in by hand back when he was working for the English Underground. The military computers in the London laboratory were not quite the same standard as the University computers which he and Allison had access to, and before they could read any of those ancient and cumbersome reel-to-reel computer tapes, he had always had to program these few translation instructions into the machine so it would know how to read the different standard. The instructions were specific to programs used in the Reich years ago and, he was fairly certain, only in England.

Standard code from years ago. From England. Typical code for Nazi documents from years ago in England.

Peter stroked his chin as he studied the familiar string of characters. Now, who would have put that there? And why? Peter leaned back and contemplated a likely scenario. The spy would somehow get access to the files and would store them on a microdisk. He would then send the microdisk and, under separate cover, a computer which could read the disk, to his boss's minions in the Reich. So, Wolf-Dietrich received his beautiful stolen computer which he had so happily shown to Stefi, and later, the American traveling under the name van Wije had, perhaps unwittingly, delivered the microdisk to Wolf-Dietrich via the inn in Lewes. Wolf-Dietrich would put the disk into the computer and read it without a problem, but there was no way that Wolf-Dietrich could pass the information on to the laboratory in that format. He would never give up or even reveal something as valuable as his new computer. So, Wolf-Dietrich would copy the files and Chandler would receive them in a more old-fashioned format, the disks that Peter had found in his filing cabinet. Those would be read by some machine – perhaps something Chandler had been secretly provided with by Schindler – and then would be copied onto the old-fashioned tapes which could be read by the sort of government-provided computer which had sat on display on Chandler's desk.

Peter closed his eyes and tried to remember what sort of machine Chandler had had on his desk. It was rather old and it probably would not have been able to read the files from a new machine. So, the translation lines were very likely necessary. In fact, instead of telling him something about the writer, those few cryptic lines probably told him more about the age of Chandler's computer. Somebody had been informed of the end user's machine and had prepared the translation accordingly. Peter hissed his exasperation as he realized he had reached a dead-end. There was virtually no information about the spy in those lines – just information about Chandler's fucking computer! And who the hell gave a damn about that?

Still, it was not a dead loss. Peter opened his eyes and looked at the lines of code again. It was familiar, but not exactly what he would have used. That meant it was probably of a different vintage than his work but not too far off. Whoever had written those lines must have worked with codes, in the Reich, no later than fifteen years ago, and almost certainly in England – in fact, in the London SS dialect. There was, of course, the chance that Wolf-Dietrich or Chandler had put them in, but that seemed very unlikely given what Stefi had reported about the former, and what Peter had observed of the latter's work. And Schindler himself was completely incapable of such things. The only other possibility that came to mind was Major Rattenhuber who had run the laboratory near Hamburg. So, it was most likely either Schindler's computer expert in the Reich – Rattenhuber, or his computer expert in America – the spy.

Peter closed the files and tapped into the library's personnel database to trace Rattenhuber's career. It didn't take long. Shortly after Peter began his visit to America and just before the existence of the sterility program was announced on that American news program, the Führer had "uncovered" the conspiracy, the laboratory had been shut down, and Rattenhuber – the presumed ringleader – had committed suicide before coming to trial. Schindler was out not only a sterility program, but also one computer expert. That left his man in America as the only likely candidate for who had written those lines of code. And now Peter knew something about him.

He left the library and went to find Marysia. If he could describe the background of the spy to her before she had told him any details about the American visitor – and if the two descriptions matched – maybe then she'd be convinced of the danger they were all in.

Marysia was in her room, and she smiled welcomingly as she opened the door to him. "Oh, good, I'm glad you dropped by. Do you want a drink?"

"Do you have a few minutes? I need to talk to you about this American visitor."

"Of course." She motioned him into the room. "It's a good time – Wanda's here. She has a brilliant idea of how we can save Ryszard. I want you to hear it, I'm sure you can help out."

"Oh, don't let me interrupt! It's not important." Peter turned to leave but Marysia had her hand on his arm and it was too late to resist her hospitality. She steered him to a seat at her table and poured him a drink. Wanda was also at the table, but did little more than grunt an acknowledgment of his presence. Her eyes were fixed on a small television that was on a cart. The television was connected to a videotape playing device and on the screen were images of Ryszard's visit to America.

Peter's eyes were drawn to the screen as well and he listened to an extract of one of Ryszard's speeches captured by an American news agency and replayed on their evening news. The words were exactly the ones Peter had suggested to Ryszard, the gestures as well. Though it was clear that Ryszard had spoken for a rather longer period of time, the sentences that Peter had planted were, as he had predicted, exactly the ones which had caught the news editor's attention: a slightly self-derogatory joke, the audience's sympathetic laughter, then the simple statement that the two peoples separated by the Atlantic had so much in common and should be able to work together for a better future. Ryszard had initially rejected using humor, but Peter had pressed the idea on him and apparently Ryszard had accepted the advice.

Wanda read a written translation that was on the table and smiled. "Look at our Ryszard!" she cooed as the segment ended. "Isn't he absolutely brilliant! What a strategist!"

Marysia nodded in agreement, "He really knows how to handle the Americans, I wonder where he learned that."

Both women glanced at Peter to hear his reaction to the tape. He hesitated only a second as he decided what to say, but that was far too long for Wanda. "Pff. *You* should be so clever! Then you wouldn't have to sleep with every Nazi who crosses your path."

"Wanda," Marysia whispered pleadingly.

"Well, go ahead and ask him!" Wanda snorted, then turned back to Peter, her gaze fierce. "How did you get out of there, Peter? Hmm? Whose bed did you slither into this time?"

The Kommandant's fetid alcohol-laden breath panting in his ear...The guards in the re-education camp hissing their hatred as they used anything they could get their hands on to...Elspeth's simple suggestion loaded with threats that did not need to be voiced...Hands clawing at him. Hands pulling him down, tearing at his clothing, binding his arms, blindfolding him – hitting, hurting, strangling, violating the sanctity of his body in any way they cared to...Blind darkness, writhing in pain, struggling to free himself, his own hands reaching uselessly, pleading for mercy, closing around nothing...No, closing around Wanda's throat, wrapping themselves around her neck, wringing the last insult out of her wretched body forever...

He saw a look of recognition and fear on Marysia's face and he forced the violent image back down, deep into that recess of his mind where such things were kept hidden. With a determined calmness, he picked up the drink Marysia had poured, downed it in one gulp and then carefully stood. "I'll talk to you later," he said to Marysia and left.

13

*R*yszard gave up on the book he was trying to read. It was pointless, he could not concentrate on it. It was "The Consolation of Philosophy" by Boethius. Quite appropriate – as it was written as the poor man awaited execution. Günter was familiar with the work. He had shown Ryszard a beautifully illustrated fifteenth century copy originally from a college library in Cambridge that had been discovered by his men, along with other "lost books", in a cave. Clearly Günter hadn't read a word of the book, but he recognized the quality of the velum and the marvelous color in the illustrations and had immediately taken possession of the work and displayed it proudly on a stand in his home library. Ryszard's version was not nearly so grand – it was just a cheap translation Kasia must have bought some time during his absence and which he had only recently discovered on a bookshelf.

He cocked his head a bit and looked out the library window. From where he was sitting, if he kept the angle just so, then he could look out without seeing the ever present sentry posted by the window or the communications detection van parked on the street. It was another miserably gray October day. Perfect for the memorial service that Günter had organized for poor Rudi. The story of the Führer's abduction and murder had been given full press coverage. The television news and radio programs were saturated with eulogies for the great departed leader, and following on from that were the quiet little items about Schindler's dignified handling of the entire situation. Tomorrow, the Party bosses would convene to decide who would lead the Party and therefore the country. They would take advice from heads of government departments and military commanders – most, if not all of whom, were themselves highly placed Party members. Günter would be elected – there was no doubt about that. What little competition he had had, was now neatly removed by Büttner's and Traugutt's arrests. His friend Schenkelhof would welcome his election, ever-loyal Frauenfeld would blindly follow, Greta's family would throw their support to him, and everyone else would recognize which way the wind had blown. No one would dare question the status quo – Schindler would be the undisputed leader. Afterwards, the Party would turn to other, more mundane business and would review the membership roster. Büttner and Traugutt would be voted off the list. Thereafter, sometime in the not too distant future, there would be trials.

Ryszard wondered momentarily what the charges against him would be. He had been told nothing at all, but Stefi had overheard someone talking about a conspiracy to murder the Führer. So, I will hang, Ryszard thought. Stefi and Olek as well. Probably Stefan, maybe even Feliks and Dorota would be implicated. If Günter was feeling magnanimous, he might leave Kasia and the younger children alone. He could probably use their lives and future well-being to elicit damning confessions. Maybe, if they were all convincing enough, Schindler would allow his victims to do the decent thing and commit suicide.

Of course, it was possible that Schindler, once elected, would see no need to press the treason charges. He might simply allow Ryszard to resign in disgrace in order to take up some mediocre position in a distant backwater of the Reich. After a few months, maybe even years, Ryszard would be quietly murdered and his death would draw no notice at all. That might be the wisest course for Schindler to take: it would cause the least fuss with respect to the Americans, but it also seemed the least likely, given the way Ryszard had conducted himself with Schindler's wife. Ah yes, poor Greta would finally be the Führer's wife – but it would not be the position she had imagined. She would be powerless, a prisoner of Günter's anger and probably spending every day in fear for the rest of her life.

Or would Günter turn against her once he was elected? She and Ryszard had made no attempt to hide their affair, and adultery was, at least technically, a crime. And adultery against the Führer? Ryszard shuddered, poor Greta! Well, she had gambled and lost – just as he had. He just wished that he had some information about what lay ahead. But there was nothing. He only had access to the news services available to the common people – and they were full of nothing but praise for the dead Führer and hints about Schindler's likely succession. There was, naturally enough, nothing about Traugutt's arrest. His absence from Rudi's memorial service would probably be the first time the pundits would have a hint that he had fallen from favor.

"Colonel?"

Ryszard looked up to see Olek standing in the doorway of the library.

"What is it, lad?" Ryszard studied Olek as the young man walked stiffly across the room. With his artificial limbs, Olek walked so well, one could hardly tell that his legs had been blown off by a mine. It had been quite generous of Peter to waste his money in such a manner. Ryszard had amassed a reasonable fortune through his activities – it was, indeed, a necessary part of his cover – nevertheless, it would have never occurred to him to offer anything similar. He smiled to himself as he realized how useless hoarding it had been – Schindler would have possession of everything within a few months, it was only a matter of how long it took the process of confiscation to go through the courts. At the end of it all, it was very unlikely that the widow Traugutt would have a pfennig to her name.

Olek stood before him, but did not say anything.

"Well?"

"It's Stefi. She's talking a bit now. But she still won't tell me what happened. I know the abortion devastated her. But it's more than that, isn't it? Do you know, sir, what's wrong with her?"

Ryszard blinked slowly. Why hadn't Stefi told Olek? She loved him, trusted him completely. And he was a soldier as well, he understood risk. Her strategy had been correct, her handling of Rudi was brilliant. She could not have foreseen that Rudi would be stupid enough to allow himself to be taken hostage, and the fiasco that followed was certainly not her fault. So why was she ashamed?

Ryszard gestured toward an armchair. "Sit down, boy." Olek seated himself and Ryszard studied his face as he let Stefi's words play through his mind. Ah yes, Peter had been quite important to Olek. A good friend, the best man at his wedding, a father-figure. Julia's son had finally found a man who could be bothered to talk to him and teach him. It should have been me, Ryszard thought. When Olek had apprenticed outside Szaflary, Julia had arranged for his mentor to be Ryszard and Olek had spent several months in Ryszard's house, working in his office, learning the ropes of infiltration. Yet, Ryszard had completely missed the hint. He had married Kasia, he had lost his chance to have Julia, but she had offered him the chance of being a father to her son. And he had completely missed the point!

Olek waited patiently.

"Peter told you, didn't he, that Karl Vogel was probably your father."

"Yes, sir."

"And you know Vogel murdered your mother."

"Yes, sir."

"Do you know how Peter found that out?"

"You told him, sir."

"That's right. Do you know how I learned it?"

"No, sir."

"Vogel bragged about it. He didn't use any names, didn't give any details of what he had done, but I knew." Ryszard leaned forward slightly. "Do you know why I immediately recognized what he was talking about?"

Olek shook his head.

"Because the details were burned into me. There is not a day in this life, that I haven't thought of Julia. Did you know that? Did you know how much I loved your mother?"

Olek shook his head again. He looked afraid, as if he feared being punished later for having heard too much.

Am I such a monster?

"Why didn't you marry her, sir? You knew her before you were married, didn't you?"

"Oh yes, we grew up together. She knew everything about me. And that, I suppose was our undoing."

"How so?"

"She knew what I wanted out of life: I wanted to do deep infiltration and be phenomenally successful at it. She was just like me though – she wanted to be successful as well. I wanted a wife, someone to support me. I needed to have a good Nazi wife in order to fit in, and she knew that if she stayed with me, she would never have more than a supporting role in our lives. She was young, only eighteen, and very idealistic. She wanted to make her own contributions, and so she went to Berlin instead. We knew she would be away for years." Ryszard sat back in his chair and looked up at the ceiling. "We quarreled. When she left, I refused to say good-bye."

"I had no idea," Olek whispered.

Ryszard brought his gaze back from the ceiling, but his look remained distant, as though he were seeing into the past. "I knew what I had to do. I needed to get on with my life plan. I wooed the secretary I had been assigned and she fell in love with me. I knew she'd be perfect for the role of a good Nazi wife, I knew that I was the only important thing in her life, so I married her." Ryszard paused, thinking about Zosia's stuttering words about her reasons for marrying Peter. Soldiers give their lives to their cause, he thought, and we gave ours. The collateral damage to other people – that was a necessary price of war. "Julia had her revenge though. She had an affair in Berlin and you were the result." Ryszard sighed heavily. "Kasia got pregnant almost immediately after our marriage. Once Stefi was born, once Julia had so clearly shown her contempt for me by mating with some Nazi pig, well, by then it was too late to undo things."

They were silent for a long moment, then Olek timidly said, "I appreciate your telling me all this, sir, but what does it have to do with Stefi?"

Nothing at all. Ryszard regretted that he had said anything. He stared at Olek long enough to cause the lad to nervously avert his gaze.

"It was just as well, you see." Ryszard's voice had grown quite cold. "There is no way I could do this job without the unconditional support of my wife. There is no way Stefi can do her job without your unconditional support. Julia couldn't give that to me, so we didn't marry. But you *have* married my daughter – now you *owe* her that support."

Olek shook his head in confusion. "But what's wrong with her? Why won't she tell me?"

"Didn't you hear me? Stefi doesn't need your questions. Just your *unquestioning* support. Give it to her. That's your job!"

Olek looked stunned by Ryszard's words.

"Mein Herr, may I have a word with you?"

They both looked up at the interruption to see Lodzia standing in the doorway of the library. Ryszard motioned her into the room. "What is it?"

"There was someone new at the bakery today, *mein Herr.* A temporary worker brought in as part of some inspection program."

Ryszard didn't even bother to feign interest. He raised an eyebrow sardonically to let Lodzia know he was not in a patient mood.

"The worker gave us an extra loaf of bread, *mein Herr*. He also told me *Die Zeit* had some interesting news today. I know it's not your usual paper, but I took the liberty of buying you a copy."

Ryszard accepted the paper from Lodzia. Doubtless it would report that there would be some idiotic parade or some other circus-event after Schindler's election – something that would interest the menial mind. Ryszard began to unfold the paper, but then he noticed Lodzia hadn't left. "An extra loaf of bread, you say?"

In the kitchen, they all watched as Leszek carefully pulled the loaf apart. The bread crumbled on the board to expose a rolled sheaf of paper. Olek brushed some crumbs out of the way. "What a charmingly quaint method of communication."

Lodzia picked up the sheaf and handed it to Ryszard. "But effective."

Ryszard reached for the papers, his heart filled with hope.

Stefi looked up from the table into her father's eyes. "I wonder whose life will be offered up for you this time?"

Ryszard glared at his daughter, but before he could formulate a reply, Olek placed his arm around his wife and led her from the room, saying, "They'll tell us what we need to know later."

Ryszard heard Stefi sobbing, but she had Olek to comfort her. He turned his attention to the papers and began scanning the information. The others watched him expectantly, waiting in impatient silence. He ignored them, returned to the library, shut the door, and sat down to read in comfort.

The American government had been told via the Governments-in-Exile that the Führer was not dead and had been advised to pass the news on to Reich officials. At the same time, the news was released to the American public, coincident with the Führer's demise being announced. Side-by-side articles carried the two stories: one the solemn Reich announcement that the Führer was dead and a memorial service was planned, the other with a photograph of the Führer holding up a newspaper with current headlines. Shortly thereafter a statement from the Führer had been released, announcing that he was in secret negotiations, would return to duty soon, and warning all officials to obey only his orders and not to allow themselves to be caught up in "illegal conspiracies or treasonable activities." At the same time there was a statement released from a high Reich official, Richard Traugutt, who had only just been visiting America, that he had certain knowledge that the Führer was alive and well, and pledging his undying loyalty to the true leader of his country and calling on all his fellow officers to reiterate their oaths of loyalty and to resist any attempt to subvert the government.

The sheaf of papers contained the entire text of Traugutt's statement and Ryszard read it carefully. He noticed that not only had someone very cleverly imitated his style – it was obviously written by someone who knew him quite well – but that the American translation was subtly different from the German text, and that both were shrewdly geared to gain maximum sympathy from their respective audiences. Ryszard recognized Peter's hand and laughed to himself that he could be so effectively imitated. He paused for a moment to light a cigarette. The English Underground had been right – Peter should have accepted their plans for him and done deep infiltration. He'd almost certainly be competing with me for the top job by now, Ryszard mused. He filed the thought in the back of his mind for later use and continued reading.

Only several hours after various Reich officials would have heard the whispered news from American or other foreign contacts, a flurry of facsimiles, telexes and hand-delivered letters showed up at every important office in Berlin or on the doorstep of every Party official. All contained the same message: the Führer was alive, it would be treason to assume otherwise, and all officers of the Reich were expected to stand by their oaths, as loyally demonstrated by Traugutt. That had happened early in the morning. Further, the publishers of certain important newspapers were convinced that it was less risky to inform the populace that the Führer was alive and well than to maintain the story which Schindler had instructed them to print. Ryszard laughed to himself as he thought of exactly how that may have been achieved: the numerous agents combing through files, the blackmail and extortion, or outright threats. Such a phenomenal effort! Ah, but he was worth it!

Ryszard laid the papers on his lap and relaxed. Doubtless numerous people were at this moment sweating over the decision of what to do, wondering which was the correct side to support in this sudden civil war. As for himself and his family, it would be a tense few hours. If Schindler moved fast to counter this assault, one of his first moves could be to have Traugutt summarily executed. It would doubtless be explained to the world as suicide, and Ryszard had not failed to note that none of Schindler's men had entered the house or removed any of the guns contained therein. Better to leave them all pathetically armed so that when it became necessary, there would be no doubt that weapons had been readily available with which they could do themselves in.

Ryszard picked up the text of the Führer's and his speeches and scanned them again. There was actually no reference to a particular plot and nowhere was Günter Schindler's name mentioned. So, they had left him a graceful way out. Perhaps, it could all be settled smoothly, with a minimal number of corpses. With no obvious conspiracy to join or defend, all of

Schindler's comrades could quietly slip away from him – congratulating him on handling the situation so well, shrugging their shoulders at the misinformation that had forced him to declare the Führer dead, and loyally picking up the business of government exactly where it had been left off.

All well and good for everyone else, but could Schindler dare leave Traugutt alive? Knowing how much his adversary must have guessed or overheard, could Schindler take that chance? Good question, Ryszard thought, then turned his attention back to the pages, to see what had been planned.

There was a knock and then Leszek entered unbidden. "Colonel Traugutt?"

"What is it?"

"Herr Schindler is approaching the house." Even as Leszek spoke, Ryszard could hear Schindler at the door, pushing his way past Lodzia. Ryszard rapidly stuffed the papers he was reading into his book and quickly placed it on a bookshelf. Then he straightened his suit jacket and awaited his guest.

One of Schindler's minions shoved Leszek aside and Schindler himself entered the library.

"Ah, Günter, welcome into my humble home," Richard greeted him sarcastically. "But haven't we forgotten our manners in all the excitement?"

"You've been treated better than any other traitor, Traugutt. You should be hanging from a meat-hook!"

"Traitor to whom, Günter?"

"The Führer! You organized his abduction! Convincing him to keep that treacherous criminal in his own residence, your daughter convincing Rudi to confront that dangerous psychopath personally!"

Richard resisted an urge to point out the incongruous choice of assignment for who the dangerous psychopath was. "Ah, I see."

"There's no other explanation for why Rudi would allow himself to come so dangerously close to a prisoner!"

Except that he's an utter idiot who truly believes in his own infallibility. Richard decided it was wiser not to say that, saying instead, "Well, it's nice to know what I'm being charged with." He cocked his head in bemused contemplation. "Pretty damn lucky, isn't it, that Halifax knew exactly what to do."

"You must have made a deal with him, during all those conversations."

"Oh, yes. Still it seems rather surprising it all worked so well – there was so much left to chance! And what, by the way, did I have to gain from Rudi's abduction?"

"Who knows? The mind of a traitor is incomprehensible to me." Schindler turned and motioned to his bodyguard to shut the library door. He turned his attention back to Richard. "Are you armed?"

Richard shook his head. "No, Günter, this is my home, I don't walk around it wearing guns."

"Is there one in this room?"

Richard nodded toward a cabinet. Schindler walked over to it, opened the drawer and removed the pistol. Richard noticed that Schindler had yet to remove his gloves.

Schindler set the gun on a table in the center of the room, then came toward Richard and seated himself. As he removed his gloves, he nodded toward the other armchair, the one Richard had been using, and said, "Have a seat. We need to talk. Alone."

As Richard seated himself, he cast a glance at the bodyguard, who stood by the door, and at Leszek, who stood where he had been shoved, by a bookshelf. Clearly, in Günter's world, neither merited enough dignity to be counted as present.

Schindler pressed the tips of his fingers together. "Herr Traugutt, we both realize the seriousness of the situation. If the government is forced to proceed in its case against you, then not only you, but your daughter, son-in-law, and aides must be prosecuted. It's also possible that your wife is involved in this conspiracy. You realize, of course, that the penalty for treason is hanging."

"Is that how you see it, Günter?"

"Yes. And I'm afraid, my dear Herr Traugutt, my hands would be tied. After public trials, there is nothing I could do to prevent your sentences being carried out."

"I see."

Schindler leaned forward sympathetically. "I see only one hope for your family."

"And what might that be, Günter?"

Schindler motioned with his head toward the table on which the pistol lay. "Do the decent thing."

"And you guarantee my family would be safe?"

Schindler nodded solemnly. "Safe? Yes."

"Even Stefi?"

"Yes, even your daughter. You have my personal guarantee." Schindler stood. "I'll leave you alone now, to think about your options. But hurry, there's not much time." Richard stood as well and he suppressed a smile as Schindler extended his hand. "It's been good working with you, Traugutt. I'm sorry it had to end this way."

Richard shook Schindler's hand, bowing his head slightly in formal acknowledgment of the fond farewell. Schindler gave a slight bow in return, spun on his heel and headed toward the door. He stopped there to pull on his gloves and Richard took the opportunity to say, "Ah, Günter. Just one little question."

"What?"

"Since the Führer is alive and returning to Berlin soon, how can you make *any* guarantees?"

The color drained from Schindler's face. "How, how do you...How can you say that?"

"Everyone knows, Günter. It's been broadcast to everyone. It's even in the newspaper."

Schindler instinctively reached toward his jacket.

Richard was faster, casually reaching into his own jacket and removing his gun. "And you know..." He glanced down at his pistol as if it were rather surprising. "In all the excitement of recent days, I'd completely forgotten that I now carry my weapon, even inside my own house."

Schindler's hand dropped back down. He threw an evaluative glance back at his bodyguard.

"Funny how that changes the perspective on everything, isn't it?" Richard mused into Schindler's confused silence. "You see, everyone knows that not only is the Führer returning, but I personally and publicly have called for complete loyalty to Rudi. If I were to suddenly die – say, in some idiotic confrontation in my library – everyone would know that a loyal officer of the Reich had been murdered. And you know what the penalty for that is, don't you?"

Schindler's eyes darted around nervously as though he were looking for an escape.

"Luckily, it won't come to that, will it?"

Schindler did not react.

"Let's avoid a bloodbath, Günter. You can only lose." Richard walked across the room to come directly up to Schindler. He smiled gently. "Dismiss your henchmen, drop the charges against me, now, *before* Rudi returns."

Schindler swallowed but remained silent.

"And we'll work together, as before, as loyal sons of the Reich. And I am sure," Richard added suavely, "that we will see eye-to-eye on every issue from now on." He put his pistol back into its holster and extended his hand to Günter.

With only the slightest hesitation, Schindler accepted it. "Just one question, Richard. How did you do it? The Americans?"

342

Richard smiled kindly. "That's not important Günter. What's important is that *you* remember that I *did* do it."

Schindler contemplated Richard for a moment, his face a mask. They finished shaking hands and Schindler withdrew his. He bowed slightly toward Richard, "I am at your service."

14

"*A*nd what makes you think he'll keep his word?" Olek asked as he watched the soldiers and vehicles departing.

Ryszard laughed, "What, don't you trust an officer's word?"

Olek looked in exasperation at his father-in-law.

"Dear boy," Ryszard soothed. "After the barrage of support I received? He's terrified of me. He doesn't know who or what or how, but he does know that next time I would not be so forgiving."

"So, you're not going to exact any revenge?"

"Why should I? I have his unconditional support now. He's more useful to me like this."

"Useful," Olek repeated bitterly. "Have you forgotten, he murdered my child?"

Ryszard was surprised. "The abortion? Don't worry about that. You'll get Stefi knocked up again. Just wait a few weeks, so the Führer is back and can claim credit."

Olek's eyes widened in horror. "Doesn't what happened mean anything to you?"

Ryszard walked over to Olek and gently placed his hands on the lad's shoulders. "Of course it does, of course it does. But what can we do? What's done is done, we must move on."

Olek stepped backward, angrily shrugging off Ryszard's hands. He looked ready to say something, but then thought better of it and, shaking his head in disgust, left the room.

Ryszard sighed. He wished Kasia was home. She would handle all these idiotic emotional issues. He just didn't have the time to deal with Stefi and Olek's anger. It was misdirected in any case – he wasn't the one who had hustled Stefi off to the hospital. Hell, they seemed to all forget that he had also been in grave danger! If Szaflary hadn't acted so quickly to rectify the situation, they would have all been dead. He was sure now that the entire rescue had originated in Szaflary – Warszawa was too distrustful of him anymore to have acted so fast. They would have spent useless days debating their response – days which would have cost him his life.

Ryszard was equally convinced that Peter had crafted most of the plan – only he could have imitated Traugutt's style, written the right words for the Americans, and guessed Schindler's moves so accurately. Not only the wording of the statements, but the entire strategy had his signature. The timing had been impeccable – and once Ryszard had had a chance to read the rest of the plan, he had learned exactly why Günter had failed to have him immediately killed.

The confrontation in the library had been a desperate move on Günter's part, a last ditch attempt to cover-up his attempted coup by having one of the few people who knew about it, kill himself. The reason Günter could not simply kill Traugutt was that all the top officials had received the same notification: the Führer would be exchanged in the presence of three senior officers: Schindler, Büttner and Traugutt. To kill Traugutt after he had been explicitly named as one of the men who was to rescue the Führer, would be a deliberate slap in the face of the terrorists and equivalent to a direct attempt on the Führer's life – and everybody would know it. So Schindler had resorted to blackmail, hoping that his prisoner had not yet heard the news, and hoping that he could therefore induce Traugutt to commit suicide.

Which is indeed what Büttner had apparently done. It was probably even genuine, given how badly he had botched his snatch at power, but that still left Richard and Günter to meet up with the terrorists. That bit of the plan had been revealed to him not only through the notes, but also through a message sent directly to his, Schindler's, and Büttner's offices. Only a few other Party leaders knew the exact details of the exchange. As for the general populace – they had been fed a completely different story: the Führer had been abducted and taken deep into mountain territory. He had bravely fought and escaped his captor, but instead of immediately presenting himself to his loyal subjects to gain transport back to Berlin, he had cleverly disguised himself and used the opportunity to learn about the life of his people firsthand and to see how his officers comported themselves in his absence. He had completed his investigations and would soon return to Berlin, even wiser than he had been before.

Ryszard sniggered at the trite crap the populace had foisted on them. They deserved nothing better, given how gullible they were. As for the high level officials who had been contacted: they were relatively few in number, but enough to be mutually competitive, and thus keep each other honest. The story they had been told was only slightly closer to the truth: Halifax had abducted the Führer and successfully taken him into the secret terrorist enclave in the Tatra mountains which he knew about from his wife. The terrorists had given him temporary shelter as they decided what to do with their unexpected guests. As a good-will gesture they were releasing the Führer unharmed and with only a few minor conditions imposed: the release of some prisoners, the closing of one particularly notorious camp...Nothing which could not be accomplished quietly, and as senior officials had given their word, the terrorists were satisfied that the conditions would be met. The exchange would take place in the borderlands in the presence of top officers from the government and at least one international delegate. The ambassador from Kivu was suggested and accepted as a sufficiently neutral witness to the proceedings.

The last of Schindler's soldiers left and Ryszard decided to take a stroll to celebrate the end of his arrest. He went into the hall, summoned Feliks, Olek, and Leszek, and together the small group left the house. The sun was out and Ryszard winced at the sudden brightness. There was a duck pond not too far away and he headed for that. Ryszard walked in the lead, Olek – recognizing intuitively that he had been demoted temporarily to bodyguard – trailed slightly on Ryszard's right. Feliks, his head shifting nervously from side to side as he constantly scanned for danger, kept pace with Olek, on Ryszard's left. Leszek walked a respectful and submissive distance behind all three, not bothering to look up, just following the footsteps of his superiors.

Despite the sunshine, there was a brisk wind, and it cut through the wool of Ryszard's coat. It felt invigorating, and enjoying his new-found freedom, Ryszard took a circuitous route to the park. He was utterly unaware of his minions, of the passing policemen who saluted briskly, of the *Zwangsarbeiter* who scurried out of his way. Most of the people out and about, those who counted anyway, were women – the men were all off working at this time of day, and Ryszard took the time to respond graciously to the greetings of each of his neighbors. So many men underestimated the importance of keeping the wives of other men happy! He didn't – Ryszard knew that although they were officially almost powerless and generally were incapable of acting in a public arena without a man to represent them, these women often wielded inordinate power behind the scenes.

Like Frau Vogel. Without her, Karl would have never made it as far as he had. She had carefully manipulated his actions, all the while playing at being an obedient *Hausfrau*. But it was she who had pushed him along, she who knew the right social moves. And it was her family connections which would have taken him a lot further if only they had not so loathed Karl. That thought brought him to Greta. With Schindler so nicely cowed into fearful submission and with Büttner dead, the time was rapidly approaching for Ryszard to make his move. And for that he needed Greta.

Though he felt fairly certain of his chances, even now, if Rudi were to suddenly abdicate, there was still the possibility of a nasty surprise. It wasn't worth the risk. If anyone else, no matter how weak, grabbed the leadership, he would know enough to get rid of Traugutt as soon as possible. Ryszard would, at the best, be assigned to some backwater colonial post and left to rot, all access would be lost and his moment would be forever wasted. No, he could not take that sort of chance, not after a lifetime of work. He needed to make sure every vote was lined up in his favor before he made his move. That's where Greta and her family connections came into the picture. He needed to marry her. He needed the loyalty of a blood relationship. So how long would that take? Each of them would need the usual year of bureaucratic wrangling necessary to divorce their spouses – assuming, of course, that both Günter and Kasia were complaisant. A month waiting period afterwards would be sufficient, then they could marry without unseemly haste. Kasia would be arriving back from America in two days, so if he gave her a day to relax when she got home that would suffice. He'd file for divorce the day afterwards.

He turned and surveyed the three men accompanying him. Feliks did little more than cast a glance at Ryszard as he was too busy diligently scanning for danger. Olek was surveying the distance moodily, clearly uninterested in their safety. Leszek huddled miserably, his thin jacket ineffectual against the biting wind. He glanced up at Ryszard hopeful that they might move on. Ryszard scowled at him and then motioned to Olek to come closer.

"I want you to handle getting me clearance from Warszawa to divorce my wife."

Olek looked up at him, quite stunned. "Divorce?"

"I believe that's the current word for it," Ryszard snapped sarcastically. "I'm going to be heading into the Tatras with the delegation to pick up the Führer, make sure the clearance is here by the time I get back. And, oh yeah, I suppose my wife will want to be met at the airport. Organize that as well."

15

"*Ah-a-ah, kotki dwa...*" It was a lullaby, Peter realized. With Madzia falling asleep in his arms, with the flickering light of the flames warming them, with the peaceful darkness settling over the woods, it seemed appropriate to sing of two kittens having nothing to do but – who? Ah, yes, of course, the words accommodated the situation: having nothing to do but play with Madzia all day long. He scanned the small group gathered around the fire and felt the warmth of belonging. He hardly knew them but they had accepted his presence immediately and made him feel welcome and at home. Madzia drew an enormous amount of interest – but then, children always did. Or maybe they had heard about him and the kidnapped child. Nobody said anything – it was an official secret, but he suspected that they all knew and perhaps even approved.

He looked down at his sleeping daughter and stroked her soft brown hair. When he had heard that Kamil and his family had returned, Peter had immediately gone to their flat. "I heard you were back," Kamil had said simply and then hugged him warmly. "I didn't tell Madzia yet – I was afraid it wasn't true." Kamil's wife, Franczeska, had greeted him with kisses and then they had both stepped back and motioned him into the room.

Peter had entered and stood in silence for a moment, watching as his little girl played with Kamil's son. Then Madzia had turned and looked at him. Her eyes had lit up, she had jumped to her feet and run to him, crying out, *"Tatu! Tatusiu!"* She had recognized him, recognized him immediately! She had not forgotten him.

Indeed, it was as though she was not at all surprised by his reappearance. After she had wriggled out of his endless kisses and hugs, she stood with her hands clasped and began to proudly recite the brief prayer, *"Aniele Stróżu mój ... "* as if she had learned it just that morning and he had only returned from a day's work.

He told her of his idea to go to the border with her, to do some camping and spend time together and she had been overjoyed. He was, however, obliged to delay their departure a bit as he had been called before the Council again. There he had been presented with Wanda's brilliant scheme and asked for his help enacting it. He was happy to allow Wanda to take the credit – it meant his plan to save Olek and the others would face little opposition and gain immediate approval, and that was the only important thing. He diligently worked with the Council on the details of the plan and wrote up several statements for their use. Afterwards, Marysia had thanked him for his contribution and exclaimed, "See, you and Wanda *can* work together!"

Peter had nodded graciously in response, then taken the opportunity to express his concerns about the American visitors again. She had solemnly listened to him, had expressed some surprise at his detective work, and had promised to relay the information to Wanda and other relevant parties for any possible action. Then she had ordered him to continue as planned, giving the American guests an impromptu interview when he accidentally encountered them at the base camp, and to await further orders.

Madzia stirred and Peter gathered her more securely into his arms. An elderly woman brought over a blanket and draped it over the child, carefully tucking it under her shoulders. "This unusual warmth won't last into the night. It will be very cold soon." The partisan stroked Madzia's hair, then, as if imparting a secret, she whispered, "You did right by her."

Peter was contemplating whether he should ask for a clarification – his command of the language was such that he occasionally misunderstood subtle concepts – but before he could decide anything, a threesome approaching the fire caught his attention. His and everyone else's.

There was a pair – a man and a woman, both of whom looked very weary, and a young man who was dressed as a local. The young man pointed toward the campfire and all three then set heavy packs down.

"It's the Americans," the woman muttered. "They don't speak Polish."

"Remember, neither do I," Peter said quickly, under his breath.

The partisan woman smiled her acknowledgment and went to greet the guests. She spoke with the young man for a few minutes and then the young man bowed slightly and walked off, leaving the pack behind. The old woman turned to the two Americans and smiling broadly said a couple of words, then turning to the others, announced meaningfully, "I will introduce our guests to the Englishman, since he also can't speak our language."

The partisan woman gestured welcomingly, saying in English, "Come, come! English!" as she pointed at Peter. She then led them around the edge of the circle to Peter. The American woman smiled hopefully.

"Do you really speak English?" the woman asked as she seated herself next to him. When Peter nodded, she continued, "Oh God! It's so good to see somebody from home!"

"I'm not American."

"Not? Oh, of course. But that doesn't matter. It's just that we had no idea that everyone's language abilities here would be so limited. No one speaks English!"

"Neither of you speak either Polish or German?"

"My husband speaks fluent German – he's a native speaker. But me, I can't speak a word! It's so confusing! I haven't a clue what's going on."

"Then what, may I ask, are you doing here?" Peter glanced at the husband: for all his fluency he had not indicated that he could say a word in any language. The woman had rather short, brown hair artificially and unbecomingly tinted with red. She moved her hands and head as she spoke as if her entire being were animated by her words. Her husband, in sharp contrast, sat almost motionless – a distant and disinterested look on his face. He was either much older than his wife or, more likely, had given himself over to a premature aging, allowing slumping shoulders and thinning hair to define his existence in some mistaken belief that this gave him an air of importance and authority.

"My husband," the woman explained, her voice dropping to a conspiratorial whisper, "is in the security service for the North American Union."

Peter raised an eyebrow at the woman's lack of caution, but still the husband showed no discernable reaction.

"They're trying to funnel some help into this area, but they need a way of doing it without arousing suspicion. Then my husband suggested this marvelous plan. You see, I..." she pointed at herself to clarify the pronoun, "...am connected with a charitable church organization, and he suggested that my organization could provide perfect cover for the government's largesse! But first we need to see the situation here first-hand. I mean, it's my husband's job to see what's going on and write a report to justify the expenditures, but I have to as well, so that I can convince my people to invest in this place – or at least set up a fund into which the government can secretly channel money. They – I mean my church – felt I'd be a good one for the job because I'm a reporter – just for the local paper, but still, I'm supposed to know how to find things out. The problem is, there's no one I can talk to here! I mean, my husband can work as translator," she gestured to the sourly silent man beside her, "but he's not all that expressive and sometimes people tell him whole life stories and he gives me just a one sentence summary! Isn't that right, dear?" She looked at him expectantly but his attention seemed to be elsewhere.

Peter stroked Madzia's peacefully sleeping face.

The woman turned back to Peter and seemed ready to explain yet more, but suddenly she drew back and furrowed her brow. After several moments silence, she suddenly exclaimed, "That's it! I know who you are! I thought you looked familiar. You're that guy who was in America – last year. Aren't you? What are you doing here?" She didn't wait for an answer, as a more important thought came to mind. "Can you help me? I need to get some personal experiences to report. I won't say they came from you. Can you help me?"

Peter sighed, looked up at the fire, and without taking his eyes off the flames, said, "It'd be my pleasure."

16

*R*ichard Traugutt looked at the tall, thin African woman as she boarded the small aircraft. As her two staff members moved unobtrusively past the first row and into the back of the plane to join the other staffers, Arieka remained standing at the front of the plane with the officer who had guided her entourage.

Unlike Günter, Richard rose to greet her, moving into the aisle so he could stand at full height. Before the officer had said anything, Richard said, "You must be Frau Ruweni, our honored international observer." He bowed to kiss her hand.

She smiled slightly in return. "You must be Herr Traugutt." She turned to look at Günter and her smile broadened slightly as if she were privy to a joke. "And you must be Herr Schindler."

While Günter grunted his greeting, Richard gestured toward the seat next to his. "Frau Ruweni, please have a seat."

"Call me Arieka."

Richard called up his best boyish grin. "Then please, call me Richard."

Günter lit himself a cigarette. "Call me nauseated," he muttered under his breath.

They were met at Krakau's private airfield by a security detail which had been sent on ahead to prepare for their arrival. Stefan was in charge of the detail and he conferred with Richard a few moments. After the passengers had had time to refresh themselves, they were ushered to a limousine which sped off southwards, toward the mountains.

Günter glanced backward at the other limousine, the one that held their staffers. "It's going the other way!"

Stefan was sitting opposite Günter, facing him. He watched impassively as the other limousine departed. "Only the four of us, our driver and our bodyguard have been given clearance to go into their territory. The others will wait for us here, near the border."

"What!" Günter screeched.

"It was one of their conditions. We had to accept it if we wanted the Führer back alive and well."

Günter snorted his disagreement but said nothing more.

Arieka peered out the dark window of the limousine. "Where are we?" The last of the villages had swept by, the road pressed ever upward and the forests closed in. There was absolutely no sign of habitation.

Stefan consulted a map he had resting on his lap. "It's the no-man's land."

"No-man's land?" Günter asked belligerently. "How can there be a no-man's land?"

"Call it what you want," Stefan answered evenly. "It's Reich territory which our soldiers do not dare enter and which their soldiers dare not live in. Both sides shoot at anyone who trespasses."

Arieka drew herself deeper into the seat of the auto. "Are we safe here?"

"Not really. The partisans have guaranteed that no concerted action will be taken against us in this region, however they are unable to guarantee that no independent actions will be taken."

"You mean someone may shoot at us?"

"I'm afraid so. There are a lot of people who are angry at the Reich and its officials. But as long as we remain in our armor-plated vehicle, behind our bullet-proof glass, we should be safe."

"Should be," Arieka repeated, as if disconcerted. In her mind she heard gunfire, felt her father's hand grasp hers, felt how he pulled her, tugged at her, literally dragged her away from her mother's body. She looked out the window at the incredibly peaceful pines. Were there rifles trained upon them even now?

Günter glowered as he stared through the glass. "It's getting dark."

Stefan leaned back and looked over his shoulder at the odometer. "Yes, but we'll soon be safe within A.K. territory."

"A.K.?" Günter asked, obviously confused.

Stefan turned back to face Schindler. "It's the initials of the terrorist army in their own language."

"Their initials? Their language?"

"When dealing with these people, Herr Schindler, it is advisable not to call them terrorists to their faces. As a compromise, I have opted for using their initials."

"You said safe?" Arieka asked, clearly indifferent to their linguistic debate.

"Safer than here. They've asked that we stay the night. They don't feel it would be safe to leave with the Führer while it is dark. We may leave at sunrise."

Günter slammed his fist into the armrest. "Who the hell are they to tell us what to do!"

Stefan seemed unimpressed. "They have the Führer in their hands, and they are asking very little for his safe return. We would do well to abide by the few conditions they have set."

"They'll slit our throats in the middle of the night."

"They have no reason to do that, they have nothing to gain from our deaths. Remember, they are gaining international recognition by this action. Our international observer is here to report to the world that they have behaved in a civilized manner. And besides, it'd be easy enough for them to kill us now. They have no need to wait for the night."

Günter muttered something inaudible and settled deeper into his seat.

Stefan turned so he could see out the front window, consulted some notes and the map, and then directed the driver to turn off the main road onto a dirt track. The limousine juddered and jolted along the track for several miles. It bounced over a series of nasty bumps, turned a curve and there, waiting for them, were two masked gunmen.

"Stop here," Stefan commanded. "We'll walk from here."

Günter groaned. "Masked gunmen? Are you nuts?"

"They have a need to keep their identity secret," Richard explained impatiently. "After all, what would be the first thing you would do if you recognized them later, Günter? Invite them to tea?"

"I'd have the bastards hanged. As they should be."

Richard ignored him and opened the door to the car. He stepped out and motioned to Arieka. "Come on, it's safe, I'm sure."

Arieka climbed out of the car and pulling her coat tightly around herself, surveyed her surroundings. Nothing but an impenetrable pine forest as far as the eye could see. Stefan climbed out as well and motioned to Günter. "Are you coming?"

Richard leaned down to peer into the car. "Or do you want us to go and get Rudi without you, Günter?"

Günter groaned again and clambered out of the car. He placed himself carefully so that Arieka was between him and the gunmen. Arieka cast a contemptuous glance at him, then marched boldly toward the gunmen, commanding, "Come on!" to the others.

The gunmen frisked them but did not remove their weapons. "You are our guests," one of them advised, "and we expect you to behave accordingly."

Günter pressed his hand to his gun, obviously reassured by the feel of the metal.

"Great," Arieka snorted, "Every idiot around me is armed!"

"Would you like my gun?" Stefan offered chivalrously.

"No!" Arieka marched off after the gunmen and the men followed in silence.

After about twenty minutes, they reached a small camp. The two gunmen indicated a tent and the four of them entered while their driver and bodyguard were directed elsewhere. Inside were two older women and a middle-aged man. Arieka surveyed them: one woman was an ancient crone, seated, who disdained to rise, the other had black hair threaded with gray and was already standing. The man was middle-aged and well built. His head was completely shaven except for a bushy black mustache. He had his arms crossed and wore a stern expression.

Arieka was disappointed that Peter was nowhere in sight. Günter turned his head down and to the side and muttered something about wizened old cows.

"Frau Kalischer!" Richard greeted the older of the two women. "So, we meet again."

"Which one are you?"

"Colonel Richard Traugutt, at your service." Richard clicked his heels and bowed slightly. "We met during the peace negotiations last January. Not even a year ago!"

Katerina scowled and turned her attention to Günter. "And which are you?"

Günter's face clouded at being treated so insolently. By an old woman! An *Untermensch*!

"That is my colleague, Herr Günter Schindler. Herr Büttner, I'm afraid, was unable to join us."

"Unable?"

Richard drew up an appropriately mournful expression. "He committed suicide."

Katerina nodded noncommittally. "And you must be our diplomat, Frau Ruweni, I presume?"

"Yes," Arieka agreed brusquely. "Where's Peter Halifax? Is he here?"

"Yes, we're holding him prisoner until we can decide what to do with him."

"Prisoner?"

"He is an interloper."

"He shouldn't be held prisoner! He's–" Arieka glanced at her companions and fell silent.

"What do you care?"

"He's a friend. I want to see him."

Katerina turned toward the middle-aged man and said something, then she turned her attention back to Arieka and said, "He'll be brought in shortly." She eyed Arieka for a moment then added, "I thought you were a diplomat in Berlin, but your German is not very good."

Arieka explained that she had only just taken up the position and was not yet very fluent in the language – which was already her fifth. They spent a few moments discussing Arieka's background as both Richard and Günter waited with growing impatience.

"Where's the Führer?" Günter finally demanded.

Katerina broke off what she had been saying to Arieka and slowly rose to her feet. She approached Schindler. Wagging a bony finger in his face, she warned, "You are on our land now. Show respect."

Günter moved forward as if intending to confront the woman physically, but Richard grabbed his shoulder. Katerina smirked and turned her attention to the entrance, gesturing to get Arieka's notice. "Here he is now."

Peter entered the tent, followed by a young man who was ostensibly his guard. Peter wore a well-tailored, military-style wool coat and high leather boots. Arieka, who was no stranger to fashion, noted that, for what were presumably borrowed clothes, they fit him remarkably well. He surveyed all of them and smiled broadly at Arieka.

Schindler reacted instinctively. "This one is not under your protection!" He strode over to Peter, raising his gloved fist threateningly. "You traitorous scum! You–" Schindler swung his fist at Peter's face.

Peter caught Schindler's wrist in midair and, without releasing it, swung smoothly around, dropping a bit so he could jam his shoulder into Schindler's chest. With a slight shift of his weight he threw Schindler over his shoulder and onto the ground. Still holding Schindler's arm, twisting it painfully, Peter placed his foot lightly on Schindler's throat. Schindler stared up at him stunned and afraid.

"Whatever our hosts here say," Peter stated calmly, "I *will* kill you if you ever try anything like that again." He released Schindler's arm, casually removed his foot from Schindler's throat, and turned his attention back to Katerina. "Frau Kalischer, may I take a walk with my friend?"

Katerina motioned toward the door with her head, indicating her approval. Arieka and Peter left, followed by his guard. Schindler rolled over and climbed slowly to his feet. He dusted off his coat and looked around, expecting sympathy, but his look of outrage was met with apathy. Even Traugutt did little more than raise an eyebrow.

Richard threw a knowing glance at Katerina which Schindler interpreted as a condemnation of the perfidy of *Untermensch* but which Katerina recognized as an *I told you so.* Yes, Ryszard had been right, there was no doubt that Peter had maintained an incredible self-control through eight years of abuse. And it was equally clear that no-one could expect he would continue with the charade.

Katerina waited patiently for Schindler to say something, but when it was clear that he had nothing to say, she addressed Richard. "Herr Traugutt, you and your companions will be shown to your quarters for the night." She sneered slightly and added, "They are lowly tents with cots – surely less than you gentlemen are used to, but it is better than you offer our people when they are obliged to enjoy your hospitality. For your own safety, you will each have a guard who will accompany you wherever you wish to go. Please be advised that there is a limit to how far you may wander. Your guard will advise you on the boundary, please do not ignore his advice. Goodnight, gentlemen."

"But what about the Führer?" Schindler demanded, regaining what little remained of his dignity.

"As I have said, you will be reunited with him in the morning and will then be accompanied to your auto. Oh, yes, there will be a few papers you will both need to sign."

"Papers?"

"Indicating your agreement to our conditions. The closing down of the Neisse camp, the release of some prisoners, a few other trivial things. Of course, as officers of the Reich, we recognize that you would never go back on your word, but if circumstances are such that you feel obliged to renege on the agreement, we will have documents with your signatures, as will Frau Ruweni. They will be an embarrassment as they will admit to these places and to abuses which you would rather not have known to the world, so you would be well-advised to adhere to our terms rather than suffer the embarrassment of having the documents publicized."

"Blackmail?" Schindler snorted.

"Not if you keep your word." With that Katerina left the tent.

Marysia approached Richard. "Herr Traugutt? I'm Marya Firlej. I have taken over Frau Kalischer's position and at any future negotiations, it will be me you will have to deal with." She waved her hand toward the man standing near her. "This is our defense minister, Konrad Jesionek, who you will remember was also at the January talks."

Schindler laughed, "Jeschonek? Any relation to Luftwaffe Chief of Staff Hans Jeschonek? The dear fellow organized the bombing of London!"

Konrad glowered. "No. *My* family knows how to spell their name."

Marysia ignored them both and spoke to Richard. "I'd like to discuss some of the details of those talks with you and their implementation. Would you please come with me?"

"It will be my pleasure," Richard replied courteously, only barely managing to suppress a smile of pleasure. Home! Home, at last!

17

"*T*hat was an impressive little demonstration you put on there." Arieka glanced behind herself. There was a gibbous moon and it was fairly easy to see that Peter's guard had fallen a respectable distance behind them. He almost looked unconcerned – or even embarrassed.

"I should have driven my heel into his throat and snuffed him out once and for all."

Arieka raised an eyebrow at the unexpected response. "I thought you were something of a pacifist."

Peter brought his attention away from the distant stars and peered at her. "If ever I was, then not anymore."

"Oh yes, your little girl."

"Yes, my little girl."

Arieka wiped something out of her eye. "I'm really sorry about that."

"Thank you. And thanks for sending that note. It really meant a lot to me."

"And the money?"

He smiled shyly and, obviously embarrassed, quickly turned to look at the path they were taking. "Yes, that too. It means my friend can walk again. And before this latest fiasco, you know, I was hoping to establish an Underground Railroad for escapees."

"I'm sorry, I didn't mean to imply anything."

"You must think of me as money-hungry. A greedy beggar."

Arieka shook her head. "No! That isn't what I meant! But I did think you might do something for yourself – get rid of those numbers or have a surgeon look at your eyes…"

"The first is pointless – I've a rather infamous face now. As for the second, well, I don't think they can do anything about that. Anyway, my vision seems pretty stable right now."

They stopped walking and Peter turned and spoke to the young man following them. Arieka did not understand a word Peter said, but the tone was hardly that of a prisoner addressing his guard. The young soldier saluted and left.

"You're not a prisoner here, are you?"

Peter gave her a self-conscious smile. "I hope you can keep a secret."

"Of course!" Arieka pondered the implications then asked, "Was this whole kidnap planned?"

"No. No, my getting arrested was a genuine cock-up on my part. But an opportunity arose to escape and once I grabbed the Führer, I headed here, to my home."

"Your home." Arieka pursed her lips in thought. "But that means you didn't need the Führer to gain entry here. And you had him alone in the woods, didn't you? After what happened to your little girl, why didn't you take revenge on him?"

Peter folded his hands behind his back and looked down at the dirt, mindlessly shoving a pebble back and forth with his boot. "He said he didn't order it."

"And you believed him?"

Peter didn't answer and Arieka wondered if he had heard her. He just kept mindlessly kicking the stone around.

"Is that why you didn't kill him?"

Still Peter didn't answer. Arieka waited, but he remained silent, almost absent. She began to feel uncomfortable and searched for something to say to draw him back. "What about the two I came here with? Schindler's obviously a sleaze, but what about that Traugutt fellow?"

356

Peter looked at her. She couldn't see anything in his expression. "He spent some time interrogating me in the *Residenz* and I've come to the conclusion that he truly wants to see things change in the Reich. I think he's someone we could work with. Keep an eye on him and if he comes to you for help, well, my guess is, he's better than any alternative."

"Is that all?" Something in Traugutt's demeanor had made Arieka wish there was something more, and likewise, she wished that Peter would somehow, magically, know about it.

"That's all I know."

"Wouldn't it be better to support someone who will make things worse – so there will be a proper revolution?"

Peter tilted his head and studied her. "Would you advise that for your own country?"

Arieka shook her head. "No. When things get worse, they just get worse. And any reaction becomes more violent and less effective."

"Then do you wish that upon us? Starvation, chaos, riots, and looting?"

"Of course not! I just thought – from what you said when we spoke in America – that you wanted a quick and complete change. Revolution. It was *your* word."

"I know, I'm sorry. It's just that…" Peter thought of his words to Ryszard in the pub in London. In exchange for a chance to go home, he had promised a change of heart, had promised to be a spokesman for peaceful evolution. "I made a promise."

"It's more than that."

Peter nodded. "You're right. When I was captured the first time, the time I was with Joanna, it was because of a bomb. A bomb that was planted by someone who was ostensibly on our side. Or at least an enemy of the occupation." The tinkle of raining glass echoed through his mind. "Near to us, there was a little girl – she was about five – and I could see that she was dead. It's funny, as far as my war is concerned, she was killed for all the right reasons: a desire for freedom, for peace, to drive the enemy out of our midst. But I'm sure her death hurt her parents no less than that of my Joanna hurt me. And was just as senseless." He thought back to the Realies, to the possibility that what they did might work. "On the other hand…"

"What?"

"I can understand the attraction of the other approach. The quid pro quo of violence. Sometimes, with some peoples, it seems to work. They have to be hurt in order to understand other people's pain. Or, more accurately, they have to be hurt before they can be bothered to care. And if they're hurt enough, they'll put pressure on their own government to stop what it's doing. That may be what the people of the Reich require, but I dare not go that route."

"Why not?"

Peter looked down to study the moonlit earth.

"Why not, Peter?"

He shook his head. "I just don't dare."

Arieka tilted her head disbelievingly. "Well, it's not because you're incapable of violence! You've certainly proved you're not afraid to kill."

"I know."

Strange. She had somehow thought he would be eager to excuse, or at least explain, that act of violence. Even stranger was how much she had hoped he would. She waited, but he said nothing more. After a moment, she simply asked, "Why did you do that? Returning long after you had escaped to wreak vengeance?"

"I had my reasons."

"Was it something to do with your position here?" Arieka turned her head back toward the camp. The young soldier had saluted and left as if responding to a superior officer. "Were you under orders?"

Peter began walking again and she hurried to join him. She felt how his hand reached down into the darkness along her arm until he found her hand. They walked in silence like that, hand in hand, into the woods.

18

*O*nce Peter had dropped Arieka back at her tent and left her in the care of her guard, he went to find Marysia. She was in another tent, about a kilometer from their visitors, conferring with Wanda and Konrad. The three of them stood around a table looking at some documents. In the corner, near the heater and almost unnoticeable in her chair, sat Katerina, her eyes shut.

Marysia looked up and smiled, "Ah, Peter, welcome."

Wanda theatrically shut the notebook they had been studying, while Konrad stepped forward to greet him.

Peter shook Konrad's hand. "Where's Ryszard? I'm surprised he's not here."

"Tending to urgent business." Marysia tapped her teeth to indicate that Ryszard was getting his tooth refilled with poison.

Peter kissed Marysia, nodded at Wanda, then, undoing the buttons of his coat, walked over to a side table. There was a coffee pot on a portable flame and some mugs nearby. He sniffed the brew, decided it was done, and poured himself a cup of coffee. "I bet he'll be relieved to have that safety net back."

"I guess. Though your experience only adds to the evidence that it's not always effective."

"If you even used it," Wanda suggested sourly.

Peter ignored her. "I made a mistake and used it too soon. They got me to a hospital right away. It would have probably worked if I had waited until I was alone."

"I doubt you would have been left alone," Konrad interjected.

"Fair point. Any new orders on the Americans?" Peter sipped his coffee, it tasted wonderful.

Marysia shook her head.

"Did you ask Ryszard if he's used the information about the spy with Schindler?"

"Give it up, Halifax," Wanda grated. "No one believes your lies."

"Oh Wanda, just…" Peter stopped himself, but then changed his mind. "Just shut up."

"Captain!" Wanda intoned threateningly.

Disrespectful treatment of a superior officer. Peter could feel her winding up for a tirade, but Marysia waved her into silence. "Wanda, we don't have time for this now." She turned to Peter and answered, "Not yet. We'll ask him…ah, speak of the devil!"

Ryszard appeared in the entryway, grinning broadly, clearly happy to be back home. He shook hands with the men, causing Konrad to laugh. "So now, you're acting English too!"

Ryszard ignored him as he quickly kissed Wanda on the cheek, then embraced Marysia and kissed her three times. He glanced at Katerina but decided not to disturb her. "Nearly the whole clan, except Tadek and my dear sister. Where are they?"

"Business trip. Out east."

Ryszard pulled off his gloves and shoved them into his pocket. "And who do I have to thank for my timely rescue from Schindler's hands?" He scanned them all as he undid his coat, but his eyes settled expectantly on Peter.

Seeing Ryszard's look, Marysia explained, "Yes, Peter wrote up your statement and the press releases, but it was Wanda's idea."

Ryszard raised an eyebrow. *"Really?"*

Over the rim of his cup Peter studied Wanda. She seemed absolutely in awe of Ryszard and anything he did. The admiration, however, was obviously not mutual.

"Well, it was really Jurek's idea," Wanda explained sheepishly.

"Ah, and who gave it to him?" Ryszard turned to Peter. "You?" The implication was quite insulting, but the others ignored Ryszard's rudeness and simply looked to Peter for his answer.

Peter sipped his coffee as he considered what he should say. "We may have discussed it," he answered diplomatically. He glanced at Wanda but there was no gratitude in her expression.

"Your work in America was brilliant, Ryszard!" Wanda enthused, suddenly changing the subject. "I watched the videos. Those speeches were fantastic."

"Peter wrote them." Ryszard stated brusquely. "He scripted everything. Even my spontaneous actions."

"What? How?"

"I interrogated him." Ryszard's tone had become harsh, though it wasn't clear if he was irritated by Wanda's fawning or by the irony of his admission. He turned his attention to Marysia. "Any news?"

"Do you remember the information Peter gave you about the sterility program in London?"

"Of course." Ryszard casually walked up to the documents on the table and, opening the cover of the notebook, scanned the first page.

"He said he thought there was a spy in the ASA."

"Uh-huh." Ryszard turned a page of the notes.

"He recognized the files he had sent to them as being exactly what had fallen into Schindler's hands, and thought you could use that information to blackmail Schindler."

"The existence of the program?" Ryszard turned another page.

With a hint of exasperation, Marysia reached over and closed the notebook. "No, the existence of a spy."

"Hmm. What about it?" Ryszard smiled at her, clearly amused that he had managed to annoy her.

"Has the information checked out?"

"What do you mean 'checked out'?"

"Did you use the information? Was Schindler intimidated? Does Schindler have a spy in the ASA?"

Ryszard tapped his fingers on the notebook as if to emphasize that he was still not really listening. "Why do you ask? Haven't you passed on the information to the Americans yet?"

Wanda snorted. "We suspect its validity."

Ryszard gave up on being distracted. "But we know the program existed."

"But not the spy."

Ryszard shook his head in confusion and turned to Peter. "I thought you said you saw the files in Chandler's office? Isn't that proof?"

360

"It was to me."

Wanda pulled herself up haughtily. "He may have added that to his tale."

Since Peter did not respond to that, Ryszard was driven to ask, "Why would he do that?"

"To make his information more important."

Ryszard let his gaze wander from Wanda to Konrad to Marysia and then back to Wanda. "You've all been in this place too long. Time to pack your bags and go home."

"Ryszard," Marysia pleaded. "Please, we need to know. Does Schindler have a spy in the ASA?"

"How would I know?"

"Did you use the information? Did he deny it?" Peter asked. At Ryszard's questioning glance, Peter explained, "As you've heard, some doubt the validity of the information I brought back, and in particular, the existence of this spy." He spread his hands in a helpless gesture. "Since I was already in possession of the files I got out of Chandler's office, I have no proof." Peter hesitated a moment, then added, "Other than my word."

"So? Let the Americans sort it out."

"It's important to *us* now. We have some Americans visiting – a husband and wife. He works for the ASA, and I think he organized this trip deliberately to gain access to us."

"Visitors? Here?"

Marysia nodded. "They're here to see about supplying arms. We can't deny them access."

"Visitors?"

Peter forgot Ryszard for the moment and turned to Marysia. "Supplying arms? That's not the story you gave me."

Marysia waved her hand at that. "I'll explain later. Ryszard, is there any information you can give us to help us decide who this man is?"

"So now we're a tourist destination?"

"Ryszard, please! You know, we've let allies in here before and we can't go denying them access now. Not when they're supplying our arms."

Ryszard pulled out a cigarette and lit it. "I don't think you should have arms."

"What?"

"Face it, unless the Americans march in and liberate us, we have no hope of overthrowing the regime. You have no use for your arms, no use for this place at all."

"Ryszard, we need to defend ourselves. You don't want to see this place overrun, do you?"

Ryszard brought the cigarette to his lips and drew in a deep breath.

Peter moved to stand next to Ryszard and, like him, looked at the others, almost as if the two of them were on safari and observing some interesting wildlife. "Whatever their hopes of armed revolt," he said, in an aside to Ryszard, "you know the main activities of this place are education, food distribution, and cultural preservation. And they provide the back-up you need to do your work."

Ryszard sighed. "I know." He closed his eyes and smoked in silence for a moment. The others waited, not daring to interrupt his thoughts. "Yes," he said suddenly. "I did mention the spy to Schindler."

"And?"

Ryszard shrugged. "Can't say for sure. It was right when Peter was arrested. He was in the Führer's custody and I was hurrying to get there before the Führer did something disgusting. I met up with Schindler in the corridor of the *Residenz* and had about two minutes to blackmail him. He was clearly guilty of the sterility program and it was clearly a secret from the Führer. That was enough. I'm fairly certain I mentioned the spy and Schindler didn't deny it, but then, we hardly had time to argue over details."

Peter grimaced.

"Still, it's obvious that there has to be someone there passing on information – how else could they have come up with a final formula?"

"Perhaps their own scientists?" Konrad suggested. "German science–"

"Went the way of German engineering and German organization," Ryszard growled impatiently.

"Tied up in a bureaucratic maze of corruption and cronyism," Peter added helpfully.

"But–"

"If you believe their propaganda about themselves…" Ryszard snorted with disgust. "You *have* been here too long!"

"And maybe you've been out there too long?" Marysia suggested softly.

"What is that supposed to mean?"

"The reports filtering back, your divorce, Leszek…We need to discuss your objectives, Ryszard."

"My objectives? *You* want to discuss *my* objectives?"

"Ryszard…" Marysia soothed.

Hoping to pre-empt a confrontation, Peter waved his hand in imitation of an eager schoolchild. "Uh, do you think you can do this school report a bit later? I've got to leave soon if I want to get back to the Americans before dawn and I'd like to know what I should do with them."

Ryszard took a deep draw off his cigarette, visibly calming down. "Kill them."

Marysia rolled her eyes in exasperation. "We can't go killing our allies!"

"But if he is a spy?" Peter pressed.

"If. What *if* he isn't? And even if he is, how would we prove that? All the Americans would know was that they had sent a trusted agent here and we kill him. That hardly makes for clever diplomacy."

"So?"

"So," Wanda answered snidely, "Follow orders. For once. Go back to your camp. If anything changes you will be informed."

"Speaking of which, what are my orders? I thought I was providing them with sob stories about our society. My society, I mean. What's this about supplying arms?"

Katerina answered. "It's not social welfare we're playing for." Peter turned to her in surprise. He had thought she was sleeping. "The bit about finding out about social problems is just a cover story in case anyone in the NAU, or even here, finds out about this visit. It's purely military. The man is here solely to check out our installation. Their government is willing to provide us with defensive arms, but they need to see our operations so that they know we aren't just a bunch of nutters hiding among the trees. We're talking millions of dollars and such inspections, in that case, are not unusual."

Peter nodded slowly – their need to get into the Central sector was suddenly clear. "Does the wife know?"

Marysia shook her head. "No. So you should keep up the charade for her and her church group and whoever else might hear about this trip." Marysia put her arm in Peter's and guided him out of the tent. Clearly she was eager to finally have her difficult discussion with Ryszard about his objectives and knew instinctively that the fewer people present, the easier it would be. Peter felt that Ryszard would welcome his presence and support as someone else who had an idea what prolonged exposure to the society was like, but he did not see any way of ignoring Marysia's not-so-subtle hint. Once they were outside and alone, he turned to her and put his hands on her shoulders. "Marysia…"

"You have your orders, Captain." She said it so tonelessly, it was as if she were reading a script.

"He might be the death of all of us."

"Isn't that what Tadek said about you?"

Peter snorted. "This is different! I was an escapee who stumbled into your midst. This is a spy who deliberately organized his position on an inspection mission. I know it!"

"Do you?" Marysia shifted slightly to indicate that his grasp on her shoulders was uncomfortably tight.

He let her go. "No. I don't know anything for sure. But you didn't about Jana either."

"We've been through that. This is an ally sent to us by the Americans. We don't have the option of removing him in that manner."

"So his life is worth more than hers?"

"Unfortunately, yes. You know the realities."

"Yeah, I know. She was one of us, so she can be condemned without proof."

Marysia nodded sadly. "For an American, we need more than suspicion. We need proof. Do you have *anything*?"

He shook his head. "No. Just a feeling."

She sighed heavily. "That's not enough."

"Marysia, we can't just–"

"Let it go."

"I *can't* let it go! I know something's not right with this guy. And his background matches exactly what I predicted from the files!"

Marysia closed her eyes, her breath formed a cloud in the cold night air. She had come out without her coat, and he could see she was shivering. He opened his coat and pulled her into him, wrapping his arms around her. She settled into the warmth. With her head pressed against his chest, she spoke. "You are very perceptive, Peter. That's why I want you down there."

"Huh?"

She pulled her head back to look directly up at him, into his eyes. In the darkness he could make out very little of her expression, just the firelight flickering in her pupils. "I can't prevent their visit, my hands are tied." She was silent for a long moment, then very softly, she added, "But *yours* aren't"

She pushed herself away from him and walked back into the tent. He knew that he was not free to ask anything further of her. Whatever action he took would be on his shoulders and his alone. But what action should he take?

19

*A*s Marysia walked back into the tent, Ryszard lit another cigarette. Marysia tiredly went over to the coffee pot and poured herself a cup. Ryszard glanced around at the group and was reminded of the stupid conversation he had had with Jung back in July. *Clueless*, that was the quaint American word for it. They were clueless. As with Jung, Ryszard decided to make sure he had control of the conversation, however unpleasant it may be. Before anyone could say a word, he gestured with his head toward the entrance and said to Konrad and Wanda, "I'il talk with Katerina and Marysia – that will suffice."

Wanda drew in a deep breath as if preparing to argue, but Marysia pre-empted her by waving toward the door. "I'll brief you later."

Konrad approached Ryszard and shook his hand, "It was good seeing you, I hope you get a chance to stop by later – before you have to leave."

Ryszard nodded his head. Konrad gathered his coat and a few papers off a chair and left. Ryszard then turned to Wanda and raised his eyebrows expectantly. She remained immobile, as if stunned by her sudden exclusion, then, without saying a word, she gathered her things and left.

Ryszard took a deep drag off his cigarette, then blew a stream of smoke into the air. "What's her problem?"

"She's fine, Ryszard."

"Fine? She must be made of glass to hold that much acid without disintegrating!" He paced to the entrance of the tent to make sure Wanda was indeed gone.

It's gone that far, Marysia thought. We're spying on each other. She cast a glance at Katerina, thinking, we were unified under her. Is *my* leadership so bad?

"And what does she have against Halifax?" Ryszard turned back to face Marysia.

"Nothing. What do you mean?"

"What do I mean?" Ryszard mocked. "She claimed Peter's strategy as her own!"

"Maybe Jurek didn't tell her he had talked to Peter."

"Tell me, sweetie, when was the last time Wanda's husband had a brilliant idea? Has he *ever* involved himself in strategy?"

Marysia was so taken aback by Ryszard's "sweetie" that she could not immediately answer. He waited expectantly and she finally managed to swallow her anger enough to answer, "No, but Ryszard, we don't have–"

"You miss the point, don't you! Wanda says something and you believe her because she's an old and trusted friend–"

"Peter's my friend as well." Marysia put a hand out toward Ryszard. "You are a friend."

"But we're not *here*!" Ryszard gestured wildly around to indicate the entire encampment. "You've grown into one amorphous mass, like an anthill – all working toward the same goal, getting your news from the same sources, experiencing exactly the same things, trusting only each other, unwilling to believe in the outside world!"

"Ryszard, it's not like that!" How, Marysia wondered had the conversation about Ryszard's methods turned into a denunciation of everyone who remained in the mountains? "It's not even us, it's HQ! They asked us to take this opportunity to talk with you."

"They're no different. They cloister themselves around Göringstadt, rather than here. They're just as blind to the realities."

"And what are the realities?" Marysia asked calmly, attempting to regain the initiative.

Ryszard opened his mouth to answer but then closed it again. "Alright." He lowered himself into a chair, and smoked in silence for a moment, making a visible effort to calm himself. "The reality is, I will not explain myself. I simply can't have that sort of constraint on my actions. You either trust me or you don't."

Marysia looked truly pained. "I'm afraid we've been informed, that's not an option. Not as long as you're receiving our support and our agents risk their lives to protect yours."

Ryszard threw his head back and released a stream of smoke toward the ceiling. "Fine."

Marysia waited expectantly, but no explanation was forthcoming. "Ryszard, it is a perfect time to pull you in. We can claim you violated one of our rules and arrest you. You can take a break here, recoup your energies."

"And leave that maniac in control of the Reich? Or worse yet, Schindler?"

"Why worse?"

"Well, Rudi is only repulsive in his personal habits, but otherwise he's happy to let things just chug along in the Reich and let me make small, but important, changes which will prepare us for a transition out of totalitarianism. Schindler would like to restructure the whole damn system and return it to fundamental Nazi values. And he's smart enough to do that. Every time we've pulled sharply to the right, he's been behind it. I think he'd even like to strike out at the NAU – kick them in the knees, just to show we're not powerless."

"Would the population support that?"

Ryszard nodded. "They'll support anything if it's presented to them appropriately."

"Wouldn't..." Marysia paced a bit and sipped her coffee nervously. "Wouldn't – maybe – it'd be a good thing for the Reich to carry out a terrorist act against the NAU? I mean, it would get them involved and they'd help us overthrow the government."

"Now you sound like Zosia," Ryszard sighed wearily. "In my opinion, fanatical governments are never a good idea, no matter what Machiavellian plans you might have. For one thing, they slide out of control all too often. For another, thousands of innocent people would be hurt – and that's completely unnecessary. And finally, if Schindler managed to provoke a hot war between us and the NAU, there'd be a patriotic upsurge within the Reich and he'd gain popularity – at least until he was defeated – and during that time he could do *anything* he wanted."

"And you think he'd senselessly waste resources on attacking us?"

"It wouldn't be senseless to him! And tell me, do you really think our NAU allies would even notice if we were ruthlessly exterminated in that little interim? Hm?"

"No, I suppose they would focus on their own losses."

"And our men would be drafted into the Reich's army – it may well go nuclear – and they would end up burned to a crisp by our allies! Those bombs can't tell the loyal Nazi from the unwilling conscript. Also, even if they managed to win without annihilating us – and remember we're big and strong enough that they would have to hit us really hard to make an impression – but even if the Reich did roll over at the first shot – even then, any peace settlement would be imposed by *them*. After all your years of fighting and surviving, you'd be out in the cold, governed by some coalition that the NAU would cobble together at the last minute and I'd put the likelihood of a bloody civil war afterwards at, say, uh," Ryszard paused as if genuinely calculating odds, "oh, about seventy-five per cent!"

"Alright, Ryszard, you've made your point about Schindler, but if you were to stay here, what about the Führer? Wouldn't he keep Schindler under control?"

"Schindler would remove him within days. You see, Rudi has alienated a lot of people."

"Oh? Then what's stopping Schindler now?"

"Me and Büttner, but Büttner's gone, so just me. He doesn't want a power struggle. He thinks I might win."

"And would you?"

Ryszard shrugged. "Maybe. I need the support of the diplomatic community – that's why I need to marry Greta Schindler. Also, I have the security services, but I don't have anyone in the military yet. Just a couple of maybes."

"I thought you had Schindler under your control. You said you were blackmailing him with the information Peter gave you, what about that?"

"It's only effective as long as the Führer is alive. As soon as Rudi is dead or powerless, the blackmail is worthless." Ryszard paused and smiled, "Though, this recent business has raised worries in Schindler's mind about my powers. He thinks the Americans are supporting me."

A quiet snort of amusement from the corner told them both that Katerina was still awake.

"Well, if Schindler is what's holding you up, why don't we just remove him now, since we have the opportunity?"

Ryszard laughed. "I almost thought Peter was going to do that for me back when Günter tried to hit him."

"Well, should we? We could even have Peter do it. That would remove all suspicions from us."

Ryszard shook his head.

"Why not?"

"A number of reasons. First of all, it would be far too convenient, right on the heels of Büttner's death. The Führer would see that and have me arrested for something, before I could arrange anything. Even if he didn't manage to do me in before I got rid of him, the others would be suspicious – they would wonder at the magical progression: Werner, Günter, Rudi all in a row. At the very least that would mean I wouldn't get elected, they'd find someone else. Anyone else. I'd probably be shuffled out of sight with a report of some serious illness, only to have my sad demise announced six months later."

Marysia looked worriedly at Ryszard. "Could they do that?"

"Of course. Jesus, Marysia, read between the lines on those political reports once in a while!"

She shook her head slightly. "Then are you in danger now? I mean, if they could organize something like that, do you think you should return?"

Ryszard laughed. "The key word there is 'they'. Rudi has really messed things up by becoming so unstable over these past couple of years. Everyone knows something has to give, sooner or later, and everyone is jockeying for position. Right now there is nothing more than a few loose alliances among mutually distrustful warlords. With Büttner's demise, nobody but Schindler has a direct interest in my removal, and a lot of people have some interest in preventing Schindler from becoming too powerful. And mutatis mutandis with respect to me. Some see their best interests in being loyal to one or the other of us, others have an interest in getting rid of both of us and opening the field up – these are the ones who are most interested in Rudi surviving. Then, of course, there is that huge group of fence-sitters, waiting to see which way the wind is blowing. As the situation changes, alliances shift."

"But you have loyal supporters?"

"There is nothing like loyalty involved! More like enlightened self-interest. And that's where my actions come in to all this."

"What do you mean?"

Ryszard leaned forward in his seat. "I mean, with so many enemies just waiting for one wrong move, I don't have time to explain myself or get clearance for my actions. Like that thing with Leszek. Legally, *I* am responsible for his behavior. If it became known that I had not punished him for such a flagrant violation of the law – and don't waste my time telling me the law is insane. If it were clear, that I – a top official and a Party member with a spotless record – that I tolerated illegal behavior, can you imagine what my enemies would have done with that? The leaks to the Party press? I might even have been brought up on ideological charges. And even if I were cleared, my career would have been ruined by the time I dug myself out of the shit."

"Peter said something like that." Marysia sipped her coffee, thoughtfully.

"Hm?"

"He defended your actions. Said you would have had no choice. I passed his comments on to HQ."

"Oh." Ryszard slumped back in his chair. "Well he would know. I'm sure he didn't fail to notice that although Vogel nearly beat him to death for his little seminars with the daughter, the incident was never mentioned to anyone else."

"So Vogel was scared?"

Ryszard sputtered. "Scared shitless by Peter's actions. If it had become known...Well, I don't doubt Peter knew exactly what sort of risk he was taking. And Leszek should have as well." Ryszard ground out his cigarette on the arm of his chair and dropped the end on the ground. He felt exhausted with defending himself. The ingrates. Maybe he should take a break and have Szaflary arrest him like Marysia had suggested. They could release him after a month or so. But what might happen in the interim worried him. He had to go back, loyally support Rudi, and continue to build his alliance. Orders, permission, clearance! Who the hell were they to demand such things from him?

"Ryszard." Marysia drew his name out, in that way she had of sounding like a mother, soothing a child. Julia had hated it, said it was controlling. Her mother, the control-freak, always presenting herself as the kind, disinterested, rational influence on all the emotional people around her. Meanwhile she was manipulating, manipulating...

"Ryszard?"

Ryszard realized that he was nearly asleep. He opened his eyes to study Marysia's face. Adam had found her concern soothing, the voice of calm in the storm. Who, he wondered, had been right? "Tell me, Marysia, what did you say to Julia?"

"Oh," Marysia moaned, "Ryszard, that is so long in the past."

"You ruined us, didn't you?"

Marysia walked over to the table. She unscrewed the cap on a bottle of vodka and poured two shots. "I told her what I thought was the best."

"You ruined us," Ryszard muttered, accepting one of the glasses from Marysia. If he fell asleep now, would Julia come to him in his dreams?

"Ryszard." Marysia's voice was matter-of-fact. "I understand your motives and I'll see that HQ clears all your actions retroactively." She poured the vodka down her throat.

"But?" Ryszard downed his shot and set the glass down on the ground.

"But I can't change their orders about what you do in future." Marysia refilled her glass and drank the shot down. "They're not going to accept complete independence of action on your part."

"So what are they going to do? Remove me?" Ryszard asked snidely. "Is my Auntie Katje going to put a dagger in my neck?"

Marysia cast a glance at Katerina, but she didn't react to the provocation. Though Katerina's days as an assassin were long in the past, Ryszard never missed an opportunity to remind her of them. "More likely, they might just stop supporting you. What would you do if those invisible hands just stopped working for you?"

"I don't give a fuck."

"Compromise." The croak from Katerina's corner surprised them. As they both stared at her, she added, "Give them something to save face, boy."

"Like what?" Ryszard was sufficiently curious that he didn't add, "crone."

"Who's running you now?"

"Tinnemann. But he's just taking orders from Stosz. And he doesn't have a clue about what's going on."

"Suggest a change."

"To what?" Ryszard stopped himself from saying that no-one would understand his work. It would sound too paranoid.

"Have Halifax be your handler."

"*Peter?*" Marysia and Ryszard spoke simultaneously, the surprise of the one no less than the other.

"You said it yourself, Marysia. He told you exactly what Ryszard was up to."

Ryszard nodded thoughtfully. "Yes, he did spend years in the Vogel household, he must have seen a lot of how the politics work. And during that time he encountered Schindler repeatedly and must have some clue as to how his mean-tempered little mind works. I imagine, too, after their long conversations and marching through the woods with the man, he is also quite familiar with Rudi and his warped psyche."

"And he lived in your household for a month," Marysia added helpfully.

Ryszard gave her a sharp look.

"You see," Katerina explained, pre-empting a scathing response from Ryszard, "he can claim to have approved anything you do – and he'll even be able to explain your motivation, probably fairly accurately."

Ryszard slowly let the suspicious anger melt from his features. Katerina made a noise which must have been a laugh. "If you could see yourself, boy! Talk about paranoia!"

Marysia glanced from one to the other in confusion.

Ryszard ignored her, but Katerina gleefully explained, "He didn't like being included in the list with Vogel, Schindler and the Führer!"

Marysia brought her hand to her mouth in embarrassment. "Oh, Ryszard! I am sorry. That wasn't what I meant at all!"

Ryszard stood and looked at his watch. "I don't have much time, I promised my mother I'd visit and I wanted to…Can I go now?"

Unused to ever hearing Ryszard ask permission, Marysia responded quickly, "Of course! I'll contact HQ and tell them of the new arrangement."

Ryszard buttoned his coat and pulled on his gloves. "And make sure you get it approved *before* telling Wanda."

"Why?"

Ryszard laughed. "Why, you ask." He walked over to Katerina and kissed her fondly on the forehead. "Take care, old crone." He went to Marysia and kissed her on each cheek. "You, too." He was already at the entrance of the tent before he stopped to look back at the two women. "Where's Andrzej?"

Marysia blinked back tears, surprised by their sudden appearance. "With Joanna and Adam."

Ryszard nodded and headed off into the darkness to visit the grave of his son.

20

*T*he waxing moon had just set and the first light of dawn had not yet tinged the horizon. The stars glowed brilliantly in the sharply cold air, and Peter stopped walking long enough to enjoy their wondrous beauty. His breath shone steamy white in the pale light, but otherwise it was disconcertingly dark and he was glad that he was nearly back to the little camp where the Americans and his guide were. He greeted the sentries who remained hidden from view, then followed the embers of the fire the last hundred meters into the camp. When he reached the remains of the campfire, he spent a moment, warming his hands over the glowing coals, then entered the small tent which he shared with the woman who was their guide, a partisan named Edyta. She woke as he stooped down next to her, but in the faint light he could discern little more than the whites of her eyes. Madzia was cuddled tight against her.

"Were you briefed?" she whispered in Polish.

"Sort of."

"Where should I lead you tomorrow?"

He described a path that took them along some cliffs. It would take a long time to climb up and then they could slowly wend their way back down through a deep forest. "If we go that way, we shouldn't cover much ground at all. Maybe three kilometers as the crow flies. Just make sure you don't accidentally bring us back to this spot again. They may recognize it."

Edyta chuckled. "They wouldn't recognize it even if we put a sign up! But I will be careful, after all, we're only, what would you say, six hours walk from your destination?"

"Yeah, about that. Shorter if we detour to the road and catch a ride."

"Well, let's hope they remain in ignorance. How long do you intend to lead them on this merry chase?"

"As long as possible, but if I don't get some word from Central that they've had the orders countermanded, I don't think we can keep it up much longer. Maybe two or three days. I want to be back by then in any case."

Edyta nodded. "And are there any further orders regarding this pair?"

Peter shook his head. "Nothing precise. If I decide to do anything, it will be on no-one's authority, but if I feel the need to take action, will you follow my lead?"

"Naturally."

"There may be consequences."

Edyta's eyes glinted. "There always are."

With Jana's fate fresh in his mind, Peter wanted to be sure Edyta understood what she was getting into. "Look, if unofficial action needs to be taken, someone will have to be sacrificed – and that's going to be me and whoever helps me."

Edyta bent her head and kissed Madzia on the forehead. "Better us than the child, no?" Peter picked Madzia up into his arms, and as he held her, Edyta added softly, "I've watched you. I've seen you with the child, I trust you completely." With that she settled back into her sack and went to sleep.

Without waking, Madzia had automatically accommodated herself to Peter's arms, resting her head on his shoulder, hugging him tightly as he embraced her. Life, Peter felt, could not be more beautiful than at that moment and the fear that their life was threatened by a spy made the moment all the more precious to him. He set Madzia in his sack then took off his coat and, rolling it tightly, placed it at the top of the bag as his pillow.

Removing his boots, he laid them under the bag, positioning them so they would not disturb his sleep but might still retain some warmth. Then he carefully crawled in next to Madzia, wrapping his arm protectively around her, careful not to put any of its weight on her. Madzia woke enough for her eyes to flutter open.

"It's me, sweetheart," Peter whispered. "Go back to sleep."

"Papa," she murmured, and pressing herself even closer to him, she closed her eyes.

After she had fallen back asleep, he made sure her hood was snugly on her head and her ears were covered, then he brushed his fingertips over her cheeks to feel the warmth. Though the sleeping bag was already warm, her face was exposed to the night air, and he wanted to reassure himself that she was not growing chill.

With Madzia's heartbeat to soothe him, Peter lay in the darkness and contemplated Marysia's last words to him. Among the usual noises of the woods at night, he could discern the light snoring of their two American guests, sheltering in their separate tent close by. He had spent the last several days in their company but despite Marysia's confidence in his perceptions, he had not managed to learn much. The woman – her name was Cathy – quizzed him endlessly, pleased that she finally had a source who could convey information directly to her in English. Her husband – his name was Albert – remained sourly silent and answered Peter's questions briefly, reiterating the details which Marysia had already relayed to Peter, but adding nothing new. Everything he said had the ring of a memorized tale and Peter had grown to distrust him more and more but had no hard evidence to work with. Indeed, Cathy was more talkative about her husband's past than he was. She would recount some story involving her husband's youth, then turn to him and ask, "Isn't that right? Isn't that what you told me?" to which he usually nodded disinterestedly.

The only time Albert showed interest was when there was any discussion of the encampment itself or its security. One such conversation had begun when his wife had asked about Madzia. Peter had explained that after he had entered the encampment with the Führer in tow, he had discovered his estranged wife and the kidnapped child. His wife, it seemed, had taken refuge within the territory once she had left him in Berlin months before. Seeing no danger in her presence, the partisans had accepted her. The two of them had reconciled and now, while she was away on business of some sort, he was watching the child.

"What sort of business?" Albert had asked with an avid look.

"Don't know. She didn't say."

"But your wife knows about this place?"

Peter had shrugged. "If she does, she hasn't told me anything."

"Is the child yours?" Cathy had asked, gently stroking Madzia's hair. Peter had answered, "She is now."

Cathy had pursued this into a discussion of fatherhood, Albert had lost interest soon afterwards.

Were they spies? Cathy seemed very nice and quite genuine. Perhaps Albert was a spy and was simply using his wife as one of the tools of his trade. Marry a native-born woman to bolster his own acceptability as a naturalized American? That would be a reasonable strategy. Albert treated his wife with a brusqueness that implied that he thought of her as little more than a tool. It reminded Peter of the way Zosia had sometimes treated him during their first years – during the time he was the centerpiece of her propaganda campaign. Of course, it would be cleverer of Albert to appear to be in love with his wife – as Ryszard fell so convincingly in love with so many of the women he used – but such cleverness and the acting ability it required were rare talents and not every spy was as gifted or devoted as Ryszard.

Indeed that had probably been the exact reason why Peter had rejected the English Underground's plans for him to infiltrate. He had not doubted his ability to live a lie – he had simply not wanted to endure years of flattering and sucking up to the very people he loathed. If Albert was a true believer in the Nazi philosophy, then he might find it equally difficult to tolerate and interact in a friendly manner with people who were, to him, nothing better than traitorous and inferior scum. Was that what left him so morbidly sour? Or was it just his personality? Was the fact that Peter found him a rather unpleasant person sufficient reason to condemn him as a spy, with all the necessary actions that implied?

Frustrated by the lack of information, Peter decided to go to sleep. He closed his eyes, thinking he might drift off, but his thoughts took that other turn – the one he dreaded. He fell into the dizzying darkness, the hands reached out for him, pulling at him…He opened his eyes and stared at the strange patterns cast on the tent flap by the dimly flickering embers of their campfire. After a moment, he leaned over to tap Edyta's shoulder. "Will you keep an eye on Madzia for me?"

"Of course." She rolled closer to the child and draped her arm tenderly over her as Peter carefully crawled out of his sack. He shook out his boots and put them on, pulled on his coat, and left the tent. He went to the supplies, found a bottle of vodka and put that in his coat, then paced into the woods and found a place to sit on a fallen log.

What should he do? The safest course was to follow direct orders – the encampment had been commanded to allow these two interlopers to visit, he should let the Council decide whether or not to follow those orders, he should let them argue with the Americans. On the other hand, there was

374

Madzia and Irena and all the other children of the encampment. There was
Zosia, and Marysia. There were his friends. It was his home. If he allowed
a spy to enter into the most guarded territory and to re-emerge with details
of the location, of faces, of the defenses – then all could be lost.

He had his orders, he should not take independent and indefensible
action. If he did, then whether he had been right or not would never be
known, but the encampment would need to punish him. Murdering an ally!
On a nebulous suspicion? How could he? They would have to sacrifice him
to the American's wrath. Yet there had been that pleading look on
Marysia's face, there were his innocent daughters' lives...Oh, God, what
should he do?

He looked back up at the sky. The lightest hint of dawn tinged the
horizon, but the stars were still gloriously bright. It was nice that everything
was so clear – his vision had been unusually stable recently and he felt
thankful that the stars were sharply defined pinpricks in the heavens rather
than the unfocussed smudges that they often were. He heard a wolf howl
and it sent a chill down his spine. What would the region be like if the
Führer's troops moved in? No wolves, certainly. Floodlights, marching
soldiers, the forests logged and looted. Deep down he felt sure Albert was a
spy, but he had no proof! Nothing but a gut feeling and the knowledge that
a spy *did* exist. But was that enough to kill someone? And what price
would he be made to pay? If the Americans found out, Szaflary would have
to, in some manner, punish him. Exile? Extradition? Execution?

He lowered his head and rubbed his face. The darkness closed in. The
hands came from all directions and started grabbing and pulling, tearing at
his clothes, his hair, his skin...He flung his arms, angrily shrugging them
off. He could not let them in here! He would never let those hands reach
out for Madzia or Irena! Never!

"Are you okay?"

It was Cathy who had spoken and she was standing only a few feet
away. Clearly she had seen his strangely defensive gesture. That annoyed
him, but even worse was that he had not even noticed her approaching. He
shook his head slightly in answer to her question. "I'm fine."

"Insects?"

"Ha. Pests, at least."

She sat down next to him. "What was it you were fighting?"

"Memories." He counted down silently to the inevitable *tell me all
about it*. He wouldn't mind so much if all the people who had said that had
wanted to hear the truth. They didn't. What they generally wanted was a
cleaned-up two minute summary upon which they could make some
trenchant comments and then be rewarded with effusive compliments about

how their brilliant words had brought everything into perspective. They wanted to effortlessly save him.

Surprisingly she did not press him to describe anything further. She reached out and touched his arm in a reassuring, yet unobtrusive manner. Peter was amazed by her gentleness, and oddly, he felt no need to pull away from her touch.

They sat that way for a while, then Cathy finally broke the silence, saying softly, "You know, some hold that it is important to delve into these things – these horrific memories. Research has shown that, not surprisingly, there is no simple answer. Some people do better discussing everything, others are well advised to ignore everything." She paused a moment, then added, "Which, I guess, is pretty useless. Sorry."

"That's alright, none of it matters anyway," he said coldly. *Please don't be so kind to me! I might have to kill you!*

"I don't believe that. It *is* important! It's your life! As the Lord Jesus Christ said…"

As she talked, Peter turned his head away and stared into the darkness. Like a dream her words drew up images of lilies dressed in fine raiment and tiny birds lovingly fed by the hand of God. *Get information out of the woman!* But he didn't feel up to it. She was genuinely trying to help him. *Use that! Gain her trust! Use her!* He shook his head at the thought.

Though in the darkness she could not see his gesture, she must have sensed it for she stopped what she had been saying. After a moment, she whispered, almost as a prayer, "You are a child of the Universe, no less than the trees and the stars. You have a right to be here."

"What?" He turned slightly to try to see her, and in so doing let her hand fall from his arm.

"And whether it is clear to you or not, the universe is unfolding, as it should."

"Is that also from the gospels?"

She laughed. "No, it's a poem, written before the war started. I've always found comfort in its words."

No less than the trees and the stars. Peter rested his eyes on his hands, but he couldn't blot out the image of Marysia, the plea in her eyes as she told him *you are very perceptive, Peter.* Find something out, he thought. Talk to the woman. He lifted his head and spoke into the night. "I was no child of the universe, I was the child of a conquered and disheartened people. Just one of thousands of unwashed and not particularly wanted faces. I knew exactly what I was worth from birth on. We all did. It was less than nothing."

"Nobody's life is worthless. Everyone has a right to their life. You included."

376

He snorted. It was as if she was begging to share confidences with him! He was having no success prising information out of Albert, he should work indirectly, through her. *Use her.* And he should do it in good conscience. It was for a good cause, he told himself. The cause, as Zosia would say. *The Cause.* Peter jerked his head up as the words passed through his mind, then he let his face rest in his hands again. So, this is what Zosia felt when she had met him. First, the divorce from all emotions toward outsiders, next the willingness to use them without regret. It sounded brutal, but when weighed against what was at stake – then there was no real choice: he had to find out if Albert was a danger to them, whatever that took.

Cathy tried again. "Why did you all feel so unwanted?"

Peter let his hands slide down his face as if pulling on a mask. He then clasped them together and rested his chin on them. Carefully imbuing his voice with an implication of confidentiality, he answered, "Our parents, mostly."

"Your parents?"

Peter nodded slowly, thoughtfully. "It wasn't their fault, you know. Most of them had grown up so deprived that they had to scramble for any shred of normalcy: housing, jobs, food, privacy. And then, when they'd have these unapproved children – everything would fall to pieces."

"How so?"

"Oh, the families would lose all sorts of privileges. Or what we thought of as privileges. Most of the kids were from dirt poor families and their birth only made their families poorer. Their parents were always trying to wring the last pfennig out of them. The girls, they had to take over all the household chores. Cooking, cleaning, laundry – doing everything so that their Mums could work. They were almost prisoners in their flats. Hell, the only time we'd see them was when they'd be lugging groceries into the apartment blocks or rubbish out. Sometimes I'd help carry sacks for this girl or that, and we'd chat a bit, but otherwise, they were almost invisible." He paused, then added, "At least the good ones. The poor things just wanted to do right and they got made into slaves as a result. As for the so-called bad girls – they'd run wild, get pregnant, get abortions, get completely used up before they were sixteen…"

"And the boys?"

"A lot of them had to earn money – somehow. Shine shoes or sell trinkets or whatever. Early in the morning, before school, and again, afterwards, they'd trudge off with their shoeshine boxes or their baubles to the edge of the government district, as close as English papers would let them get to the offices…"

"Kids carried papers?"

"Of course, but nobody had to check them. The police could tell by looking – or if you like, smelling – who was from the seedy neighborhoods. So, these kids would shine boots or flog their wares, all the while keeping an eye out for the grown men who were doing the same job to support a family."

"Why?"

"What would you do if some snot-nosed brat was stealing food from your family's table?" Peter asked, almost impatiently. "Even though the men could do a better job shining boots, the officials always favored the kids, partly because they looked winsome, partly because they'd do a better job telling the customer what a marvelous Aryan he was."

"I see." Cathy's voice sounded wistful and distant, as if she really were seeing into a faraway land, into the past.

"Also a lot of the boys were employed by the Underground selling contraband, and sometimes they'd skim a bit of the profits for their families, so they'd have something to take home to their parents, so they could earn a bit of love." Peter remembered how he would sometimes even distribute some of his pocket money because the kids looked so desperate to have something they could take home. He chose not to mention that and said instead, "It was fairly dangerous – they could get in big trouble doing that." He sighed, realizing that he had begun to engage himself in the conversation. That would never do.

They continued to talk for some time and as Peter told Cathy about his life, he leaned into her, as a close friend might. She begin to tell him about her life and slowly they moved through her childhood and into the years when she met Albert. Peter pressed her with questions about what Albert was like back then, what he did, what she knew of his past, his present, his friends, his colleagues, his habits. Did he make unofficial trips? Was he secretive? Strange phone calls? Did he seem distracted? Easily angered? Cathy answered willingly, confiding secrets and emotions along with simple facts. "He seems so cold sometimes anymore. Not like when we first met..." She hesitated a long moment before adding, "And sometimes he says things that are disturbing – not at all what I expect. Like before we got on the plane to come here, Albert–"

"What are you saying about me?" Albert's voice asked accusingly from behind them. Peter twisted around to see him, coincidentally putting a few inches between himself and Cathy as he did so. The hint of morning light now formed a band of gray behind the trees and against it, Albert's silhouette looked threatening. Peter swore quietly at the ill-timed interruption.

"Goodness, it's turning into a party!" Cathy giggled.

378

"Good idea." Reaching into his coat, Peter pulled out the bottle of vodka and motioned with it toward the log. "Have a seat, Albert, join us!"

Albert sat down and reluctantly accepted the proffered bottle. He brought it to his lips but did not seem to drink any. Handing it on to his wife, he asked Peter, "When did you get back? Why were you called away?"

Peter dismissed the questions with a wave of his hand. "I had to answer some more questions about my abduction of the Führer. Why I didn't shoot the bastard dead, that sort of thing." Peter tried to see if Albert had any reaction to the harsh suggestion, but the light was too dim to discern such subtleties.

Cathy put Peter's bottle to her lips and happily downed a bit, then snorted and coughed. "Geez, that's strong!" She giggled again and handed the vodka to Peter.

Peter accepted the bottle, took a swig. "I was just telling Cathy about life in London when I was a kid. But you grew up there as well – why don't you share some of your experiences? Surely they must be relevant." He pressed the bottle into Albert's hands.

Albert did not even pretend to drink. "Not really. You see, my mother was English, but my father was German. I was raised in the rebuilt part in the north of the city – in 'Little Berlin'. Consequently, I had very little experience with English London." He handed the vodka on to his wife.

Cathy took another swig then passed it back to Peter. "At least not until you ran away from home."

Peter accepted the bottle but didn't drink. "Why'd you do that?"

He listened to Albert's answer, although he already knew, from what Marysia had told him, exactly what Albert would say. Everything up to that point in Albert's life fit the mold of an up-and-coming Nazi official: a hard-working, loyal father, a turncoat mother, appropriate schooling, two years military service as an officer. Then, suddenly the good little Nazi had taken offense at it all, and, at the age of twenty, he had disappeared from view and lived underground for two years. He had then stowed away on a ship and after working his way through various neutral countries, had turned up on American territory spouting loyalty to the NAU and seeking asylum.

As his military service had included some fairly sensitive positions, Albert had been welcomed by the American Security Agency as a defector with useful information. He told them everything he knew, worked diligently for them for decades, and finally won their complete trust.

A stranger in a strange land, Peter thought, as Albert patly relayed his tale. Distrusted and watched for years, that could make anyone bitter and sullen. So, too, could being forced to live among people he loathed as he awaited his opportunity to serve his country. There was only one weak area that could be tested in all this. Those two years living underground in London. It was unlikely that a spy would have actually lived those two years among the London underclass – not when the time could be well spent learning his trade. He would instead memorize a few details already known to the Gestapo about the criminal underground and would trust to the fact that his story could not be checked out in great detail as that part of it happened far away among people who were unidentifiable or unreachable.

"That's amazing!" Peter enthused, "It's so wonderful to share experiences with another home-boy! We lived in London at exactly the same time. Tell me, what do you remember best?"

Albert hesitated, then answered, "I suppose the concert hall in Kovent Garten."

"Um-huh. Neat architecture, what?"

"Yes, I heard it even won an award."

Nobody thought the architecture was anything other than disgusting, neo-brutalist rubbish. Indeed its nickname had been *the Rubbish Bin.* "It had a nickname…" Peter snapped his fingers as if trying to recall the name.

"Really?"

"Yeah, but I can't remember what it was. Did you live near there?"

"I lived all over."

"But never in the area of Kovent Garten?" Peter casually took a swig from the vodka bottle as he waited for Albert to confirm this detail of his original cover story. Would he claim to forget where he had lived?

Albert seemed to be deciding something, then answered carefully, "I took a room in a pub across from the concert hall. One could make a lot of contacts there."

"Which pub was it that you stayed at?"

"The Goose and Bull. A lot of people congregated there. They shielded me."

"I'm sure they did." It was *Goebbel's Ball.* Nobody who knew it called it the Goose and Bull. Now, was it really possible that Albert had lived there, had congregated with the English who frequented the pub, had been helped by them, and did not know the Londoners' name for the place? And how could he not know that everyone who was not a loyal Nazi hated the concert hall? Surely he would have been better prepared in his background story. Or would he? The Americans would be completely unaware of such subtleties and it was for them Albert would have been prepped. Nor was there any guarantee that the people who schooled him had been competent. Indeed, the Underground had even had a saying about competent Germans: *they could be found in the dust of Dachau.*

Nevertheless, such suspicions were not enough to murder a man. Especially an important ally. Peter chewed on his knuckle a moment and then decided to dive in full force. He thrust the vodka bottle at Albert, suggesting jovially "Drink some, you've hardly had any!"

With a tight little smile that was barely visible in the dim light, Albert handed the bottle back to Peter without drinking anything. "I think I've had enough." He stood and added, "I'm going to get some more sleep before that stupid cow takes us marching again. I'm really getting fed up. First all our personal equipment gets stolen, then getting guided by this moron who, I swear, is taking us in circles!" With that, he headed back to his tent.

21

"*O*h Richard, oh Günter, oh my dear, loyal lieutenants!" The Führer was almost weeping with joy. His eyes fell upon the tall, thin black woman and he looked momentarily confused. "Who's this?" Before anyone could answer, he turned back to his dear, loyal subordinates. "You have no idea what I have suffered. Look at what they've done to me! My hands bound as if I were some sort of animal! They're such swine! Brutes! Pigs!"

Richard threw a pointed glance at the Führer's captors. Günter chose to be more straightforward. "Rudi, they understand what you say."

The Führer glared at Günter, infuriated by the familiarity in front of strangers. "As well they should."

Schindler bowed his head in an obsequious acknowledgment of the Führer's wisdom. "Yes, *mein Führer*."

The Führer's outburst was nothing more than what Richard had expected, but he wondered why Günter had chosen to immediately provoke Rudi. Richard turned his attention from both to address Marysia, who stood to the side of the Führer's guards. "Would you please instruct your men to release our Führer?"

"But of course, Herr Traugutt. Have you and Herr Schindler signed the documents?" Marysia pointed to the table in the tent and the papers on it.

Richard stifled a yawn. "Yes, we've both signed. All copies."

Marysia said something to one of the guards and the Führer was released from his bonds. Stefan offered his arm to his Führer and guided him to the safety of his dear, loyal lieutenants.

Marysia turned to Richard and said, "Herr Traugutt, please instruct your Führer that he must sign as well."

The Führer looked in confusion at Marysia. Was it a sign of respect that she chose not to address him directly? He was so taken aback by this unexpected submissiveness that he followed Richard's guidance and signed as directed without even reading the documents. "What do they say?" he asked, as he straightened.

"They're just some minor conditions we agreed to for your release," Richard answered quietly.

"Conditions? You negotiated with these..." The Führer shook with revulsion.

"We've negotiated with them before."

"Yes, but then I didn't realize what they were! I will never treat with these subhumans again! The way they abused me!"

Richard hid a yawn behind his hand, "Of course, *mein Führer*. Let us discuss this later, back in Berlin."

Marysia, ignoring them, walked over to the table and picked up the papers. She studied the signatures, comparing them with samples that she had brought. "Fine, you may all go. Our soldiers will lead you to your automobile." She separated out two sets of papers and walking back over to the group, handed one set to Arieka and the other to Traugutt. "Here, so you have a copy of what you signed." Then she turned to the Führer. "I wish we had had the time to re-educate you."

The Führer drew himself up, "You are but an inferior being. There is nothing you could teach us."

Marysia smiled. "I suppose that is our essential difference. I believe that every human is worthy." She reached up and stroked the Führer's cheek. He flinched so visibly that she laughed. "But maybe for you, I would make an exception." Suddenly businesslike, she turned to the guards and ordered, "Get them out of here."

It took Marysia several hours to get back to the bunker, but the nausea still had not dissipated. She went down the dim hallways, pausing outside Peter and Zosia's dark and empty flat. She missed them, Peter especially. She wanted so much to talk with him – he would know what to say. He would probably find some way to blame himself and she would readily agree, just to feel better about herself.

She opened the door and looked into the dimly lit room. No Zosia, no Peter, no Madzia, no Irena. No Adam or Joanna either. It was as if the world had deserted her. She turned on a light and went over to the cabinet where Peter kept his mother's diaries. Marysia opened the drawer and gingerly picked one up. Still standing, she opened the book and began to read. After a few minutes she glanced at the front of the diary to remind herself of the woman's name. Peter had pronounced it for her, and as she looked at the signature, Marysia let the strange syllables roll through her head. Catherine Sinclair Chase. How very odd. If she had lived, Catherine would be only a few years older than herself, yet she seemed to be from an entirely different universe. Catherine's words of hope, her desire to cooperate and fit in, her belief that the end of hostilities might usher in an era of peace were so alien. And in the end she had experienced the terror of being arrested and the horror and hopelessness of a slow death in a concentration camp.

Marysia closed the book, stroking its cover as if to offer comfort to its author. "You are a lucky woman, Catherine," she whispered. "You did not live to see your grandchild murdered." She carefully placed the book back in the drawer and shut it. Then she went over to the cupboard and found a bottle of vodka. She poured herself a large glass and sat down. She took a deep gulp, coughed slightly as it caught her by surprise, then drank some more. After a few minutes the glass was empty and she began to feel the alcohol. She looked at the ceiling as if addressing the heavens and said, "I let the bastard walk free. I let Joanna's murderer walk away." She lowered her gaze to the table, and muttering, "I'm sorry, Adam. I'm so sorry, son," she refilled the glass and continued to drink.

22

*P*eter awoke to the sensation of someone trying to pry his eyes open. He carefully raised his lids but something blocked his vision. He shook the hands away from his face, squinted, blinked and finally brought his focus in to the right distance. About three inches in front of him was Madzia's grinning eyes. "Good morning!" she sang.

"So early?" He was exhausted.

"Good morning!"

He reached up, tenderly stroking her face as he carefully maneuvered her back a few inches. "Good morning, *Mäuschen*." He blinked the last of the morning muck out of his eyes and focused on Madzia again. This time, he was able to see her entire face and that brought a smile to his. He glanced over where Edyta had been but not even her sack was there. The flap of the tent was up and when he looked out, he saw Edyta's sack, already neatly rolled and set next to her pack. A few feet beyond that he spied her, sitting by a fire, sipping from a mug.

She smiled a hello, then motioned toward a little pot on the fire, "It's boiling. Do you want a cup?"

"It might help." Peter wriggled his way out of his sack, then crawled out of the tent. Madzia clambered onto his back and rode to the fire with him. "Dismount," he announced, rising enough to gently slip Madzia off his back. She giggled and clung to his neck. "Please," he groaned.

Edyta threw a handful of loose coffee grounds into the bottom of a tin mug, then using a rag to protect her hand, she grabbed the pot and poured boiling water into the cup. "I didn't let her wake you until now. I figured there was no real hurry."

"Thanks. What time is it?" Peter finally managed to free himself from Madzia's embrace and sit properly.

"Nearly nine." Edyta handed Peter the cup of coffee then passed him a spoon.

He carefully turned the grounds on the bottom of the cup so that the boiled water could soak through. He watched the speckles of coffee swirling on the top, waiting impatiently for them to drop back to the bottom. Not quite three hours of sleep. Ugh. After a moment, he decided he could wait no longer and sipped the muddy concoction. Edyta brought her fist up to her mouth to hide her laugh.

"You better not laugh at me! Or you'll get freckles!" It was a game where one spit out the loose coffee grounds at an opponent's face.

"Beware! I am not unarmed!" Edyta raised her own mug in a mock threat, but then lowered it and gestured with her head behind Peter. "Good morning," she called out in English. "Coffee?"

"Oh, yes!" Cathy smiled her thanks. Albert accepted a mug in silence. They spent a few minutes, drinking their coffee, and Peter and Cathy fell into a lively conversation in English with much gesturing. Edyta sat in polite silence, but eventually asked what they were talking about and Peter switched to German and explained that they were discussing the landscape, and the geography of the region and the reasons for their convoluted route.

As Peter talked with Edyta, Cathy went to her pack and returned with a yellow notepad and a pencil. She began sketching and Peter interrupted his conversation with Edyta to see what Cathy was doing. It was a portrait of Madzia, done in simple lines, but extremely cleverly.

Peter shook his head in amazement. "That's astonishing! You've caught so much of her character in so few lines."

Cathy blushed and murmured, "Thanks. I like to draw and she was sitting there so prettily, I just couldn't resist."

Peter continued to stare at the notebook, but his attention was drawn from the penciled lines of Madzia's face to the pale green lines which ran horizontally across the yellow paper. "That's an interesting choice of paper for portraits."

Cathy giggled with embarrassment "Oh, I had a proper little notebook, but it was in the pack that went missing – the one with our electronic equipment. After we went through the trouble of smuggling all that in, it

384

was such a nuisance—" She smiled an apology for implying the encampment had lax security and thieves. Tapping the yellow notepad, she explained, "This belongs to Albert. It's for his notes. He prefers the legal pads."

Peter ran his fingers down the length of the pad. "Yes, the longer of your two sizes. Fourteen inches, isn't it?"

"Yeah, he does everything that length. Drives his colleagues nuts – especially if they want to copy something." Cathy added a few lines to the page and then stopped to compare her work with Madzia.

Her curiosity piqued, Madzia clambered over Peter's lap so she could see the paper as well. "*Mein?*"

Cathy nodded and, carefully removing the page from her notebook, handed it to Madzia. "Yes, yours."

Madzia gleefully accepted the paper. She held the picture in front of herself and grinned at it. "*Mein, mein!*"

"You know," Cathy commented as she set the pad and pencil down next to herself, "I think that's the first time I've heard her say anything."

"Breakfast?" Edyta offered, using one of the few words of English that she knew.

They all readily agreed. As Edyta rose to fetch the food from her pack, Madzia tugged at Peter's arm. "*Darf ich helfen? Darf ich helfen?*"

"*Natürlich, Mäuschen.*" Peter helped her to her feet and she ran off after Edyta to help her.

"She speaks German to you?" Cathy asked.

Before Peter was able to answer, Albert said, "But of course!" Cathy looked at her husband in surprise, but he was completely oblivious to her confusion.

The sign of a true believer, Peter thought. In Albert's view Madzia was the pure-blooded daughter of Karl and Elspeth Vogel. *But of course* a pristine Aryan girl would speak the language of the *Übermensch*. Deliberately side-stepping Albert's comment, Peter turned to Cathy. "Yes, it's our common language."

"But she said, 'mine' just a moment ago. Does she use English too?"

As Albert laughed at his wife's ignorance, Peter explained that the word "mine" sounded the same in both languages and then added, "I haven't managed to teach her much English yet. Maybe that's why she's been so quiet when you're around – she's probably confused by the language."

Cathy nodded, but didn't say anything. Peter noticed that she had reddened at her husband's laughter, so he gave her a moment to compose herself. He picked up the portrait which Madzia had dropped, folded it, and carefully tucked it into his coat pocket. Madzia returned to the circle with a packet of heavy rye bread and Peter smiled fondly at her and called her over to him. Taking the bread from her hands, he whispered in her ear, "The nice

385

man wants to hear your prayer. You know, the one about your guardian Angel."

Madzia smiled broadly and turned to Albert, who had only just managed to stop laughing at his wife. Madzia waited until she was sure she had his attention, then she made the sign of the cross and very solemnly recited, *"Aniele Stróżu mój, Ty zawsze przy mnie stój..."* As she proudly continued reciting the little prayer, Peter watched Albert closely. Madzia's recitation lasted only a few seconds and throughout Albert said not a word, but his face told Peter everything he needed to know.

"I really can't hold it any longer," Cathy whispered desperately to Peter. "Why haven't we taken a break before now?"

Peter didn't tell her that he had instructed Edyta not to stop. Instead he pointed to the rough terrain – a wall of rock on one side, a steep drop into a rock-strewn gully on the other. The edge of the trail was slippery with shale, the crevices in the wall, few and far between. "I think because there's no opportunity for privacy here. She knows you like your privacy."

Cathy reddened. "Well, I'm past that now. Could you tell her I need to stop?"

Though it was exactly what he had hoped for, indeed, planned on, Peter nevertheless hesitated. Did he really want to do this?

"Please."

"I have an idea." Peter set Madzia on the ground next to Cathy. "I'll go on ahead with your husband and Edyta can help you find a safe place off to the side. I'll leave Madzia with you, I'm sure she could use a little break. Albert and I will wait for you ahead."

"Oh, would you do that? Oh, that'd be great. Thanks, so much!"

"It's nothing," Peter muttered, and then strode ahead to catch up with Edyta. They conferred and Edyta waved her arm, indicating that the path was obvious. She then turned and walked the few paces back to Cathy, taking Madzia's hand in her own.

Peter motioned to Albert and the two continued alone. They climbed steadily upwards for a few moments, then suddenly Albert stopped. "This is far enough, we can't see them."

Peter tugged on his arm. "The guide said there's a good place to stop up ahead. Much nicer since it's at the top."

"I'm not going any further," Albert panted, shrugging off his pack.

Peter scanned the terrain. "Fine." He took his pack off and set it next to Albert's. "It's a nice view anyway."

Albert looked out over the ravine. "Rocks," he grunted.

Peter slipped off his coat and set it on top of his pack. "God, climbing in this sun. I'm sweating." He pushed up his sleeves and ran his fingers through his hair, wiping the damp off his forehead as he did so. He clasped his hands behind his head and stretched. It gave him a moment to close his eyes and reconsider his plans. When he opened his eyes, he saw Albert staring at him. Peter followed Albert's gaze and looked up at his left forearm. "You didn't see them before?" Peter asked, referring to the identification numbers tattooed there.

Albert shook his head slowly. "So you really are one of them?"

"So they told me." Peter lowered his arms and stepped to the edge of the trail, sending a few lose pebbles clattering noisily down the ridge. He watched them as they tumbled to the bottom, finally losing sight of them as they fell between some huge boulders about ten meters below. The bottom seemed to contain the detritus from an earlier rockslide. He leaned a bit further out and surveyed the distance. Though time was short, he still took a moment to gather himself, then, carefully imbuing his voice with a reasonable amount of excitement, he exclaimed, "Look at that!"

"What?"

"I think it's a bunker. Or an arms depot." Peter pointed downward along the ravine.

"I don't see anything."

Peter straightened and took a step backward so that he was behind Albert. He placed his arm around Albert's shoulder to guide his view. Albert glanced down at Peter's arm, shuddering as if in disgust at its touch, but Peter ignored that and urged Albert closer to the edge. "Right there. See the concrete corner sticking out?"

In his eagerness to view what Peter was pointing at, Albert overcame his revulsion and turned his attention back to the rocks below. Deep down Peter hoped Albert would recognize the danger and retaliate. If Albert turned on him, tried to throw him over the edge, then it would be a fair fight, a matter of self-defense. But Albert simply scanned eagerly in the direction Peter was pointing.

But of course. A true believer, Peter thought. A true believer would underestimate his enemy. A true believer would feel no danger in the presence of an *Untermensch*. A true believer would be oblivious to risks that even an innocent man would notice. A true believer would look at Madzia with utter abhorrence as she recited her prayer in the enemy's tongue.

Twisting imperceptibly, Peter shifted his weight and then swung his shoulder into Albert's back, simultaneously slamming his hand into the back of Albert's head. As Albert screamed and fell forward, Peter jumped back out of reach. Albert's arms revolved desperately in an attempt to catch his balance or grasp something, but there was nothing, and he pitched forward and tumbled downward, his body making sickening thuds as it repeatedly bounced against the rocky slope, his yowls of pain echoing through the air. At last he came to rest in a crevice among the boulders.

Peter carefully lowered himself over the edge and clambered down the slope as quickly as possible without falling. He skidded to a stop near Albert then carefully approached the body. Albert was gasping noisily, his arm bent at an unnatural angle behind his head. Peter lowered himself between the rocks and reached for Albert's face. He turned it toward himself, then curling his fingers against themselves and arching them backward to keep his palm flat, he slammed his knuckles up against Albert's nose, sending the bone directly into the brain.

"What's happened? Are you down there?" It was Cathy, calling from above.

Peter looked up the escarpment, but he couldn't see the trail from where he was. He climbed out from among the rocks and called upward. "It's Albert, he's fallen. He's badly hurt."

"I'll come down."

"No, no! It's too dangerous. Stay up there." Peter switched to German and added, "Edyta! Can you radio for help? It's Albert, I think he's dead."

23

*T*he boy waited expectantly. Peter read the note, then glanced down at his watch. Six hours. Six fucking hours! He and Edyta had so carefully staged everything, spontaneously choreographing their moves to inform the Council as quickly as possible about what had happened, arranging for Peter to return with the body without betraying his links to Szaflary, carefully shuffling Cathy off to a nearby cabin where Edyta could console her and keep her safely away from witnessing the fallout...And all for nothing. Six hours before Wanda had deigned to summon him, and now, suddenly, it couldn't wait until morning. "Tell her I'll be right there."

Timidly, the boy responded, "I was told to accompany you."

"I'm not going to run away! Tell her I'll be there as soon as I get someone to watch my daughter. Now go."

The boy hesitated, then nodded briefly and returned the way he had come.

Wrapping a blanket around her, Peter picked up Madzia and carried the sleeping child next door to Marysia's, but she wasn't home. He tried Kamil's rooms next, but all was dark and he chose not to wake them. Hania was obviously home and awake and greeted him warmly.

"I didn't know you were back from your camping trip." She pulled the blanket from Madzia's face and peered at her. "They are such angels when they are asleep."

Peter smiled down at his little angel, nodding his agreement. "Even when she's awake."

"So what brings you here?"

"I've been summoned to talk with Wanda."

Hania made an appropriately apprehensive noise. "You want me to watch her for you?" She stroked Madzia's nose.

"If you don't mind."

"Of course not. How long will it take?"

"Either I'll be back soon, or..."

Hania looked up at Peter, worried by his tone.

He shrugged apologetically. "If I'm held, Marysia will watch her until Zosia gets home."

"Held? What's happened? Is this to do with the Americans?"

Peter nodded. "He's dead."

"Dead? And you had something to do with it?"

"There are suspicious circumstances, at the very least."

"I see. And Wanda is handling this alone. Hmm." Hania's face darkened. "You know, whatever happens is a Council decision. Why haven't I been informed?"

"Perhaps it's considered solely a security issue. You know, arresting murder suspects."

"She can't possibly intend to arrest you!"

Peter laughed. "Yes, she can. With the American woman still around, we have to be seen to be doing the right thing." He looked ruefully at Madzia. "I can't imagine why I would be denied the opportunity to see her, but anymore, with Wanda, I just don't know what to expect. Anyway, if I am detained or moved to the border regions, could you please explain to Madzia what's happened? Or at least something plausible. I don't want to say anything right now – I'm afraid of waking her up for no reason."

"I understand." Hania went up on tiptoe and kissed him on the cheek. "Don't worry, you'll be back within an hour. And if not, I'll make sure she's taken care of. And...Whatever happens, don't worry. I'll make enough of a stink that any stupid decision will be reversed. I promise."

"Thanks."

"Not just on your account. I'm tired of these clowns running things like it's their personal fief. We're supposed to have a proper government here, not a dictatorship." As if embarrassed by her outburst, Hania quickly turned and strode purposefully back into her room. "Now let's settle the little one."

Hania made a bed for Madzia and Peter laid her on it and tenderly draped a blanket over her. He kissed his daughter, thanked Hania and then bid farewell. As he trod the hallways toward Wanda's office, he reviewed what he might say to her. All told, he had no hard evidence, nothing at all to prove Albert had been a spy. A history and a preference consistent with a few lines of code, minor details missing from his knowledge of English London, a careless assumption about innate language, a brief look of horror as a pure Aryan girl recited a prayer in Polish, a shudder of revulsion when touched by an *Untermensch*. It would never do. There was no point in mentioning any of it.

He arrived at the office, knocked, and entered when bidden. The small room was crowded – not only Wanda, but Marysia, Konrad, and Katerina were there. The usual gang of four, he thought. "You rang, *Gnädige Frau?*"

Wanda scowled. "None of your sick humor."

"Of course not, *Gnädige Frau Oberst*. I leap to answer your call whatever the hour, no matter how long I am made to wait."

Wanda pointed at some papers which Konrad held. "The coroner has reported on the death of the American. He said that the American was killed by a bit of his nose-bone being shoved into his brain. He was of the opinion that this injury was typical of that sustained by someone attacked by a trained killer and would have been a very unlikely injury to have occurred during a fall – especially since the victim had a reasonable amount of internal bleeding from his other injuries. This would indicate that he was alive for some minutes after sustaining his initial injuries and before he received this final, fatal blow. Such a scenario is unlikely for the victim of a fall."

Konrad held the coroner's report in the air. "The evidence would indicate the American was murdered."

Peter raised his eyebrows but did not comment.

"You were the last person to see him alive," Marysia softly pointed out. "Do you have any explanation?"

Peter shook his head.

Konrad fingered the report nervously. "Was he alive when you ran down to see him?"

"Does it matter?"

"Did you kill him?" Marysia asked bluntly.

Peter scanned each of their faces. They remained silent, awaiting his answer. "He would have been the death of us all."

"Peter, did you kill him?"

Peter nodded. "Yes."

They exchanged glances but did not say anything. Marysia looked back at Peter, her face reflecting a mixture of relief and fear. Peter remembered that she had never really felt comfortable with Adam's choice of career and perhaps she was dismayed to see him following the same path that her son had taken. But that didn't seem to be the case – her fear was more primitive than that. She looked genuinely afraid of him. "Why?" she asked at long last.

"He would have been the death of us all."

"So you think he was a spy?"

"Yes."

"What evidence do you have?"

Peter shook his head slightly. "Nothing substantial."

They fell silent and Peter wondered if they were communicating telepathically or if they had strenuously argued about what to do with him if he admitted the crime. Perhaps they had hoped he would refuse to confess and save them from making any decision. Or had they hoped for some irrefutable evidence? Here, he should say, it's his Party membership card! Or Schindler's home phone number in his address book! Or a signed photograph of the Führer, stating, "To my ever-loyal spy, Albert!" Peter sighed, he wished it had been that clear.

"Thank you, Captain." It was Katerina who had spoken.

Peter was not sure whether it was gratitude or a dismissal.

Marysia smiled slightly. "It was very cleverly done. The wife is unaware that it was anything other than an accident. And so it shall remain."

Konrad walked over to the shredder in the corner of Wanda's office and fed the offending document into it. There was silence as the little machine whirred away. When it had finished, Konrad explained, "A new one will be prepared."

Peter nodded. "Where is she?" Though he was asking about Cathy, it was Wanda who worried him. She stood with her arms crossed, studying the floor of her office as if she no longer had anything to do with the proceedings.

"The wife is still down at the cabin where the body was initially brought. She's being tended by Anna, since she speaks some English."

Peter tore his attention away from Wanda. Apparently she had accepted a majority decision. "Will she – the wife, I mean – come up here?"

"We see no reason for that. She may stay for the burial, we'll put him down near the border, then we'll send her back."

Peter nodded. With the wife's testimony, it would be unlikely the Americans would bother sending anyone all the way to Szaflary to do a post mortem. "Do you think anyone in the ASA will want to see the body? Have it shipped back?"

"It's not really practical," Konrad said, as if planning his response to the American request.

"Better if they don't even ask," Katerina suggested. "Peter, you know the wife. Go down to the cabin tomorrow and convince her that the only dignified thing to do is have him buried here. And no exhumation. Can you do that?"

"Yeah, I can do that. I think she trusts me."

"Yes, Anna relayed to us that she thinks of you as a friend," Konrad confirmed. "That was quite clever of you."

Peter nodded. He heard Cathy's uninhibited giggled echo through his mind. She had told him he had a right to his life. And he had taken her husband's. Again he was on that barren trail, the sun hot despite the chill air. Rocks below and a clear sky above. And Albert had not resisted. He had suspected nothing. Standing on the edge of a cliff, he had accepted a guiding arm thrown over his shoulder. *He had not resisted.* What if he was innocent?

"Peter?" Marysia said it as though it was not the first time.

Peter shook off his ruminations. "Is there something else?"

"I need to speak with you about Ryszard." Marysia suddenly stopped. She looked at Wanda, then back at Peter to say, "But that can wait until tomorrow. Could you drop by before you go down to see the wife?"

"Of course. May I go now?"

Marysia nodded, but Wanda snapped, "No!" She raised her gaze from the floor. "I wish to speak to my subordinate." She paused only slightly, then added, in a much lower tone, "Alone."

With a groan Katerina raised herself from her seat and motioning to Marysia and Konrad to follow, she headed to the door. Wanda had returned to staring at the floor, but once they had left she raised her head, uncrossed her arms so that she could clasp her hands behind her back, and theatrically approached Peter. "Orders, Captain. Once again, you've disobeyed orders."

Peter thought of Marysia's plea – *my hands are tied, but yours aren't* – but if Marysia had not confided in Wanda, then he did not dare either. "I did what I thought was best for us all."

"Best!" Wanda nearly screamed. She brought her face uncomfortably close to his.

Your sons, Peter thought and awaited the inevitable, confused denunciation.

She surprised him, though. "I've been outvoted on this and, unlike you, I will abide by my orders. Nevertheless, you are no longer on the Council, you are under my direct command, and you disobeyed your orders! I will not forget this."

"Colonel, I am sorry. I did not undertake this task lightly. I know you think little of me, but I am *not* a cold-blooded killer. It was a very difficult–"

"Shut-up!"

Her breath on his face made him uncomfortable and though he did not back away from her, he chose to look off to the side, at the files lining her wall.

"I can't take any action against you for what you have done, but you know, there will be those in the ASA with their suspicions. They won't be able to prove anything, but they'll get their revenge. I'm sure this man had friends, and even if they can't do anything officially, they can make our lives miserable. And they will. And believe me, Captain, I'll make sure you know about it, because I can make your life miserable, too. And I will."

Peter continued to stare at the files.

As if aware of how unprofessional her words sounded, Wanda pulled back slightly, making the distance between them more comfortable. "We released the Führer this morning, and one of the conditions he signed was that you could stay here, under our protection, without his taking revenge upon us or our people. That means, you stay *here*. No more outings. None. And that means, you can forget all your stupid little projects."

Peter directed his gaze back at Wanda. "I understand." That restriction would be easy enough to work around.

"You will be assigned back to the cryptanalysis office, to work under Jurek."

"Under?" Peter kept his voice deliberately low. "You know, he doesn't know anything."

"He knows how to follow orders, which you, obviously, do not!"

Peter nodded disinterestedly. Handling Jurek would not be a problem either.

"You will spend every minute of your workday going through each and every intercepted message and noting all information contained therein."

"Yes, Colonel."

"You will spend any remaining time updating and reorganizing our database."

"Fine." No more politics, just cool, rational analysis. Wanda's punishment was a welcome relief.

"I am not seeking your agreement, Captain. These are your orders."

"I understand, Colonel. Thank you for the information, Colonel."

Wanda's eyes narrowed as she weighed his tone and demeanor against his words.

"May I go now, Colonel?"

Wanda frowned. After a moment, she answered, "Yes, alright. But don't forget, I'm going to keep my eye on you."

"I look forward to it, Colonel."

24

"So?" Hania pulled her robe around herself and tied the belt. "How did it go?"

Unsure of what position Marysia would take with respect to the other Council members, Peter chose his words carefully, "The coroner's report makes it clear that it was an accident. Just like I said all along." He smiled at Hania so that later she might interpret what he had said as a jest.

Hania stepped back and motioned him into the room. "Will you be rejoining the Council?"

Peter walked over to where Madzia lay. "I don't think that's an option." He carefully lifted the child into his arms. "Thanks for watching her. I'm going to go home now and get some sleep."

"Good idea."

As Peter headed for the door, Hania suddenly stepped in front of him. "Peter…"

He looked down at her questioningly.

"You know, I haven't had a chance to talk to you since you got back. Not really, anyway." Hania stopped speaking and nervously fingered the knot on her belt. Peter waited patiently. The heavy breathing of Hania's husband as he slept on their folded out bed filled the silence.

"It's just that…" Hania dropped the knot and looked up at him. "I'm really sorry about what happened in that interview, you know, the one with the Council. We were so taken by surprise, we…" Again the knot seemed to need adjusting. Her fingers worked feverishly untying the knot and retying the belt tighter. With her head bowed over her work, she muttered, "We acted like idiots. I'm really sorry."

"It's okay."

Finally satisfied with her belt, Hania looked up and smiled slightly. "Will you rejoin the Council? I could use your support."

Peter shook his head. "I don't want to."

Hania pressed her lips together as she considered this response. From Peter's tone it was clear there was no point arguing and after a brief moment, she stepped to the side, allowing him to leave. "Good night."

By the time Peter had reached his apartment, Madzia had awoken. "I'm hungry," she announced, her eyes still half-closed. He decided she'd be more likely to sleep well if she had something to eat, so he warmed some boiled wheat, added honey and set that before her. She insisted on sitting on his lap to eat, so he held her and fed her, occasionally taking a spoonful for himself as well.

To Peter's dismay, instead of making Madzia sleepy, the warm cereal seemed to make her more awake. Madzia slipped off his lap and began tugging at his arm, insisting he play with her. Peter yawned. "I'm sleepy, *Mäuschen*, it's the middle of the night, I didn't get much sleep last night. Let's go to bed."

"Play horsie! Horsie!" Madzia insisted over and over, her voice rising almost to a screech.

Peter swept her into his arms and carried her into the bedroom. "No, tickle monster!" He flung her onto the bed and as she giggled and begged him to do it again, he tickled her. She squirmed and kicked and struggled to get away but he gently pulled her back, interspersing genuine tickling with monster-like noises and threats. When her whole body shook with laughter he stopped to let her rest.

She needed no rest. She launched herself at her father, yelling, "More, more!" and poking him mercilessly in an attempt at tickling. Peter indulged her for a few more minutes, sure that at last she would be tired. When it became clear that he was the only one who was tiring, he changed tactics and raising his hands in surrender, called out, "No more. Daddy needs to sleep. I'm really tired. Let's go to bed."

Madzia was having none of it. Peter tried negotiating, suggesting that if she rested for just five minutes, he would play some more. It took fifteen minutes of haggling, but finally Madzia agreed to pretend to sleep "for two minutes!" She held up two fingers to emphasize the number.

Peter numbly agreed. If only he got her to lie down and stay quiet for just a minute, he was sure she'd fall back asleep. He put her into the middle of the bed, and not daring to delay long enough to remove his clothes or turn off the light in the front room, he crawled in after her. He wrapped himself around her to quickly warm her and encourage her to sleep.

"Enough sleep?" Madzia squeaked after a few seconds.

"Not yet, *Mäuschen*. Pretend just a bit longer."

She grabbed his hand and brought it to her mouth so she could suck on his finger. He saw that as a hopeful sign and lay very still, not daring to move or otherwise disturb her. As he waited in the darkness, he heard the door of the flat opening and he wondered if he had fallen asleep and was dreaming. There were voices as well and he listened to them. One was Zosia's, the other belonged to a man. That was nice, Madzia must have fallen asleep and now I'm dreaming, he thought. It had to be a dream, Zosia wasn't due back until tomorrow. He let the voices rise and fall through his dream, but then he realized that it was tomorrow.

Peter opened his eyes but the voices had disappeared. Still, he was sure someone was in the flat. Carefully, so as not to wake her, he removed his finger from Madzia's mouth and slid from the bed. He walked silently to the doorway and stood there, somewhat confused, dazed by the brightness. When he finally blinked the scene into focus he could see Zosia and Tadek, their bodies wrapped around each other, kissing.

Zosia pulled back from Tadek. "We did a great job!" she announced and kissed him again. "And it's so good to be home!"

"We make–" Tadek began, but then he spied the shadowy figure in the doorway. *"Adam!"*

Zosia spun around, expecting to see a ghost. She was not disappointed and the color drained from her face. "Peter," she whispered. "Peter?"

If only they hadn't been kissing like that, it would be so much easier! Peter's overwhelming joy at seeing Zosia again was offset by his confusion at what he had just witnessed. Friends celebrating the successful end of a mission or a tender moment in a de facto marriage? Peter's eyes left Zosia's confused face and wandered over to the couch. There was a bundle there, and he guessed it was Irena, sound asleep under her blankets. He looked back at Zosia. "No one told you?"

Zosia shook her head slowly from side to side. "We came straight back here. We haven't seen anyone yet." She glanced at the light and added, "I wondered why that was on. I thought maybe a sentry had told Marysia or..." Her voice dropped off as she realized how strangely stilted their conversation was. As if suddenly aware that Tadek's arm was still draped over her, Zosia stepped forward, shrugging his hand off her shoulder as she did so. "That wasn't what it looked like..."

What did it look like? But Peter didn't ask. He smiled welcomingly and stepped forward, raising his arms in invitation. "I missed you."

As if waking from a trance, Zosia rushed forward and threw herself into Peter's embrace. "Oh, God, you're safe!" she sobbed. They hugged and held each other, Peter stroking her hair, whispering how much he loved her, how much he had missed her. Zosia buried her head in his chest, alternately sobbing and laughing, her tender words of undying loved interspersed with questions and explanations.

"Later," he whispered, in answer to all her questions. "Later."

Words became superfluous and they fell silent, their bodies pressed together, the warmth radiating directly from one to the other melting the months of loneliness and fear. Peter closed his eyes, pressing his face against Zosia's hair so he could smell her scent, feeling her heartbeat as it pulsed through her skin.

There was the slight noise of someone clearing his throat, and Peter opened his eyes to see Tadek still standing where Zosia had left him. He was studying the wall of the flat as if he had never seen it before. Peter had pity on him, and releasing his hold on Zosia slightly, said, "And welcome back to you as well, Tadek. Did the mission go well?"

Tadek drew his attention away from the wall. "Yes, fine." He started looking around the apartment as if trying to find something and muttered, "I should get going."

"Going?" Zosia released her hold on Peter and turned around to face Tadek. "Where are you going?"

Still scanning the room, Tadek shrugged. "I'll find somewhere. I just need a few things..." He seemed unable to find any of these things. He finally stopped looking and in response to Peter's questioning look, explained, "There's a family temporarily in my room."

Zosia looked from Tadek to Peter. "Tadek was staying here before we left on our assignment."

"I just need some clean clothes." Again Tadek scanned helplessly around the room.

Peter was amused by the charade, Tadek's clothes were exactly where Tadek and Zosia had left them. "They're in the bedroom, on the top shelf of the closet." He pointed helpfully toward the dark room. "But don't go in there now, I just got Madzia back to sleep. Why don't we sit down and have a drink first – toast our reunion?" He went to the cupboard and pulled out the vodka, but the bottle was inexplicably nearly empty. "That's odd," he muttered, putting it back and digging deeper. He found some whiskey and used that to pour three drinks.

They sat at the kitchen table and drank a toast to Peter's safe return, then another to Zosia and Tadek's. "Now," Peter said, as they raised their glasses a third time, "rather than a toast, a suggestion."

Tadek raised his eyebrows questioningly.

"Why don't you stay here the night. Or rather, until your room is free again?" Peter waved at the couch. "We have plenty of space."

Tadek turned slowly in his seat to look at the couch Peter had indicated. Zosia took the opportunity to move her eyes theatrically toward the door.

"It folds down and is very comfortable." Peter hesitated only slightly before adding, "As I'm sure you know."

"Of course, of course," Tadek agreed all too readily.

Zosia widened her eyes in a desperate bid to get Peter to rescind his invitation. *"Our privacy!"* she mouthed.

Peter ignored her. If Zosia had seen to Tadek's comfort to the extent that his clothes were stored in the bedroom, it was the least he could do to welcome her friend into their living room.

"I don't think I should." Tadek nodded his head toward Zosia. "You two need to be alone."

"Nonsense!" Peter laughed, echoing the word Zosia once had commanded him to say. "Heaven forbid that my return should make you homeless. Stay here!"

"Peter," Zosia intoned softly.

"And besides," Peter interrupted whatever Zosia was planning to say. "If it were known that you moved out the minute I came back, well, don't you think it would look like Zosia was trading husbands?" Peter picked up his drink and sloshed the liquid around a bit. "Why feed rumors that aren't true?"

Deciding it would be embarrassing to make Tadek pretend that he knew how to unfold the couch, Peter did it for him. His desire to be hospitable was genuine. Tadek had come through for him numerous times: helping to ferry Madzia out of Berlin, rescuing him when he was imprisoned in the hospital, welcoming him onto the Council. Yet, during Peter's absence, Tadek had not only moved into Peter's apartment but, apparently, his bed as well. *I should feel threatened,* Peter thought. *Or angry.* But he didn't feel either.

He paused in his efforts long enough to look at the two of them. Zosia was wrapped up in tending Irena, Tadek sat uneasily at the kitchen table, finishing his drink. Peter wondered at his own lack of emotion. He remembered how hurt he had been back in January, when he had returned from London and Zosia had invited Tadek for dinner the first evening that they could spend alone together in months. Then, he had been overwhelmed by jealousy and fear. Now, he welcomed the same man into his home.

His friendliness toward Tadek was, Peter supposed, not only sincere, but a reasonable strategy. Why, after all, should *he* play the role of monster? Why should *he* be the one to cast a comrade and friend out of the house? If Zosia found the crowding in the apartment and the lack of privacy annoying, let *her* show Tadek the door. And if Zosia found something in Tadek's company which Peter could not provide, then why should he deny her that? He might even, eventually, lose her to him. At one time that thought would have terrified him, but it no longer did.

Perhaps he was just more confident than before. Not only that Zosia would prefer him to Tadek, but also that his life, even without Zosia, was worth something. Though he still loved her, he no longer needed her to need him. So he could relax, and as a result, he could be a much more pleasant partner. Let her have her doubts and play her games, it just wasn't that important to him anymore.

Peter finished making the bed and with a wave of his hand, presented it to Tadek. "Voila! Now, if you'll excuse me, I'm going to bed – I'm absolutely exhausted."

Tadek stood and shook Peter's hand. "Good night. And thanks."

"Peter." Zosia motioned him back to the chair where she was sitting, nursing Irena.

He walked over to her and kissed her forehead. "Good night, love."

"Please wait."

Peter stroked Irena's hair. "I'll wait for you in bed."

"You'll be asleep."

Peter yawned. "I'm sorry. I didn't get much sleep last night. And today...Oh, I'll tell you about that later." He bent down and kissed Zosia, straightened and turned to go into the bedroom.

"I have some news."

"What?"

Zosia glanced at Tadek as if hinting he should leave. He folded his arms and returned her look with one of irritation. "It's not like I don't know."

Zosia sighed. "Alright." She smiled up at Peter. "I'm pregnant."

"Pregnant?" Peter pointed at Irena as she hungrily slurped at Zosia's breast. "I thought that was supposed to prevent–" He stopped as he realized how stupid that sounded. "Pregnant?" He looked at Tadek.

Tadek shook his head vigorously in answer to the implied question.

"Yes, pregnant." Zosia giggled. "You should see your face." As Peter turned his attention back to her, she added, "Though I must admit, I was surprised as well."

"How? When?" Peter only just stopped himself from asking, who?

Zosia bent her head down to look at Irena. She stroked the baby's downy hair as she answered, "Don't you remember? The day you were arrested. Before you went to see Konstantin. I was so happy we were finally together, I didn't think about..."

A smile played across his lips as he remembered. How could he forget? He had replayed that afternoon in his mind every day for the months that followed. And now there would be a child to commemorate their love-making. How very wonderful! The smile turned into a grin and Peter stooped down at Zosia's side so he could hug her. As he held her and kissed her and congratulated her, he felt the chains wrapping themselves around his heart yet again. Once again, she had captured him. Once again his soul was alive.

25

"*G*ünter told me that Halifax tried to kill him," the Führer mentioned, almost casually.

"Oh? I must have missed that." Since the Führer was still standing, Richard remained on his feet as well. He paced over to one of the ornate windows that looked out from the Führer's private rooms onto a garden below. The view, though, was obscured by the heavy mist which had hung over the city since the morning. November, grim and gray. November first. Wasn't that All Saints' Day?

"He said you did nothing to help him."

"Me?" Richard turned from the window to face the Führer. So this was what was on Rudi's mind? Affairs of state be damned – there was politicking to do. Rudi only felt safe if his subordinates were at each other's throats.

"Yes, you. He said you just stood there as that *Untermensch* attacked him."

Richard laughed. "Oh, that." He turned back to look out the window some more. *You're welcome*, he thought sarcastically. On top of his irritation at the Führer's complete lack of gratitude, Richard could not remove the image of Andrzej's grave from his mind. Beneath the dirt lay his son's body, and here, in the very same room with him, was the man ultimately responsible for Andrzej's death.

"How come Halifax didn't attack you?" The Führer joined Richard at the window and stared out at the fog with him.

"I didn't try to hit him."

"Huh?"

"Günter started swinging at him the moment Halifax entered the tent. Halifax reacted and dropped him to the floor." Richard snorted his amusement. "So much for Günter's vaunted military training."

"How come you always stare out the window, Richard?"

Richard snapped his head around to look at the Führer. "I'm sorry, *mein Führer*. I intend no disrespect."

The Führer saved Richard from deciding if he needed to cast his eyes downward, by turning suddenly and pacing away. He stopped in the middle of the room, his back still toward Richard. He clasped his hands behind his back, and maintaining a pensive tone, asked, "Richard, did you know Halifax before he helped you with your American interviews?"

"I told you. He served at the Vogels and I was there for dinner. I saw him then."

"I said, Richard, did you *know* him?"

Though the Führer's back was to him, Richard shook his head. "No."

"Then why, Richard, did you save his life?"

The repetition of his name worried Richard. "*Mein Führer*, I've explained that. The plot–"

"No, Richard, that's not what I mean. I mean, why did you save his life the *first* time?"

"The first time?"

The Führer turned around to face Richard. He smiled in a manner that caused Richard to shudder. "The first time, Richard. Back when he was in re-education."

Richard allowed his face to betray complete confusion. "Did I save him?"

"Yes, Lederman told me. You were on an inspection tour and he showed you an English prisoner. He said that he knew the prisoner was not ready to be released, but you insisted that he was. He even noted what you said."

"And what was that?" Though his instinct was to glance at the guards in the room to see if they were preparing to move in on him, Richard was careful to keep his full attention on the Führer.

"That the prisoner should be placed with someone important."

Richard reached into his pocket to pull out his cigarettes. He approached the Führer to offer him one. "Well, if it's in Lederman's notes, then it must be true. He was always a very precise officer."

The Führer accepted Richard's cigarette and leaned in slightly as Richard lit it for him. "So you don't deny it?"

Richard pulled out a cigarette for himself. "I haven't a clue. That must have been years ago."

"Why did you do it?"

Richard lit his own cigarette. "Can't say. If you give me the date, I'll consult my diary and see if I made a note about it."

The Führer nodded but did not then order any of his men to seek out the date. Richard wondered if the incident was going to be forgotten, or if it was being saved for later use.

"Tell me, Richard, what happened to Büttner?"

"I was told he committed suicide."

"But you don't know."

"I wasn't there. I was under house arrest."

"Yes, Günter seemed to think you were involved in Büttner's plot." The Führer smoked for a moment in a manner that indicated Richard should

401

remain silent. Eventually, as if emerging from deep thought, the Führer added, "I'm glad you two sorted that out. I don't like to see my lieutenants bickering."

Bickering. Like children. Richard bowed his head slightly in acknowledgment of the Führer's wisdom.

"Do you think…" The Führer drew out the words, indicating how high a compliment he was paying his subordinate. "Hmm. Do you think Büttner was planning to betray me?"

"The evidence would seem to indicate that. I have reason to believe that he was behind my arrest." Realizing how ambiguous that was, Richard added, "Back in July, I mean."

The Führer nodded. "And his daughter was engaged to Günter's son. Isn't that right?"

"Yes, *mein Führer*."

"But Günter told me that he grew suspicious and called off the engagement some months ago."

Richard studied how the end of his cigarette glowed. "Yes, I've heard that Wolf-Dietrich–"

"Who?"

"Günter's son."

"Oh. What about him?"

"He's supposed to get engaged to Ulrike Vogel."

"Elspeth Vogel's daughter?"

"Yes, *mein Führer*."

"Hmm. That's a powerful family. Despite her poor choice of husband, may he rest in peace." The Führer sucked on his cigarette and blew a stream of smoke into the air. He watched the smoke swirl toward the ceiling and again it was clear he was thinking and Richard should not interrupt. When he brought his gaze back to Richard's face, it was not particularly reassuring. "Your son is also involved with the Vogel family. Or so I'm told."

"Yes, I believe Paul has developed a friendship with one of the daughters. Teresa is her name."

"Do you approve?" The Führer smiled slyly at Richard.

Richard shrugged. "He's too young, I think."

"How old is your boy?"

"Paul? He's just turned eighteen."

"And how is your other child?"

Which other child, Richard wanted to ask, but he wisely refrained. "Stefi? She's recuperating."

"Bad business with that miscarriage. She must have been terribly upset by what happened to me."

Richard sighed. "Yes, *mein Führer*. Devastated."

"Have her visit me."

Richard lowered his head in a gesture of submissive regret. "As soon as she has recuperated, *mein Führer*. She's still in a terrible state." He restrained himself from adding, *and you're the last person she wants to see*. It probably wasn't true anyway – besides Günter, Stefi's anger was directed at her father. He couldn't seem to get through to her what would happen if the Führer found out about the forced abortion. Schindler would be immediately arrested, and with Büttner's suicide, that would leave Traugutt as the only obvious successor, a dangerously powerful subordinate. And Rudi was not stupid enough to allow such a situation to last for long.

"A terrible state…" The Führer placed a hand warmly on Richard's shoulder. "Your grandchild, Richard, but my son." He waited until Richard looked at him appreciatively, before adding. "This is hard on all of us and I want to see her."

"Of course, *mein Führer*. I'll relay your concern."

Satisfied, the Führer paced away and ground out his cigarette in an ashtray. "You and Günter seem to be working together quite well, recently."

Richard took a drag from his cigarette before answering. How much longer would he be forced to dance to Rudi's suspicions? "Yes, *mein Führer*. We are united in our loyalty to you." Deciding to prove his point, he added, "As can be seen by how we worked together to rescue you."

"Rescue?"

"I mean, *mein Führer*–"

"The Führer is the natural born ruler, Richard. The Führer does not need rescuing."

"Of course, *mein Führer*. I misspoke. Forgive me."

The Führer walked back up to Richard and stood far too close. Richard lowered his head again, waiting for the Führer's words. Would they be "arrest him?"

I should have had him killed, Richard thought, angry with himself. *I should have taken the risk. Remove Günter, remove Rudi and declare myself Führer. I had the perfect opportunity and I let it go. It probably would have worked.* But he knew that wasn't true. The others, individually weak, would have united long enough to defeat him before breaking back into squabbling factions, fighting over the throne to the Reich.

Again, the Führer placed his hand on Richard's shoulder. "Forgiven."

"Thank you, *mein Führer*." Richard's anger was overpowering, and he could not suppress a quaver in his voice, but he was safe, for the Führer naturally recognized it as awe. After a moment, he dared to add, "Is that all, *mein Führer*?"

403

The Führer glanced at him sharply. The hand slid from Richard's shoulder. "Are you in a hurry to leave?"

"No, *mein Führer*, it is always a pleasure to be in your presence." Richard took a step to the side so that he could grind out his cigarette. The slight distance it put between him and Rudi was an absolute relief and he was able to moderate his voice much better. "Unfortunately, there is much business which has not been handled properly over the past week and I have much work to do."

"You and Günter both." The Führer walked over to one of the armchairs and sat down. He motioned for Richard to join him, but did not indicate that he should sit. Richard stood uneasily awaiting the Führer's command, and at long last he did speak. "I've decided that my divisional heads should spend more time in their sections. Don't you think that's wise?"

"Yes, *mein Führer*."

"Günter will be heading to London for a long stay. I expect you'll be in Göringstadt."

"As you wish, *mein Führer*."

The Führer waited a moment, eyeing Richard, waiting to see if he would ask. As Richard remained silent, he volunteered, "I need some new blood in this office giving me advice. Seppel Frauenfeld will be taking over your job as personal advisor on internal security. Only temporarily, of course." With those words, the Führer watched Richard avidly, awaiting his reaction.

Richard smiled and nodded his head in acknowledgment of the Führer's wisdom. "It's a good choice, *mein Führer*." It was a good choice. Josef Frauenfeld was an intelligent and, given his high position, a surprisingly humane man. He also had limited ambitions and was truly loyal to the Reich and whoever led it. Rudi could sleep easily with such a man in his office.

"And I'll hand off Günter's duties here to Lederman."

"*Heinrich* Lederman?" Richard only barely managed to mask his horror.

"Yes, I know he's quite young, but he's very perceptive. I had some very interesting discussions with him, while you were away."

Richard nodded numbly as the Führer told him about his talks with Lederman. Heinrich Lederman. Lederman, the torturer. Lederman, the true believer. Not quite the boss, that was true, but in a position where he could influence the Führer directly. Combining the Führer's power with Lederman's sadistic beliefs, Richard could foresee a rough time ahead for the downtrodden of the Reich. He nonetheless recognized the cleverness of Rudi's move. Neither he nor Günter had been demoted, they were simply being shuffled off to the side, to cool their heels for awhile, far enough away that they would have difficulty keeping their support in Berlin but not cast so low that they would openly revolt. Meanwhile a loyal son of the Reich would handle advising the Führer, while Lederman provided the necessary counterpoint – an ideological purist on whom any future mistakes could be blamed.

If he held the Führer's ear, Lederman was likely to destroy all Richard's attempts at restructuring and he would cause thousands of people untold misery. Richard weighed the expected suffering against the likelihood that any word against Lederman would have an effect, and as the Führer finished speaking, he heard himself say, "Yes, he's also a good choice. From a good family, I've heard. A very cultured young man."

"Good, good. I'm glad you approve, Richard. You don't know how much I value your opinion."

They should have hanged you. Richard smiled, "Thank you, *mein Führer*."

"Now, I'll expect you'll need to start packing up your household."

Richard shook his head. "If it pleases, *mein Führer*, I'll be heading to Göringstadt without my family. I'll be separating from my wife and would like to divorce her."

"Divorce? But she's such a wonderful woman!"

"Yes, *mein Führer*. I don't deserve her. Beyond that, her life is here, in Berlin. I would like to ask your approval of the divorce."

"Richard, you are a free man and you are free to divorce according to the law."

"Yes, *mein Führer*. But I am also your loyal subject and do not wish to go against your wishes in any way. Not even in my personal life."

The Führer smiled his approval. "You know, it goes against our values to break up good German families."

"My wife is Polish."

"*Volksdeutsch*, Richard. She has German blood. And her family has worked undercover so loyally for you all these years!"

"Yes, *mein Führer*. Unfortunately, though, that means we are unable to interact socially with her family. They must maintain a show of enmity toward us at all times. And vice versa. It has been a strain on us all these years and I would like to end it. I wish to marry a German woman who is proud of her blood and whose family I can interact with in a normal manner."

"Who?"

Richard hesitated. Should he admit he already had a wife lined up? Well, it would be obvious soon enough. "Greta Schindler."

"Günter's wife?"

"Yes, his *third* wife. They plan to divorce." That had been the easy part. Günter was more than happy to grant his wife a divorce in exchange for Richard keeping Stefi's abortion a secret.

The Führer rubbed his chin thoughtfully. "With Günter and Greta, I see no problem. There are no children, it's obviously a mismatch. But you, Richard, how many children has your wife borne for you?"

"Six, *mein Führer.*"

"Don't you think she deserves your loyalty?"

"Yes, *mein Führer*. But she wants this divorce. In fact, it was her idea. I have simply conceded to its wisdom."

The Führer looked thoughtful, somewhat like a wise uncle. "Your wife wants to divorce you. Hmm. Well, I guess if you are both agreed and, well, there is that blood issue. I must admit, you made a mistake marrying her in the first place. Someone with your background – you should have never…Well, never mind, there's no accounting for young love."

"So you'll approve the paperwork?"

"I don't know, Richard. There's always mutterings among the common folk that the rules are different for the ruling élite. You know, we should set them a good example."

"This is something my wife truly wants, *mein Führer.*"

"Will she be properly supported?"

"Of course, *mein Führer*. I will not leave my children in poverty."

"Good, good. That's important. We must never forget our duty to uphold German society. The German family is sacred…"

Richard looked entranced as he listened to the Führer wax poetic about the Germanic folk. He waited patiently throughout the exposition, varying his expression from agreement to admiration at the Führer's unique wisdom. When the Führer reached a natural break in his lecture – and it was after only twenty minutes, Richard smiled adoringly. "*Mein Führer*, you have such insights! I never thought of things quite that way."

"But you are young, Richard. You have much to learn. Much to learn."

"Yes, and I will miss being in Berlin, where I can study at your feet."

The Führer sighed. For a moment it seemed possible he would rescind his order. He studied his subordinate, smiled fondly. "Ah, I will miss your insights as well. But duty calls. Both you and Günter have spent far too much time in Berlin – one would think you two were running the Reich rather than your own regions. It will be good for you to get back in touch with your duties."

"Yes, *mein Führer*." Richard waited, but there was no indication that the Führer had anything more to say. Rudi slumped back in his seat, exhausted by his efforts, apparently forgetting Richard's presence. It would have been the natural point for Stefi to take over and Richard missed her help. He felt awkward standing there, but his last attempt at leaving had provoked such a virulent response, that he did not dare try again.

Rudi's eyes began to close and in panic, Richard found his voice. "You carry the cares of the world on your shoulders, *mein Führer.*"

The Führer opened his eyes. "You're still here? Leave already, I'm tired."

Richard snapped his heels and bowed slightly, "As you wish, *mein Führer.*"

26

"*L*et's see your papers, boy."

Leszek stopped dead in his tracks and reached into his jacket to pull out the tatty bundle which contained his papers. Just how many times had he walked this particular path? Didn't the idiots know him yet? The patrolman approached and Leszek risked a quick glance at his face. It was somebody new, somebody who didn't know the local servant population yet.

Leszek kept his head and his eyes down, watching the finely gloved hands page through his documents. Gloves, now there was an idea! The cold damp mist made his fingers ache – what a great idea gloves would be! Indeed, when he had started working for Frau Traugutt, she had immediately noted the problem and bought him an acceptable pair of gloves. Still, though there was no explicit law against his wearing such things, it was clearly not the convention and the Colonel had ordered Leszek not to wear them when he was out in public.

"Let me see your face."

Leszek looked up at the patrolman. A young lad. They were almost always young, either that or old enough to be a grandfather. The old ones were alright, they were just marking time until retirement, but the young ones – well, they were different. Almost always from poorer families – those with better blood did their apprenticeships in offices – this was the first time they had been handed any authority. Their ears freshly filled with ideology, their eyes trained upon a brilliant future, this was the first time they were giving orders, rather than taking them, and they reveled in their new-found power.

As the lad compared the photograph on Leszek's document with his face, Leszek studied him in turn. The patrolman's hair was straight and brown and cut short. He had wide brown eyes and pale skin that blotched red with the cold. His features were far from mature, and in compensation, he scowled fiercely.

"What are you looking at?" the boy snapped suddenly.

A little pig eager to get its nose in the trough. But Leszek only thought that. The new ones were the most dangerous and if he felt insulted, the boy could do a lot of damage before the Colonel would be able to intervene. *If he intervened*, Leszek thought bitterly. Keeping his head up as had been ordered, Leszek lowered his eyes. With an effort, he managed to murmur, "Nothing, *mein Herr*. Sorry, *mein Herr*."

"The stamp on your pass is out of date."

"Is it, *mein Herr?*" Leszek recognized the mistake in that and immediately amended, "I'm sorry, *mein Herr*. There have been unusual events in the past week, *mein Herr*, and our routine has been disrupted. I'll remind Frau Traugutt as soon as I return to the house and I'm sure she'll see to updating it immediately."

The name meant nothing to the boy – he was clearly fresh from the country. "Come with me."

"*Mein Herr*, I don't think that it is wise–"

"Silence!"

Leszek sighed and fell into step behind the patrolman. Fortunately, the boy was also quite earnest and led Leszek not toward some private corner where justice could be summarily executed, but toward a local guard post. The lad tapped on the copper-colored glass and an unseen presence slid part of the window open. The elderly man who sat inside furrowed his brow in confusion. "You're new, aren't you? Where's your partner?"

"He's out sick."

The old man frowned at the lack of respect in the boy's answer. "So they send a pup like you out alone. What have you got there?" He tilted his head to get a better view. He recognized Leszek immediately. "Oh, God in heaven! That's Traugutt's boy."

"Yes. His stamp is out of date." The boy shoved the papers at the older guard, trying to show him the relevant section.

The old man ignored the papers. "You're an idiot."

Outraged, the boy pulled himself to his full height. "Your conduct is unprofessional."

The older man looked as if he was going to say something to that, but then glancing at Leszek, changed his mind. "Comrade, this servant is well known to me. He works for Colonel Traugutt – whose name may be unknown to you, but believe me, he is one of our most upstanding and important citizens. Colonel Traugutt is a very busy man and I am sure it was just an oversight that caused his servant's stamp to be out of date. If I were you, I'd release him now with a warning."

The boy hesitated.

"And I'd be sure not to make a similar mistake in the future. Colonel Traugutt does not take kindly to unnecessary disturbances."

The young patrolman sheepishly handed the papers back to Leszek. "You may go." His voice had become very soft. "And make sure your papers are in order next time."

Leszek simply turned and walked away, not even giving the boy the satisfaction of a submissive nod. He heard the older patrolman talking to the boy, but his voice was too low for Leszek to discern the words. A few streets away Leszek was finally able to stop gritting his teeth. He felt nauseous. God, what he would give to have a gun! To be in the mountains shooting at the bastards rather than this, this…Words failed him.

By the time Leszek reached the house, his nausea had abated, leaving only a miserable headache. Lodzia gave him a cup of tea and set about unpacking the bags as he stood in the kitchen drinking it. He looked over the edge of the cup at his wife, breathing in the steam, hoping to clear his head. "We've got to get out of this assignment."

Lodzia set down the bag of flour and walked over to her husband. She kissed him on the cheek, "Rough day?"

Leszek sighed heavily. "Neither dead nor alive, Lodzia. That's us, neither dead nor alive."

"What do you mean?"

"We just exist, waiting for something to happen. We're helpless. We can't influence events, we can't fight, we can't even live our own lives! I'm twenty-four, in the prime of my life, and what am I doing? Nothing. Absolutely nothing. My God, don't you realize, this could go on for years!"

Lodzia kissed him again. "We're doing our part. HQ appreciates our work and we'll be moved out of here soon."

Leszek shook his head. "They'll never move us. We're trapped. We'll be stuck here until the Colonel gets us all killed. And all we can do is wait."

Lodzia frowned. "Do you really think he'll take us down with him if he's arrested?"

"I suppose it depends on the manner of his fall. If he goes down without breaking cover, they'll probably leave his wife and family alone. In that case, we should be okay. Nobody would be surprised if Frau Traugutt moves out of Berlin, and after a while, we could just disappear from the public eye. Move abroad, or a tragic boating accident, or something." Leszek stroked his wife's face. "That's the only way we'd ever be free."

"Is that what you want?" Ryszard leaned in the doorway, his arms crossed, his face a mask.

"Colonel, I didn't hear you come in."

409

"Obviously." Ryszard smirked. "Pack your bags, Leszek, I've been ordered back to Göringstadt."

"My bags? What about–"

"And mine, of course."

"Colonel, does that mean you intend to leave your family here?" Lodzia asked worriedly.

"I don't intend to make my move out of Berlin permanent," Ryszard snapped. "Kasia and Olek and Stefi will remain here to make sure that is clear. And you, Lodzia, are needed here to help with the children and the house."

"I should stay as well," Leszek interjected hurriedly. "The house is large and the family – your family is important. You should have two servants here."

The look Ryszard gave Leszek caused him to almost cringe. "A man in my position without a servant?"

"HQ should assign someone else to you. Explain–"

"HQ is not being particularly cooperative of late." Ryszard tilted his head bemusedly. "It seems someone has been feeding them stories about me. So, I'm afraid, dear boy, *you* are my only option."

"Colonel–"

"It's an order." Ryszard left Lodzia and Leszek to their chores and returned to the living room.

Kasia was sitting on the couch. She looked up expectantly as he came in. "Did you tell Leszek?"

Ryszard nodded. "Stefan's leaving for Göringstadt tomorrow so he can locate housing for me. I've told him that I want nothing longer than a three-month lease."

"Renewable?"

"Of course. I have no idea how long it will take for Rudi to calm down. There's some Party-owned furnished flats in the inner district, I imagine Stefan will find something for me there." Ryszard walked over to the window and stared out at the neat suburban street. "I guess I should tell him to find himself a room as well."

"So you're only taking Stefan? What about the rest of your staff?"

"I'll take Feliks as well. Dorota can stay here to protect my family. My lifestyle is simple enough I should be able to get away with just one bodyguard. I'll be provided with plenty of security at official functions. As for the rest, I don't need anyone else. There's staff on the ground in Göringstadt. As usual, a complete duplication of bureaucracy. Olek will stay here, so he can influence things."

"And so Stefi will stay as well?"

"Naturally."

"Ryszard…"

Ryszard took his attention off the street only long enough to give Kasia a warning glance. "I don't want to hear it, Kasia. She's deep into enemy territory, she can't just turn her back on the conflict now. I need her."

"What about your flat in town?"

He fingered the drapes as he answered. "The lease is expiring soon. Whatever Leszek doesn't pack, I'll store here. When I come back, Greta and I will rent something in town. Or, if it's gone that far, I can move into her house."

The silence lasted long enough that Ryszard finally turned around. "Oh, Kasia, don't cry, for heaven's sakes!"

"So you're really going through with it?"

"Of course! Do you realize that if I had been married to Greta, I could have seized power during this latest crisis? The only reason I have to jump to that lunatic's commands is because…"

"Because you're married to me?"

"Because I don't have enough weapons. Greta will add to my arsenal, Kasia. It's just strategy, that's all."

He walked over to her and sat down on the couch, twisting so he could face her. He grabbed both her hands in his. They felt so cold! "*Kochana Kasiu*, please don't make this harder than it is. I can't fight this battle alone. Everyone is abandoning me. Stefi won't see the Führer, Leszek is plotting my demise…I need you!"

Kasia pulled a hand free so that she could dab at her eyes. "I'm trying, Ryszard. I really am. But I just feel that with Greta it's more than strategy. You're just using that as an excuse. There's something about her that excites you."

Ryszard stood, brusquely releasing Kasia's hand. "Oh, to hell with you." He walked back over to the window and stared at the street. "Why don't you just grab a knife and stab me in the back like everyone else?"

"Ryszard, we're not against you. Leszek isn't plotting anything. Stefi's just hurt…" Kasia's voice trailed off as she neglected to mention herself. She finally found enough courage to add, "It's just that you don't make it easy for us."

Ryszard spun around to face her, he was livid. "So giving more than twenty four years of my life to this charade isn't enough?" He gestured angrily around the room. "Now I have to make it easy for you all! Who the hell makes it easy for me? Tell me that!" He stopped suddenly. He was so angry he was shuddering. He turned his attention back out the window and repeated softly, "Tell me that."

Kasia wet her lips, but she could not bring herself to say anything.

"What the hell?" Ryszard tilted his head to look further down the street.

411

"What is it?"

Ryszard did not answer. He continued to stare into the street. "Shit!" Kasia rose in alarm. "Ryszard, what is it?"

Ryszard strode away from the window, grabbed Kasia's shoulders, "Tell Stefi to jump into bed. She's ill. Have Olek sit with her. Get Lodzia to warn the children and go through the house making sure there's nothing suspicious around. Jan and Pawel can watch the young ones, keep them out of the way. Leszek will answer the door, you read a book, here. I'll be in my study."

"Ryszard, what is it?"

"The Führer."

Leszek was appropriately awestruck as he opened the door, and it was no act. The way a small army of guards were stationed outside the house, the way the Führer's men swept into the house and inspected it, the way they were each carefully frisked, the way all the weapons in the house were locked in a room for the duration, it was enough to terrify even a law-abiding citizen. The only small pleasure Leszek found in it all was watching Traugutt's face as he surrendered his gun and submitted to being frisked in his own home. There wasn't a trace of emotion, and anyone who did not know him better would have said that he was not at all bothered by the search, but Leszek did know better and he knew the Colonel was seething at the humiliation.

When they were all cleared, the Führer emerged from his limousine and entered the house, greeting his hosts with smiles and modest apologies at his intrusion. As Leszek took his coat and Lodzia was sent to the kitchen to make up a tray to serve to their esteemed guest, the Traugutts fell over themselves welcoming their beloved Führer and explaining that he was welcome at any time – *any time* – into their humble home.

"It *is* rather humble." The Führer looked around curiously. "Not at all what I expected."

Kasia bit her lip, unsure what to say. To explain that they had no old money to rely on, would imply that the Führer's fortune was undeserved. To say that Traugutt lived modestly, solely off his legitimate salary, would not do at all.

"*Mein Führer*," Richard gushed, "I am but a tiny part in the vast workings of our great State. I am pleased that I have been granted this much – it is far more than my worth."

"Oh Richard, don't underestimate your wealth." The Führer smiled at Frau Traugutt as he spoke. "To have two beautiful women in one household is more riches than most men could dream of."

Leszek cast a meaningful glance back toward the kitchen, but he imagined that Lodzia had not even been entered into the count of women in the household, much less among those who might be considered beautiful. When he looked back at the little group in the hallway, the Colonel caught his eye and with only the slightest movement managed to convey his absolute fury at such recklessness. Leszek was still shuddering in reaction even as Richard was smiling and enjoining the Führer to come into their sitting room.

Leszek offered cigarettes but as the Führer refused, no one smoked. Richard suggested sherry and the Führer accepted. Leszek poured that, was sent to fetch a good bottle of wine from the cellar, decanted the fine red, and then took up a position by the door, where he could wait on any further needs of his masters. Lodzia entered with a small tray of food, offered it around, then immediately returned to the kitchen to prepare something more substantive. Unobserved and unimportant in his corner, Leszek watched the drama unfold.

"Frau Traugutt, do sit down." The Führer was already relaxed in an armchair and he gestured toward the couch.

"*Mein Führer*! I am so enthralled by your visit, I'm afraid I'm just…" Kasia gestured helplessly. "I'm just too excited!" She cast her eyes downward, blushing becomingly, and added, "And perhaps you've come to talk with Richard. I don't want to burden you with a woman's unwelcome presence."

"Nonsense, Frau Traugutt, you are always welcome in my presence. Indeed, I came to talk with you, not your husband."

"*Me?*"

The Führer did not take offense at Kasia's poorly concealed fear. He knew how powerful and overwhelming his sheer presence was, especially for the weaker sex, and he smiled kindly in response. "Do not fear, my dear lady, I only wanted to talk to you directly about this divorce idea."

Kasia's eyes widened and she looked to her husband for help. As the Führer had not yet invited him to sit, Richard stood casually to one side, his hands clasped loosely behind his back. "I explained to the–"

The Führer silenced Richard with a brusque gesture. "I am talking with your wife!"

Richard immediately fell silent, submissively ducking his head as a sign of remorse at his presumptuousness.

Kasia looked from Richard to the Führer and smiled uneasily. "What would you like to know?"

"Simply, why? It pains me to see good German families broken up." The Führer diplomatically avoided mentioning Kasia's mixed blood. "If it's

413

inevitable, well…But I think you and Richard make a wonderful couple and I'd like to know that this is truly necessary."

Kasia took a deep breath, gathering clues from the Führer's question. She glanced again at Richard, but he remained obediently silent. "I think," she began hesitantly. "I think it is for the best."

"But why?"

Kasia wondered if she was supposed to enumerate Richard's reasons, but conversation with him had been so strained of late, she was not even sure what they were supposed to be. Finally, in desperation, she said, "I don't want to stand in the way."

"In the way? In the way of what?"

Kasia cast her eyes downward. The Führer rose and walked over to her. He placed a hand under her chin and gently raised it. "Dear, dear Frau Traugutt. I am so sorry to embarrass you like this, but you can tell me. Trust me. Like an uncle."

"I think, *mein Führer*," Kasia stammered, "I believe there is another woman."

"So *he* wants the divorce. Not you."

Kasia simply did not react to the assertion and the Führer turned away from her and walked over to Richard. He stopped in front of Richard and surveyed him menacingly. "You haven't lied to me, have you?"

"*Mein Führer–*"

The Führer raised a warning finger. "No lies, Richard. I don't like lies."

"*Mein Führer*," Richard implored, "I would never deceive you. I *could* not deceive you. You are far too wise and I am loyal to you with my entire being."

Placated the Führer lowered his finger and waited expectantly.

"I told you that my wife wanted a divorce. I myself was unsure of the reasons why. Now, with just a few words, you have managed to clarify a situation which has mystified me. Once again, your wisdom and insight overwhelm me."

The Führer smiled and turned back to Kasia. "Frau Traugutt, did you hear that? It's all just a misunderstanding. Richard thought *you* wanted the divorce! Shall we call this whole thing off?"

Kasia looked at her husband. Since the Führer's back was to him, Richard allowed his guard to drop for just a second, and Kasia read the plea in his expression. She licked her lips, her expression pained. Then she vigorously shook her head. "No, *mein Führer*. My husband has betrayed me and I do not want him in my house anymore. Please grant us the right to a quick divorce."

"So you *do* want the divorce?"

"Yes, *mein Führer*," Kasia answered decisively. "There is nothing that man could say or do to make me want to take him back. I thought it was unseemly for a woman to feel this way toward her husband, and I wanted to hide this from you and lay the blame at Richard's feet for this decision, but it is mine. Please, he has humiliated me with this woman. Please, grant me the dignity of a quick and quiet divorce."

The Führer raised his eyebrows and pursed his lips. He turned toward Richard, still maintaining his almost comical expression. "The lady seems adamant, Richard, I'm afraid I have no choice but to grant her this one small favor." He turned back to Kasia and smiled. "I'll personally see that the paperwork is expedited."

"Thank you, *mein Führer*," Kasia breathed.

"Now that we've cleared up that little problem, I'd like to visit your daughter. Is she at home?"

"Yes, she's resting upstairs. She's being tended to by..."

Lodzia entered the room with another tray of food and as she set the tray down, Richard ordered, "Lodzia, show the Führer to Stefi's room."

Lodzia nodded her head and walked to the door. The Führer followed, but then turned back to Kasia. "By?"

"By her husband."

The Führer winked as he headed into the hallway. "I'll be tactful."

They remained frozen in their respective places long after the Führer had left the room. Although, for the moment, they were alone in the living room, no one dared move. Eventually Leszek overcame his stupor and walked over to the Colonel and taking his arm, gently pulled him toward a chair. "Come on, *mein Herr*. I think you need to sit down."

Richard did not resist. Leszek picked up Richard's untouched sherry and placed that on the table next to him, then he lit a cigarette and handed it to him. Richard accepted the cigarette, but he did not smoke it. He stared into the distance, unmoving and silent.

Kasia came over to her husband and touched his cheek. Richard closed his eyes. "Thank you," he whispered. It was unclear whether he was thanking her for her inspired performance or just for her gesture.

Leszek was not surprised that he took no joy in the Colonel's humiliation – the situation had been far too deadly for any possibility of *Schadenfreude*. He was surprised though that he wished to say something – something to excuse his earlier carelessness. "Colonel, if I may..."

Richard shook his head slightly. "It's not over yet."

"Of course, *mein Herr*."

Leszek paced back to his post by the door. Kasia retreated to the other armchair and sat down. Richard sipped his sherry and they all awaited the return of their Führer.

415

27

"**C**ongratulations, Richard, you pulled that off in record time." Greta perused the divorce papers, nodding approvingly. "Faster than Günter, even. How did you manage it?"

Richard walked away from her to pour two drinks. He placed one by Greta and then walked over to the window to look out at the city street. It was a nice flat, small and comfortably furnished, right in the heart of Göringstadt. "I had my wife ask the Führer personally."

"Ooh! And whose baby did she have aborted?"

Richard shot an angry look at Greta, but she was still looking at the documents. "I promised her the house and a good income."

Greta looked up in alarm. "Your house? Part of your income?"

He nodded, pleased for some reason. "You didn't tell me you wanted me for my money."

Greta snorted. "As if you had any."

"I have enough."

"Not now. Goodness, what inspired you to give up your property to her?"

"She has my children to look after. I owe them something."

Greta made a little noise of derision. "Oh well, I have enough. I will, of course, expect you to sign certain documents before we tie the knot." She picked up her drink and held it up.

Richard walked back to her and they tapped their glasses together. "Of course, my dear. I'm not marrying you for your money either."

"Just my family."

Richard leered at her. "Do you really think so?"

Greta made an attempt at shyness, turning her head to the side, but her sly smile ruined the effect. She gave up and, reaching to the top of her blouse, undid a single button. "Tell me, Richard, are you still going to lust after my body after we're married?"

"You'll have to wait and see, my dear. It'll be a while yet before everything is finalized – do you think you'll be able to bear the suspense?" He set down his drink and undid the second button.

"Hmm. I guess, what I'd rather do is accumulate a sufficient store of data before the wedding so that I'll have something to compare with afterwards." Greta set her drink down and undid the third button.

"Good idea." Richard undid the fourth button. He pulled back the material and laid a trembling hand on the exposed skin of her chest.

Sometimes, it really didn't matter that he was stuck in Göringstadt, sometimes, when he was with Greta, it was simply enough to be alive. "Welcome to Göringstadt, my love. I've missed you."

"I've missed you, too." Greta glanced around the flat. "I was surprised you picked me up alone. Where is your man?"

"Leszek's out buying dinner. I figured it'd be nice to eat in."

Greta nodded. "I meant your bodyguard."

"Oh, I left Feliks at the office with Stefan – he's handling some business for me."

"Didn't Rudi assign someone to keep an eye on you yet?"

"Feliks reports to him regularly." Richard's hand strayed a bit, feeling the warmth of Greta's skin.

"But you haven't gotten anyone else?"

"No." Richard removed his hand and picked up his drink. "I guess Rudi thinks my being here is enough. Anyway, he's probably busy listening to Lederman's hare-brained ideas. Meanwhile Frauenfeld is running the entire Reich."

"Günter's been assigned a new keeper. Although I guess he managed to convert this one, just like the others." Greta made a motion with her fingers indicating the money which regularly passed from Günter to his bodyguards.

"Figures. I think Rudi feels more threatened by Günter. He is, after all, older than Rudi and qualifies as a senior statesman." Richard walked back to the window and looked out.

"Whereas you?"

"Me? I don't have enough connections."

Greta came to stand by Richard. "And losing what few you have while you're stuck out here."

"It's only been a month."

"A lifetime for *homo politicanimus*. Are you doing anything?"

"I'm having my son-in-law talk to some people."

"Any luck?"

Richard shrugged. "Some. Schenkelhof is adamant in his support of Rudi, and, as a successor, he'd prefer Günter, or, as I think he put it, 'anybody but Traugutt'. And with him goes the entire *Wehrmacht*."

"What about Lang?"

"He's more amenable. But Schenkelhof is his superior."

"As long as there are no unfortunate accidents." Greta swirled her drink and stared pensively at the eddy.

Richard looked at her but did not say anything. If only he could trust her!

"What about the *Luftwaffe*?"

"Better. They're open to any possibility should Rudi suddenly be incapacitated." Richard snickered. "Anyone but Günter – they're still smarting from his comment about 'effeminate pansies'."

Greta laughed. "He was drunk, you know. And I fed that line to him."

Richard smiled at her. "To my sweet genius." They clinked their glasses and drank.

"You need to get back to Berlin."

Richard sighed. "I know, I know. I visit every weekend, to see the children."

"And?"

"And on the occasions the Führer bothers to receive me, he makes it clear that he expects me to return to Göringstadt by Monday." Richard gazed out at the street. "I need Stefi."

"Is she still refusing to see Rudi?"

Richard nodded.

"What about Paul, how old is he?"

"Eighteen, why?"

"Maybe you could get Rudi interested in boys?"

Richard glared at her.

Greta laughed. It was a light, sweet sound that enlivened the little flat. "Richard, I was joking!" She reached up and stroked his cheek to soothe him. "I heard the Führer even came to your house to see his dear princess."

"Yes. Once."

"What did she say to him?"

"Nothing. She was in bed, her husband was there. Rudi just kissed her forehead and wished her a swift recovery."

"She shouldn't play with him like that. He's not a patient man."

"I don't think she's playing. I think she's genuinely quite ill." There was a chair near the window and Richard lowered himself into it, he didn't feel so well himself.

Greta stroked his hair fondly. "You should take a vacation. Go skiing. We could go to Switzerland, I could show you my home–"

"I need to spend the holidays in Berlin."

Greta moaned.

"I've been invited to the *Winterfest* at the *Residenz*. I don't dare miss that."

"No, of course not." Greta fell silent, she continued to stroke Richard's hair. "And how are things here? In Göringstadt?"

"Well enough. I got some laws pushed through that I wanted. The initiative to decriminalize various nonviolent activities has helped to lower the violent crime rate."

Greta climbed onto Richard's lap. "Really?" With her finger she traced a pattern down his face.

He grabbed her hand, brought it to his lips and kissed it. "Unfortunately, I can't advertise that success very much since we don't actually acknowledge the existence of violent crime."

"Hmm." Greta leaned in and brushed her lips against his cheek. He felt himself growing warm.

"Otherwise I let Stefan handle most things. He's very competent."

"And you?" Her lips moved close to his ear. "What do you do?"

"Like every high-level official, I plot."

His skin tingled as he felt her teeth gently taking hold of his earlobe. "And what are you plotting now?" Her words were barely distinguishable.

"Umm."

She didn't really need to ask.

"*Mein Herr? Mein Herr?*" Leszek gently nudged Richard's shoulder.

"Oh, God." Richard unwrapped himself from Greta and rolled onto his back. "What do you want?"

"Dinner will be ready in a few minutes, *mein Herr*." Leszek stood stiffly, his head raised so that he was staring across the room, not at the two of them. "You left me with instructions to have an evening meal ready by seven. When I returned, you were, uh, asleep, and I did not wish to disturb you to ask if there was a change of plan. So, I followed your orders, and the meal is nearly ready."

"It's seven?"

"Almost."

Richard groaned. This life in Göringstadt was destroying his discipline. He could saunter late into the office, take entire afternoons off, get blind drunk – there was simply nothing to do. The district ran itself quite nicely, the low-level bureaucrats carried out their work without instruction, and there was no one he could work on. He needed to get back to Berlin! "Okay, fine. We'll be at our seats in a few minutes."

Leszek nodded crisply and left. Richard raised himself up and leaned over to kiss Greta. "Good morning!"

"Morning?" Greta rolled toward him, her eyes remaining closed.

"So to speak. It's time for dinner. Come on, wake-up sleeping beauty."

Greta's eyes fluttered open. She looked up at Richard dreamily. "How long do we have?"

"Five minutes?"

"Long enough." Her hands reached down and he felt himself being stroked.

"Greta…" Her fingers strayed and he moaned. "Not there!"

"No?"

"Oh, Greta." He shifted, but her hands followed. "Okay, but we shouldn't take too long…"

"Why not? Are you worried what your servant will think of you?"

He couldn't even say no.

28

*K*asia knocked lightly on the door and entered at Olek's reply. Olek turned to look at her and smiled faintly. He was fully dressed in his uniform, his cane in his right hand. Stefi was sitting on the edge of the bed, still in her nightgown, and Olek turned from Kasia to his wife. "Stefi, sweetheart, I've got to go to work now."

Stefi nodded, her head moving slowly up and down as if she had only just learned the motion.

"I'll be back late tonight. You know that?"

Stefi nodded again.

Olek bent down and kissed his wife's cheek. "Take care, darling." As he left the room, he caught Kasia's eye and shook his head slowly. Kasia watched as Olek limped down the hallway, his cane tapping against the wood. He looked exhausted, and so lonely! He reached the steps and began his careful descent on his two artificial limbs. Kasia turned away, unable to watch.

"Stefi – we need to talk."

Stefi looked at her mother, blinked slowly, then looked away.

"I'm not putting up with this anymore."

Stefi stood and went to her vanity. She sat down and began to brush her hair. Kasia studied her daughter as she sat there, so beautiful, so pale. "You need to at least step outside and see some daylight. You're going to make yourself very, very ill."

Stefi continued to brush her hair as if unaware of her mother's presence.

"Stefanuszka, if you don't tell us what's wrong, how can we help you?"

Still Stefi ignored her, as she had done since Kasia returned from America nearly seven weeks ago.

Kasia stood by the door and watched as Stefi brushed her hair. She knew that Stefi sometimes spoke to Ryszard when the two were completely alone, though apparently only to denounce one or the other of them. Ryszard had grown impatient with the exchanges and no longer bothered to try to talk with his daughter. For Olek, Stefi would nod and sometimes say a word or two. For her mother, though, the silent treatment was complete. *What have I done,* Kasia wondered. *What have I done?*

"I need to go out and Lodzia is busy. I'm going to leave Piotr in your care."

Again Stefi acted as though she had not heard. It had been a desperate attempt on Kasia's part, leaving the baby with Stefi on a previous occasion. It had worked only in that Stefi had taken care of the child. She did not react to her mother's leaving or returning, she simply took adequate care of the baby. Sometimes, with Genia, Stefi managed a smile, but most of the time, she neither smiled nor frowned.

Kasia finally ventured into the room. She walked up behind Stefi and stroked her hair. "Don't ignore me."

The brush barely missed her fingers.

Kasia opened a drawer and drew out a pair of scissors. She grabbed Stefi's hair in her fist and pulled harshly. Stefi's head jerked backward and Kasia was pleased to see a surprised look on her daughter's face. "If your hair is such a diversion, I will cut it off." She opened the scissors and began to cut.

"*No!*"

Kasia stopped. "So, you are there." She released her hold on her daughter and set the scissors down. The few strands of hair she had cut glided to the floor. "Then let's stop this nonsense and talk."

"Alright." The voice was so hoarse that Kasia barely recognized it, but she did not pause to comment on that, not when there was hope of communication.

She grabbed her daughter's hand and urged her to her feet. "Come, child." She guided Stefi to the bed and had her sit on the edge, then she sat next to her, placing her arm around her daughter's shoulder. "Now, tell me, what happened."

Stefi shook her head.

"Is it something the Führer did?"

Stefi shook her head again.

"Your father?"

Still Stefi shook her head.

Kasia paused and then carefully asked, "You?"

Stefi did not move.

"Did it have something to do with your baby?"

Stefi shook her head.

"With the Führer's kidnap? With Peter?"

Almost imperceptibly, Stefi nodded.

Kasia stroked her chin. She put together all the hints she had picked up over the past weeks and asked, "Did you tell the Führer to go to Peter?"

Stefi nodded.

"To kill him?"

Stefi closed her eyes and nodded emphatically.

"To save your father." Kasia did not even bother to make it a question. After a moment, she said, "It turned out alright, honey."

Stefi looked at her, tears in her eyes.

"I know, sweetheart. I know, they took your baby. I'm sorry." Kasia pulled Stefi in towards her and tried to hug her, but Stefi was stiff. "Wait here a minute, honey. I'll be right back."

Kasia returned a few minutes later with a small ornament, a clay angel hanging from a worn red ribbon. She pressed it into Stefi's hand. "I want you to have this."

"Your Christmas angel? I don't understand."

Kasia felt awash with relief at Stefi's words. "Between you and Pawel, there was a pregnancy. I miscarried. No terrible reason, it was a completely normal event. Your father didn't seem to think it was at all important, nobody really did, but to me it was. Still, I didn't want to make a fuss. It was near to Christmas and we were at Szaflary for a visit. I went to a mass and after the mass, some village children were selling these ornaments they had made. I bought one as a memorial to my lost angel." Kasia was horrified to realize there were tears in her eyes. After all these years!

"Oh, Mama."

"Every year, I hung my little angel on the Christmas tree and remembered that there was somebody missing. But – and this is important Stefi – I got pregnant very soon after that miscarriage. The result is Pawel. I look at him and realize that if my little angel hadn't left when he had, I wouldn't have Pawel. *He* would be my lost one – and I wouldn't even know it."

Stefi shuddered a sigh. "So, you think I should get pregnant again."

Kasia nodded. "If that's what you want. If you want to have a child with Olek, you can't let this horror, you can't let what Schindler did to you stand in your way."

"Oh, Mama, it's worse than that. It's more than just a lost possibility!" Stefi slumped into her mother's embrace.

Kasia stroked her daughter's hair. "I know, it's terrible what that man did to you. And you can't even say anything." She felt Stefi sobbing in her arms. "Do you need to get away for awhile? Do you want to go to Szaflary? We can arrange a break there."

"Mother, I can't go there! I gave him up to be tortured and killed. What if Rudi told him that? What if he knows? How can I ever face him?"

"Peter?"

"Yes! My God, what if he knows?"

422

"Stefi, whether he knows about what you did or not, you need to make it up to him. You offered up his life as if it were yours to offer."

"I know! I'm horrible. Worse than Schindler, worse than Rudi. My God, they don't give up their friends!"

Stefi looked on the verge of collapse again and Kasia grabbed her shoulders to pull her upright. "Listen to me! You offered him up to be tortured to save your father, to protect his position, to push forward our goals!"

"I know."

"And so does Peter! Stefi, think about it. He had the Führer alone, in the woods. The man who ordered Joanna's murder! And he let him go! Do you know what that means?"

Stefi shook her head, confused by her mother's intensity.

"He gave up Joanna's murderer for the same reason, to protect Ryszard's position! He didn't do that lightly – he knows what's at stake. You lost your child, he was nearly murdered, he gave up Joanna's murderer, all for Ryszard's position."

"Yes! All for the stupid cause!"

"Not stupid! For Christ's sake, child! You don't make such sacrifices and then denigrate them by throwing it all away!"

"Throwing it all away?"

"Yes, that's what you're doing now. Make it up to Peter, show him that you're willing to make sacrifices, too. Show him that you didn't offer his life lightly."

"I didn't–"

"I know you didn't. But the way you're acting now, makes it look like you did. You're the only one who can get Ryszard back to Berlin. If he spends much longer out of the capital, he'll be ruined. He won't have any prospect of becoming Führer. He needs you, he needs you to influence Rudi."

Stefi closed her eyes and breathed heavily. "Oh God, not him."

"You were willing to have Peter tortured, but you're not willing to tell sweet lies? You're turning your back on the Führer because you find your work distasteful? For heaven's sake, distasteful is hardly a legitimate excuse given all that has gone before!"

Stefi opened her eyes and looked at her mother. "Do you know what I do with that monster?"

"I know, Stefi. I've feigned ignorance because I am weak. But I've known all along. And I've admired your courage." Kasia shook her head as if trying to rid herself of the images which had come unbidden to her mind. "Do you think shooting someone is tasteful? It's not a pretty sight. We call that war and we feel that somehow it is justifiable and that our fighters are

423

brave, heroic even. But to fight this war in the manner that you do – that is much harder. No fancy guns for you to shoot in the air to show your bravery – just lies and…" Kasia shuddered. "No one acknowledges such sacrifices. No one recognizes such bravery. But that's what it is. Please don't lose heart now. Not after all you have given, not after what others have given."

"Such as you?"

"Me?"

"You begged the Führer to allow you to divorce a man that you love."

Kasia sighed. "It's strategy, my dear."

"Was it strategy that made you reject Dad's attempt to return home after we rescued him?"

Kasia shook her head sadly, "No. Just my pathetic attempt at revenge."

"And was it strategic to have him use the guest room once the Führer insisted he return home?"

"Stefi, child, I am not as brave as you. You already know that. Please don't shame me with my weakness."

Stefi smiled gently and stroked her mother's cheek. "It's alright, Mom, I understand. I love Olek – and if he did to me, what Dad has done to you…" Stefi leaned in and kissed her mother's cheek. "Let the Führer know I'm recuperating and will be able to attend his *Winterfest* activities."

"He asked Olek if you would be willing to co-host."

"What about his wife?"

Kasia shrugged. "I think she's planning to visit relatives. In the Alsace, I believe."

"Okay. I'll do it. And could you make sure Szaflary knows about it? I want Peter to know."

"I'll make sure of that."

29

Stefi had chosen well, she looked stunning. Whereas the other young women had opted for too much skin – bare shoulders and slit skirts, Stefi had kept with the theme of the festivities and worn a flowing, dark blue gown, almost medieval in its dropped waist, tight bodice and ornate sleeves. Her dark hair, swept up and pinned with diamonds, only emphasized the delicacy of her neck and white skin. She looked so graceful, and though she was not dancing, her steps fell in time with the music, as if the waltz was being played only to accompany her movements. Wolf-Dietrich watched her as she glided across the room, smiling and greeting the Führer's guests, and felt his loins aching with desire.

He wasn't the only one, he noticed. Lederman was nearly drooling. He stood off to one side, talking with Frauenfeld. Poor little Frauenfeld listened courteously, his head turned upward, his bald pate shining like a party decoration, as Lederman pompously droned on about something even as his eyes followed Stefi across the room.

Ulrike tugged on Wolf-Dietrich's arm and he turned to smile at her. She looked pretty. A sweet face with eyes that longed to please him, ruddy cheeks and bleached blond hair. Unlike many of the other young women, she had chosen to wear a dress that made her look proper, and unfortunately, that was exactly the effect. He had trouble imagining making love to her without feeling that he was somehow defiling all of German womanhood.

Playing the part of gracious escort, Wolf-Dietrich asked, "Do you want a drink?"

Ulrike pointed at the servants with the trays of *Sekt*. "They'll come around."

"No point waiting, I'll get you something." Before she could object, he had left her side. He glanced back – she looked hopelessly lost, standing there alone, and he felt a twinge of regret, but if he took long enough, somebody would grab her to chat and he would be free to mingle. It wouldn't do to spend their time at the party together – that was not the point of these social occasions.

When he returned, he was horrified to see that, of all people, it was Stefi who had chosen to rescue Ulrike. He tapped his heels together and bowed his head slightly, then handed Ulrike her drink. Rather than excusing himself to mingle, Wolf-Dietrich chose to stay with the women in the hope of controlling, or at least counter-acting any unfortunate exchanges of information.

Ulrike gestured at Stefi. "Frau Karlsson, here, was good enough to welcome me personally to the party. This is my fiancé–"

Stefi offered her hand. "Wolf-Dietrich needs no introduction. We are already acquainted."

Wolf-Dietrich bowed to kiss the proffered hand. He hoped Stefi did not notice how hot his lips had become.

Ulrike stiffened. "Are you feeling alright, Wolfi? You've grown flushed." Her voice carried wifely overtones of concern.

"Of course. I'm fine." Wolf-Dietrich scanned the room. "An impressive crowd. I see the Führer. Where is his wife?"

Stefi smiled sweetly. "Visiting family. I've agreed to fill in as hostess."

Ulrike glanced over at the Führer and then back at Stefi. "How are you and Wolf-Dietrich acquainted?"

"His father and mine both work closely with the Führer. We meet occasionally at social gatherings."

Wolf-Dietrich glanced at Stefi. There was something in her tone that had caught his attention.

"Your father? Who's he?"

"Richard Traugutt."

"Oh, Traugutt! You must be Paul's sister. My sister Teresa has spoken of you. She–" Ulrike fell suddenly silent. She turned to Wolf-Dietrich for help, but he was busily scanning the crowd.

"Ach, and there's Frauenfeld and Lederman." Wolf-Dietrich waved his hand toward the two men.

Stefi and Ulrike looked where Wolf-Dietrich had gestured. Frauenfeld was in the process of waving the smoke from Lederman's cigarette away from his face. "You know," Ulrike intimated, "Frauenfeld – I've heard of him – he's been around for years, but where did this Lederman come from? I never heard of him before."

Wolf-Dietrich shrugged.

"You're right, my dear." Stefi sipped her drink before continuing. "He's spent most of his time outside Berlin. Used to run a re-education camp. He was called in by the Führer to handle a special case, and I guess he grabbed the Führer's ear."

"A special case?"

"Yes, have you heard of Peter Halifax?" Stefi brought her hand to her mouth. "Oh, but of course you have!"

"What about him?" Ulrike's voice had taken on a strange tone – a mixture of anger and something else.

"That man there." Stefi pointed at Lederman. He was looking at her and, noticing the gesture, smiled broadly in response. "He's the one who tortured Halifax."

"Tortured?" Ulrike stared at Lederman. Seeing that both women were looking at him, he winked at them.

"Yes, for months apparently. He's very proud of his work, described it all in detail to the Führer. Gruesome things, absolutely horrible." Stefi shuddered, and it was not faked. "I know, I heard it all."

"He tortured Peter." Ulrike continued to stare at Lederman as if she could not fathom the existence of such life forms. "What did he do wrong? Peter, I mean."

Stefi shrugged. "I believe it was all for trying to leave the Reich. To seek a new life in another land." She had taken her attention off Lederman and was studying Ulrike, watching as the color drained from her face.

"He wasn't lying." Ulrike seemed to be speaking to herself.

"I gather our dear Herr Lederman thought Peter needed to be broken." Stefi had decided to refer to Peter by his first name, in keeping with Ulrike's obvious familiarity. Watching Ulrike closely, and choosing her words accordingly, Stefi continued, "Lederman's the sort of man who feels that such things are justified when dealing with lesser beings."

"That's not proper."

Stefi tilted her head. "No it isn't. Is it?"

Ulrike shook her head slightly. Lederman had detached himself from Frauenfeld and was making his way toward their group.

Stefi glanced at Lederman to gauge his progress across the room. Not much time, but she could probably manage it. "Ulrike, he's coming to us now. Take the next dance with him."

"Dance with him? Wolf-Dietrich–"

"Won't mind. Your future husband will be an important man, and it is necessary for you to get to know the people with whom he will work. That is, if you want to be useful to him in his career advancement. You do, don't you?"

"Oh yes, of course!"

"Then dance with our dear Heinrich, find out about him."

"Find out what?"

There was no time to answer Ulrike's question. Stefi turned to Lederman and smiled graciously. "Heinrich! How charming of you to join us. Have you met Fräulein Vogel?"

As Stefi finished the introduction, Lederman bowed deeply, then grabbing Ulrike's hand kissed it warmly. "Charmed."

"And you know her fiancé, Wolf-Dietrich Schindler."

"Yes, of course!" Lederman snapped his head in a slight bow, then shook Wolf-Dietrich's hand. "Though I've never had the pleasure of meeting you socially."

Wolf-Dietrich bowed slightly in return but did not say anything. The orchestra finished the waltz they had been playing and started another.

"Oh, Strauss! That's wonderful for dancing," Stefi enthused. Lederman smiled at her and began to bow in invitation, but Stefi pre-empted him. "What a good idea! You must dance with Fräulein Vogel! You need to get to know Wolf-Dietrich's intended!"

Lederman turned deftly in mid-bow toward Ulrike. "May I?"

Ulrike cast a nervous glance at Wolf-Dietrich. He nodded almost imperceptibly. Ulrike accepted Lederman's hand and together they walked toward the dance floor. Stefi and Wolf-Dietrich stood side-by-side watching the two of them as they disappeared into the crowd.

Stefi kept her eyes on the crowd and spoke softly. "We need to talk."

"You betrayed me."

427

"Like you, I am nothing more than my father's tool."

"So you left me to work directly with that…" Wolf-Dietrich's caution caught up with him and he amended, "With the Führer."

"And you have been advising your father. I recognized your imprint on my father's arrest."

"My ally abandoned me. I had no choice but to work with my father."

"And did you have no choice about the abortion?"

"*No!*" Wolf-Dietrich risked looking directly at Stefi. "You must believe me, I would never do such a thing to you. That was my father's idea. He thought…" Wolf-Dietrich turned back toward the dance floor. "He was a vindictive fool, and he's paid for it. Greta forced a divorce out of him using that information. My God, could you imagine what would happen if the Führer had found out?"

"Yes, I can."

"So why didn't you tell him? Certainly that would have served your father's purposes."

"Not really. You can see for yourself, removing one competitor only allows another to step into his shoes. My father can work with Günter. This Lederman – he's beyond the pale."

Wolf-Dietrich nodded his head. "He is sleazy. But the Führer – I've heard he's so inclined anyway."

Stefi turned to look at Wolf-Dietrich. He felt her eyes upon him and could not resist looking into her eyes. They stood that way for a long moment. "We do no one any good by encouraging Rudi's baser predilections. The people he hurts are real," Stefi whispered. "And, if someday, he must step down, we would be well-advised to avoid making the same mistake again."

Wolf-Dietrich glanced nervously behind himself but there was no one nearby. God, Stefi had spoken treason! His surprise at her blind trust in him battled with his well-honed survival instinct and he only just managed to stop himself from swearing that the selection of the Führer could never be mistaken. He realized he was trembling.

"We have to get rid of Lederman. For the sake of the Reich." Stefi paused, then added with a smile, "And as dutiful children of ambitious fathers."

Wolf-Dietrich turned his attention back toward the dance floor. The waltz was still playing, nobody was approaching them. He should say something in response, but he was afraid to open his mouth.

"And you realize…" Stefi was also watching the dancers. "If both your father and mine are back in Berlin – we may well see much more of each other."

"Oh, Stefi..." Wolf-Dietrich moaned. He shifted position, trying to relieve the pain in his groin. To have such desire and be so afraid at the same time! "You're the Führer's..." He coughed and dug his hand into his pocket to find a handkerchief. After he had finished with it, he pressed it securely back into his pocket. That helped a bit.

"Will you help me?" Stefi raised her chin, in the manner of a hostess observing the effectiveness of her party preparations. Was there enough food? Were the drinks well distributed? Was anyone standing alone?

"What do you plan to do?" Wolf-Dietrich noticed how long and slender her neck was. What would it look like if the Führer put it in a noose?

"I'm going to say Lederman behaved indecently toward me. I need you to corroborate my evidence. The Führer will take care of the rest."

"Oh, God, Stefi. That's dangerous!"

"You once complained of being bored, Wolfi. Now's your chance to change that." The music ended and Stefi looked expectantly toward the dance floor. She smiled broadly as she spied Lederman returning with a flushed Ulrike. They stopped to talk to another couple who had also stepped off the dance floor. "Are you with me?"

Wolf-Dietrich's answer was barely audible, but it was yes.

Lederman was gesturing. Ulrike looked pleased that she was being introduced in the company of someone important.

"Good, here's what you have to do..."

30

*P*eter grunted quietly to himself and leaned forward to look at the computer screen more closely. He stroked his chin wondering if he had left out a step or missed something. Nothing worked with this particular message. Although it had been sent along normal channels using the normal protocols, when he tried to read it, he got nothing but gibberish. Was it just a corrupted file? Or had they intercepted a private message inserted into the usual Reich traffic?

He thought back to the last time that had happened. Rather than ignore the message, he had privately worked on it, gnawing on the problem for weeks. When he had finally cracked the code, he still had to beg the Council to pass on relevant background information to him. And once he had pinpointed a possibility for them to infiltrate Schindler's sterility program, he had been ordered to go. Not as an officer, not as a member of the government. No, they had forced him to wear the uniform of a

Zwangsarbeiter. All so that they could keep him on a tight leash. And as a result he had fallen into the hands of those policemen and been beaten under interrogation. And then later, on the train, he had been helpless when Karl had found him...

Peter frowned. Still, whatever discomfort had resulted from the last time, the message he had uncovered had been genuinely important. It could be this time as well.

"Are you napping, Captain?"

Only Wanda insisted on his title and only Wanda would walk into the office unannounced and automatically assume a momentary pause in activity meant something was amiss. Peter shook his head, but kept his eyes on the screen. "No, just thinking."

Wanda stood behind him and looked at the strings of characters on the screen. "What is that?"

"Gibberish."

"I can see that!"

Peter looked up at her and then back at the screen. "It's probably just a corrupted file. When I get the new system installed–"

"Have you finished that yet?"

"Not yet, Colonel. I've been working on it whenever I have a spare moment." He typed in a command to save the file he had been inspecting then, still staring at the screen, ventured to say, "You know, it is a complicated endeavor, if I could work uninterrupted on it–"

"You have twenty four hours in a day, Captain, just like everyone else."

"I realize that, Colonel. What I'm suggesting is..." But he did not bother to finish. He turned in his seat so that it was clear he was giving Wanda his full attention. "Is there anything I can do for you, Colonel?"

Wanda slapped down a thick folder of papers. "These need to be transcribed and sent to the American Security Agency as soon as possible. Stop what you're doing now and get on this right away."

"Yes, Colonel." Peter opened the folder and picked up the first sheet. "What is it?"

"None of your business. Just send it."

"Word for word?" He already knew the answer. Though word-for-word transcriptions were really only necessary for treaties, and technical documents, Wanda would insist on this much more time-consuming and tedious approach to encoding the document.

"Yes." Wanda pointed at the stack. "How long?"

Peter paged through, looking at the density of type and the frequency of non-standard text. "Is there an electronic version?"

"No. Just that."

"Eight hours, give or take."

The Führer's Wishes

"Can't you do it faster?"

Peter shook his head. "Not word-for-word. Are you sure there are absolutely no passages that can be summarized?"

"Are you afraid of the work, Captain?"

Peter sighed. "Wanda…" The name had slipped out before he had realized it and as he mentally scrabbled for a way to undo this disrespectful familiarity, he could feel Wanda winding herself up.

"Captain, just because you're Colonel Król's husband, gives you no–"

"Who's my husband?" Zosia bounced cheerfully into the office, her nicely rounded belly protruding as she stood with an exaggerated sway. "Oh, you!" She brushed passed Wanda and kissed Peter hello. "Hey, sweetheart, how 'bout a break?"

"Colonel Król!"

Zosia waved her hand impatiently at Wanda. "Where the hell did all this formality come from, comrade? It's lunch time, Peter's going to take a break. Do you have a problem with that?"

Wanda glowered, but then seemed to realize that her position was bordering on silly. With a gesture of disgust she dismissed Zosia's question and pointing at the stack, snapped at Peter, "I want it done by day's end."

He saluted her back as she stomped out of his office.

"Geez." Zosia stood with her hands on her hips and looked from the now empty doorway to Peter. "Doesn't she get on your nerves?"

"A bit."

"What a slave-driver!"

"I've had worse bosses." Peter motioned toward his lap. "Come, sit down. Take a load off your feet."

Zosia dropped onto his lap with a loud "Oomph." She kissed Peter, then patted her belly. "Next time, it's your turn. I swear, they get bigger each time."

Peter stroked her tummy. "Do they?" He hadn't known Zosia when she was pregnant with Joanna, and during her pregnancy with Irena, he had been in England. It was wonderful this time, watching their child grow within her. Life was so marvelously normal – working through the day, coming home to wife and children in the evening. Madzia was hitting that charming age where speech was blooming, Irena's personality was emerging from beneath the cocoon of infancy, Zosia was buoyant and happy. Even Tadek somehow fit into the routine.

Zosia placed her hand on Peter's on her belly. "Everybody tells me, it's going to be a boy."

"What makes them say that?"

"Because I'm carrying it all up front." Zosia looked down at their clasped hands, raised so unnaturally high. "I must agree, this one feels like a boy."

"Is that possible? Do you think you could really tell?"

"Well, I don't know. I just felt pretty sure the last two were girls, and this time, I feel it's a boy. Sounds silly, doesn't it?"

"No." Peter stroked Zosia's hair with his free hand. "Nothing you say sounds silly. So, what would you want to name a boy? Adam?"

Zosia shook her head.

"Why not? I thought that's what we agreed last time."

"If I remember correctly, you weren't too pleased at the idea."

"Ach, I was just jealous. I'm alright with the name now."

Zosia turned in his lap so that she could look at him. "You really are alright with that." She sounded surprised and perhaps even a bit disappointed. "You know, sometimes it worries me…"

"What?"

Zosia shook her head. "Nothing. I just think that the baby should have its own name. If it's a boy, how about Walenty?"

Peter shook his head.

"Okay, how about Kazimierz?"

"Kazimierz? Sounds like you're clearing your throat."

"Kaz for short?"

"Mmm."

"Krzystof?"

"Gesundheit."

Zosia giggled. "You could call him Krys."

"Krys? Yes, I can get my English tongue around that one. Nice and short – I like that."

"Okay, Krzystof it is, and since you've been so nice, you can give the next child some proper English name."

Peter grinned at the thought that Zosia was already planning another child. Where in heaven's name did she think they were going to put them all? "Now, before we start planning the next decade, should we have that lunch you promised?"

"Oh, that was just an excuse. Marysia sent me down to get you, she wants to talk with you and she said not to let Wanda know."

"Must be about Ryszard."

"Yep, looks like he's running wild again."

"Okay, give me just a moment." Peter called up the file he had been working on, but then his fingers remained poised over the keyboard. It was very unlikely the file was anything more than a corrupted encryption of mundane matters. It would certainly be nothing more than a wild goose chase…Still, his desire to find out, to unravel the mystery was overwhelming. There might be something truly important hidden inside those inscrutable characters.

"Peter?"

"I'm thinking." He had to know – whatever the cost, he had to know!

"Is something wrong?"

Still staring at the screen, Peter shook his head. No, everything was absolutely perfect and it was going to stay that way. Unbridled curiosity was no less dangerous than any other passion and was therefore just as forbidden. Everything had to be kept in balance – it was the only way. He tapped in a command and followed it with a confirmation.

"What are you doing?"

"Oh, I just irrevocably deleted some garbage. Come on, let's go."

Zosia slid off his lap and stood up. Her movement caused one of Wanda's papers to drift to the floor and as Zosia bent to retrieve it, Peter could not help but notice her curvaceous buttocks. He smacked Zosia's fanny lightly and she jumped around in surprise. "Peter!"

He smiled broadly and raised his eyebrows hopefully. "Do you think we should detour a bit before finding our way to Marysia's?"

"You're sweating." Marysia stroked Peter's cheek quizzically. "Are you sick?"

He shook his head. "No, just a bit of exertion." Peter slid past Marysia into her room. "From climbing the ladders." Madzia leapt off the couch and ran to him, wrapping herself around his leg.

Marysia made a face as Zosia entered the room, also a bit flushed. "It seems to have taken you some time to fetch him, dear."

"Wanda was there." Zosia cleared her throat. "She was making a fuss about some…Something or other."

Marysia nodded her head. "I guess she's getting flak from some of the people at the ASA. They've talked to that American's wife about what happened and they're telling Wanda that they're suspicious of you, Peter. They think we should investigate the accident a bit more thoroughly."

"Do they know I'm working here?" Peter limped across the room with Madzia on his leg and picked up Irena.

"No. But they know you're under our protection. Of course, everyone knows that now."

He nuzzled Irena, then set her down on her feet. She toddled to Zosia flapping her arms excitedly. "Is that why you called me up?"

Zosia swooped Irena into her arms. "Madzia, let your daddy go. Come on, Sweetie" Zosia pulled at Madzia, finally freeing Peter's leg. "I'll leave you two alone."

Marysia waved Zosia and the children out the door. "No. It's not that. We need your help. It's the French, they're furious."

"Don't tell me, somebody's finally told them that they have garlic breath?" Peter went over to Marysia's kitchen and began looking for food.

"Why do you always pick on the French?"

"Do I need reason?" Peter looked back at Marysia and winked.

Marysia gave him an exasperated look.

"I'm English, it's our tradition. Our *culture*." He turned his attention back to the counter and noticed some pickled beets.

"They have been our good allies for centuries."

"And with friends like that…" He picked up a piece of beet and dropped it into his mouth.

"Peter, such chauvinism is unbecoming. And not helpful."

"Oh, my French friends would know I'm just teasing. Do you mind?" He picked up a knife and pointed at a loaf of bread, but didn't wait for an answer.

"Do you have any French friends?"

Peter sliced the bread and put it on a plate, then puts some of the pickled beets on the plate as well. "There was a French section to the labor camp I worked in. And back when I was in the English Underground, I liased with a few. Shared information and whatnot."

"Which doesn't answer the question."

"No, it doesn't. So what's up?"

Marysia gave up. "Sit down. Let me get you something to drink with that, and then I'll fill you in on events."

She offered a glass of wine, but Peter rejected it, explaining that he didn't want to have to tell Wanda why he had alcohol on his breath. "Water will do fine."

Marysia made a face but poured him water. As Peter ate his lunch, Marysia told him how Stefi had returned to being the Führer's mistress and how she had specifically asked that Peter be told that.

"Why?"

Marysia shrugged. "All Ryszard's children are a bit weird, but Stefi is definitely the oddest."

Peter shook his head but didn't argue. "When was that?"

"Two months ago – during the Winterfest season."

"So did she get Ryszard back to Berlin?"

Marysia nodded. "Yes, but first she got rid of one of the replacements."

"Which one?"

"Lederman."

"Ah, good." Peter shuddered as if he had tasted something disgusting. "That creep being so close to power…"

434

"Apparently you weren't the only one who felt that way. Stefi told the Führer he forcefully propositioned her. He's married, she's married, so it was clearly inappropriate and illegal. It seems Schindler's son Wolf-Dietrich even stumbled upon them as he – Lederman, I mean – attempted to assault Stefi."

"Did that really happen?"

"I gather not quite. Stefi set Lederman up and Wolf-Dietrich was in on it. Anyway, given the Führer's relationship with Stefi, he was not in the mood for tolerating inappropriate behavior."

"Good. Did he string the bastard up?"

"No, just sent him off to a menial assignment."

Peter groaned. "I wonder why he decided to be restrained with that guy, of all people."

"I think Lederman has some connections the Führer doesn't want to alienate. He's getting very nervous of late."

"Rightly so." Peter refilled Marysia's wine glass, then poured himself a bit more water.

"He recalled Ryszard to Berlin – again, Stefi organized that, but as a counterweight to Ryszard, he also recalled Günter Schindler."

"Yes, the two are about equal and opposite. What about Frauenfeld?"

"He's maintaining his role as security advisor to the Führer. I gather the Führer finds his loyalty reassuring."

"Then what's Ryszard?"

Marysia downed the wine Peter had just poured for her and refilled her glass. "He's been appointed advisor on internal economics or something idiotic like that."

Peter's eyes were drawn to Marysia's glass, but given how obnoxious he had found her unsolicited advice about alcohol, he decided not to comment. "So what's this have to do with the French?"

"I'm getting to that!" Marysia drank more wine and calmed down. "Okay, so the three of them are in Berlin advising the Führer. Günter's got his supporters, Ryszard has his, and Frauenfeld is nobly loyal. Ryszard is divorcing Kasia–"

"As approved."

"Yes, as approved, and marrying Greta Schindler as soon as it'll be legal, pulling in most of the diplomatic circle with her. Meanwhile Schindler has been gathering his remaining forces – especially those who support the programs he's running in England."

"Any information on those?"

"Yes, your brother has been very useful. Surprisingly so. Most importantly, he's been telling us who has been with Schindler every time an inspection sweeps through." Marysia paused to empty her glass.

435

"And?"

"And there have been some very important people visiting him there. Schindler's still powerful. In particular he has the *Wehrmacht*. Or rather, had."

"Had?" Peter noticed how Marysia hesitated to refill her glass. He poured another for her.

"Thanks." Marysia smiled at him fondly, obviously relieved to have escaped an overt judgment. "Have you heard of Schenkelhof?"

"Of course."

"Well, with him goes the *Wehrmacht*, and apparently he has always supported Günter over Ryszard in any upcoming election for Führer. Indeed, he's been of the opinion that anyone is better than Traugutt."

"What does he have against Traugutt?" Peter finished the beets and began using the bread to mop up the sauce.

"A while back – maybe you remember – Ryszard pushed through a measure to increase the cost of forced labor to the industrialists. He was of the opinion that if the *Zwangsarbeiter* were more expensive, they might not be wasted so brutally."

Peter nodded. "Yes, but the wages went to the government, not the *Zwangsarbeiter*."

"That's how he sold the program – it raised revenue for the State. Anyway, one of Schenkelhof's industries was hard hit by the extra costs. Schenkelhof never forgave him for that."

"Ah. So what has happened that has everyone so upset?" With the last bit of bread, Peter wiped his plate clean and pushed it aside.

Marysia picked up her glass, but then set it back down without drinking anything. "Schenkelhof has been severely injured by a bomb. A briefcase exploded in his face when he opened it."

"Oh. That is bad. Unapproved, I assume."

"Worse than unapproved. Ryszard didn't even ask."

Peter rested his chin on his hands. "Hmm. A bomb. I wonder why so messy?"

"I guess because he had to arrange it himself."

"How badly is Schenkelhof injured?"

"Badly enough. He'll have to be replaced. Lang will take his position – and he's amenable to Ryszard's succession." Marysia picked up her glass again, this time drinking from it.

"So why are the French upset?"

Marysia peered into her glass as if the answer were there. "Ah, it seems Schenkelhof was in their pay."

"In their pay? They had an agent that highly placed?"

"Not exactly. There were some deals between him and the French resistance. Apparently part of his support for Schindler came from the fact that he thought he could manipulate Schindler much more effectively as Führer, and the French wanted that access to power. They were hoping to use Schenkelhof to arrange a secret agreement between Schindler – as Führer – and themselves. They wanted certain rights restored, an improvement in the status of Reich subjects…"

"But only in French territory?"

"Yes, I think it was supposed to apply only to those with 'French' as the nationality on their identity papers. Those, at least, who had not already gained reasonable rights by assuming citizenship."

Peter shrugged. "Then why do we care if they're upset?"

"It's not really that. It's that Ryszard did this without checking with anyone. Without clearance."

Peter motioned toward the half empty wine bottle. "Do you mind if I have a glass?"

"Of course not!" Marysia rose and fetched a clean glass for him. "But what about Wanda?"

"I'll tell her my wife ordered me to have a drink with her. Wanda's very big on orders, she'll believe that."

Marysia laughed. Peter filled his glass and topped up Marysia's. When Marysia had reseated herself, he held his glass up. "Here's to you, Marysia." They clinked glasses. "And your endless courage."

"Courage? My God, I'm an absolute coward." Marysia turned her head away and muttered, "And ineffectual."

"You're very effective, and doing a great job holding this fractious group together."

"I've sent my children, even my grandchildren, off to die or be maimed and I do nothing but sit here and arbitrate bickering officials. If you think Wanda's bad, at least she's forthright. You wouldn't believe the back-stabbing and duplicity. The, the…" Marysia shook her head. "It's my fault. I'm worthless."

"Don't denigrate your work. What you do is important, and difficult. And you do it well."

"Katerina managed better. Konrad would be better. They're both more decisive."

Peter reached out to touch her hand. "That's not your style, but the way you handle things works. And, don't forget, Katerina had a lot of discussions and bickering and arguments to oversee. Just remember how my appearance here was treated. If she had been decisive, I'd be dead."

Marysia closed her eyes and smiled at the image his words had conjured up. "I remember what a wretch you were. Poor thing. And Katerina gave in to me and Zosia pleading for your life just because you reminded us all of Adam." She laughed lightly. "That, and I think I gave her a bottle of Goldwasser. Quite coincidentally."

"See? Don't worry if you feel pulled this way and that. It's part of the job. You're doing well."

Marysia looked at him, earnestly seeking his approval. "Do you really think so?"

Peter nodded. "And I know how much it must have hurt to let the Führer go. That's why I wasn't too bothered by your accusations when I arrived with him."

"You weren't? I don't understand. Why not?"

"I didn't realize it at the time, but I wanted to be righteous, I didn't want to be the one to kill him. I wanted you all to do that – for it to have some basis in law. Somebody's law. I wanted to see him suffer, but I didn't want to think of myself as the sort of monster he was, so I put the burden on you, on the Council. And for you, Marysia – with all that you've suffered because of that man and his regime – that was like me waving a cup of water before someone dying of thirst. I held it out and then–" Peter suddenly froze, his expression blank. Marysia looked for that rage she sometimes saw, but it was not there. Instead she recognized a distance in his expression, as if he had retreated into another world. Was it the same world in which anger and hatred ruled him? Before she could say anything, Peter shuddered as if shaking off a vision. He blinked and wet his lips. "I held it out and then cruelly pulled it away."

As was her habit, Marysia politely ignored Peter's strange pause. "You didn't pull it away. It wasn't your decision."

"No, but I did waste the only real opportunity to punish him."

Marysia nodded. She looked off toward the wall with the photographs of her children. "If I had been you, Peter, I would have strangled him with my bare hands."

"I know. And I'm sorry I didn't do that."

Marysia looked as though she was going to say something, but then changed her mind. She sipped her wine thoughtfully. "So, what do you think we should do about Ryszard? Do you have any ideas on how we can retroactively approve his actions?"

"How come the French suspect the Home Army had anything to do with this assassination attempt?"

"Oh, they don't know anything for sure. They're just screaming bloody murder to all the representatives of the Governments-in-Exile in New York. Alex got an earful."

"So they admitted Schenkelhof was working for them?"

Marysia shook her head. "Not even they would do something that stupid! They just raised a ruckus about all these uncoordinated resistance actions in Berlin. You know, there's an agreement among the governments that none of them will take unilateral, unapproved action in the capital."

Peter nodded. "So their sudden concern emerged with the attempt on Schenkelhof?"

"Yeah. Alex has his own contacts with the French in New York and he picked up the rest of the story from them. He also found out that the Home Army fell under particular suspicion because this assassination attempt so obviously works in Traugutt's favor."

"But they don't know that Traugutt is one of us, do they?"

"No. Not at all." Marysia took another sip of her wine. "What they do know is that we favor Traugutt for more obvious reasons. He's been running the Göringstadt region humanely, and the local A.K. has made several informal agreements with him. Even most of them are unaware that they're dealing with one of their own."

"Then you would think the French would be happy to work with Traugutt as well."

"Maybe we can eventually convince them of that. Right now, they seem to think he's based too much in the east to make any improvements in the west."

"That's the way to handle them. Get Ryszard to make some statement or do something that will calm their worries and at the same time organize a propaganda campaign for Traugutt in the western Reich. I can even handle organizing something in England. In fact, that part will be easy. They hate Schindler."

"Good idea. But what about Ryszard's action? How do we explain that to HQ?"

"Maybe we should be sure it was his action. Has anybody asked him?"

Marysia shook her head. "Not yet. He's not all that accessible to us. But who else would do it?"

Peter smiled. "Lots of people, believe me. Before we panic about Ryszard, let's pin down the blame."

"Do you think Ryszard will tell us the truth?"

Peter nodded. "Yes. Mainly because I don't think he did it – he knows it goes against the rules, and there'll be hell to pay."

"Whose rules?"

"Theirs. Rule number one: the big guys don't try to kill each other. It's a gentleman's agreement."

"What about Ryszard's arrest in July?"

"From what I've heard, that was Büttner – and the first sign that he was losing his grip. He was getting desperate because he was being excluded.

An insider wouldn't have taken that sort of risk. Also, an arrest is not a direct assault – it's more acceptable. Especially if you can make the charges stick."

"I see."

"The other reason Ryszard wouldn't have done it is that Schindler and Schenkelhof are friends–"

"How do you know that? Has Ryszard been talking with you?"

Peter shook his head. "Don't forget – I have my own information. Remember, I spent nearly three years among these people. I may have been invisible, but I certainly wasn't blind. Sometimes, early on at least, I'd be especially alert so that I could report useful information in case I ever escaped." He smiled to himself at the insane hopes of those early days. "I worked at the Schindler's parties more than once–"

"You didn't belong to him."

"No, Vogel. But he'd loan me out to Schindler, and others, to curry favor or sometimes to repay a debt. Anyway, you can tell when two men talk as friends, and it was clear Schindler and Schenkelhof were genuinely friends."

"Which means?"

"Ryszard would never try to kill the friend of someone as powerful as Schindler – not unless he was desperate, and he isn't. In fact, this attack on Schenkelhof may well work against Traugutt. No one will want to support somebody who is that blatant and treacherous."

"Who did it then? Do you have any candidates?"

"One or two. Possibly Greta Schindler. She might be trying to help Traugutt, but didn't realize the damage it would do his reputation. In any case, whether she did it or not, she's a good one to pin the blame on. Wait a day or so and then tell HQ that we have an idea who did it and Ryszard is not to blame. Have Zosia poke around with her computer and see if she can find some evidence – a transfer of money from Switzerland or something like that."

"And if she doesn't find anything? What do we tell HQ then?"

Peter winked. "I'm *sure* we'll find something, as necessary."

Marysia picked up her glass and tapped it against Peter's. "Will do." She took a sip from her glass. "You know, Peter, Zosia seems a bit distracted of late, maybe it'd be better if you did it. Can you do that? Without Wanda noticing?"

Peter nodded. "Sure. I'll work on it at night." He drank the rest of his wine and stood up. "Speaking of work, I'd better get back. Thanks for the lunch." At the door, he paused to add, "Make sure someone talks to Schenkelhof's servants. If it isn't political, they're very likely to know who did it."

"Won't the police do that anyway?"

Peter shook his head. "Probably not if they're *Zwangsarbeiter*. After all, their testimony is inadmissible. But even if the investigators are thorough enough to talk to them, they won't get any sense out of them – they'll hear exactly what they expect to hear."

"Why?"

"Because the servants will say whatever is necessary to avoid being beaten up. What we need to do is have Leszek or Lodzia contact them and see what gossip there is. That's the only way to get a straight story."

Marysia nodded. "Okay, I'll pass that on."

31

*A*s Günter Schindler emerged from his office, it was obvious to Wolf-Dietrich that the news was not good. He waited, sitting stiffly in the Louis XIV chair, as his father paced angrily back and forth. Wolf-Dietrich eyed the delicate vases and fine mirrors and wondered if his father was going to send one flying into the other. Not only had the telephone call clearly angered him, but everything in the room belonged to Greta and would remain in her possession after the divorce. Too bad the law didn't allow her to throw her husband out of her house immediately: a lot of mischief could be done in the interim.

Günter picked up a vase and inspected it. Wolf-Dietrich had an appreciation for it as a work of art and not wanting to see it destroyed, decided it was time to speak. "So, what's the news?"

Günter set the vase back down unharmed. Clearly even he was hesitant to destroy such a fine object, even if it did belong to Greta. "Helmut is dead."

"Schenkelhof?"

Günter drew in a deep breath, absent-mindedly fingering the vase. "They say he suffered terribly – all those burns. Death was a mercy."

Wolf-Dietrich lowered his head in respectful sorrow.

"That bastard killed him! I'm going to get that son of a bitch!"

The sudden change in tone scared Wolf-Dietrich and he looked up worriedly. "Traugutt?"

"Of course. And you told me I could work with him!"

"I thought you could."

"Not now. He's gone too far this time. Murdering an officer of the Reich! And my friend."

"I'm sorry, Father. I really didn't expect this."

"Don't worry, I'll get that son of a bitch."

Wolf-Dietrich watched his father's hands as they continued to stroke the vase. It looked strangely threatening. "Father, be careful, he has friends."

"And enemies too. Especially now after this perfidy."

"Are you so sure he did it?"

"Who else?"

Wolf-Dietrich risked standing. He carefully approached his father. Damn, if his father destroyed everything now in an act of vengeance, after all his hard work! And if his father and Traugutt went at each other's throats, then he would lose Stefi forever! Wolf-Dietrich approached close enough to touch his father, but he did not dare. Instead he lowered his voice so that the bodyguards and servants could not eavesdrop. "Father, if anything happens to Traugutt, everyone will know it's you. The Führer will take it as a direct challenge. And the others will see it as a power grab."

"Oh, don't be stupid, I'm not going to assassinate the bastard. But believe me, I will make him pay. First I'll wait and see if the Kripos don't find any evidence against him."

"They won't."

"Of course they won't. It wouldn't do to air our dirty laundry to the world. Still, I have a few contacts among them – they may at least have an idea who's at fault."

"And then?"

"Then I'll bring down Traugutt. It's well past time."

Wolf-Dietrich moved in closer, daring to place a consoling arm around his father's shoulder. It struck him as odd that his father was smaller than he – when had that happened? Dropping his voice even lower, he asked, "What about the abortion? He might tell the Führer about it."

Günter glanced around. The two bodyguards in the room had stayed loyal to him during Rudi's kidnap and therefore had taken part in all the actions, including Stefi's arrest. They were as guilty as he and so there was no need to whisper. As for the servants, they were meaningless. With a slight shift of his shoulders he freed himself from Wolf-Dietrich's embrace. "He can't say anything – it's way too late for that. Rudi will wonder why he was lied to in the first place."

"But I thought Traugutt had information on the lab in London. He could tell the Führer about that."

Günter shook his head. "The laboratory was destroyed long ago, too long for Rudi to believe Traugutt would suddenly have information on what it was being used for. And if Traugutt claimed he knew something about it all along – well, then I think he'd have a lot of explaining to do about why he kept his mouth shut."

"And your programs?"

"I've abandoned the sterility program – that *would* infuriate Rudi if he learned it was ongoing." Günter dropped his voice. "I'll pick it back up once I'm running things. As for the others, I've transferred them to the Institute. The security is better there anyway."

"And are you going to admit that you have your own personal source in the ASA? If you don't, Traugutt will hold that over you as well."

Günter smiled. "I'm going to tell Rudi everything."

"But then you'll lose your ability to use the spy – Rudi will insist on his people having control of the information."

"That's not a problem anymore." Günter made a strange face. "You see, he's been terminated."

"The Americans discovered him?"

Günter shook his head. "No, he managed to get himself inside that resistance enclave bordering the south of Traugutt's territory – Schaf-something-or-other. The place that held Rudi. Somehow or other, they worked out who he was and had him killed."

"Wow." Wolf-Dietrich turned away from his father, to the vase that his father had been stroking so threateningly. It was quite beautiful. "Did they tell the Americans?"

"No. In fact, they passed his death off as an accident. But here's the interesting part – they might even believe it was an accident."

Wolf-Dietrich picked up the vase and looked at the bottom. Meissen. "How so?"

"You remember, we left Halifax in their protection?"

Wolf-Dietrich nodded and carefully set the vase back down.

"Well, my man was alone with Halifax when he 'fell' to his death."

Wolf-Dietrich looked at his father in surprise. "*Halifax* killed him?"

"Yes. That goddamned *Untermensch* took out my best agent!" Günter had grown quite loud and it was with some effort that he dropped his voice. "And he managed to make it look like an accident."

"Do the Americans know?"

"That their agent was an infiltrator for the Reich? No. That he was killed? Well, they believed the accident report – the wife corroborated it. But there are some who have their suspicions, and they're pretty upset. They don't know he was a spy, they just think that Halifax is a psychopath." Günter smiled evilly. "Fits the profile – kidnapper, murderer, criminally insane. His very existence defiles the purity of our nation…"

As his father ranted, Wolf-Dietrich recalled the bemused, intelligent expression he had seen on the face of the man pictured in the American magazine. He saw Stefi gracefully pointing toward Lederman as Halifax's torturer, he heard Ulrike's appalled report of what she had learned.

443

Kidnapper, murderer, criminally insane. None of it made sense, none of it fit with what Ulrike had told him about the man.

Wolf-Dietrich turned away to look at the fireplace. There were flowers placed in a basket inside it, where the wood should have been. The firebrick had been painted a pristine white to match the white stone mantel. Greta refused to have smoke in the room with all her precious possessions and so the fireplace was never used to make fires. It looked terribly cold to Wolf-Dietrich, cold and somehow silly – as if it felt insulted by the use to which it had been put. Flowers. Doubtless, next there would be bows or something asinine. As asinine as this vendetta his father was planning. Traugutt hadn't killed Schenkelhof, and doubtless Günter knew that. It was just an excuse in his mind to finally rid himself of the man.

"Father…" Wolf-Dietrich cringed at the look his father gave him for interrupting, but he forged ahead nonetheless. "Doesn't Traugutt have some American support? You said, after the way he pulled off that propaganda stunt while under arrest, you know, while the Führer was being held–"

"Even if he does have some mysterious backing in the NAU, I have my supporters now too! There're those men in the ASA who are angered by their co-worker's demise."

Wolf-Dietrich furrowed his brow in confusion.

"I'll let it be known that I am unhappy with Halifax being allowed to remain in the protective custody of the A.K. Don't you see? Those American spooks and I have the same goal: bring Halifax to justice. We won't be able to charge him with the murder of the American, but he's still guilty of Vogel's murder and I can demand that he be given up!"

"And so this group of Americans will support you?"

"Yes, especially when they realize that Traugutt wants to leave him in peace. Peace for a murderer!" Günter walked over to the fireplace and ran his fingers along the stone filigree of the mantel, inspecting it for dust. "And that's the most interesting thing, you see, because it was Traugutt who originally pushed for Halifax to be brought to trial, now, all of a sudden, he says we should just forget about him."

"Didn't you all sign an agreement that he could stay there?"

"It was signed under duress. It means nothing."

Wolf-Dietrich nodded.

"Besides, I'm not so sure Traugutt has any secret support in the American security services, after all, my agent never heard anything."

"Then how did he pull off that barrage of press releases that got him and Rudi freed? He was under house arrest at the time."

"Yes, he obviously had help, but I don't think it was the Americans. I think Halifax had something to do with it. He somehow convinced the A.K. to mobilize their people to save Traugutt."

It was the second time that his father had used "A.K." rather than "terrorists" when referring to the enemy and Wolf-Dietrich wondered at this sudden concession to political niceties. Had he somehow been impressed by the professionalism of the people he had seen in the mountains? "But why would Halifax care about Traugutt?"

"Good question, and one I'd like Rudi to ask Traugutt."

"But you can't tell him about what happened in his absence!"

"No, of course not. But I can tell him lots of other things. Did you know, for instance, that Lederman said it was Traugutt who convinced him to release Halifax from re-education?"

Wolf-Dietrich shook his head.

"Lederman had Halifax lined up for eventual liquidation, but Traugutt saved him. Now why do you think he did that?"

Wolf-Dietrich thought of his father's distress at how much Schenkelhof had suffered before dying. "Maybe he just doesn't like torture. Most of us don't like to see a human being suffer."

"Nonsense! We're not talking about a human, he's an *Untermensch*."

"Of course, Father."

"Halifax is Traugutt's agent. Traugutt thought he could gather evidence on his competitors by having Halifax placed in their household."

Wolf-Dietrich shook his head slightly. Kidnapper, murderer, criminally insane, and now an agent for a rival politician? None of it made any sense. "I've heard those re-education camps can be pretty brutal – why would Traugutt risk his agent's life in one of them?"

"Perhaps he didn't value it very highly." Günter seemed suddenly annoyed by Wolf-Dietrich's questions. "Anyway, who cares what his methods are? What matters is, there's some connection between those two and whatever it is, it's going to be Traugutt's Achilles' heel."

"How so?"

"I'm going to point out to Rudi what a scandal it is that his kidnapper lives in peace in the mountains. He murdered an official of the Reich and went unpunished and so he's become bolder. I'm going to suggest he had something to do with Schenkelhof's murder."

"Do you have any proof?"

"No, but once we have him, I'll interrogate Halifax – properly – like we should have done last time. It won't take long before he'll give away his master, after all, he isn't Aryan, so he won't be loyal."

"So you think he'll point a finger at Traugutt for Schenkelhof's murder?"

"Yes! And for Vogel's too! You told me yourself that you thought there was something odd about his returning to murder Vogel. Doubtless, he did it under orders from Traugutt."

"But why?"

"Karl Vogel must have somehow discovered the connection between Halifax and Traugutt. Maybe he tried to blackmail Traugutt with the information."

"Hmm." Wolf-Dietrich had to admit that his father's wild scheme did have a certain logic to it. "So, the idea is that Traugutt has an agent who for some reason or other ends up in a re-education program. After a reasonable amount of time has passed, Traugutt convinces the head of the program to release his man and has him placed as a *Zwangsarbeiter* in an important family." Wolf-Dietrich stopped to think about that. "You know, that's a pretty nasty position to put someone in. Does it make sense that–"

"You're talking about a man who has pimped his own daughter to the Führer."

Wolf-Dietrich reddened. And to himself? "Okay. Okay." After a moment, he collected himself and continued, "Okay, Traugutt then uses his agent's position as a domestic worker to collect information on Vogel and others. He uses that to advance his own position…" Wolf-Dietrich paused again. "You know, that part's a bit weak. I mean, what good is–"

"Doubtless he has other agents as well."

"Okay. So, at some point, Halifax escapes and then…Well, what was all that stuff in America? Did Traugutt organize that, too?"

"No. Traugutt's always trying to cozy up to the Americans. He had no reason to ruin the Reich's reputation. I think what happened is that Halifax got fed up with being kicked around and quit his job, so to speak."

Indignation was an *Übermensch* response, but Wolf-Dietrich knew better than to say that. Once again the terribly heretical thought ran through his mind that maybe there really was no racial hierarchy.

"I think the story Halifax told after that point is essentially true. He was captured in the Balkans and his services were sold to the Governments-in-Exile in New York. Once Halifax returned he realized he needed Traugutt's protection, so he contacted him and re-established a working relationship."

Wolf-Dietrich nodded pensively. "You know, actually maybe Traugutt contacted him. After all, there was that miraculous escape from the hospital. Perhaps Traugutt was afraid Halifax would betray him then."

"Oh yes, I had forgotten about that." Günter smiled. "That would explain yet another mystery. In fact, Halifax even screamed something on that videotape about making some sort of deal. Maybe he had in mind selling out Traugutt. So Traugutt has to rescue his erstwhile agent before he talks and then offers him another job."

"One which doesn't require him to be a slave."

"Yes, instead he became Traugutt's assassin. That explains why Traugutt didn't want him to be questioned once he was arrested the second time, in Berlin. He knew that Halifax would try to make a deal once the fun and games started in earnest."

"Oh, I see. Then Halifax escapes – this time without help – and heads toward the mountains and once he learns that Traugutt has been arrested, he convinces the A.K. to organize the exchange of the Führer. But how did he manage to enlist their aide on behalf of a Nazi official?"

"Doubtless in exchange for the Führer himself. You'll notice, they're the ones who made all the deals – not Halifax. All he got out of the proceedings was the right to remain in the mountains. No money, nothing."

"And he's still working for Traugutt?"

"Yes, and at this point, I would guess he's being handsomely paid, having proved his worth."

"You know, Father, it all sounds pretty believable." Wolf-Dietrich ignored his father's petulant glance. "But there are some weak points in it all. How are you going to present this to the Führer? You can't just accuse one of his top aides of multiple murders of Reich officials without some sort of proof. How are you going to handle this?"

Günter glanced at his watch. "You'll see. Come with me. I've arranged a meeting with Rudi about the security of his top aides in light of the attack on Schenkelhof, and I've asked that Traugutt be there. We're meeting at the *Residenz*, in Rudi's private suite. It's time we go."

"We?"

"Of course, you're my aide, aren't you?"

"Yes, Father. I appreciate your including me." Wolf-Dietrich felt himself flush with pride. But not just pride: Stefi might be there as well.

32

"*G*ünter, ach, my dear friend." The Führer absolutely beamed with pleasure as he heartily shook Günter's hand. "And who have you brought with you?" He extended his hand to Günter's companion.

"I'm Wolf-Dietrich, Günter's son."

"Ah, we have met, haven't we?"

Only about thirty times, Stefi thought. She stood behind the Führer playfully giggling at Wolf-Dietrich.

The Führer turned around. "And what has you so amused, *Mäuschen*?"

"Wolf-Dietrich's face. Look, he's blushing!" Stefi pointed at Wolf-Dietrich.

The Führer turned to see and nodded his head in agreement. "Indeed. So, Günter, how are you doing?"

"Not very well. Have you heard? Schenkelhof has died from his injuries."

"Yes, I've heard. Terrible business, terrible." The Führer shook his head in dismay.

"And I suspect it's only going to get worse."

"What do you mean?" The Führer walked them over to the living room suite, motioning to Traugutt and Frauenfeld, who stood together, off to the side. "Richard, Seppel, come join us."

They did. Frauenfeld extended a hand to Günter and then Wolf-Dietrich. Traugutt, who was out of reach of the two, bowed marginally. "Günter, Wolf-Dietrich."

Wolf-Dietrich returned the greeting with a similar bow. Günter remained stiffly erect. "Colonel Traugutt."

The Führer exchanged a surprised glance with Richard but did not comment on Günter's sudden formality. After Rudi had seated himself, he gestured for the others to sit down. A servant brought them drinks and offered cigarettes. Once everyone was settled, the servant bowed and withdrew a discreet distance.

Rudi swirled his drink lazily. "So Günter, what's this all about?"

"Peter Halifax."

Richard groaned audibly. The Führer sat upright. "What about him?"

"*Mein Führer*, after what that man has done, allowing him to remain alive *anywhere in the Reich* is a mistake. We're sending the wrong message, and we are emboldening a known killer."

Richard blew a stream of smoke into the air. "Günter, give it up, already. The man is in exile and he's just not worth the trouble."

"Colonel Traugutt, I find it interesting that you think the Führer's abduction and the horror he suffered is 'just not worth the trouble'."

"Don't be stupid. That's not what I said." Richard leaned forward, resting an elbow on his knee, and shook a finger at Günter. "You're making a mountain out of a molehill. The man's not important. He's a ridiculous distraction from the business of directing the Reich, and I'm wondering why you think the Führer's time is so unimportant that you bother him with this trivia. What are you trying to do, Günter?"

"Me? I'm just worried about the safety of Reich officials."

"Then do something about it! There's a whole Reich out there!" Richard gestured broadly toward the window. "And Rudi hardly has the time to waste on one idiotic criminal!"

The Führer patted the air with his hands. "Calm down, both of you. You're acting like children."

"*Mein Führer–*"

"No, I mean it. You, Richard, you must admit that man is an evil being. He lives contrary to the natural law, flaunting his subhuman traits. He took me prisoner and marched me through the woods for days. He bound my hands with a rope! Me! And now he roams freely through the mountains, his very existence an insult to my dignity."

"Yes, of course, *mein Führer–*"

"And you, Günter! Think about what you're saying! I am not going to dishonor myself by hunting down this gnat. Soon enough his friends will grow weary of him and trade him for one of their own. It's just a matter of time. Until then, why do you rub salt in my wounds?"

"*Mein Führer*, these people are dangerous. We ignore them at our peril."

"Who?"

"The people who hold those mountains, the Armia Krajowa."

Richard drew himself up at Günter's use of the proper name of the Home Army. Where had he learned that, and why?

The Führer was equally confused. "What are you talking about, Günter?"

"You must have seen it for yourself, *mein Führer*, they have–"

Richard decided to interrupt. "Günter–"

"Silence!" The Führer gestured angrily at Richard.

"As I was saying, *mein Führer*, before our dear Colonel Traugutt chose to interrupt, they have an impressive organization there. We saw only the smallest part of it, but the way we were intercepted, the governmental structure, even the control they exercised over their own people were all very impressive. Do you realize that we were not disarmed? They were that sure of themselves."

The Führer was nodding. "Yes, I didn't get to see much, but you're right, there's more there than just the bandits we always assumed we were dealing with."

"There's enough to form a government. A rival government." Günter drew the word *rival* out as though it were poisonous. "And they made sure there was an international witness. She's been in the NAU since then and has published several articles about their efficiency and organization. She's even spoken with American politicians about them."

Richard decided to try again. "*Mein Führer*, if I may–"

"I told you to shut-up. Let Günter speak."

"Yes, Richard, let me speak. Or are you afraid of my words?" Günter leered at Richard, but did not give him a chance to answer. "What I suggest is, we must assert our right to try Halifax for murder. The agreement we signed is worthless, it was signed under duress. We cannot give up our right to try our own criminals!"

The Führer was nodding. "But what if the mountain people won't surrender him?"

"Then we invade. They are a danger to us! We should never have tolerated their existence and it's time to put an end to this nonsense."

The Führer turned to Richard. "What do you think?"

With an effort, Richard unclamped his mouth. "*Mein Führer*, I think if we demand Halifax, the A.K. will think that he is somehow important and will not give him up. I believe that if we are patient they will eventually exchange him for some of their own. In the meanwhile, I would like to point out that we freely signed agreements to negotiate your release and that very little was asked of us. As civilized gentlemen, we would do well to honor our signatures and what little we did agree to. They have much that might embarrass us if it is publicized and if we violate this one agreement, they may well feel we've reneged on everything."

Stefi stroked the Führer's shoulder. "And you know, Rudi, our own men would die if they tried to invade that place. Our beautiful Aryan soldiers. There would be so much German blood shed for no good reason."

"Nonsense!" Günter harrumphed. He looked at Wolf-Dietrich. "You'd be happy to die for the Fatherland, wouldn't you?"

Wolf-Dietrich looked around in alarm.

"Rudi," Stefi cooed. "We don't want to send Günter's son to die, now do we? Not for something as silly as one stupid man!"

"The place should be invaded in any case! They are a danger to us! And what I want to know..." Günter paused to look meaningfully at Traugutt, "Is why do you want to tolerate a foreign government and a foreign army on Reich soil? Right in your own backyard, Richard."

"They were there before he took over that region," Wolf-Dietrich interjected helpfully. He visibly withered under the scowl he received from his father in response. "But of course," he added, timidly, "that's no excuse to continue to tolerate them."

"If you were truly loyal, Richard, you would insist on their annihilation!" Günter smiled in triumph.

"Günter, I am truly loyal, and I know that there is more to this Reich than one miniscule group of mountains."

"But what about Halifax?" the Führer asked suddenly. "We don't need to invade, if they give him up to us. It's not that much to ask."

"*Mein Führer*, we did sign an agreement–"

"Richard, you're not going to defend him again, are you? You know, I'm still wondering about why you had Lederman release him. And why did you insist I not have him properly interrogated when we had him under arrest?"

"*Mein Führer–*"

"Not a third time, Richard. You know, I would worry if you defended this man a third time."

"Exactly." Günter was nodding vigorously. "He should have been interrogated when we had him. Properly, I mean. And we need him back so that we can interrogate him properly this time."

Richard set his cigarette down in the ashtray. "Why? We know he murdered Vogel."

"Yes, but did he also murder Schenkelhof?" Günter looked meaningfully at Richard. "Maybe, he's even working for someone in Berlin."

The Führer tilted his head. "Is such a thing possible?"

Günter leaned toward the Führer, his face a mask of sincerity. "*Mein Führer*, we'll only know if we can question the man. We *must* interrogate him. We must demand that he be handed over to us."

"And if they refuse?"

"Then we invade. It's time to destroy that nest of vipers in any case. We kill them all and bring Halifax back to Berlin."

"It'd be a bloodbath!" Stefi hissed. "Do you wish to spill German blood on useless adventures?"

Though the question was directed at Günter, it was Rudi who answered. "Ah, *Mäuschen*, soldiers are meant to die. We must blood our troops, and this would be a good opportunity."

Richard weighed the Führer's words and the general tone of the conversation and decided to offer a compromise. "*Mein Führer*, might I suggest that we return to the original idea we had of extraditing Halifax for trial in a neutral country. There was a great deal of support for that in America and–"

"No!" Günter's booming objection caused them all to look at him in alarm. "Then we'd never be able to interrogate him."

"Günter, he has nothing we want to know anyway. If you think his continued free existence is an assault on the Führer's dignity, then this would solve the problem. He would be tried for murder and doubtless found guilty and imprisoned for life or executed."

"We must try him here!"

"Let the international community do it."

Günter's eyes narrowed threateningly. "What about Schenkelhof's murder? We'd never get to the bottom of that. We must find out why he did it and who ordered it! Or are you afraid of his speaking, Richard?"

"I'm not afraid, Günter." Richard sounded weary. "I just know he won't have anything useful to say. We'll ruin our reputation for nothing. If you want to see justice done, then insist on an international tribunal."

"And how do you know he'll have nothing useful to say about Schenkelhof's murder? Huh?"

Richard sighed. "Because he didn't do it."

"How do you know?"

"Because I know who did."

Everyone looked at Richard, and in response, he rose and went to his briefcase. He opened it and pulled out a sheaf of papers. "Here are the details."

The Führer was amazed. "Richard, how did you find this out? The Kripos have come up with nothing. And the Gestapo have no real suspects either."

"Neither of them bothered to ask Schenkelhof's servants. Or rather, the Kripos didn't bother and the Gestapo simply terrified them into stuttering nonsense."

"And what did you do?"

"I visited Frau Schenkelhof and took my servants with me. While I talked with her, my servants talked to her servants. Because they did not feel threatened, they talked freely."

"Why did you do that?"

"Because," Richard looked pointedly at Günter, "I knew there were some people who might want to blame me for this horrible crime, so it would be in my best interests to find out who really was guilty."

Rudi shuddered his distaste. "Yes, but to use servants. *Untermensch, um Gottes willen!*"

"I know, their testimony is worthless, but they gave me leads which I could follow up and here," Richard laid the sheaf of papers on the coffee table, "is what I found."

"And?"

Richard clasped his hands and bowed his head, gathering his thoughts. He looked up and addressed his audience as if beginning a lecture. "The Italian Autonomous Region has seen fit, under certain circumstances, to transfer a number of its treasures from museums in Italy to museums in the Reich. As we all know, Roman artifacts and whatnot are as relevant to our history as to theirs – certainly as far north as the Teutoburger Wald. Indeed, we are the heirs of the Roman Reich, are we not?" The group all nodded their agreement.

"Under an agreement with the Italian authorities, these transports are guarded by the *Wehrmacht*, to avoid theft by the local population. Nevertheless, it seems there is always a small portion of the transports that do not arrive intact into the Reich proper." Richard paused to pick up his cigarette from the ashtray. "The evidence I have uncovered indicates that there is a reason for this. The local criminal organization – the mafia, I believe some call it – had an arrangement with Schenkelhof–"

"Impossible! An officer of the Reich would never–"

The Führer silenced Schindler with a gesture. "Let Richard finish."

"I'm sorry to say that there is every reason to believe that Schenkelhof ordered the soldiers away from certain shipments, thus leaving them open to theft. The mafia paid Schenkelhof for the privilege of skimming off certain art treasures, which they, naturally, sold on the private market."

"Richard, if this is true, it still doesn't explain why…"

"I realize that *mein Führer*. But first, let me assure you, it is true. I have some bank statements from an account Schenkelhof held in Switzerland. You'll see that there are regular transfers of money from southern Italy." Richard peeled off a few pages from his sheaf and handed them to Rudi. "The problem came about when Schenkelhof decided to up the ante. He demanded more from the mafiosi, but they refused."

"What happened?"

"The mafia attempted to remove certain items from a shipment and instead of it being undefended as usual, they were fired upon by the soldiers. Unbeknownst to Schenkelhof, one of the young men killed in the melee was the son of a mafiosi boss. He, naturally enough, ceased to care about the profit and loss aspect of the business, and turned his thoughts solely to revenge."

"And?"

"He admitted that they had been wrong to refuse the higher fees and agreed to pay Schenkelhof everything he had demanded. The money would be sent to him directly, in gold coin, just to show their contrition at having rebelled. It was to arrive in a briefcase."

The Führer raised his head in recognition. "I see! So, it was a bomb!"

"Yes, revenge for the death of a son."

"And you have proof of this?"

"Of course." Richard handed over the rest of the papers. "Here's the trail. Give it to the Gestapo and I'm sure they can fill in the blanks."

Rudi held the papers in both hands, clearly excited. "How fascinating! What great detective work!"

Richard smiled at the thought of telling them all that Peter had suggested Leszek's and Lodzia's involvement and then afterward had traced the details via computer. Sometimes he truly regretted the silence under which he had to live. He also regretted not having removed Schindler when he had had the chance. As soon as they had all returned to Berlin from Szaflary, he should have told the Führer everything – Stefi's abortion,

Günter's power grab. Günter would have been arrested and Richard would have been reinstated as the sole senior advisor. He would have been rid of this continuous thorn in his side!

Instead he had been cautious, fretting uselessly about the Führer's reaction to having only one very powerful subordinate and worrying that HQ would not adequately support him. He had also banked on Günter's caution. And his word. How long had he kept his word? Richard could still remember Günter's slight bow and his "I am at your service." That was early November, and here it was only March and Günter was scheming yet again. He was right though, all the information that Richard held over him was dated and therefore worthless for blackmail. Richard supposed he could use the existence of the research programs in London which Günter had moved into the Technological Institute as new blackmail material, but it was unlikely that Rudi would object to those anyway. Especially since the sterility program – the only one which could generate genuine negative publicity – really and truly was dead. After all, every country had the right to develop bacterial and chemical weapons along with their usual nuclear arsenal. If Günter did the Führer a favor by keeping such things under his responsibility, then it would hardly do to denounce him for his devotion.

The Führer was showing the records to Günter, pointing out the transfers of money, the trips made and the telephone calls to numbers in Sicily. He looked up at Richard appreciatively. "An impressive research effort, Richard. You should have some of your people working with the Kripos."

Richard accepted the compliment with a crisp bow of his head as he reseated himself. "I'll suggest it to them." As Günter grumpily scanned the pages, Richard decided he could risk bringing it all to an end. He smiled at the Führer, "So, *mein Führer*, I think we've dealt with Günter's issues, perhaps it's time we move on to more pressing business. I've recently received information about nuclear material possibly being smuggled into the Reich via–"

"Not so fast, Richard." Of all people, it was Frauenfeld who had chosen to interrupt. "I am still concerned that we have allowed a murderer to escape justice. I don't think we should agree to such things. And this region in the mountains – that is a scandal. I had no idea they were such a threat to our security."

"They're not, and–"

"How can you say they're not?" Günter snapped. "You were there, Richard! And do you know, they are a source of information for the American Security Agency – not just from their region, but from throughout the Reich."

The Führer raised his eyebrows. "How do you know that Günter?"

"Because I had managed to get one of our agents into the ASA." Günter leaned forward as if imparting special knowledge, "And do you know – it was Halifax who found him out and killed him."

"How?"

"My agent managed to get inside that resistance enclave – after Halifax took refuge there. It was meant to be a surprise for you, Rudi. I know how much those people have hurt you." Günter sat back and closed his eyes in dismay. "Unfortunately Halifax must have found him out because that treacherous snake murdered my–" Günter caught his mistake and amended, "your man."

"I think…" Frauenfeld paused thoughtfully to make sure everyone was listening. "I think we should test how much of a threat these people are to us. We should demand Halifax be sent to an international tribunal – like Richard suggested – and if they refuse or claim he's fled, then they are obviously too strong and we should invade. If they agree, then they are not a challenge to us and we can bide our time with them."

Rudi smiled at Frauenfeld. "Good idea."

Günter nodded. "Except it should be Berlin. We still need to question him."

Frauenfeld shook his head. "No, not Berlin, I think Richard is right about what holding him here will do to our international reputation. But if we demand a neutral country – say Switzerland – then no one can object. Indeed, isn't there support in the NAU for him being sent to Switzerland, Richard?"

"There was. But now, I think we should drop this whole thing. It's a waste of time."

"Richard…" The Führer leaned forward, his eyes glistening. "Are you saying that your own idea was a waste of time?"

"No, *mein Führer*. What I mean is–"

"Or are you defending this man yet again?" Günter interrupted to ask.

Richard shook his head.

"It was, after all, your idea, this international tribunal."

"I know."

"And I think it works perfectly!" Frauenfeld pounded the coffee table excitedly. "We can test the strength of the enemy by demanding something perfectly reasonable, something they have no reason to fear. After all, why do they want to harbor a murderer and a kidnapper? They'll be assured that he'll be tried by international standards, people in the NAU support his extradition, and if they reject the idea, we'll know they are far too strong and we'll invade and crush them now, before they grow stronger!"

The Führer looked thoughtful, Günter nodded his head excitedly. "And we should demand they hand that child back as well!"

Stefi glanced at her father, but he was staring down at the coffee table and didn't say anything. She looked at Wolf-Dietrich. Madzia was his fiancée's sister, but that seemed insufficient to prod him into voicing his opinion. It was Frauenfeld who disagreed. "We don't even know if she is there. Besides, I think Halifax or his wife would publicly fight for custody. I don't think we want to go that route."

"What about Frau Vogel? It's her daughter." The Führer turned to Richard. "Has she said anything to your wife?"

Richard shook his head slightly. "My son speaks with Teresa Vogel – she seems to be of the opinion that her mother is resigned to the loss." He hesitated, then added, somewhat reluctantly, "And I don't think our child custody laws would withstand international scrutiny. We would do well to avoid that topic."

Stefi was surprised that her father had thrown away such an extraordinary propaganda opportunity. Was it possible he had sacrificed a strategic advantage in order to spare Peter further pain?

Frauenfeld was vigorously nodding his head. "And if we waste resources squabbling over the child, the focus will shift off Halifax and his crimes."

"Yes, that's what we want to focus on," Richard said quietly, without looking up. Stefi looked from him to the other men in the room and decided her father's surrender made sense.

The Führer smiled that a consensus had been reached. "Richard, it was your idea in the first place. Why don't you organize everything? Let them know what their choices are."

Before Richard could answer, Günter volunteered, "I can handle publicity in the NAU. I have a few contacts there. And Wolf-Dietrich's fiancée will be very helpful in generating positive publicity for us."

"Very good, very good, Günter. It's great to see you all working together. What do you say, Richard? Can I count on you?"

Richard's cigarette was nothing but a trail of ash in the ashtray. He reached down and ground out the end. "Of course, *mein Führer*. I'll let the A.K. know that they must hand over Halifax. I'm sure they'll be more than willing to cooperate."

33

"Shallow? Then you do it!" Kamil called out. With one arm, he was hanging onto a tree trunk that leaned out over the stream and with the other, he was desperately reaching with his fishing rod for his cap as it approached, merrily floating along.

Tadek, who had made the suggestion, set down his fishing rod and boldly skidded down the bank, but at the water's edge he hesitated. March waters were icy, and after all, it wasn't *his* favorite hat that had landed in the stream. Of course, it was his fault that Kamil's hat was in there, but...As the cap floated past Kamil's rod, Tadek took a tentative step into the water. Even through his leather boot he could feel the bitter cold, and it would only take a few seconds for the water to soak through. He withdrew his foot and looked up the bank. "What are you doing?"

Peter continued walking downstream. "You'll see." A few meters further on he found a stony section free of undergrowth and he waited, not even bothering to scramble down to the water's edge. When the distance was right, he cast his line and the hook landed nicely on top of Kamil's hat. He carefully reeled it in, pulling it to the bank and Tadek walked over and picked it up.

"Show off!"

Kamil joined the two, gratefully taking the wool cap into his hands. "Thanks, guys!" He carefully smoothed the feather. "This belonged to my dad. Man, I would have hated to lose it."

Peter finished reeling in the line, too distracted by the approaching hook to say anything. He tensed as the hook swung into reach. Very carefully, he raised his hand and caught the line above the hook between his finger and thumb.

Tadek observed the ritual bemusedly. "I've always meant to ask you, is that how they do it in London?"

"Huh?" Peter kept his eyes on the hook, slowly moving his hand down the line, closer to it.

"Why do you do that?"

Peter didn't look up, all his attention was focused on the hook. "Do what?"

"Approach the hook like that. I mean, like it's covered in poison."

Kamil nodded his head in agreement at Tadek's observation. "Maybe in London they are. I've heard the river is really polluted."

Peter ignored them as he concentrated on his task. He managed to finally close his fingers around the treacherous slip of metal and with a trembling hand, tucked it safely away. Only then did he look up, replaying their questions in his mind. His confusion was evident in his face. "There're no fish in the Temms."

Tadek persisted. "Then where'd you learn–"

With a sudden recognition, Kamil jammed an elbow into Tadek's ribs to shut him up. Placing his still damp cap on his head, Kamil started to walk,

457

motioning to his friends to follow. "Come on, the women will be missing us. Let's get back and show them the wonderful fish we've snagged."

Tadek took the hint and suppressing a grunt of disgust at the nauseating scenarios that flashed through his mind, followed Kamil's lead. Kamil was right – he didn't want to know! But even the implication was enough to make Tadek want a drink, and, he reasoned, it might well aid him in the task ahead. He had put it off all day, there wasn't much time remaining.

As the three walked back, he pulled out a bottle and passed it around. Once they had all imbibed a bit, he began singing and Kamil and Peter joined in, pausing every now and then to take a swig from Tadek's bottle. They covered the rest of the distance back to the bunker that way, singing, drinking and eventually laughing a bit too much.

Before they reached the entrance, Tadek stopped to tuck away his bottle and then pulled Peter aside, explaining to Kamil that he needed to have a private conversation. He waved Kamil on, then led the way into a copse, where he set down his equipment and sat on a log.

Peter followed, but remained standing, leaning against a tree. Only a moment before he had been laughing at Kamil's joke, but now he remained tensely silent, clearly unnerved by the unexpected detour.

Tadek pulled out a pack of cigarettes. "Want one?"

Peter shook his head and Tadek put the pack away. Tadek stared off into the woods, wondering how best to phrase his question.

After a long silence, Peter was finally driven to ask, "You wanted to ask about something?"

Still looking off into the woods, Tadek nodded.

"Fishhooks, maybe?"

Disconcerted, Tadek snapped his head around to look at Peter. He thought he and Kamil had nicely sidestepped that one! "No! No, not that."

Peter raised an eyebrow derisively. "Then *what?*"

"It's...not that. I've been asked if I could..."

Peter crossed his arms and stared off at the sky. A flock of geese heading north flew overhead, honking noisily.

"The Council..." Tadek sighed.

"I'll make you a deal, Tadek. I'll answer your uncomfortable question, if you answer one of mine. Okay?"

Tadek nodded.

"So, spit it out already."

Tadek took a deep breath. "Okay, here goes. Are you aware of the fact that you occasionally seem to black out?"

Peter nodded. A slow, overtly patient nod.

"Has it become a more common occurrence recently?"

"That's more than one question."

"Please, Peter. It has caused some worries among members of the Council–"

Peter looked in the direction the geese had flown, but they were no longer visible. "Just think of it as deep thought."

"It isn't that, though, is it. You're having flashbacks aren't you?"

"Maybe. Why does it matter?"

"Have they become more frequent?"

Peter shook his head. "I don't think so. I think before I kept more to myself, so they weren't noticed as much."

Tadek nodded in agreement. He didn't bother to mention what they both knew – that at that time not only did Peter keep more to himself, but many people, Tadek chief among them, actively shunned him. "So, they're not getting worse?"

"No, but why does it matter? I'm not going to do any infiltrating. And I'm hardly likely to hurt anything if I pause in front of my computer screen."

"We – that is the Council – just needed to know in case you go anywhere else, the NAU, for example."

"Wanda's made it clear I'm not leaving here, and I like it that way. I'm not taking any trips, so what's this about?" Peter walked over to the log on which Tadek was sitting and sat down next to him. "The truth, Tadek."

Tadek laughed. "I must be a lousy liar."

"Yes, it's your only charming characteristic. Now, what's their problem?"

"Oh, a couple of people were afraid that, well, you know that sometimes you black out and your face is a blank, but other times, it looks like…"

Peter worked a chip of wood loose from the log and flung it into the trees. "Like I'm capable of mass murder?"

"Or at least murder."

"Ah-ha! Wanda's worried I'm going to strangle her." Peter laughed heartily. "Good!"

Tadek found the image funny as well.

Eventually, Peter calmed down and explained surprisingly gently, "Tell her I'm quite safe. Tell her that even though my mind is elsewhere, a part of me is still rooted in reality and that I am always aware enough not to react to my visions. That's why I simply freeze."

Tadek nodded, satisfied. "I've seen that look, you know, and it scared me."

"Scared the Führer, too. But even him, I didn't harm, now did I?"

"Fair enough." Tadek stood. "Shall we go?"

"No. You owe me a couple of answers now." Peter motioned toward the log.

Tadek reluctantly sat back down. "Alright, what do you want to know?"

"Why haven't you remarried?"

Tadek gave Peter a sharp look. "You know my wife is still alive."

"Yes, I know she was taken to a brothel and quickly worked her way out as somebody's mistress. You tried to rescue her and lost a number of men. And as far as I can tell, she showed no interest in going with you."

"We didn't get a chance to discuss it."

"She lives as the housekeeper and nanny of an SS officer but everyone knows she's his de facto wife and mother to his children. Why don't you divorce her and get it over with?"

"Because she didn't have a choice. She deserves to have a choice. *You* of all people should understand that."

Peter picked off another bit of rotted wood and tossed that into the distance. "Maybe."

"But why do you care anyway?"

"I should think that's obvious. Tell me, how long have you and Zosia had your special relationship?"

Tadek hesitated, then opted for complete honestly. "Almost since I arrived."

"That long! But why? I mean, I see what you're doing. You don't want to abandon your wife but you don't want to be entirely alone either. You're in some miserable limbo with respect to marriage. But didn't Zosia know Adam then? Wasn't she in love with him? Why did she pick up with you?"

Tadek laughed slightly. "I think she just wanted to add a trophy to her collection."

"I don't understand."

"Insecurity."

"Zosia? Insecure? *Zosia?*"

Tadek smiled at Peter's naïveté about Zosia. Despite everything, he was still blindly in love with her! "That's my guess. I wasn't here, but you know, she was the sixth of six children. Her brother, Ryszard, is almost ten years her senior and you can imagine what it was like growing up with him around. And you know Alex – he's hardly the warmest of men. I imagine Zosia only got her share of attention when she started accomplishing things. So now, she wants to hedge her bets. There was Adam, whom she adored, then me – I provide the necessary reassurance when she's feeling insecure."

"And me?"

"You're still a work in progress." Tadek rubbed his chin. "You know, I think her love for you is more deeply rooted than what she felt for Adam."

Peter raised his eyebrows in surprise. "But she still needs you?"

"Is that so awful?"

There was only a slight hesitation before Peter shook his head. "Not anymore. My entire worth is no longer wrapped up in the reflection I see of myself in her eyes."

"So you're not going to kick me out?" Tadek regretted the plea he heard in his voice, but it was too late – Peter had heard it as well.

Instead of the cutting remark which Tadek expected, Peter shook his head in commiseration. "No. I'm not going to deny Zosia what she obviously needs. And besides, the bunker is overcrowded – it's our duty to provide you with space."

Tadek clapped his arm around Peter's shoulder in a spontaneous gesture of gratitude and friendship. Peter flinched in response and Tadek laughed at that. "Don't cringe! I'm not going to kiss you."

Peter responded with a weak smile. "Good, I can handle your and Zosia's non-standard relationship, but I'm definitely drawing the line there."

Unable to resist, Tadek teased further, pulling Peter into a hug. Obviously perturbed, Peter shrugged off Tadek's arm, then quickly stood, trying to make the gesture look natural. "Shall we go?" he asked, with casual cheerfulness.

But Tadek wasn't fooled. He remained seated and looked up at Peter, laughing at his sensitivity. "You're funny."

Peter nodded, a tight smile on his face. "Yes, it's all hilarious. Now shall we go?"

Tadek stood and picked up his equipment. As he grasped his rod, he noticed the hook, tucked snugly against the pole. He stared at it a moment, at the very sharp, curved metal.

It's all hilarious.

All hilarious. Even fishhooks. Fishhooks? Tadek shuddered. Embarrassed, he muttered, "I'm sorry, Peter. I didn't mean anything by all that."

"I know. Let's go." Peter started up the incline out of the copse.

"Peter?" Tadek called out hesitantly. "Do you remember? I mean, do you know why…"

Peter stopped. Without looking back, he nodded.

"And?" Tadek prompted, then wished to God that he hadn't said anything.

"Come on, let's go," Peter suggested and resumed the climb.

They continued in silence the rest of the distance to the bunker. At the entrance they were met by a sentry. "Oops, looks like a Council meeting," Tadek guessed, relieved by the promise of a distraction. But the sentry turned to Peter and informed him that Marysia needed to see him immediately.

"Doubtless Ryszard again." Peter handed his equipment to Tadek. "I'll see you back at the flat. Could you tell Zosia I've been called away?"

"Sure. But I won't be there by the time you get back. I've been invited out to dinner. So – you two will have some time alone." He winked at Peter.

"Ah, yes, privacy with a toddler, a baby and a big squirming lump in Zosia's belly!"

"Do what you can." Tadek walked off grinning.

Marysia greeted Peter with a brief smile and a kiss. She looked terribly strained, her face was drawn and her hair, though pinned back, hung in strands around her face as if she had been pulling it loose. "Sit down, we need to talk."

He immediately felt very worried. "What is it?"

"We've received an ultimatum."

"A what? From whom?"

She poured him a drink. "Sit down. I'll explain everything."

They sat next to each other, at her kitchen table. As she began explaining the situation, Peter placed his elbows resting on the table and stared down at the wood. His fingers curled around the drink she had poured for him, tightening their grip on the glass, but he did not bring it to his lips. Marysia watched for some reaction, but he didn't move and he kept his eyes lowered. She finished speaking and waited for him to say something but he remained silent. "You understand what it means that it came from Traugutt," she added, just to provoke some response.

"Of course."

"Ryszard is warning us – they're serious. The wording is unequivocal."

"I understand."

"Peter…" She reached over and touched his hand. He gently slid it out from under hers and used it to push his hair back. It was such a natural gesture that she was unsure if he had meant to reject her consolation.

"What about Madzia?"

"They didn't mention her. They only want you."

"Good."

She touched his shoulder. He adjusted his position, straightened in his seat, and, quite naturally, his shoulder fell out of her reach. She did not try again to touch him, instead she used words. "I'm sorry. I know you were just following orders."

"It's okay."

Marysia shifted so she could look into his face, he turned his head a bit in response. She simply could not catch his eye. "Peter, if you're angry – I understand."

"Why would I be?"

462

She didn't know what to say to that. She could think of a million reasons why he should be furious and she had been ready to respond to each, but not to this complete withdrawal. "Look, do you have any better ideas?"

"You've already made your decision, haven't you? I mean, the Council met on this, didn't they?"

"I haven't brought it to the full Council yet, but I have consulted with Katerina, Wanda, and Konrad. They're agreed…" But she didn't say on what they had agreed. "Zosia knows as well. She says we shouldn't allow ourselves to be blackmailed, and in general, I agree with that. But we can't afford to risk our existence over…"

"Over one man. Especially one whose actions we've advertised as being personal and criminal. I understand."

Marysia found his complete agreement unnerving. Deep down she had hoped that when she presented him with the ultimatum, he would casually suggest an alternative strategy or even explain the necessity of war. The counterweight was missing and she worried that with it, they were missing the way out of the mess. She realized, too late, that she should have told him that it was someone else being demanded. Then he would have turned that brilliant mind of his to strategy, but it was clear that on his own behalf, he had lost the will to fight. "Peter, maybe there's something that can be done. I was hoping you…"

"I'll see if anything clever suggests itself." He stood and she studied his expression, eagerly looking for some sign of what he felt or would do. But he looked as though she had told him nothing more than the upcoming weather forecast. She even hoped for that flicker of anger, of unmitigated hatred that sometimes marred his face, but even that was absent.

A wan smile flitted across his features then disappeared back into the void. "Thanks for not making it an order." With that, he leaned down, kissed her on the cheek and left.

34

*A*s Peter headed to his apartment, he knew he should be plotting an alternate strategy, some complicated scheme to protect his freedom, but all he could think of was that boy Dennis saying to him, "Sorry, kid, bloody unfair. Now off with you!"

Zosia was in the flat, sitting on the couch alone, reading a file. The bedroom was dark, so he guessed the children were napping. He set down his equipment, hung up his coat and gun, then walked over to the couch.

She looked up from the page she was studying and seeing his expression, guessed, "Marysia told you?"

He nodded.

"Damn it! She just found out this morning, why didn't she wait a bit?"

He ran his fingers absently along the material of the sofa, as if memorizing it. There was so much to memorize before it would all disappear. Irena's and Madzia's and the baby's entire childhoods! They might be adults before he came back. And Marysia – she might well be dead by the time he returned. If he returned. "I guess she wanted me to know what was going on immediately," he said, in vague answer to Zosia's question.

"Yes, but the Council hasn't even met on this yet. Telling you even before a decision has been taken – that's unfair. She's looking for you to volunteer so she doesn't have to bear the responsibility!"

He nodded slightly. "I suppose." He closed his eyes as he traced out a pattern. Magdalena, the cryptanalyst perhaps. He imagined her working with devices he could not even name. And Irena? Would she be an assassin like her mother? Or an infiltrator? Or would everything have changed by then? Would it all be over, a new society he would neither recognize nor understand? And what would the baby look like? Would he be able to walk up to a strange young man or woman and say, "Hi, I'm your father." Would he know anything about any of them? Would he receive photos and letters? Or would their security demand he remain in ignorance the entire time?

"Peter, do you understand what this could mean? You can get a death sentence for murder, you know."

"We'll make sure that's not an option," Marysia stated from the doorway. Zosia stood to confront her, but Peter did not even look at her. "We will refuse extradition if the death penalty is an option."

Again Peter simply nodded. Would Zosia wait for him all that time? Would it be fair to even ask that of her?

Zosia was less controlled. "Great! Then all we're looking at is life in prison! Jesus Christ, Marysia, he did it for us, for Ryszard, with our approval, at our request. At your command!"

"And are we going to tell the world that?"

"We don't have to tell them anything! We owe them *nothing!* Why should we hand *anybody* over to them?"

"You know the realities, Zosia. You know the Führer will invade if we don't hand Peter over."

"The ingrate! We let him go – we should have hanged him. Tortured him first, then hanged him on a meat hook for all to see."

"That would not have been politically expedient." Marysia sounded as though she was tired of saying the same words over and over. "The Führer

464

does not understand gratitude – in fact, he feels rather annoyed that our existence has been so blatantly rubbed into his face. I don't think he understood what our independence meant before. Now he's angry. Angry that Peter's been allowed to stay here, angry that we're here at all, and he wants to destroy both him and us."

"Let him invade. We fought them off last time."

"No." Marysia drew the word out like a tutor trying to teach a very stubborn child. "We *held out* last time – until Ryszard convinced him to give up on the idea. Last time they weren't serious. We have no idea what sort of suicidal tactics he'd insist on this time – but one thing I do know is that it will cost a lot of lives, both ours and theirs."

"So you're saying we won't fight because we don't want soldiers to die? Bit pointless having soldiers, isn't it?" Zosia asked sarcastically.

Marysia looked at Peter but he had remained quietly contemplating the fabric of the couch the entire time. She approached him, but he did not look up. She sighed heavily. "You know it's more than that. You know Ryszard has built an entire edifice upon being able to hand Peter over to the international community for a fair trial. And I'll remind you – that was at your request."

"That was when Peter was in the Führer's hands!"

"Nevertheless, the groundwork was laid. Ryszard pushed strongly for the idea, staked his reputation on it. You also know the damage that's been done to our cause by this scandal. We're harboring an accused kidnapper and murderer."

Zosia snorted. "Describes the whole damn Reich government."

"I know that, you know that, but we've painted ourselves as the guys in white. We do no wrong and our line has been to deny any knowledge of Peter's actions. They had to be personal so that Ryszard wouldn't be implicated." Marysia tugged at Peter's sleeve. "That was *your* suggestion. This was all *your* plan."

"Oh, Marysia!" Zosia spat, "Why don't you just say it's *all* his fault! You not only betray him, but you're a coward about it!"

Three children. Irena, Madzia, the baby. Would they greet him on the day of his release? Would Zosia be there? He should divorce her before he left. It would give her the freedom to marry Tadek. She shouldn't spend the time waiting. That would be silly.

Frustrated by her attempt to draw him into the conversation, Marysia turned her attention back to Zosia. "We can't suddenly claim that Peter's actions were political. We can't defend him! We can't harbor him without harming our cause. It's already cost us a lot of support! And you know that the ASA have their suspicions about their agent's death here. They've kept quiet so far, but they could go public with that."

But a divorce wouldn't be enough. Not for Zosia. She'd need an annulment. Could they claim the marriage wasn't valid? Based on false pretenses – yes, that was true. She had lied to him from the moment they met. He smiled at the thought – she'd never accept that: he'd have to make it his fault. Well, that'd be easy enough. He'd have to talk to one of the priests, see what he could arrange. And Tadek needed a divorce as well, he could be convinced to stop waiting if Zosia were truly available…

"…that support was never really there in the first place," Zosia was saying. "We got what we wanted from the bastards – their money. Now we should forget about them."

"I wish we could. We thought this stupid thing would go away. But someone's constantly fanning the flames and we can't ignore it any longer."

"Marysia! You're talking about Peter going to prison, probably for life!"

Marysia touched Peter's sleeve again. He took a small step away from her, and she let her hand drop.

How many years of his life had he spent imprisoned? Should he count school? It had certainly felt like prison. Prepared him for the rest of his life. So four years at that horrid school, a few months here and there for misdemeanors, four years in a labor camp, half a year under interrogation and re-education, altogether about three and a half years with the Reusch's and the Vogels. So, just over a dozen. Twelve years – some of it in intense pain, most of it under threat of death – and his greatest crime had been wanting to be free, wanting to be an individual, wanting to be human.

"Maybe they won't find him guilty," Marysia was suggesting, somewhat hopelessly.

Twelve years. Was that any way for a person to spend his life?

"They'll have to, if he sticks to his story." Zosia sighed heavily. "Besides, they have a witness, a confession and material evidence. You know he deliberately avoided covering his tracks!"

"Maybe he could use the defense…"

It'd be better that way. He was meant to spend his life alone. Anytime he had struggled for anything else, it had led to disaster. He didn't want that to happen again. First his sister, then his parents, Allison, Joanna…It was enough. Better not to get close to anyone. Better to leave the children safe and untainted by his presence. They would be fine without him. Surrounded by love, they'd be alright. "Alright," he whispered, looking up at Zosia. They'd be alright without him.

Surprised by his words, Marysia stopped in mid-sentence. Peter replayed what she had just said, then turned to her and said, "No, I'm not going to plead insanity. Temporary or otherwise." He grinned at her impishly. "It's too close to the truth."

"Peter…"

"It's time to stop arguing. How long do I have? Can we delay my departure until after the baby is born?"

Marysia nodded. "I'm sure we can. Since there will have to be NAU involvement, it will take some time until everything is agreed upon and you should stay here until that point. In fact, if we delay long enough, maybe this whole thing will blow over."

"Maybe, but I won't bank on it. I'll finish upgrading the system here, but I'm resigning from all other work, okay?"

"Effective when?"

Peter pursed his lips as he thought about working even one more day with Wanda as his boss. "Immediately." She would still outrank him though, so he added, "And I'm resigning my commission."

"Your commission? But why?"

"I'm going to be a completely free man – for the duration. I'd like to arrange a few things, too. A divorce for Zosia – an annulment if possible."

Zosia furrowed her brow angrily. "What are you talking about?"

"Your freedom, dear. I'm going to be pleading guilty to first degree murder and kidnapping. I'll probably get life. That means at least twenty years before there's any hope of parole – if they have such things."

"But what does that have to do with our marriage?"

"What are you going to do during that time? The same thing you did the last time I was away?"

Zosia narrowed her eyes and cast a meaningful glance at Marysia. Peter ignored her warning, but Marysia suddenly cocked her head. "I think I hear the baby." She disappeared into the bedroom.

Peter dropped his voice to a whisper. "I know you're not violating your own morality – and that's fine with me. Your body is yours to do with as you please, but we live in a society here, one that disapproves of such things." He nodded his head toward the bedroom, "Or feels embarrassed by them. For the sake of the kids, I think it'd be best if you and Tadek didn't have to go sneaking around or defying convention or whatever. If you're divorced from me, then you could express your love for him openly – and the children could be raised by you both."

"You've wanted this all along, haven't you?"

Peter shook his head. "You must know that's not true, but I can't deny reality. I'm going to be gone too long to be anything other than a name to them – and to you. You can't love a name. They shouldn't have to wait years and years and years for a name. Let them have a father who can be here for them. Tadek will be a good father to them. And you'll take care of all of them, won't you?"

"Yes, of course."

"Madzia included?"

"Of course!" Zosia said it without thought, too busy being insulted by the implication.

That worried him – he knew her so well, he knew it would someday be an issue and he hoped she would shrug off the insult and seriously confront it before that day, but he also knew that there was no realistic possibility of forcing her to think about her future feelings. He would simply have to hope that Zosia's sense of fair play would overcome her natural predilection to favor her own flesh and blood. "Zosiu, will you treat Madzia *as your own*?"

"I said I would."

She hadn't, but he ignored that. "You swear?"

Marysia re-emerged from the bedroom. "I must have been wrong. They're sleeping peacefully."

Zosia ignored her. "By all I hold sacred."

Marysia returned to standing by Peter. "Your children will be cared for, Peter. Madzia included."

"No matter what happens?" Peter looked from Marysia to Zosia. "No matter whom you marry?"

Zosia shook her head, "I will not marry anyone else! We *will* wait for you!"

"Please don't. It's bad enough I'll be locked up for years, there's no reason for you and the children to be imprisoned by–" He heard a door slamming and the noise confused him because it shut out the light. The room was damp, and his skin grew clammy. No windows, there were no windows and no lights. It was pitch black. Oh God, no! He wanted to reach out to find the walls, but he was afraid of moving, afraid to discover that he was bound and gagged, afraid to find the walls of his coffin were only inches away. Rats crawled over him and he could not stop them. Their eyes glittered at him through the darkness, their tiny claws gouged his face. He twitched in revulsion at their touch.

"Are you alright?" Marysia stepped over to him, grabbed his arm, fearful that he would fall.

"Alright?" Zosia snarled. "You've implied that the only alternative to his surrender is hundreds of deaths, Marysia. And you want to know if he's alright? You shouldn't have even asked this of him! It's totally unfair."

"It's an unfair world. I have asked, and he's accepted it." Marysia reached up to touch Peter's face. "As I knew you would."

The glittering eyes were Marysia's. Zosia stood a few feet away, tears rolling down her cheeks. She was whispering something. Peter listened, heard her say, "Prison will kill him."

Kill who? He looked from one woman to the other, confused by the bright light, by their concerned faces. Marysia was holding his arm. He freed himself from her grasp. He was at the door, had put on his holster and was reaching for his coat, before he realized he should say something. He turned and smiled gently at the two women. "I'll be back, I just need some fresh air."

Part III

No Regrets

1

*H*ow long would Ryszard need to become Führer? And once he was, how long would it take until he could issue a pardon? But he couldn't, could he? It was an international tribunal which would convict and pass sentence. To whom did one appeal to overturn or nullify that?

"Are you paying attention?" Alex whispered.

Peter shook his head. "There doesn't seem much point. I'm going to be convicted." And then, would he get a life sentence? Interestingly, though the NAU and the Reich both had legal executions, the tribunal had ruled out any possibility of his getting a death sentence. That had been one of the Home Army's conditions for handing him over. Apparently it had not been too difficult to get agreement on that condition in America – he had a lot of support among the general populace and even among some politicians, and the country which had agreed to host the trial – Switzerland – had also insisted that no greater punishment than life imprisonment be possible.

Still, life could be a rather long sentence and he didn't want to spend his life rotting in a prison – especially not for Vogel's murder. It hardly stood as a great cause around which he could rally support. He could present it as understandable, merited even, but without giving away Ryszard's position and the Home Army's involvement, he would be obliged to spend his time as a violent criminal, not as a freedom fighter, not as a soldier. Who would have thought, in a country full of politically inspired murders, that a simple assassination would ever evoke such a response? Who would have thought that America, which consistently ignored the slaughter of innocent political prisoners worldwide, would fall prey to this propaganda effort and would be incensed by the killing of a cruel official of the Reich's security apparatus?

"...unprecedented opportunity to reawaken interest..." Alex was saying. Peter did not listen, he had heard too much of it already. He did not listen to the expert witness talking about post traumatic stress syndrome, nor did he listen to Alex's intense whisperings about how they should proceed. The presiding judge cast a warning glance at them, and Alex fell into silence. Peter was relieved. He did not need to have it all laid out in gruesome detail – he understood Alex's points, didn't even really disagree with them, he just didn't have the heart to go through with it all.

Peter's lawyer was speaking now. He was a decent fellow – uninformed about the genuine reasons for the assassination, or even that it was an assassination, he did his best to defend his client's actions. There were tedious discussions about the psychological state which could lead a person to commit such a crime so long after he had escaped. Was it possible that it was all due to temporary insanity? A delayed self-defense mechanism? Had the cruelty of those years been so great, that the chance sighting of Vogel had driven Peter to a desperate and irrational act?

Despite Alex's pleas, Peter refused to testify either on his state of mind or on what his years with the Vogels had been like. Yes, it would highlight, once again, the justice of their cause. Yes, it would add salacious details to an otherwise dry proceeding, thus raising audience interest in the televised portion of the trial and providing the anti-Reich coalition with much needed publicity. Yes, it would even raise the possibility of an acquittal, or at least a lower sentence upon conviction. But it would all be complete lies. He had killed Vogel because Vogel's assassination had been required to keep Ryszard safe. It had been done under orders. And if complete secrecy was necessary to protect Ryszard and all those involved, then so be it. Peter would remain quiet about his motives, but he would not lie. It was not that he was incapable of lying. God knew that he had lived entire false lives and could convincingly present almost any face he wanted to the world, nor would most of what he'd need to say be untrue – he *had* suffered horrendous brutality at Karl's hands – it was simply that he did not want to present himself as an irrational man. He would not plead insanity – temporary or otherwise.

A screen was illuminated and the series of surveillance photographs which Ryszard had unearthed were shown to the courtroom. Peter looked at them with interest. Though he had never seen them, he had been told that this incident had been captured by a security agent assigned to keep tabs on Vogel during a politically sensitive shift in the *Reichsicherheitshauptamt*. The fact that the agent had managed to capture Vogel as he carried out an apparently unprovoked and vicious attack on his *Zwangsarbeiter* was serendipitous. Or was it? The set of three photographs captured an entire incident: Peter on the ground looking under the car with Karl standing nearby, Peter looking at Karl in expectant horror, and then Karl kicking at Peter's head. Ryszard had once explained that it was standard practice for the security services to keep embarrassing information about their own people or even evidence of criminal behavior on file. Thus, with a body of evidence kept in storage, anyone, at any time, could be brought down, forced to resign, or even imprisoned. Peter tilted his head to get a better view of the pictures – had the photographer thought Karl's behavior was embarrassing or illegal?

"...unprovoked assault on a defenseless man..." the lawyer was saying.

But it wasn't unprovoked. Peter remembered the incident quite well. He had been checking for explosives under the car, a standard precaution before he drove Karl into town. Karl had asked if there was anything there and Peter had replied that everything was fine.

"Did you check carefully?" Karl had asked worriedly. Perhaps he was privy to some knowledge denied Peter.

"Of course I have." Peter had replied, and then incautiously added, "Hell, I'm going to be in the car too!"

Even before Karl had rumbled, "You insolent bastard!", Peter knew his little joke had not been appreciated. He had not been surprised when Karl aimed a kick at him and had ducked back down to protect his face, feeling Karl's shoe lightly impact the back of his head. Ruthlessly violent, yes, but unprovoked? No.

That was the problem with Alex's defense strategy. Though the brief overview which Peter had presented the American people had left them believing his life as a *Zwangsarbeiter* was chaotic and inconsistently cruel, there had been a logic to it all – and if his life with the Vogels was laid out in too great a detail, then it might become apparent that there was little in what happened that came as a surprise to Peter, and therefore, little reason for him later to be suddenly shocked and irrationally violent. It was the system that should be on trial – not Karl's treatment of his slave, nor Peter's response to that treatment. Violence was a natural outgrowth of giving one group of people too much power over another group. Whether it was men over women, aristocrats over serfs, owners over slaves, or *Übermensch* over *Untermensch*, it was all the same – someone with too much power, and someone with too little.

Of course, as the imbalances were redressed and the violence faded away, the next stage was disbelief and denial. For some reason, it became hard for following generations to believe that such violence had ever been a part of normal life. And that was a problem as well – for though the panel of judges was meant to be impartial, they lived in a world that was completely different from the brutal hierarchies of Nazism. They would have trouble believing what they saw was in any way normal – and therefore, they might well believe it was in some manner merited. They might well think that Peter's later criminal behavior proved that Karl's treatment of him was justified.

The court moved on, but Peter's thoughts remained fixed on that point. Not in the judges' world, but perhaps in his and Karl's world, it *was* justified. Even with the best intentions, a man like Karl would have had difficulty controlling his temper year in and year out when there was such a convenient method of blowing off steam constantly to hand. Nor did Karl have the best intentions – what he had was an upbringing that told him he was effortlessly superior and a reality that painfully conflicted with that view. His chattel was uppity and insulting, lacking discipline and loath to carry out his duties. Karl's own superiority was brought into question and nothing was as it was supposed to be. The serf refused to doff his cap, the courtier refused to bow. Societies crumbled when such discourtesies were tolerated. What else could Karl do but lash out violently in defense of the status quo?

And what other incentive was there to force obedience other than violence? There was no monetary incentive, no promises could be made about the future. There was nothing that could be used by all the people with *Zwangsarbeiter* under their control other than the threat of violence. Even the Reusch's, as kind as they had been to Peter, must have realized that. There, the threat had been that if Peter were seen to misbehave, then he might be seized by the authorities and taken back to re-education. The Reusch's had never mentioned it, had never once said, "Do as we say, or else…" They did not need to – Peter had been as aware of the threat as they were. So, they could feign innocence and behave kindly even as the threat of torture had kept Peter under control. Was then, their blackmail any less cruel than Karl's direct intervention?

"And where did this take place?" the prosecutor asked.

Peter turned his attention to the witness stand. A young man with a fleshy, pale face looked earnestly at the court audience and answered, "At England house, in Manhattan. There was a party there, to honor contributors to our cause, and he was in attendance."

"He?"

The young man jerked his chin to indicate Peter. "Mr. Halifax."

"And what happened at this party?"

"Mr. Halifax approached a member of our group – a friend of mine named Graham – and started saying odd things to him."

"Odd?"

"Yes, I don't remember exactly what. They were just very off-the-wall comments."

"And what did your friend do?"

"He greeted Mr. Halifax as if they knew each other from a previous occasion. He mentioned some personal details that appeared to embarrass Mr. Halifax."

"Like what?"

"Objection!"

Peter studied the young man as the lawyers and judges debated the merits of the testimony. Eventually the prosecution was allowed to continue with a reworded question.

"What exactly did your friend say to Mr. Halifax?"

"Something about knowing that his story wasn't quite true, that Mr. Halifax had not been married to the woman that he had described as his wife."

"He was having an affair with this woman?"

The young man nodded, "That was the implication."

There was another objection and again the prosecution won the right to continue.

"Did Mr. Halifax deny these allegations?"

The witness shook his head, then realizing that he should speak, said, "No. Not at all."

"Tell me," the prosecutor asked patiently, "What happened next?"

"I'm afraid we – that is, the rest of us – realized it was a rather personal exchange and so we did not listen in. The next thing I know was that Mr. Halifax was threatening our friend."

"Threatening?"

The young man nodded. "He seemed to say he would kill Graham."

"Kill?" The prosecutor twisted around so that he could study the accused with a mixture of fear and loathing. He looked back to his witness with sympathy. "That's an extremely strong threat. How did your friend react?"

"Nervously. But he calmed Mr. Halifax down and eventually he – Mr. Halifax, I mean – left."

"You are a supporter of an anti-Reich resistance movement based in America?"

"Yes," the young man answered proudly.

"And therefore you are not in any way connected to the Reich or its government?"

"No."

"Nor do you sympathize with Nazism?"

"No, of course not."

"So your testimony about this man is not in any way tainted by your political sympathies?"

"No. I've sworn to tell the truth!"

477

"Why then, have you come forward? You realize that Mr. Halifax is an ally, yet you have portrayed him as an adulterer and someone who threatens to murder a friend."

Again an objection and the prosecution was warned against making such statements, but the damage was already done and no instructions from the presiding judge could erase the imagery from anyone's mind. Bored, Peter picked up his pen and muttering, "Let there be light," wrote down the integral form of Maxwell's equations. As he used them to derive the wave equation for electromagnetic radiation, he saw out of the corner of his eye how his lawyer's assistant made some notes. Yet more damage control would be necessary, but whatever they said, it would come too late. An adulterous past and threats of murder. And that from an ally.

Peter began refining his equations, adding the background proofs for each step that he used. He really liked playing with the elegant mathematics that had been developed by the physics of the nineteenth century and had felt quite cheated when he had been obliged to turn his attentions to cryptanalysis and its tedious reliance on numbers and computers. As he spent the rest of the day with his esoteric symbols and graceful symmetries, the prosecution spent the rest of their day in a painstaking destruction of his character. Each time the defense attempted to object to hearsay and gossip, the prosecution was able to point out the unusual nature of the case: there was nothing else available and since the accused had confessed to the crime, everything hinged upon his motives and his state of mind – therefore his character up to that point needed to be established. Thus the story Peter had presented in the NAU was analyzed in great detail. The changes which Alex and Zosia had insisted upon fell apart under scrutiny and each minor discrepancy was blown out of proportion to make Peter appear to be an unscrupulous and pathological liar. The defense attempted explanations, called witnesses to rebut the assertions, but that only underscored the importance of the prosecution's accusations.

As the testimony dragged on from one day to the next, Peter continued messing with his equations, ignoring everything else. He did not bother to listen as words were read from the confession he had signed after his escape from the work camp. The signature on the paper was his, and no one could see the pain and despair which lay behind his admissions. It was a legal document presented to a people governed by rational laws – how could they not take it seriously? How could they know that the signature on the paper was as meaningless as the interrogator's inevitable, initial question, "Are you comfortable?"

An admitted homosexual affair with the *Kommandant* of his prison camp! The prosecutor read further, quoting from a police investigation that occurred shortly after the accused's illegal exit from that camp: the same *Kommandant* with whom the prisoner had an affair is brutally murdered by the accused's best friend! The implications were clear: a love triangle, jealousy and a murder. Peter knew exactly the parallel that would be drawn and he shuddered at the humiliating prospect of being convicted for killing Karl out of jealousy over Elspeth.

Peter shook his head slightly at his lawyer's questioning look. He had never explained to his American audiences the reasons for his escape from the prison camp nor had he seen any reason to tell them about the eventual fate of the Kommandant. Now, whatever he said would sound like the desperate lies of a man scrambling to cover his tracks. There was no point in rebutting the accusations and he turned his attention back to his scribblings.

Alex leaned over and spoke directly into Peter's ear. "Did you hear that?"

Peter shook his head.

"Conspiracy to murder! You signed a confession that says you conspired to murder the *Kommandant*!"

"Did I?"

"Didn't you?"

Peter didn't look up from the page he was writing on. "I don't know what I signed. I didn't read it."

Alex looked momentarily thoughtful. "*Did* you conspire to have the *Kommandant* murdered?"

Peter snorted. "No. But I should have done."

Alex moaned quietly. "You're going to have to explain what happened."

Again Peter shook his head. "I'm not on trial for the *Kommandant's* murder."

Peter's lawyer leaned in toward him and tapped the copy of the confession which he had just been handed. "Well, it *is* in the document. We're going to have to fight this, even if it means rehashing everything. We can't have you labeled as a murderer."

"I'm rehashing nothing."

Alex looked ready to explode but Peter's lawyer pre-empted him. "Do you have any other suggestions?"

Peter took the confession into his hands and looked at it for a few moments. It wasn't the words that intrigued him, it was the dark blotches at the bottom, near where he had signed. He remembered that the worst of the interrogation had ended days before, but when they demanded his signature, he didn't doubt they would have knocked him around a bit – enough to open old wounds. He would have been exhausted and hurt. He would have bent close to the document, his face would have hovered just above it, his hand may have rested on it. It came from either his face or his hand. He handed the document back to his lawyer and pointed at the spots. "There. Make them show the original. You'll see, those are bloodstains. You can do some tests to show it's my blood. That should let the court know how seriously to take this thing."

That evening, as Peter sat on his cot in his cell, he watched the evening news on the little television which someone had provided for him. The trial was no longer headline news, but it was still reasonably prominent on the local news. Alex was getting his long sought after publicity – too bad it wasn't quite as positive as he had wanted. There was a shot of the accused as he sat through the testimony. "Stony-faced" was the description used by the news reader and Peter had to agree that the words seemed apt. More appropriate, however, might have been "fatigued." His attempts to ignore all the virulence that had been spewed about him throughout the days had only partially succeeded and he had found himself inexplicably exhausted by it all.

An interview with Alex came next and Peter leapt up to turn the television off before he could hear what Alex was going to say. He paced away from the set to the cell's window. No bars, just thick glass woven through with metal fibers. Narrow and tall. He let his hand brush over the concrete-block walls and onto the glass surface. There was no transition from the one to the other, no sill, no change in temperature or dampness. As if the window were nothing more than an illusion painted into the concrete. He would have preferred something less modern and antiseptic. Bars. He could wrap his hands around bars and feel their strength denying him his freedom. He could fight uselessly against them, dissipating the energy which built up as frustration inside him.

He turned away from the window, trying to ignore the tightness in his chest, forcing himself to breathe deeply and calmly. After a moment he returned to the television and turned it back on.

2

"*F*ather?"

Ryszard looked up from his desk to see Stefi and Pawel standing tentatively in the doorway. "How'd you get in here?"

Stefi motioned with her head toward the front door of Ryszard's flat. "We rang the bell. Leszek let us in. Didn't you hear?"

Ryszard shook his head. "No, I have bodyguards to hear things for me now."

Stefi smiled. "Where are they?"

"I gave them the day off. I'm not planning on going out."

Pawel shifted uneasily and glanced toward the kitchen. "What about Leszek?"

"There's nothing I can do about him."

"You could have sent him over to our house with a package or something. Then he could have at least visited with Lodzia."

Ryszard surveyed the two of them standing there in the doorway. Was he supposed to be organizing everyone's social life as well? Before he could say anything though, Stefi asked, "Can we come in?"

"Of course." Ryszard shook off his mood and stood to welcome his children into the room. "I'm surprised to see both of you. Can I get you something?" He motioned to them to sit down as he went to the doorway.

Before he could call Leszek though, Stefi assured him, "Leszek's already getting a tray." Ryszard nodded and came to sit down. He felt oddly ill-at-ease with his children.

Pawel looked around the room. Although his father had been back in Berlin more than half a year, it was the first time Pawel had visited the new flat. "Is Greta here?"

Ryszard shook his head. "She's visiting relatives."

"But she lives here, doesn't she?"

"Sometimes. She maintains her official residence at her house, but since Günter has yet to move out, she often finds it more comfortable to stay with me." Ryszard felt annoyed that he felt an urge to apologize. "Are you still seeing that Vogel girl?"

"Her name is Teresa, Father. And yes, I'm still seeing her."

"Do you trust her?"

Pawel bit his lip at the harsh tone of his father's questions. "I trust her, Dad, but I will never take unapproved action. You know that, don't you?"

Ryszard pulled his head back slightly in surprise. Was Pawel implying...?

"I see that Greta's putting more of her touch on your place." Stefi gestured toward a series of photographs mounted on the wall.

"It's Switzerland. Her mother's home village."

"Very pretty."

Ryszard stood and paced to the door again. Where the hell was Leszek?

Stefi stood as well. She walked over to a large vase set in the corner. "And the dried flowers, too."

481

"Yes, those are hers."

Stefi turned away from the vase to examine the room. "And I see the furniture has been rearranged."

"What are you here for? Neither of you visit me, what's this about?"

Before either of them could answer, Leszek entered the room with a tray full of food and a bottle of wine. Stefi primly reseated herself on the couch, Pawel shifted uncomfortably in his chair. Ryszard moaned quietly at the amount of food and the implied length of the visit as he rejoined them.

Leszek picked up the corkscrew. "Would you all like wine?"

They all agreed wine would be fine. As Leszek pulled glasses out of the cabinet and opened the bottle, the three of them sat in silence. Leszek poured the wine, then set the bottle on the coffee table. "Would you like me to leave?"

Ryszard made an impatient gesture toward the door. With a slight, ironic bow, Leszek left the room.

Stefi looked into her glass as if reading the future. "And how is life with your little Gretalein?"

"Fine." Ryszard lit a cigarette, then realized the ashtray had been put away. He glanced at the one on his desk but decided instead to get a clean one. He stood and went over to the cabinet and pulled one out of a drawer. He set it on the cabinet and remained standing there to smoke his cigarette.

Stefi gave Pawel a knowing look. "Father, we have an idea about Peter..."

"Oh for Christ's sake, that's over with. The trial has already started."

"And is going on, even as we speak."

"Yes." Ryszard tapped the ash off his cigarette. "Face it, we lost that round. But maybe it's for the best."

"How so? Do you think Peter should spend years of his life in prison?"

"Not particularly, but it's better than the alternative. You were there, Stefi, you know. Now, maybe we can put a line under this whole messy business and get back to work." Ryszard held his cigarette up and looked at it, watching as the smoke curled upward. "Nothing has been going right recently. Not since...Not since I was arrested last year. It's been one damn thing after another. My arrest, Peter's arrest, Rudi's kidnap, my being arrested again–"

"You mean, us."

"Yes, us! Your abortion, then Lederman mixing it in and Schenkelhof's murder and Schindler using that as a provocation..." Ryszard sighed heavily. "God! It's been an entire year of non-stop shit. Maybe once this trial is over and Peter's in prison, then Rudi will finally settle down and we'll be able to move forward with our plans."

"Which are what?"

Ryszard gave his daughter a withering look.

"What I mean is, what do you want to do next? What's the next move?"

"Well, if Schindler doesn't pull any more stunts and if there are no other nasty surprises, I'd like to wait until Greta and I are married and I have her family's support. In the meanwhile, I'll see if there isn't anyone else I can gather into my fold of supporters. I need to start spreading the largesse a bit lower down as well. When push comes to shove, it is the Party members who get the final vote, and each and every one of them needs to feel, uh…"

"Loved?"

Ryszard laughed. "Yes, loved."

"And after that? Do you want to get rid of Rudi and assume Günter will lose the election? Or do you want to shuffle Günter out of the way first, before offing Rudi?"

Ryszard was surprised that Stefi spoke so openly. Even with a loyal staff and with the apartment being regularly swept for electronics, they were never so bold. It was an unnecessary risk. He glanced at the windows. Apparently it was possible to bounce microwaves off them and read the vibrations in the panes and that was sufficient for an external eavesdropper to understand everything that was said. Luckily such technology was used only on foreign embassies. His own flat was probably secure. In any case, the damage was done, Stefi had spoken and there was no point in not answering her.

"I would prefer to somehow politically cripple Schindler without physically removing him. That way, my election would be secured but I also would not become an obvious target for Rudi's or anyone else's paranoia. You saw what happened with Schenkelhof. If I hadn't found out exactly who had done it, I would have been brought down simply by the suspicion."

Stefi nodded. "Well, Pawel got some information from Teresa and he has an idea on how we can use it against Schindler. It has to do with Peter's trial."

"Oh. So you weren't looking for me to intervene?"

Stefi shook her head. "No, not at all. I know that would be not only risky, it'd be pointless."

Ryszard smiled fondly at his children. He ground out his cigarette and went to sit down with them, then turning to Pawel asked, "So, son, what's your idea?"

3

The next morning the court continued where it had left off and Peter continued his elaborate treatise, barely paying attention to the long sequence of simple facts and outrageous innuendo. Alan Yardley, that had been his name in the English Underground at the time of his arrest. Not only had he not been married, but the woman whom he had referred to as his wife had been married to another man. And not only she was arrested, but every member of the cells that Yardley managed. All but Yardley himself.

The prosecutor turned toward Peter and eyed him suspiciously before continuing. "Interesting, isn't it?" he asked the panel over the loud protest of Peter's own lawyer. After another round of bickering, the sealed records from Toronto were presented with all the strong implications of Yardley's betrayal of his own people.

Who, Peter wondered, had given them that?

As Alex leaned in toward him to say something, Peter pre-empted him. "This time it's up to you and your allies to speak. Explain that I was scapegoated to save some royal arse from scandal."

"You know they won't do that. It would show cracks in our unity."

Alex was right. No one in the British government-in-exile would come to his aid on this point. Well, maybe one person would. It would give him the chance for absolution. Peter scribbled a note to his lawyer.

Graham looked nervous on the stand. He swore to tell the truth, the whole truth and nothing but the truth and Peter was able to catch his eye as he did that. Graham began by explaining about his encounter with Peter at England House. "My friends didn't realize that we were old comrades. We always said those sorts of things to each other – black humor, you know, to counter the stress of constantly being on a war footing."

"So did Mr. Halifax threaten you or not?"

"What he said was...He..." Graham stopped and took a deep breath. Peter could see how he weighed up the various options in his head. If Graham spoke the truth he would lose his position and ruin his own career, yet anything he said would not prevent Peter from being convicted – so why not follow the party line and let his friend swing?

"I repeat, did Mr. Halifax threaten you or not?"

Graham looked at Peter and said, "I'm sorry, Alan, I'm really sorry."

Peter closed his eyes at this warning that he had lost his gamble. Graham would renege on his promise to Peter's lawyer and protect his government and his job.

"What are you sorry about?" the lawyer asked gently.

"They…, we…I. I followed orders. I risked all their lives so that we could find out if there was a spy among us. We suspected someone high up, someone with a lot of clout, and we didn't dare act against him without firm proof. Yardley and his group were used as bait. I knew that and I didn't warn them." Graham looked down at his hands. "And they all were killed, all except Alan. He managed to disappear, but we didn't know that. We thought he was dead, too. So, to avoid a scandal, the government implied he was to blame. We did bring the spy to trial, perhaps you can subpoena the records and that will prove I'm telling the truth. But maybe not. They really did want to bury this thing." Graham sighed heavily. "At England House, Alan – I mean, Mr. Halifax – learned all this for the first time. I don't remember exactly what he said to me after that, but anything he said was justified."

Graham's testimony did not stop the prosecution's attacks, but their impact was considerably weakened. After that the testimony turned to Peter's possible motives. Again Peter buried himself in his maths, but even the most convoluted derivations could not shut out the defense witness who testified to the trauma he must have suffered at seeing his beloved daughter murdered. Like a deer frozen in the headlamps of an oncoming car, he stared at her, his pen poised in mid-equation. It may well have triggered a delayed reaction on any number of fronts, the woman explained.

But none of it would have brought Joanna back. The little girl with the big grin, daisies woven into her hair, all messy and full of leaves and twigs. Trying to tell a joke and then laughing so hard she couldn't finish what she was saying. Those blue eyes with their long lashes, full of trust and hope, looking at him, begging him to help her, to somehow get them both out of danger. The word *Daddy* just barely emerging as those hands closed around her neck…Alex touched his shoulder and Peter broke out of his trance and turned his attention back to what he was writing.

As a counterpoint, the report of the Reich investigation into Joanna's death was presented by the prosecution. It stated that the Neu Sandez police had established that a number of children had been injured and killed in the bomb blast which led to Halifax's arrest and that he did seem to hold an association with one of these children, though, since he was using false papers, it was not clear what his association was. When presented with the body to identify, Halifax had become overwrought and physically violent, accusing the doctor in attendance of murder. It had been necessary to restrain him, and it was these pictures which were shown in the video. All interrogations were filmed as a matter of course, as part of an anti-corruption drive and to protect suspects from false confessions. The behavior of the interrogator seen in the videotape was explained by the fact that his own child had been murdered in the bomb blast and he held the suspicion that Halifax had set the bomb. He had been acting outside of orders and had been duly punished, but the minor injury he had inflicted on the suspect was understandable. The voices on the tape were completely faked, there was no child in the room, and no murder had taken place. The prisoner had simply become hysterical when confronted with photos of the mayhem he had caused. It was in the interest of elements hostile to the Reich to accuse them – and particularly the Führer – of barbarity, but the accusations were totally false and the fact that the prisoner had been subsequently released when insufficient evidence against him had been found was proof of that.

The tangible evidence was sufficiently sparse that it could be made to fit this grotesque version of events and Alex moaned aloud with that painful realization. Peter stared unmoving at the paper in front of him, but the equations were an unreadable blur. He rubbed his eyes wearily, trying to maintain his composure. So, now even Joanna's murder was brought into question. They had miscalculated, he realized, miscalculated badly. Ryszard, Alex, Marysia – they had all thought the trial could be used as an opportunity to highlight all the cruelties and inequities of Nazism, but instead of awakening interest in their cause, they were losing what positive publicity they had previously generated.

The police report spurred a long debate over what exactly had occurred visually on the tape which extended into the following days. Without the sound, there wasn't much to differentiate Peter's desperate words to try to save Joanna from the ravings of a lunatic spewing hatred and threats. No one else's face was visible and what little he had said could easily be misinterpreted by a lip-reader working in a foreign language. Rather than suffer through a repetition of Joanna's murder as this was all hashed through, Peter chose to remain in his cell throughout that part of the trial.

When he returned it was unclear what the effect of the prosecution's initiative had been. Alex and his lawyer assured him that no one believed the prosecution's idiotic reinterpretation of events, but Peter could see that doubt had been cast, even on this most painful aspect of his story, and even a shadow of a doubt was enough to damage his defense. He also wondered who had organized this plan of attack, and why? After all, denying the reality of the videotape was not in any way necessary to secure a conviction. So why the gruesome display? Was it more personal than legal tactics? Did someone simply want to cause him to suffer again the agony of Joanna's murder? With that question in mind, Peter scanned the audience in the courtroom, but whoever was advising the prosecution, had chosen not to attend the trial personally. Instead he caught sight of one or two friendly faces and they offered him reassuring smiles and nods of encouragement.

The final witness in the character and motivation phase of the trial was called and Peter smiled as his friend Roman took the stand. The calling of witnesses from the Reich had been problematic from the very beginning and the subject of intense negotiations. Who, after all, would dare to testify in defense of a known enemy of the Reich? Who could Peter even admit to knowing? In the end it was decided that the main body of evidence would be composed of Peter's words in America, his confession to the Reich authorities and testimony from character and expert witnesses from outside the Reich. Only two material witnesses from the Reich itself would attend the trial, and Roman was one of these.

The lawyer asked Roman to identify himself and how he was acquainted with the defendant. Peter listened directly with one ear to the exchange, while holding a headphone to his other ear so that he could check that the English translation that was provided was accurate.

"It is stated that your legal status is such that you are not in possession of a passport. How is it that you are able to attend this trial and speak on behalf of someone who has been declared an enemy of the Reich and of the Führer?"

If Roman found anything odd about the wording, he did not show it. Quite formally, and with no indication of sarcasm, he stated, "I was granted a release from my contract and a passport to attend the trial on the understanding that I would not return to the Reich afterwards. I was promised that I would be granted residency here in Switzerland or possibly in America. I don't know why."

Peter, however, did. He had suggested Roman as a witness for the defense since Roman was already known to the Führer and thus in grave danger of arrest. Ryszard had then managed to convince the Führer to release Roman by pointing out that no one would ever take seriously the word of such a lowly man, and in exchange for Roman's testimony, they could send a witness for the prosecution of their own choosing. Having absolutely no interest in the man, the Führer had agreed.

Upon questioning, Roman explained the details of his own life and how he knew Peter. Even though he had no inkling about public relations or propaganda, he was a very effective witness – not so much for Peter's defense, rather as an indictment against an entire system that would leave so many people so effectively cut off from any hope. Through the defense lawyer's careful questioning, it slowly emerged that though Roman had suffered neither imprisonment nor torture, he was nevertheless obliged to follow conventions which were intended to keep him in bondage forever, rules which allowed him no hope of improvement or wealth, rules which he had not created nor could he change. He had been told that obedience was the only option, indoctrinated into a hierarchy which placed him firmly and permanently at the bottom, and warned that questioning the status quo was evil and therefore merited punishment of the most severe kind. He may have even believed it, and many of his acquaintances supported it as a means of maintaining civic order, but the one thing he had not lost was his sense of being human. And so, when he had met Peter, he had befriended him.

As Roman's words turned to what he had witnessed of Peter's suffering at Karl's hands, Peter found he could no longer listen. The memories provoked were too painful, the imagery of his impotence – too humiliating. He placed his elbows on the table in front of him and rested his head in his hands, shielding himself from the curious stares of the court.

A sudden silence brought Peter back to the courtroom. The prosecutor was doing the questioning now and Roman was looking at the judges as if confused. The presiding judge returned with a patient, encouraging nod.

Roman turned back to the prosecutor and repeated incredulously, "The authorities?"

"Yes, did you report any of these incidents to the authorities?"

Roman shook his head in confusion. Peter felt sorry for him – Roman probably thought the prosecutor simply misunderstood the situation. Finally Roman managed to stammer, "Don't you understand? That's not possible."

The prosecutor feigned confusion. "What do you mean? Certainly, in your opinion, a criminal assault had occurred. And by your own testimony, you knew that the victim had not reported it. Did you, then, report it?"

"To whom?"

"To the authorities!"

Again Roman shook his head. "I'm sorry. I don't understand."

The prosecutor's voice took on a hard edge, as if questioning a very unreliable witness. "You said that your friend, Mr. Halifax, had clearly been assaulted, possibly with a weapon. You further stated that he showed no interest in explaining the crime or reporting it. Therefore, it was your duty to report the crime." There was a pause, and then the prosecutor added slyly, "Unless, of course, you've exaggerated the severity of this incident."

The defense objected. Before the presiding judge could react, the prosecutor cast a doubtful glance at Peter, and added, "Is it just possible that your friend was in a brawl in which his opponent got the better of him and perhaps he was embarrassed to report that fact? Um?"

The defense loudly repeated its objection. After a brief conference, the prosecution was allowed to reword the question. "Did Mr. Halifax ever explicitly tell you what happened?"

Roman had to admit that he did not.

"Did you personally witness anything?"

Again Roman had to admit that he did not.

"So you have no idea what happened, do you? It could just have easily been a street fight, could it not?"

Roman shook his head. "No," he whispered desperately. "That's not the way it was!"

"Maybe he was caught sleeping with somebody's wife – we know he was quite a lady's man – and there was a bit of a scuffle?"

"No!"

"I know, I know," the prosecutor agreed kindly, "Your friend is in trouble and you want to help him. You don't want people to know what a violent man he is. I understand."

"Objection!"

"I withdraw the statement," the prosecutor quickly responded. "No more questions."

"Headache, Alex?" Peter's question echoed around the small consultation room.

Alex brought his hands away from his face and surveyed Peter gloomily.

"You should have let me plead guilty."

"Shut-up or I'll have them put your shackles back on!"

Peter leaned back, ostentatiously folding his arms and crossing his legs – exactly the sort of free movement that had been impossible on the first day of his consultations with his lawyer and his advisor. But it hadn't been Alex who had protested. Incensed, the lawyer had left the room only to return half an hour later with a court order to allow Peter to consult with his counsel without such restraints. Peter turned to his lawyer. "What do you think, Gerhard?"

Gerhard stroked his chin thoughtfully. He was a Swiss German, short, with dark curling hair and a moustache, and he maintained a strange formality, always referring to Peter as "Herr Dr. Halifax" in court. He had a perpetually sorrowful look that had only grown more mournful as the trial had worn on. "There's not much left. They're going to present your confession to the authorities and then the final witness and...I had hoped to offset the effect of your confession before we reached this point, but I'm afraid we've been outmaneuvered." He studied Peter, searching for the missing pieces of the puzzle. "You know, without your testimony, we have nothing to contradict the signed confession that the prosecution will present."

"I know."

"Would you please consider testifying for me?"

"I'd do more harm than good."

"The prosecution will call you in any case, why don't you let me question you as well?"

"Because it'll look natural if I am hostile to the prosecution's questions, but there'd be no sound reason for me not to answer yours."

Gerhard considered this for a moment. "Then maybe you'll satisfy my curiosity. Off the record." He waited, raising his eyebrows expectantly, but no answer was forthcoming. He leaned in toward Peter. If it had been anyone else, the move would have looked threatening, but with Gerhard, it was obviously a plea. *"Why?"*

Peter shook his head.

"None of it makes sense. That's why we've taken a hammering in there." Gerhard jerked his head toward the courtroom. "All that bullshit we're presenting, it's as if..." He looked at Alex suspiciously, then concluded, "As if you're satisfying a different agenda rather than defending yourself."

Peter shrugged.

"I haven't known you very long, but I can tell this isn't the sort of thing you'd do. Why did you do it? *Did* you do it? Are you covering for someone else?"

Peter shook his head again, though it was unclear whether it was an answer or just a rejection of the questions.

"Don't you care whether or not you have to go to prison?" Gerhard asked angrily. He was clearly excited because he bounced slightly with each word.

"Yes, I care. But I care about other things even more."

"Dr. Halifax..." With an effort Gerhard stopped bouncing. "Peter, it's your life to do with as you please, but it doesn't make sense for you—"

Alex cleared his throat. "If I may interrupt, what are your plans now?"

Gerhard motioned helplessly with his hands. "I'll present what you've given me. Or if you think I'm not doing your cause justice, one of my associates will step in."

Peter shook his head. "No, you're doing fine. Let's just get this over with so you all can go home."

Nobody commented on Peter's chances of going home.

4

*T*he prosecutor waved the document in the air as if its simple physical existence were proof of its veracity. "Then I stabbed him in the neck," he quoted, appalled by the words he read. He turned to the panel of judges and repeated dramatically, "Then I stabbed him in the neck."

Peter sat in the witness box waiting patiently for some words to be addressed to him directly. Since it was an international tribunal with a negotiated protocol, the laws were mixed. He did not have the American right to refuse self-incrimination, but, of course, he could simply refuse to answer. Contempt of court was hardly a charge which carried much weight in his current circumstances, and he debated with himself how much he cared to say.

The prosecutor turned to him and asked, "Are those your words?"

"No." Before the prosecutor could express his disbelief, Peter explained, "I did not write them. My hands were bound and I was not permitted to write in any case."

"But you said them?"

"I don't know. You see, I was injected with some drug – after that, I have no idea what I may or may not have said."

"Mr. Halifax–"

"All I remember was some sort of device. They gave me electric shocks whenever I said something they didn't like."

"Mr. Halifax, that was not the question."

"Oh, I'm sorry. What was? Did you want to know if I had an attorney?" Peter shook his head emphatically. "No. No attorney."

Titters from the audience clearly annoyed the prosecutor. "That was, however, in keeping with the laws of your land," he remarked defensively. "This confession was legally obtained according to Reich law and you put your signature to it."

"Indeed!" Peter leaned forward, pleased that the prosecutor had taken the bait, "All that was done, was done in accordance with the laws of *my* land. The torture of a suspect, the lack of a defense counsel, the killing of a person. It was all carried out under the insanity that passes for 'legal' there." He gestured angrily as if toward the Reich's border. "That's what happens when a gang of bullies is given the status of a government – whatever their ideology! And that's what happens when the rest of the world accepts anything as long as it's *within* some self-declared borders."

"The killing of Karl Vogel was not legal, not even under Reich law."

"But the killing of others was." Peter relaxed back into his seat. "If Hitler hadn't attacked outside his borders, if he hadn't declared war on you, you would have never gotten involved—"

"Mr. Halifax—"

"You would have happily let him murder every so-called unfit person in Germany. Just like you let the Soviet Union murder tens of millions of people. Maybe it was too risky to help them – that's a fair decision – but then you should not dare to judge those of us who defend ourselves." Peter finally stopped as the presiding judge's gavel was slammed down and he was being drowned out by calls for order. He listened patiently to the instruction to only answer the questions put to him and not to lecture the court on politics, but he saw, with some pleasure, that a number of people in the audience were nodding their heads in agreement.

The prosecutor looked down at his notes, collecting himself after such a tasteless scene. "Did you kill Karl Vogel?"

"Yes. I took the law into my own hands, because somehow *you* weren't available to bring him to justice."

This admission should have been enough, but the prosecutor could not prevent himself from responding to the personal accusation in Peter's statement. "Whatever injustices in a system, you had no right to murder and it is only fair that we bring you to justice now."

"Fair," Peter repeated sardonically. "It would be even fairer if I had no *need* to kill. If our people were supported in their fight against these murderers, then we could bring them to trial and show the entire world the heinousness of their crimes." Peter gestured dramatically around the room. "Certainly the money and effort wasted on this charade could be better spent fighting the genuine criminals who are raping an entire continent!"

There were muted cheers and grunts of approval from the court audience and Peter could see Alex nodding his head excitedly.

"The government of the Third Reich is not on trial here—"

"That's right! You don't have the power to bring them to trial, or even to stop them from carrying out their crimes. So in frustration at your impotence, you reach out and grab one weak individual and self-righteously apply your judgment in a vacuum—"

"Mr. Halifax," the presiding judge intoned warningly.

With a gracious nod toward the bench, Peter stopped.

The prosecutor stepped back to gather himself. Though the forces which had brought Peter to trial had been intent on his destruction and the negative publicity for the resistance which would follow a personal attack on their spokesman, the prosecutor was not a party to that. His job was to gain a conviction according to international law against someone accused of murder. A good conviction – and that meant allowing for no excuses.

"That's a very interesting opinion, Mr. Halifax," the prosecutor carefully stated, "but a debate on our willingness and ability to enact justice outside this courtroom must be deferred to a more appropriate time. Right now, we must deal with the facts of this case. And the fact is you admit to killing Karl Vogel."

"Yes."

The prosecutor was taken aback by the brevity of Peter's answer. It took a moment before he found his next statement. "You deliberately sought him out, broke into his house, and murdered him in his sleep."

"I woke him up first."

"Nevertheless he was still defenseless."

Peter shook his head. "He had an entire military dictatorship supporting him."

The prosecutor looked annoyed. "You know what I mean."

"I'm afraid I don't. He was a brutal man capable of and – I am certain of it – guilty of murder. He was a danger."

"But not to you! He was no different from many other security police officials–"

"You said it."

A few quiet laughs punctuated the silence of the courtroom. The presiding judge raised his gavel but resisted calling for order.

The prosecutor glowered as he realized what he had said. "I mean, it was a personal vendetta!" he hissed angrily. "You weren't enacting justice. You sought him out and killed him in his own bed. Nor can you claim it was self-defense. He was not a specific threat to you."

"Yes, he was."

"What?"

"He specifically threatened me."

"What? When?"

It was a stupid question for the prosecutor to have asked, for it allowed Peter to speak uninterrupted. He explained how he had stumbled across Karl on a train more than a year after his escape. Of course, he did not mention Zosia or that he was carrying out undercover work at the time, but he described in detail how Karl had held him at gunpoint and Karl's ranting threats. "I managed to escape him that time, but I had no doubt he would track me down and carry out his threats. It wasn't enough what I had suffered at his hands. It wasn't enough that he had beaten and starved me. It wasn't enough that I spent years slaving for him." Peter shook his head sadly. "I had never harmed him or his family. I escaped with nothing more than the remnants of my shattered life. Yet *he* wanted revenge. After all he had done to me, *he* wanted revenge! I lived in fear for my life – and in fear for those dear to me – every day. When I happened to sight him again years later, I knew that eventually he'd find me and then…" Peter let his voice drop off, but finally managed to stammer, "I knew he would carry out his threats. I had already seen what they are capable of and I was afraid."

The prosecutor opened his mouth to say something but no words emerged. The silence emphasized the raw emotion of Peter's testimony and realizing that, the prosecutor decided to cut his losses on the murder charge and quickly snapped, "Did you kidnap his daughter?"

"No."

"No?" The prosecutor's voice nearly squeaked with incredulity. He picked up the copy of Peter's confession. "In here, you state—"

"Oh, that." Peter waved his hand derisively at the document. "We all know how confessions like that are obtained and what they're worth."

"Are you saying you did not take Magdalena Vogel?"

"No, I'm saying I did not *kidnap* her. It is well established in the legal system of *my* land, that children may be taken into custody if their parents are deemed, in some manner, unfit."

"But you were not acting on behalf of the legal system of the Reich."

"No, I wasn't. Their criterion for snatching children is that the parents have broken some petty law or been denied a slip of paper by some vindictive bureaucrat. I deemed Karl Vogel unfit as a parent based upon the brutal upbringing I had seen him inflict on the other children in the family."

"What about Magdalena's mother?"

"The mother never interfered. I feared for the child's safety. I feared that due to the time of her birth and the timing of my escape, that Vogel would one day decide she was my child and he would harm her."

The prosecutor, busily steering clear of the obvious question – Magdalena's parentage was a subject both sides had reason to avoid, missed the inconsistency. Instead he asked, "What about your wife?"

"My wife and the people she knows had nothing to do with the abduction."

"According to your testimony, your own wife called your action 'cruel' and left you."

"My own testimony, as you call it, is nothing more than the words written by a security official as I was being held – handcuffed, drugged and with an electroshock belt strapped around my waist. It has no basis in reality."

"So what did your wife do?"

Peter had no idea how much information about Madzia's presence in the mountains had filtered back to Berlin, so he answered carefully, "I sent her with the child to seek safety. I didn't go with her because I knew the Führer was still seeking me and my presence would endanger them. Indeed, several months after my wife left, I was arrested in Berlin on charges of treason – for what I had said in the NAU during my interviews. For telling the truth." Peter paused to let the word sink in, then added by way of emphasis, "You see, it seems I had been convicted without a trial and had been sentenced to torture and death. Even in my land, that is not legal, but the legal system is something the Führer does not choose to abide by." Peter had struck a careful balance there, impugning the Führer's reputation without attacking the entire government structure. He wanted to maintain Traugutt's pristine reputation in the NAU and therefore had sacrificed the opportunity to denounce the entire Reich as well as the Führer.

The prosecutor attempted to bring the subject back to the criminal charge. "So you kidnapped the child never to see her again?"

"It wasn't the child that I kidnapped – it was the Führer. He threatened me personally during my stay in his residence, and so I grabbed him and used him as a hostage to make my escape. I went to the Tatra mountains and gave the Führer into the custody of the government there. They, as you know, released him safely back into the Reich. The Führer rewarded me – and them – for our restraint by demanding my extradition from their territory." Peter leaned forward again and let his eyes bore into the prosecutor's. "You will remember that this was the man who ordered the murder of my daughter. *And I did not harm him.* I handed him over to a responsible government. You see – I am not the sort of man to carry out vendettas – not when there is *any* chance of justice being served legally."

The prosecutor, realizing that he had lost the initiative, bluntly asked, "But you freely admit killing Karl Vogel and abducting Magdalena Vogel?"

Peter took a mental inventory of the panel's patience and quickly calculated what he could say before that gavel came hammering down. He took a deep breath. "Not as you mean it. You in the free world have your legal systems you can rely on, you have your statements of human rights – but you limit that to humans born within your boundaries." The prosecutor began to interrupt but Peter simply spoke louder and faster, "The rest of us are cattle. As long as there are some maniacs willing to tell you they are our rightful government, you give them carte blanche. You deal with them, you sell them arms, you turn a blind eye! And it's not just that you fear the consequences of any action against them – I know because you support even murderous little regimes that could be toppled overnight. Just for the sake of *stability*. Stability bought with our lives!"

"You are not answering the question!"

"What you fear are your own intellectuals who hypocritically claim that these so-called cultures with all their terror against their own population must be respected! Who think freedom and human rights are something they alone should have and who piously condemn the rest of the world to

495

live under tyranny. They want peace, they say! But it's peace bought with *our* lives, not theirs!"

The prosecutor threw both hands up in irritation at the presiding judge's inaction.

Peter continued unabated, "You fear your strength, you fear being called cultural imperialists if you try to impose basic human rights on anyone else, and in doing so you say a human life has value only if it is bounded by your borders. Then deep down you realize that your philosophy is no different from the Nazis or the Communists."

The presiding judge roused himself. "Mr. Halifax, you are not answering the question."

Peter ignored him. "The Nazis define worth by blood, the Communists by class and *you* use borders! Anyone not fortunate enough to be born within the free world's borders are the *Untermensch* of your world and you refuse to acknowledge they have human rights worth fighting for!"

"Mr. Halifax, answer the question!"

"I can understand if you hesitate to intervene directly, but at least you could support those who do!"

"Mr. Halifax!"

"You can stop propping up murderous regimes just because they are politically convenient and you can stop playing political games like this trial!"

The gavel came pounding down. *"Mr. Halifax!"*

Peter looked up innocently. "Your honor?"

The presiding judge took a deep breath and let it out slowly. "The witness is instructed to answer the question."

"Yes."

"Yes?"

"Yes. The answer is yes."

The prosecutor was probably the only person who actually remembered what the question had been. He decided though to spare himself and the court a repetition. "There you have it!" he thundered. His words echoed unconvincingly around the courtroom.

Peter allowed himself one final observation. "Yes, justice was served."

5

"*W*ell that was a fine little show you put on in there!" Gerhard didn't even wait until they had closed the door of the conference room. "Are you *trying* to get convicted?"

Peter seated himself at the table and gave himself a neck rub. "Conviction's always been a certainty."

"But the sentencing is not!" Gerhard angrily slammed his files down on the table. "Do you remember the trial rules that were agreed on? Do you? *No politics!* No political speeches! You had a chance there – the judges were clearly sympathetic to you and you had to go and blow it! You're lucky you weren't cited for contempt of court. They're not going to cut you any slack now."

Peter shrugged. He had decided at the last minute to speak and given how little time he had had, he was surprised he had managed to say anything. Certainly there was a lot that should have been worded more politely, or at least more coherently. And certainly too, with his call for support of armed rebellion, he had not done Ryszard's cause any good, but at the moment he was not feeling particularly pleased with Ryszard or his strategy of blithely sacrificing his allies.

Alex calmly took a seat. "What Peter did was exactly right. Though I'm not sure you should have included that bit comparing the free world to the Nazis and the Communists."

Gerhard raised a finger to Alex, preparing to reply, but changed his mind and turned to Peter. "Does he *always* have to be here?"

Peter looked up at Alex and motioned with his head toward the door. "I'll handle this."

"Peter, I don't think that's wise."

Peter shut his eyes as if in pain. "Please, Alex."

Reluctantly Alex stood and left. As he shut the door behind himself, Peter and Gerhard remained in silence. Gerhard was clearly struggling to control his anger. He picked up the files, tapped them against the table to straighten them. "Herr Dr. Halifax...Peter, look, I'm going to have to hand this over to someone else. I don't like not knowing what's going on, and I don't like seeing my efforts sabotaged – not by my own client. One of my colleagues will take over. Do you have a preference?"

"I prefer you. Please, bear with me."

Gerhard shook his head. "No, it's gone too far. Your little theater in there – that was the last straw."

"*Please*. I promise, I won't do anything like that again. And there's not much more – can't you see the case through to the end?"

Gerhard sat down, despondently resting his forehead on his hand. "We spent all that time convincing them that you were under enormous stress and that Vogel's killing was an impulsive act, then you go and basically state to the judges that he deserved it and you would happily do it again. What can I possibly say now? There's nothing left to throw at them."

"There's Frau Elspeth Vogel."

"She's a witness for the prosecution!"

"I understand, but I think we can use her."

Gerhard looked at him suspiciously. "How?"

"Well, I blew the distressed victim aspect of my defense, but there's still the possibility that I worked under orders. Indeed, that I was blackmailed and was protecting somebody else."

"And still protecting that person?"

Peter nodded. "That could be implied. It would explain my…"

"Lack of cooperation with your defense lawyer?"

Peter smiled enigmatically. "Maybe."

"So who are you protecting?"

"Obviously – assuming my blackmailer is still alive – I could not say that, now could I?"

"Then who blackmailed you into this?"

"Again, I could never say – not even to you. But what I can do is tell you exactly what happened that night that I killed Karl Vogel. Frau Vogel will present a very well practiced version of events, but if you cross-examine her, given what I've told you, then she'll recognize that I want her to tell the truth."

"Will she do that? I mean, do you think she'd be inclined to say anything that might help you? You did, after all, kill her husband."

Peter rested his chin on the heel of his hand, looking thoughtfully into the distance. "I think so."

"Were you two in love?"

Peter laughed. "Come visit me in prison some day and I'll tell you all about our sordid little relationship."

Gerhard looked dubious, so Peter opened his mouth and tapped two false teeth near the back. "These two here – I have Frau Vogel to thank for those. Fractured my jaw as well. Not being a masochist, I did not find that sort of behavior lovable."

"She did that?"

"It was my fault really. I was stupid enough to mouth off while she was holding a rolling pin."

peated the answer I had given her then.

"Geez." Gerhard looked truly embarrassed. "Why would anyone do anything so..."

"Stupid? Thoughtless? Counter-productive? I think she lived in a never-never land where violence..." Peter paused, wondering how to briefly express Frau Vogel's strange relationship with reality. "I don't think she...She never seemed to realize that her actions would have consequences."

"As a criminal defense attorney, I can assure you, she's not all that unusual."

"To give her credit she was shocked by the damage she had done. When I screamed and started spitting blood, she dropped the pin, walked me over to the sink and then gave me some antiseptic to rinse my mouth with. And after that, she never used such a heavy weapon again."

Gerhard sniffed derisively. "How very considerate! So, tell me, what happened that night?"

Peter gave Gerhard a summary of his conversation with Elspeth, being sure to include the important phrases. A lot he had to reconstruct, parts of it he judiciously edited, but some of it he recounted word-for-word.

When Peter had finished, Gerhard looked at his notebook. "What did she mean 'Your behavior is totally inappropriate' and why did you say she wouldn't have it any other way?"

Peter laughed quietly. "She probably didn't realize it, but that phrase was something she had said to me about three months before I escaped. So I repeated the answer I had given her then."

"Why? I mean, why was it so memorable?"

"Ah, because I always regretted that interchange. It convinced her I had..." Peter looked off into space as he tried to find the right word. "Well, with horses, they call it *spirit*."

"I don't understand."

"A lack of proper submissiveness in an inferior creature that makes it perversely attractive to its master. You see, after I said that, she decided to have me perform certain household services for her."

"Oh, I see." Gerhard reddened and quickly bowed his head to study his notes. "Well, if you don't mind my asking, why would you want me to bring up that phrase?"

"Oh, because she'll recognize it. She always used it any time she wanted to say something else."

"And what did she want to say on the night you killed her husband?"

Peter stood and went to the wall. He leaned against it, his arms casually crossed. "That's not important. What's important is that she does recognize that I have spoken to you about that night. I think then, if you press, you'll get her to admit the relevant detail."

"That you knew her husband was in political trouble and not long for this world in any case?"

"Yes, and most importantly who told me that."

Gerhard tapped his notes with his pencil. "Who is this Frau Schindler?"

"Frau Greta Schindler is the wife of the second most important man in the Reich."

"Oh, *that* Schindler. And did she get the information from him?"

Peter pushed himself away from the wall and paced the length of the small room. "Ask Frau Vogel that."

"I'm asking you."

Peter reached the opposite wall and leaned against that. "And I'm not saying. What I need is for Frau Vogel to admit – without prompting – that Günter Schindler's wife was the one who informed me of Karl Vogel's political situation. You can leave it up to the court to draw their own conclusions about why I was informed of such a thing."

Gerhard furrowed his brow. "He wanted you to kill Vogel and you didn't want to do it, even with some sort of threat being held over someone dear to you. So he gave you this information as added incentive – to convince you that Vogel was going to be removed in any case." Gerhard looked at Peter questioningly, but Peter did not react to his conjecture. "Okay, but if Vogel was deadmeat anyway, why was Schindler in such a hurry?"

Peter walked back across the room and again took up a position leaning against the wall.

Gerhard made a face as he guessed, "He didn't want Vogel to be questioned? Vogel had some information that could hurt Schindler?"

"I can't say."

"Why not? Why don't you testify about this? It could save you!"

Peter shook his head. Frau Vogel's testimony would bring Schindler under suspicion, but Peter knew if he said anything, the Führer would surely suspect a conspiracy. "It wouldn't save me. In the legal utopia of an international criminal court, there is no acceptable reason for killing a man in cold blood. The crimes of extant governments are considered irrelevant while the actions of an individual are judged in an unreal light–"

"Please! No more!"

Peter smiled at his poor beleaguered lawyer. "Sorry. The point is, I'd still be guilty."

"But it might lead to a reduction in your sentence!"

"It would cost too much. Trust me, I can't say a word. All I can do is hope that Frau Vogel says enough that the implication is clear without me having said anything. And for that, I need you. Can you do it?"

"Without your telling me what this threat against you – or whomever – is?"

Peter nodded.

"On blind trust?"

"Please?"

Gerhard sighed heavily. "Okay. Don't worry, I'll get her to remember. But why didn't you tell me all this earlier? We could have slanted our whole approach toward this moment." He didn't need to say that it would have spared everyone a lot of tedious testimony.

"It would have been too obvious. You see, if there is even the slightest suspicion that I am at the root of this revelation, then all will be lost." Peter returned to the table and sat down. He looked pleadingly into Gerhard's eyes. "I'm talking about people's lives, you understand."

Gerhard closed his eyes and nodded, his whole body bouncing slightly with the movement. He remained with his eyes closed, as if replaying everything that had gone before. When he opened them he gave Peter a twisted, self-deprecatory smile. "You know, I feel pretty used."

Peter laughed. "Welcome to the club."

6

*P*eter picked up the letter Alex had brought him and read it again. It was thick – Zosia had taken the time to give him a day-by-day description of the children's growth. When he finished reading it, he pulled out the pictures and looked at them. Madzia and Irena had not changed much, but Krys looked completely different. He had been born on May second and had been two months old when Peter was handed over to the international delegation. So now, the baby was four months old. So many changes in such a short time! Or was it a long time? The trial, with all its hearings and delays and recesses was still going on. And here he sat, locked in a cell, staring at photographs as his children changed and grew with each passing day.

And himself? He supposed he was simply growing older. He furrowed his brow and thought about the date. Oh, yes, he had just had a birthday, he had finally reached the date that meant he had lived as long as his parents had. The date which had disappeared from everyone's records with Niklaus Chase's demise. The date that only Erich might remember. He wondered if his brother had thought of him. What they might have accomplished if they had not been set in opposition to each other so early on! Erich the fulfiller of his parents' dreams, lording his privileged position over his brother, and Niklaus, the extra burden determined not to be ignored – even if it meant being nothing better than a thorn in the side.

Peter looked at the pictures of his children again. How dearly he hoped they might make something better out of their relationships. He stared at the photograph that had all three of them together. Madzia sitting on the floor with Irena on her lap and Krys's head resting on Irena's legs. They all had enormous smiles on their faces, obviously caught in mid-giggle. He wondered momentarily if Krys was really laughing. Did a four-month-old know how to laugh? He counted on his fingers from January, when Irena had been born, to May. So, he had been around when Irena was four months old, but still he couldn't remember whether she had truly laughed then or not.

He went through the small stack of photos yet again, looking at the background, trying to see a glimpse of home. Zosia was nowhere to be seen. He had brought no photographs of her and none would be sent. Given that a prisoner had no right to privacy and that his possessions would undergo multiple inspections by completely anonymous guards and officials, it had been decided that it was simply too dangerous for Zosia's photograph to be among Peter's possessions. Even Madzia would soon have to disappear as she reached the age where she would be taken into town. Peter sighed as he looked at her smiling face. At least that would be another year or two.

He spread the photos out on his cot and laid Zosia's letter next to them. He picked up Tadek's letter and decided to read that again. Before leaving, Peter had arranged for Madzia to finally be baptized and he had asked Tadek to be her godfather. In that way, Peter had hoped that though Madzia had no blood relatives in the camp, she would at least be provided with someone who would feel uniquely protective of her. Unlike Zosia, Marysia or even Kamil, Tadek was also unrelated to anyone within the encampment and therefore he could pay special attention to his little goddaughter. And indeed he did. He took his responsibility very seriously and sent Peter a separate report on how Madzia was doing, including drawings that the child made and some attempts at handwriting. Peter smiled as he saw that the word Madzia had attempted to write was *Tata*, and realized, somewhat sadly, that by the time he returned, his child would view English as a foreign language.

Tadek explained, as if only by chance, that Madzia had complained of being cold and lonely in her cot, and since Zosia already had Krys and Irena in her bed, there was no room for another, so Madzia had taken to sleeping with him on the fold-out bed. Peter laughed to himself at the coy way Tadek had implied that all was within the bounds of propriety in the tiny flat. It was a nice fiction and for everyone's sake, he would play along. Zosia had categorically refused to divorce and vehemently stated that she would await Peter's return – however long that took. What she had not said, and Peter had not requested, was that she would remain untouched. Zosia *needed* physical contact and though Peter knew he could survive years without the slightest hint of human kindness, he also knew such deprivation had never been easy, not even for him, and would certainly break Zosia.

He heard one of the guards approaching and he hurriedly gathered together the letters and pictures and placed them safely on the table. As the guard unlocked the cell, Peter took a last glance in the small mirror over the sink to make sure he looked presentable.

"Show time," the guard announced jovially and led the way back down the hall toward the exits. After passing through several security gates, Peter was handcuffed and escorted to the van that would take him to court. He sat in the back, the only passenger other than the court security guard who accompanied him. Though the court had refused Alex's petition to release Peter into his custody during the trial for fear that Peter would flee, there clearly was no great concern about the likelihood of his being freed by anyone else.

Peter studied the cold metal that bound his wrists and thought about Zosia. He had misread her all along. She was so sensual, he had always thought that her need to be touched and held and stroked was part of her natural exuberance, an expression of her lust for life. But it was the other way around. Her exuberance and lust for life were a way of bringing people near to her so that she could feel their touch, so that she could physically experience their love, and so that she could satisfy an insecurity that had hounded her since childhood.

He twisted his wrists and the metal glittered with reflected light. The two of them were more alike than he had ever realized. Both had lived their lives in fear of being ignored or forgotten. But whereas he had grown up in virtual isolation and therefore had sought protection in an ability to cope alone with the world, molding his personality to fit his circumstances, Zosia had been surrounded by people and had thrown herself whole-heartedly into the fray, embracing any who would have her and taking comfort in her power to break hearts at will. His golden girl, loved by all, yet needing to be loved even more. He supposed the years during which she had tormented him with her rejection had been as nothing compared to the one cool refusal he had once handed her. And for all the cruelty of her treatment of him and the pain he had suffered as a result, he imagined that she now suffered more from the simple fact that he no longer adored her.

They drove directly into the building through a subterranean entrance and Peter was taken up to the conference room. His handcuffs were removed, he shook Gerhard's and Alex's hands, they spent a few minutes discussing strategy and then they made their way into the courtroom. Before sitting down Peter surveyed the audience and saw that Elspeth was already there, seated in the front row. Their eyes met but neither made the slightest attempt to acknowledge the other. Peter's tongue probed to the two false teeth he had shown Gerhard and it occurred to him that he had forgotten to mention that Elspeth had been unaware that she had broken his teeth. Indeed, they had remained cracked and intermittently painful in his mouth until the dentist at Szaflary had recoiled in horror at the jagged, rotting remnants and immediately removed them.

Next to Frau Vogel was her daughter Teresa, and Peter was surprised to see that she smiled warmly at him. He gave her a slight nod of acknowledgment then immediately averted his gaze so that their interaction would not be captured by any of the cameras. If all went according to plan, the Führer would view the proceedings very closely and Peter wanted to avoid any hint of collusion between himself and any member of the Vogel family. Next to Teresa sat a man whom Peter recognized – more from photographs than memory – as Frauenfeld. The row behind Frau Vogel was almost entirely filled with Reich officials, some of whom had been in attendance all along, some of whom were a new presence in the courtroom. Clearly, the Führer was taking no chances on the proceedings – whatever Frau Vogel said would be recorded and sent to him and whatever nuances the camera missed were sure to be reported by one of these witnesses. Peter wondered if Elspeth felt intimidated.

After the panel's arrival, it didn't take long until Frau Vogel was called to the witness stand. She took the oath and was questioned first by the prosecutor. She repeated the story which Peter recognized as the one he had taught her. She woke up and saw Peter in her room. She wanted to scream but he threatened her. He killed her husband, told her "an eye for an eye, a daughter for a daughter" and then after warning her not to move, he left.

"So he broke into your house, came into your bedroom, and murdered your husband as he slept," the prosecutor summarized.

"Peter woke him up first."

The prosecutor rolled his eyes at the repetition of this trivial detail. "Yes, of course. But your husband was defenseless, was he not?"

"Yes, his gun was in the drawer next to the bed."

"And he did not in any way threaten Mr. Halifax?"

Elspeth looked momentarily confused. "Oh, Peter," she murmured.

"I repeat, did your husband in any way threaten Mr. Halifax?"

"No, I mean, not more than usual."

That caused a few chuckles and Elspeth looked at the audience in surprise. The prosecutor ignored the laughter. He asked Elspeth if anything else had happened and after she admitted that she did not recall anything else, he again summarized what she had said, thanked her, and left her to the defense.

In a manner that was quite charming, Gerhard gave Frau Vogel a slight bow and explained effusively that he understood how difficult it must be for her to talk about that night but he only had a few questions and he would be pleased if she would do her best to remember everything she possibly could. "After all, we realize that up to now you have only summarized what happened. I'd like to know, if you could possibly recall some specifics. For instance, did you in any way protest at Dr. Halifax's behavior, did you, for example, tell him that his behavior was *totally inappropriate*?"

Elspeth's eyes widened slightly. "I may have done."

"Did you have any sort of discussion with him, maybe to try to distract him?"

"Discussion?"

"Well, for instance, did you talk about a trip you once took to Dresden?"

Elspeth snapped her head around to look at Peter. He gazed at her calmly in response, willing her to understand.

Elspeth turned her attention back to Gerhard. "I may have done. It was the middle of the night and I was terribly confused."

"Of course, we understand. It must have been very traumatic for you. But this is important, so I'm going to ask you to think back very carefully. You said that Dr. Halifax woke your husband and then killed him. Certainly your husband did not remain silent throughout. Did he say anything when Dr. Halifax woke him?"

"His name is Peter!" Elspeth snapped.

There was a sputter or two from the back of the courtroom where some Americans sat listening to a translation on headsets. Gerhard paused theatrically, clearly implying they all should gain a great deal of knowledge about his client's situation from that single comment. Then he turned to Peter and raised his eyebrows questioningly. Peter nodded his consent.

"Certainly, Frau Vogel, I have no wish to make you uncomfortable. Let me repeat the question. Did your husband say anything to Peter when he was awakened?"

"Yes, I believe he expressed surprise. And anger."

"Did Peter at any time explain his actions?"

Elspeth nodded. "Yes, as I said, he told me an eye for an eye and a daughter for a daughter."

"And did your husband have something to do with the murder of his daughter?"

There was the obvious objection to that and Gerhard agreed to withdraw the question. His tone of voice became quite conversational as he asked the next question. "Frau Vogel, I'd like to step back just a moment. Is it true that you found it necessary to occasionally punish Dr. Hal–, Peter when he was in your service?"

"Discipline is always necessary, in any work. We are an orderly people."

"I see. Did you at one time slam a rolling pin into his face, breaking two teeth and cracking his jaw?"

Peter drew himself up in shock. This was certainly not the approach he had expected! He had wanted Elspeth to be cooperative, not defensive! Elspeth was equally surprised. She shook her head slowly. "My discipline was always appropriate to the situation."

"Naturally, but did you do that?"

There was an objection and the lawyers and judges spent a moment quietly discussing the relevance of this line of questioning. At last Gerhard was permitted to continue and he repeated his question.

Elspeth looked this time, not at Peter, but into the audience. Teresa mouthed something to her mother. Elspeth looked thoughtful. "I may have hit him with something more than my hand," she finally admitted. "I am only a weak woman, and he is a strong, healthy man."

"Did he remain healthy?"

"I'm sorry, what do you mean?"

"I mean, while in your household, was his situation such that he remained healthy? Or was he denied adequate food and sleep and forced to spend his nights working in a factory?"

Elspeth straightened. "We demanded nothing unusual of him."

"Was he paid a salary?"

"Of course not."

"Was he beaten?"

"There was discipline, as necessary."

"Did your husband use a shovel to try to break Peter's legs?"

Elspeth looked again at Teresa.

Gerhard turned around to follow her gaze. His voice became soft, almost understanding. "Did your daughter witness it?"

"My husband had a temper," Elspeth muttered.

The prosecutor rested his forehead on his hands so his expression wasn't visible to the court.

"Did your husband flog Peter senseless because he spoke to your daughter about history?"

Elspeth breathed deeply. "There was some incident, I don't remember exactly what."

"Now, I understand this was all in the interests of keeping a well-organized household, but Frau Vogel, would it be safe to say that Peter was quite seriously physically injured at various times during his years in your household?"

Elspeth pursed her lips. "I wouldn't call it serious."

Somebody sputtered loudly.

Gerhard stroked his chin thoughtfully. "Do you think Peter might have thought his injuries were serious?" Before the prosecution could object, Gerhard refined his question. "For instance, did he ever need a physician?"

"He did ask for a doctor once."

"Did you get him one?"

"Of course not."

There were a few groans from the back of the courtroom and again Elspeth seemed surprised by the response. The prosecution took the opportunity to object to the long digression, but the line of questioning was allowed. Peter stared down at the table, annoyed with himself. He had wanted Gerhard to get Elspeth to incriminate Schindler and in carefully setting up that situation, he had forgotten that Gerhard was only interested in defending his client. Of course, Gerhard would rather spend his time establishing a justification for Peter's actions. Once Peter had indicated that Elspeth might in some way regret her earlier behavior, Gerhard had grabbed the bit in his teeth and was running with a new strategy. And in the process, he might well forget the entire blackmail scenario and completely miss the chance to implicate Schindler!

Alex leaned in toward Peter. "I thought you said you could handle it."

"Give him time. He does believe, after all, that he's being paid to defend me."

Gerhard paced away from Frau Vogel, giving the court time to contemplate her statement. When he turned back to her, he smiled sympathetically. "Frau Vogel, when Peter left your house, did he in any way harm anyone?"

Elspeth drew herself up. "He took some valuables. He stole my husband's car."

"I see. But did he harm any member of your family? Your husband, for example?"

"No."

"So he did not carry out any acts of revenge?"

"Why should he have?"

Gerhard's smile became even more understanding. "Indeed. Yet more than two years later, according to your testimony, he returns – at great personal risk. Did he give a reason for this strange action?"

"As I have said, he told me 'an eye for an eye, a daughter for a daughter'."

"Did you understand what he meant?"

507

Elspeth shook her head.

Gerhard noted her gesture for the record and the prosecution objected to the relevance. There was another conference and then Gerhard was allowed to ask, "Did you ask him what he meant?"

Elspeth remained silent.

"Frau Vogel, I want to remind you that you are under oath." Gerhard caught Elspeth's eyes and drew her attention to Peter. "You told him his behavior was inappropriate, you talked about Dresden. What else was said? Did you ask him what he meant?"

Elspeth scanned the row of officials from the Reich. Her eyes came to rest on Teresa and she spent a moment contemplating her daughter. Teresa looked pointedly at Peter, then back to her mother. "Not again," she mouthed.

Elspeth took a deep breath. "Yes. He told me his daughter had been killed."

"Did you believe him?"

"Not at first. He said I should ask my husband, that he would know."

"And did you?"

"I didn't want to, but he woke Karl up, so I asked him if he had murdered Peter's daughter."

"What did he say?"

Yet another objection interrupted the proceedings, but eventually Gerhard could repeat, "What did your husband say?"

"He said that he didn't have anything to do with it. He only watched the videotape." Elspeth hesitated, then added, "He started to say that it had been good for a laugh, but then he noticed that Peter held a gun."

"What happened next?"

Elspeth shook her head. "I'm afraid I really don't remember. Peter whispered something to Karl that shocked him. He said 'How?' or 'Why?' or something like that. I didn't hear the reply. The next thing I know was that Peter had stabbed Karl and he fell forward. Peter pulled him back into a lying down position and closed his eyes." Elspeth shuddered. "He looked like he was asleep."

"How did Peter react?"

"React?"

"Yes. Was he triumphant? Threatening? Did he do anything that might imply he felt sated or avenged?"

Elspeth shook her head. "No. Nothing."

"Were you surprised by his action?"

"What?"

"Before your husband was awakened, you and Peter talked about a number of things. Did he tell you what he planned?"

508

Elspeth's mouth worked through a number of expressions before she finally answered, "Not exactly."

"Did he mention anything about your husband's political situation?"

"He said that Karl was in deep trouble and would be forced to..." Elspeth glanced at the row of officials again. "He told me Karl was in deep trouble."

"Did he say why?"

"No. He seemed to think I knew what was happening."

Gerhard glanced at Peter then back to Frau Vogel. "Did he tell you how he knew so much about your husband's political situation?"

"He said that Frau Schindler told him."

"Who is this Frau Schindler?"

"He meant Greta Schindler. She's the wife of the Gauleiter of the London region."

There was a murmur of surprise in the courtroom. Gerhard raised his eyebrows, as if astonished. "How did Peter know this woman?"

"I don't know. We had him work for them a number of times. At their Berlin residence."

"Anything else?"

"You know, Peter was from London – maybe there was a connection from further back." Elspeth stroked her chin thoughtfully. "In fact, I remember that Günter – that's Frau Schindler's husband – he always seemed to take a special interest in Peter anytime he visited. He even mentioned him in dinner conversations at his own residence." Elspeth paused, then added, "That always struck me as a little bit odd. I mean, he was a servant. One doesn't talk about servants – not by name, anyway. I never understood why the Schindlers were so fixated on him."

"And then they're passing on information to him about your husband's political situation as well. Long after Peter was no longer in your, um, employ."

"Yes, so it would seem."

There was an objection at this blind speculation involving a witness but Elspeth had already agreed. The presiding judge noted that the comments should be struck from the record and, with a reminder to Gerhard to maintain proper procedure, the court moved on.

"Tell me, was Peter a vengeful man?"

Elspeth did not hesitate. "No. Not at all."

"Frau Vogel, how did he behave with your children?"

"He was very good with the children. Nice to them."

"Would you even say he was kind?"

Elspeth nodded. "Very kind. He paid attention to them. Listened to them." Again Elspeth's eyes fell upon her daughter and she added softly, "They loved him."

"Did it make sense to you that he returned, years later, for what seemed like a senseless act of vengeance?"

Elspeth shook her head. "No."

"Did it make sense to you that he knew your husband's political situation so well?"

"No."

"Do you think there may have been some other motivation for his actions?"

The prosecution objected to this question, but Elspeth was too busy contemplating the idea to notice. "I...I had never thought about it," she said softly. It was clear to all that she considered it very likely and so Gerhard happily accepted the presiding judge's admonition and after a pro forma apology, he thanked his witness and ended his questioning.

Peter breathed a sigh of relief and smiled at his lawyer as he took his seat. He leant toward him and whispered, "Thank you."

7

"*I* never talked to that horrid man!" Greta Schindler stomped around Richard's flat as if it were a cage. She went to a window, scowled at the view, turned and walked to the cabinet.

Richard came over to her and selected a bottle. "How about some cognac, darling?"

"I gave him instructions, of course. And had to berate him all too often. But I never *talked* to him! Why would I? He was..." She shuddered at the thought of having interacted with such a nobody. "He was a disgusting creature. God, why would I have talked to him?"

Richard poured two glasses of cognac and handed one to Greta. "Well, I tried conversing with him once."

"Really?"

"Yes, you were there. It was at the Vogel's. It was the first time I met you." Richard looked at her lovingly. "Don't you remember?"

Greta drew herself up. "Oh, then. Yes, I remember meeting you. Was he there?"

Richard laughed. "He served the dinner. Coughing and choking the whole time, if I remember correctly."

Greta looked confused and Richard furrowed his brow in thought. "You know, actually, I don't think you were there – I met you the following night, at your house. I came with Beate, the archivist. But even then Günter managed to talk about Halifax. Elspeth Vogel was at least right about that, it was odd that he seemed so fixated on Halifax's behavior."

"He did it to embarrass Vogel." Greta smiled wickedly. "I tormented Elspeth about him as well."

"How so?"

"Oh, it was obvious she wanted to get him into her bed." Again Greta shuddered. "Can you imagine?"

Richard shook his head. "No."

Greta looked thoughtful. "You know, though, maybe if I had gotten stuck with Karl...You remember what he was like, don't you?"

Richard nodded.

"Well, I mean, at first, earlier, before you met him, he was actually quite handsome. Full of himself, but then again, what man in Berlin isn't?" Greta smiled at Richard to exclude him from her harsh judgment. "But then, all of a sudden it seemed to all go to his head. He got disgusting – both physically and mentally. Fat and lazy. Boring too."

"And Elspeth Vogel?"

"She's always been an arrogant bitch. It was quite fun watching as her little Nazi star began to crash. I mean, after all, with her connections, she could have married anyone. But she had to oppose her parents and elope with Mr. Blond-Hair-and-Muscles and then he goes and loses everything! Not only the political game, but his physical appeal as well! Hah! You know, when I first met her, I think she thought that she had made the better marriage."

"And later?"

"Later! Hah, she's lusting after servants. What a loser."

"Indeed. But Greta, you know, this is a godsend. Are you sure you never talked to Halifax?"

"As I said, I sometimes had to correct his behavior. Elspeth was terribly lax." Greta shook her head. "But after he ran away? Of course not!"

"Hmm. I wonder why Halifax told Elspeth you talked to him. Do you think he might have meant another Frau Schindler?"

"I suppose. It is a common name."

Richard swirled his drink in its glass. "You know, we should take advantage of this misunderstanding."

"How so?"

"Well, whether or not you actually talked to Halifax, what's important is that everyone thinks you did. And they think you did it at Günter's

511

request." Richard looked at Greta meaningfully. "And that would mean that Halifax was his agent."

"Is that possible? Do you think Halifax *was* working for Günter all along?"

"The question is, do we care?" Richard leaned into Greta and tenderly kissed her cheek. "Maybe you should remember speaking with Halifax, at Günter's direction. You would be guilty of nothing except being a dutiful and obedient wife. Whereas…"

Greta's eyes sparkled with possibilities. "Whereas Günter would suddenly fall under serious suspicion." She pulled back a bit and looked at Richard. "Is that fair? I mean, I have no reason to believe Günter is guilty of anything so horrific as ordering Karl Vogel's murder."

"My dear Greta, when Rudi was kidnapped, your innocent husband forced Büttner's suicide and was planning to have me hanged. When he realized that his plan was crumbling, he tried to trick me into suicide."

Greta nodded as she remembered those difficult days, then she frowned in confusion. "Once Rudi was back, why didn't you tell him about what Günter had done?"

"Several reasons – one of which was that I had very little proof and Rudi was already excited and paranoid. God only knows how he would have reacted to a spate of accusations from his most trusted advisors."

"And the other reason?"

Richard grunted. "Was possibly mistaken. I still need time to organize things and I thought, during that time, it was necessary to keep Günter as a counterweight so that Rudi didn't get too scared of me."

"But he did anyway." Greta sipped her drink. "Well, I guess you can thank your daughter that you're back in Berlin."

Richard nodded.

"So why do you think you can take Günter out of play now? Don't you still need him as a counterweight?"

Richard shook his head. "There's Frauenfeld now. We've already had several public disagreements, no doubt that's enough to convince Rudi that we'll keep each other in line. Besides, this is simply too good an opportunity to pass up. You know Günter tried to pin Schenkelhof's murder on me and said that I had Halifax do it for me. Now the tables have been turned."

"But everybody knows that Günter had no reason to want to hurt Schenkelhof and was truly upset by his death."

"Yes, but not by Vogel's."

"I suppose you're right. And whatever one thought of his personality, he was, after all, a pure Aryan and an official of the Reich. It was quite a heinous crime."

"And there's always the question of why Günter would want to have Karl killed. What did Karl know?"

Greta walked back over to the window and looked at the street. "Do you think Rudi will have Günter hanged?"

"No. No matter what Rudi suspects about Günter, I don't think he'd have him brought to trial. Partly because there really is no hard evidence, but mostly because it would detract from the proceedings in Switzerland. After all, I convinced Rudi that an international tribunal would be the best way to destroy Halifax's reputation and therefore negate anything he had said in America, so the last thing Rudi would want to do is draw attention away from Halifax's guilt of Vogel's murder."

"He might do it in secret."

Richard joined Greta by the window and gently rubbed her shoulders. "Don't worry about Günter, darling. He's too highly placed for Rudi to do anything to him without it drawing international attention. And since Rudi doesn't want that, he won't do anything. Günter will be declawed, that's all."

"How?"

"Oh, I think Rudi might find it necessary for him to go back to London and stay put for a long while." Richard continued to give Greta a massage, hoping to soothe her. He wondered why she was so worried about Günter's well being, but didn't want to ask. Perhaps it was simply that although she felt her chances for power were better as Traugutt's wife, she felt no particular animosity toward her estranged husband. Indeed, she often seemed quite upset any time things turned a bit nasty. He remembered Greta's reaction to Mathias punishing Leszek and amended that thought. Greta simply didn't like low-class behavior among the élite, violence amongst and against the lower orders was an entirely different matter.

Greta rolled her head, enjoying Richard's touch, and purred lightly. "So how is the trial going? Is Rudi pleased?"

"Very pleased. He's getting reports from our observers, and they are all very positive." But of course, they would be, wouldn't they? Who would want to bring the Führer anything other than good news? As for the taped version, Richard was sure that Rudi would see only good news since Olek had volunteered to oversee the delicate task of editing the tedious weeks of trial testimony into just a few hours of tape. The only difficult portion would be the presentation of Frau Vogel's testimony. Richard was truly annoyed at Peter for allowing his defense attorney to spend so much time on justifying Peter's actions rather than simply getting to the point of having Frau Vogel mention the Schindler name, but he felt relatively sure that Rudi would be too busy untangling the hints of conspiracy to even notice that Peter was portrayed rather sympathetically throughout that part.

Richard kissed Greta's exposed neck and whispered, "Rudi's waiting until the closing arguments to view the entire trial. He won't see the bit I just showed you until tomorrow at the earliest. After that, he may well have some questions he'll want to ask you. Do you think you could give him some useful answers?" He moved up to her earlobe, caressing it gently with his lips.

Greta shuddered at Richard's touch. "I'm sure I can."

8

"*A*h, Richard, so glad you could come!" The Führer embraced Richard.

Richard was so taken aback by the Führer's familiarity that it was all he could do not to pull away. "*Mein Führer*," he stammered, as he attempted to return the hug in a manner which would be sufficiently warm and deferential at the same time. He wasn't sure if he got the balance right, as he was simultaneously fighting an almost overwhelming urge to defend himself. After all, such warmth from a man like Rudi seemed most appropriately followed by a dagger between the ribs.

"So good to see you!" The Führer pounded Richard's back heartily.

Richard winced but managed to turn it into a smile. As the Führer released him, he maintained the self-conscience grin, knowing that Rudi would take it as a sign of his pleasure at being so flattered. "*Mein Führer*, you honor me."

The Führer good-naturedly waved the comment away and turned to Richard's companions. He bowed deeply and kissed Stefi's hand. "Frau Karlsson, it is always a pleasure." He squeezed her hand lightly before releasing it and turning to Olek. Olek bowed deeply and the Führer returned with a slight bow of his head. "And Herr Karlsson, thank you so much for coming."

Olek was going to reply but suddenly noticed the Führer had extended his hand. Olek quickly reached for the Führer's hand. The Führer grabbed Olek's hand in both of his, shaking it warmly. "I want to thank you in advance for all the work you've put into organizing this tape for me. To summarize everything that happened over the past several months in four hours – that really is an accomplishment!"

"It's always an honor to serve you, *mein Führer*." There was silence at his words and Olek realized he needed to add something. In desperation he resorted to quoting a school verse which had been as effectively pounded into him as it had been into any true Nazi schoolchild. "*Der Führer kennt nür Kampf, Arbeit und Sorge. Wir wollen ihm den Teil abnehmen, den wir ihm abnehmen können."*

Stefi bit her lip to hide a laugh. Poor Olek, quoting nonsense about lightening the Führer's many burdens! The Führer looked pleased though – clearly, despite his panic, Olek had chosen his words well. The Führer motioned them all into the room. "Come on in! Sit down, make yourselves comfortable. Nobody else is here yet, except my wife, of course."

Stefi and Olek exchanged a surprised glance as they followed Richard and the Führer toward the suite of furniture near the television. The Führer's wife stood forlornly near the couch. Fifteen years earlier, when Rudi was still organizing his bid for power, he had seen fit to marry. His bride, Gertrud, a reticent eighteen-year-old of little promise and even less beauty, was nevertheless very attractive to him as a member of the Goebbels family with all the connections to power that that implied. Her parents had welcomed the opportunity to marry off their dismal progeny and were overjoyed when Rudi ultimately obtained Party leadership several years later.

For his part, Rudi had dutifully paid attention to his wife for a few years, but no children were forthcoming. The progressing years did nothing to enhance Gertrud's limited charms and as Rudi's less salubrious personal habits began to emerge with his ever-growing personal power, he had grown bored with her. He never mistreated her, was never publicly rude to her, nor did he dare divorce her – for her family still held the keys to vast political support – he simply ignored her. She uncomplainingly accepted her lonely role as the only one available to her and lived her life in a purgatory of neither being married nor being free. She maintained her own apartment in the *Residenz*, visited her family frequently, and lived an almost entirely separate life, making only intermittent public appearances with her husband simply to prove she was still alive.

Stefi was therefore quite surprised to see her at a private gathering, but decided that perhaps it had something to do with the fact that Olek had also been invited. She had met Gertrud several times, but always at a large gathering and now, as she watched her father indulge in a deep bow and kiss Gertrud's hand, she wondered how she should greet the Führer's wife.

Richard and Gertrud exchanged a few pleasantries and the color returned to Gertrud's cheeks. Olek repeated Richard's performance and then Stefi approached. Gertrud stared at Stefi icily for a moment, the edges of her mouth trembling with tension, but then her will broke and she resignedly offered her hand. Stefi took Gertrud's hand, at the same time curtseying slightly and exclaiming, "My most esteemed First Lady! How kind of you to receive us."

The Führer smiled benignly, pleased that Stefi was so gracious. His little Stefi shone like a diamond compared to the cloudy bit of quartz he had married; nevertheless, it was only right for Stefi to show an appropriate level of respect to Gertrud – she was, after all, the wife of the Führer.

Gertrud nodded lightly in reply. "Frau Karlsson." There was obviously more, but Gertrud took her time finding the right words. She swallowed, smiled slightly, then added, "It is, as always, a pleasure to see you and your family."

Any further conversation was interrupted by the announcement that the Schindlers had arrived. There was another round of almost formal greetings with Greta playing particularly coy with Richard. The Führer smiled to himself. Whereas he, with his power and virility, was able to keep the incredibly young and beautiful Stefi always at his side, poor Richard was left with Greta Schindler, a headstrong woman of his own age who could torment him at will by whimsically withholding her favor.

A moment later Herr and Frau Frauenfeld arrived – the pair of them looking like a matched set: both short, rounded and homely in their appearance. Irmtraud Frauenfeld, with her pinned up hair and her rolling accent, reminded everyone of a favorite aunt and with her arrival the atmosphere lightened considerably. Again more greetings, drinks were served – the Frauenfelds both taking only mineral water – and then, finally Rudi chose to sit down, placing himself on the loveseat. He motioned to Stefi. "Frau Karlsson, why don't you sit here, next to me? I would love to hear your commentary on your husband's editorial efforts."

Stefi smiled demurely and sat next to Rudi. Gertrud sat in a corner of the couch. Günter Schindler sat in an armchair, and quite surprisingly Greta Schindler perched herself on the arm of his chair. The Frauenfelds took the two remaining places on the sofa, with Irmtraud in the middle, comfortingly near Gertrud. Only one armchair remained, and Richard graciously motioned his son-in-law toward it, on the assumption that hierarchy gave way to Olek's status as crippled.

"Um Gottes willen!" The Führer jumped to his feet to yell at his servants. "Can't you buffoons count?" As the servants hurriedly brought over more chairs, the Führer snarled at Günter. "And you, Günter, are you so old that you must take a seat while a young man who gave his legs in the service of our country remains standing? What's wrong with you?"

Casting a quick but meaningful glance at Frauenfeld, Schindler stood, apologizing profusely to Olek. But it was too late, the Führer had already turned his attention to rearranging the seats and Olek was too embarrassed to listen. Richard smirked his satisfaction. It was a perfect start to what he hoped would be a miserable evening for Günter.

Olek and Richard sat in the chairs that had been brought over, the disputed armchair remained empty. Schindler continued to stand, not knowing what to do. Almost kindly, Greta reached out and urged him to resume his seat. He frowned at her. Why was Greta being so solicitous?

Finally they were all settled to the Führer's satisfaction and he addressed them from his seat. "You know, of course, that I magnanimously surrendered Halifax to be tried by an international court so that his supporters in America will have no doubt about his guilt and in that way we can destroy his reputation in the NAU and undo some of the damage he has done to our reputation." Nobody dared ask if *our* meant the Reich or the Führer himself. It was a moot point in the Führer's mind. "I've only received summaries of each day's events from my observers, but the entire proceedings of the trial have been filmed up to the verdict and sentencing, which, of course, has yet to happen. Herr Karlsson–" At this point Rudi motioned toward Olek, "–has selflessly dedicated himself to the task of editing these hundreds of hours of trial proceedings down to only four. And I have invited you, my dear friends...and wife, to share these hours with me."

The small group applauded and the Führer pressed the button to start the video player. Initially, they watched in silence, but eventually Rudi began to make comments and the others followed suit. It was trivial for all of them to maintain an interested air: for the men, the proceedings were far better than a Party speech – which also could easily last four hours, for the women, the trial was more engaging than their long-winded husbands. Only the Führer was showing signs of flagging as the hours went on and Richard worried he might well be asleep by the time the important part was reached.

"He was having an affair with this woman?"

"Immoral scum, sleeping with someone else's wife!" Schindler directed his comment not at the prosecutor who had spoken on the tape, but at Halifax. He smiled up at Traugutt, enjoying the implied insult of his colleague. The connection was obvious! Traugutt smiled back. Indeed, it was. Günter reddened as he realized what he had said, but luckily the Führer had failed to notice. Frauenfeld and his wife exchanged a worried glance.

"You realize that Mr. Halifax is an ally, yet you have portrayed him as an adulterer and someone who threatens to murder a friend."

"Perfect," the Führer purred, reaching over to Stefi to hold her hand. "Threatens to murder a friend!" He grew even happier with the charges of homosexuality and bizarre love triangles. "This is great!"

The next segment gave Yardley's complicated background and the strong implication of his complicity in the arrest of his comrades. Somehow

Graham's testimony and his salvaging of Yardley's reputation did not make it onto Olek's edited version of the trial.

"Betraying his own people..." Frau Frauenfeld murmured, apparently genuinely appalled.

"Only clever thing he did," Schindler commented. Again, from the looks he received, he realized that he had somehow missed the mark.

As the prosecution turned to an infamous videotaped incident, Stefi excused herself to visit the toilet, quietly insisting that the tape not be stopped on her account. She missed a long segment on how Halifax's little girl had been killed by a bomb which he himself had set but presumably mistimed. That was followed by a description of his hysterical reaction to being arrested – all of which had been caught on the usual police videotape and later cynically used by the opposition. There was no counterargument on the tape and Stefi returned at the point where Peter's friend Roman was being sworn in.

"Rather a waste of time, isn't it?" Günter looked around to see if this time someone would agree with him.

It was Greta who agreed. "Yes, their simple minds are incapable of understanding the subtleties of testifying, much less presenting uncorrupted testimony."

"Luckily, I think that becomes obvious to the court." Olek shifted slightly in his seat, proud of his role-playing.

Richard nodded his agreement. "And we received a wonderful quid pro quo for this in having Frau Vogel speak personally about that violent man."

Even as Richard finished speaking the prosecutor could be heard saying, *"Your friend is in trouble and you want to help him. You don't want people to know what a violent man he is..."*

The entire room nodded their agreement. The Führer turned off the tape and suggested a small break. They went en masse outside to take the evening air and enjoy some refreshments in the garden and returned an hour later, ready for more.

Peter's testimony to the prosecutor came next, but it seemed rather short and was mostly limited to the prosecution's initial statements as he read from the confession followed by his direct question asking if Peter had killed Karl Vogel. Olek had deftly edited out Peter's comments in between and jumped immediately to his straightforward acceptance of guilt.

"From his own mouth!" the Führer trumpeted in time with the prosecutor's own triumphant words. "From the villain's own mouth!" With that he stretched and yawned ostentatiously. "I'm not sure we need more."

With his next yawn, he missed the number of panicked glances that shot around the room. But before any of the conspirators could say something, Irmtraud Frauenfeld spoke up. *"Mein Führer,* I have so looked forward to hearing Frau Vogel's testimony. I think we owe it to her after all the poor woman must have suffered. And besides, so far we've not heard the testimony of one good German!"

The Führer pursed his lips as he considered her words. Olek ventured, "There's not much more, *mein Führer*."

"Shall we finish the tape?" Stefi suggested brightly. She settled herself more comfortably in her seat and quite coincidentally brushed up against Rudi.

He perked up perceptibly. "Of course, of course. It would be a disappointment to stop now."

Elspeth's testimony to the prosecution played out almost uncut. It was followed by the defense's questioning of her. For brevity, Olek had cut through the preliminaries of that and jumped in near the end as Elspeth explained that Peter had stolen some of her husband's possessions upon leaving their household. The Führer seemed oblivious to Frau Vogel's statement that Karl had watched Joanna's murder on tape, possibly losing the importance of that statement in the convoluted series of questions and answers that followed. He sat up, intrigued at the admission that Peter knew Karl's political situation and glanced pointedly at Greta Schindler when her name was mentioned.

Greta smiled and looked down at her husband almost simultaneous with his name being evoked. Günter had his eyes closed and seemed to be snoring quietly, but somehow he sensed the sudden tension, for his eyes snapped open. "They're speaking about you, dear," Greta cooed.

"Do you think there may have been some other motivation for his actions?" the lawyer was asking.

"Talking about me?"

Frau Vogel's voice was thoughtfully answering, *"I...I had never thought about it."*

"Thought about what?" Günter looked around confused.

"Good question, Günter." The Führer picked up the remote control and handed it to Olek. "Could you replay that section for Günter? I think he's missed something important."

It was Frauenfeld who led the attack. He quite clearly remembered the meeting where Schindler had drawn him into spurious accusations against Traugutt and he was genuinely angered at having been so manipulated. Now it was clear why! The whole Traugutt as Halifax's protector scenario had been a simple dodge to hide Schindler's own involvement in something quite sinister. He grew so excited he was obliged to stand, pacing angrily around the room. "This is really unbelievable, Günter, really too much! First unknown agents of yours just happen to be in the A.K. hideout in the

519

mountains, and now we're finding out that you're passing on political information to Halifax himself!"

Günter had risen to his feet as Frauenfeld spoke and now he turned and angrily gestured at the television. "She was lying!"

"Frau Vogel? Why would she lie?" Irmtraud asked innocently.

"Then he lied to her! Isn't that right, Greta? You didn't talk to him!"

Greta seemed to be undecided. She slipped off the arm of the chair and looked from her husband to the Führer and then back to Günter. "Darling, I know you're my husband, but really, in the presence of the Führer, my duty is clear. My loyalty is to my country and my Führer. I must tell the truth."

"Greta? What are you talking about?"

"Günter, surely you haven't forgotten? Is that it, dear? Have you forgotten?" Greta was exquisite, playing the concerned wife. Could it be senility that would allow her husband to survive this political explosion?

"Forgotten what? What are you talking about?" Schindler's face had become a dangerous shade of purple.

"Frau Schindler, Greta..." The Führer rose to his feet to approach the two of them. Behind him the others found it wise to stand as well. "Can you please tell us what is going on?"

"*Mein Führer,* I am so sorry! I didn't realize it at the time, but now that I've heard Frau Vogel's words it's all becoming clear to me." Greta continued in her effusive manner, telling how, obedient to her husband, she had done a favor for him and gone to a café in Berlin to meet with someone. A man had joined her table and given her the password. She hadn't recognized him as the Vogel's servant so he must have been wearing a disguise, or perhaps...At this she stopped to remember, "Perhaps I wouldn't have recognized him anyway. After all, I would have never guessed it was Peter Halifax! My husband had me explain Karl Vogel's political situation and told me to emphasize that he was in very deep trouble. He..." At this Frau Schindler indicated her husband, "He didn't tell me why I was doing this, but I was a dutiful wife and did as he requested. This was very shortly before Karl Vogel was murdered and I remember thinking what an odd coincidence it was." Greta sighed heavily. "But now it's clear it was no coincidence. Oh, this explains so much!" She collapsed into the chair Günter had vacated.

The Führer ignored her. "Günter, is this true? Did you have something to do with Halifax murdering Vogel?"

"Of course not! Rudi, this is utter nonsense, why would I organize Vogel's murder?" Günter spread his hands helplessly, simultaneously confused and desperate.

"Maybe he knew something about you?" Frauenfeld guessed. "Maybe he knew of a connection between you and Halifax?"

520

"It was Traugutt who was connected to that man! It was Traugutt who had him freed!" Günter nearly screamed, his finger trembling and pointing at Richard. The others turned to Richard.

"Indeed, that is what I suggested," Richard agreed calmly. "But if you ask Lederman, even he will tell you that *he* selected the prisoner I was to see. I was shown an anonymous and starving wreck of a man and told that he was thoroughly broken. If Lederman tells me later – years later – that that man was Peter Halifax, I won't disagree with him, but I won't take responsibility for his mistakes, either." Richard paused and looked at Günter curiously, "Or tell me, Günter, was it a mistake? Were you already setting up somebody to cover your tracks?"

"What are you talking about? I didn't even know the man!"

"Neither did I. But you knew Karl Vogel long before I was even in Berlin."

"That's right." The Führer drew the words out in a sing-song as he turned back to Günter. "You were implying a connection between Halifax and Traugutt but it was *you* who was in Berlin at the time Halifax was brought there. It was *you* who worked with Vogel for years before Traugutt was transferred to Berlin! You could have told Vogel to go and get Halifax from Breslau." The Führer paused and squinted his eyes as another strange coincidence finally dawned on him. "And *you* were Gauleiter of London when Halifax, a.k.a. Yardley, was declared dead!"

Günter shook his head slowly. "Rudi...I had nothing to do with that...This is insane..."

"Silence!" The Führer placed his fingers on his forehead, gathering the threads together. "He betrays his entire Underground cell to *your* police. He's listed as killed resisting arrest by *your* security apparatus. He turns up later, working for one of *your* competitors whose fortunes spiral downward from that point on..." The Führer paced away, rubbing his forehead. "I have a headache." He walked over to the window and stared out into the night. The others remained behind in silence. Irmtraud turned to Gertrud, gesturing toward the Führer, indicating that she should go to him. Gertrud simply shook her head and sat back down. Irmtraud sat down as well and folded her hands on her lap. She was not unfamiliar with the Führer's moods and she knew it could be a long wait and there was no point in being terribly uncomfortable. The men remained standing, staring off into space. Only Stefi dared move. She left the group to stand next to the Führer by the window.

She touched his shoulder lightly and when he turned to look at her, she smiled hopefully, but maintained the silence he had commanded.

"Oh, *Mäuschen*, is there absolutely no one I can trust?" Rudi turned his gaze back out the window. "They all betray me. All they are interested in is their plots and schemes. I should do away with them all!"

"We are all stricken, my love. Look behind you, see how the others are shaken by these revelations!" Stefi paused as the Führer looked back at the little group. He turned back to the window and the darkness. Stefi let her fingers trail down his sleeve. "Don't you see, you can trust my father, and my husband, and Frauenfeld. Only Günter has betrayed you."

"I don't even know what he's done! How am I going to get to the bottom of all this?"

Stefi let her fingers twine into his. She could feel how he trembled at her touch. "Is that something you want to waste your valuable time on? You know Günter has been up to no good. It is clear he has lied to you for years and that he's still lying about something. But it's also clear that whatever he does is unimportant – he's grown old and confused. He has too many responsibilities. Remove him from his advisory roles, appoint different Gauleiters for the northwest Reich. He's grown too powerful, and with his power he has become arrogant."

"I can't strip him of all his power. Not without proof of something."

"Let him keep London. Let him keep all of England, but remove everything else. Get Ireland and Wales and Scotland out of his hands. It never made sense to combine all those jobs in any case. And he shouldn't be heading up *Niederland* security. He needs a rest and he needs to pay attention to his duties in London. Get him out of Berlin and keep him out." Stefi lightly squeezed the Führer's hand. "That will keep him out of trouble."

Rudi smiled down at Stefi. "What would I do without you, my dear?" He did not wait for an answer but grabbing Stefi's arm in his, went back to his minions. "I'd like you all to leave. Frau Karlsson has agreed to stay and give me a neck massage, to relieve my headache. As for you, Günter, I've decided to rearrange a few things in the western territories. Please contact my office tomorrow. My secretary will have your orders. Understood?"

Günter's lips trembled. "Rudi..."

The Führer shook his head. "Don't push me, Günter. Just go."

Schindler nodded. Without even waiting for his wife, he clicked his heels, bowed sharply and left. The others took their leave as quickly as possible though Olek did pause long enough to hold Stefi's hand in his, squeezing her fingers in his warm grasp.

As they were finally out of the room, the Führer turned expectantly to Stefi. "Now, my dear, I believe I could use one of your marvelous massages."

Stefi smiled sweetly and led the Führer to his bed.

9

*G*uilty. There were groans from some sections of the courtroom, quiet cheers from others. Peter stood next to his lawyer, trying hard not to react to the word. It was no different than he had expected; nevertheless, there was an ache deep in his stomach that would not go away. He would go to prison, he would spend years, maybe decades behind bars and fences and barbed wire. Somehow the miracle he had hoped for had not happened. Guilty of pre-meditated murder. Guilty of kidnapping.

He felt the cameras on him, recording his reactions. He would not give the reporters what they wanted: that was the last bit of freedom left to him – to deny them that glimpse into the depths of his despair. The presiding judge was talking now, explaining that although he had been found guilty, the panel had indicated that they were aware of unusual extenuating circumstances and recommended the minimum sentence possible. The presiding judge noted, however, that the seriousness of the charges left little room for discretion.

Twenty years was the minimum for the murder charge. The kidnapping carried ten but could be served concurrently. However, it did affect the awarding of parole, and though it was unclear exactly whose laws Peter's life would be governed by, Gerhard had warned him that the absolute minimum time he would have to serve if found guilty of both charges was twelve years.

Twelve years. Adequate food, no beatings, no torture. Visits and packages. Regular mail delivery. So what if he was surrounded by concrete walls or barbed wire? There would be some level of security, his life would not be continuously threatened. There would be no ranting propaganda forced down his throat, no shackles worn twenty-four hours a day. It would be okay. They even had libraries and gymnasiums in modern prisons. He would get fresh air and be able to...His thoughts faltered. Twelve years. Madzia would be fifteen, Irena thirteen, Krys twelve. His children would know next to nothing about him. Twelve years, Allison had been dead that long. Twelve years since his life had skittered out of control, landing him here, once again before a court, once again, being sentenced for something which – in his own mind at least – was not a crime.

His thoughts strayed to the times he had spent in prison before. Not to the fiasco that had marred so much of his life, not to Allison's death twelve years ago – but to earlier times, to short sentences he had served for curfew violations or for being caught up in a pub brawl. Those were easy sentences to get, easy to serve. Whenever there was a bar fight between English and German patrons, the police always swept through arresting anyone with English papers. Guilt was assumed and the standard sentence was three months. Usually Peter had managed to get out of such situations before the police got him, but once or twice he had gotten caught in the crush while trying to pull out his friends, and been trapped in the dragnet. If one behaved, the three month sentence was often reduced, so one spent the time, often with friends, in a barracks, working through the day at some idiotic labor and spending the evenings smoking and playing cards. The weeks passed, a line was added to one's papers under the "Convictions" section and then one was released to rejoin society and repeat the idiotic process.

Curfew violation was a bit different. A series of warnings were received and recorded on the violator's papers. Fines were issued. Eventually, when the warnings and fines had grown too numerous, the miscreant was issued a summons. It was a serious crime not to report, so most people went along to their local police station and gave themselves up to serve short sentences of a week or two. Multiple convictions of an indeterminate and varying number would be interpreted as a sign of asocial behavior, at which point the culprit, after he had reported to the police station, would be sent away to a camp for a longer stay and sometimes even a re-education program. Though the stays in the camps could be quite short, they often were extended into years as the prisoner inadvertently added violation upon violation to his record.

Peter supposed the same thing could happen to him now if he was not careful. In all the prisons, he had been told, there was a great deal of trouble keeping the pro and anti Nazi factions from fighting each other. He would naturally fall into the anti-Nazi gang by virtue of his background – that was unavoidable and in many ways necessary for survival – but he would have to be careful not to get involved in any gang activities which could prolong his sentence. This would not be like the labor camp where they had all been incarcerated for the same reason and therefore had some esprit de corps. There would be no shared nationality, no shared hatreds. He was going to be thrown into a much more dangerous milieu and he would have to be very careful about his associations. To as large an extent as possible, he would try to keep himself to himself.

Gerhard was talking now and Peter listened to his words. They seemed polite and sensible and said about everything anyone would want to say in such circumstances. Peter was asked if there was anything he wanted to add, but, keeping his promise to Gerhard, he declined the invitation to speak. The court adjourned, the judges left and the bailiff approached Peter. Several other people tried to come forward to talk to him as he was led away, but he ignored them and they were kept back so he did not hear their words. He didn't want to talk to anyone right now, he just wanted to be alone with the unending ache that was strangling his gut.

Once they were through the doors and in the privacy of the hallway, Gerhard shook Peter's hand. "This is as far as we can go. I'll be in touch to see about appeals and the like." He looked slightly chagrined. "As soon as I work out who to appeal to. Anyway, good luck."

"Thanks."

"Oh, yeah. I want you to take advantage of the medical care available to you. Initiate a petition from inside – make up new symptoms if you have to – and I'll make sure something gets done."

Peter was stunned by Gerhard's words. "That's...Yes, I'll do that. Thank you."

Gerhard looked at Alex expectantly, but Alex seemed tongue-tied. He stared entranced at Peter's wrists as the bailiff put the handcuffs on Peter. Finally Alex managed to move. He began to reach forward to shake Peter's hand, but the bailiff had already begun to pull Peter toward the door.

Gerhard tapped the bailiff's shoulder. "Just a few seconds."

The bailiff nodded and Alex stepped forward. He grabbed Peter's hand and held it sandwiched between both of his. "I'm so sorry," he whispered in Polish.

It was the most emotion Peter had ever heard from his father-in-law. He smiled at Alex. "You know what to tell everyone for me. Okay?"

Alex nodded and they parted company.

10

"*H*e says he's getting very good at solitaire." Zosia laughed, then aware of the noise she had made, she stroked Madzia's sweaty hair soothingly. The little girl lay with her head on Zosia's lap, sleeping uneasily.

Tadek was on the floor of the kitchen, wiping up Magdalena's vomit. He made a face as he wrung out the cloth, "Any other news?"

"I'll read you some." Zosia brought the sheets of paper closer to her nose and changing the tone of her voice to that appropriate for quoting, read, "After I arrived, I established a routine of sorts, but I haven't managed to settle in. Maybe I'm just hoping that it's all a big mistake and there's no point getting comfortable (ha, ha). I know, I know. I should be using the time wisely, learning something or other, but I just haven't managed to do that yet – unless you count the fact that I'm getting very good at solitaire.

When I first arrived, I put my name on the jobs list, just for something to do and to earn a bit of cash, but I'm not working right now."

"I wonder why not."

Zosia shrugged and read on. "There are some early preparations for the holidays, but I'm not taking part." Zosia glanced at the top to look at the date. "Oh, yes, he wrote this in November."

"So it took more than two months to find its way here." Tadek did a last swipe over the floor and stood up to admire his work.

Zosia hefted the sheets. "Or he spent weeks writing it." Still that didn't explain why it was only the second letter. Admittedly, it was a long letter, but why the great silence? Did he think the letters wouldn't get through?

Tadek spread his arms dramatically. "Ta-da!"

Zosia looked at him confused, and then at the floor. "Oh, yes, beautiful. Thanks." Having cleaned the floor about a hundred times that day already, she felt rather annoyed at needing to thank him. But they were not *his* children and he remained very much a guest in *her* flat, helping out with *her* family. "Could you glance at the babies and see if they're okay?"

Tadek nodded and disappeared into the bedroom. He re-emerged within seconds. "They're fine. Both monsters sleeping." He sat down next to Zosia on the couch and gently tousled Madzia's hair. "Any more?"

Zosia bowed her head over the letter and continued. "When I do get some work, I would prefer something outdoors like picking up litter (putting my talents to their fullest use), but not surprisingly that's only done in the summer. I guess, in the winter, one can volunteer for emergency snow removal, and I'll do that as soon as possible. Until then, I'll spend my time playing cards and working out in my cell. Why in my cell, you ask?" Zosia's voice dropped off and she read silently for a few minutes. "Oh, oh dear," she muttered.

"What's up?"

"It seems there was some sort of incident. One of the Nazi sympathizers in the prison tried to stab Peter. There was a fight—"

"Was he hurt?"

"No. He managed to get the knife off the attacker and stabbed him with it. When the fight was broken up, the knife disappeared." Zosia read aloud, "It was obvious that I had not started the fight, but I did stab the other guy in what was perhaps not entirely self-defense, so I'm afraid I've already managed to violate prison rules and, as a result, I've been disciplined."

Zosia looked at Tadek in alarm and then back down at the page. "Don't laugh," she read, "that's the word they use. It conjured up really nasty images in my mind, but all I got was solitary for three months. That'll take me through January. Thank God! My cellmate was an absolute idiot, chattering all the time about his girlfriends and how much they all missed him. With luck, I can get the sentence extended and remain here indefinitely."

"Maybe he should be sentenced to scrubbing up baby vomit and listening to three squalling brats indefinitely." Tadek smiled broadly, trying to show that he meant his comment as a joke.

Zosia continued reading, "I'm sorry I haven't written in so long. I started lots of letters, but there's so little to say that I haven't said before, and I felt kind of embarrassed to admit that the first thing I managed to do here was get in trouble. Luckily the incident didn't affect my sentence or parole chances, but I'm pretty limited in what I can do right now. Various privileges have been cut, et cetera. Anyway, once I've finished the three months, I'm going to organize something here, to keep myself from going insane–"

"As if that's an option."

She looked up at Tadek. "He put a 'tell Tadek I heard that' in parenthesis." She laughed at Tadek's expression and then continued reading, "I'll get a degree in something. It will be the first time I'll have official recognition for something I know. There's all sorts of career opportunities posted – auto mechanic, laundry assistant..." Zosia's voice trailed off as she realized Peter was joking. She looked up at the ceiling, biting her lip. "I guess he'll be out of solitary next week. I hope he does do something when he gets out. It's such a waste of his life."

Tadek snorted. "We all waste our lives. I mean, what do you or I have to show for our years of work?"

Zosia thought of her children but, sensing Tadek's ill-temper, decided not to mention them. "Not a whole hell of a lot."

"And at least he's safe. Safer than us anyway."

"I think there's more to life than being safe."

"Yeah, like cleaning up baby vomit. Ugh."

Holding Madzia carefully in place, Zosia twisted in her seat so she was looking directly at Tadek. "If it's too much, maybe you want to find somewhere else."

Tadek stood and went into the kitchen. "Do you want a cup of tea?"

"Sure."

Zosia turned her attention back to the letter, reading silently now.

Peter told her how much he missed them all and how lonely he felt then wrote, "As far as appeals, my lawyer has run into dead ends and has given up for the moment, and Alex has left Switzerland so I don't see either of them anymore. Before I got solitary, I was surprised by a visit from Arieka – she's that woman I met on the late night TV show and now she's the ambassador to the Reich for Kivu. Oh, that's right, you know all about that. Well, I won't scratch the words out. Anyway, she's been very kind and has purchased some things that I'm allowed to have in my cell. Best of all though, is that she leaned a bit on the administration..."

Zosia read of how Arieka, in conjunction with Peter's lawyer, had first made sure that he had access to an eye specialist and, as Peter put it "phenomenal medical technology – equipment that makes Frankenstein's laboratory look tame." The two of them then followed that up with political pressure to make sure the specialist's advice was followed. Peter wrote, "All at the expense of the international tribunal and every visit got me out of solitary for a while. (There are exemptions for medical stuff. Amazingly humane. I'm going to have to recommend this resort to all my friends.) Anyway, they discovered that some of my problems (mostly the headaches and dizziness, but also some blurred vision) are caused by brain damage due to repeated head injuries. I guess there's some memory loss associated with that, too. Uh, what was I saying? (Ha, ha.) Oh yeah, my brain essentially got bruised and scarred by being slammed into my skull (Szaflary's quack told me that much) – and that, I guess, cannot be artificially repaired (with current technology) but may heal over time. (Or the functions relocate – amazing organism, the brain.) And there's all the stuff from those pesky spinal injuries – you know, the jackboots into the small of the back. They're tricky as well. (Painful, too, I can assure you). But never mind all that, the real news is that they also determined that I have a detached retina and some problems due to badly healed fractures to the bone around the edge of my eye (the orbit?) – and that, apparently can be fixed! They can smooth the bone and reattach the retina – and I've even been assured they're not going to pop my eyeball out of my skull to do that! I'm scheduled for surgery in a few days – which I guess will be long in the past by the time you read this. Cross your fingers. I'm told that if it's not the central region of the retina that's involved my vision will improve enormously and, at the very least, will stop deteriorating. So, here's to hoping the surgeon doesn't drink as much as I would like to!"

Zosia brought her hand to her mouth, overwhelmed by hope, fear, and guilt simultaneously. They had never even tried to do anything about his sight! They had used the money to buy weapons! And his lawyer and that skinny African woman...Oh God, was she jealous? She looked down at the letter, scanning ahead a few lines and saw that the date changed. So, it was written in pieces. She read on, eager to find out if everything had turned out okay.

His words under the new date reassured her immediately. "God, I wish I could see your face. I've had my first check-up and was told that all is progressing marvelously. I have to minimize my activities for a time, but that's hardly a problem given my current circumstances. The doctor chided me for having left things untended for so long – she told me I had been toying with blindness and I was a complete cretin and how could I possibly have been so cavalier with something so precious. I didn't even mind being scolded – I was so happy. I am so happy! Who would have thought something good would have come out of this mess? It's wonderful. If only I could see you now. I wish you could visit, but I know that's not possible." He wrote on at length about how much he missed her and everyone else and Zosia's heart calmed as she realized not only that there was no more surprising news, but that he missed her despite Arieka's help and visits.

Zosia paused long enough to tell Peter's good news to Tadek, as he stood in the kitchen, waiting for the water to boil. Tadek's response was pleased but she felt vaguely disappointed that he wasn't more excited, so she read on in silence. Under a later date, Peter told her that despite the eye operations and his new clarity of vision, he still occasionally suffered "pretty bad" headaches from bright light. "This place isn't a stellar tourist site – the mountains are distant and across the highway from us is some light industry and manufacturing, but even so, when a fresh snow falls and the sun shines, it looks phenomenally beautiful. Just too bright. My lawyer, bless his little cotton socks, took it upon himself to get me special permission to wear sunglasses, so now, when I get done with solitary, I can stand around the prison yard looking as cool and tough as all the guards. Man, I'll be the envy of the other prisoners, having something so personal!" Zosia smiled at the image and the light tone and read on as he wrote about the passage of time and remembered to wish Irena "happy (belated??) birthday" well in advance of the date. "I've enclosed a little present for her. I hope it isn't late, but I don't imagine this got to you all that fast since it has to go to Alex first. Maybe we'll work a better system soon. I'm sorry the present's so little but I didn't figure much else would make it through..." Zosia pulled out the enclosed page and studied it.

Tadek looked on curiously from the kitchen. "What's that?"

"It's his birthday gift for Irena. He drew some pictures for her to color and wrote a silly poem. Look, he even wrote down the chords so I could sing it to her!" Zosia laughed at the thought that she would be able to sing a song based on so little information. "He says he didn't think anything more substantial would make it through." She resumed reading. Peter described his daily life, sketching the personalities of some of the "characters" he had met, and giving the details of his routine and the results of further medical work. It was a long letter, and Zosia read page after page without looking up, without noticing Tadek placing the cup of tea next to her and sitting down beside her. She barely realized that he had put his arm around her and rested his head against her shoulder, tenderly stroking Madzia's brow with his free hand. He remained silently holding her, warming her with his presence, as she reluctantly read the last lines of Peter's letter.

529

Zosia sighed and set the letter down on the table next to her. "He sends you his greetings."

Tadek felt so sorry for her, he offered the only thing he could think of. "I got a letter as well. Do you want me to fetch it so we can read it?"

Zosia shook her head. "Let's save it for tomorrow. It will be awhile before the next ones make it here."

"I'm sorry, Zosia."

Zosia looked at him, surprised. Tears glinted at the corners of her eyes. "For what?"

"That he's the one who had to go. I wish I could have taken his place."

She smiled sadly at his words. "He said something like that to me once."

"What do you mean?"

"Peter once told me he was sorry that Adam had been killed instead of him. He said it would have given some meaning to his life if his death could have at least let me and Adam be together." The tears wouldn't stop and in desperation Zosia blinked wildly. "Oh Tadek, what's wrong with me? Why do the men I'm with make such offers?"

"Because it's what you want. And we'll do anything for you."

Tears streamed down Zosia's cheeks. "Why can I never be happy with what I have, when I have it?"

"You were happy with Adam, weren't you?"

She sniffed noisily. "Only when I was sure he loved me – and that wasn't as often as I would have liked. I loved him so desperately."

"Maybe that's the secret." Tadek assumed a conversational tone, hoping to calm Zosia down. "You need to feel in danger of being rejected in order for a man to be worthy of your attention. Maybe, that's what I should do."

"What?" Zosia stroked Madzia's hair and her hand met Tadek's.

"Go see my wife. Before he left, Peter tracked down her location for me and gave me the address."

"He told me he had done that, but I forget: where is she now?"

Tadek looked at the bookshelf as if reading the location there. "Belgium, at least as of last June. It seems her man keeps being transferred, though it's not clear if that's a sign of progression or decline."

Zosia's fingers twined into Tadek's. "Maybe his relationship with her hurts his career."

"Maybe. Maybe it's a sign of how deeply he loves her that he keeps her with him anyway."

"But if he's truly in love, he could research her background and find out she has appropriate bloodlines somewhere in the past, and get her status changed so that he could marry her."

"Only if that's what she wants as well, don't you think?"

Zosia twisted her fingers so they wrapped around Tadek's now. She squeezed his hand gently. "Oh Tadek, don't give yourself false hopes. She's not waiting for you."

"Then I should ask her that and end this thing once and for all."

Her hand crept up his arm. "And what would you do if she *does* want to go with you? Do you think you'd get permission to bring her back here?"

He shook his head. "No way. There's no way she could be vetted now." Madzia stirred and both of them reacted. Zosia whispered soothing words as Tadek wiped Madzia's feverish brow.

"So what would you do?" Zosia whispered once Madzia had calmed.

He shrugged. "We'd go somewhere. I have friends, connections...I'd find a way to get her and me out of the country."

Zosia's hand had reached Tadek's shoulder, and she massaged it. "Do you really want to talk to her?"

He nodded as he wiped the last of the tears from Zosia's eyes. "Yes, I really want to find out if she's waiting for me."

"Do you think you'll get permission to go to Belgium?"

Tadek laughed quietly. "Good one, Zosia." He leaned in to kiss her.

Zosia's hand moved behind his neck and she pulled him in to prolong the kiss. When their lips parted, she asked, "So what are you going to do?"

Tadek pulled back enough to look at her. "Like always, I'll take a ticket and wait in line."

11

*T*here was a freshly fallen snow and it looked quite nice except for all the mud and slush that had been thrown up by the vehicles. Peter stared out through the barred window of the bus at the mountains, but it was still too dark to see beyond the floodlit parking area. The last group of prisoners boarded, their restraints making that unmistakable clanking noise. Peter shuddered and looked down at his own chain, threaded around his ankles. He only had to wear it about half an hour – from the time he left the secured area of the prison until he was safely ensconced at his unit in the furniture factory. It was light and almost unobtrusive – just there to fulfill the security requirements for transporting convicts along open roads. Yet it was enough to jar extremely unpleasant memories, and he was seriously considering giving up the work just to avoid wearing them.

He laughed to himself. The others would have said he was crazy to even think of quitting. It was a good job, relatively well-paid and generally awarded only to prisoners who had a long record of good behavior. Peter clearly did not and had needed a special clearance from the prison officials to allow him to do the work. Someone had obviously had some sympathy for his cause and had done him an enormous favor, and here he was ready to throw it all away.

He was still debating the merits of quitting as the last of the prisoners were seated and locked into place. A very young man was placed in the seat next to him, but Peter didn't even turn his head to say hello. He loathed his companions, all of them. He knew he shouldn't. Though many were simpletons and others were too easily excited into violent action, the majority seemed fairly normal. He didn't want normal though, he didn't want his life to be whiled away in mindless work and tedious conversation. He just wanted to be left alone.

"You're that guy, the one whose trial was on television, aren't you? You're on my wing, I've seen you in the mess."

Peter grunted to let the boy know he wasn't interested in chatting.

"I need your help."

Peter turned his head to look at the lad. The youth was overweight and carried it badly – like some overgrown cherub. "Go away," Peter snarled quietly, before turning his attention back to the window.

"I heard you're queer, they said that at the trial. I'll be your boyfriend, if you want. If you protect me, I'll do what you want."

Early on, Peter had been obliged to turn down some rather forceful passes, and he had made it a point to be extremely threatening in his response. Since the first months, word had gotten around that whatever had been said at the trial, it was not a good idea to approach him, so he was exceedingly annoyed by the young man's suggestion and the implication that he would again have to go through a process of educating his fellow inmates. He turned his head deliberately to look menacingly at the fat young man, then speaking in a low but clear voice, said, "If you ever say anything like that again, I will kill you. Do you understand?"

His eyes wide with fear, the young man nodded. But it was not enough to stop him. "Please help me. They won't leave me alone. I need someone to protect me. I'm not in any of the gangs, I don't have anyone."

"Go to the authorities."

"You know I can't do that. Maybe you could, you have a special arrangement with them, don't you?"

"No, I don't," Peter grated. "It's your problem, handle it yourself."

"I *can't!* You can do it! You've got authority. You knifed one of them. The other guys respect you, they're afraid of you, they'll listen to you!"

If there was any truth in his words, Peter was unaware of it. He had done everything he could to stay out of the politics of the prison and remain as isolated as possible given his situation. Indeed he had only been released from solitary two weeks earlier. He shook his head.

"You've got to help me! Please!"

The young man had the same desperate look of that boy who long ago had confessed what had happened to him at the *Kommandant's* hands in the prison camp. Peter had helped then, without any power or official authority, he had gone to the *Kommandant* and demanded an end to it all. Everything that followed stemmed from that moment of insanity: the forced sodomy leaving him no option but a risky escape, the recapture and terrifying journey back into the Reich, the weeks of brutal interrogation, the kangaroo court and the sentence of death. Only to find out it was not over...If he had not helped, Joanna would still be alive. If he had not helped, Jana would not have been killed. "I said no." Peter turned his attention back to the window.

"Please!"

He felt the young man's hand on his shoulder and before he could stop himself he had swung his arm from the elbow, landing his fist in the lad's face. "Keep your fucking hands off me!"

The guard at the front stood to see what the commotion was, but Peter was already staring disinterestedly out the window and the boy did not make a move to report the assault. The guard reseated himself and they finished the rest of their journey in silence.

Peter stared out the window at the outlines of the mountains as they became visible in the faint dawn light. As he watched the beautiful ghostly forms emerge behind the bars of the bus window, he wondered, once again, if there was some way he could be released earlier, pardoned perhaps. The problem was that nobody knew what the mechanism would be. The Swiss had accepted responsibility for seeing that the sentence was carried out, and with only a few special instructions, he was governed by their laws within the prison system, but that was the extent of their involvement. The Americans had forgotten about him as soon as the cameras were packed up, and the Reich had stripped him of any official status whatsoever. He was stateless and therefore, once the international tribunal had closed its proceedings, he had been left in a political limbo. So *who* could pardon him? The Führer? An international tribunal convened just to review his case? Nobody would bother with that! Both Gerhard and Arieka had indicated that they would make inquiries among the notables that they knew, but Peter did not hold out much hope for their success. His case had been dealt with and the powers-that-be had turned their attention to much more important things.

He supposed there was escape. The Home Army would have found it fairly trivial to remove him – the security at the prison was not that tight – but he knew they wouldn't do that. Any hint of support for his actions from them would be disastrous and he knew even Zosia, even in her most unruly mood, would not consider violating the hands-off policy. He might be able to organize something on his own, or with the help of other friends, but it was unlikely that Szaflary would allow him entry and so there would be little point in being free. Maybe Zosia would take the children and go somewhere with him into exile. A ray of sunlight broke through and momentarily blinded him. He winced at the unexpected brightness and with it blinked away the insane daydream that Zosia would give up everything: cause, family, home – just to hide with him in bitter poverty in some distant and utterly alien land.

He had to face facts, he was stuck, at least for the foreseeable future, and he'd have to deal with life as it was, not as he would have it be. It was time to pick up his cards and play the game, and even as he made that decision, an idea began to coalesce.

Three weeks later, he was sitting in the outer office of the prison governor. He had been here a number of times before on account of his special status but also because of various incidents, one of which had been the knifing that had happened several months prior. Each time, Peter had taken pains to be friendly to the secretary, but she was wary and had been slow to respond. He was making progress though, this time his warm greeting and broad grin had been rewarded with a timid smile and a muted invitation for him to sit down and make himself comfortable. At least, that's what he thought she said, as her dialect was nearly incomprehensible to him.

When he finally entered the governor's office, the director politely stood and extended his hand. As was his habit, he spoke English and used the title that Peter's lawyer had insisted upon throughout the trial. "Dr. Halifax, always a pleasure."

"I appreciate your seeing me, sir." Though Peter found the habit of using a title with his name rather odd, he also recognized that it carried some advantages, so he never debated its merits. Likewise, he had learned that military-style politeness went a long way towards easing negotiations and he was careful to deal with the prison officials accordingly, using their titles frequently and generously inserting the English *sir* into his speech even when speaking German.

They shook hands and the director sat back down, indicating a chair to Peter as he did so. "You know, an important man like me can't afford to give this sort of time to every prisoner here."

Peter recognized the self-deprecatory humor, but he also knew that despite the director's egalitarian demeanor, he was an extremely hierarchical creature and so Peter tempered his response accordingly. *"Herr Direktor*, I will be sure to pass on your wisdom to my fellow prisoners and thus the few minutes of time spent with me will be magnified a hundredfold."

The director laughed approvingly. "As if they'd understand! I guess, though, I must admit I enjoy our occasional interviews. It's a pleasure to speak with someone who is educated."

He had switched into French for that last part and Peter took his cue and answered in English, "But not as educated as you. I'm afraid I can understand only a bit of French."

"Ah yes, I had forgotten. Shall we use English or German, then?"

"German, please. You know I'm not as linguistically talented as you, sir, and I'm not sure my English vocabulary extends to all the technical words I wish to use." That last part was a complete lie, but Peter found it wiser than saying that even the director's Swiss-accented German was easier to understand than his unique version of English.

"Good, German it is. So, what can I do for you?"

"It's what I can do for you, sir." Peter gestured at the terminal that sat on a side table in the office. "I've noticed that your computer system here is rather outdated. I also know you've applied for a systems upgrade but have been denied the monies."

The director suppressed a look of surprise. "I didn't realize you read the political budgets for this region."

"What I'd like to do, sir, is offer you my services. I will update your systems and design in compatibility with the other government systems so that you can communicate data without so many corruptions entering your files and records."

The director leaned back in his seat, crossing his arms. "How do you know about our system problems?"

"I hacked into your records using the computer in the library."

The director's eyes widened. "What?"

"Herr Direktor, what would you like to know? Your salary? Your boss's salary? Do you want to read the private communications between various government offices? Sensitive budgetary records?"

"You did this with the computer in the library?"

Peter nodded. The computer in the library was not actually available to prisoners and stood behind a locked door, but the director was either unaware of this fact or did not wish to dwell upon the point. Nor did Peter, and he quickly added, "As part of the redesign, I can separate the network used by the library from that used by your office and if you wish, construct a better security system for your office records and communications."

535

"Where did you get such expertise?"

Peter smiled, "It was part of my training in the English Underground. That's why I was awarded the doctorate in Manhattan." That wasn't entirely true, he had been given the honorary doctorate while visiting Manhattan for his resistance work in cryptanalysis, but it was close enough – everything he knew about systems design had stemmed from the same work.

"But that was a long time ago, wasn't it?"

"Yes, but I've had an opportunity to keep up to date on things."

Peter was spared having to use the elaborate story he had constructed since the director did not ask how he had managed to keep up to date. The director chewed his lip thoughtfully. "You know my salary?"

"And your wife's birth date. Don't forget to buy her a present before next Thursday, sir."

The director looked balefully at the terminal sitting innocently on its little desk. When he turned his attention back to Peter, it was clear he had decided to take the bait. "Alright, Halifax, I'll bite. But tell me, even if you were to offer all this expensive expertise for free, what about the equipment? Won't that cost a bundle?"

"Not really, sir. What you have isn't so bad."

"But–"

"I know, the bids you got included both redesign and expensive new hardware. But that was from salesmen – and why would they offer one product when they could sell you two? The hardware you have will be adequate, with the purchase of just a few extras. Here." Peter pulled a piece of paper out of his pocket, unfolded it and put it on the desk in front of the director. "I've written up a list and taken the liberty to price the items."

The director picked up the sheet of paper and scanned it. "Not too bad. We could probably find this sort of money." He stroked his chin. "And what do *you* need?"

"I'll need complete access to the system for the duration of the redesign. I would guess that will take about six months, depending on how tangled things are. I'd also like to be paid for my work – the usual prison rate for labor."

"The usual rates? Fifty marks a day? That won't even buy you a pack of cigarettes!"

Peter rolled his hands outward to show his empty palms in a gesture of powerlessness. "I'm not really in a position to ask for more. And that way it can be entered as working in the library – cleaning or filing or whatever."

"Why not put down exactly what you're doing?"

Peter shrugged. "If you want, but I wouldn't. I think you'd run into trouble with giving a prisoner that sort of file access."

"But you already have that sort of access, don't you?"

"Yes, but do you want to explain that?"

The director nodded his head in recognition of the problem. "Alright. Library work." He waited expectantly, but as Peter said nothing more, he asked, "So how do you really want to be paid?"

"I'd like a private cell. Solitary confinement without the daytime restrictions."

"Protective overnight confinement," the director amended. "I can arrange that, it's not so unusual for foreigners or infamous prisoners. In fact, we've recently released a gentleman from the south. You can have his cell. It's been nicely outfitted."

"Thank you, sir. I also have a list of books I would like the library to acquire." Peter pulled out another sheet of paper and unfolded that. "They're not that expensive."

The director glanced at the list and nodded. "That won't be a problem. What else?"

"One of the computers on that list that I gave you – I'd like it to remain in the library. Once I'm done redesigning your system, I'd like to continue my 'library work' and have use of that computer."

The director looked suspicious. "What would you be doing?"

Peter smiled enigmatically. "Studying."

The director pulled his head back signaling that he was dubious. Peter recognized that he had overstepped the limits of familiarity and so he hurriedly explained, "*Herr Direktor*, it will be years before I'm released. By then, I'm hoping that many things have changed – and I'm looking toward how I can contribute to society–"

"Which society?"

"The Reich, sir. I'm planning to study economics and constitutional law. I'm hoping that maybe I can learn enough to offer my help to the government that is in power when I am released."

"Big plans, Halifax."

"I have nothing but time, sir. There are some universities in America that offer courses via computer–"

"Yes, I've heard about those."

The director sounded vaguely annoyed that such things were being explained to him, so Peter skipped the details. "I'm hoping that I can link up with one of their networks and work with someone there to study their constitution and their government."

"And that's all you want? To study? How long would you want to keep up this studying?"

"*Herr Direktor*, I'll leave it to your discretion. When you feel I've received sufficient compensation, you can reassign me."

The director raised his eyebrows in surprise. "You would trust me to make that decision?"

I have no choice, Peter thought as he glanced down at his prison uniform. He would have no mechanism for enforcing any agreement and so rather than demand something which could be arbitrarily reneged upon, he had chosen to use flattery. "I trust your judgment, sir. You are an honorable man, and one who recognizes the value of knowledge. You will understand the worth of what I've done and I know you will not deny me adequate recompense for my efforts."

The director breathed deeply, turning his attention to the window as he mulled over all that had been offered. He stroked his chin with his thumb and forefinger then turned back to Peter and smiled. "I think we can arrange something of mutual benefit, Dr. Halifax."

"Thank you, sir."

"Is there anything else?"

"Yes, sir. A favor."

"Oh?"

"There's a young man on my wing. I don't know his name, but I've written down his number." Peter handed the director a slip of paper. "He seems to be having some difficulty with the men around him. If you could see your way to having him moved to a safer location – quietly, so that no one thinks he's complained..."

"If he can't bring the complaint to me himself..." The director shook his head.

"He's afraid, sir. If word got out–"

"Then he'll have to deal with it himself. As they say, if you can't do the time, don't do the crime."

Peter knew he was destroying all his hard work, but he decided to press the issue. "Sir, forced sodomy is torture. No conviction in this country calls for torture as the punishment, does it?"

"What happens among the prisoners–"

"Is supposed to be controlled by the prison officials. The boy was not sentenced to torture and it is your duty to do whatever is in your power to see that he is not."

The prison director stared at Peter. It reminded Peter of that dangerous moment when he had confronted the *Kommandant*, and Peter shuddered in response. He lowered his head into his hands. God damn it! What was his problem! He had destroyed everything for the sake of some stupid fat boy he didn't even know! "I'm sorry, sir," he said with his head still bowed. "That was totally out of line. Please forget I mentioned it."

"No, Halifax, you're right. Sometimes the rhetoric that surrounds my profession blinds us to our duty and to the basic human rights all of us have, even those who have been convicted of violating society's laws. I'll see that he's moved to somewhere safer. And I'll get back to you about this work we've arranged. Report for duty in the library starting tomorrow morning. Tell the secretary on your way out about the reassignment."

"Thank you, sir." Peter rose.

He was surprised that the director rose as well. The director came around the desk to shake his hand and walk him to the door. They stopped at the door and the director pursed his lips as if weighing something up in his mind. Finally he asked, "You read my personnel file, didn't you?"

"Yes, sir. I am sorry, sir. I apologize for the intrusion into your privacy. I only wished to make a point about—"

The director waved him into silence. "Were you able to access *all* of it?"

"You mean, for example, your superiors' reviews of your work?"

The director nodded.

"Yes, sir. All that is available. And various inter-office communications as well," Peter added, hinting that he would be able to tell the director exactly who had been hindering his career progression.

"You know, before you fix everything, do you think you could find out some information for me?"

Peter nodded. "Of course, sir. It will be my pleasure."

"Good, very good." The director clapped him jovially on the back, keeping his hand there in a paternal gesture. "You know, Halifax, you have an incredible background. Lots of knowledge, lots of experiences."

"Some would say so, sir."

"And now you're here. For what is essentially the rest of your life."

Peter raised an eyebrow, waiting for the question to be made explicit.

"You've thrown away everything. Everything for someone or something you won't – or can't – name. Was it really worth it?"

It was the sort of question that could kill his chances for parole a dozen years down the line. "Off the record?"

The director nodded solemnly. "Off the record. Any remorse?"

Peter shook his head. "No. I had my reasons."

The director looked surprised, as though he had thought his words would open Peter's eyes. Incredulous, he asked again, "No regrets?"

"No regrets," Peter reiterated quietly, but firmly.

He left the office, stopped by the secretary to tell her of his work and cell reassignments, and then went into the hall to pick up his guard. They passed in silence through the various security checkpoints and back into the prison proper. Only when he was returned to his unit and had a few seconds alone did Peter allow himself a small smile of triumph.

12

"*T*hose bastards set me up!" Günter Schindler growled as he paced angrily back and forth in his office. He stopped at the window, looking out at the wrought iron fence and beyond that the park grounds. Just across the park, occupying a huge corner of it, was Gestapo Headquarters for England and next to it, hidden behind a wall, the execution grounds. "They wanted me to get rid of that."

"Huh?" Wolf-Dietrich came to the window to see what his father was talking about. The bastards had set him up and wanted him to get rid of what?

Günter pointed toward the execution grounds. "We're supposed to start executing criminals indoors – to make it quieter. Sort of misses the point of making an example of them, I say."

"Yes, but since the executions aren't public in any case, maybe they should move indoors."

Günter shook his head. "I like the public to hear the shots. Sometimes I have the boys fire off a few rounds for no reason at all – just to keep the locals wondering." He laughed. "Nothing like the sound of gunfire now and then to keep these cretins mindful of who's boss here."

Wolf-Dietrich nodded absently, wondering if his father had called him to the office just to gossip about the execution grounds. Ever since they had been forced to move to London last autumn, his father had been acting stranger and stranger. He had managed, with his arbitrary arrests and fanatical enforcement of the laws to alienate nearly everyone in the city and things had only gotten worse since someone had taken a shot at his motorcade several weeks back, during the Winterfest. No one had been injured – at least if one didn't count what had happened to all the detainees who had been taken into custody afterwards, but the incident had fueled Günter's anger with paranoia, and now he spent most of his time sulking in his office, endlessly plotting. Wolf-Dietrich wondered if Greta's absence was a factor in his father's deteriorating mental state. Wolf-Dietrich had never liked the woman, but there was no doubt that she had known how to handle her husband. Maybe Ulrike could step in as the calming influence. Wolf-Dietrich smiled fondly at the thought of his young wife. She had loyally accompanied him into exile and now did her best to make London home to them all. He should have a word with her about perhaps offering soothing advice to her father-in-law. Somebody had to.

"Father, Ulrike was wondering if you would consent to eat dinner with us some evening."

Günter gave his son an incredulous look. "We have important business to conduct and you're asking me about dinner?"

"Sorry."

"Listen, I have a plan."

"About the execution grounds?"

Günter threw his hands into the air. "Forget the execution grounds! I mean about those bastards in Berlin!"

Wolf-Dietrich nodded and waited patiently. It was his father's favorite subject and his harangues about the Führer, Traugutt, Frauenfeld, Greta, and Stefi often lasted hours. Worst of all was when he fixated on Halifax. He would begin by wondering if Frau Vogel had told the truth in her testimony – this was especially painful when the conversation took place in front of Ulrike – and then he would move on to how Halifax's lies to Frau Vogel that night had destroyed his career and how he would one day take revenge upon that insolent *Untermensch*.

After one evening when Günter had carried on in this manner in front of Ulrike, she had later that night confided to Wolf-Dietrich what had happened five years before when Peter had been caught by her father speaking to her about history. "It was my fault," she had explained, "I kept badgering him. I even went into the attic late one night to talk with him and then got mad at him when he begged me to leave. I had no idea what my father was capable of." She had looked off into space at those words and then shook her head vehemently. "No, that's a lie. I knew, I just pretended not to know. I've always done that."

She had continued, sobbing, "My father made me come down to the cellar to see him mete out a punishment. I just sat there, on the steps, watching. It was so horrible! I finally just ran back up the stairs and left Peter alone…Then afterwards, I avoided him. My father kept going at him, using any excuse to hit him or hurt him, and I ignored it all, trying to pretend it wasn't happening! I wanted to believe it was his fault."

She had lowered her head onto Wolf-Dietrich's chest and he felt tears on his bare skin. He had comforted her the only way he knew how, saying, "Lots of people do that honey. If they don't like the way things are, they pretend it isn't like that or blame the victim." And then attack those who speak the truth, he had added mentally, thinking of himself rather than Ulrike. "You were just a child then, it wasn't your fault." He did not mention the tearful videotape that she had made later, when she was no longer a child, where she had denounced Peter and defended her father's actions. Wolf-Dietrich knew it would be unfair to blame that on her – Ulrike had made that tape out of love for him, not knowing he had already sold her services to his father. God, how despicable he was, using a girl's love to destroy a man just to curry his father's favor!

"Are you listening to me, boy?"

"Of course, Father." Wolf-Dietrich let his father's last few words run through his mind. "You're right, the Führer's treatment of you was appalling, especially after what you went through to save his life after he was kidnapped."

"Let's go for a walk."

Wolf-Dietrich drew himself up and glanced around the room. Good Lord! His father had long ago abandoned normal caution – perhaps with good reason, given his power base and well-trained security force – so this sudden burst of secrecy must be rooted in something truly frightening. Wolf-Dietrich shuddered. "Father, it's February. A walk in London in February – at your age – I don't think that's very healthy."

"Coward. Put on your coat!"

They tromped straight across the muddy grounds surrounding Green Park prison and then into Hyde Park. Wolf-Dietrich only half-listened to his father, too busy wondering how it could feel colder in London than Berlin. Must be the damp, he thought, it creeps into the bones, making even relatively mild temperatures and slight breezes feel more bitter than the iciest cold. God, how he hated this place! He stepped onto some grass and his boots sunk several inches into miserably cold water. He swore quietly. The boots were leather, but not particularly waterproof, and now he would have to spend the next several hours not only listening to his father rant, but with damp, freezing cold feet as well!

Günter, who had somehow managed to stay on firm ground, stopped to look at his son and laughed. "You can't even keep your feet dry and here I am, trusting you with this mission."

Wolf-Dietrich froze with fear. What mission? My God, what had his father been saying? "Father, the wind took your words. Could you repeat that last bit?"

Günter snorted. "Let's go over to the bandstand so your feet can dry. I'll explain it all to you there."

At the bandstand, Wolf-Dietrich stomped his feet a bit, trying to get the water off his boots and some warmth into his toes, but it was hopeless – he could feel how damp his socks were and knew his feet would not be warm again until they were inside, in front of the fire that Ulrike would have the servant make for him.

"Stop that stamping, you idiot. The wood's rotten! Do you want the damn thing to come down on us?"

"Sorry." Wolf-Dietrich forced himself to remain still. "So what is your plan?"

"Have you heard of the English Republican Army?"

Wolf-Dietrich nodded emphatically, pleased that the conversation was on a firm footing. "They're a minority member of the overall English so-called Freedom Movement which makes up the bulk of the political underground here. They support a democratic England without a monarchy and have representation in the Toronto-based British government-in-exile and a small number in Manhattan, attached to the delegation at England House. About two years ago, the more activist portion of the group, calling for an immediate uprising, split off to form their own, independent movement, called the *Real* ERA. For several months after that, they indulged in civilian bombings in and around London as they tried to stir up some response. Our suppression of the group must have been successful because they ceased their activities sometime during that summer." Wolf-Dietrich had heard rumors that it had not been their efforts, but a cease and desist order from Halifax, whose name they had used, which had caused the abrupt termination of their activities, but he knew better than to tell his father that. Any hint that Halifax had ever been in London would only provoke a violent denial from his father. He continued carefully, "They've been quiescent for a while, though every now and then, there is an indication that they are still around."

"Yes, yes." Günter sounded genuinely pleased. "They are still around, and constantly plotting. A while ago, after that incident with my motorcade, we arrested a man named Fowler, who, it turned out, is second-in-command of that splinter group and directly responsible for some of the bombings – in particular that messy one around Pikadilly Platz."

"Oh, I remember that. That was nasty." Wolf-Dietrich shook his head in disgust at the memory. Body parts everywhere interspersed with shopping bags and ladies' shoes. "Has he been executed?"

"No, I've had him released on lack of evidence."

Wolf-Dietrich tilted his head at his father. "Lack of evidence?"

"I had a little discussion with him – after he had been interrogated for a bit. He agreed to work for me, or rather, as I explained it to him, with me."

"With you?"

"Yes, we're in a collaboration. I'll provide the materials, papers, and transport passes, and he'll supply the labor."

"To do what?"

Günter smiled broadly at his son. "I'm going to blow them up!"

Wolf-Dietrich drew in his breath very slowly. "Who?"

Günter laughed. "Rudi and his entire crew! A nice big bomb placed in the *Residenz* during the Solstice party and boom! Ha, ha, ha! They won't know what hit them!"

Wolf-Dietrich turned away from his father to survey the grounds. Was his father serious? Or was it just a fantasy, played out to relieve his irritation? Or was it all an elaborate joke? "Father," Wolf-Dietrich intoned softly, still looking away from him, "if you're serious, you know there would be horrendous casualties. There would be numerous officials and their wives there. The *Residenz* staff. Completely innocent people – Germans, good Germans, all of them – would be killed."

"Eh, never hurts to blood the *Volk* now and then. They've gotten soft. You see, once they feel the pain of genuine resistance, once the fat and overconfident Berliners understand what the noble German colonists must put up with each and every day, then they will be prepared to take action! The ensuing chaos will require a leader with strength and vision, and once I'm anointed, there will be such a surge of patriotism that you have never seen. No sacrifice will be too great! We'll be able to purge this land of all the resistances and terrorists and criminal vermin! We'll find a connection to those traitorous bastards in the NAU and then we'll have carte-blanche to attack them even as they cower in exile! We'll have control! Total control!"

Wolf-Dietrich cleared his throat. He really didn't know what to say. Eventually, he managed to rasp, "But how?"

"Ah, that's the beauty of it. The Real ERA will do all the dirty work. And of course, afterwards, I'm going to wipe them out. There won't be a single witness left. I know the names and addresses of each and every member of the organization."

"But how are they going to do it?"

"Like I said. Fowler will convince his people of the wisdom of targeting the *Residenz* – and from what I can gather, that won't be hard, they've been chomping at the bit. He'll be the only one who knows that we're providing them with help. He's a good man, it's a shame we'll have to kill him." Günter laughed. "But before that, we'll see that he or his representative gets the necessary materials and separately we'll pass on the instructions for how to build the bomb, and I'll make sure that it has an easy crossing – the customs boys are used to receiving instructions about not inspecting certain trucks…"

As Günter carried on, Wolf-Dietrich found himself moaning quietly *Oh God, oh God*, under his breath until he heard the words, "…and that's where you come in."

"What am I supposed to do?"

"As I said, the rest of the Real ERA are unaware of our involvement, so we'll have to cover our tracks. The materials are coming out of Southampton, but the plans will originate here, in London, from the Institute. All you have to do is find some sucker who works in the Institute who will be a reasonable go-between. He has to have some sort of believable reason to sell secrets to the Underground. Go through the personnel files and see if you can find someone for the job. Someone with an English background, or heavily in debt, or with a grudge, or whatever. Just make sure it's not a secretary. I don't trust women."

Wolf-Dietrich nodded. Rid the Reich of their mad Führer. He had to admit, there was a great deal of appeal in the idea. The lecherous snake should never have been elected to such a high office! And his father was right, the top brass had gotten complacent and arrogant. They needed shaking up. It'd just level the banquet hall and maybe a room or two of the *Residenz*. Only high-level officials and a few others would get killed. Possibly Stefi. Well, he could make sure she and her family did not attend. Ulrike's family too. And once his father finally had power, then he would calm down. The Reich could be governed correctly, not erratically. Rather than a bloody civil war that could last years, they could overthrow Rudi's demented regime with one well-aimed blow. The civilians killed would be small in number compared to outright war. They could win so easily. He, Wolf-Dietrich Schindler, would be a central figure, the power-broker, the brains behind the throne. Hell, if he played his cards right, he could end up running the show!

A bomb in the *Residenz*, hundreds of loyal Germans dead. Loyal Party members! Oh God! Oh God, what should he do?

13

*Z*osia stumbled into the flat and threw herself onto the sofa, oblivious to all of them. She wearily dropped her head back onto the cushion and closed her eyes. Tadek studied her from the kitchen as he handed Madzia a finished potato to put in the pot and accepted an unpeeled one from Irena. Krys hung onto Madzia's waist and waddled behind her, trying to walk. Tadek pushed the accumulated peels out of the way and picked up the knife, all the while waiting for Zosia to look up at him. *Cooking! God damn it, but that woman was good at getting people to do for her! And Halifax – the bastard had been clever, leaving me nicely ensconced in the apartment to take care of his wife and his children!* But Tadek was unable to maintain a mental diatribe for long. Before being called away, Zosia had read aloud another letter from Peter and despite his valiant attempts to report only cheerful news, it was obvious that the concrete walls and the guard towers and the razor wire were wearing him down.

Peter hadn't said a word about nightmares or flashbacks, about headaches or pain, but somehow Tadek knew all those things were still there. Claustrophobia as well. He remembered Peter's early years at the encampment and how he would so frequently leave the confines of the bunker, even sleeping outdoors, even in misting rain. Tadek had laughed at Peter then, using his restless need to walk freely as the butt of a number of ill-tempered jokes, but now Tadek thought about what he knew of Peter's past – the terrifying near suffocation in the crate, the months locked in abysmal cells, the chains that never came off, and he wondered how long his friend would be able to cope with imprisonment. Tadek paused, his knife poised over the potato. Peter as his friend? He snorted with amusement. He supposed it was true. Despite their best attempts to the contrary, despite Zosia...

And what about Zosia? She seemed so tired of late. Though she was officially beached at the moment, taking care of three children, she seemed to always be on call. Wanda constantly had her down in the cryptanalysis office sorting things out for Jurek. Zosia had no expertise in the field, but Peter had left some notes which she seemed better at interpreting than Jurek – not that that was saying much – and she was adept at computers. Still, it was clear that Wanda was being made painfully aware that with Barbara's and Olek's and finally Peter's departure, they had lost all their analysts. She should have taken Peter's offer to spend his last months of freedom training someone rather more seriously, but it was too late for that now. They were sending nonsense to Warszawa for decryption, important files piled up undeciphered in the office, pandemonium reigned.

Tadek was just debating whether he should delay cooking so that Zosia could nap when she suddenly said, "Tadek, do you remember what you said about visiting your wife? That you'd await an opportunity."

Tadek was amazed that Zosia had spoken. Her head was still thrown back, her eyes still closed. "Yes, I remember, what about it?"

"I might have one for you."

"Does this have anything to do with Wanda calling you out?" Tadek turned the potato Irena had given him and inspected it for rot.

"It was Marysia this time, and yes, it does." Zosia lifted her head and opened her eyes. "Do you remember, Peter recruited his brother Erich to do some snooping in that laboratory he works in?"

Tadek nodded. He dug the knife into the potato and sliced off a blackened bit. Remembering Peter's warning, he was careful to wash the knife and slice off a good bit of untainted potato just to be safe. *Damn that bastard – he knew I'd be doing everything!* At the time Tadek had wondered why Peter had insisted on telling him so many stupid things before he left.

"Erich uses a dead-drop, so all we know is the information that he passes on to us, but he has been surprisingly useful. Apparently he's getting to know various people inside the laboratory sections that are of interest to us and has gotten those people to talk to him."

"Yes, I know. I'm still on the Council, you know." Tadek cradled the maimed potato in his palm. Madzia was tugging at his sleeve, demanding it, Irena was offering the next victim. "At least, that's my hobby when I'm not chief cook and bottle-washer." Tadek glanced down at the children. They formed a human chain, Krys using Madzia as a walker, Madzia tugging at Tadek's sleeve, Irena holding onto his shirt on the other side. *I'm falling behind,* Tadek thought. "Hold on, comrades, I'm slow today!"

Zosia continued as if he hadn't spoken. "A few weeks ago, Erich left a note saying that he had very important information and that he had to speak to Peter personally. He apparently was unaware that Peter was out of the country and in prison."

Tadek removed the eyes from the potato. "Well, his extradition and trial weren't mentioned in the Reich press, so I guess that's not surprising."

"No, the Führer certainly wasn't going to highlight Peter's existence now – not with all the background that would have to be explained. Anyway, Barbara finally contacted him – Erich, I mean – and told him his brother was in prison. He still insisted that he had very important information and would only pass it on to Peter. She explained how impossible that would be and tried to get him to tell her. For some reason, though, he refused to trust her – I guess she had not been very friendly toward him the first time they met."

Tadek held the potato up to inspect it and laughed quietly as he remembered the account of Erich's first mission with Barbara, Mark and Peter. "She threatened to shoot him, didn't she?"

"Something like that. So, Erich's insistent he has important news but does not want to trust anyone other than Peter with it, but Peter's unavailable. Barbara asked if there was someone else he might trust and he said Peter's wife."

"He knew Peter was married?" Tadek set down the knife and picked up the peeler.

"I guess it was mentioned at some point." Zosia brushed some hair back from her face. "Obviously we could send any woman there – I don't think he's seen a picture – and she could claim to be Peter's wife, but I suspect

Erich will be clever enough to ask a lot of personal questions. And Peter might have told him something about me."

"But are we even sure he's worth talking to at all?" Madzia and Irena had started tossing a potato back and forth, Krys was on the floor picking up a stray peel and shoving it into his mouth.

"No, of course not. He has, however, been feeding us very high quality information and has never before insisted on anything like this. It may be truly important. Marysia's asked if I'd go and talk to him. I'll have a limited authority to make a deal with him, if that's what he wants."

Tadek set the potato down, bent down and extracted the peel from Krys's mouth. He picked Krys up and transported him to the pile of toys near Zosia. "Will you take the children?"

"No, since Krys has weaned himself there's no need. But I still need a husband along. Would you do it? We could travel overland. An overnight stop in Belgium wouldn't be so hard to arrange. You could see your wife. What was the town?"

"Löwen." Tadek handed the peeler to Zosia. "I've done my share."

Zosia inspected the device then handed it back. "Do you want to go?"

Tadek accepted the implement with a sigh and went back into the kitchen to pick up where he had left off. "Sure." He pointed at the two little girls hovering around him. "If the bosses are willing to give me the time off."

Four days later they stood in front of a church in the center of the town – Leuven, Louvain, Löwen – whatever it was called. Tadek looked admiringly across the way at the incredibly ornate town hall. "Wow, that's really something! Nice that it didn't all get bombed."

"Nothing here worth targeting. Not unless you count the university – but I guess they looted that separately. The library was moved en masse to Leipzig."

Tadek turned to his right and looked down the widened street at an endless row of ugly concrete buildings. "Ah, but I see the New Order Architects have given it their best shot. I'm surprised they didn't take out this fiddly medieval monstrosity." He twiddled his fingers derisively at the town hall in imitation of a typical bureaucrat. "A bit of concrete slapped over those statues and we'd have something truly worthy of the Third Reich!"

"They probably decided it was *gemütlich*. Anyway, it's not medieval, it's all fake."

"Which way?"

Zosia looked to her left, back at the train station and then at the map. She pointed straight ahead, along a narrow cobblestone alley. "Through there. Our hotel is over the pub."

They checked in, had a delicious pub meal and then returned to their room to plan. "Did you pick up any extra information on her?" Zosia asked, as she changed clothes.

"No, we're going to have to wing it." Tadek studied the map. "Let's walk over to where they're supposed to live and check the nameplate. My guess is the children go to school here." Tadek stabbed the map with his finger. "So, we can swing by the school and check out the hours. Maybe tomorrow we can get her coming or going from there. If not, we'll have to ring the bell."

"Do you want to do that tonight?"

Tadek checked his watch. "Too risky, her husband might be home already. Let's leave it until tomorrow."

"You're not getting cold feet are you?"

"No! I just don't want to take any stupid risks, okay?"

The address was still valid and the following morning, they sat at a nearby bus stop to observe the house. Two children emerged and headed off to school. A few minutes later the woman of the house emerged with two smaller children and took them toward the nursery school. Tadek and Zosia followed. After dropping the children off, the woman stopped at a café and Tadek and Zosia followed her in. They took up a table near her and ordered coffee.

Tadek chewed his thumbnail and observed the woman, trying to get a glimpse of her face.

"Is it her?" Zosia's back was to the woman and all she could see was Tadek worriedly looking over at the other table. "You know, if she hasn't changed her papers, it's illegal for her to be in here."

"I know that."

"Why don't you go talk to her? Just introduce yourself as the friend of a friend. Once you see her face, you'll know for sure."

Tadek heaved a sighed and stood. "Cover me," he muttered then walked over to the woman at the other table.

Zosia switched seats so that she could see what was going on. The woman looked up when Tadek spoke to her, and it was clear she recognized him because she half stood. He said something to calm her and she sat back down. Zosia saw how Tadek seated himself, pulling the chair out without taking his eyes off his wife. Their voices were low and she could not make out a word though it was clear they were speaking German. At one point the woman turned in her seat and glanced at Zosia. Before Zosia could smile or in any other way react, the woman had turned back to Tadek.

The waiter delivered a coffee and a small piece of cake to Tadek's wife and then brought two little pots of ersatz coffee over to their table. Zosia sent one over to Tadek. When the waiter placed it in front of Tadek he looked up at Zosia in panic. She smiled a reassurance. It was an innocent conversation in a café, no one was going to take notice.

Again Tadek's wife turned to look at Zosia and this time Zosia could see she was genuinely annoyed. Oh, so that was it. *She* didn't want him to get comfortable at her table! Tadek leaned forward to speak more intensely and his wife turned her attention back to him. They spoke for another five minutes or so, their voices never getting louder than a whisper, but Zosia could see that the conversation was growing heated. All at once Tadek stood. He gave a slight, formal bow and said good-bye. He came back to Zosia's table but did not sit down. "Let's go."

"We haven't paid."

Tadek walked over to the waiter, handed him a note and then returned to Zosia's table. "Okay, let's go. Now."

As they strolled away from the café, Zosia waited for Tadek to speak, but he didn't say anything. A light rain began to fall, but neither took notice. Eventually they came to a canal and turned to walk along the water's edge. Moss grew on the slimy bricks lining the canal, gnats swarmed around them. They stopped by a lone tree, its branches hacked off so that only the tall stump remained like an angry fist rising out of the bricks. The top was crowned by a spray of tender shoots with fine green leaves. Tadek reached up and tore off one of the thin new branches. He ran it through his fist, stripping the leaves, so that all that was left was a supple switch. "I think they used to grow them like this as building material. They could weave them into walls." He flicked the switch and hit the tree with it.

"What did she say, Tadek?"

"She's staying."

"Does she love him?"

"No, but she loves her children and they love their father."

"Oh, Tadek…"

"Let's go to London, Zosia. We have work to do." Tadek threw the switch into the canal and they watched to see if it would float away, but it remained motionless in the still, fetid water.

14

*T*he two of them walked quickly along the busy London street. Zosia turned to Tadek and smiled encouragingly. "Have you ever been here?"

Tadek shook his head. "Why would I have been?"

The city looked depressingly like so many other large cities in the Reich – ugly gray buildings lining both sides of the street, sudden open parade grounds completely paved over and devoid of anything other than a few flags, some areas of damaged housing that still had not been repaired or removed, ubiquitous flags and posters. Like most of the cities in the western Reich there were still some concessions to bilingualism, though whenever only one language appeared, it was always German. Zosia stopped to read one of the posters – it was issued by the London authority and had both languages on it. "I've heard that Schindler and the Führer argue about this all the time."

"What are you talking about?"

Zosia pointed at the poster. "The Führer wants the population to speak German. You know, one country, one language."

"And?" Tadek peered over Zosia's shoulder at the poster. It announced a change in curfew regulations.

"Well, Schindler wants to promote English as a language."

Tadek set down their luggage and wiggled his fingers to get the blood flowing through them. "I thought he hated the English."

"He does, and he doesn't want them to integrate and mess up the pure German bloodlines. He figures if they keep their language, that'll be one more way of keeping them separate – and to him that means in an underclass."

"He could just annihilate them. Like they're doing to us, out east."

Zosia sniffed. "I think if he had his way…"

Tadek looked at the people walking along the street. "Eh, no great loss, I'd say."

Zosia elbowed Tadek. "Hey, none of that. Remember, we're supposed to be the good guys. Love, peace, racial tolerance…"

"It was a joke." Tadek picked up the bags. "Come on, let's get going."

After they had checked into their hotel, they headed to the bookstore. Zosia was annoyed because she had wanted to ride the Tube but the line she had planned to use was shut for repairs which were scheduled to be finished nearly a year prior. So, she and Tadek took the bus across town and eventually, after having done an inadvertent tour of the northwest quadrant of the city, found the address. Barbara had been expecting them and when they walked into the bookstore, she gave them a broad smile. Then, remembering herself, she immediately donned a dour expression and continued her dealings with a customer. Once she had finished, she came over to them and handed Zosia the keys to the flat. She told them how to get in and advised them to make themselves comfortable while she finished work and closed the shop.

Zosia noticed a toddler playing in the back office, tearing up a notebook that looked like it might be important. "Where's Mark?"

Barbara smiled ruefully. "Out. Go on ahead, I'll close up early today, so I won't be long. Can you take the baby?" Without waiting for an answer, she rushed to the office, picked up the baby and brought it to Zosia.

"It's a boy?"

"Yes."

"What'd you name him? Peter?" Tadek asked sarcastically.

Barbara shook her head. "Mark would never have allowed that! We called him Edward. After Mark's father."

"Ah. Nice name." Zosia handed the child to Tadek. "We'll see you upstairs, Barbara."

It took longer than they expected, but eventually Barbara joined them. She looked exhausted but neither Zosia nor Tadek thought to offer her a cup of tea. Barbara sighed a greeting and went into the kitchen nook to put on the kettle. Even though she had never considered either of them a friend, she looked forward to conversing. She hadn't had a good conversation since Peter's visit nearly two years before. Then, she had opened her heart, telling him all about her life and her problems and her loneliness. Now, he was rotting in prison, and she felt, so was she. She could confide in no one here! Mark's friends were chummy enough, when he was around, but they were his friends, uncomfortable with either of her two languages, uncomfortable with the presence of a woman in their group. She knew no one. No one with whom she could speak German or Polish, no one who could know her secrets. And Mark was always busy, doing deals, out with his mates, sleeping off hangovers...

Barbara finished making her tea and came into the living area. She seated herself on the couch, next to Tadek. "Can I top up your tea? I made a fresh pot."

Zosia shook her head vigorously. "No, we've wasted enough time. When have you arranged our visit with Erich?"

Barbara's mouth opened as she tried to begin to answer, but she was so embarrassed to admit that nothing was arranged yet, that she could only stutter a noise before shutting it again.

"You *did* make arrangements?"

Barbara shook her head. "I'm sorry, Colonel. I didn't know you'd be in such a rush."

Zosia rolled her eyes, then looked petulantly at her watch. "Where will he be now?"

"Probably still at work."

"Take us there, we'll snag him on the way out."

When Barbara caught up with him and tapped his shoulder, Erich visibly jumped. *Subtle*, Barbara thought sarcastically. Erich stopped dead in his stride and gaped at her.

"I've brought Niklaus's wife. You can call her Sophie." Barbara gestured with her head toward a man and a woman standing near the bus stop. The man was holding a toddler who was crying and squirming, but neither of the two took any note of the child. "The man with her is an associate. He'll stay nearby to guard against trouble. I'll leave you alone with them." With that, Barbara walked over to the two, took the child from the man's arms and left.

As Erich looked at the two people, he suddenly wished that Barbara had stayed – despite his fear of her. She was a lot less threatening than Niklaus's wife and her associate! The man was tall and lean with dark hair and pale eyes that stared at him menacingly. The woman had wavy, dark blond hair, a very fine face with high cheekbones, and a curvaceous figure. Erich would have congratulated his brother on the beauty of his wife if only the woman didn't have such a dangerous look in her eyes.

Erich knew he should go over to them, but he found himself unable to move. The woman seemed to recognize this and she approached. Her steps were graceful but hinted at a deadly physical strength – like those of a cat, and Erich worried that if he somehow drew her suspicion, he might well not live to see the morning. Suddenly panicked, he wondered why he had embarked on this course. He should have done exactly as he had been told! Or handed the documents to Barbara! It had been curiosity – he had wanted to see his brother, and when he had discovered that was impossible, he had been determined to meet his brother's wife. But no one had told him about the risks!

"Hello. I'd like to introduce myself, my name is Sophie." The woman spoke softly, in English, and she extended her hand in a manner that was not at all fiendish. "May I call you Erich?"

"Yes, of course." Erich shook her hand. "Your English is very good."

"Niklaus has taught me a lot. But if you don't mind, I'd prefer German."

"Oh, that's fine!" Erich replied, relieved.

"Let's go somewhere where we can talk. Do you have any suggestions?"

Erich led them to a café where they found a table in a private corner. Once they had settled into their seats and ordered, Erich studied his companions, waiting for them to begin their interrogation.

"Well?" the woman prompted.

"Well what?"

"Do you have any questions?" She reached into her purse and pulled out a photograph. "I brought this – I thought it would help convince you I am indeed Niklaus's wife."

Erich took the photograph in his hands. It was a picture of his brother, his sister and himself, taken when he had been twelve, or maybe thirteen. No, it had to be twelve, since Anna was dead before his thirteenth birthday. He turned the picture over and looked at the date. She only had a few more months to live.

"I gather Niklaus gave you some of the photos he found, but he kept this one for himself. This is a copy, you can keep it, if you wish."

Erich nodded. He didn't know what to say. Do you have any questions, she had asked. Hundreds! Thousands! But she was only interested in proving who she was, not in a family reunion. "You...You have a daughter?"

Sophie smiled. "Yes, and now there is another child. A boy."

Their drinks arrived. As Erich sipped his wine, he slowly began to relax, and as he found his questions were not considered impertinent, he asked for more and more details. She told him no current names, no locations, but she did describe her husband in detail, told Erich of his habits and bits of his past that Erich would recognize. Erich enjoyed hearing it all and began to join in, adding details to stories and anecdotes of his own.

"Enough." It was the man who had spoken and it drew Erich back to the present. "She's proved who she is. Now tell us why we are here."

The woman cast an annoyed glance at her companion, but did not disagree. She looked expectantly at Erich.

"It all started about a month ago, at the beginning of March. I had noticed that there was a heightened tension in the Institute, so I was doing the rounds, talking to people, picking up gossip, trying to work out what was going on. I couldn't find out anything though and I returned to my workstation empty-handed. When I got there, I saw that a message had been left that I was to see the unit director. There wasn't anything too unusual in that, so I went over to his office without a thought. But all he did was send me up to the director's office. That worried me and I thought maybe I should just leave the building and make good my escape. Still, there were no security guards or anything, so I thought maybe I should just go and see what it was all about."

The woman nodded interestedly. The man snapped his fingers and indicated that their table needed another round of drinks. Erich continued, "There were a bunch of people in the director's office, waiting to see him, but when I reported to the secretary, she immediately sent me into a conference room. It wasn't the director's office and no one else was there. I waited about half an hour, and then Schindler, the younger, showed up. I jumped to my feet when he came in, and I was sure his first words were going to be 'you're under arrest', but all he did was wave me back into my seat. He was alone, and he had a file in his hands. He sat down next to me at the conference table and opened the file. I saw then that it was my personnel file."

The drinks arrived and Erich fell silent. Once the waiter had wandered off, the woman prompted, "And?"

"He said that he had noticed that I had a very good record and had been very loyal over many years. I didn't know what to say, so I kept quiet. Anyway, after going through my record, he went into my background, pointing out that I had English parents who had been arrested while I was quite young. Before I could say anything to that, he said that he knew that was not my fault and should not affect me, but it had probably held me back a bit and that he would do what he could to amend that. I mean, this was Schindler's son speaking! I had no idea why he would be interested in someone like me. He said though, that in return, he needed me to do him a favor."

Erich paused and the woman raised her eyebrows encouragingly.

"He wanted me to deliver a package. He asked if I had ever heard of the Real ERA and I said yes, they were responsible for some pretty gruesome bombings in London some time ago. He agreed and said that they particularly liked to target English Conciliators – people like me who were willing to work with the system and were rewarded accordingly. He said that they knew that the Real ERA was active again and was planning to use chemical weapons on commuters using the Tube. He said that the group had been trying to get all the necessary information for nerve agents and a dispersion mechanism and he was afraid that sooner or later they would succeed, that someone from abroad would sell them what they needed. Schindler's plan was to prevent this catastrophe by selling the agents information that had been neutralized."

The man frowned in confusion. "Neutralized?"

Erich looked at him, surprised that he had spoken. "Yes, he meant that it would be a believable production plan and would take up a considerable amount of their time, money and energies to produce, but the end product would be harmless. They would be flushed out into the open when they made the attempt and arrested, but no one would be hurt. He said though, that the only way they could convince the Realies that the plans were genuine was if they were sold to them by someone who could convince them he was on their side. He said that my background was perfect and that they'd trust me because I was ethnically English, and they'd believe I had a motive for betraying my country since my parents had been arrested when I was young."

The woman nodded. "So what did you do?"

"I agreed, of course. I didn't think I had much choice, but also, I didn't want those bastards killing innocent people on the Tube just to prove they were upset with the occupation. A week later Schindler gave me the plans in a large envelope. They were coded documents and when I asked, he said that they had to be coded in order to convince the Realies that they were truly stolen files and not to worry, that they'd be able to decode them. He gave me a meeting time and place and told me they would expect me. I was to give them the envelope and accept money in return but I was not, under any circumstance, to talk about their plans or how I had acquired the documents or what was in them. I could, if they asked, answer questions about my background, but that was all."

"And did you deliver the documents?"

"Yes. But before I did, I made a copy."

The woman sat up, interested. "Why?"

"I wasn't sure Schindler was telling the truth and I was worried about what I might be passing on. I didn't want to tell the English Underground about it though, because they might well have some infiltrators who would let Schindler know what I had done. Or somebody might pass the word on to the Realies that I was working for Schindler. Either way, I'd be in deep shit. That's why I wanted to talk to my brother. I knew he could decode them, and I also know that he's not in any way connected with Schindler or the Realies."

The woman smiled as if Erich had said something quite humorous. "Why didn't you just pass this on to Barbara when she contacted you?"

Erich looked down at his glass. "That guy she was with, when I met her. He was English. I figured he had connections to the English Underground, and I was afraid she'd tell him. I just wanted to talk to Niklaus. I figured he'd know what to do."

The woman nodded her understanding. "I'm sorry he couldn't be here. Will you give me the copies?"

"Yes, I can get them now, if you come with me."

15

Zosia paced back and forth angrily. The cryptanalysis office was tiny and crowded and she could take no more than two steps in either direction. She knew her movements were annoying the hell out of Jurek, but she was equally annoyed and had no interest in catering to his sensibilities.

Jurek hammered his fist onto the desk. "Would you stop that already!"

"Have you translated it yet?"

"No! I haven't a clue what to do!"

"How did I know you'd say that?" Zosia gave Jurek a shove. "Move over, let me look."

He stood. "Go ahead, if you're so damn smart."

"At least I don't claim to be able to do a job that I have no clue about." Zosia studied the screen for a moment and then began busily tapping at the keyboard. They had spent countless hours painstakingly entering all the code into the computer so that one of Peter's programs would decipher it, but nothing worked!

"If your stupid husband had left things in a better state, I wouldn't have all this trouble."

"My stupid husband – as you put it – isn't here because he's saving your worthless hides. And if you had bothered to listen to him before he left, you might know enough to actually do something here other than create chaos." Zosia stopped her tapping and looked at the screen. Utter nonsense. She deleted the entry and called another program. Jurek sat down, smugly patient. After an hour or so Zosia stopped and rubbed her temples. "I don't even know where to begin. Do you want to have another go, Jurek?"

The answer came softly out of the corner where he sat. "No, I don't know what to do. I'm like the proverbial monkey trying to bang out Hamlet."

Zosia was surprised by Jurek's tone. It reminded her of the man she once knew – Wanda's reticent husband who never had an unkind word to say about anyone. The man who had joked with her and Adam all those years ago at a border camp, the evening before Wanda's sons were killed. She looked up at him. "You miss him, don't you."

Jurek nodded. "He did good work. Quietly too. He kept trying to teach me, but I'm too old to learn. I was so embarrassed that I asked him not to tell anyone. So he just did most of the work and let everyone think I knew what I was doing." Jurek smiled wistfully. "That's why Wanda dismissed his idea of training someone else before he left."

"So why were you always so brusque with him?"

Jurek sighed heavily. "I was ashamed. And Wanda…"

"What is it with her? I mean, ever since Maciej and Marek, she's been a bit off, but it's just gotten worse and worse and she seemed to focus so much of her anger on Peter. He had nothing to do with it!"

"Do you know what happened to the twins' father?"

"He was killed in action."

Jurek slowly shook his head. "That's what we tell you younger ones."

"Then what did happen?"

Jurek straightened as if preparing to tell a long story. "Wanda was rounded up when she was twenty-four and was put to work in a factory. About a year later, an officer came through the factory and had all the young women stand in a row. Wanda was one of them and he selected her out of the row to come to his house and be his housekeeper."

"Was she his slave then?"

"She didn't know. No one ever told her what her status was. Things were a bit different then, not so organized. All she knew was that she wasn't allowed to travel without permission – but that had been the case at the factory too. She got room and board and I think even some money from him. As far as I know, he never mistreated her."

"So he didn't rape her?"

"No. But after a few years she got pregnant."

"Then what?"

He shrugged. "As she tells it, she left and hid at her brother's. She had the twins there and then her brother got her into the Underground. She moved up from there."

Zosia tilted her head. "What does this have to do with Peter?"

Jurek sighed heavily. "I never asked her why she got pregnant by that man. Indeed, I never asked if it was that man or someone else. I thought maybe if it was someone else, that would explain why she felt it was necessary to leave…"

"Now you think something different?"

"After that Council meeting where Peter spoke to you all, asking if he could stay among us, Wanda came back and told me that she had been swayed by Peter's eloquence into voting in his favor, but when Tadek was ready to shoot him, she changed her mind. She said – and this is really odd – that you simply can't trust anyone who worked so closely with *them*."

"But–"

"Exactly. It was as if she had forgotten that she had worked for years in that officer's household. *Or* as if she knew, from her own experience, the sort of deals that one might indulge in. I think she made a deal with that fellow to be his mistress and she did it entirely voluntarily just to better her situation. When she got pregnant, there must have been some sort of confrontation. Maybe he said that he loved her and she found that abhorrent. Maybe she loved him and discovered he had only been using her. Or maybe their illegal relationship became obvious and she had to flee prosecution. If he helped her leave, that might explain how she got away so easily. I don't know. Whatever happened, I think she feels guilty about it."

"There's no reason for that."

Jurek raised his eyebrows. "That doesn't sound like the Zosia I know – the one who screamed so loudly at her husband that everyone on the wing heard it. The number of times you called him *collaborator* – I mean, you didn't really help him to make friends here, you know."

Zosia turned away, chagrined. "I've calmed a bit, since then..." And, she had to admit, it had been useful to keep him isolated from the others, all the better to manipulate his actions.

"Well, Wanda hasn't. When she learned that he had been sleeping with Elspeth – that was the last straw for her. She came back from the meeting where that had been made public absolutely ranting, saying that she had known it all along. I think she wants to punish him for being a collaborator–"

"You would think she'd be the last to want to punish him."

Jurek shrugged. "She was punished. The twins were killed. Maybe in some wretched way, she's trying to save Peter from God's judgment by pre-empting it."

Zosia shuddered. "Oh, Jurek, please don't say things like that. It makes Wanda sound insane!"

Jurek looked down at his hands which he had clasped on his lap. "You're right," he said, speaking to the floor. "We're all completely sane here and none of us have any experiences that would make us act in any way that was other than completely rational. And..." He looked up at Zosia and smiled wistfully, "As long as we believe that, we're safe."

Zosia shook her head, angry at his sarcasm. "Jurek, it's not like that."

Jurek motioned toward the screen. "Hand it on to Warszawa, they'll decrypt it, or someone in the NAU will. It's probably not all that important anyway."

"No! This is our catch, and we're going to keep it. I just need to find someone to decrypt it. Damn, I wish Peter was here!"

"Why don't you go see him? You must be able to come up with an adequate disguise."

"Oh, I can disguise myself, but then I have no reason to be allowed to visit him. You can't just randomly go in and ask to see a prisoner. And I need to be someone official, so that I have a chance to hand stuff to him..."

"Why not be a reporter or something like that?"

Zosia rubbed her chin, "I think I have a better idea. I won't need anything more complicated than standard Reich papers, and I might be able to kill two birds with one stone."

So it was, two days later, armed with all the necessary documentation, Zosia and Tadek were in Berlin across from the pension that they used as home base and in front of Arieka's embassy. Tadek presented his papers to the secret policeman who guarded the entrance and was allowed to pass as a minor government official with his secretary. Inside, he presented his papers to the clerk and explained that he had an appointment. They were shown to Arieka's office and she stood to greet them. As Zosia and Arieka curiously eyed each other, Tadek opened his briefcase and pulled out a detector.

"That's not necessary," Arieka began, but stopped herself. She turned to Zosia and the two made light conversation as Tadek inspected the room. He stopped by a little box which contained the junction for the telephone line, and flicking off the plastic lid, motioned to Arieka.

Zosia was busily discussing the weather as Arieka bent down to look into the little space. Tucked nicely among the phone wires was a small round device. She nodded her recognition of it, just as Zosia was saying, "Frau Ruweni, perhaps you and *mein Herr* would like to take advantage of this beautiful spring day. I'll have no trouble taking notes outside."

Tadek grinned. "What a lovely idea. Do you think we could have our meeting in the park?"

Arieka agreed and they left together. It was clear they were followed – Arieka always was – but their tail would not be able to hear their discussion and that was sufficient for their purposes.

Arieka snorted with disgust. "I thought only our conference room was bugged! For heaven's sake, we're so unimportant, how in the world can they find the manpower to watch us!"

Zosia sat on a bench and motioned to the others to join her. "They can't. Everything said in your office goes onto a tape and is filed for later analysis along with thousands of others. They're years behind and I think a lot gets archived without anyone hearing a word."

"What about him?" Arieka nodded her head toward the man who had followed them and now sat on a bench a short distance away.

"Ah, that's just a social welfare program. Keeps the unemployed busy. He has virtually no training and not much idea what he's supposed to do. He's there more to intimidate the natives from talking freely to you. The real agents get used for more important things."

Arieka sniffed.

"Sorry, didn't mean it like that." Zosia pulled out a notepad and began writing. "But I should at least put on a show."

"What's this about? All I got was that note that was handed to me. Pretty cryptic stuff."

Tadek glanced around, then turned to Arieka. "My secretary is named Zosia, she's Peter's wife." Arieka snapped her head around to look at Zosia, but Tadek continued speaking. "My name is Tadek, I'm an associate of his. Please look like you're talking with me, while Zosia speaks. Afterwards, if anyone asks, we talked about sending an experimental pesticide to your country for testing."

Arieka nodded and as she looked interestedly at Tadek, Zosia explained her idea. As Zosia finished, Arieka nodded again. "I think I can manage that. I go to Switzerland periodically just to get out of here anyway, and each time I've made it a point to visit your husband."

"I know, he's written to me about your visits. Do you think you could convince the prison authorities to give him the files or are we going to have to smuggle them in?"

Arieka put her head back to contemplate the unusually blue sky. "God, I hate this city. The whole place feels like a prison. A gloomy, gray one at that!"

"Why did you come?"

"Heh. I was curious." Arieka dropped her head and looked again at Tadek. "I don't know, Zosia. They're pretty strict about things like that. We'll have to see. What you should do is hand your resume over to the clerk as soon as we go back. I'll tell him to put it on my desk and if you show up tomorrow, I'll have a job for you as translator and personal assistant. I'll check my calendar, but I think I can book time in Switzerland for next week—"

"Can't you do it earlier?"

"Afraid not."

Tadek jabbed Zosia with his elbow to remind her that she was asking a favor and not to demand too much, so Zosia let it rest and after a few more minutes planning, they headed back to the embassy.

16

*P*eter folded his arms and leaned back, grinning. "Well, well, two for the price of one! When they told me my girlfriend had come to visit, they didn't tell me I'd have my choice of chocolate or vanilla."

"*Peter*," Zosia hissed, annoyed by his banter. "Don't you recognize me?"

Peter smiled at Arieka and spoke softly, "Yeah, I recognize you, but I'm not going to show anyone that, now am I?" He leaned forward, still looking at Arieka. "Let's just talk normally for a little while and they'll lose interest. We lucked out, you know. They're installing more secure communications, but until it's done, we have this nice old-fashioned face-to-face."

Zosia glanced down at the table between them. Running along the center was a simple board, about ten inches high, separating them with a virtual wall. "Can I touch you?"

Peter shook his head. "Didn't you read the rules?"

Zosia couldn't stop herself from reaching for him anyway.

Peter drew back in response. "If you do that, they'll end the interview. Please, don't do anything impetuous, Zosia. Please?" He allowed his eyes to stray to her face. "I have no freedom."

Zosia knew he said it only to explain his request, but the sad truth of his words tore at her heart.

The guards were already taking up positions lounging against the walls, the neighboring couples were intent on their own personal revelations. Peter gave Zosia a quick, encouraging smile before turning his gaze back to Arieka. "I'm really glad to see you. How is everybody?"

Zosia told him about home, about the children and Marysia and everyone else. She rushed her words, intent on telling him everything before getting down to business. She had so much to convey, words were insufficient. She added unspoken detail with the tone of her voice, her expressions, her gestures…

"You're moving too much," Peter whispered suddenly. "Please don't draw attention to yourself. They might be keeping an eye on who visits me, and I don't want them to think I know you other than as Arieka's aide."

Zosia glanced around at the various guards stationed throughout the room and at the cameras in each corner. "Do you think the Reich has agents here?"

Peter shrugged. "They had someone in that government office I went to when I escaped years ago. I don't want you to risk it." He nodded his head toward the other prisoners. "Besides, about half these guys are convinced Nazis. They're always looking for information to sell later, when they get out."

Zosia pulled herself erect to sit primly, as a personal assistant might. "How are you doing?"

"Me? I'm fine. You got my letters?"

"Yes, and they worry me."

"Why? I've told you everything's okay."

"I know. It's just that your words are so..." Zosia faltered. "So calm," she whispered at last.

Peter shook his head ever so slightly. "I'm fine. Really."

"Don't worry about him," Arieka confided to Zosia, though she kept her attention on Peter. "I can see, the fighter still remains."

Peter smiled at Arieka. "I like your new girl. Gonna keep her long?"

"Ah, I don't think our budget is up to it. She's a rather expensive proposition. Getting me involved in..." Arieka's tongue darted out of her mouth as if snatching the forbidden word from the air to swallow it. She closed her lips and held them firmly shut, with a broad smile turning up the corners of her mouth.

"So, what's the real reason you visited?"

As Peter and Arieka carried on the pretense of a conversation, Zosia dropped her voice low, shielded her mouth and, looking disinterestedly at the wall behind Peter, explained about Erich, his files and Jurek's and her unsuccessful attempt at translating them. "Is there any way you could work on them? I mean, if I can get them to you?"

He almost had to laugh. "Yeah, put them in an envelope and address it to me care of the governor. Don't put in any personal messages. Take it to his secretary and tell her it's part of the work I'm doing in the library. They'll see I get it."

"What are you doing?"

Peter explained about the computer access he had organized for himself.

"But why?"

"I was bored. And I thought I might be able to contact you and offer my help. It's all being done on the cheap, so if I tell the governor I've managed to get some important information for free, he'll let it pass. Oh yeah, make sure it's in the macrodisk format – we can't read anything more high-tech than that. Then once I have it, I can analyze it, but I'll need some information from the Szaflary office. And that's the next thing you have to do. I need you to create a window in the system back home. I'll tell you how – write this down, it's a bit complicated." He described in detail the steps she should take to dismantle the security and hook the computer directly into the phone system and the problems that might arise as well as their solution. "I won't be able to communicate with you until you do this, but after that, I can handle things from here."

Zosia looked down at the pages of notes, nodding. But then her eyes caught sight of the clock. "Oh my God!" she moaned. "It's almost time to go."

"There's something else I want you to do."

"What?"

"It's about the escape route I was trying to set up. It's just an idea and maybe you two could work together on it for me?" Peter looked at Arieka. Zosia knew he did not doubt her participation, but Arieka was not part of their organization and would be taking a huge risk for people who were meaningless to her.

Arieka glanced at the clock. "Let's hear it."

Still looking at Arieka, Peter directed his words to Zosia. "I'm assuming your brother will be supplied with a completely new staff soon, courtesy of his new wife."

"That's right – the old staff will be staying where they are."

"They aren't both needed there. Have the man reassigned, the woman can stay. The woman can take Roman's place in my plan, directing people to the first stage of the route via word of mouth. She can start by contacting the people I knew." While Peter spoke a buzzer sounded, and he began to speak more rapidly. "Meanwhile, the man will get a new identity and if Arieka agrees–" and here he threw her a pleading glance, but continued to direct his comments to Zosia, "he can be hired in as a janitor. Organize it so he just uses the building – an external entrance to the cellar – one which the minders won't watch since there's no access to international territory through it. If you can't arrange that, get a tunnel into a neighboring cellar. Keep him totally disconnected from her staff so if he's ever caught, there won't be any implication of her involvement–"

"Even if there is," Zosia interjected, "she'll have extra protection as a foreign dignitary and the worst that will happen is she'll be thrown out."

"I have no problem with that," Arieka chuckled.

Peter rushed on. "The embassy building can be the first stop where the escapee can get clothes, papers, a bit of training on how to behave, and can be directed to the next location. That will be in Home Army territory, so we can vary the destination and have our people handle them. I think they should generally be sent over the mountains and out via the south, but that can be changed according to current conditions." Peter stopped and took a deep breath. A second buzzer sounded and the guards moved away from the walls toward the prisoners. Some of the prisoners stood as they took leave of their visitors. "Contact Roman – he's got asylum here. He can give you some indication of where to start, and I can send more details once you open up that window." By raising his eyebrows, he managed to let Arieka know the next question was for her. "Would you do it?"

Arieka nodded. "Sounds exciting. And I'm pleased you trust me."

Peter let his eyes catch Zosia's for a split second. "I think the other two will be happy to do it. What do you think?"

"It sounds good to me. We'll work on it."

Peter turned around to see the clock. "It's time. I have to go. If you stay in the area, you can visit again next week. Can you do that?"

Arieka glanced at Zosia and then back to Peter. "I'm sorry, I just can't stay that long."

A third buzzer sounded and the guards moved along the row, tapping the shoulders of those still sitting. The other prisoners began to rise.

"Peter…" Zosia almost reached for him.

He stood, shaking his head. "Tell Krys happy birthday. And Madzia, next month. I've sent them some stuff in a letter – maybe they'll get it. And kiss them all for me. Hugs too. And Marysia. Tell everyone I love them, my wife especially, okay?"

One of the guards tapped Peter's shoulder with a fist. "Move it."

"Peter…"

"I gotta go, ladies." He backed away from the table mouthing the words, "I love you. Miss you." Then he turned and exited with the others.

"I love you, too," Zosia whispered, but it was too late for him to hear. She watched him disappear through the door, and then, giving up any pretense of her secretarial role, she dropped her head in dismay onto Arieka's shoulder. She felt Arieka's thin arms wrap around her shoulders and she felt how the material of Arieka's blouse grew wet with her tears.

17

"*A* bit over the top, don't you think, her wearing white?" Rudi directed his comment at Gertrud since nobody else was near. As he expected, Gertrud did nothing more than nod mutely. God, what he would give to have that tedious woman drop dead naturally! He could mourn with the extended Goebbels clan, keep up contacts as a dutiful relative, and finally be free of her. Every now and then the thought occurred to him that he should arrange something, but he always rejected the temptation. It wouldn't do to have even a hint of suspicion about her death and besides, she was easy enough to shuffle out of the way while still alive.

Out of the way so that he could fall into his dear Stefi's arms. My God, but she looked radiant there with her husband. Sooner or later this tedious wedding would be over, Traugutt and his new bride could disappear for a brief honeymoon and…He felt lonely, he missed his *Mäuschen*, he hadn't seen her in days! This wedding had consumed everyone's time, his dear Stefi included. Now all he had to do was make it through the evening and he could be with her. She had promised. But what a long evening it was proving to be. Just as well he had fortified himself with half a bottle of whiskey. That dulled the senses enough to make the tedious little people all around him slightly more tolerable. Only slightly though. Rudi glanced down at his watch. Goodness, it was almost time to start.

Though Richard and Greta's marriage had gone through the necessary bureaucratic channels and was therefore final, they had nevertheless asked Rudi if he would say a few words in front of their comrades, friends and family. The Captain of the great ship of the Reich, marrying two of his loyal subjects. It seemed appropriate, and Rudi relished the role, going so far as to invite the pair to celebrate their wedding in the great hall of the *Residenz*. Motioning to one of his officers to gather the crowd together, Rudi stepped up to the podium and called the happy couple before him.

He spoke eloquently of love and duty, of the leading role of the husband as Führer of the family and the devoted role of the wife, supporting her husband and providing children for the future and greater glory of the Reich. He noticed a slightly pained look on Greta Schindler's face as he mentioned children. Yes, she was already in her early forties, children would be a bit of a stretch, and Greta had never come across as the motherly type in any case, but that did not stop him from praising her in her future role as mother.

Rudi did not use notes as he spoke, it was one of his talents that he could talk for hours on end without them. This time, he decided not to speak too long and ended his speech after an hour. The audience broke into spontaneous applause and Rudi surged forward to embrace the bride and congratulate the groom. He felt awash with the folkish spirit, his great people warmly applauding his words, his loyal subjects uniting under his leadership. The warmth translated through his body downward and he scanned the crowd to find Stefi's face.

He saw his dear little *Mäuschen* talking to her husband. She had told him she was pregnant again and he grinned at the thought of finally becoming a father. His son would lead the Reich, the first time that the leadership would pass from father to son! There would have to be someone in between, he supposed, like the Americans did with their presidents. But maybe not – he could easily lead for another thirty years, retiring gracefully in his nineties, and by then his boy would be ready to take the reins of power.

Rudi noticed suddenly that he was being spoken to. It was Seppel and his wife. What a tedious little man Frauenfeld was, standing there drinking his fucking mineral water. But loyal, Rudi reminded himself. He was handed a glass of champagne and he drank it absent-mindedly. Loyal. Yes, that was a good characteristic, one which too few had. He nodded at Seppel's comment and let his eyes stray around the room. There was Traugutt, chatting to Lang. As incidental as Schenkelhof's murder had been, it had been quite a godsend for Traugutt – everybody knew that Schenkelhof had loathed him. Now there was his successor Lang happily gossiping with Traugutt. The empty glass disappeared almost magically from Rudi's hand and with only the slightest nod of agreement, he was handed another. Next to Traugutt was his new father-in-law, Johann Graf vom Stein. Retired, but still very well connected in the diplomatic services. Rudi continued to nod thoughtfully as Irmtraud Frauenfeld said something, but his gaze had moved on, to the other side of the room. He drank the champagne in his hand and felt the bubbles rolling through his head. Richard's son Paul was in attendance with his girlfriend Teresa Vogel, daughter of Elspeth Vogel nee von dem Bach. He knew that during Karl Vogel's life, Elspeth had been almost shunned by her family, but now, he wondered, was she in contact with them? Was Teresa Vogel yet another influential connection for Richard? Oh, good Lord, there she was, Frau von dem Bach talking warmly with Paul and Teresa.

"Yes, yes," Rudi agreed, oblivious to what had actually been said. He downed the champagne and handed it to the faceless servant, accepting another without even noticing. Now with Günter gone, there was only Seppel as a counterweight to Richard. He had thought it was enough, but as he surveyed the room, he began to have his doubts. Could loyal little Frauenfeld hold his own against the waxing power of Traugutt and his connections? His eyes fell upon Traugutt's widowed mother, Anna, whom he had only just met. She had come from Göringstadt for the wedding and there she was, conversing warmly with Gertrud's father! Rudi ran a quick mental calculation and guessed that Anna must be about seventy years old. Gertrud's father, whose wife had died three years ago, was seventy-four. Rudi groaned as he realized that being married to Gertrud was useless if her father's loyalties were with someone else. Though it was Gertrud's mother who had carried the Goebbels connection, her father was truly integrated as a member of the extensive clan and could sway their preferences as a result!

The entire party was nothing less than Traugutt's consolidation of his power. *And in my Residenz*, Rudi thought angrily. He slammed the empty champagne glass to the floor. There was a momentary silence as everyone looked at the source of the noise, but they quickly realized that it was not deliberate and turned their attention away. *I'll kill the bastard!* A servant was under his feet, sweeping up glass. *So misusing my hospitality! I will kill him!* He had an urge to kick the nonentity underfoot, but Irmtraud said something.

Making it appear accidental, Rudi stepped on the hand of the servant sweeping up the glass. Out of the corner of his eye, he saw the man silently recoil in pain. That felt better. He took a moment to smile at Irmtraud and then he excused himself to talk to some other idiot who had approached. Ah yes, Frau So-und-so. Also useless. My God, he was surrounded by useless sycophants while Traugutt was hacking away at his legs! He would fall, and fall soon, if he didn't act quickly. Where was the crowd that usually surrounded him? Where was everybody? Like magic, his beautiful Stefi appeared at his side and took his arm. She said something which sent the moronic Frau So-und-so away and then she gently led him across the room to a chair. He hiccupped. *Damn those stupid bubbles.*

Stefi took a seat next to him, but seemed to understand that he didn't want to talk. His mind worked feverishly. Richard had the Eastern Reich under his control. Those parts which he did not directly control were run by cronies and friends. Security. He was highly placed in the *Sicherheitsamt*, and from all accounts, well-liked as well. The old Nazi élite – well, his mother seemed to be working on that. The *Wehrmacht* – he already had Lang in his pocket. The *Luftwaffe* were amenable to anybody other than Schindler. The diplomatic services – Greta's father. Damn, the bastard had it nearly sewn up!

A servant approached and Rudi accepted another glass of champagne. Why did Traugutt serve French champagne? What, Rudi wondered, was wrong with good German *Sekt*? He downed half the glass and stared glassy-eyed across the room. There Traugutt was, trim, fit, charming, young. *Thirteen years younger than me*, Rudi thought grumpily, and then it dawned on him: that was the age he had been when he had taken over the Party leadership! He felt a sudden desperation. First, he had to find out who was on his side, and then – immediately – he had to rid himself of that man! *But how, how?*

Rudi drank the rest of the champagne and looked around. Stefi caught his eye and smiled sweetly. She would know what to do, he would talk to her. Yes, she would help him. His little *Mäuschen*, his loyal Stefi. He made a slight motion with his head and Stefi nodded her understanding. Rudi stood and sought out Richard.

"Ah, my dear, dear Richard, there you are!" Cleverly hugging Richard to hide his venomous intent, Rudi whispered in his ear, "You and your friends stay here as long as you wish. I have a headache and am retiring for the night."

Richard and those near him expressed their regrets that he was abandoning them so soon, but Rudi was adamant. He needed to see Stefi! On unsteady legs he made his way out of the room and with the usual entourage returned to his chambers to await her arrival. She would need about half an hour to discreetly remove herself and he decided to spend the time scanning the weekly reports. It was all trash – informers reporting on union meetings, suspect theater productions, soldiers' and servants' gossip. He sighed heavily at the burdens of his office and lazily perused the pages.

Stefi waited until Rudi had left the room and then approached her father. He leaned down to kiss her cheek and whispered, "He's in a vile mood, be careful."

Stefi only nodded. After she had spent an appropriate few minutes chatting in his group, she sought out Olek. The two of them did nothing more than hold hands and exchange a solemn look. They had made their plans well ahead of this evening. It was necessary for Traugutt to bring together his support under one roof so they could be aware of each other and make the necessary tacit agreements among themselves that would bear fruit in several months, or perhaps a year. That was why Richard had opted for a showy wedding, that's why they had delayed until May, even though the divorces had become final months earlier. There was only one flaw in the plan, and that was Rudi's reaction to such a show. So, it had been decided that Stefi would find time alone with him during the evening or immediately afterwards. She would gauge his mood and carefully shift it away from suspicions. He didn't have to be strung along for much longer, but it wouldn't do to have him slip into wild paranoia before all the players had taken the stage.

Olek knew all this and he also knew exactly how Stefi would manipulate the Führer. Knowing the reasons and importance of her actions did not make them much easier to accept, though. It hurt every time he had to let her go, and now it pained him especially because the Führer was so obviously drunk and angry. Would he, in a fit of irrational rage, take it out on Stefi? Was this, Olek wondered, the last time they would see each other?

He turned his attention away from the small group they were in and kissed his wife lightly. "I love you," he mouthed. Stefi smiled sadly and Olek added quietly, "Please be very careful."

She nodded, then placing a hand on his shoulder she leaned into him so that her lips were next to his ear. He shivered as he felt her warm breath. "Remember, I will always be with you," she whispered, and then she was gone, walking away toward an exit, to go to her Führer. Olek felt himself trembling with fear for her and the child she carried within her, and it was all he could do not to run after her and drag her away. Far, far away. To safety.

18

"*M*ǟuschen."

Stefi was disconcerted to see that Rudi had switched back to whiskey. He was never particularly easy to handle, especially when he was jealous or suspicious, but when his paranoia was combined with alcohol – then he was truly unpredictable. Stefi smiled sweetly as she approached him. She supposed that paranoia was not the appropriate word for what Rudi felt since they *were* all out to get him. Without saying a word, she sat on the couch and cuddled up against him. He stroked her hair and continued drinking.

Poor lad, he had started out so well! There had been such great hopes when he had assumed the office, young and strong and promising to restore order. In the wake of the chaotic years of inflation and unemployment following the Freedom Movements, Rudi had applied a reassuring firmness. He had expanded government employment to absorb the disgruntled youth and insisted on a return to the old values to satisfy the terrified middle classes. With the return of properly enforced racial laws came a sense of order and security. With the revival of ancient festivals and holidays, came a sense of belonging to the *Volk*.

Among the general population the mood had not changed much. Rudi kept order. He kept a lid on the turbulent youth, he kept the lower orders in their proper place. The never-ending increase in taxes was borne mostly by *Nichtdeutsch* and was, to the citizens of the Reich, only fair given that it was their constant troublemaking that required all the extra police and expansion of the army in the first place. It was among the élite that Rudi had slowly begun to lose favor. With the years, Rudi's less respectable characteristics had emerged – for example, his obvious enjoyment of some of the more unfortunate aspects of keeping the lower orders properly subdued. Camps, prisons, interrogations and punishments were all necessary to the running of the State, but it was rather unseemly to be seen to enjoy such things. It also slowly made an impression on international opinion, and Rudi's inept handling of the public relations fiasco of recent years did not bode well for the entire Reich.

More important, though, was Rudi's penchant for humiliating his own people. Only so many times could an officer of the Reich be brusquely told to shut-up before he would turn his thoughts to plotting against his dear Führer – even if he had sworn an oath of undying loyalty. This was a subtlety that seemed quite beyond Rudi. Though he was not hindered much by ideology on the mundane level of running the Reich – the racial laws were a convenience, not a conviction – he did seem to believe that he had been anointed by the deities. When he chose to be friendly, he was quite charming, but when he stepped onto his pedestal, he managed to endlessly offend.

"They all hate me, *Schatzi*. Why do they all hate me?"

Stefi twisted her head so she could look at Rudi. Her usual response was to insist that he was well loved by all, but she suspected that was not appropriate this time. "I love you, darling."

He eyed her as if he would question her statement, but then said, "You're the only one. Do you know, my father always thought I wouldn't amount to anything. He was still alive when I was elected Führer, and do you know what?"

Stefi shook her head.

"He didn't even say 'well done'. Not even then."

"I'm sorry."

"All my life I struggled to find someone to love me, all my life!" Rudi looked into Stefi's eyes, he stroked a strand of hair out of her face. "When I was a child, I trapped a stray cat in our garden shed and I decided I was going to make it mine, it was going to love me! I tried feeding it and holding it, but it kept wanting to get away. So I put it on a leash. But you know what cats are like – it just lay on the ground making a strange guttural noise. I tried to teach it to be mine, but it kept trying to get away. So I decided to discipline it. I began beating it – first with a piece of rope, but it didn't seem to feel that what with all its fur. It just stayed low on the ground making that awful noise. So I switched to a stick and hit it."

"What happened?"

"It just pulled harder on the leash. I stopped and tried to hug it, to show it how much I wanted it to love me and then it scratched me."

"What'd you do?"

Rudi smiled. "Not what you think. I gave up. I decided that I would try a different approach the next day and so I put it in a cage for the night. There wasn't anything like a cage in the shed though, so I used a box. I put it inside the box and put a heavy stone on the lid to keep the cat inside."

"And?"

"It was an old, insulated ice box. When I came back the next morning to find my friend, it was dead. It had suffocated." Rudi paused, tilting his

571

head slightly. "I had killed it. I had killed the only thing in the world which might have one day loved me."

Stefi wanted to ask Rudi what he thought the significance of the story was, but she feared delving too deeply. The one thing he was unlikely to forgive was her knowing embarrassing secrets about him. Indeed, in these few moments, she had probably passed a point of no return. How, she wondered, could he tolerate her continued existence once he realized that she knew these deep secrets of his soul?

She quickly ran through a number of possible responses wondering which would work. Another assertion of her love? A reassurance that the whole world loved him? "I'm sorry," she said with heartfelt sympathy.

He stroked her fondly. "It's alright, little one. Do you want to know what I did?"

"Yes."

Rudi put his hands behind his head and leaned back against the cushion. "I told my mother that the gardener had killed my pet cat. She had him beaten for that." He laughed. "That's when I knew my destiny was not to be loved, but to lead. I could do anything as long as I didn't worry what others thought."

"And you are indeed a great leader. The greatest."

The Führer sat erect and lifted Stefi's chin under his hand. "Come to bed, my little one, and I'll show you my powers."

The thought that anything would happen in Rudi's current drunken state was laughable, but Stefi did not laugh. This was exactly what she had been waiting for and she was relieved that Rudi's mood had been assuaged by a simple discussion of his past, rather than his ranting about how he would kill his insubordinate and disloyal minions. Pleased that it would be over with so quickly, she rose to her feet and extended her hand to help him up. Once he had grunted and panted himself to sleep, everything would be back to normal.

Rudi stood and stretched ostentatiously. Holding her hand, he led Stefi over to the bedroom and made a motion which she knew meant he wanted her to undress. As she began to remove her dress, he opened a drawer of the bedside table and Stefi moaned silently. Unfortunately, tonight would not be the schoolmistress and her naughty pupil. Tonight, Rudi was the great leader, and that meant he was in control.

Stefi had prepared herself for her evening's work and was well-outfitted with stockings and garter and lacy corset. But Rudi wasn't interested, he indicated with a wave of the hand that he wanted her totally naked. Once she had undressed, he bound her hands behind her with thin leather strips and then, grunting and wheezing, lifted her onto the bed. He lost his hold and Stefi dropped the few inches onto the mattress and then lay there like a virgin waiting to be sacrificed on some heathen altar.

As was usual in this particular scene, and to Stefi's great relief, he did not remove most of his clothing. He did however need some help getting warmed up and since her hands were bound, Rudi indicated that Stefi should use her mouth, so he stood next to the bed while she lay close to the edge, trying her damnedest to breath some life into his limp member. Remembering to moan intermittently with pleasure, Stefi let her mind wander, trying to come up with apt analogies to the physical sensations she was experiencing. A wiener, cooked and then left on the counter to wilt. And she was tasting it, deciding whether or not to bite deep into the limp little sausage or spit it into the garbage. Ah, that was too apt – it wouldn't do to burst into laughter.

Despite any genuine physical response, Rudi seemed to think he was ready for something. He crawled into the bed, removing the rest of his clothing as he did so. Stefi deftly rolled out of the way. She lay facing him and he reached out and stroked her skin, following the curve of her body from her breasts to her hips. He looked ludicrous, his skin pale, his chest hair sparse and gray, his muscles flaccid with age and inactivity, his eyes glazed with alcoholic fervor. He pressed a kiss on her and then pushed her onto her back. Stefi opened her legs invitingly, praying for a quick end to the scene, but it was not to be. "I need to warm you up a bit, you naughty wench!" the Führer exclaimed, as he reached for the riding crop.

Stefi played her role well, moaning with feigned excitement as he laid the whip across her breasts and stomach and thighs. He rolled her over and applied it heavily to her backside, causing her to whimper with genuine pain and not a little fear. Something was different about him tonight and she grew quite worried. Suddenly he stopped hitting her and climbed onto her. He straddled her waist, trapping her arms beneath him, and slid the riding crop under her throat, lifting her head with it so that the thick leather bent painfully against her neck.

"Now *Mäuschen*, it's time you answered some questions for me."

Stefi stiffened with terror. Oh God, he was going to kill her! Would the servants or guards stop him? Would they even realize what he was doing? "Rudi, darling." Her voice was a barely audible hiss. "That hurts. Please stop."

"I learned that you didn't have a miscarriage, my little whore, you had an abortion!" He pulled the riding crop higher.

"Oh, Rudi," she croaked. "Please stop!"

"Not until you tell me the truth, you bitch!"

The pain was intense. Stefi's vision faded in and out with the labored pounding of her heart. Catching her breath in noisy, painful gasps, she struggled for air by trying to bend her back upward but the Führer's weight held her down. He tightened his grip and she gave in. "It was Günter!" she wheezed. "He forced me. I didn't want you to know! I knew it would break your heart!"

"What? Break my heart?" The Führer dropped the riding crop down a bit.

"Yes," Stefi moaned. She felt a desperate need to swallow. "When he arrested my father and me, he had me taken to a hospital and had our baby aborted! You can ask the hospital staff, they'll tell you that I had to be held down and anesthetized."

Again the riding crop dropped a bit lower. "Why didn't they report this to me?"

Stefi coughed and gasped. "They didn't know whose baby it was! They thought I was just hysterical. They were just following Günter's orders. He told them I had been raped by some *Untermensch* and the pregnancy was the result of that."

"I'll kill him."

Stefi squirmed slightly, trying to move her head forward so she could swallow, but the Führer suddenly tightened his grip again. "Why didn't you tell me?"

Stefi struggled to answer despite the pressure. "I knew how it would hurt you. I was devastated and couldn't speak to anyone for weeks, and by then, it was too late." She felt a strange pulsing in her head, as if it were going to explode.

"And why didn't your father tell me this?"

"The damage was already done," she squeaked. Immediately Stefi wanted to recall the words and claim her father hadn't known, but it was too late. She gulped a bit of air. "So he kept it quiet in exchange for Günter divorcing Greta."

The Führer dropped the whip and Stefi's head dropped heavily to the bed. "He could have widowed Greta by telling me."

Stefi gasped and panted. She swallowed repeatedly, choking and coughing, before she answered. "He didn't want to burden you, right after your return."

The Führer lifted the riding crop slightly – not enough to hurt, just enough to threaten. "Don't lie to me, little vixen. I want the truth about your father." He pulled up on the whip and Stefi choked noisily in response. "No, first I want to know whose side you're on."

"Yours, Rudi. My God, I love you! It was my baby too! Do you think it was easy for me?"

"Good. Then if you're on my side, you're not on your father's. Do you understand?" He jerked upward.

Stefi sputtered. "Yes, yes. I understand. I love *you*."

Rudi lowered the riding crop and with it, Stefi's head. He climbed off her. She coughed and rolled onto her side. Her face grew hot as blood rushed into her head. Saliva drooled from her mouth as she choked and sputtered.

The Führer lay down next to her, breathing heavily. "I want to trust you, darling. But you must understand, you can only have one master."

"And you *are* the one," Stefi rasped. Slowly the bright flashes of black that followed each heartbeat began to deteriorate, the edges grew more diffuse and the center narrowed until her vision was nearly back to normal.

"Your father is trying to displace me."

Stefi decided it was wiser not to disagree or argue. It was clear Rudi would allow her only one option and that was being his ally against her father. To try to argue her father's loyalty would only bring her own into question. "I didn't realize that," she said softly. She coughed again as quietly as possible. Her neck was so sore and her head still felt cloudy.

"Yes, and we have to stop him."

"But how?"

"He was complicit in the murder of my child. Both he and Günter will be arrested and tried. The hospital staff and your testimony will be sufficient to convict them: the one for murder, the other for conspiracy. I'm going to issue the order right now. In fact, I'll go back into the great hall myself to see to it personally that my orders are carried out."

Stefi glanced into the darkness of the room. Nobody was near enough to hear their conversation. As Rudi began to rise, she slid her shoulder onto his. "My God, you are so forceful!" With her hands still tied behind her back, it wasn't easy, but she managed to wriggle her body onto his. "Oh, *mein Führer*, you must take me. Take me now! I can't stand waiting any longer!"

She lowered herself onto him, working her legs around him as best she could. He was flat and limp, but with thigh muscles and determination, she made him feel that he was entering her. She saw him smile and she knew that her flattery had won him over to a short delay. She pressed herself against him, burying her head against his shoulder. With her face turned away from him, she twisted her jaw so that her upper teeth came down at an angle onto the lower teeth, putting all the pressure on one tiny area. All the while she twisted herself erotically over Rudi's body, her legs clenched themselves around him, trying to convince him that he was irresistible. She felt the cap of her tooth crack and very carefully she separated her teeth. This wasn't what the system had been designed for and, acutely aware that a wrong move would mean her own death, Stefi carefully worked her tongue into the gap and rolled the tiny bead into her mouth. She pressed it against her gum with her tongue and held it there. Once she felt its position was secure, she raised her head.

The Führer had turned his head to the side and with her hands tied behind her back, Stefi was unable to move it, nor was she able to say anything. She turned and jostled her head so that her hair brushed his face and he looked up at her. She radiated adoration and brought her lips down to kiss his. She opened her mouth and thrust her tongue into his, dropping the tiny bead in as she did so. He looked slightly confused, but she gyrated her lower half and he seemed to forget the strange sensation of something dropping into his throat. She kissed him passionately, forcing him to gasp for air and with that, she hoped, he swallowed the poison. She waited a moment and saw his expression change. He began to shudder and jerk convulsively, his eyes opening wide with horror or pain. The poison was intended for her body size and weight and Stefi feared it would not be effective against the Führer, so she kissed him again, pressing down with her entire body to shove her mouth over his, forcing her face into his nose. She held him that way as he juddered and thrashed as if in orgasm. Even at his age, even drunk, he was quite powerful, but she was also strong and her legs clamped mercilessly around him and she remained with her face suffocatingly close throughout his throes.

All at once he stopped moving. Stefi gasped for breath and looked at him. He had squeezed his eyes shut and it was possible he had simply passed out. She kissed him again, holding her face pressed against his, but it seemed he wasn't breathing. She bent her head against his neck and could find no pulse. She slithered downward a few inches and rested there, exhausted and sweating, her ears over his still heart. She noticed she was trembling and wondered if it was from cold, fear, or triumph.

I must look ridiculous, she thought. Her hair was spread about her, sticking to everything, her hands were tied behind her back, she was naked and lying atop an elderly, naked, dead man. She felt a warm wetness between her legs and she realized that in the throes of death the Führer had either ejaculated or urinated. *Good God, what a way to earn a living!* It was, she supposed, of some comfort to know that the ridiculous scene was probably in no way unique to the history of mankind.

She waited until she was sure he could not be revived, and then she raised her head. "Somebody! Can one of you help me? It's the Führer. I think he's had a heart attack!"

The servants rushed over but stopped at the bedside, not daring to touch the great man without his permission. The head officer in the room had been by the door and it took him a moment longer to reach the scene. He pushed his way through the servants and gingerly touched the Führer's shoulder. *"Mein Führer?"*

"Can someone untie me?"

A rather handsome young man stepped forward, one of the Führer's bodyguards. He gently lifted Stefi off the bed. "Can you stand?" he asked solicitously.

She nodded her head shakily. "I think so."

He noticed the footstool and set her on that, then quickly untied her hands. Somebody else brought her robe and Stefi slipped into it. She realized that nobody was trying to revive Rudi. The senior officer ordered someone to call the Führer's physician, but he added quickly that it should be done quietly. He turned to Stefi. "You should put your clothes on and leave. It'd be better for all concerned if you weren't here."

Stefi nodded and quickly pulled on her clothing, discarding the time-consuming and uncomfortable corset into the closet. There were plenty of clothes in there that she imagined she might never see again, and she was happy to add that to the stack. As she headed for the door, she gave the bed a last glance. Somebody had thrown a sheet over Rudi's body, covering even the face. *So, he's gone*, Stefi thought. Despite the efforts of all those powerful and arrogant men to remove their great leader from his job, it had been left to her, an unimportant woman, to enact a change of regime.

Stefi heaved a sigh, did up the last button on the front of her dress, tucked her hair back and went into the hall. She passed through the security without saying anything – they were used to her silent departures – and found a ladies' room near to the ballroom. There she stopped and sitting on a toilet, she used toilet paper to clean between her legs. In the adjacent lounge, she inspected her dress and tidied her hair. In the bright lights of the lounge she could see her neck was red and she left quickly before any other guests came in. She went directly to the cloakroom and picked up the light shawl that she had worn. It matched well and she could wear it as part of the dress without drawing any notice. She wrapped the shawl stylishly around her, lifting it a bit so that it covered her throat, and then entered the great hall.

Olek saw her as she walked into the room and he rushed over to her. He held her as if he would never let go. Stefi leaned her head against Olek's chest and whispered. "I'm tired, would you take me home?"

19

*K*ittens, playful kittens running around the room chasing balls of wool. Stefi picked up one and put it on her shoulder, it ran down her back. The baby reached for another, stroking its fur. They were all mewing, playfully attacking each other, rolling on the floor. The mother cat climbed onto Stefi's lap and curled up, satisfied that her babies were safe. Olek sat down next to Stefi and placed his arm protectively around her shoulder. The music started up and the kittens began dancing a quadrille, executing intricate steps with uncanny precision...

She awoke to the slamming of her bedroom door against the wall and bright light from the hallway streaming in. She looked up to see her father looming over her.

"Why the hell didn't you warn me?"

Stefi turned her head to see that Olek was in bed next to her. He was sitting bolt upright, his expression one of unconcealed anger. "Colonel! This is our private bedroom in your ex-wife's house. You have no right to come barging in here!"

Ryszard ignored him. "I asked you a question! Why didn't you tell me what had happened?"

"You were no more surprised than anyone else there, Father," Stefi replied lazily. She turned her head away from him and closed her eyes, as she added, "And I'm sure you handled it marvelously."

"Why the hell did you kill him? You did, didn't you? Was it an accident? Was it really a heart attack?"

It gave Stefi a great deal of satisfaction to see her father so confused and at her mercy for information. She peeked through her eyelashes and saw that Olek was utterly shocked as well. Ryszard roughly shook her shoulder. "Answer me, damn it! Stop playing games!"

Stefi sat up and turned on the bedside lamp. She grabbed the top of her nightgown and jerked it down a few inches and then histrionically leaned her head back, exposing her neck.

"God in heaven, Stefi!" Olek exclaimed. In the dim light of the party and the darkness of their bedroom, he had not noticed the marks on her neck.

"It looks like I'm going to have to wear high collars for a couple of days," Stefi commented, deadpan.

Ryszard sat down on the edge of the bed and reached out to touch Stefi's face, gently stroking her cheek. "What happened?"

* * *

As Stefi explained to her father and husband the events of the evening, Kasia was confronted with entertaining her ex-husband's new wife in the middle of the night. Why, she wondered as she wrapped her robe more tightly around herself, hadn't Ryszard sent the woman home? She supposed though that Frau Schindler, or rather, Frau Traugutt – oh, that sounded silly – Greta then...Yes, Greta would not take orders as easily as she had. Perhaps Greta had simply insisted on accompanying Ryszard. Poor Ryszard, he would have his work cut out for him, having a wife who was not also his military subordinate. Kasia suppressed a laugh at the thought of Ryszard jumping to this shrill woman's commands and asked Greta if she might like a glass of wine.

Greta clearly had already had a reasonable amount to drink and dropped wearily into one of the armchairs as Kasia gave Lodzia instructions. When Lodzia had returned with a tray, Kasia suggested she should offer something to the bodyguards and servants who had waited in the hall. "Take them into the kitchen so that they can sit down," Kasia ordered, then added, "and stay with them, I'll take care of Frau..., er, Greta here."

Kasia handed Greta a glass of wine and seated herself on the couch near to her guest. She sat primly, sipping genteelly from her own glass while Greta remained slumped in the armchair, her legs sprawled indelicately. After an uncomfortable moment of silence, Kasia asked, "So, could you tell me what brings Richard here on this – your wedding night?"

Greta was clearly not amused. She set down her glass and yawned expansively. "The Führer is dead."

"Goodness! How did that happen?"

Greta grunted. "Heart attack. It seems he had imbibed too much and then indulged himself in some pleasurable pastime before collapsing in his bed."

"Did they say what sort of pleasurable activity?"

Greta yawned again. "No, and no-one asked. That's not the sort of thing that anyone wants to have spread around. In fact, they didn't give any details. At least not to us. The big men all left the party to go discuss things, the other guests left, so it was just me and some of the other important wives who got to sit around and guess what was going on." Greta glanced meaningfully at Kasia's robe just to make sure that Kasia got the point. Though Greta may have been denied a chance to join in the political discussions that had followed the Führer's death, at least she had been in the ante-chamber and not at home sleeping!

"Would you like some pâté or cheese?" Kasia indicated the tray with a wave of her hand, but Greta had put her head back and was already snoring lightly.

* * *

Ryszard paced the length of the room and leaned against the far wall to face Stefi as she lay in bed. "Well the timing is lousy, but you were right. My career would not have survived another arrest. Especially not for conspiracy to cover-up the murder of Rudi's child. I can see you didn't have any other choice."

Olek was holding Stefi. "Are you *sure* you're alright? Why didn't you tell me? Oh, God, he almost killed you!"

Stefi leaned into Olek's comforting embrace, but it was her father she was watching. He was still wearing the full military regalia he had donned for his wedding and he looked quite dashing with the high black boots, black uniform and medals. Funny, Stefi thought, that in his twenty six years of existence, Richard Traugutt had never picked up a rifle in anger, yet he had so many fancy medals! Prior to Traugutt's existence, Ryszard had certainly seen his share of action, yet none of the medals reflected that. Or did they?

Stefi couldn't restrain herself from asking. "Dad, did Traugutt ever see any fighting?"

Ryszard glanced down at his uniform and sniffed his amusement. "Yeah, before he – I showed up in Krakau, there was some action in the Hebrides, against smugglers and terrorists. That's what this one's for." He tapped a medal. "And this one here – that's for when I was injured. You know, when I was sixteen, I took a bullet in my shoulder."

"For real?"

"Yeah, for real. We translated that into Traugutt's history. Explains the scar, plus it gave me another medal." Ryszard returned to her bedside and looked down at his daughter. He reached out and tentatively touched Stefi's neck. "I'm glad you're okay, sweetheart. You did a good job."

Stefi smiled at her father's unusually excessive praise. Her throat must really look awful!

Ryszard sat on the edge of the bed. "We need to plan."

"What can we do?"

Ryszard stroked Stefi's hair away from her face as he thought. "Not much really. We'll just have to hope things go our way at the Party meeting. I just wish we had had a bit more time – I hadn't even begun bribing the electors. The wedding was a good start, but a lot of those connections are so new and tenuous. And no one has had any time to get the word out to their subordinates."

"I'm sorry, Dad."

He smiled at her. "Don't worry, sweetheart, I'll do a bit more politicking at the funeral and then we'll just have to trust to luck."

"Do you think you'll get it?"

Ryszard nodded. "I think so. Günter's out, Seppel is a non-entity, and the rest are all second-stringers." He sighed. "But it's not unknown for them to pull someone out of a hat. A compromise candidate or someone that they feel can be easily manipulated. After all, Rudi got in when nobody thought he would."

Olek finally broke his silence. "Hopefully they learned from that mistake."

"Is there anything I can do?"

Ryszard shook his head. "I think it's best if you lay low for a bit. Go with your mother to the funeral–"

"When is it?"

"Sunday." Ryszard glanced at his watch, it was already four o'clock Saturday morning. The birds were singing. "Tomorrow, that is."

"Is there going to be an autopsy?"

Ryszard shook his head. "No one suspects anything other than a well-deserved heart attack."

"Too bad he didn't suffer," Olek commented.

Ryszard ignored him. "After the funeral, why don't you and Olek take a little holiday? Go to Switzerland. Greta has a nice cabin in the mountains there, and she's already ordered the servants to get it ready for us, for our honeymoon. We won't be able to go now – I need to stay in Berlin, but there's no reason you two shouldn't go."

Olek made a face at the idea of using anything of Greta's but he knew better than to protest.

Stefi didn't comment on the idea. "Who's running things now? Are you in charge?"

Ryszard shook his head. "Not quite. We had an emergency meeting after the announcement and it was decided there should be a coalition caretaker government. Seppel, me and a few others have been empowered to meet and make decisions. Short of someone invading us, it's not likely we'll need to do much until the Party has chosen a new leader."

"When will that be?"

"The first meeting will be called for Tuesday. There might be an immediate decision, but more likely everyone will need to talk for a few days before they vote."

"Then what?"

"Then the coalition will approve the leader, we'll all swear undying loyalty to the person and the office, he'll be elected Chancellor, and it's back to business as usual. Much cleaner than American elections."

"Are you going to be okay if Olek and I go away?"

Ryszard recognized that she was not asking about his political future and he was quite touched. He stroked some hair off her forehead and then let his fingers stray back to those ugly red marks on her throat. "Doubtless I'll smoke an extra carton of cigarettes this week, but otherwise, I'll be fine. And it will ease my mind to know that you are safely out of harm's way."

"You know, it would ease my mind if you gave up smoking."

Ryszard smiled and stood up to leave. "Not this week, sweetheart. Not this week."

20

*F*irst the funeral and then all this blathering. My God, but his head ached! He wasn't the only one smoking extra packs – the air in the rooms was so thick it was like fog and even Richard was finding it hard to stomach. He made his excuses and left one of the subcommittee meetings. As he walked down the hall of Party headquarters, he was wondering what more could possibly be said. Oh, there were the merits of this candidate for that job, and of that candidate for this job. There were the pompous jackasses who jumped up and blew their own horns because no one else would. There were idiotic discussions on staffing the foreign embassies – everyone putting in his bid for the plum positions. And why did they have a day-long discussion of foreign policy? So that everyone could show his wares, advertising himself for a high position in the next regime.

Richard had lost track of how many implicit promises he had made, he had no idea anymore who was going to get Teheran or Tokyo. All he knew was that his head was pounding. He reached the entrance, and automatically accumulating a crew of bodyguard as he went, he stepped outside. When all the big boys were gathered together in one building, security was extraordinarily tight, but as a top candidate for the leadership, he merited special protection.

There was a light wind which was drying the rain off the sidewalks. Overhead there was a momentary clear patch but the next set of rain clouds were already marshalling on the horizon and Richard could feel one or two drops on the breeze. It would help if Greta were more supportive at home. She greeted his late return with nagging questions and shrill suggestions. Oh, for Kasia's quiet patience! He glanced back into the building. He was bored. Tired and bored. God, if this election didn't put him into power, he didn't know if he had the strength to continue the charade. Arrested twice in the past year alone, nearly arrested a third time, and now this – death by tedium! Just how many stupid bureaucrats could one empire support? Too many, it seemed. Far too many.

He felt daunted by the task ahead. Great inroads had been made into the power structure that held the Reich together, but there were still so many faces he did not know, men with whom he had no connection, men he could have no hope of influencing! And he was alone here. The Home Army could do nothing for him at this conference. No little surprises to bolster his chances, no convenient deaths. Nor did he have what *everyone* else had: a real background. Old school mates, college buddies, old pals from the military, relatives. Even the years he had lived as Traugutt had been so busy and so cautious, he had made virtually no genuine social connections. He had no friends among these people. How could he? The entire impressive edifice of his rise to power was nothing more than papier-mâché. He couldn't do it alone. He needed help! Why, he wondered sourly, did the Home Army not have more people floating around in the Party apparatus? Why was there so little communication between allies? Why, for example, had Schenkelhof not been notified to support Traugutt instead of Schindler?

The thought of Günter brought a smile to Richard's face. He was there, milling around, trying to slot himself back into the important ranks, but everyone was united in turning their backs. His star had faded and he was left to circle at the fringes, like a vulture, waiting to see what carrion he could have after the predators had had their fill. Poor Günter, he might not even get to keep all of Britain. Maybe the London region was enough for him – he was, after all, getting on in years.

Richard shook his head. Pointless planning such little revenges when he didn't even have the position yet. Let such things wait until after he was elected. *If* he was elected. It was, at this point, entirely up to that amorphous mass of élite Party members who were inside. It was their one chance at power, the only time that their whispers could make a difference. And whispers it would be – from one nonentity to another until suddenly the amorphous mass would harden into an immutable decision. He and Frauenfeld and the other candidates could push and shove, shaping this bit or molding that, but in the end it was up to the polis, up to the middle-managers, up to blind luck.

He should have spent more time courting them. He had wasted too much time on the big boys. They, of course, all had their constituencies, and it was impossible to be elected without them. Indeed, they usually stopped someone by not even allowing his candidacy. Now that he had passed that barrier, now that his name was approved, Richard regretted that he had spent so much time with them. He should have been making promises to the little guys. To the voters. It was all a matter of time, and he had not had enough. Just a few more months and it would have all been so much more secure!

A car pulled up at the base of the long flight of steps. Richard looked with interest at which politician had dared to arrive so late, but it wasn't a politician, it was his son. Paul presented his credentials to the security agents at the base of the steps and before Richard could descend to him, he had cleared the first hurdle and was bounding up the steps to his father.

"Glad I didn't have to find you inside!" Paul panted, stopping a few steps shy of his father.

Richard walked the several steps down to his son, motioning to the bodyguards and security staff to remain behind. "What's up?"

Paul waited until his father was close, waited for an approving nod to indicate he could talk freely, then began speaking in a low voice. "Tadek came to the house. He's been awaiting Zosia's return from Switzerland. She was due back yesterday, but with the Führer's funeral on Sunday, and everything being shut down for two days, he thought she was just delayed. When she didn't come back this morning, he checked at the Kivuan embassy—"

"Why there?"

"She went to Switzerland under the ambassador's protection – as her aide and translator."

"To visit Peter?" Richard scowled at his sister's lack of professionalism. Indulging in a personal visit!

"Yes, she had some business she needed to conduct with him. The ambassador left a message that her aide had been arrested at the border and that she was staying with her to make sure she remained safe."

"Oh God, that's all I need right now. Where is she?"

"They took her to Bregenz."

"Do we know anything else?"

Paul explained everything he knew about the mission that Tadek had relayed to them, but said that they had no further information on what had happened at the border, other than Arieka's message to her embassy. "Mother thought Tadek should go back and get a rescue team organized, but since Bregenz is so far outside our area of operations, that's going to take some time."

"It'd be likely to fail as well." Richard glanced back up the steps to make sure no-one was close. "Okay, here's what you need to do. Cancel any rescue team. We'll use your mother's sister Sofia – Zosia knows enough about her to play along and the coincident name is helpful. Have HQ take Sofia into hiding and amend any government documents on her to fit Zosia. It doesn't have to be perfect, just whatever they can do quickly and quietly. Your mother can handle that. I want you to go straight to my office and have them issue an order to have their prisoner sent up to Berlin.

I'm going to say she's my agent – there's precedent for that since Stefi introduced Dorota and Feliks to the menagerie."

"But Dad, they almost certainly picked her up because of her visit to Peter. They must suspect a personal relationship with him. Maybe they even guessed she's his wife. How are you going to handle that?"

Richard smiled. "My boy, you have no idea what a wide network of agents I have! I've even managed to work one into the A.K.'s mountain encampment. It is, after all, Traugutt's area of operation. And one of the things my girl there did was to meet up with this Halifax fellow."

"Why did she go see him?"

"Good question." Richard stroked his chin thoughtfully. "This Kivuan woman, Frau Ruweni. I met her when we picked up the Führer. Have someone contact here – she's not under arrest is she?"

Paul shook his head. "No, they don't dare touch her, and I gather, Zosia's safe as long as Frau Ruweni refuses to leave."

"Okay, have someone contact her and tell her that one of my men – Tadek in fact, get him all the papers he'll need to fit this story – one of my men got in touch with her and asked her to take Zosia on as an aide. I knew that Frau Ruweni visits Halifax periodically and I wanted my girl to get in touch with him."

"Why?"

Richard scratched his head. With Rudi dead, what would be a good line to take? If Rudi were still alive he would have invented something to do with revenge, but now the game was different. Richard turned to look at the building where so much political debate was taking place. Restructuring. It was consistent with what he had been saying all along. And maybe this could even be a useful start...He turned back to Paul. "The ambassador agreed to the plan because I promised to try to help Halifax out of prison – she doesn't need to know my motives. My agent was told to sound out Halifax's views on non-violent change. She was told to establish a friendship with Halifax, building on their previous experience in the mountains. That's why she was less than restrained in her behavior and why whoever observed her thought she might be his wife. See if you can get any of that through to Zosia. And make sure the directive to have her sent to me includes the order that she *not* be questioned and that she be treated well. Understood?"

"Understood." Paul waited a second to see if there was anything more, then turned and headed back down the steps to the car. Richard sighed, then wearily climbed the steps back into Party headquarters. It was going to be a long, long day, but with luck the full congress would meet that evening and maybe, finally, come to some decision.

21

*N*aturally, the party afterwards was extremely crowded and everybody hovered around Josef Frauenfeld clinking their *Sekt* glasses against his mineral water, offering their congratulations, and putting in their bids for jobs. Richard stayed aloof, listening politely to someone who still thought he was worth knowing and sipping a whiskey which had been specially procured at his request. He planned to stay only long enough to make it obvious he was not completely crushed, but he had no interest in approaching Seppel to beg for his old job or indeed for anything else. How, he wondered, had it gone so horribly, horribly wrong? He could still feel that strangely calm panic that had slithered through his spine as he realized that the voices in the corridors were increasingly singing Frauenfeld's praises. His unquestionable loyalty to the Reich, his maturity and sturdiness. It went unsaid, but it was there as well: his lack of arrogance, his clean image, his morality and his long-lasting stable marriage.

Richard rubbed his brow, trying to wipe out the thoughts of where he had made his mistake. Too many possibilities, too many what-ifs. He would go insane if he let himself stew over this. But he had no choice, twenty-six years of playing this game, twenty-six years of plotting and conspiracies. The support from unseen hands, Stefi's efforts, his tireless maneuvering, all necessary just to get this far – but also, damaging. There were those who hated him, who would support anyone to keep him from being elected. And there were those who feared him – those who recognized too many convenient *incidences* in Traugutt's background. And beyond that, no one *knew* him. Traugutt had arisen out of thin air, with a paper-perfect background, but no real human connections. And it was, in the end, humans who had carried out the elections. Men who had worked with Frauenfeld, men who had felt he was funny and self-effacing and trustworthy. Men who had thought *this is someone we can keep under control*. Seppel had made promises that were believed, he had shaken hands and talked about old times, he used a nickname that was the epitome of boyish chumminess. Seppel scared no one, he had no opponents – not even among Traugutt's supporters. So, a tiny push away from Traugutt and Frauenfeld was the obvious compromise candidate – someone about whom everyone could breathe easily.

For all his self-effacing loyalty and bonhomie, Seppel had won the highest position in the Party and in the Reich. Seppel the pudgy as Führer. Seppel with his silly southern accent. Oh, better not make fun of that,

Hitler's idiotic accent was much worse. Richard took a swig of his drink and wondered idly what his chances of survival were. Not only politically but literally. Would Seppel dare take the chance of letting him bow out gracefully on the assumption that he would never again enter the fray? Seppel would have to be certifiable to do that.

Richard thought about retirement. He could walk up to Seppel right now, say congratulations once again and then explain that he would like to make the transition period easier for his dear Führer and was planning on resigning from the Party and retiring to Switzerland. Then he could simply disappear back into the mountains, leave Greta, live with his family. The Underground certainly owed him a place there, he could work intermittently on this and that, give advice and training to new infiltrators, but he would never again have to say, *mein Führer*. Oh, God, it would be so nice to just quit.

Finishing his drink, Richard nodded a few more times and began to take his leave when one of his companions tapped him on the shoulder. "I think the Führer is trying to get your attention."

Richard turned and saw Seppel smiling at him, pointing toward a private annex and gesturing with his head. Richard excused himself from his little group and made his way, sighing, to the door that Seppel had indicated. Seppel stopped at the door and politely asked for a moment of privacy and then he and Richard went into the room alone and Seppel closed the door behind them.

Richard stopped next to one of the armchairs but chose not to sit down. "Again, my congratulations, Sepp."

"Ah, it's not official yet. The coalition has to approve it." Seppel seated himself and indicated that Richard should do likewise.

Richard remained standing. "You know we will. You are, after all, the best man for the job."

"Maybe, maybe not. But I have been elected and I take my duties seriously. I will assume this responsibility and do my best for the Reich."

Richard nodded disinterestedly. He supposed now was as good a time as any for Seppel to break the news to him that he was no longer needed in Berlin.

Seppel set down his mineral water on the table next to his chair. "Now I know, in contested elections, such as this, that it is traditional for the new Führer to consolidate his power to make clear to all and sundry that he is the sole power in the city."

Richard pulled out a cigarette. "Do you want one?"

"You know I don't. And I'd prefer if you didn't have one."

Richard sighed and put it away. "So, do I at least get to keep Göringstadt or is it absolutely essential that I represent the Reich to outer Mongolia?"

Seppel smiled in recognition of the joke. "Richard, of course you can keep the Göringstadt region."

"But next year, some time, one of my children will be mysteriously abducted and released several days later, several hundred kilometers from home, only a bit worse for wear." Richard smiled bitterly at the incident which both he and Seppel remembered well enough from Rudi's early days. The targeted official had been slow in getting the hint and the next abduction had ended in murder.

"Richard, I assure you, your children are safe."

"So we're going the unfortunate auto accident route?" That was the Führer before Rudi.

"Richard, that isn't my style."

"Ach, then it must be I contract a terminal illness and disappear into a sanatorium." Sudden chronic illnesses were epidemic at the beginning of each new Führer's reign.

Seppel sighed with exasperation. "No! Nor is there going to be a sweeping anti-corruption drive! Look, I am not naïve, but I think it would be a waste to lose a man of your talents. And despite the advice of many other people, I would like you to stay in Berlin. I want you to take over your old position as internal security advisor – as well as keep your other duties."

Richard pulled his head back in surprise. "And in exchange?"

Seppel pointed to the other chair. "Please sit, Richard. You're making me nervous."

"What do you want, Sepp?"

"Please, Richard." Again Seppel motioned to the chair.

Richard finally sat, but he felt more uneasy than when he had been with Rudi in his worst mood. Seppel certainly had a reputation as a reasonable man, but he had not reached this level of power by being soft-hearted. What game was he playing?

"What I need from you, Richard, is..." Seppel gestured helplessly. "Well, I think it's clear to many people that you are less than elated at the outcome of this Party conference. If you were to stay in Berlin, you might naturally become a focus of any disgruntlement. And I can't have that, not as I am establishing myself. What I need from you is a show of loyalty."

"Loyalty? I'll swear the oath with everyone else tomorrow – my complete and undying loyalty to the Reich and to you personally as the embodiment of our great land and as our Führer."

"Yes, I know, but I need something more."

"Such as?" Richard suppressed a laugh as he remembered Americans wearing tee-shirts with their favorite sports team or whatever printed on it. He could wear such a shirt saying *Property of Josef Frauenfeld.*

"Well, I think you should refer to me as your Führer. Even in private gatherings. It would give the right signal to the others."

That you're a pompous arse? Richard only replied with a tight smile.

"Can you do that?"

"Even Rudi didn't insist upon such formality."

Seppel spread his hands. "Rudi had his own way, I have mine. It's not for me, it's showing respect for the office. You understand, don't you?"

"Of course. And you'll refer to me, even in private, as Colonel Traugutt?"

Seppel looked annoyed. "Richard, I think you're being deliberately problematic. Do you want to stay in Berlin or not?"

"Yes, *mein Führer.*" The answer had come out without Richard's even thinking about it. So much for dreams of retirement!

"Good. Secondly, I'd like you to conduct your personal life in a manner more befitting a high-level official."

Richard grit his teeth.

"You have a bit of a reputation with the ladies, you know. Now that you are married to Greta, we would hope you could remain loyal to your wife."

We? Richard wondered if Seppel had a tapeworm, or had he decided he was royalty?

"And there is entirely too much smoking and drinking. We must set a healthy example for our people. Like Hitler did."

Richard threw a glance at Hitler's portrait. "So we'll be giving up meat as well?"

Seppel grimaced. His love of sausage was famous. "There's no need to get carried away, Richard. Now, what I also need–"

"There's more?" Richard let a moment pass before he sarcastically added, "*Mein Führer.*"

"Yes, Richard. I know you'll be swearing the loyalty oath with everyone else, but I don't think that will be a strong enough signal to the others. I want you to take a special oath, alone, on stage in front of the entire Party congress. If they see that, then they'll know I have your loyalty since you are a man of honor who would never violate his word."

Richard laughed. "Sure, I'll dance on the table naked if that's what you want." He paused again, before adding with a hiss, "*Mein Führer.*"

"Oh, Richard, perhaps I've made a mistake, I didn't expect this level of resentment–"

Richard stood. He had no idea what his strategy was, he simply let his anger and frustration have free rein. "Don't give me that shit, Sepp! You won this election by a hair and you want to make sure you have a firm grip on my leash. Fine! I'll serve the Reich and the wishes of the Party as a loyal Nazi, but goddamn it, let's skip the farce. You're the Führer and I will give you the respect due your office. If you want proof of that shown to the membership, I'll give it to them. But please, enough of the pious crap. You're a politician and you know exactly what you're doing." Richard pointed angrily toward the door, indicating the crowd behind it. "You know they elected *you* because they think they can control you! You know they *will* control you! You want me in Berlin because you need help and you don't know who to turn to. I'll give you that help, but I can't work through a smokescreen. At least in private, we'll need to be honest with each other. Otherwise I will be useless to you and you may as well go ahead and organize my demise."

Seppel's eyes widened, but then he breathed heavily and leaned back in his chair. "Okay. You're right. I need help. Will you give it to me?"

Richard nodded. "For the sake of my country and the people I serve." Then, because he knew he'd have to get used to it, he added, without sarcasm, "*Mein Führer.*"

22

Zosia was shown into Richard's office the evening of the following day, her hands bound by handcuffs, her eyes kept low. Arieka came in with her looking tired and disheveled but defiant. Richard ground out his cigarette and stood to greet Arieka, bowing and kissing her hand. He indicated to the guard that Zosia should be shown to a seat and that her handcuffs should be removed and then Richard dismissed the guard from the room.

He turned back to Arieka and spoke English, "Frau Ruweni, welcome back to Berlin. I am most sorry your trip has been so unnecessarily eventful. Please, accept the Reich's apologies."

Arieka nodded.

"I heard you slept in the reception of the prison?"

Again Arieka nodded.

Richard smiled kindly. "Please, be assured that your aide is safe in my care. No harm will come to her. You can return to your embassy now."

Arieka drew herself up to her full height. "Colonel Traugutt, I may be tired, but I will not leave while my aide is in your custody."

Richard's smile grew even gentler. "Frau Ruweni. She is a Reich citizen in Reich custody. You are a guest in our country and though we are honored by your presence, we have no obligation to you with respect to our own subjects. We have thus far allowed you to remain with your girl so that you could feel reassured–"

"And because you knew I'd raise an international stink about this if you hadn't!"

Richard nodded. "And doubtless you will, even now, if I eject you from the premises. I am aware that with your fame in America, you have more than the usual clout and can make things unnecessarily difficult for us and I have no desire to rouse you to action. But I would like to speak with your aide in private. I will leave the room and let you have a word with her. I think you will see she is safe here."

Without waiting for Arieka's reply Richard left, closing the door behind him. Arieka went over to Zosia and stooped down so that she could whisper in Zosia's ear. Before she said anything though, Zosia turned to her and whispered, "It's okay. I don't know what Traugutt is up to, but he used a codeword in there. My people must be in contact with him. Doubtless they've worked some sort of deal. I'll be okay. Thank you for your protection."

"Are you sure?" Arieka glanced around the room wondering what would happen to Zosia after she left. It looked like a normal office. No rubber truncheons, no cattle prods…

Zosia nodded. "It's best you go. Thank you. Thank you for everything. And I'm really sorry I screwed up like that. I can't believe I was so unprofessional. I hope it doesn't affect your career here."

Arieka waved her hand in dismissal of such a silly idea. "You love each other." She kissed Zosia's cheek. "Take care. Come back to the office, if you can, so I know you're okay."

"I'll at least have a message sent."

Arieka nodded, kissed Zosia again and then opened the door to the secretary's annex. No one was there. Traugutt stood outside the annex, in the outer office, leaning against the wall. The only other person around was the guard who had brought Zosia in, and he waited even further down the hall. When Arieka told Traugutt she was ready to leave, he directed the guard to escort her from the building and she felt reassured as she saw Traugutt return to his office completely alone.

Ryszard felt sorry for Zosia, so much so that he decided to spare her the humiliation she deserved. She would get enough of it back at Szaflary. Besides, he had had enough humiliation for one day. It was only a few hours ago he had sworn his specific allegiance to Seppel, alone, in front of everyone. Afterwards, at the reception he had organized in honor of the new Führer, Ryszard had used Frauenfeld's new title frequently and exclusively, and the others had followed suit. Ryszard had refrained from smoking and had drunk only mineral water, and most of the others had as well. The only thing Ryszard hadn't done was take off his clothes and dance naked on the table, but only because Frauenfeld hadn't asked that of him.

He sat at his desk, facing Zosia. "So, our little Zosienka is in love."

She looked up and around at the walls questioningly.

"I had Stefan clean it out after Rudi died. It's been guarded ever since. But anyway, I'm too powerful for anyone to violate my privacy. It's *my* office that listens in on *other* people."

Zosia nodded, apparently unconvinced.

"Little sister, if you had wanted to be cautious, you should have conducted yourself professionally in the prison."

Zosia dropped her head into her hand. "Peter even tried to warn me," she groaned softly. "He said I was too expressive, and all I could think of was why was he acting so cold!"

As tempting as it was, Ryszard decided not to harass Zosia. She was, after all, one of the few who had never been judgmental about his actions or passions. "Never mind, I can use your presence here. Do you want a cigarette?"

Zosia looked up and shook her head. She looked curious, but did not ask anything.

Ryszard lit himself a cigarette before explaining. "I've given you Kasia's sister's identity – that's how I know you."

"Kasia's sister? Sofia?"

Ryszard nodded.

"That's convenient."

"You're like Dorota, been working underground for me, infiltrating. My stroke of brilliance was to use a woman so you were not as suspicious as a Nazi agent and therefore you've even worked your way into Szaflary."

Zosia drew herself up. "I'm going overt?"

"Yes. You've managed some minor position in Szaflary, have learned that the deterrents they talk about are for real, and therefore that's one of the reasons I am so against an invasion of that region. I kept your presence a secret during Rudi's rule because he was less than stable about certain issues and I didn't want to upset the balance."

Zosia laughed. "Less than stable. That's a good way of putting it."

"I requested you organize a position with Frau Ruweni so that you could go see Peter Halifax in prison. Frau Ruweni was convinced to help because you told her that you had a message from Halifax's wife. Tadek will convey that information to her eventually. I guess he didn't get a chance to do that yet, but luckily no one's interested in your case. There's too much going on with Frauenfeld's election."

"Yes, I heard. Sorry about that."

"Pff. Next time." Ryszard gave Zosia a sly glance. "And you know, with Stefi unable to form the same sort of liaison with this one, I might need your services eventually. So, you're being overt will help in that respect."

The color had returned to Zosia's face. "I look forward to being of service."

"Good. At this point, though, you need to return to Szaflary. I'm going to release you – it will be generally known among the top here that you're my agent, but the official reason will be lack of evidence with the implication that Arieka's threat of international pressure played a role."

Zosia nodded her understanding. "Why was I sent to visit Halifax in the first place?"

"You were told to sound him out about his views on non-violent change."

"Is that what you are going to say to the Führer?"

"That's none of your business. Just do as you're told." Ryszard paused, then added, "Remember, I have your solemn oath of obedience and I expect you to keep your promise."

Zosia noticed that Ryszard had pressed his fingertips together in the classic gesture of impatient power. Whether Ryszard was right or not, she had to admit, he held the strings and she would dance accordingly. "Okay, whatever you say. What's my role?"

"First, finish your mission. Did the police seize anything you need?"

Zosia shook her head. "I had some notes, but Arieka was carrying them, so I'll just go to her embassy and pick them up. Once I get back, I should be able to communicate with Peter regularly. He convinced the prison governor to give him access to their computer systems, and he gave me instructions on how to open a window in the security on Szaflary's computer."

"Good." Ryszard seemed bored by such technical details. "I also want you to get the message through to HQ that I need more people here. They shouldn't know who I am, but get their resumes onto Stefan's desk so he can hire them in. I need to have people I can call on at a moment's notice. At least fifteen, twenty would be better. I'll have Stefan pass on the appropriate positions they can apply for and the backgrounds they'll need."

"Ryszard, I think–"

"Don't think. Just go pound on a few desks. If that doesn't work, use threats. Tell them I know where the deterrents are in Berlin, and I'll have them defused. Or tell them that I have the names and addresses of every major figure in Göringstadt and I'll hand the list to the Gestapo if they don't

593

co-operate. Whatever. I'm fed up with being undersupported while I fight for them."

"*Are* you fighting for us? Or are you just consolidating your own power?"

That caught Ryszard by surprise and he looked at Zosia as though she were a cockroach he had discovered unexpectedly in his food. Zosia thought for a moment he would have her dragged down to the cells for half an hour or so just to teach her a lesson, but then his expression softened. "Ah, little sister, if you had any idea what my life is like, you wouldn't say such stupid things."

"I'll get you those people," Zosia promised timidly.

"Tell Mother she's to move permanently to Berlin. I need the family background again. It would be helpful to extend my family connections, maybe some relatives for Olek as well. Whoever they can find loyal enough to have all the necessary details."

Zosia nodded.

"Once you do that, organize a firm legend as Kasia's sister and a life for yourself here – bring the children and a husband – Tadek, I suppose. You'll be in for the long haul."

"How so?"

"I'm going to convince Seppel that we need a special ministry for women's affairs and I'll want you to head it."

"What? Me? A woman? Have you lost your mind? No-one will ever agree to that."

"I think they will. I've had Olek and Stefan doing some canvassing for me, and the women of the Reich are ready for a few more rights. We've put them in work anytime that's been convenient, and we need loyal skilled labor now. They'll be a liberalizing influence on the society."

Zosia shook her head in disbelief.

"Again, this is not without precedent. Lots of so-called traditional societies manage to put a woman in power. It will be a positive signal to the NAU. And anyway, the woman's ministry will be viewed as toothless and unimportant."

"Thanks."

Ryszard shrugged. "What matters is that you'll be able to attend cabinet meetings and therefore can influence other issues as well. Sooner or later, I'll get a majority stacked in my favor, then I can pretty much run the show."

Zosia nodded thoughtfully. Rather than overthrow the government, simply usurp it. Though Ryszard had been preaching the idea all along, she had never expected him to work it in this manner. A ministry to herself, how very odd! "I always thought you were going to wait until you were Führer to make the big changes. Do you really think you can do all this?"

Ryszard sighed heavily. "I might never get to be Führer, so I've decided to start now, while Seppel still wants my advice. And as to whether or not it's all possible? Who knows, I can only try."

"Ryszard, what if you're discovered? With each new person you bring in, you're raising the possibility of eventual betrayal."

"I know. It's probably inevitable. I'm hoping that by the time that happens, it will be irrelevant. It will be so obvious that I am a loyal son of the Reich, even if my origins are from within the armed opposition..."

Zosia laughed. "You've lost your mind! We were *born* into the resistance! Even without that against us, we have an aristocratic Polish mother and our father's father was Jewish – have you lost track of what this ideology said was supposed to happen to us? That is, assuming we were even born?"

"Quarter Jews served in the Wehrmacht throughout the war, and Poles could become *Volksdeutsch* with only a bit of bureaucratic manipulation. Anyway, although the nastiest of Hitler's policies were tolerated by the populace, it's never been clear to me that they were whole-heartedly supported."

"No, just ignored." Zosia rolled her eyes in exasperation. "For heaven's sake, that is their way of accepting the unacceptable!"

"That's all in the past."

"Then look around at what's going on *today*! Ryszard, as a non-German, you'll never be accepted!"

"Well, we'll try out the premise on you."

"Me?" Zosia squeaked.

"As Kasia's sister, you will have only the most tenuous connections to claiming *Volksdeutsch* status. We'll have you do that before you head up your ministry, but it will be clear to all and sundry that your roots are in a minority group. We can offer up your presence in the government as proof of our inclusion of oppressed minorities."

"I don't want to be an oppressed minority!" Zosia wailed. "Isn't it enough I'll be the only woman? No one will listen to a word I have to say."

"You don't have to say much, you'll just need to agree with me."

"Great."

"Besides, even though Seppel probably won't take on any mistresses, you can be sure that he'll still be amenable to a smile now and then from his prettiest cabinet member."

Zosia groaned. "Oh for Christ's sakes, that's not fair! Why should I have to flutter my eyelashes at him?"

"Because you're a woman in a man's world," Ryszard snarled, "and if you want to succeed you'll use every goddamn weapon at your disposal! Grow up, Zosia. We all have to sometime." He stopped and breathed deeply to calm himself, but it didn't work. Ryszard flung his hand in the direction of the door. "What the hell do you think I was just doing if not the equivalent of fluttering my eyelashes! On stage, in front of thousands of Party members, swearing my sincere loyalty to that pudgy clown and the diktats of that idiot!" He finished by pointing at the portrait of Hitler on the wall.

Zosia looked up at the picture of Hitler. "Oh, dear." She shook her head as she contemplated their incredibly evil founding father. "Ryszard, it's hopeless. This empire is based on *his* ideas. We can't just go and turn it all around. It will never work..."

"Nonsense! Look at the reforms the Soviet Union has managed to undertake recently. If you believe what they're saying, everything is changing there–"

"I think it is. Tadek and I were there not long ago."

Ryszard pounded his desk angrily. "See! And with NAU support. Yet on the body count they beat us by *millions*!"

Zosia noted Ryszard's use of the word "us", but did not comment.

"Change is not impossible, we just need support for our reforms, instead of this blind opposition that we always face."

Zosia pursed her lips. "Perhaps the Reich's *current* human rights record–"

"There are plenty of places that have ongoing use of prison slave labor, torture and secret executions but then manage to be favored trading partners with the NAU whereas *we* are pilloried for our human rights record."

Zosia nodded as she thought about what she knew of other governments in the world. She had gathered most of the information while in the NAU, so there was no doubt it was accessible to Americans, yet somehow the standard for acceptable behavior varied radically. It defied logic that regimes which denied all civil rights – even the right to be seen – to half their populations, which suppressed ethnic minorities, which indulged in torture, maiming and public executions could be well-supported NAU allies, yet that was exactly the world situation. "It's not rational," Zosia muttered, mostly to herself.

"The world isn't rational, but what we need to do is turn that to our advantage for once. We need to reform this country from within. It will be a lot less bloody that way. We need to get the NAU's support for our reforms and for that, we need to make a show of reforming on our own."

Zosia had a sudden inspiration and her eyes lit up with hope. "What about Peter?"

"What about him?"

"How about getting him released? You can convince Frauenfeld to use him as proof of your efforts to help oppressed minorities."

Ryszard frowned.

"You could convince Frauenfeld to let you introduce some new laws that will finally grant rights to the *Zwangsarbeiter* and eventually phase them out altogether and for that you'll need a new department to handle the transition. Peter would be perfect to head the department and he would add a voice to your chorus."

"We're not exactly at the point of inviting the opposition into government."

"But that's the beauty of it! Peter's a free agent. None of the Undergrounds claim him. He's not a part of the opposition, yet he has a following in the NAU and could easily establish a reputation here as an honorable man, someone the lower orders will listen to and respect. And if he throws his lot in with peaceful transition, then doubtless others will as well."

Ryszard shook his head. "I've thought a bit about something like that Zosia, but–"

"There's plenty of precedent! Worldwide there are any number of former freedom fighters, and even terrorists, who are now respected world leaders. In fact, for new countries, it seems to be almost requisite."

"Zosia, think about it. He's been convicted of the murder of a Reich citizen. A Party member." Ryszard leaned forward and folded his hands together in the manner of a patient schoolteacher. "Seppel's not the sort to let that pass unremarked. My excuse for your visiting Peter will be that you, as my agent, were trying to convince him to speak for non-violent change from within prison. But there's no hope of us getting him out."

Zosia wilted visibly. She licked her lips and looked around the room helplessly. "But if you suggest him as a spokesman for the *Zwangsarbeiter*, then we can mount a campaign to get him released."

"Peter is not going to be invited into government, not as long as Frauenfeld is running things."

Zosia stopped looking around the room and turned her eyes upon Ryszard. He could see the glint of tears in them. "Then not in government. But surely with Rudi dead, we can organize his release. Can't we?"

Ryszard smiled sadly. "It wouldn't be proper." At Zosia's horrified look, he added, "That's not my opinion, it's just what I would hear."

"But Ryszard…"

"If I ever get power, then we can think about it. But Zosia, keep in mind that politically I've only just barely survived this transition. Seppel is showing an unprecedented magnanimity by letting me stay in Berlin and so close to the top. He knows I'm a danger to him and he's not stupid. He's going to keep his eye on me and any changes I suggest are going to have to be natural and to the obvious benefit of the Reich. I'm in no position to help Peter."

"He did it for you," Zosia whispered almost inaudibly, then finding her courage, she asserted, "You can't leave him rotting in prison!"

Ryszard's voice hardened. "He knew the rules of the game when he signed on – prison is always a risk the opposition faces, you know that! He isn't the first person who will spend years of his life behind bars because he annoyed the powers-that-be. Tell your husband to make himself comfortable – he's going to be there for a while yet."

"Ryszard, we've always arranged better for *our* people."

Ryszard closed his eyes as if in pain and breathed heavily. He looked unnaturally pale.

"Ryszard? Are you alright?"

He shook his head and then rested his face in his hands. "Nothing has gone right this year and I have no idea what I'm doing now or where it's going to end. I'm exhausted." He opened his eyes to smile wanly at Zosia. "I'm sorry I can't help you. And I'm sorry I can't repay Peter for all he's done for me. I *am* sorry, Zosia, but that's just the way it is."

Zosia was so worried by Ryszard's pallor that she almost missed the incredible fact that he had expressed regret. Eventually, she managed to stutter, "It's okay, Ryszard. He knows you're grateful." She brightened as she remembered Peter's plan for Leszek. "There is a way to repay him – it won't be hard, and he will appreciate it."

Ryszard nodded, obviously uninterested. "Fine, tell me about it tomorrow. It's time you go now. I'll have one of the guards get your papers for you and escort you out of the building. Come back tomorrow at eleven – you'll have an appointment. We can discuss things further then." He stood and Zosia recognized a transformation that meant he was changing his persona.

So that was it. "You know," Zosia muttered, "this isn't a very satisfactory outcome from the Führer's demise. I thought it'd be better."

Ryszard looked down at her contemptuously. "Alright. A fairy appears and sprinkles magic dust, the Reich collapses, democracy is established, and we all go off to live happily ever after." He tilted his head at her as if seriously considering the likelihood of that happening. "In fact, why don't we have Joanna and Andrzej and Adam – oh yeah and Julia too – they can all return from the dead. Hey, what the hell, let's–"

"Ryszard, please. You know that's not what I meant. It's just that I don't feel we're any closer to our goals. It's like we're going in circles!"

"At least we're still going."

Zosia sighed. "I thought somehow things would work out once Rudi was gone. Oh, it's so depressing – the prospect of Peter spending years in prison, and you still have to work through someone. I thought things would be more positive."

Ryszard smiled down at Zosia, one of those big brother smiles he used to give her when she was much younger. "It's up to us to make them positive. Consider this: Peter is safe and alive – did you expect that when he was captured by the Führer? He's not being regularly tortured or beaten – I'm sure *he* appreciates that subtlety. And you truly love each other – that's a wonderful and rare thing in this world. Plus your children are healthy and safe – they're not going to suffer Joanna's fate. Indeed, even though he's less than perfect, the Reich now has a Führer who isn't a sadist – that's a real plus. Günter's been declawed – the Reich's been spared the pain of another psychopath, a more dangerous one, in power. I'm still in this office – all the rules of politics would have said I should have been removed the day after Frauenfeld took power. And Stefi is free – you have no idea what she went through."

"I can imagine," Zosia assured him quietly.

"If our expectations are too high, we'll always be disappointed. Life isn't like one of the Reich's propaganda posters."

"Or a Hollywood film," Zosia added with a laugh.

"Indeed, it just goes on. And luckily for us, we're here to go on with it. As long as we're alive Zosia, we have a hope of making a difference."

"Jeszcze Polska nie zginęła, Póki My żyjemy?" Zosia asked, quoting the first lines of their national anthem.

"Indeed, *while still we live.* Isn't that enough?"

"It'll have to be." She stood up. "Thank you, Ryszard. I didn't know you were such a philosopher."

"Neither did I, but necessity is the mother of invention."

"I can still hope for the fairy with magic dust, can't I?"

Ryszard smiled indulgently. "Sure, but meanwhile I'll expect perfect obedience from my little sister and her husband – when you finally establish that connection with him."

"I made a promise, but what makes you think Peter will obey you?"

Ryszard's smile broadened into a grin. "I extracted a promise from him as well. And I'm going to collect."

Zosia grunted, "God, I had no idea we both made a deal with the devil."

"Not the devil, Zosienka, just your big brother. Come on, I'll escort you to the guard."

23

*P*eter heard the normal sounds of morning and opened his eyes to look up at the concrete slab ceiling and the single bulb centered in it. The sensation of closeness, of air too thick to breathe crept through him and he pointedly turned his thoughts away from the walls around him. He had been dreaming of when he had been at the Reusch's, how he would rise early in the morning and raise the shutters of the shop as quickly as possible to get rid of the horrendous gloom they caused. Now there was nothing to be done about the gloom – the window was thick, small and secure.

Well, at least there was one.

He heard the electronic bolt being thrown on his cell and shortly thereafter a guard turning the key and opening the manual lock. Peter tilted his head and looked at the heavy metal of his door and the face he could see through the grate.

"Running a bit late?" the guard asked jovially as he pushed the door open.

Peter swung out of bed, greeted the guard by name and replied with the usual banter. With this one, he talked about cars. It struck Peter as odd that a twenty-something prison guard could afford to own a car – even a lousy one that was always breaking down – but he didn't say that. A good many of the guards were decent blokes, and he did what he could to maintain friendly relations with them. Some of them were even quite sympathetic to his cause, one guard going so far as to suggest that Peter should have killed "that cow" as well, then he would have never been caught.

There were, naturally enough, others – those who were offended by his crime and they were accordingly less friendly. With them Peter maintained a formality that showed his respect for their position as his keepers and also evinced some level of contrition for his crimes. Among the guards there were also the obvious Nazi sympathizers, those who felt that Switzerland, too, belonged *Heim ins Reich*. Some of these were fairly dangerous and, as far as possible, Peter avoided being alone with any of them.

Peter made his way to the mess for breakfast. It wasn't too bad – the food tended to be heavy and greasy, but there was no lack of it, and wherever he sat, he always had company. Even if he selected an empty table, somebody would sit down near him and begin conversing. It was in stark contrast to his days in school, where he had been so shunned that even if someone was forced to sit next to him due to the crowding, they still managed to pretend he wasn't there. In response, Peter had learned to ignore everyone and everything in such situations, and he had to fight quite hard against that tendency to remember to answer the questions and comments directed at him as he shoved down mouthfuls of greasily fried eggs.

After he had breakfasted, Peter requested permission to go to work and though the man behind the desk was a devout Christian and frowned at the thought of anyone voluntarily working on a Sunday, Peter was granted the necessary chit to pass from one section of the prison to another. He turned that in at the door to the library, showed another pass to have the office unlocked for him, and sat down at the terminal he had confiscated for his personal use.

Waiting next to it, just as he had hoped, was coiled the cable he had organized and as he inspected it, he smiled with pleasure. It would be perfect. He turned everything on and tapped at his keyboard for a quarter of an hour, solving a minor technical problem, as he waited for the guard who sat outside the office door to relax again. The guard found the girlie magazines which had been stacked near his usual seat and picked one up. When Peter saw that, he quit working at the keyboard and climbed under the desk with the cable.

He plugged one end into the computer into a circuit board he had previously installed, and then shoved the other end into a hole he had cut into the carpet. He worked the cable under the carpet toward the wall and then along the wall. It was tedious work and he glanced up regularly to see if the guard was taking much notice of him, but the guard was wrapped up in his magazine.

The cable snaked invisibly around the room up to where the telephone junction box was located. Peter pulled it through the edge of the carpet and ran it up the wall to the box, wrapping it into the other cables so that it would be less obvious. He got up, went to the secretary's desk and removed the screwdriver he had secreted there and used that to open the box. When he had wired up the cable, he closed the box and put the screwdriver back.

He heaved a sigh of satisfaction at his work. There were now remote devices that would do exactly what he had done without the need for a cable but they were very expensive and he had already pawned everything he owned to purchase the card, cable, magazines and tools. It had probably been an unnecessary precaution, he could have gotten most of it directly through the governor's office, but if someone other than the director read the list, Peter had wanted to be sure that he had left no trace of his intentions. Once he was in communication with Szaflary, it would be much easier – he could request they smuggle in the little extras he would need to do his work.

Peter spent the next several hours sitting at the computer, configuring the system and hiding his work as well as he could. A clever and knowledgeable systems administrator would doubtless be able to find what he had done – that was unavoidable given the constraints. Fortunately, though, the prison budget did not extend to having its own administrator and Peter had ascertained that the bureaucrat who intermittently visited was not particularly thorough.

"What is all that stuff?"

The guard's voice made Peter visibly jump. "Damn, don't creep up on people like that! You scared the shit out of me!"

"Sorry. But what are you doing?" There was nothing more than simple curiosity involved.

"I'm trying to organize the library system so that archived material can be accessed along with shelved books. That way, you won't have to do separate searches to find if something is here."

"Oh." The guard wandered away, repeating the word *archived* as if savoring it.

Peter turned his attention back to the keyboard, but his fingers remained still. His heart was pounding. For reasons that were completely unclear to him, he felt more fear at being found out here than when he had been hacking around government offices with Allison back in London. Then he had everything to lose: his freedom, his love, his life – now, there was so little they could do. Doubtless his punishment would involve his being denied simple privileges and he would be obliged to spend many more hours locked in his cell, but that was as nothing compared to what he had already experienced. So why, he wondered, was he so afraid? He rubbed his forehead, trying to calm himself, but he could feel the room closing in on him. Stop it, he yelled to himself, this is pathetic!

It didn't stop and to cut out the image of the walls moving inward, he squeezed his eyes shut. The darkness was even worse, like in that crate, where the air had been so foul with his own breath...He opened his eyes and stared downward, shielding his view of the wall with his hands. If only he could just get up and leave. Just ten minutes outside the gates, his view of the mountains unobscured by fences or bars or barbed wire. Just ten minutes...

One of Joanna's prayers came to mind and he repeated it to himself. The words were meaningless to him – he did not believe in angels or virgin births or any of it, but it *had* meant something to Joanna and the image of her face as she had solemnly recited her prayers, kneeling at her bedside – that *did* mean something to him. She would have told him that no prison could hold him, that his spirit was free. She would have told him that his life was not being lost in meaningless confinement – that he had eternal life. When she was alive, he would have smiled fondly at her and not wishing to hurt her feelings, would have remained silent. Now, he sent her a mental thank-you. He could not find it within himself to take comfort in his own beliefs, but he could find refuge in hers, and in so doing, his heart calmed and the walls grew steady and he was able to return to his work.

He finished setting up the connection and then began searching for the window that Zosia should have created. He couldn't find anything and he started changing parameters, hoping that maybe it was just a small error in the protocol. Still nothing. In some ways, he wasn't surprised, though he was dismayed, in that strange way his work had of bringing him down. It was a peculiarity of his work that it was possible to go backwards – that an error could compound itself as it was being tracked and that hours, days, even weeks could be sacrificed just to get back to the state things had been in before it all went wrong. He rubbed his forehead and prayed that he wasn't on that backward-running treadmill before he started his checks.

First, the hardware. He sought out and found other connections, into the NAU, and that reassured him that the cable and circuitry were sound. Then he went through his programming, checking line by line. He found two small errors that should not have made a difference. He corrected them and tried again. Still no luck. Had he forgotten something? The machine was not what he was used to, was there something buried deep inside its bowels that was screwing everything up? What about the telecommunications junctions? Had the security services changed things? Had he messed up on what he had told Zosia? Did he leave something out? Had she even gotten back yet?

His mind worked through various schedules. She had visited on a Friday, the Führer was announced dead on Saturday and Reich transit had been shut down through Monday. So, she might not have left for Berlin until Tuesday, even Wednesday. He counted on his fingers, four days. She should have been able to reach Szaflary and make the changes. Had she stayed in Berlin to take care of some business? But she had implied she was in a hurry to return to Szaflary. Had something happened? Had she been arrested? It had broken his heart to have to keep his attention on Arieka, only watching Zosia through the corner of his eyes and in his mind he could still see the way she had gestured, leaning toward him, her hands flapping in circles as she described Krys's antics, a broad smile on her face. Had somebody else observed the odd familiarity of Arieka's aide and sold the information? He felt suddenly very ill as an image of Zosia in the hands of the Gestapo flashed through his mind. *Please, no!*

Peter stood and paced uneasily. Was there any way he could find out? It would not be in any newspaper, nobody could contact him with the news. Police files? Would an arrest be entered so quickly? He sat back at the computer and began a frenzied search. After three hours had passed he accepted that it was worthless. There were ten different places she could have crossed the border – assuming that she had gone straight back into the Reich – and each had three or so nearby towns and a city or two that might have handled her, she might be held by the border police, the local police, inland security, the Gestapo, or even the criminal police, and he didn't even know what name she had been using.

He looked up at the clock. He had worked through lunch and it was already time for dinner. Soon, he'd have to report back to his cell. He sighed, shut down the machine and found the guard so that he could check out of the library, sign his timesheet, and go get something to eat before it was too late.

On Monday there was still no sign of Zosia. Against his better judgment, Peter decided to distract himself from his fears by searching through American news reports to see if there was any reference to his case. Not a word – he had vanished without a trace with the end of his trial.

He welcomed the anonymity. Genuine criticism had always been hard enough for him to accept – and that was one reason he had preferred to work alone most of his life, even giving credit to others for his ideas and effort, simply so that he could avoid unwanted feedback – but what he had experienced during and immediately after the trial had been so much worse! The virulent opinions of morons! The nonsense about his motives, his psyche, his past – all given out as indisputable fact. It went against the precision of his training and had irritated the hell out of him, and he had found himself envying Alex's wonderfully irrational thought processes and marvelously thick skin. Now, at last, he could read the news without wincing. The worst was over and there was only a blessed silence.

By Tuesday, he found the window, exactly along the path he had expected, and he groaned aloud with relief. As soon as he could, he sent Zosia a message and the reply came within an hour. Together they established two levels of communication – one for personal messages and another, secure route, for business. If his illegal connections within the prison were discovered, Peter would point to the personal messages as proof that his actions, though not strictly permitted, were harmless. He was simply a husband and father who wanted to communicate with his family and if he had bent a few prison rules to do so, that would be understandable.

Zosia told him of her arrest, adding that once she had spoken to some official in Berlin, she was released due to lack of evidence. Peter recognized Ryszard's hand and did not ask more, even via a secure communication. There was, he felt, no point in tempting fate.

In the middle of his endeavors, Peter was called away by the prison governor. He followed the guard to the administration offices and, after an appropriate amount of time waiting, he was shown in to the director's office.

The director did not waste time on the usual pleasantries. He shoved a heavy envelope across his desk at Peter. "This was handed to my office last week with the request to pass it on to you."

Peter saw that the envelope had been opened and so he removed the contents. There was a macrodisk and a thick sheaf of pages. He flipped through the pages, wondering why the director had waited so long to hand it on to him, but not daring to ask.

The director politely waited a few seconds, then asked, "What is it? Why was this given to you?" There was the hint of an accusation.

"You remember, sir, I said that I would improve communications between this prison and other government offices?"

"Yes, what about it?"

"This is the system code for those offices. With it, I can make our system compatible with theirs and reduce the number of communication corruptions."

The director shook his head in confusion. "But there isn't a single word in that! It's just letters and numbers and symbols."

Indeed, lots of *different* letters and numbers and symbols, rather than the accursed 0's and 1's he had expected. How very odd. "Yes, sir. It's computer code. Just a copy of what's on this disk, no doubt." Peter weighed up the wisdom of elaborating with invented technical details. In the end he decided it was wiser not to volunteer too much information.

The director stood and reaching across the desk, removed the file from Peter's hands. "Look, here." He paged through until he found what he was seeking. "Look, diagrams. What are those for?"

Good question, Peter thought, as he leaned over the desk to inspect the drawing. "The wiring of certain junction cards," he answered smoothly. "We probably won't need those, but I'll know after I study this a bit."

"Where'd you get this stuff? Is it secret? Are you breaking some law?"

Peter shook his head. "No, it's not secret, and no law has been broken, but you know, even public information is sometimes hard to acquire directly." He let the meaning of that sink in, then answered the director's first question. "A friend of mine knows somebody who works in a government office and acquired the information as a favor for *us*."

The director nodded, apparently not wishing to know more. He handed the files back to Peter. "And how is it going? I've noticed you've spent a lot of hours working at your terminal. You do know, you're being paid by the day, not the hour?"

"Yes, sir."

"Then why are you spending so much time working?"

Peter shrugged.

"You feel more at home with your machine than among people," the director suggested condescendingly.

Peter smiled shyly, then looked away, appropriately embarrassed by the director's keen insight. "Very perceptive, sir."

"Well, don't let me keep you from your work." The director waved Peter to the door.

Peter thanked him and left with the files, going directly back to the library and his computer. He responded to the confused questions Zosia had sent at his sudden absence and they continued their communication. Zosia's final message for the day was some decryption files which Peter had asked her to send. He only had time to complete the reception, hide the files and shut down before having to return to his cell for the night's lock-down. As the electronic bolt on his door shut with its familiar, nerve-wracking clang, he realized that in his excitement at contacting Zosia, he had missed dinner. He grabbed an apple and sat on the edge of his cot. Outside a spring rain was pounding down. His cell's thick window, though it muffled the noise somewhat, did not prevent an overall dampness in the room, nor did the apple do much to alleviate his hunger, but as he sat there chewing thoughtfully, he felt strangely sated, warm, and at peace.

24

*P*eter was still in a contented frame of mind when he approached the work he had set himself for the evening. He filled a bottle with water from his sink and put some music on. Even though it would be a few hours before silence was required, it was always better not to draw attention to oneself and so he set the volume quite low. Then he sat down at the small table which served as a desk, put on his reading glasses, and drew the documents out of their envelope. It was probably a waste of time, looking at coded documents without the use of a computer, but he had nothing but time to waste and he was curious about what Erich had passed on to Zosia. In particular, he thought he might be able to determine something about their content from the diagrams.

A cursory glance told him something that quite surprised him. The earliest mechanized codes had been based on the typical typewriter keyboard, and to a large extent had remained so. Because English keyboards had not contained umlauted letters or the β which were special to the German language, the English Underground had never added these characters to their substitution set. Since Erich's document contained a multitude of characters, but only those typical to an English language machine, Peter guessed it had been encoded using an English algorithm. And given that it was not binary, it was also probably old and therefore insecure. That struck him as extraordinary.

According to Zosia, Erich had said that he had been assured the end-user would be able to decode the document – so, that would be a reason for choosing an English code, but if Schindler had wanted to be sure the documents were read, why have them coded at all? A "Top Secret" stamp and a few dire warnings across the top would have been sufficient to indicate the documents had been stolen. Was the encryption just camouflage? Had they been encrypted only to hide their contents from Wolf-Dietrich, Erich and any other couriers involved? Were the documents something more than what had been advertised? If so, that might mean the end-user was himself involved in a conspiracy with Schindler. How very interesting.

Peter tried to reconstruct what Schindler's actions might have been. He's got a sheaf of documents that he wants the Real ERA to get their hands on, he needs to hide their contents from the couriers and perhaps a few others, but needs to know that the end-user will be able to read them. Communication with the end-user is either non-existent or minimal. So, he goes to his communications office and asks for an encryption that could be easily cracked. But what are the capabilities of the Real ERA? They are a small breakaway group, probably with minimal technical support. The security service suggests using one of the old English codes that were available to just about everyone for mundane communications. They have a machine from an appropriate time – just before the Real ERA broke away, back when many in the group were still in the proper English Underground. All they'd need to do was give the receiver a password and the rest would be trivial. Possibly, too, they would suggest translating the documents into English in order to help hide their origin if they were ever discovered.

That would explain why Zosia and Jurek had not been able to deal with the files – there was nothing in the office in Szaflary set up to deal with mundane interoffice communications between various branches of the English Underground. But if Peter was right about what Schindler had done, all he needed was the password and he could have Barbara feed it through one of her decrypters, or she could just send the algorithms and he could do it himself on the computer.

Peter put his hands behind his head and leaned back. His gaze fell naturally on the wall in front of him, but his focus was elsewhere. Where would the end-user get the password? Perhaps Schindler had given it to him directly or passed it on via another route. More importantly, Peter wondered, how could he get the password? If he hammered at the documents long enough, he could back it out using the structures that would naturally reveal themselves, but could he, he mused, do it faster and more intuitively? In his cell, while the light lasted, without a computer? Probably not. It'd be a waste of time to even try, but he smiled and reminded himself, that as long as he was locked in the cell, he had nothing but time to waste.

He paged through the files to find the diagrams and began to study them. Try as he might, he could not imagine how they could represent chemical structures. He tried to work out if they depicted the dispersion mechanisms – some device to quickly and lethally spread the chemicals through a subway system, but they didn't look like that either. In fact, the diagrams looked strangely familiar and he searched his memory, trying to work out what they reminded him of. As the rain beat reassuringly against the window, Peter lost himself completely in his work, immersed in a world where he could wander wherever his thoughts took him. A world where he was free.

25

*R*ichard felt unusually nervous. This was his first private meeting with the Führer since Seppel's election, and Richard had no idea how he was going to handle the man. The security at the *Residenz* was cursory – Seppel clearly did not suffer from Rudi's paranoia. Richard was even allowed to keep his sidearm, and as he walked the hallway to the Führer's private office, he wondered what other changes had been instituted. The décor was already in the process of being changed. Gone was the imperial court look and in its place light colors and nondescript art. The door to Rudi's old private apartments was open and as Richard passed by, he could see workmen inside, removing the heavy wood paneling and stripping the wallpaper. Frauenfeld would probably have the whole thing painted white and furnished with plastic chairs.

Richard reached the Führer's office and leaving his bodyguard in the annex, he went into the outer office alone. He greeted the secretary by snapping his heels, giving the Nazi Party salute and intoning *"Heil dem Führer."* She responded appropriately and with sufficient enthusiasm to warn Richard that it was a ritual that was not going to disappear quickly. He wondered if at some point they would all be saying "Heil Frauenfeld" but he doubted it. No one since Hitler had actually managed to get his name into the mythology and even if Frauenfeld insisted upon it, "Heil Frauenfeld" sounded too stupid to survive in colloquial speech.

"I'm here to see the Führer." Richard smiled at the secretary, but the gesture was wasted. She was a sour-looking and unattractive woman – doubtless one of Irmtraud's hand-selected staff. Clearly no temptation was going to be placed in Seppel's path and he would remain pious and proper throughout his tenure. The secretary buzzed the Führer and announced Richard's presence. Surprisingly, Richard was told he could go in immediately.

Not bothering with the usual too-busy-to-notice-you nonsense that most officials indulged in upon the entrance of a subordinate, Frauenfeld looked up immediately. "Richard, glad you could come!"

Richard bowed his head in a crisp acknowledgment of the Führer's greeting. "*Mein Führer*, I am always at your service."

Frauenfeld grinned, clearly pleased that Richard had maintained a respectful formality. "Come, have a seat. I'd like to discuss some policy changes with you and I need your opinion on reshuffling my cabinet and on who to appoint to some positions."

Richard approached Frauenfeld's desk, but remained standing. "*Mein Führer*, it must be an extremely stressful time, with all the changes necessary during this transition. I hope I can be of genuine help to you." Richard almost meant what he said – he knew Frauenfeld would feel momentarily overwhelmed. "You might wish to use this unique opportunity to get new blood into the executive, but scanning new resumes is an extremely time-consuming process, and with all the other pressing issues, you might not have time to take full advantage of this opportunity. Might I suggest, *mein Führer*, that I handle the first screenings of new appointments?"

Frauenfeld looked suspicious.

Richard smiled and seated himself. "With your final approval of all candidates, of course."

"What do you want to do?"

"I thought we might draw in people from the regional offices, new officers. There's a lot of old blood in Berlin and they all have their power bases. If we let the old boys gracefully retire on full pensions and appoint new, unfamiliar faces, then we can dismantle some of the old networks and cut down on corruption without having to go through the risk of purging the Party."

"You think corruption is that widespread?"

Richard wondered if Frauenfeld was only playing at being naïve. "I know it is. You only need to look into almost any major official's finances. It's strangling our economy."

Frauenfeld nodded thoughtfully. "And I suppose all this 'new blood' would be your old cronies from the Göringstadt office?"

609

Richard shook his head. "No, I would search throughout the Reich for competent officials. It would be a very time-consuming process, but I think it'd be worth the effort. Naturally, if you already know of some good people, it would be very useful to be given their names, but beyond that, it would be an open selection."

"Interesting, interesting." Frauenfeld suddenly remembered his manners and indicated the bottled water. "Would you like a glass?"

"Yes, please." What Richard really wanted was a cigarette, but that wasn't possible. He hadn't been in the office five minutes and already it was dominating his thoughts! That wouldn't do. He had to face it – if he wanted to be effective in Frauenfeld's presence, he would have to give up smoking altogether.

Frauenfeld got up and got a glass off the shelf and poured Richard some water. At Richard's surprised look, he explained, "I see no reason to keep servants standing around waiting to do little things I can manage well enough on my own."

Richard nodded, somewhat shocked. He looked around the office and noticed, for the first time, that they were alone. Not alone in the sense of no other important persons, genuinely alone! "Not even bodyguards?"

"They're outside. You're the only one in this office and you're not a risk to my life, are you Richard?"

Richard shook his head. "Of course not, *mein Führer*. Nevertheless I..." Richard was about to advise against such folly when Frauenfeld dealt with others, but then changed his mind. "I am honored by your trust."

"It's time some things changed here, Richard. Don't you agree?"

"Yes, *mein Führer*. I agree heartily."

The two men conferred for hours. Lunch was brought in and they continued their discussions as they ate. They reached agreement on the directions that should be passed on to a number of ministries and on the reorganization of several others. As the hours wore on, Richard began to congratulate himself on how easy it was going to be – Frauenfeld was nearly a fellow traveler, willingly adopting the policies which Richard would need to completely restructure the government and eventually overthrow the National Socialist's stranglehold on society. It was even possible that Richard would not need to become Führer. The possibility intrigued him, and with it, he felt a mixture of relief and disappointment. To be able to finally work on his real goals! To finally see some of his plans come to fruition – these were wonderful prospects. On the other hand, he had spent so long scheming for power, it was quite a letdown to think that he might never achieve more than the status of a loyal and hard-working lieutenant. His name would be known only for the few years that it was relevant and would be immediately forgotten with his departure from government. And would his accomplishments be equally ephemeral? That could be a problem.

"...one of the easier ministries to deal with."

Richard looked up in surprise. Frauenfeld had just dispensed with an entire department while he had been daydreaming! Richard did not waste another second on chiding himself. "*Mein Führer*, is this a conclusion of a long study, or just your impression?"

"Hmm? Oh, no, I haven't organized a study, but you must admit, the legal code is pretty well established. I see no need to mess with it."

Richard realized his fingers were twitching nervously with a desire to hold a cigarette. He forced himself to stop by balling his hand into a fist. "Perhaps, *mein Führer*, it'd be worth considering removing some of the capital crimes currently on the books."

"What? Like what?"

Like what? Something obvious, something undeniably unjust. "Well, for instance, it's still a capital offense to teach without explicit State approval. Certain languages and subjects are completely banned, and if a person is convicted of teaching these subjects or in that language, he or she may be executed."

"Every country controls its education system. It determines the thought-processes of the citizens and hence the future of the State."

"I realize that, *mein Führer*, but certainly you don't believe the death penalty is an appropriate response to such trivial violations of the law. It's a leftover from the forties, when we were actively at war with these people. It's no longer necessary."

"If it's no longer necessary, then that means it's no longer used and there is no reason to remove the crime from the books."

"I'm only suggesting that we lower the penalty, *mein Führer*, not that we decriminalize it." Adam, and the mangled mess that must have been left of his body, came into Richard's mind. He hurriedly suppressed the dangerous image of his friend and colleague, but the damage was done, he was trembling.

"Richard, are you alright? What's wrong with you?" Frauenfeld's questions were sharp, accusatory.

"Excuse me, *mein Führer*." Richard stood and walked over to the window, cursing himself. As he stared out, working to gain control, he explained, "I've just quit smoking and I'm afraid the physical effect is quite disturbing. Please forgive me."

"You've quit? High time, I say."

"Yes, *mein Führer*." Richard knew he should return to the desk, but he gave himself another few seconds by the window.

"What about the alcohol? Are you giving that up as well?"

Frauenfeld made it sound like Richard was regularly inebriated! "All in due time, *mein Führer*. I'm not as strong-willed as you." Richard threw a glance over his shoulder, accompanied by a flattering smile which quite nicely hid the venomous thoughts that swirled through his head. Frauenfeld's porky little body and his penchant for swallowing small sausages whole spoke well of his strong will!

Richard was spared Frauenfeld's response by Irmtraud's entrance into the room. She walked in unannounced and Richard could not hide the surprise on his face, but she didn't notice as she devoted her attention to greeting her husband and setting down a plate of *Lebkuchen*, which she announced were fresh from the kitchen, but not, she added regretfully, from her own hand. "I know it's not really the season," she added apologetically, turning her attention to Richard, "but Seppel loves them so much! Would you like one?"

Richard gave Irmtraud a slight bow, wondering as he did so, what he should call her. Since her husband insisted on a formal title, would she as well? *Frau Führer?* Or given her ability to manipulate her husband's actions, should it be *Meine Führerin?* Richard straightened and smiled, "Frau Frauenfeld, your presence alone is enough for me."

She beamed and came over to him, offering her hand. Richard bowed again and kissed it.

"So, Richard, how are you doing?"

"He's given up smoking, dear," Frauenfeld interjected, spewing a few cookie crumbs as he spoke.

"You have! Goodness! I'm sure your wife will be pleased."

"I don't think Greta minds my smoking."

"Oh!" Irmtraud covered her mouth with her hand in a gesture of embarrassment. "I'm sorry, I had forgotten! I meant...Well, never mind, it's good you're doing it. Following Seppel's healthy lead?"

Richard looked at Frauenfeld as he shoved another piece of gingerbread into his mouth. "Yes."

"Our dear Richard here thinks that we should go easier on criminals in the Reich." Frauenfeld sent crumbs flying across the carpet. "What do you think, *Schatz*?"

"Oh, dear, oh dear me, no!" Irmtraud shook her head vigorously.

"I think *mein Führer* has slightly overstated my position," Richard responded irritably. Now he no longer only wanted a cigarette, he wanted a drink as well. "I only suggested that the death penalty is rather too blunt a weapon for petty violations such as teaching children to read."

Irmtraud furrowed her brow. "But we have teachers for that, trained and licensed by the State. All children go to school, so if anyone is teaching children illegally, then it can only be for anti-State purposes."

Richard shook his head. "All children do *not* go to school. Only children of legal marriages are entitled to schooling. The others are not admitted."

"And indeed they shouldn't be! Otherwise state resources would be used to educate bastards! Products of miscegenation! We'd be stating that out-of-wedlock children were acceptable as full members of society, as if such liaisons which created them were to be condoned. That would destroy the fabric of our society!"

"As in the Weimar Republic," Seppel added helpfully.

"Certainly you can understand that interracial and extramarital relationships are an abomination and..." Irmtraud fell silent. She held her mouth clamped shut, clearly determined not to apologize for her faux pas this time around.

Seppel stood and walked over to join the group. "Under Rudi's leadership, there were many things which were tolerated." Seppel clapped his hand on Richard's back. "And we all made mistakes, I'm sure. But now, things will change. We are going to clean up this government and instill a sense of order into the Reich. All of us here know we have upstanding backgrounds and we will endeavor, from this point on, to show that to the people."

Richard knew he should cut his losses and fight this battle another day, but he felt too annoyed to bow to his better judgment. "And exactly how does killing schoolteachers contribute to a sense of order in this society?" He waved his hand angrily toward the window. "Don't you know what such outdated laws do to our society? The criminalization of harmless actions causes nothing but fear and hatred of us – and that leads to violence."

"Richard, calm down," Seppel soothed. "It's violence that we're trying to avoid. You know these laws are applied only to the inferior members of our society and even then, only rarely. As such they serve as a warning to the lower orders. You see, they don't understand subtlety, they only barely grasp the need for government, and they need harsher punishments than the *Übermensch* in order to encourage good behavior. It's not their fault, it's just the way of the world."

Irmtraud nodded her head vigorously in agreement. "Yes! And if they follow the rules and faithfully fulfill their roles in society, then all of us benefit. We're doing them a favor, keeping them from sliding back into chaos and savagery. We lead and they are led, and God's good order is preserved. It may be hard for us to understand – being pure, good Aryans as we are – but we must do our best to comprehend the rules used to keep these people in order. Order is everything."

I'd kill for a cigarette, Richard thought. For all his loathsomeness, Rudi had never insisted on such physical torture. Richard felt himself shaking and he did not know whether it was anger or a nicotine fit. He took a deep breath to calm himself. "*Mein Führer*, perhaps this isn't the time to discuss this issue. Maybe later—"

"No, Richard. We're *not* going to discuss it later. The laws of this land were developed by the best legal minds with the true National Socialist philosophy in mind. They have been refined over decades of use. I am not going to toy with this great inheritance – it is the strongest pillar of our society! I have no interest in changing, refining or exploring the criminal code or the racial code. Is that understood?"

"Yes, *mein Führer*." Richard knew he should add some blandishments, but he couldn't find the appropriate words. Instead he felt an almost overpowering urge to tell Seppel and his wife what his true ethnicity was – and then to ask them to explain how he could have reached the highest levels of the *Übermensch* government if he was so incapable of subtlety or reason. Of course, they'd be able to do it. He had taken parasitical advantage as any inferior might, he had used deceit and slyness as was typical for his sort. And look, his less than pristine private life was proof that his spirit was inferior and unclean. Doubtless Seppel would visit him in prison and as Richard sat there drooling blood through broken teeth, Seppel would clap him on the back and magnanimously forgive him for his duplicity. Richard pushed the urge back down from where it had come and grit his teeth.

"Richard, are you alright?"

"Yes, *mein Führer*. Just a momentary pain here." Richard touched his right temple. "Let's get back to work and I'm sure it will go away."

Irmtraud took her leave and the two men returned to the desk to continue their discussions.

Rather than have the limousine take him directly to the house – Greta's house – Ryszard chose to be driven into town. Greta would be home, ready to interrogate him on the events of the day, and he wasn't quite ready for that yet. He needed a few minutes alone. Just a few. He got out at the edge of the Tiergarten and, with Feliks following, walked up to the gate that let into the wooded section.

The sentry recognized him, clicked his heels and nodded respectfully. "I'm sorry, Colonel, this section of the park closed at sunset. It's currently not guarded."

"Let me in."

The sentry nodded and stood aside. When he saw that Ryszard intended to go in alone, he politely suggested that the Colonel be accompanied by his bodyguard, warning, "It can be dangerous at night."

Ryszard shook his head. "No, I'll take my chances with the wildlife. Thanks." Dangerous, Ryszard laughed to himself. What monster hiding among the trees could possibly compete with the danger he faced in the *Residenz*? He strode along, diving deep into the darkness, chiding himself for his inept handling of the Führer. Damn! Why had he allowed himself to fixate on one capital crime? How could he have let Adam's death penetrate his thoughts? It was inept and idiotic. He would convince Frauenfeld to modernize the criminal code, it would just take time. Why had he tried to bludgeon him into action so quickly?

Ryszard realized he was shaking again. He reached into his pocket and pulled out his cigarette case. Just one, he thought. Just one to calm this idiotic shaking. No. One would lead to another and he would have to start all over again. He simply could not allow himself the disadvantage of suffering cravings while in Frauenfeld's presence. He had to overcome this thing.

He stepped off the trail and headed deeper into the trees. He had at least managed to recoup some of his losses during the long afternoon. He had even gone so far as to propose a Ministry of Women's Affairs, though he had refrained from suggesting that a woman might head it. Frauenfeld had promised to consider the idea.

Traffic along the avenue could still be heard, and through the leaves the lights of some of the buildings could be seen, but still it felt wonderfully isolated. Twigs and debris crunched underfoot, weeds tangled around his legs as he walked. Here and there the ground was squelchy with mud. It was a "wild" section of the park, deliberately unkempt to imitate woodlands that no longer existed around Berlin. It reminded him of home and as he walked along, Ryszard let himself relax and think freely. He pulled out a cigarette and held it up to his lips. He inhaled the sweet fragrance of unlit tobacco, then exhaling heavily, he removed the cigarette and with a show of determination shoved it back into its case. He would have to give up smoking – at least for as long as Frauenfeld was Führer. Damn, but he'd kill for a cigarette. Now, there was a thought.

If I kill Frauenfeld, then I can smoke, Ryszard mused. It was tempting. Bring the little porker a plate of sweets laced with poison and he'd be dead on the floor within minutes of schnurfling them up. Or force mineral water down his throat until he gagged. Ryszard kicked lazily at a piece of dead wood and snickered to himself. Unfortunately, it wouldn't do. Too soon. Too convenient. Too suspicious. He was stuck with the little twerp for the immediate future. *Mein Führer*, Ryszard thought sarcastically. *My leader. Bleh!*

A twig snapped and Ryszard immediately spun around, drawing his gun as he did so. Two eyes glinted at him, wide with fear.

"*Mein Herr*, don't shoot, don't shoot!" The words were slurred with drink but the accent was native Berlin.

Ryszard looked at the grizzled beard and the tattered clothing. A tramp, a good old-fashioned German tramp. How quaint. All the asocials had been cleaned out of society decades ago, but always there were these new ones turning up. How, he wondered idly, did they manage to blow their chances even when given every possible advantage?

The tramp looked Ryszard up and down. "Do you have some food, *mein Herr*? I'm hungry. Or a little money, maybe?"

"Parasite." Ryszard felt a cold power pulse through him. "Superhuman trash." He could kill the man and walk away from the crime with no one the wiser. He'd simply tell the guard that he had been attacked by a vagrant and had shot him. He wouldn't even bother to add that it was in self-defense. It would do both society and the tramp a favor – the man was working his way toward death quickly enough anyway. And it would be so cathartic! The parasite would finally serve a purpose in his miserable life. Ryszard raised his gun and pointed it at the man's heart. "You were planning to jump me, weren't you. Give me one reason not to kill you."

The tramp raised his hands in a pathetic attempt at surrender. "Please, *mein Herr*. Don't."

"Why not? One reason. Give me one reason why I should let you live." Millions of deaths, untold destruction, Joanna, Andrzej, Adam, Julia...What was one worthless life in the grand tally?

It was more than the tramp could handle. Tears rolled down his cheeks. "I don't have one, *mein Herr*."

Not a symbol, not a representative of oppression or hatred. Nothing but a pathetic individual. *Like the rest of us.*

Ryszard motioned with his gun into the woods. "Go away." As he watched the tramp vanish into the darkness, he felt the sense of isolation and freedom disappear with him. Once the tramp was safely gone, Ryszard headed back toward the entrance, assuming his persona as he did so. It was time to go home and face Greta.

26

"**Y**ou're back awfully late." Greta approached down the hallway as the servant took Richard's briefcase. Setting that down, the servant then helped Richard out of his uniform jacket. Richard breathed a sigh of relief and loosened his tie. Though Frauenfeld himself was not military, he had casually suggested that government officials with military rank should wear their uniforms more frequently. So now Richard wore his SS uniform, not even bothering to wonder what Frauenfeld's motivation was. Perhaps he simply liked looking at the slim black figure presented by his subordinate. Richard shuddered at the thought.

The servant offered a cigarette, but Richard waved it away and looked down at his watch. "Late? Are you nuts?"

"Richard!" Greta cast a meaningful glance at the servants. "You told me it would only be a few hours."

He smiled an insincere apology and sat down to have his boots removed. "Sorry. I went into town before coming home. Ugh!" One boot off. "I stopped at the Tiergarten and had a brief walk in the woods. Ah." That was the second.

"Why?"

Once his house shoes were in place, Richard stood, and the servant turned away to pour him a drink. "I wanted a chance to relax and think."

"What's wrong with relaxing here?"

"Nothing, darling. Shall we retire to the living room?" Richard accepted the drink from the servant, then kissed Greta on the cheek.

"Dinner's waiting." Greta turned and walked back toward the dining room. The command in her action was unmistakable.

Richard stood in the hallway, holding his drink as he contemplated what he should do. Kasia would have never been so brusque! And he had told Greta that he had an appointment with the Führer that *might* last a few hours. Did she think he would jump up and say to the Führer, "Sorry, but the wife's waiting and your time's up?" Did she really expect he would keep the sort of schedule where she could have dinner waiting and could be irritated that he was not there on time? And was he to be prevented from saying "Are you nuts?" just because the servants would overhear and think it disrespectful? Richard let his breath out in a quiet hiss. He noticed the servant waiting, looking at him. The boy's face betrayed no emotion, but Richard was sure he was amused. Richard gestured toward his briefcase. "Put that in my office!"

The servant responded promptly, moving quickly to pick up the briefcase, giving Richard a wide berth.

The boy knew I knew what he was thinking, the bastard. Just as well he stayed out of reach. Richard watched the servant carry the briefcase into his office. *Not really a boy, is he.* Richard thought back – he was fairly certain that this was the same servant who had helped serve dinner the first time he had visited the Schindler's, the elder of what had appeared to be two brothers. That was about six years ago. At that time the servant had appeared on the verge of manhood. *So, he must be well into his twenties and not a boy at all.* Richard smiled to himself. At least, for all the disappointments he had suffered over the past years, he had not spent the time silently serving Greta!

As Richard thought her name, she poked her head out from the dining room. "Well, are you coming?"

"Yes, darling. I just need to wash my hands." Richard downed the rest of his drink, set down the glass and strode down the hall to the guest toilet to wash his hands. Without his even noticing it, he was joined by the servant who then handed him a towel at the appropriate moment. As Richard dried his hands, he studied the boy's, or rather, the man's face. Though the servant was quite clearly not looking directly at him, Richard's curious gaze obviously made him nervous, for he turned his head slightly in an instinctive and useless attempt to be unnoticeable. *Coward, show some spirit!* Richard flung the towel back into the servant's hands and headed toward the dining room.

Ach, but it's rather unfair to expect a show of spirit. From all accounts, Günter had kept his staff in a state of almost constant terror, and why would any of them assume that things would be better with Greta's new husband? Inferiors who showed spirit were treated the way Peter had been. It was simply asking for trouble – after all, the new aristocracy had not achieved its power by being kind and forgiving. Indeed, such traits in any Party member were rewarded by a permanent position in a low-level job. *Noblesse oblige* could come later – after generations of well-established power and the confidence that came with it.

The servant was right. The aristocracy was not yet hereditary and anyone who achieved Richard's position did not get there by being nice. None of them were innocent – not Schindler, not Vogel, not even Frauenfeld, for all his jovial pretenses. And that was a problem. If Frauenfeld were really the country bumpkin that he seemed to be, then he would be in the country doing whatever bumpkins do. He had not stumbled into the leadership, that was impossible, every step of the way he must have been plotting. All of it, even the humility and loyalty shit, had been an act.

Greta noticed his expression, for even as Richard was seated at the table, she asked, "What are you scowling about?"

The servant opened a napkin for Richard and placed it on his lap. With a flourish an appetizer was placed before Richard and, after he had nodded his agreement at the label, a bit of red wine poured. Richard swirled it around, tasted it, and nodded. He set the glass down to be filled. "Frauenfeld." Richard picked up the filled wine glass. "I've underestimated him. We all have."

"Zum Wohl." Greta picked up her glass. She had white, and Richard knew it would be sickly sweet.

"Zum Wohl." Richard drank some wine, wondering how much he could say in front of the servants. They probably posed no threat. There would be a great deal of risk in betraying their masters' confidences, and not much prospect of reward. More problematic was Greta herself. Richard did not doubt that if she lost interest in him or his chances of success, she would move her loyalties elsewhere, with devastating effect.

He looked up and noticed Feliks standing unobtrusively by the doorway. He was the only person in the entire household aware of the constant charade, yet the two had never spoken as comrades. Since he had been assigned as Richard's bodyguard, Feliks had shown not only an unflinching loyalty but had maintained a respectful distance, as if in awe of Richard and what he had achieved. *Or maybe*, Richard thought, *he's waiting for me to make good on my word.* Long ago Richard had said he would follow-up on Rudi's promise to locate Feliks' and Dorota's stolen child. He had gone so far as getting a description of the child, but upon learning that the babe had been blond-haired and blue-eyed, he had let the inquiry drop. It was unlikely such a child would have ended up in service; he would have been adopted by a family and his discovery at this late stage would serve no purpose other than to ruin his life and his chances for betterment.

With a slight movement of his head Richard caught Feliks' attention. "You can relax now. Go into the kitchen and have them get you something to eat."

Feliks nodded and left.

"You should get someone else."

Richard looked at Greta in surprise. "Huh? What do you mean?"

"He's not one of us, you know. I don't trust him."

"He saved my life, Greta."

"He's your ex-wife's brother-in-law! And there's not even a hint of German blood in him."

"He was my loyal agent for years and he gave up his cover to save my life. Since then he has put himself in the line of fire more than once. He's staying."

Greta made a slight face.

I have one lousy person in this entire household loyal to me, and she wants to remove him!

"I can arrange a better bodyguard for you. Someone well trained."

"He's staying." Richard glanced around the room. "How many servants do we have?"

The change of topic seemed to work for Greta drew herself up as she did a mental tally. "Well, I have six contracts here and then there's two in Switzerland, seeing to the property there."

"They don't run away?"

"The Swiss ones are *paid* employees," she stated with some irritation. "Beyond that I have four people who come in on an occasional basis, depending on the season, parties, and so on. Two of those are German hirees, two are foreigners on work visas." Before Richard could again misinterpret, she added, "All four are salaried."

Richard nodded.

"One is the head gardener. He's a German – quite expensive I find. I've been thinking of firing him and using one of my people."

Though he and Greta were now married, it was clear they were *Greta's* people. Richard took a sip of wine.

"Richard! I was asking your opinion."

Richard looked up at his wife. "Of course, darling. I think that's a good idea." He ate in silence for a moment, before casually mentioning, "Do you know, the Führer poured water for me himself." He used Seppel's title deliberately with Greta, since she was even more annoyed than he by his failure to be elected to that position.

"Himself? How odd."

"I think he was making a statement. An important one."

Greta looked confused.

"Don't you think six full contracts is a bit..." Richard searched the ceiling for the right word. "Ostentatious?"

Greta indicated to the servant that she wanted some buttered bread. "We're not poor. Your churchmouse *ex*-wife may have survived on two, but your house was *tiny*."

Richard nodded noncommittally. "I've never stumbled across a woman here. How many of your workers are female?"

"None. It's extremely difficult to get women nowadays. I think they're kept in industries where their social life can be more closely regulated." Greta tilted her head at Richard. "But why do you ask? Are you worried?" Before Richard could answer she added, "No need to fret, my dear. I'm not going to sink to Elspeth Vogel's level."

Elspeth Vogel, Peter, Magdalena..."Tell me, did Günter know about that – you know the thing between Elspeth and her boy? I mean..." Richard glanced at the servants and switched to French, hoping none of them spoke it. "Did Günter know about what Frau Vogel was up to with her servant *before* Karl Vogel was killed?"

"You mean before it became obvious with the kidnapping?" Greta pursed her lips. "I would suppose so. I mentioned it more than once in his presence." She furrowed her brow. "Yes, yes, he actually commented on it once or twice. Yes, he knew. Why do you ask?"

"No reason." Richard pushed his appetizer away. Something was percolating in the back of his mind, but he wasn't sure exactly what. A servant removed the plate and then offered him a cigarette. Richard shook his head.

"That's the second time you've done that. Are you ill?"

Richard watched as the box was closed and set back down on the table. With an effort he pulled his attention off the cigarettes and back to Greta. "No, dear. I've quit smoking. It will help if we clear the house of cigarettes."

"You've *quit?* Why?"

"The Führer has requested I don't smoke in his presence, and if I'm going to spend hours consulting with him, I'd rather not have the distraction of a constant urge to light up." Richard found it difficult not to turn away from Greta to stare at the box. Addiction. It was a fascinating thing. That's what Seppel lacked – that strange yearning for power, the symptoms of addiction. The only thing he seemed genuinely attached to – other than his sausages – was his pudgy little wife. So how did he get so far? Why the excessive show of loyalty – even to someone as loathsome as Rudi, someone who "made mistakes?"

A plate appeared before Richard, but the food looked unappetizing. Always a slab of meat – usually beef, sometimes pork – and then salted potatoes, sometimes fried with onions. "Doesn't the cook have any other recipes? How about chicken?"

"Poor people eat chicken."

Hence the ridiculous slab of meat every evening. Richard smiled at a childhood memory of mushroom picking and the wonderful mushroom *barszcz* they later had as their evening meal. The mountains towered around them, the fresh smell of the pine forests, the hot creamy soup…

"Richard?"

"Hmm?"

"I asked you what was so funny."

Richard shook his head. "Nothing, darling." Damn, he was losing control! "I was just thinking that the French do some wonderful things with chicken. Nice sauces and whatnot."

"The French," Greta drew the word out in a sneer, "*have* to do things to their meat – it's old and tough and cheap! If those peasants could afford proper meat, they wouldn't have to drown it in wine. We in the aristocracy are not afraid to taste our meat."

Not afraid. It had been fear! Frauenfeld had reacted with *fear* to the proposed change in criminal penalties! But what did he have to fear? He was so willing to restructure everything else, why not that? And he was now Führer, what could he possibly have to fear? God, Rudi had certainly shown that almost anything was acceptable in their leader, so why was Frauenfeld afraid? Why were criminal penalties a sacred cow? And, in particular, which ones? Teaching? Crimes against the *Volk*? Racial crimes? Extramarital affairs? *Miscegenation?* How had they come to that juncture? Richard pushed his plate away and stood. He needed time to think and the dark of the bedroom, before Greta joined him, seemed perfect. "One of the servants can have my dinner. I'm not hungry – the Führer had some snacks brought in – and anyway, I'm exhausted. Good-night."

"Good-night? But Richard, you've only just gotten home."

He walked around to her side of the table and kissed her forehead. "Sorry, love, it's been a rough day."

Greta looked at him meaningfully, her eyes narrowing. "Richard, that is rude. Please take your seat and wait until the dinner is over."

"I'm tired, Greta. This is my home now and I can retire for the evening when I want to."

"Richard." It was no more than a whisper, but there was some unnamed threat in it.

No sex? No political support? Betray those of his secrets she knew? It wasn't worth the risk. Richard drew a smile out from somewhere. "I'm sorry dear. I didn't mean to be rude." He went back round the table and sat down, pulling his wine glass to him so that he could drink as she ate.

His new home, he thought, was not unlike prison.

27

*B*eyond the first fence was a second. Both were topped with untidily coiled razor wire, and it looked not only intimidating, but ugly. Peter let his gaze wander along the fence until it reached the tower. Rifle toting guards patrolled at the top of the tower, keeping a vigilant eye on their charges below. The sun glinted strongly off the tower, hurting his eyes and threatening to provoke a headache. Peter reached into his pocket and pulled out his sunglasses, and with their protection, he was able to look past the tower, to the muddy cleared field beyond. There was another fence past this extended dead zone and then the landscape returned to normal – a highway, beyond that some factories, and, in the distance, mountains. If he turned his head just so, focusing his eyes carefully so that the fences blurred, and if he simply wiped the image of the tower from his consciousness, then he could – just barely – imagine he was outside and free.

"Halifax, do you have a cigarette?"

Peter turned toward his fellow prisoner and shook his head. "Gave them all away already." It was a complete lie, but though he never smoked any, they were useful for bargaining, and he saw no point in sharing his limited supply with someone who was not even remotely an ally, much less a friend. It would only be interpreted as weakness.

"I heard the governor gives you cartons in exchange for buggering you," the prisoner sneered.

It was nothing more than mindless provocation and Peter responded in kind. "I heard it's your mother who spreads her legs for yours."

"You motherfucker, you take that back!"

The prospect of fighting – either verbally or physically – seemed singularly unappealing to Peter, so he readily conceded. "I take it back. Your mother is a wonderful woman and deserves our complete respect."

The prisoner eyed him suspiciously. Not quite believing the concession, he decided to prod a bit. "Your mother–"

"Is long dead." Peter turned away to look back out at the distant mountains. It was a bit risky, turning his back on someone like that, but mercifully, his fellow inmate accepted his victory and walked away.

Once the inmate was far enough away that it wouldn't seem like relief, Peter took a deep breath, filling his lungs and savoring it. Fresh air was important and he had made a point of not missing the opportunity to go outside. Immersed in his work, he had foregone the privilege since Tuesday and it had taken quite a toll, leaving him doubting his competence and the results which he had uncovered. Now, as he restlessly paced the packed earth and breathed deeply, he was able to focus much better and he ran through the discoveries of the past several days, trying to work out what it all meant, and more importantly, what he should do about it.

Though he had yet to check his work, he was fairly certain that what he had was accurate. It was not chemical weapons that Wolf-Dietrich had given to Erich to pass on, it had been the plans for building a single nuclear device. A simple, small atom bomb. Even with the intense censorship of the Reich, it was the sort of thing which any determined and well-connected Underground could have found out for itself, but there was no indication that the Real ERA was either. Still, it was not the plans themselves which were surprising, it was that Schindler had passed them on. There would be no point in doing so unless he also intended to supply them with the necessary materials – the weapons-grade plutonium and explosives to detonate it all. With the instructions and the materials, the Realies would possess a genuinely powerful weapon, and given what Peter could remember from his earlier training and from what he could uncover via his computer, there was every indication that the plans Schindler had passed on were accurate.

The bomb would not be a dud.

More interestingly, the plans were in English and had a number of indicators that implied they were from America. Either Schindler had been clever enough to pass on genuine American plans or had faked up the indicators. In either case, if the Realies detonated the bomb and their guilt was uncovered, there would be every reason to believe that the Americans had been behind their actions.

Which led to the most interesting of Peter's discoveries. For, after all, why would the Americans be involved in a bombing of the London Underground or indeed, anywhere in London? No one would suspect them of complicity in that, even if the plans were in American English. They would however be suspect if Berlin had been targeted, and buried at the end of the coded documents had been the real gem: directions for an approved transit route leading across the channel and into the *Altreich*. The route ended outside Berlin, near Potsdam, and after that there was a detailed description of the area with an appropriate supply warehouse highlighted. The warehouse, on the edge of the *Residenz* grounds was about a kilometer from the Führer's private residence – and that would almost certainly put it within the zone of total destruction.

So Schindler wanted to blow up the leadership. Clearly he would step into the breach, seize control and implicate the English Underground and the Americans in this heinous crime. The former would be sufficient to allow a horrific backlash against the resistance, the latter would provide a pretense for war, if that was his desire. It could all turn into a very bloody mess.

Of course, with Rudi now gone, perhaps Schindler no longer desired revenge against the Berlin hierarchy. But it was too late – the plans had already been passed on, and Peter had little doubt that the Real ERA already had the necessary materials as well. If Schindler wanted to pre-empt the disaster he had planned, he could arrest everyone involved in the conspiracy, but that would be risky – doubtless one or two of them would be aware of his involvement – and it was also unlikely that a dragnet would catch everyone. More unlikely was that Schindler would *want* to stop the plan. Even with Rudi dead, he remained shunned and isolated in London, and doubtless seething as well. So, the die was cast, the Real ERA could blow up the Führer and his leading officials. And there was no doubt that they would.

The bastards would finally be made to pay. That one, directed, fantastic strike against the leadership of which they had all dreamed. Blow them to oblivion, the entire government! Peter quivered with excitement at the thought. How long had he dreamed of this day? How many hours blindfolded, gagged and bound had he spent, reveling in their imaginary destruction. Now, finally, at last, revenge! *Real revenge!* All those years of suffering, all the murders, all the hatred would finally come home to roost. The endless destruction, the soul-destroying oppression, the millions murdered in cold blood would be repaid. In the name of the *Volk*, they had spread hatred and earned it in return. The hatred of millions, the hatred of one brutally tormented soul...*Revenge at last!*

The hatred flooded into Peter, spreading through his arms and legs and mind. Freeing him as it used to, from chains, from handcuffs, from pain, from despair. His vision narrowed and darkened and the prison walls loomed over him to blot out the daylight. The blind anger and mindless strength that had freed him from the Führer's grasp now wracked him with a lust for vengeance, and he had no desire to stop it. The devastation would be enormous. The ruins of charred buildings obliterating the flags and swastikas and gun-toting police. Ashes raining down on the *Residenz*, symbols of power toppled in the hurricane of wrath, the tormentors learning what it means to scream in agony as flesh melts from bone...

Daylight penetrated, sending his gruesome thoughts scattering. Peter blinked and focused on the fences surrounding him. *Control, boy, get control.* He breathed deeply and began to feel more normal, but not entirely. Something still churned inside him. He ignored the sensation and focused his thoughts, trying to realistically assess what the fallout of such an explosion might be. The *Residenz* was far from the center, so Berlin and its people would be spared. Distant suburbs, in particular where Kasia and her family lived, would almost certainly be safe. Of course, the radiation would be high and it would be best if they were out of the region entirely, but even if they weren't, they would have time to flee to safety. Was there anyone within the ring of devastation whom he cared about? Possibly Ryszard, but he could be warned. Anyone else?

Peter shook his head at his thoughts. For all its distance from the center, the *Residenz* was near villages and sprawling suburbs and the staff that worked inside the complex was huge. God almighty, thousands of innocent lives would be sacrificed! What was he thinking? And what of the A.K. deterrents buried throughout the region? Was there one near the *Residenz*? Would the explosion set it off as well? The devastation could be phenomenal – back to the sort of destruction that had been common in the forties and early fifties. And the retaliations. Oh God, it had to be stopped!

Or did it? Peter wove his fingers into the mesh of the fence and leaned against it. If properly managed, this could lead to the revolution that he and Zosia had always advocated. Forget Ryszard's infinitesimal progress toward normalcy, they could rid themselves of the Nazi scourge in a few months of violent upheaval. Yes, thousands would die but wouldn't their quick deaths be better than the slow attrition of decades? Weren't the prisoners who were to be executed over the coming years worth saving? Why should their lives, why should every hope of freedom be sacrificed for the safety of a few thousands? Like always, they would be the innocent and regrettable victims of war. But a just war. A war that had to be fought. A war that had remained unfought for far too long.

Peter rolled away from the fence, leaning his back into it. Oh God, nothing was simple anymore! It had been so clear in 1938, or at least 1939. Stop Hitler and his evildoers. But even then, the Soviet menace loomed and had, up to that point, proved to be much more deadly. Who would have sanctioned Hitler's murder? Who could have guessed what would follow? Who could have conceived that Stalin's murderously psychotic regime would lumber into a sort of normalcy that was perhaps preferable to the Reich's current blundering mess? Who would have guessed, after tens of millions of people had fallen victim to Soviet excesses that the Reich, stymied in its efforts to exile its Jewish population, would resort to slaughter and that the Soviet Union would become a haven for some of them?

Violent overthrow. Let the Real ERA bomb the *Residenz*. If they got the timing right, setting it off during the Solstice when the *Residenz* would be absolutely overflowing with top brass, then the government would have to collapse. The Undergrounds could seize control of their various constituencies in the ensuing chaos. Ryszard could step into the power vacuum in the heartland and rule Germany, skillfully letting the other regions slide off into autonomy and independence. Power would devolve back to the national governments. The colonists would be sent home or obliged to assimilate. Europe could regain its diversity and culture. The clock could be turned back to the 1920's and fledgling democracies could be re-established. New constitutions written, parliaments established. Oh God, was it possible?

And even more disturbing – was it his decision to make? If he withheld the information from Szaflary and released only enough details to Ryszard to save his and his family's lives, then he could decide history. Peter scanned the prison yard and the various miscreants who sloped around him. He had to laugh. There were only two types of uniforms in sight – prisoners and guards. He looked down at his own uniform – prisoner, of course. As usual. The dregs of society – yet here he was, in sole possession of truly important information. His laughter grew louder and one of the inmates nearby turned to him.

"What's so funny, Peter?"

"Ach, I'm deciding the fate of Europe!"

The inmate nodded noncommittally. Everyone knew it was wiser not to provoke the crazier prisoners. Up to this point he had never counted Halifax among them, but now he knew better. With an indulgent smile, he carefully backed away.

Peter watched him walk away and thought, I should pass the information on to Szaflary – let them or HQ decide. Or to the English Underground, or the Governments-in-Exile or Zosia or Ryszard. But why? Each of them would jealously take possession of what he offered, completely secure in their right to own it. Yet he was no less capable of analysis than any of them. He had desires and plans that were no less important, no less respectable. If he gave the information to any one of them, they would automatically assume complete control of it without respect to anyone else's wishes. At best he might be thanked, but in any case he would become irrelevant. Having slavishly done his duty, he would be ignored and left to rot in isolation. And if he gave it to all of them, they would do nothing but endlessly bicker.

But if he kept it to himself, releasing details as he saw fit – well, with his ability to communicate via computer and with his network of contacts, he could stage manage whatever he wanted. Indeed, with a bit of manipulation, he could even take over control of the Real ERA. They were looking for a spiritual leader and had never fully accepted his renunciation of the role. He could run the show. From prison, wearing a number, locked in a cell, the lowest of the low, he could run the whole damn show! He would have power. For once, he would have real power and could make the decisions. Peter smiled at the thought and nothing, not the fences, not the guards carrying their rifles, not even the razor wire could dampen his mood.

28

"*W*hat have you found out?"

Stefan set down two boxes of files near Ryszard's desk. Olek tapped at one of them with his cane. "Nothing. He's clean as a whistle."

"I know he's clean!" Ryszard stood and, pointedly turning his back on Olek, walked to the window. He was not being deliberately rude, he just felt such an intense desire for a cigarette that he needed to move. He stared out at the traffic below and wondered what it was he had been looking for. "Is there any hint of anything?"

"No, sir." Olek looked down at the boxes of files. "We've set everyone on tracking down absolutely everything about the man. These are the details, but as far as I can see, there's just nothing there."

Fear. Teaching, extramarital affairs, miscegenation...How had they come to that juncture? Ryszard turned to Olek. "How was your holiday?"

"Wonderful, sir. Stefi seemed really happy. Like her old self."

Ryszard nodded. "Did you get information on Frauenfeld's wife?"

"Yes, sir. It's contained in this one." Olek tapped one of the boxes. "Her complete background."

"Everything?"

"Yes, sir. Even her baptismal records."

"Hmm." What was it he was looking for? Ryszard's eyes strayed around the room. Olek stood by the desk, Stefan was off to the side and there was Feliks standing silently by the door. *Waiting for me to find out about his child...*"Feliks, what would you do if I told you I had found your son and he was living with a good German family as their adopted child?"

Feliks' face lit up.

"It's just hypothetical!" Ryszard snapped.

The bland mask returned. "I would go to my son and tell him the truth."

"Why? It could well ruin his life."

"I can't let their actions become justified by my inaction. My son deserves to know the truth."

"With such knowledge, he might well spend the rest of his life in fear of discovery."

Feliks' face remained a mask, but a slight edge crept into his tone. "He deserves to know the truth and make his own decisions."

"What if I were to order you not to contact him?"

"I'd disobey the order."

Ryszard did not respond to that and there was a momentary silence. Feliks' expression slowly altered and as the bland mask dissolved, a look of pleading hope came into his eyes. "Have you learned something, sir?"

Ryszard shook his head. "No. But I wouldn't tell you if I had." He turned back to the window before he could see Feliks' reaction to his blunt assertion.

Fear, fear of discovery. Don't mess with the very thing that could bring you down. Indeed, show an excessive loyalty to it to deflect suspicion. *Criminal penalties.* Criminal penalties for teaching, for teaching illegal children. Children born of unapproved parents, children whose parents were something other than they say. *Blood fraud.*

Ryszard turned back to address Stefan and Olek, "Go through Irmtraud's background and see if there are any inconsistencies in her early youth. Check her parents, grandparents and great-grandparents as well. I want every detail verified, down to the addresses of their churches and the names of the priests who baptized them. Everything." He pointed at the boxes. "Start with what we have, work in the annex. If you need more information, track it down. Meanwhile, I'm going to sift through Seppel's legislative initiatives."

Four hours later Ryszard had discovered only one incident to support his thesis – shortly after marrying Irmtraud, Seppel had sought to introduce a change in the Aryan classification scheme used in his district. The initiative had been rejected by his immediate superior never to be resurrected. All very interesting and consistent with the picture that Ryszard was building, but certainly not enough to sink his teeth into. He needed something more. He turned to reading through the evaluations that Seppel had accumulated throughout his career. Due to his election as Führer, all such files had been removed from access, but Ryszard kept his own personal library and the Home Army had a huge archive of historical documents.

Time and again the same words were used: loyal and hard-working. Yet, in each case, Seppel had gone on to eventually outrank his boss. Interesting. Perhaps blind loyalty was such a rare trait anymore that it was disproportionately rewarded and Seppel leap-frogged through the hierarchy so that he could be unfailingly loyal to the next tier. Certainly that had been the case with Rudi, and the fact that Seppel had never once given offense in his rise to the top had made him irresistibly electable as Führer once the position was open.

"Dad?"

"Come in, sweetheart!" Ryszard stood and smiled as Stefi stepped into his office. "Did you just get here?"

Stefi shook her head. "I came to pick up Olek for lunch hours ago, but I found him hunched over files in your annex and so I decided to help out instead." She smiled and it brightened the entire room. "You certainly have that boy under your thumb!"

"It's not *my* thumb he's under." Ryszard was so pleased to see Stefi. She looked absolutely radiant, full of life and energy. "Did you enjoy Switzerland?"

"Not just! Oh, Dad, I feel human again." Stefi patted her belly. "And that's good for both of us."

Ryszard put his arm around his daughter. "You're not showing.

"It's not even two months." Stefi looked up at him, her eyes glinting. "Do you realize that the other one would be about a year old already?"

Ryszard shook his head slightly. "Don't think about that." He pulled Stefi into him and held her protectively. "You're safe now, the baby's safe."

Stefi pressed herself into her father's embrace, enjoying the unusual sensation.

"And how's your mother?"

"She's fine. She misses you."

"I miss her too."

Stefi looked up in surprise but it was as if she had imagined the words, her father's expression was completely businesslike. He released his hold on her and stepped back. "Have you discovered anything?"

"Of course!" Stefi laughed. "Why in the world you set your boys to this task is beyond me. You should have called me in immediately!"

Ryszard smiled with pride, Stefi's instincts were impeccable. "You're right, of course. But how did you sift through all that stuff so quickly?"

Stefi grinned. "I used a secret weapon."

"Oh?"

"Rather than go through all the details and checking each, I told Pawel to contact Hania and had her send me a list of our favorites."

"Favorites?"

"The places we used to use for *our* legend writing, before we got infiltrators and forgers in place. You know, anywhere that had floods or fires in their town halls or churches, where the records were destroyed and had to be replaced by hand."

"Ah, yes. Good idea. I should have suggested that. And?"

"Irmtraud's mother. It seems all the important details about her were lost."

"Where?"

"Slovakia. Her mother was one of the ethnic Germans living in a village near Bardejov. Her records were reportedly destroyed in the flood of the Topl'a in 1926. She was already living in Munich by that time, so she didn't do anything about it until she married in 1933, when she petitioned to have them replaced."

"And the source of information for the details?" Ryszard already knew the answer.

"Herself, of course. Everything was on paper then and replacing lost files was essentially impossible without the cooperation of the people involved. It was a rather casual affair since everyone knew each other."

"But with a little money changing hands, details could be changed."

"Or invented altogether. Hitler had just taken power in Germany and everyone knew his agenda. It may have been a deliberate act of defiance on the part of some Slovak clergyman or town hall official, or it may have been simple bribery."

Ryszard nodded. If anyone else had attempted to tutor him like this, he would have been annoyed, but not with Stefi.

"By the time Reich officials were nosing around the archives, the records were already five years old and not in any way dubious. And by the time Irmtraud was born, it was well-established that her mother, grandparents and even great-grandparents had been born and baptized

630

Catholic in Slovakia. Of course, it may all be true, but I think it's a little too convenient."

Ryszard rubbed his face. A cigarette would be so nice! "Well, it'll probably do. It'd be nice if we could firm up the evidence."

"Not likely after all these decades. The trail is pretty cold. And I'm sure that over the years Seppel has carefully purged anything left in Vienna or Bratislava or wherever."

"I guess I'll have to stick with innuendo when I use this." Ryszard reached into his jacket pocket but there was nothing there. Damn, no one said it would take so long!

Stefi saw his gesture and grinned at him. "I heard you gave up smoking."

Ryszard grunted.

"Congratulations."

Again he simply grunted.

Stefi saw that her father was in no mood to discuss smoking and so she kindly switched topics. "What do you plan to do with the information?"

Ryszard shrugged. "I don't know yet. It won't do to bring Frauenfeld down, but maybe, if I use it wisely, I can get something out of it."

"Like what?"

"Oh, maybe I could get him to set up a commission to rework the criminal code." Ryszard's face brightened. "Would you like to be on it?"

"Me?"

"Why not? You're schooled in the ways of government, smart, well-connected—"

"Female."

"Women are affected by laws as much as men. You could be the token woman."

"If you can organize it, I'd love to be on it!" Stefi kissed Ryszard on the cheek. "Thanks, Dad."

"Least I can do for all your good work."

"Speaking of which, shall I tell the boys to stop working?"

Ryszard shook his head. "Let them sweat a bit – they may even find something else. Meanwhile, why don't you sit down and tell me all about your holiday." He sat in one of the armchairs in a corner of his office and gestured toward the other. "I'd enjoy that."

Stefi poured coffee for them both from the carafe and then seated herself. "Where shall I begin?"

29

*A*s there was a national holiday which closed the library on Monday, Peter was denied permission to work there on either Sunday or the Monday. Master of Europe's Fate, he laughed to himself, but still prisoner to the whims of surly officials. Time was short, there was only a month to the solstice, and he could ill afford the delays to his plans. He shrugged off his irritation and used the time to better organize what he would do. He paced the prison yard restlessly, turning down an invitation to join a side in football, and debated with himself about how active a role he should take. Certainly if he tried to take control of the Realies, he was tainting himself with a great deal more guilt than if he simply remained aloof and let fate take its course. On the other hand, the more he managed, the less violent and bloody the aftermath was likely to be.

A buzzer sounded and Peter joined the queue with the other prisoners to return inside. After dinner, as he was on the way back to his cell, he checked the post and was surprised to find that he had received a letter. It had the postmark of an international sorting office in Switzerland, but it was addressed in Zosia's hand. Peter guessed that while she was still in Berlin, Zosia had given the letter to Arieka to send through her diplomatic post. Thus, the letter could pass freely and quickly out of the Reich, though it would still be subject to the prison censors. Overjoyed by the surprise, he returned to his cell, pulled the letter out of the already opened envelope and sat down on his bed to read:

My dear love,

I'm hoping that soon we'll be able to communicate more frequently and directly, but that might not work as expected, so I wanted to take this opportunity to write.

First of all, I had a conversation with R. and he is of the opinion that nothing can be done about your situation for the time being. I felt overwhelmed with grief and frustration, but R. reminded me of how much we have achieved and how lucky we are to have what we do. He's right, you know. His words set me to thinking, and I realized that I need to tell you some things.

Most importantly are some words I failed to say before. I failed to say them so long ago when we had that confrontation outside the Council chamber. I failed to say them later when I tried to convince you that I loved you. And I failed to say them even as you left to face trial and imprisonment. With each omission, they became harder to say, and even now I hesitate to write them – not because I don't mean them – but because I don't think I've ever done this before. You know how it is with new things and in this respect, I'm a virgin. So, here goes and forgive me if I'm clumsy: I'm sorry.

Phew, glad that's over with! You don't need me to explain what for, do you? Suffice it to say I know that it should be said more than once, for more than one thing, but beggars can't be choosers and I'm sure you're pleased I managed even the once.

Or are you? I realize that in the past I've sometimes forged ahead without listening. I've been trying to change. I've started asking about other people and actually listening to the answers. I've talked to T. about his wife, I've heard what W's husband had to say about her, and I even made time to listen to B's endless complaints. (I wasn't going to, but then at the last minute, before leaving the city, I thought of you and went to see her, and I don't know, but I may have saved her from drinking herself into a stupor and letting the baby fall out of the window or something horrible like that). M. often stops by to chat. She's obviously looking for you, but then she remembers that you're not around and she talks to me.

Do you have any idea how many people miss you? You were always there for them and I don't think they realized that until you were gone. I certainly didn't. With each absence it got worse, first those months that you were sent away – at that time I was convinced my loneliness was due solely to Joanna's death. Or at least that's what I tried to tell myself. Then when you were captured by the Führer, then I knew how much I needed you. And now, each day without you is a day of my life lost. But I can't think that way. Each day of knowing you – even from a distance, is a positive experience.

God, this sounds like a love letter! I don't think I've ever written one before. But you're worth it! You have taught me so much. You seemed to understand the importance of simply being human. You always knew how to keep a private life through all the madness around you. You found time to gaze at the stars and plant a garden and pick wildflowers for me and cook nice meals and be kind to a little girl. I'll never forget how you mended her clothes, though you could barely see to get the thread through the needle. Or how you taught her how to play soccer, though you winced with the pain. I remember how when you were busy working on a stack of stuff, you handed all your notes to your helper so you could be with Joanna because she was sick. And everyone assumed he was

633

due all the credit! Nobody else knew how much work you had done. And I saw how your eyes strayed toward your unfinished research as you read her one of her books for the zillionth time, yet you never let on. You always found time for us. You never lost sight of the important things. Even in the worst years of your life you planted trees and sang songs and talked with the Vogel children.

Despite your devotion to your work, you never became a fanatic. Despite your passionate love of freedom, ideology never enslaved you. Despite what you suffered at their hands, hatred never took control. You remained human. And that is all we are and the most we can be.

You taught me so much. I miss you so much. I love you. And I really mean that.

Yours always, Z.

When Peter finished the letter, he read it again from the beginning, then leaned back against the concrete block wall and closed his eyes. His beautiful Zosia had once again underestimated herself. *She* had been *his* inspiration from the moment he had met her. Such strength, courage and resolve! And so much love. It was obvious that she truly loved Joanna and had loved Adam with all her heart. And though she had used him, Peter knew that she had at the same time selflessly done everything in her power to help him heal.

"She's a great mom."

Peter opened his eyes to see Joanna sitting contentedly on his lap. She was as light as a ghost. "I must be dreaming."

"Do you mind?"

He shook his head. "Of course not, I'm always glad to see you, even if I do invent you. I'm sure though, the psychiatrists would have a negative view of all this, if I were to tell them."

Joanna pursed her lips in what looked like the beginnings of a pout.

"I take it back. You're as real as love. And we both know that exists, don't we?"

She smiled and hugged him. She had grown over the years and now she looked the eight years that she would have been. Still with her messy blond curls, though now they were a tiny bit darker. Peter pressed his face into her hair, happy that his dream included a sense of touch.

"You're not really going to let them do it, are you?" With her face still buried in his chest, it was hard to believe that she had spoken.

"Of course not, baby. That's not like me." He stroked her hair.

"Good," Joanna murmured. "I saw the hate in you. Sometimes it controlled you."

"Only briefly."

She pulled back to look at him. "I'm glad it's gone."

"Oh, it's still there, child. I'm just not going to let it own me." He smiled at her. "I'm stronger than it."

There were tears in her eyes. "I was scared, I didn't want you to become what you hate."

"Don't worry, honey, I won't." He pulled her back into his embrace. "Is that why you came to visit me?"

Her answer was softer than an angel's whisper. "Only you can answer that question."

He didn't say anything more, fearful that he would break the fragile threads of his dream. She was already beginning to fade, so he closed his eyes and held her close to him and let his fingers trail down her silky fine hair.

The cells had been locked and the lights turned off by the time he awoke. His hand rose instinctively to stroke Joanna's hair, but she wasn't there. Still, she had left him with a sense of peace. He knew what he had to do. So much for his brief fantasy of power. It wasn't in his heart to kill indiscriminately or even to stand idly by as others carried out such plans, no matter how effective the result might be in promoting his aims. Tomorrow he'd get a pass to go back to the library and then he could send Zosia the details. Everybody would be informed, the plot would be foiled and Ryszard might even be able to turn the whole thing to his political advantage. Thousands of lives would be saved, the streets would not flow with blood, there would be no quick overthrow of the government. They would continue to follow Ryszard's painfully slow path of evolution.

And I'll sink back into obscurity, stuck for years behind these bars and concrete walls and razor wire. He wasn't bothered though. It was the right decision, it was the human thing to do. That part of him that Zosia loved, that part that survived re-education and torture, that endured through slavery and the loss of his loved ones – he would still have it. Neither free nor powerful, but at peace with his conscience. And that was enough.

30

"*I* want a full report of what's been going on!" Frauenfeld's screech, even filtered through the telephone receiver, made Richard wince.

"Right now?"

There was a silence and Richard realized that in his sleepy state, he had forgotten to add "*mein Führer*."

"Would I be calling you now if I wanted it some other time?" Frauenfeld asked in far too calm a tone.

"No, *mein Führer*. My apologies. A great deal has been happening and..." Richard rubbed his face. "Are you sure, *mein Führer*, that you wouldn't rather wait until morning?"

"Richard, do you want to answer to me or to my investigators?"

"I'll be there as soon as possible, *mein Führer*."

"What the hell is all this supposed to mean?" Frauenfeld sat behind his desk and shook a handful of papers in Richard's direction. Richard pulled the door shut behind him and looked around. They were alone in the room, and the Führer had, mercifully, seen to it that a carafe of coffee was available. He didn't, however, give Richard time to pour himself a cup. "I return from my little holiday in Greece, tired from the travel, looking forward to my bed, and what do I find here? This!" He slammed the papers onto his desk.

"I'm sorry, *mein Führer*. Your private retreat has no communications–"

"Deliberately! My God, Richard, I've been working eighteen hours a day, seven days a week since I was elected. Do you begrudge me a few moments rest?"

"No, of course not, *mein Führer*. It's just that right after you left, things happened. I had a courier sent to the island to tell you about events, but I guess you had left by the time he arrived."

Frauenfeld's face darkened. "To *tell* me? Not to get my permission?"

"I had to act quickly."

"Act quickly about what? Taking over an entire section of the Reich on your own initiative? Arresting people, conducting massive searches, evacuating villages? What the hell did you think you were doing? You've repeatedly overstepped your authority and invoked my name without my permission! You better have a good story, Traugutt." Frauenfeld held his thumb and forefinger about a centimeter apart. "You're this close to being arrested."

Again. But that wasn't a useful concept to impart to the Führer, so Richard waited for a question.

"Was this all a plot to unseat me?"

"No." The coffee was on a side table near the wall and Richard walked over to it and poured himself a cup. It would be quite ironic to be arrested the one time he had actually acted in the best interests of the Führer and the Reich.

"Don't try my patience, Richard."

Richard approached the Führer's desk and indicated the chair. "May I sit down?"

As he sat in the chair, sipping his coffee, he told the Führer everything he knew about the Realie plot. Immediately upon Schindler's name being mentioned, Frauenfeld interrupted. "Are you just making this up to ruin Schindler?"

"Why would I do that?" Richard motioned with his hand in a gesture of exasperation. "He's already been ruined. And if I was going to invent something against him, don't you think I'd come up with something simpler?"

"Where'd you get this information?"

"I have an agent I managed to get into that Carpathian stronghold of the Home Army. She's been there several years and worked her way up."

"Oh? You never mentioned that before."

Richard shrugged. "You know what Rudi was like."

"All too well. But I thought you said that it was an English group behind all this."

"It was. You see, Peter Halifax got wind of the plot."

"Halifax?" Frauenfeld drew back in consternation. "That name again! Isn't he in prison? In Switzerland? How did he find out about all this?"

"He was a member of the English Republican Army back when he was in England. I imagine he still has ties to them and to the breakaway group. One of the breakaway's members must have seen the plans and had his suspicions about the group's intentions. The problem was, the plans were coded, so whoever it was sent Halifax a copy. Halifax then decoded–"

"How'd he do that?"

"I gather that's his field of expertise." Richard left unanswered any question of how Peter had been in a position to use his expertise. "Halifax decoded the documents and, not trusting anyone in England with the information, passed it on to the Home Army hideout in the Tatra mountains."

"He's in communication with them?" Frauenfeld sounded angry at the breach of Reich security.

637

"I imagine he sent it via that fellow in New York. We can't control communications between Switzerland and the NAU, and the Governments-in-Exile have their ways around our censors. Everyone knows that."

Frauenfeld nodded, satisfied. "And your agent found out about it?"

"Not directly. The A.K. decided that this sort of action was beyond the pale and the Reich should be informed. They looked for someone to relay the information and my girl volunteered. She contacted me, here in Berlin, and I went through the plans that she had, then I checked with the transport ministry and learned that there were any number of candidate trucks approved to follow the indicated routes with uninspected cargo. That combined with some recently missing plutonium in the London area–"

"How'd you know about that?"

Richard smiled wanly. "I'm afraid I had to overstep my authority. I made contact with the ERA – the original group. That's the sort of information they collect to keep an eye on what the government is doing. In exchange for a couple of pardons – granted under your authority – I was given the details."

"I see."

"What I found out was enough to convince me that the threat was real. I had no idea which side of the channel the truck would be on and it was possible that they were anywhere in the Reich. I feared that as we moved in on the bomb, the Real ERA might find out and detonate it prematurely, so I acted to simultaneously arrest all of them. Since I had no legal right to act in the greater London arena, I invoked your authority and put Schindler under temporary detention while your personal security forces carried out the action." Richard took a deep breath. He had already confessed to enough crimes to merit a long prison sentence. "I also figured it was possible the bomb had already reached its destination and so, as a pre-emptive safety measure I had the villages near the *Residenz* evacuated, while your security forces searched the warehouses."

"And you found the bomb?"

Richard nodded. "In a warehouse near the *Residenz*. It's still there, defused and under guard, of course. I can show it to you tomorrow if you wish." Remembering Frauenfeld's angry impatience over the phone, Richard added, "Or even now. We should move it somewhere safer and have it deconstructed as soon as possible. I'm told that the scientists will be able to find all sorts of information that will give clues to its source. We can also test the arrested suspects for radiation exposure. I'm sure some of them mishandled the materials and I wouldn't be surprised if we lose a few to radiation poisoning."

"Near the *Residenz*?" Frauenfeld seemed incapable of moving beyond that fact.

"Yes. It would have leveled the entire *Residenz* complex and everything around. The destruction would have been phenomenal."

Frauenfeld looked thoughtful. "Yes, I remember what those cities were like. I was just a boy back then – I guess you're too young to remember." He didn't wait for Richard's response, his gaze was elsewhere. "It was horrible. Our cities and theirs all smoking ruins and charred bodies. And then you couldn't go anywhere near those places. And the people who came out, their flesh dropping off. Those who survived were so sick, dying. The children..." Frauenfeld's voice trailed off.

Richard waited quietly. When Frauenfeld brought his gaze back into focus, he looked ready to hear more and Richard explained, "The whole thing was supposed to be set off during the Solstice festivities – when there would be a full house."

"But not Schindler," Frauenfeld added distantly. "What evidence do you have against him directly?"

"Not much. His office approved the transit, but there is no proof that he had anything to do with it personally. Relevant materials went missing from a reactor within his territory, but I'm sure, by now, any paper trail has been destroyed. We could interrogate every employee, but we'd never know if we had uncovered the truth or just got the answers we wanted. I suppose you could have his son questioned, but that might look like pure vindictiveness. Indications from the conspirators are that a man named Fowler had made contact with Schindler personally, but Fowler himself–"

"Was killed resisting arrest."

Richard nodded wearily. "You guessed it. It seems Schindler's people got to some of the Real ERA before I could." Richard ran a hand through his hair then added. "I'm sorry about not consulting with you, but you had disappeared and by the time I had established the existence of a genuine risk–"

Frauenfeld waved his hand. "Oh, don't worry about that. What you did was right." He leaned forward, resting his chin on his hand. "It's amazing, isn't it – you had the cooperation of the English Underground, the Home Army, that fellow Rudi so hated...Everyone working together to prevent this disaster."

Richard went over to the sideboard and poured himself another cup of coffee. He had a terrible craving for a cigarette and was exhausted, but the opportunity was too good to pass on. "I wanted to talk to you about that."

"About what?"

"We need to bring representatives from these people into government. We need to start talking with them. As it currently is, the established Undergrounds and the Governments-in-Exile can no longer offer their own people anything, and in frustration, the people are turning to these more

639

violent breakaway groups. This was the first big incident, but there will be more if we don't–"

"But they couldn't have done it without Schindler."

"Yes they could, he just speeded up the process. The fact that they were willing, shows the level of anger out there." Still holding his coffee, Richard began pacing as if expressing the people's frustration personally. "There is such an undercurrent of violence, I suspect just one incident – like this bomb – will be enough to plunge the whole Reich into chaos. We've got to prevent that."

Frauenfeld pursed his lips. "Do you think offering advisory roles to select members of the various Undergrounds would be enough? Some sort of non-Party advisory council?"

Richard came to a stop at the far wall and casually leaned against it. "If it has any power, yes, it's a start."

"I don't know, Richard. It seems rather risky, letting our enemies in among us. They have sworn to destroy us and if we let them in – it's like accepting the Trojan horse."

"We don't need to drop our guard entirely. The Home Army one would be easy. They still don't know that my girl is one of us. She could 'represent' them."

"A woman! Nonsense!"

Richard shrugged. "We need to bring women into the process as well. It's time. And by including them, we could strengthen our own hand."

"But, but…" Frauenfeld shook his head. "That would be so unsettling to the social order!"

"The social order is *already* unsettled. Just think of Frau Vogel and her servant. She's not unique." Richard took a deep breath then plunged in. "There are many examples of people who live apparently perfectly upstanding lives, but have something to hide. If not in their behavior, then in their past. The social order has never been what it seems. We all have skeletons, don't we?"

"Irmtraud and I don't."

Richard nodded. He'd try again later. He was ad-libbing, and that was always difficult, but he had prepared well over the past weeks and even if he hadn't yet collated everything in his head, he felt the time was right. "I think my girl–"

"What's her name?"

"Sofia."

"Where'd she come from?"

"She's my ex-wife's sister. Like Dorota, I had her working for me for years. I think she'll be perfect. She's put years into her role and can offer us genuine insights into what these people want and at the same time, we can convince them that they have real representation in our government."

"But they will."

Richard pushed himself away from the wall and returned to the Führer's desk. "What do you mean?"

"Everyone knows your ex-wife isn't really German. She and her sisters are Poles! Your girl is *not* one of us."

He hadn't expected that one. Richard took a sip of his coffee, set it on the edge of the desk and sat back down. He leaned forward slightly, as if sharing a confidence. "*Mein Führer*, everyone knew *my* wife's background. There was absolutely no duplicity or blood fraud involved. She applied for *Volksdeutsch* status and received it."

"Because of you. She didn't have any German blood."

"*Not* because of me. Because she was one of us!" Richard deliberately let his tone harden. "Whatever the failings of our marriage, I will never let anyone suggest that my wife was anything other than perfectly loyal. She was one of us because she wanted to be! And I suggest that that is more important than any other criterion. If for instance..." Richard scanned the ceiling theatrically as if looking for the wildest idea possible, "Say, Irmtraud's mother was Jewish. Say her mother had her family records re-established in a neighboring jurisdiction just to hide that fact–"

Frauenfeld had drawn himself up but Richard held his eyes with a penetrating look. "Just hypothetically, of course. Would you say that such a distant and unimportant fact should be enough to bring into question Irmtraud's loyalty? Should that have been something to have ruined your career in the Party? Should that be enough to bring you down as Führer?"

Frauenfeld had pulled back slightly, his eyes wide, his hands gripping the edge of the desk.

He's wondering if he needs to have me silenced, Richard thought. "*Mein Führer*, I only use the example because Irmtraud is so *obviously* a part of the *Volk*! And I think *that* should be our definition. You see, even if such nonsense were true," and here Richard stopped to give Frauenfeld a significantly knowing look, "then I believe it should be irrelevant. We are all individuals and the group we belong to is *our* choice and *our* responsibility."

Richard pulled back slightly to lower the intensity of his words and in a much calmer tone, like a lecturer in a university, he continued, "Those who first formulated our philosophy were looking for a unification of the *Volk*, something to give them a sense of identity and strength after great national loss. They believed that blood was the answer, the unifying principle, but since then science has discovered many things. We know now that the concept of blood doesn't even make sense. Humans are defined by many things, by their genes, by their environment, by random chemistry! Our biochemical make-up is astonishingly, overwhelmingly complex. Our bloodlines are mixed and mixed and mixed again. All we pathetic lay people can do is give up on scientific definitions of who is superior and who is inferior and instead use common sense and wisdom." Richard took a breath and added softly, "And I think it would be wise to include more people in the definition of *us*. If we expand the concept of citizen to include any who would undertake the responsibility of working for the betterment of our country, then we would be a much stronger land." He smiled. "And, *mein Führer*, a lot fewer people would be driven to live lies."

Frauenfeld looked stunned. He motioned without looking toward a cabinet. "There's a bottle of whiskey in there, Richard. Pour me a glass. And one for yourself, of course."

Richard did as the Führer requested and poured the whiskey. When he returned to the desk, Frauenfeld looked much more composed. "I think you made some good points, Richard. I will think about what you said."

Afraid that he might lose the initiative if he let the Führer mull over everything, Richard raised his glass. "Good! So we can ask the Home Army if they will enter into a dialog with us and suggest my agent as their representative. As for the other Undergrounds, I don't have anyone – maybe we can let each suggest several candidates."

Frauenfeld looked surprised. "I didn't..." He stopped and looked at Richard, as if deciding just how far Richard would go with the information about Irmtraud. Then, sighing heavily, he gave in. "Very well. They did after all help us prevent this disaster. A council of *nichtdeutsch* advisors reporting directly to the Führer, is not unthinkable. Do you think you can convince the Cabinet of that?"

"Yes, *mein Führer*, leave it to me."

"Fine, I will. I'm sure you have something on everyone by now." Frauenfeld sipped his whiskey and coughed slightly at the raw sensation. "It's been a while."

Richard knew he should stop there, he had accomplished a phenomenal amount, but Zosia's suggestions about Peter rattled through his mind. "Now about Halifax."

"What about him?" Frauenfeld narrowed his eyes as if annoyed. "God, I wish Rudi had just killed him and been done with it."

"Without his work the *Residenz* and everyone around would have been incinerated. You and I would have become charred corpses. We owe him a debt of gratitude."

Frauenfeld took another sip from his glass but didn't say anything. He looked very suspicious.

"Not only that, but he's aware of what went on and who was behind it. He could broadcast the information and cause us a great deal of embarrassment."

"You mean about Schindler?"

Richard nodded.

"What should we do about him? Schindler, I mean. Can we try him?"

"I'm afraid there's probably not enough hard evidence. Besides, I don't think we want the international embarrassment of trying one of our own top officers for attempting to set off a nuclear weapon in his own land. I think he should be forced into retirement and sent somewhere, and we could hush-up this entire humiliating affair. His boy, Wolf-Dietrich can be promoted – I've heard he's trustworthy – and also that will make Günter's retirement look more natural."

"Hmm." Frauenfeld took another sip of his drink. Though he had drunk a tiny amount, it already seemed to be affecting him.

"As for Halifax, I think he'd make a good spokesman for the *Zwangsarbeiter*."

"The *Zwangsarbeiter*?"

"Yes, he was one. Classified *Untermensch* as well. You can't get better credentials than that." Richard was joking, but Frauenfeld didn't seem to appreciate that fact.

"What I meant was why would we need a *Zwangsarbeiter* spokesman at all?"

Richard finished his drink and went to refill his coffee cup. As he poured, he explained, "For the same reason as the Undergrounds. We need to pre-empt any violence by offering them a nonviolent outlet for their frustrations." He turned toward the Führer. "They are the most oppressed group and therefore the urge to violence is the strongest." It was plausible, but he had no evidence whatsoever that what he said was true. From all his observations it seemed that the lowest orders of the Reich were actually the most effectively pacified, but Richard certainly had no interest in telling the Führer that. So Richard returned to stand opposite the Führer as he sat at his desk and, with heartfelt sincerity, lied. "My studies of that level of society have shown that they could explode at any time. And with people from that group integrated into every high-level household – well, you can imagine the mayhem they may wreak."

"Hmm. So you think we need someone to speak on their behalf and you think that Halifax would do that?"

"Yes, I already put my agent in touch with him to sound him out, and he'd be willing to speak out for a nonviolent approach to change."

"Putting aside whether or not I like your idea, there is a flaw in your plan, Richard."

643

"Yes, *mein Führer*?"

"He's in prison."

"I know. I think in gratitude for his work in uncovering this plot, and to prevent any embarrassment with regards to it, we should petition to have him pardoned. He already has strong support in the NAU, and if we were to remove any objection to his release and ask for his pardon, I'm fairly sure it would be granted."

Frauenfeld came out from behind his desk and walked up to Richard. He tilted his head back so he could look directly into Richard's eyes. "Tell me, Richard, why do you care what happens to this man?"

Richard raised an eyebrow as if asking himself the same question and took a sip of his coffee.

Frauenfeld waited expectantly.

"He saved our lives."

Frauenfeld shook his head slowly. "It's more than that. What is it?"

As if coming to an important decision, Richard put down his coffee. "*Mein Führer*, a long time ago, about nine years, I guess, I inspected a new camp that had been set up to re-educate prisoners. I had been one of the prime movers behind setting up such places, in the interest of lowering the number of executions the Reich carried out."

"Even then you were fretting over our criminal justice system."

"Yes, *mein Führer*. As you once did, shortly after your marriage."

"Hmm."

"Anyway, I was given a tour of the camp by its director, a man I myself had chosen – Heinrich Lederman. You know him."

Frauenfeld shuddered. "Yes, he does not impress me."

"Well, to impress me, he showed me a new recruit to the program. The man had already spent weeks under interrogation and had then been condemned to death by a court. There was some sort of melee at his sentencing and he ended up being knocked unconscious. He woke up in a completely white cell, naked, shaven, soaking wet, manacled and tattooed. Everything was set up to maximize his disorientation and denigration. We – Lederman and I – stood above on a catwalk, looking down on him the way you might view an animal in a cage. Despite that, he looked up at me, not like an animal at all. He looked right at me and his expression said, 'I am human, I am sane. What about you?' I had to smile."

"I don't get it."

"It was a good question, don't you think? I mean, any outside observer would say it was we who looked like the beasts in that drama."

Frauenfeld smiled wryly.

"Months later I was shown the same prisoner. Lederman was in the process of torturing him to death. I could see he had been repeatedly beaten and was starving. He had a filthy piece of rope tied around his neck that looked like it was used as a leash, or maybe to choke him now and then. He wore chains and was filthy and covered in sores, but worst of all, he was dying of thirst. There, before our eyes, in a land awash with water, he was dying of thirst." Richard paused, giving Frauenfeld a moment to absorb the appalling ugliness of the scene. "I was shown how obedient the prisoner was. When told to remain still he did so even though faced with what seemed to be certain death. The man who had looked into my eyes was gone. There was nothing left of that human I had seen earlier. This was National Socialism's vision of a remade society, and it was horrifying."

"And the prisoner was Halifax?"

"Yes."

"What had he been convicted of? Rudi said he was in the Underground. Had he been involved in a bombing or something?"

Richard shook his head. "No, no one knew about his Underground connections then, and in fact, what we found out later indicates that he was in their intelligence branch and did nothing but gather data."

"So why the death sentence?"

"He had been convicted of escaping a twenty year term, with all the fraud and deception that involves."

"But no violence?"

Richard shook his head. "No, no violence, no one hurt."

Frauenfeld rubbed his chin. "Hmm. Death."

"People have been killed for less."

"Hmm. And why had he been sentenced to twenty years? Was that at least a real crime?"

Richard laughed slightly. "Seems his papers were out of order. No proof of having done his labor service, no residence documents, and so on."

"Papers?"

Richard nodded. "Back then Schindler had just taken over the Greater London district and had decided to take a tough line against the native population. When you're born into the wrong social group, it's easy to get yourself stomped on. What, for a colonist would have been a minor infraction, was, for the natives, a serious felony."

"And you thought that the treatment of this prisoner reflected badly on National Socialism's vision of the future?"

"Don't you?"

"It wasn't National Socialism's vision, it was that *sadist's* vision."

Richard raised his eyes to the portrait of Hitler on the wall, but that was not who Frauenfeld was talking about. Nor was he talking about Rudi. He meant Lederman. "Lederman was being promoted within the system. He was successful and that told me what it meant to succeed in our system. It opened my eyes. I determined then to do whatever was in my power to change the system – or at least that part of it."

Frauenfeld seemed impressed. "And that's been your goal all along? That's what motivated your climb to power?"

"Yes." Richard didn't feel too bad about adding yet another layer to the deceit that defined his existence, for in some ways this convoluted lie summarized a deeper truth. "I feel a debt to that man. And to know now that Lederman walks free and has not even been accused of a crime, while the man I saw serves a prison sentence for killing someone who everyone knew was a murderous pig–"

"Murderous?"

Richard nodded. "Vogel was responsible for at least two deaths to my knowledge. One was Halifax's predecessor, the other a woman he killed in Paris."

"And he was never charged?"

"The servant was on lease, so Vogel was fined for beating him to death, but killing an *Untermensch* is not legally murder."

"What about the woman?"

Richard closed his eyes as an image of Julia came to mind. Beautiful Julia, so full of life! He opened his eyes to see Frauenfeld's curious face and he smiled ruefully in response. "Vogel confided that to me while drunk. I had nothing but his own word."

Frauenfeld shook his head. "All very interesting, Richard. But still, Halifax is a murderer – he voluntarily returned to Vogel's house just to kill him. He didn't *have* to do that!"

"I don't think it was voluntary. There is nothing in his behavior before or afterwards to suggest that he is a killer."

"He admitted to the crime! Frau Vogel said she witnessed it!"

"She also said that he had been told sensitive political information by Frau Schindler."

"Your wife."

"Yes, but Günter's wife at the time."

Frauenfeld furrowed his brow. "Do you really believe he was Günter's agent the whole time?"

Richard shook his head. "No, I think that's unlikely. I do think though that he did on that occasion act as Günter's agent. You see, I've talked to Greta and she said that Günter was aware of Elspeth Vogel's affair with her servant. So Günter must have known that Magdalena Vogel was Peter's daughter. I think he threatened to harm the child unless Halifax carried out his command to kill Karl Vogel. Or maybe he just told Halifax he'd tell Vogel who Magdalena's father was – that would have been enough. He probably told Halifax about Vogel's troubles just to make it easier for

Halifax to accept the assignment. Afterwards, Halifax took the child with him to make sure she wouldn't be harmed and to prevent Günter from blackmailing him again."

Frauenfeld nodded thoughtfully. "But why did Günter want to kill Vogel?"

"If I knew that, Günter would have had me killed as well."

"Hmm. So you think Halifax isn't really guilty of murder."

"No. He was just carrying out what he thought was a justified execution in order to save someone close to him from harm."

"Hmm. Put that way..." Frauenfeld paced away to the sideboard and poured himself a glass of water. He stood with his back to Richard as he drank it. Richard remained silent, letting Frauenfeld work through it all. After a moment, Frauenfeld asked, "If this is all true, why didn't Halifax explain it all at his trial?"

Though Frauenfeld still had his back to him, Richard shrugged. "Fear? Günter does, after all, control London. There could be any number of people there that Günter might arrest in retaliation for Halifax speaking out."

"I suppose." Frauenfeld continued to sip his water, still facing the wall. He was facing Hitler's portrait, but he didn't seem to be looking at it. After several moments had passed, he said, "You realize, this could set us on an entirely new course."

"*Mein Führer*, I believe that is best for the Reich, and what we both want."

"There will be resistance."

"I know, but I believe that under your leadership, we can handle it."

Another few minutes passed in silence then Frauenfeld turned to face Richard. "Alright, Richard. Organize whatever you can. Clear with whomever you think necessary."

"Thank you, *mein Führer*."

"Understand though, that I'm only giving you permission to pursue this. I'm withholding my own judgment on this man, so I will not, under any circumstances, make a personal appeal on his behalf."

Richard snapped his head in a gesture of precise acknowledgment. "I understand, *mein Führer*."

31

*D*rizzle. Endless gray clouds and perpetual dampness. Peter stood with the other prisoners under the roof of the yard and looked out at the depressing day. Two weeks of continuous rain and drizzle, only occasionally broken by heavy cloud cover. Already July and still lousy weather! It wouldn't be so bad if they were surrounded by woodlands, or even an interesting cityscape, but there was nothing but muddy fields and dripping razor wire.

It was telling on everyone and the area under the roof was alive with verbal sniping and childish aggression. Out of boredom, Peter passed on a few "dumb Nazi" jokes to his nearest neighbor. The fellow chuckled and left to tell them to his friends. The jokes would only add to the tension under the roof as the Nazis would sooner or later overhear and take retaliatory steps, but Peter didn't care. Let the guards swing their sticks a bit – the exercise would do them good. He stepped out into the drizzle and walked over to the fence where, though wet, he could be relatively alone.

A year to the day. A year ago, he had been handed over. He had walked out of the woods with only Marysia at his side. Behind him, hidden among the trees were the snipers of the Home Army, before him was the international delegation sent to receive him, and lurking in the distance, the soldiers of the Reich. Marysia had shaken his hand in farewell, then one of the representatives of the Swiss police had stepped forward and handcuffed him and had led him away to the vehicle that was to take him into Switzerland to detention and trial.

One year to the day since he had been taken into custody. Upon his conviction the court had given him credit for time served, so that meant he only had nineteen years to go. Not eleven, nineteen. At some indeterminate time he had decided to discount the parole date, figuring that he would not be able to avoid serious trouble for that long, so now he counted down the entire sentence. Twenty years. One down, nineteen to go. He wove his fingers into the links and let his weight rest against the fence in the classic pose of a detainee, bored and despairing.

He had been right. Once he had passed on the information about Schindler's and the Realies' plans, he had become irrelevant. There was a lot of work to be done to foil the plot and in his circumstances, he could offer no help. Zosia had tried to keep him informed of what was going on, but since she had to be out of Szaflary most of the time, her messages had been intermittent. Once all the conspirators were arrested, she had returned to Szaflary and communication had been re-established, but then she had to leave on a mission that would keep her out of touch for a long while, possibly months. Don't worry, he had been told, she would be safe, just unavailable.

Arieka had also dropped out of sight and he guessed that she had traveled home to either Kivu or Manhattan. Perhaps she had given up her diplomatic position altogether – she had only organized it out of curiosity and the Reich had clearly not been to her taste. Berlin, she had said, was "cold, gray and full of white men with guns. What more could a girl want?" He couldn't blame her if she had headed to sunnier, friendlier climes, but he regretted that she had not been able to stop by on her way out to say good-bye.

Nor had he heard anything from his lawyer. That was not surprising – the money had run out long ago. Gerhard had promised, nevertheless, to keep his eyes open for an opportunity to appeal the sentence and told Peter he would contact him if something came up. No word, no news.

Peter untangled his fingers and turned around so that he could lean against the fence and look at his fellow prisoners. A fight had broken out and the guards were busily separating the relevant parties. One of the guards had to use a chokehold to drag a prisoner out of the fray. The uninvolved backed away, crowding themselves even more to avoid being caught up in any disciplinary action. Just nineteen more years of this shit, Peter thought as he watched the little theater, I'm going to get old here.

He laughed quietly to himself. He'd be alright, and everyone he cared about was well. Despite being bored and a bit depressed, he also felt at peace with himself. It had been the right decision, he had maintained his humanity. That would have been the only unbearable thing – to become what he hated.

As the fight was finally broken up, Peter thought about what had caused it. The proximate cause was irrelevant, the genuine cause was boredom. A funny way to deal with people who were already at odds with society: remove the need to do anything except follow rules, limit social interactions to the most basic and brutal, surround them with unhealthy ugliness, and then tell them they were being reformed. He wondered if there was anything he could do for his fellow inmates. A lot of them were quite uneducated, some didn't even know how to read. He could try teaching them – after all, he had some experience from before. His approach would have to be rather different from simply offering the opportunity – there were a number of activities on offer which were often ignored by the men because they felt embarrassed to admit any weakness or in any way be seen to cooperate with the system. Peter rubbed his chin thoughtfully. It could be quite a challenge, he'd have to work on a good approach. But what the hell, he had nineteen years.

He stretched against the fence and looked up to let the rain splash into his face. Or maybe something more worthy. Maybe he could organize an environmental movement within the Reich. Different groups in each region, each with an appropriately local agenda, newsletters and publications sent via computer. That was possible now. He could do a lot of research, make each target relevant. Barbara could help distribute information and recruit members. Maybe someone from Szaflary would help, the Kindergarten teacher, Basia, perhaps. He could even work out of Berlin if he got Pawel and Teresa involved...

One of the guards emerged from under the roof and approached him. *Bloody hell, what now?* Had one of the fighting prisoners claimed that Peter had started it all? Peter ran his hand through his hair to remove some of the water and waited, ready to argue his innocence.

"Halifax, the director wants to see you. Come with me."

Peter furrowed his brow. "What about?" Oh God, had the director discovered all the hacking he had been doing? Was he going to lose the use of the computer? His private cell? He had already passed on all the personnel information that the director had requested, so he had nothing left to bargain with. *Shit!*

The guard shrugged and led the way out of the prison yard. As they walked the corridors toward the administrative section, Peter brushed the water off his face and clothes as best he could. Wouldn't do to look like a drowned rat. His mind churned with the accusations he might face and the best way to deflect them. Admit everything and beg for understanding? Invent explanations? Shit! He had hoped his virtual freedom would have lasted just a little longer.

The guard took him into the director's secretary's office and she buzzed the great man. Peter heard the disembodied voice say "Show him in." He got no hint of the director's intentions from his tone and as he approached the door, he felt himself stiffen with a combination of fear and a desire to fight.

The director was not alone in the room – Gerhard, Arieka, Alex and Zosia were there as well. *Zosia?* The other three were plausible, but Zosia? As Arieka's assistant perhaps? But why?

The director stood and shook Peter's hand. "Dr. Halifax, as always, a pleasure." He picked a sheet of paper up off his desk. "This time, more than usual."

"Sir?"

Arieka spoke up. "It's a pardon, Peter."

"What?"

Alex gestured toward Zosia. "This woman was sent as a representative of the Führer's special commission set up to investigate your conviction. Upon the recommendation of the commission, the Führer asked that the international tribunal reconvene and consider a pardon. Frau Ruweni and I organized a quorum and your lawyer presented your case. With the Reich's support, the decision of the tribunal was quick and unanimous. A pardon was granted effective upon the anniversary of your incarceration. That's today."

Peter felt he couldn't trust his senses. Why hadn't he read anything about this in the news? "Was the decision public?"

Alex smiled. "Yes. But you're yesterday's news – hardly anybody picked up on it."

Arieka seemed to understand Peter's confusion. "We didn't tell you what was up, because we didn't want to raise false hopes."

Peter nodded slowly. He felt almost sick with the knowledge that in a moment he would awaken back in his cell, or worse yet, by the fence. A dream was one thing, but hallucinating? Oh God.

"You're free, Peter."

He looked at Arieka, saw the happiness in her face. He turned to the director. The director nodded. "There's no reason you can't leave immediately. You can go gather up your things, sort out whatever you have to with the work you've been doing, and then check out at the main gate any time you like."

"Free," Peter repeated, his eyes moving from one to the other of them. "Free."

Gerhard came forward to shake his hand. "Congratulations." He beamed and added, "I'll send you the bill!"

Peter did not get a chance to respond as Arieka surged forward to hug him. She kissed him on each cheek, then whispered into his ear. "I'm so happy for you! For both of you."

Though it was only a dream, Peter allowed himself to reply, "Thank you, thank you for everything."

Alex stepped forward and extended his hand. As Peter shook it, Alex explained, "There's a car waiting for us out front."

Peter nodded but his eyes strayed to Zosia and she stepped forward. "Herr Dr. Halifax?" She extended her hand and for the first time in a year, he was able to touch her. The charade was solely for the director's and Gerhard's sakes and Peter wondered if it was really necessary. He so much wanted to pull her into him to hug and kiss her before she vanished into the dawn.

"Herr Dr. Halifax, I have been empowered to reinstate your status as a subject of the Reich and return to you the right of residency within its borders. You will be granted a residence permit for either your native region in the Greater London Administrative District, or for Berlin." Zosia drew the word Berlin out to emphasize its significance. Peter could only look at her in confusion.

"I have also been asked to extend to you an invitation to join the Führer's special non-Party, *nichtdeutsch* advisory council as the *Zwangsarbeiter* representative and to help establish a commission which shall be charged with studying the current racial segregation laws and suggesting appropriate modernizations to reflect the diversity of the Reich's population while maintaining the high standards of our National Socialist German Worker's Party philosophy."

It was too much and Peter coughed to hide his sputter. If it had been anyone else, he would have said *fuck off*, but Zosia was clearly having fun with him. She stood so properly, wearing some sort of idiotic N.S. woman's uniform, her hair pulled back into a tight bun. No dream would have invented such a wonderful farce, it had to be real. As he stared at her, unable to summon up an appropriate answer, she gave his hand a gentle, familiar squeeze.

"You will, of course, be required to sign an apology for your crimes against the State and its citizens and a declaration that you have renounced violence as a political tool. Are you willing to do that?"

So, together they would work under her brother's direction, keeping their respective promises. No bloody revolution. No revenge. Ryszard's strategy had won out, and Peter felt very pleased with that fact. He smiled and gave Zosia a slight, formal bow in return. "I consent to the conditions and would be honored by the position offered to me."

Three hours later all the formalities had been fulfilled and Peter walked out the front gates of the prison to join his friends. Alex led him to the car, but before he got in Peter looked around. The rain had stopped but still a heavy veil of gray hung in the air. Nevertheless, he could see them clearly – no fences, no razor wire, no guard posts – just the mountains, and they were beautiful.

About the Author

J. N. Stroyar is a theoretical physicist living in Germany and has also worked in America, Belgium, and England. Her extensive research for her books included visits to Poland, the former East Germany and the USSR, as well as studies of Nazi Germany, resistance movement archives, family accounts of slavery and concentration camps, and personal interviews with torture victims, Holocaust survivors, and former Nazis.

Printed in the United States
47141LVS00003B/6